MISTRUNNER
BOOK 1

MISTRUNNER

BOOK 1

NICHOLAS SEARCY

Podium

Thanks to all of my friends, family, fans, and Patreon supporters. Without you all, none of my work would be possible.

All rights reserved. No part of this publication may be reproduced, stored in a retrieval system, or transmitted in any form or by any means electronic, mechanical, photocopying, recording, or otherwise without prior written permission from Podium Publishing.

This is a work of fiction. Names, characters, places, and incidents are either products of the author's imagination or used fictitiously. Any resemblance to actual events, locales, or persons, living, dead, or undead, is entirely coincidental.

Copyright © 2023 Nicholas Searcy

Cover design by Paul Ghezzo and Pius Bak

ISBN: 978-1-0394-3336-6

Published in 2023 by Podium Publishing, ULC
www.podiumaudio.com

Podium

MISTRUNNER

BOOK 1

CHAPTER ONE

A WORTHY PURSUIT

I will never forget the day the world changed. A bright flash of light, a sudden feeling of impending doom, and then all hell broke loose. I survived. Others didn't. I'm not sure who was luckier.

—Jeremiah Braddock III

I tore through the alley, ignoring the trash piled against the walls as I clutched my ill-gotten gains to my chest. Behind me, my pursuers' steps pounded against the pavement, splashing through the puddles of water and who-knew-what-else that had gathered in the alley. As I passed, I dragged a nearby trash can behind me, and I was rewarded with the sound of a man tripping over the aluminum barrel. The others were not so easily deterred, though.

Not that I expected such a thing to work, of course. The men behind me were all at least Tier 2, and they had cybernetic enhancements to boot. If I'd known they would chase me, I never would have dreamed of stealing from Farooq in the first place. I glanced down at the package in my hands, realizing just how inaccurate that thought really was. Even if I ended up getting caught, it was worth it.

Of course, that wasn't plan A. Or plan B. Or really, any plan in the alphabet. I guess what I'm saying is that I didn't want to get caught. But then again, who does? It's not like any thief sets out to be caught, right? Sometimes, though, it's unavoidable.

Like right now.

Before I could get to the end of the alley and blend in with the crowd of pedestrians walking alongside the main street, I felt a meaty hand clamp down on my shoulder. I tried to duck away, but his grip was like iron. No—wait. Upon further reflection, it wasn't just *like* iron. It was literal metal. Which was my first hint that I'd made a huge mistake.

Or maybe like the third or fourth hint, following closely after Farooq screaming at me and a trio of hulking mouth breathers chasing after me. So, third hint. Either way, I was screwed because I knew just whom that hand belonged to.

With those metallic fingers digging into my shoulder, I skidded to a stop, then promptly fell on my ass. Water and—*oh God, that doesn't smell like water*—splashed, covering me in muck.

"Ow! Fuck. Shit! Ow!" I sputtered, trying not to think about what, exactly, the semiliquid was. I looked up at the figure who'd suddenly topped my list of most-hated people in Nova City. Once, it had been called New Orleans, but that was almost a century ago. Now, almost everyone just called it Nova.

I turned to glare at my nemesis, and even though I was still furious and annoyed that I'd been caught, that fire lasted for only a few seconds before it was quelled by the sheer degree of trouble I was in. Instead of some nameless mook, I found myself looking up at Turk James, a veritable mountain of muscle and metal who any sane thief would avoid like Mist rot. And judging by the look on his face, I'd gone and put myself on his bad side.

"Give it back," he growled, one of his eyes glowing red. His other was mostly black, though instead of an iris, it had a white skull. Original? No. Not even the least bit. But it was definitely intimidating enough to send a shiver of fear up my spine. "Now."

I clutched the package to my chest. After spending the last five minutes sprinting through the Garden—so named because it was home to the Silos where most of the city's food was grown—I was in no mood to give up my hard-won treasure. Even if it meant getting my legs broken by some edgy asshole with a fetish for metal appendages.

"No!" I spat, pushing myself away. I only got a few inches before his metal hand found my hair. Damn me for unbraiding it, right? But at least it didn't stink. Most of the time. You know—when it wasn't covered in muck and being used as a leash. "Ow. Fuck! Let me go!"

He didn't. Because, obviously, right? He'd been chasing me for a half dozen blocks; he wasn't going to let me go just because I threw a few swears his way.

"Uh . . . boss?" said one of the men who'd followed Turk. He was just as tall as the man who had a death grip on my hair, but he was probably half his weight. Like Turk, though, he had a cybernetic appendage—this time, a leg. Then and there, I labeled him Pegleg. "You recognize her, right?"

Turk dragged me to my feet and then onto my tiptoes. My feet were barely scraping the pavement, and it set my scalp on fire with the pain. Hair wasn't supposed to support a person's entire body weight, apparently. Good to know, but if

I'm honest, probably not the most important thing to consider, given the circumstances. Said circumstances being that I had an angry cyborg staring me in the face.

"What's your name?" he growled. Did he have any other tone? Or more importantly, had he ever heard of dental hygiene? Because his breath was terrible, and that was me being nice. The other way would've had me using words like *rotting corpse* or *sewage mouth*. Then again, considering that his teeth were entirely metal—and probably his jaw, too—I had to wonder if he even had to worry about cavities. If push came to shove—and shove was right on the horizon, from what I could smell—he could just replace the whole thing.

"Uh . . ."

"Go on, girl—spit it out," he ordered, his metal teeth clacking together with every word. I hated that I was close enough to hear it. The sound wasn't so bad, but being so close meant that it came with the smell. And like I said, gross.

"That's the Wraith's little girl," supplied Pegleg. "You know what he'll do to us if he finds out . . . you know . . ."

My heart leaped into my throat. The last thing I needed was for them to run off and tell my uncle what I'd been doing. Whatever they had in mind as punishment couldn't have been as bad as what he would do to me. But then again, the moment I thought back to the package still in my hands, I thought it was worth it.

"That so, kid?" he asked, a slight smile playing across his face. God—he knew, didn't he? He knew that I was way more afraid of my uncle than I ever could've been of him. And rightly so, given that the cyborg, as obviously powerful as he was, was probably just as scared of my uncle Jeremiah—or the Wraith, as he was colloquially known—as I was.

"Just . . . just let me go," I said, summoning every ounce of courage I possessed. It was probably enough to fill a thimble. "And I won't . . . I won't tell anyone about this . . . uh . . . this misunderstanding. Got it?"

For a moment, I thought my bluff would work. After all, everyone in the Garden was terrified of my uncle. Was it right to leverage that into getting away? Maybe not. But I was still a week away from my sixteenth birthday, when I would get my Nexus Implant, so it was the only reasonable thing I could do to escape.

"Maybe we should just let her go," said the third member of the chase-a-teenage-girl-through-the-streets club. He was short and a little pudgy, with a bald head and the dubious distinction of having no obvious cybernetics. I bet they made fun of him for that. You know, when they weren't threatening teenagers. "I don't want to get on his bad side. You know what they say about him, right? You've heard the stories."

"I ain't scared of Jeremiah," Turk said. "Besides, he'll probably thank us for bringing this little street rat back home. I heard he's been lookin' for her."

"For why?" asked Pegleg.

"Rumor is that she done run off," said Vanilla. Yes—I'd dubbed the guy without cybernetics Vanilla, on account of him being a vanilla human. In my defense, his skin was kind of white, too. And he probably liked ice cream, I guess? And I was doing everything I could not to have my hair ripped out of my skull. So, I think I should get a little bit of slack.

"Run off? From where?" was Pegleg's next question. Clearly, he wasn't the brains of the operation. Turk wasn't, either. And Vanilla? Please. Maybe nobody was the brains, which kind of explained how an Unawakened teenager was able to elude them for more than six blocks.

"From her uncle, idiot," Turk said, slapping Pegleg on the back of the head. Immediately, the man reacted, his arm exploding into moving parts that resolved themselves into the barrel of a gun. All around the metallic cylinder were the splayed parts of Pegleg's left arm, held in place by various rods and wires.

"I told you not to hit me no more!" the man spat, his weasellike features distorting with anger. Perhaps I should beneficently bestow a new moniker, changing his name from Pegleg to Weasel. I wonder if he'd be grateful. Probably not.

Turk rolled his inhuman eyes. I couldn't help but wonder if they had any special features; likely, they were just cosmetic, though. Even if he was Tier 3, he was just some midlevel mook, and there was almost no way he could afford functional optics. In any case, he followed his eye roll up by slapping the man's arm gun away. Pegleg—or did I decide to call him Weasel? Moreover, why do I even care?—tried to resist, but he clearly wasn't on Turk's level because he couldn't stop himself from tumbling to the ground. I was satisfied to see that he was soon covered in the same disgusting liquid that coated my own legs. Served him right, as far as I was concerned.

Obviously, all wasn't right in the land of mooks and cyborgs because, with a growl, Vanilla launched himself at Turk. As he did so, a pair of blades extended from his forearms. Despite being on the wrong side of a pair of cybernetic swords, Turk didn't panic. Instead, he dodged Vanilla's first swing, then blocked the next. Vanilla had no intention of stopping there, though, because he let out a wordless battle cry before redoubling his efforts. Metal blades clashed with Turk's free arm, which turned out to be cybernetic, as well, albeit with a thin coating of Realskin.

Not to be left out, Pegleg climbed to his feet and backed away, his arm gun aimed at Turk. I heard him mumble something along the lines of, "Ought not hit people no more . . ."

Then, he fired. In the narrow confines of the alley, it was like a cannon had gone off. The puddles of liquid erupted, spraying into the air, and the sound rattled the fire escapes dangling above us. Windows shattered, raining plasti-glass down into the alley, and most importantly, a ball of molten metal tore across the alley to slam into Turk.

The impact sent me flying in one direction while Turk went in the other. Notably, he took a good portion of my hair with him. I didn't have any time to curse him, though, because a millisecond later, I found myself slamming into a concrete wall. My breath left my chest, and I thought I felt at least a couple of ribs crack before I fell to the ground, landing in a pile of garbage. Hopefully, nobody had left any used needles lying about.

Over the next few seconds, I lay there, my thoughts slow and muddled. In retrospect, I'd hit my head pretty damned hard, and I had a not-so-light concussion. But in the moment, I was in no shape to properly assess the damage. In any case, I had more important things to worry about.

No—not the trio of idiots who'd forgotten I even existed. Both Pegleg and Vanilla—who wasn't so Vanilla, now that I thought about it—were engaged in a pretty impressive brawl. Every now and then, Pegleg would shoot Turk again, but he'd clearly spent most of his Mist on that first shot. And given that it had torn a hole right through Turk's midsection, it was a fairly impressive attack. Not that it did much good, of course. Despite having had his insides splattered across a wall, Turk was as functional as ever—the benefit of being more machine than human, I guess. And more importantly, Pegleg had thoroughly pissed him off.

I knew how that fight was going to end, and it probably wouldn't be much longer until Turk had the others subdued. Or dead. Probably dead. So, I focused on the only thing that really mattered—my ill-gotten gains. Luckily, the package hadn't been damaged, and I dared to hope its contents would be similarly unaffected.

Seeing that I had a chance to escape—after all, Turk was way more focused on establishing dominance to care about little ol' me—I scrambled to my feet. Or staggered. Definitely staggered. Whatever the case, I grabbed the package and ran from the alley-turned-war-zone and into the flow of pedestrians.

The street itself was mostly empty, but that wasn't so surprising. Not many people in the Garden District could afford any more transportation than their own two feet, so only a few cars or bikes, both vehicular variants hovering on what looked like cushions of air, passed by. One day, I would get my own bike. I already had the perfect one picked out, too. But I had to wait until after I got my implant, at least. Otherwise, I wouldn't have the skill to control it. That was for another day, though. For now, I needed to focus on escape.

At first, I moved with unhurried purpose, trying to seem like just another pedestrian. Sure, I was coated in foul-smelling muck, had bits of trash clinging to my jeans and there was blood trickling down my forehead, but that wasn't so uncommon. Even the fight between Turk and the other two mooks hadn't really drawn any attention, despite its destroying windows and rattling the ground. Most of the city's natives had seen much worse, and they all knew to stay in their own lanes; otherwise, they might end up on the wrong end of something like Pegleg's arm cannon. And most people couldn't just shrug something like that off. Worse yet, it was only a matter of time before the Enforcers showed up. When that happened, things would get really ugly.

Turk was Tier 3, and he'd clearly trained quite a bit. He probably hadn't reached his limits, but few people ever did. My uncle, for instance, was a positively ancient Tier 5, and he probably had the attributes to prove it. Or that's what I'd heard. Without an implant, I didn't have access to any skills or optics, so I couldn't be sure. For his part, Uncle Jeremiah didn't like to talk about things like that. No matter how many times I asked.

After a few minutes of weaving through the crowd of pedestrians, I veered off into another alley. I didn't stop there, though. Instead, I took off at a jog, turning this way and that through the maze of backstreets that ran through the massive concrete buildings. Every now and then, I would pass a bum or a drug addict—probably glitter fiends or dustheads, though my uncle had kept me away from those sorts, so I couldn't be sure what their drug of choice was—but I ignored them all. So it went for a little more than an hour until, finally, I reached familiar territory.

I reached the head of an alley and looked back and forth before crossing the broad street. It was the edge of the Garden, so there were a lot more cars and bikes on the road—all with angular designs and going almost too fast to track with the naked eye. Again, I had to rip my thoughts away from the bike I planned to get the moment I turned sixteen, got my implant, and saved up enough money. I didn't think Turk or his mooks, if they had survived the infighting, would still be on my tail, but they weren't the only people to worry about. Nova City was full of dangers, especially for those of us who hadn't gotten our implants. It was one of the reasons my uncle had kept me locked away at the top of our megabuilding for most of my life.

But that would change soon for me. I was only a few days away from turning sixteen, which meant I could report to the public Confluence and get an implant. It wouldn't be top-of-the-line, but anything was better than nothing. Besides, maybe I'd get lucky and make it into one of the specialty programs. Or perhaps I could even become one of the mysterious and powerful Templars.

I almost chuckled at the thought. Me? A Templar? No chance there.

After waiting for an opening, I darted across the street and into another alley on the other side. Back on my home turf, I didn't even have to think as I traversed the twisting turns. The buildings here were a little smaller, but they were constructed of the same sturdy concrete as the rest of the city. Sure, in places like King's Row, the concrete was usually decorated with fanciful facades, but those weren't for the likes of me to even look upon. I'd only been in that vaunted district a single time, but even that small taste was enough to tell me that I didn't belong.

"Fancy assholes," I muttered, eyeing a nearby drainage grate. I crossed the alley and, with a heave, levered it out of the way. Then, I climbed inside before pulling it back into place behind me. My ribs twinged at the motion, but it wasn't too bad. Perhaps I'd avoided breaking anything, after all. I dropped down into the tunnel; it didn't smell great, but it was still better than whatever I'd fallen into earlier. Or maybe I was just used to it by now.

My feet splashed in the shallow stream of water at the bottom of the tunnel as I walked the familiar path back to my home away from home. Ever since I'd run away a month before, I'd been living beneath the city, and it had begun to feel more and more comfortable with every passing day. Sure, it wasn't luxurious, and it was a pain in the ass to get to, but that wasn't so bad—especially considering the alternative.

It took me about half an hour to reach my destination, and when I did, I relaxed at the familiar sight. At one point, it had been a cistern, but for whatever reason, it had been bypassed, resulting in a dry chamber. The decor wasn't much to look at, either. Just an old discarded couch, a few boxes, and a nano-generator I'd found on one of my infrequent treasure hunts. But with power, somewhere to sleep, and blessed solitude, it was enough.

Of course, the moment I stepped into my humble abode, I knew that I'd lost one of those things. I wasn't alone. Worse, I knew precisely who'd found me.

I glanced into the corner, saying, "Hey, Uncle Jeremiah. Long time, no see."

I couldn't see him, but I still knew he was there. Call it intuition. Or maybe there was some subtle shift in the air, a smell, or a sound I'd subconsciously cataloged. I have no idea. It was probably just as likely that I was talking to an empty room. But every instinct I had screamed at me that someone was nestled in those shadows. That it was him was just the most logical guess. After all, who else could find me down here? Who else would want to?

A soft chuckle came from the shadows, confirming my suspicions. Then, my uncle—or great-great-uncle, I suppose, but who's really counting these days?—emerged. He looked no older than fifty, with a shiny bald head, full black beard, and a build that suggested athleticism. Like me, he had dark skin, full lips, and lively eyes. He wore a black tank top, loose faux-leather pants, and a coat that dangled down to midcalf.

"You smell like shit," he said. "But at least you haven't forgotten everything I taught you."

"Nice to see you, too," I muttered. Then, under my breath, I added, "Asshole."

CHAPTER TWO

BACK TO REALITY

We fought so hard to survive the Initialization, so when we finally reached equilibrium with our new and far more dangerous world, we thought we'd won a great victory. In reality, the fight had yet to even begin.

—Jeremiah Braddock III

"Don't try to run off," my uncle said, reading my intentions like a book. When your guardian is a man who borders on the omniscient, it makes it difficult to get away with anything. "You won't make it."

"I wasn't going to," I lied. There was a part of me that thought I was close enough to the exit to get away, but that thought lasted only a moment before it was completely destroyed by reality. My uncle, for all I'd grown to resent him, was a Tier 5, and a well-developed one at that. I wouldn't even make it one step before he closed the gap, and that was being generous. There was a reason he practically ruled the Garden, and it definitely wasn't because of his sparkling personality.

He smiled, the expression never touching his eyes. How long had it been since I'd seen him genuinely happy? Years, certainly. Maybe not since before my parents had died, leaving me in my uncle's care. My mother's death had hit him almost as hard as it had hit me, and that was saying something. Since then, he'd tried to take care of me as best he could, but he'd never been the fatherly type. Usually, his parenting strategy boiled down to locking me in the apartment at the top of our megabuilding and keeping me busy with games, entertainment streams, or training. Or taking me to the range, where he'd throw constant criticism at my shooting form.

"It's time for you to come home," he said, sitting on my ratty couch. He ran his finger over the faux-leather. "Why did you choose this spot to set up shop?"

I chose to ignore the question. "I'm doing just fine on my own," I said—another lie. I'd already lost almost ten pounds since running away—ten pounds that I really couldn't afford to lose. It wasn't that I didn't know how to survive; rather, it was more that survival without skills was incredibly difficult to pull off. Even the poorest among the citizenry had some means of contributing. For my part, I could only steal what I needed, and even that was harder than it should have been. Anything worth stealing was worth paying a couple of thugs to guard, hence my recent brush with Turk and his subordinate mooks.

"Maybe," my uncle allowed. He stepped forward, and in only an instant, he'd covered the ground between us—at least fifteen feet. He gripped my thin arm and inspected it. With a derisive tone, he said, "Maybe not."

My uncle was Tier 5, but that by itself wasn't a guarantee of power. I wasn't exactly sure how it all worked. Being Unawakened, nobody had bothered to explain it to me. However, I knew that a person's tier was only an indicator of their potential. Without the right skills or training, it would be useless. Jeremiah wasn't like that. He was just as dangerous and powerful as his lofty tier might suggest.

I tried to jerk away, but he held on to my arm with a viselike grip. It wasn't like Turk's, which was aided by a cybernetic. As far as I knew, my uncle only had a couple of implants—optics, an arsenal implant, and a skeletal enhancement that made his bones almost unbreakable—so his grip was powered almost entirely by his own stats.

Jeremiah looked down at the package I was still clutching to my chest. It was just a box, though its logo doubtless told him that it wasn't something I'd just found in one of the alleys. "What did you take? And more importantly, who'd you take it from?" he asked, ripping the box out of my hands.

"That's mine!" I protested, but what was I going to do? If he wanted something of mine, he was going to get it. I just wasn't strong enough for it to be otherwise.

"And now it's mine," he said, letting me go. I knew better than to challenge him. He wouldn't hurt me—not permanently—but I wasn't eager to learn another lesson in dominance. I'd been on the receiving end of plenty of those, and I wasn't prepared to endure yet another. "What did you steal, I wonder? Let's see."

I held my breath as he ripped off the top of the box, revealing the contents. For a moment, a look of confusion crossed his face. Then, he smiled—this time, it was a genuine expression of amusement. He looked up at me as he retrieved my prize from its box. He raised a heavy eyebrow, saying, "Really? A pair of boots?"

My heart sank into my stomach. I knew good and well that I'd been stupid to target the boots, especially when my efforts would have been better directed at getting food or some other necessity. But in my defense, these weren't just any boots. They were *the* boots. Almost knee-high, and with a chunky heel, they were made of black leather and covered in a wide range of straps and buckles. Highlighting the black leather were splashes of neon green—my favorite color.

I'd wanted them from the very moment I had found them, and I was willing to risk just about anything to get them. So, I'd hatched a plan to set up a distraction in Farooq's store while I snuck in the back and snatched them right out from under his nose. It was only because I tripped on my way out that he'd even known I was there, but the moment he saw me with the box, he'd sent his goons after me.

"Tell me how you got them," he said. "Walk me through it."

I groaned, rolling my eyes. He didn't care that I'd stolen them. Jeremiah wasn't too keen on obeying laws. No one was, really. So long as the city didn't erupt into a war zone, the powers that be wouldn't descend from their ivory towers in wealthy districts like King's Row or Lakeview. As far as they were concerned, everyone could fend for themselves. If they weren't strong enough to protect their interests, then they didn't deserve them. And Uncle Jeremiah was a perfect example of the kind of man who thrived in such circumstances.

After sighing, I told him how I'd set up a pair of harmless bombs—little more than noise, really—to distract Farooq's and his goons' attention. Then, I recounted how I'd snuck in through a vent on the roof, found my quarry, and snatched it. He frowned when I admitted to tripping and alerting Farooq, but he actually seemed proud that I'd managed to escape from a known Tier 3 and whatever Pegleg and Vanilla were.

"You know what you did wrong, don't you?" he said.

I nodded. "I tripped, and—"

"No. You went wrong the moment you decided to target someone stronger than you," he said. "Farooq recognized you. So did Turk. Tell me—what are you going to do about it? They won't let this lie."

"You could—"

"I've already taken care of it," he said with a sigh. Showing the first real sign of humanity, he ran his hand over his bald head, saying, "I swear to God—you're more trouble than you're worth sometimes. Your real sin is not having enough power. I don't care that you tried to steal from Farooq. He's an asshole, and he probably should have been put in his place a long time ago. But listen to me, Mirabelle. You can't go through life without power. Not now, and not with what's coming."

"What are you talking about?" I asked. "And don't use my full name like that. It sounds wrong."

I hated my name, which was why I went by the shortened version. Mira sounded so much better than Mirabelle. Jeremiah didn't agree, probably because

I was named after his sister, my great-times-however-many-grandmother. He didn't care about many people, but family had always been incredibly important to him.

"You're not going in for the public evaluation," he said. "I've set everything up. Now, gather whatever you can't live without. We're going home. I've got a lot to tell you and not much time to do it."

"W-what?" I asked, surprised. "But everybody goes."

That wasn't an exaggeration, either. Literally everyone went in for the public evaluation before being assigned a Nexus Implant at the Confluence. Some people came out higher-tiered than others, but that was just a natural expression of someone's innate power.

"Not everyone," he stated.

I narrowed my eyes in annoyance. It would have been so much easier if he'd just explained everything to me.. But no—according to him, that wasn't possible. If he revealed too much, he would be sanctioned by the system. Then, suddenly, a thought came to mind.

"Are you a Templar?!" I blurted, putting it all together. Jeremiah was one of the strongest men in Nova City, and what's more, nobody ever messed with him. On top of that, I knew that Templars didn't have Nexus Implants. I wasn't sure how it worked, but they were definitely superhuman, even when compared to Tier 3 people like Turk. It made so much sense that Jeremiah would be one of them, and the moment that thought crossed my mind, I knew it was true. More than that, I just knew he was going to turn me into one, as well.

My hopes were dashed when he erupted into a great guffaw of laughter. Jeremiah didn't often show any emotions other than anger, annoyance, or stoic patience, so the outburst took me by surprise.

"Me . . . a Templar . . . oh, that's a good one," he said, dramatically gasping for breath as he slapped his knee. He wiped a tear from his eye, adding, "That made my day, Mirabelle. Really. Thank you for that. It almost makes up for what you did."

"Glad I could amuse you," I muttered.

He stood, saying, "Come on. We've got a lot to do."

"Wait!" I said, reaching out to grab his arm. I missed because of course I did—if he didn't want to be grabbed, he wouldn't be. "Please. Can I show you why I moved to this spot?"

He sighed. "Fine," Jeremiah said. "But then we head back. No more questions until we get home, either. There are ears everywhere."

"Oookay," I said, rolling my eyes. "C'mon."

With that, I took off back the way I had come. I didn't bother slowing my pace; Jeremiah could keep up without even trying, and despite having lived down here for a while, I couldn't ignore how disgusting it sometimes was. The water wasn't that bad, even if it was a little dirty. But everything else about it was, as Jeremiah had said, disgusting. First, there was the ubiquitous scum that coated everything. I wasn't sure if it was algae, fungus, or something inorganic, but I did know I didn't like it because, well, who would, right? It was just green-brown gunk, with no redeeming qualities. Then, there were the occasional carcasses. I'd only ever seen one human body down here, but there were plenty of animals—mostly birds and various reptiles—to make up for the lack. And where there were dead animals, there were live scavengers. Giant roaches the size of toddlers, rats just as big, and various other creepy-crawlies that made me glad I could shut my cistern off from the rest of the drainage tunnels.

Anyway—that's all to say that I didn't want to linger long, especially knowing that I would soon be topside and in the comfort of my uncle's place, which occupied an entire floor of the Garden's tallest megabuilding. But a housing project was still a housing project, right? Even the undisputed king of a place like the Garden was nothing to the real people in charge.

Finally, I closed in on my destination. I turned back to make sure that Jeremiah hadn't lagged behind, and predictably, he hadn't. He didn't even look like he'd gotten his feet wet. The asshole.

Grumbling, I continued on, turning a couple of times before finding a ladder that descended even farther. I climbed down without hesitation, and the moment I dropped into the next corridor, I was buffeted by a strong wind that carried with it a host of unfamiliar smells. After living in Nova for my whole life, I was used to the scents of the city. Human body odor, garbage, waste, and stagnant water mixed with the aromas of the food carts, the heady perfumes of so many of the women—and more than a few men, too—preferred, and the distinct smell of a hover car's Mist exhaust to give the city a unique odor. But the wind carried with it something else, something new. It was one of the reasons I loved the spot so much.

Without stopping, I strode down the tunnel, ever watchful for an aggressive insect. They weren't that common, but I'd found myself on the wrong end of a pair of pincers often enough that I didn't want to take any chances. Especially with Jeremiah there, watching my every move. Despite the fact that I knew he cared about me, I'd never been able to shake the feeling that he was always evaluating me, but for what, I had no idea. Given his cryptic words from earlier, I thought I might soon find out.

Eventually, we reached the spot that was my destination.

"I should have known" was Jeremiah's response.

I barely heard him as I looked through the metal grate and saw the world outside the city. The delta was far below, but the green vegetation and murky water seemed so mysterious to me. Often, I would come to this spot and just imagine exploring the swamp, having adventures, and seeing the world beyond

Nova's boundaries. It was a pipe dream, of course. Almost no one was allowed outside the city. But the world so far below had captured my imagination like nothing else ever had.

"There used to be a city down there, you know," he said, sitting next to the grate. I joined him. "New Orleans. Not directly below us. South of us. But it's almost all underwater now."

"I know," I said. Everyone knew at least that much, but few knew the whole story. "It was a tidal wave or something, right?"

"After the nano-cloud hit Earth, all our old technology quit working," he said. "Including the pumps and levies that kept the city from being flooded. At first, it was fine, but when the storms started coming, the city was lost. Until we built Nova City. Back then, it was just a single pylon. Now, it's one of the biggest cities in the world."

As I listened, I looked out at the environment; clearly visible were the city's support pillars—giant cylinders of nano-reinforced concrete that held Nova aloft. It was a necessity, given the nature of the environment below, but I still regretted that I would never get to experience true wilderness.

We sat there for a long time—an hour, at least. Neither of us said anything else. We just enjoyed the view. Or I did, at least. I never got tired of it. However, I got the feeling that Jeremiah was lost in thought; he was one of the few people still around who'd lived through the Initialization, and I knew he'd lost a lot of friends during that transitional period. Doubtless, he was thinking about the years of struggle he—and everyone else back then—had been forced to endure.

Finally, he let out a tired sigh, then said, "Okay. Playtime's over. Like I said before, we have a lot to talk about."

I mimicked his sigh—not my fault; I was raised by the man, so it was only natural that I'd pick up some of his mannerisms—and said, "Fine. Let's go home, then."

CHAPTER THREE

LESSONS LEARNED

I tried so hard, but we were all alone in the wilderness. Seventeen kids, me, and one other adult. None of them had even a semblance of survival training. Only me. I did everything I could to protect them, but the world had changed overnight. I had to become intimately familiar with failure. With loss. Otherwise, I would have gone insane.

—Jeremiah Braddock III

My uncle took the lead as we climbed through the drainage tunnels and back to the surface. Neither of us spoke because we didn't really need to. I'd spent so much time with Jeremiah that silence had become more comfortable than endless chatter. I had been living with him since my mother had died when I was only four years old, and so, he had come to fill that role for me. My father had lasted a couple more years than my mother, but he'd never really been interested in being a parent. Jeremiah was the only parent I really knew.

Not that I didn't sometimes hate him, of course. Like when he'd grounded me for getting my hair cut and dyed into a green mohawk; I'd been forced to spend an entire week at home, with no company or, more importantly, access to the cybernet. He already restricted my access, but to be cut off completely? It was beyond the pale. After that, he'd forced me to go to someone with a barber skill, and I'd had my hair returned to its former glory before long. Which is to say that it went back to being a mass of unruly black curls that seemed to defy my every attempt to corral it into some semblance of order.

"Took out your braids, huh?" he asked, his eyes scanning the area. Someone would have to be an idiot to attack Jeremiah, but Nova City had no shortage of morons who thought they were more powerful than they really were. And if Jeremiah was attacked by the wrong person, even he could fall. By force of habit, I mimicked his wariness; he'd drilled a certain paranoia into me, and one that my time on the streets had only enhanced.

I shrugged. "They started to stink" was my answer. An understatement if ever there was one. My curly hair—a feature that had come from my mother—might be unruly and uneven, but at least it was easy to clean. The same couldn't be said for the braids Jeremiah insisted I wear. Often, I dreamed of cutting it all off just to spite him.

Or maybe getting that mohawk again. That would be so cool.

He snorted, but he didn't say anything. He didn't have to, either. If I hadn't run away, I would have had all the tools to properly take care of my hair. Instead, I'd chosen to live in the sewers like a vagrant. It was no surprise, then, that I'd come to look and smell the part.

After a few minutes, we made our way to the main street. I ignored the concrete-and-steel monstrosities that were the surrounding buildings, unfazed by the ubiquitous neon signs and giant holographic billboards. Most were advertisements, hawking various products via sexually suggestive material. I was used to it, though, and I hardly even noticed the depictions of half-naked men or women slurping on the latest, greatest soft drinks or pushing some popular virtual reality experience on the cybernet.

Finally, he led me to a gleaming black hover car with chrome accents. It was all sharp angles and clean lines—an expensive machine that showed anyone who cared to look that Jeremiah was someone important. Of course, in King's Row, such vehicles were common to the point of mundanity; my uncle was rich, but to them, he was just another thug from the Garden. Stuck-up assholes, the lot of them, as far as I was concerned.

Hearing a buzz overhead, I glanced up to see a pair of drones whiz by. I shook my head in disgust. Despite ubiquitous surveillance, what passed for government in Nova City rarely utilized their power to instill law and order in places like the Garden. They only responded to the worst of the worst—when gunfights threatened the stability of the entire district's farming output, usually—ignoring the chaos in favor of sitting in their ivory towers and looking down on everyone who hadn't been born with a silver spoon.

Of course, given that I'd been raised by one of the most powerful men in the district, I didn't really have much room to talk. Still, I didn't go around imposing my will upon the masses, did I? I didn't walk around with my nose in the air, either. Not like them. I was just another girl from the Garden.

I thought back to a few years back when one of the council members deigned to descend upon us, coming down to the Garden to redistribute food that had been grown in one of the district's own silos. Back then, I had been so excited—someone from that side of the city was finally doing something to help. My nine-year-old self couldn't have been more wrong. It was all just a photo op. An effort to show that he was a man of the people.

Ostensibly, we had elections. And everyone voted, too. However, no matter how the people cast their votes, the same stooges kept getting elected. It was telling that everyone in the government was from the more upscale districts, like King's Row, Lakeview, or Uptown. Those of us in the Garden, Bywater, or, worse, Algiers, comprised the vast majority of the population, but none of our candidates ever got elected. It didn't take a genius to figure out that the fix was in and that the elections were a farce. Still, I'd been surprised to learn that such a ruse actually worked on most of the population. They thought they had a choice, and even believed the drivel that came out of those politicians' mouths. It was disgusting.

In any case, it wasn't as if the politicians had any real power, either. Sure, they managed the mundane, but the people in charge were more akin to my uncle than the pristine officials who spent their days arguing about taxation or managing trade with other cities. At the very top were the sorts of people who could, if they wanted, destroy the entire city and everyone in it. They were the ones who made Jeremiah look like a common thug in comparison.

Could he come out on top in a fight? Maybe. I had never really seen him fight, nor had I seen the legendary founders of the city in action. Or at all. They didn't come down to the Garden District, after all. But they also had armies of Tier 3 and 4 soldiers at their disposal, well trained and completely uncompromising. I had seen them before, and it was an experience I never wanted to repeat.

"You coming?" asked my uncle, sliding into the back seat of the car. "Or are you just going to stand there staring at a couple of drones all day?"

I jerked my attention from the sky and climbed into the hover car. The faux leather was luxurious and comfortable, and the back seat was spacious enough to swallow me whole. My uncle was a big man, and the car's interior had been tailored to fit him. Such was one of the benefits of being on top.

I remained silent as the car accelerated on its cushion of air. Or was it nanites? I knew that most of our technology ran on the microscopic machines we referred to as Mist, but like most people—especially those who had yet to receive a Nexus Implant—I'd never gotten any details. I'd tried, of course, but anything more than the most basic facts was thin on the ground. Perhaps I'd learn more when I got my own implant.

"Wait," I said, pressing my face against the window as I saw that we'd passed by the quickest route to the megabuilding that contained Jeremiah's penthouse. "Where are we going?"

"We've got a stop to make on the way," my uncle said. "And no, it's not optional, so don't complain."

I gave a dramatic sigh and slumped back against the seat. Crossing my arms, I settled down to wait. However, as I looked out the window, I couldn't help but notice familiar territory. My heart started beating faster as I recognized one landmark after another, and then, finally, when I saw Farooq's shop looming in the distance, I felt my insides twist into a thousand knots.

Farooq's business sported a holographic sign depicting a beautiful and mostly naked woman putting on a pair of high-heeled shoes. The name of the shop—Hot Heelz—kept appearing in cursive script beneath the woman. I hated the sign, but then again, it wasn't anything new. I was used to being bombarded by such depictions as they tried to convince me to part with my hard-earned credits.

Well, sort of hard-earned. Because I wasn't even integrated into the system yet, I was entirely dependent on Jeremiah to give me an allowance. But as soon as I got my Nexus Implant, my identity and account would be integrated into the implant. For now, though, I had to wear a Juvenile Account Bracelet that wouldn't be removed until I became an adult and received my Nexus Implant.

In any case, the car glided past Hot Heelz, and at first, I was relieved. I had gotten it into my head that Jeremiah was going to force me to return the boots and apologize to Farooq or something. However, my breath caught when we pulled to a stop half a block down the street, where I saw the results of my handiwork.

The concrete walls of the building sported marks of blackened soot that were in the process of being cleaned by the utility drones that were responsible for removing graffiti. Apparently, the evidence of my distraction qualified because they were hard at work spraying the walls clean. However, the soot marks weren't what drew my eyes. Instead, I stared at the bodies.

"What . . . w-what happened?" I muttered.

Seven corpses were lying in the street, riddled with massive bullet holes. Blood pooled on the ground, and bits and pieces of flesh decorated the sidewalk. The only concession the city had made to the grisly scene was to use holographic caution tape to warn people to go around.

That there were dead bodies on the street wasn't too surprising. If it was in King's Row or Lakeview, they would have been immediately disposed of, but the Garden wasn't exactly a priority. Eventually, someone would get around to it, but by then, the bodies would probably already be gone. Sometimes, the families of the deceased would claim the corpses, but usually, it fell to the scavengers to pick through the bodies for anything valuable. When they were finished, they would dump the bodies into the delta far below.

"That little bomb you set off drew the Enforcers," Jeremiah said.

My breath caught in my throat, and I felt like I was going to vomit. The Enforcers were, nominally, a peacekeeping force. They were what passed for law enforcement in Nova City. But instead of investigating and filing paperwork, they responded to any threat by swooping in with guns blazing, taking out criminals and victims alike. As extensions of the powerful elite, they didn't care about right or wrong. They only wanted to promote some semblance of order. And apparently, a tiny bomb—little more than a flash of light and a loud bang—was enough to get their attention.

"This is on you," he said. "Remember this scene. I want it burned into your brain. Actions have consequences, Mirabelle. You wanted something, and you chose to act. You probably thought your plan was perfect, that no one would get hurt. But sometimes, no matter how much you plan, innocent people are going to suffer."

I stared at the dead bodies, tears in my eyes. I was no stranger to death. It was part of life in Nova City. But I'd never directly caused anyone to die, and it didn't feel good.

"What do I do?" I asked, my voice barely more than a whisper. I wiped my eyes. "What can I do?"

"Nothing," Jeremiah said. Then, he handed me the box containing the boots, adding, "There. Seven people died so you could get these. It would be a shame if they went to waste. Make better choices next time."

Guiltily, I took the box. However, I wasn't as excited about the boots as I had been before. All I saw when I looked at the box was seven dead bodies. I knew I hadn't killed them, but I also knew that those people would still be alive if I hadn't stolen the boots. Or if I'd chosen a different distraction. Or made any number of other decisions. I hadn't pulled any triggers, but that didn't mean I wasn't at least partially responsible.

"The second lesson of the day is this," Jeremiah said, holding up two fingers. "You didn't kill anyone. They did. They created the world the way it is. You just made a mistake, and one you're not going to repeat. Remember who's really responsible."

"Who?" I asked. "I didn't have to—"

"Those assholes at the top," he growled. "They could have made Nova City into a utopia. They could have made this place a refuge. They had the means. Still do. But instead, at every turn, they've made choices based on selfishness. The rest of us are just trying to survive in the world they chose to create."

I didn't really agree with his assertion that I wasn't ultimately responsible. I didn't want to pass that off on someone else. However, I didn't argue because I really didn't know what to say.

After Jeremiah told the driver we were ready to move on, the hover car accelerated away from the scene of my crime, eventually looping around toward my uncle's penthouse in the heart of the Garden. The closer we came to the megabuilding that had been my home since I was four years old, the less prevalent the drones became. Eventually, they disappeared altogether, and with their lack of attention, the buildings that comprised the city became far more colorful, more decrepit, and populated by people in a wider variety of clothing. Graffiti decorated almost every cracked wall, and as I looked around, I couldn't help but feel a little jealous of the diversity of outfits on display.

There were four basic types of pedestrians walking in front of the building. First, there were the workers. Most were dressed in drab coveralls—or something similar—as they trekked back from their mundane jobs at one of the Garden's Silos or in one of Nova City's factories, most of which were in Algiers. One and all, they had that defeated—or maybe exhausted—look about them.

Second, there was the younger crowd. In many cases, they barely wore clothing at all. It didn't matter if they were male, female, or anything in between. Short shorts, tiny skirts, and tops that barely covered a person's chest were the norm. And in some odd cases, even that was too restrictive. No one went strictly nude, but there were quite a few that might as well have been. Even though I could never walk the streets like that, there was a part of me that envied them. But one facet of their appearance, above all others, drew my eye.

It was the hair.

It came in every color of the rainbow, and it seemed like the variety of styles didn't lag too far behind that lofty number. I almost let out a sigh. Most of those styles were completely out of my reach. My wild, tightly curled hair just wouldn't cooperate with a proper sidecut or hang down to my back in a glorious mane. Instead, it grew out rather than down and, without significant effort, would frequently decide to do its own thing as opposed to what I wanted it to do. That was why I usually wore it in braids, but as I'd told my uncle, life on the street hadn't given me many opportunities to clean them properly, so they'd quickly gained a pretty terrible aroma. I'd unraveled the braids, cleaned my hair in one of the public fountains, and then just let it roam, wild and free. The result was a giant ball of curly hair that was almost assuredly lopsided.

I told myself I didn't care, but with my return home, I was beginning to dread the looks of my uncle's hangers-on. Especially Heather, who tried to mother me at every opportunity. Of course, her hair was perfectly straight and enviably blonde, so she had no idea what it was like for me. I'd hated her from the very moment she moved into Jeremiah's apartment.

Was it rational? Nope. Not one bit. Still hated her.

In any case, there was a third type of person walking the streets, though I hardly paid attention to them because they were so uncommon. Dressed in cheap suits, they were the professionals. People who were trying to climb their way up to a more prosperous district. They eschewed the fashion so prevalent among the denizens of the Garden, favoring the styles you'd usually find in Uptown or Lakeview. Of course, the clothes were knockoffs, made of cheap materials by unskilled laborers in sweatshops. It made them look like they were wearing costumes. Or maybe it was just my own biases peeking through; I considered them bootlickers and traitors, and I wasn't the only one.

Finally, there was the fourth type of person, and those were far more familiar to me. The warriors. The fighters. The Operators. Like my uncle and his men, they wore practical clothes, though not without their own sense of style. Faux-leather jackets adorned with spikes, elbow pads, or chains were common, and they were usually paired with matching pants and heavy boots. Some of them had visible cybernetics, but others seemed entirely flesh and blood. Vanilla had taught me the error of assuming that just because I couldn't see a cybernetic enhancement didn't mean it wasn't there.

But it wasn't the way they were dressed that made these people stand out. Instead, it was the way they moved. All predatory grace that told anyone who knew anything that they could handle themselves. Most moved in groups of two or three, but every now and then, I'd see a lone wolf. Stupid, suicidal, or confident—those were the only reasons anyone traveled alone through the Garden. And sometimes, it was a combination of all three.

There was a parking structure connected to the megabuilding, and the driver directed the car up the ramp, twisting and turning until we finally reached the top. Once again, my stomach twisted when I saw a crowd of people waiting for us. Four were standing, and each of them carried some sort of firearm. I recognized a couple of them as my uncle's underlings, but the other two must have been new. Either way, I immediately dismissed them as unimportant, instead focusing on the other three.

Kneeling, two were fairly average sized, but one was quite a bit bigger. What's more, I didn't need to see Pegleg's cybernetic leg or Turk's creepy eyes to recognize who the captives were. And they were definitely prisoners, as noted by the Mist-infused shackles clasped around their wrists and ankles. They were made specifically for people who were Tier 2 or above, designed to siphon the power from the nanites that gave skills their power. The prisoners could still display superhuman strength, but that was what the guards were for, I suppose.

"What . . . w-what's going on?" I asked.

"Cleaning up your mess," my uncle said. And when the car pulled to a stop next to the men, he said, "Remember—actions have consequences. People know you. They know you're one of mine. And I can't allow anyone to attack my people without responding in kind."

He opened the door and got out. I followed without a word.

"Mr. Braddock, we didn't mean nothin' by—"

Jeremiah didn't allow any more begging, and in the space of an instant, a pistol appeared in his hand. Without a moment's hesitation, he aimed the weapon at Turk's head and pulled the trigger. A bright-blue bolt of energy erupted from the barrel, and a nanosecond later, Turk's head exploded. Blood splattered, and what was left of his head sizzled and smoked. Turk's lifeless body fell to the pavement with a thud.

With that, Pegleg and Vanilla tried to scramble away, but they only got a few inches before identical bolts of energy tore through their craniums. In the space of two seconds, there were three new corpses at the top of the parking structure.

"Erik, Nora—you two head over to Farooq's," he said. "He deserves reparations. I think two thousand each for the guards, a hundred for the boots, and five hundred for his trouble should do. Lacy and Brock, do something with these bodies."

"Yes, sir," said Nora—a strapping woman who bulged with almost as much muscle as any man I'd ever seen. And she liked to show it off, too, opting for a sleeveless leather jacket with spikes at the shoulders that left her thick arms on full display. Beneath that jacket was a top that covered little more than her breasts, leaving her impressive abdominal muscles bare. Finally, she had on a pair of fuchsia pants that looked like they'd been painted on. Despite her obvious femininity, she'd spent so much time in the gym that she could give just about any man a run for his money, at least in terms of raw musculature.

I'd always found it to be a bit much, but judging by the fact that she rarely spent a night alone—and almost never let one of those nights go by without a good deal of bragging about it later—some people must've found it attractive. As much as I hated to admit it, I wanted to be more like Heather—slim but athletic. It was too bad, then, that I ended up like neither. Instead, I was short and compact. Apparently, another feature I'd inherited from my mother. In any case, if Nora was happy with her bulging physique, who was I to judge?

Besides—I was a little too preoccupied with the fact that my uncle had just killed three men. And though they'd clearly had it out for me, I hadn't wanted them to die.

"Why?" I asked, glaring at Jeremiah.

"Because you are my niece," he said. "And nobody hunts my family. Even when they deserve it."

CHAPTER FOUR

THE GREAT LIE

We thought we were at war, and we mistakenly believed we had a chance. Little did we know that we'd already lost before the first shot had even been fired. Earth was never meant to win. The best we could do was survive.

—Jeremiah Braddock III

My uncle stepped away from the bodies, and I stared at the pool of their mingled blood in horror. Death in Nova City was not an uncommon sight. Even at the tender age of fifteen, I'd seen my fair share of dead bodies—my father's included in that number. Some were old and rotting in some out-of-the-way nook or cranny where the utility drones weren't programmed to look. Others were fresh, victims of the ubiquitous violence that seemed so commonplace in the city. But I'd never seen anyone executed so casually, and the event had hit me like a bag of bricks.

Nora reached out to knuckle my chin and push my mouth closed. "Not your fault," she said, her voice surprisingly high-pitched. She was my uncle's right-hand woman, so I'd known her for most of my life. "They knew better. They made their choices."

I shook my head, looking away. Tears gathered in my eyes, but I stubbornly refused to wipe them away as my thoughts dwelled on my actions. When I'd set out to steal the boots, it had felt like an adventure. Like a game. But now? A handful of people were dead, and it was all my fault. My uncle always talked about actions and consequences, but until that moment, I'd never really understood. Now, though, I'd seen firsthand the costs of acting without considering how it might affect other, innocent people.

Not that I considered Turk and his mooks to be innocent. Likely, they'd earned their deaths a hundred times over. But with me, they'd just been doing a job, and one they never could have expected to cost them their lives. It was a depressing end to equally depressing existences.

As I stood at the edge of the parking structure, I saw Nova City in all its glory. The sun had set, but the city had plenty of artificial sources of light. Not only were there holographic displays for every business, but there were enough streetlights that the city never really slept. Even in the middle of the night, traffic would barely wane. Such was life in Nova City. Everyone scurrying around, trying to make the best of a bad situation. The city wasn't fair. I had discovered that when I was orphaned, and for no other reason than because my parents had made a few bad decisions. It was kill or be killed, and I intended to survive.

I set my jaw, wiped the tears flowing down my cheeks, and turned back to Nora. By then, she'd already begun to bundle the bodies into a black sack, which she'd use to carry the corpses away. They'd eventually end up in the delta, forgotten by anyone that mattered.

"Do you need help?" I asked, squaring my shoulders. It was my mess, and it only made sense that I would help clean it up.

The muscular woman gave a harsh chuckle before saying, "Naw. I got this, peanut. Your uncle's expecting you."

It was only then that I realized that Jeremiah had disappeared from the parking structure. I knew he'd found his way to the penthouse that he called his home just as I knew that I'd better not tarry. He would put up with a lot—like me running away for a little while—but there were lines I just didn't want to cross. If he told me he wanted me to do something, I'd better do it, or else there would be consequences. And his punishments usually involved me spending weeks up to my waist in the foul-smelling muck that accumulated in the water-filtration system beneath his building. Ostensibly, he'd send me down there to help clean, but I knew that it was just meant to be unpleasant. How the actual workers stood it, I'd never know. Whatever the case, I wasn't going to keep him waiting.

Nodding at Nora, who had already gathered two of the corpses, I hurried across the parking structure and past a couple of old and rusty vehicles. It didn't take me long to find my way to the elevator that would take me to the top floor. I stepped inside, pulling the chain-link door closed behind me. Then, I slapped my hand on the control pad, saying, "Ninety-third floor."

"Identity confirmed," came a robotic voice. Then, the elevator shot up, rattling and clanging in all the wrong ways. Every time I used the elevator, I thought I was on the verge of plummeting to my death. I knew it was kept in good repair and that the sounds were meant to unnerve intruders and distract from the high-tech security system, but that didn't mean I was comfortable with it. I leaned against the wall, sighing as I glanced up at the twin domes in the ceiling. If the wrong person found themselves in the elevator, a pair of auto-turrets would descend and rip them to shreds. I'd seen the results, if only from a distance, and even the memory was enough to send a shiver up my spine.

Finally, the elevator slowed to a stop, and I saw the outer doors slide open to reveal my uncle's domain. It was both familiar and disconcerting, walking into the lobby. Calling it a penthouse was a bit of a misnomer, given that his personal living quarters only took up a very small portion of the floor. Instead, with how huge the megabuilding was, a single floor was enough to house his entire organization. Row upon row of domiciles, a massive conference room, a market with various shops, and lodgings for his trusted lieutenants were only the beginning, and the floor would've been better characterized as a small village. But then again, the megabuilding was home to at least a quarter of a million people, so that was really only a drop in the bucket.

Still, everything about the place screamed low-cost housing. The rooms were almost all exactly the same size, and without any real adornment. The ceilings were too low, the layout was uninspired, and the amenities were nearly nonexistent. Sure, individuals had the latest entertainment options, and there was even a brothel and a couple of bars. But everything was a little too tacky, with a bit too much gold, and far too many animal prints. Jeremiah called his people "ghetto rich," and I couldn't really argue with that assessment. Refined taste was the prerogative of the truly wealthy, not a bunch of Operators who courted death every time they left the building.

After traversing the floor's depressing corridors, I entered the apartment, closing the door behind me. Looking around, my shoulders slumped as I felt the tension I'd felt for the past couple of hours melt away. I was finally home. Even if I often rankled at my uncle's rules, I'd lived with him for years. He'd treated me well, and he had tried to make me feel welcome. It had worked, too.

"Go take a shower," came his unmistakably gravelly voice. I flinched. I hadn't even seen him in the doorway. "You stink. When you get done, come into the living room. There's a conversation we should have had months ago."

"Is it about my Nexus Implant?" I asked.

He grunted, "Take a shower."

Then, without another word, he strode off toward the communal area where he often met with his most trusted subordinates. Knowing I wouldn't get anything else out of him, I went in the other direction. Plus, now that I was home, I'd become well aware that he was probably being a bit generous by only saying that I stunk. In my defense, I'd been living in a glorified drainage pipe for the past couple of months. Down there, cleanliness wasn't exactly high on my list of priorities.

In a few seconds, I found my way to my bedroom, and when I passed through the door, I felt myself relax even more. Nothing had changed. My discarded clothes still decorated the floor, various holo-posters depicting my favorite bands were affixed to the wall, and a sizable bed dominated the relatively small room. The furnishings weren't enough to disguise the utilitarian concrete walls, but they definitely did some heavy lifting when it came to making it feel like my personal space. Resisting the urge to collapse onto the bed and wrap myself in the soft blankets, I made my way to the connected bathroom.

After stripping down, I looked at my dirty and stained clothing. Before I'd left—or run away, I guess—I'd chosen not to wear my best clothes. Even then, I had known I would be back. I had also known that being out on my own wouldn't be kind to my wardrobe. So, I'd chosen all my oldest stuff—a good decision because everything was ruined. I quickly threw them into the trash chute that would lead to the incinerator far below and stepped into the shower.

It was a while before I was satisfied with my cleanliness. I was far dirtier than even I had suspected, and there was plenty of grime in all the wrong sorts of places. Eventually, I managed the small feat of cleaning myself before stepping out of the shower. I dried off, then wiped my hand across the mirror. The reflection I saw was familiar, but I could see that my foray into independence had changed me.

For one, I was skinnier than I'd been in years. On the streets, I'd had to claw and scrape for every meal, and that showed. My ribs were clearly visible, my cheeks were hollow, and my eyes were sunken into their sockets. Even so, I knew that I was, at the very least, pretty. I'd gotten that from my mother, I think. I'd only seen a few pictures of her, but even those were enough to tell me that she'd been a beautiful woman.

Predictably, the biggest eyesore was my hair. I didn't hate it—not really. Jeremiah always told me to be proud of it, that it was part of my racial heritage, but I only saw it as a pain in the butt. Other girls could just run a comb through their silky hair, and they were fine. But me? I had to spend hours just to make it presentable.

Almost in protest, I left it wild. Anyone who didn't like it could go to hell.

After I brushed my teeth, I went back into my bedroom and got dressed. I chose a soft pair of pajama pants decorated with pink unicorns—my obsession with the mythical creatures was a holdover from my youth—and a teeshirt emblazoned with the logo of my favorite band, Leviathan. I'd gotten it at an underground show, and it was probably my favorite possession. Leaving it behind when I ran away had been one of the hardest things I'd had to do.

Once I was dressed, I gave in and tied my hair back into a giant poof, then padded down the hall and into the living room, where my uncle was waiting patiently. Regrettably, he wasn't alone.

"Ohmigawd!" exclaimed Heather, my uncle's blonde bimbo of a partner. She was tall and slim, and so top-heavy that she looked like she would topple over at the slightest breeze. And at that moment, she was clamoring toward me, arms outstretched. Before I knew it, she'd wrapped them around me, pressing my face into her surgically modified chest. Thankfully, the hug ended quickly, and she held me at arm's length, saying, "I've been worried out of my mind, young lady! Do you have any idea how dangerous it is out there for a pretty young girl like you? You're lucky someone didn't pick you up and force you to pick up a pleasure skill!"

"Ugh," I groaned, rolling my eyes. "I know how to avoid people like that. And nobody can force you to take skills, anyway. Those are choices."

She narrowed her eyes. "No. You're right. But they can make it the easiest choice you can make," she said, frowning. Her sudden change of expression was a good reminder that no one in Nova City had it easy. Clearly, she'd seen some terrible things, and I briefly regretted my insensitive comment. "Anyway, what's important is that you're safe."

"Let her breathe, Heather," Jeremiah said.

Heather cut her eyes at him, then made a scene of making sure I was okay. Only then did she back off, saying, "I'll leave you two to it, then."

When she'd left the room, I took a moment to look around. The communal area wasn't much different than those I'd passed along the way to my uncle's living quarters. The furniture was secondhand, but it was well-made and comfortable, and any decorations were, to my untrained eye, gaudy and a little tacky. That was Heather's influence because, left to his own devices, my uncle would have lived in a bare cement room not much better than a jail cell.

There was only one feature that had been there ever since I'd moved in. On one wall was a gun. A rifle, in fact. But it wasn't just any firearm. Instead, it was one of the most powerful sniper rifles from before the Initialization—a Barrett M82A1 50 BMG. I had no idea how it would stack up to the more modern nanotech guns, but it certainly looked deadly. That might have been due to me knowing its history, though. Everyone in Nova City—at least in the Garden—had heard about my uncle's exploits with that gun.

"Sit," he said. "It's story time."

"Uh . . . okay."

I sat on the overstuffed couch across from him and curled my bare feet under me. Once I was settled in, he began, "I know you know some of this, but don't interrupt. It's going to be difficult enough to get through this as it is."

"O-okay. Sure." He fixed me with a withering stare, and I realized I'd just done precisely what he'd asked me not to do. "Sorry. No more talking from me. Not a word."

He sighed. "You're so much like your mother," he muttered, shaking his head. After a second, he said, "Before the Initialization, I was a soldier. You know that, right?"

I nodded, and he jerked his head toward the gun on the wall. "That was my weapon," he said. "I was a sniper, and I was good at it, too. Twenty-three confirmed kills, which was a lot before things went to shit."

That didn't seem like so many to me. I knew of at least three Operators whose kill counts were triple that. But I didn't say anything. Instead, I continued to listen as my uncle went on, describing his life before the Initialization. I knew most of it. Back then, the world was different. It was freer. There was no Mist tech, and everything was more civilized and a good deal safer.

"I got hurt," he said. "Broke my back. I was lucky that I wasn't paralyzed. But my days in the army were done. So, I went home, and I wallowed in my own depression. I'd have probably stayed there, too, if it wasn't for Helena. She was another veteran, and she'd started this outreach program for underprivileged kids."

He sighed. "I thought I was in love with her for the longest time," he stated. "She's gone now, though." After a short pause, he added, "Everyone is."

Jeremiah was silent for a long moment, and I could only guess what was going through his mind. I didn't dare break the silence, though. My uncle, for all he cared about me, wasn't exactly an open book. He played his cards close to his chest, and he almost never talked about his past. It was one of those persistent mysteries that I'd long accepted as unsolvable. And now, it looked like I was going to get the whole story; I wouldn't do anything to mess that up.

"I decided to help out," he said. "I'd spent a lot of time surviving in the wilderness. Even before the army, I was always in the woods. Hunting. Fishing. Having BB gun fights with my friends."

"What about the monsters?" I asked. Nobody left Nova City. It was too unsafe. Even with my limited view in the drainage tunnels, I'd seen hulking monsters wading through the delta. Going out there was suicide.

He chuckled. "No monsters back then," he said. "We had gators and such, but it wasn't bad. Anyway, I took a group of kids up to a state park. It was a few hours away from where I lived, and most of these kids had never really been out of the city. It was supposed to help them reconnect with nature.

"How was I supposed to know that the Initialization would happen while we were out there? In the space of a couple of hours, everything changed," he said, his voice cracking with more emotion than I'd ever heard from him. "None of us knew what was going on. All I knew was that the animals were acting rabid, attacking without any provocation, and I had seventeen kids with me. And Helena."

I didn't know how to respond. I could hear the pain in his voice, so I could infer what had happened to these kids. Even ninety years after the Initialization, it was obviously still raw. I leaned forward, wavering between eagerness to learn more and dread concerning the inevitable next part of the story.

"We lost three kids in the first two days," Jeremiah said, his voice cracking as he tried to keep the emotion from his voice. "Two more a couple of days after that. Then, I found a gun store, and things got better. With a rifle, I could protect them. I thought. I was... I was wrong. It happened while I was out hunting. We'd been surviving on stuff from a vending machine, and I thought I could go out and find a deer. And I did. I had to range a bit farther from our base, but it was going to be worth it.

"When I came back, everything was gone," he went on. "The store was destroyed. The cars in the parking lot had been flattened. It was destruction on a level I hadn't seen since the war. And the kids were gone. Helena was gone."

He buried his head in his hands. "I don't talk about it," he mumbled. "I found bits and pieces of her, sliced apart with surgical precision. Someone had done it on purpose. They'd done it for fun. It took me a while to come to that conclusion, but eventually, it seemed like there was no other choice. I sat there for a few hours, not knowing what to do. I wanted to give in. I wanted to give up. Back then, I wasn't in the best mindset to begin with, and then this? I almost lost it. I almost just ended it, then and there."

Obviously, he hadn't. Otherwise, he wouldn't be sitting across from me telling the story. But I could feel the despair in his voice. After a few seconds, he started up again.

"I don't know when I saw the tracks," he said, shaking his head. "They were so obvious. They didn't even try to hide. And it only took a few minutes of studying the tracks for me to realize that they'd taken some of the kids with them. That, more than anything else, lit a fire under me. I tracked them for miles, and when I finally saw who'd attacked us, I was taken aback."

He looked me in the eyes. "Aliens," he said. "Later, I would discover that they were smugglers. They weren't supposed to be on a newly initialized planet. But where there are rules, there are ways to break them. And these assholes had done just that, setting up a mining operation and manning it with captured humans."

"W-what did they look like?" I asked. Everyone knew about aliens. Most of our technology had come from them.

"Big and purple," he said. "But they died just fine after a bullet to the brain. Over the next couple of weeks, I waged a guerrilla war against them, and eventually, I killed them all. I had no idea how lucky I was that they were low-tiered. Otherwise, the hunting rifle I'd found wouldn't have done a damned thing.

"Not that it mattered," he said. "The kids were dead."

I gasped. I'd hoped that he had saved them. "Why? You said they were using them as slaves," I said. Slavery was illegal in Nova City, but that didn't really stop it. Half the girls and boys on Bourbon Street were pleasure slaves, and nobody seemed to care.

"Not the kids," he said. "They were being prepared as sacrifices or subjects for an experiment, as far as I can tell. I don't know how it worked. All I know is that, after I killed all the aliens, I found a Confluence."

Nova City had a Confluence, and everyone knew that was where people got their Nexus Implants. It also provided access to the Intergalactic Bazaar, which was where humanity had obtained the advanced technology necessary to survive.

"It was a surprise, getting my Nexus Implant," he said, rubbing his neck. "Five skill slots. I didn't know how rare it was. Eventually, I would learn that most people got only one, and three made someone an elite. I had no idea how lucky I was. All I knew was that it gave me a chance to kill more of what I considered invaders.

"And I did. God, I did," he went on. "I picked up skills. I leveled. And I murdered any alien I found. There were a lot of them. It was only after I found my way here that I started to settle in. I helped build this city, hoping that it would be a bastion for humanity, but it was all a farce. The private war I'd been fighting had already been lost. The aliens, they propped up the people who could protect their eventual interests. I was down here, fighting tooth and nail to maintain our independence, and those assholes were up there, making backroom deals to sell out their entire species."

He looked up and smiled. "But it wasn't all for naught," he said. "After I killed one of the puppets, I stole this."

He held up a small, pink cube. I couldn't really see many details from where I was sitting, but there were seven distinct symbols on each side. "Is that what I think it is?" I asked.

"If you think it's a Tier 7 Nexus Implant," he said. "Then yes. Yes, it is."

CHAPTER FIVE

GIVE AND TAKE

Losing Helena nearly broke me. When it didn't, my grief was replaced by fury. After spending years in the military, I thought I had seen the depths to which a man could sink. I hadn't. Not until my rampage was through.

—Jeremiah Braddock III

I stared at the Nexus Implant, transfixed by the shimmering colors inside. Each of sides bore the same seven symbols, tiny but eminently clear. I had no idea what they meant, but in that moment, I felt a level of greed I'd never even considered. It was as if I'd spent my entire life rolling around in the back alleys of Algiers, all the while looking for my next hit of dust. And now, the biggest, most potent stash to have ever existed was sitting right in front of me. It was need on a level I'd never experienced.

"You want it," Jeremiah said. "I've seen that look before."

"W-what . . . what's going on?" I managed to croak. I reached out, slowly and with trembling fingers. I couldn't stop myself. And then, just as suddenly as it had appeared, it was gone. For a second, I wondered if it had just been a hallucination. Had it ever existed at all?

"Power," he said. "Pure and unadulterated. That's what that cube represents, and your body—or more accurately, the Mist that suffuses every single one of your cells—knows it. That craving is a natural by-product."

I didn't speak. Instead, I swallowed hard. It went down like a ragged ball of sandpaper, scraping its way along my throat and leaving it raw. My body felt like one giant, cramped muscle, and despite the climate-controlled penthouse, a sheen of sweat clung to my forehead. I didn't bother wiping it away.

"Where did it go?"

"Away," he said. "How does that make you feel?"

Like launching myself at him and ripping it away from wherever he'd stashed it, that was how I felt. But then realization washed over me like a bucket of cold water. In only a second, I clawed my way out of whatever state the cube had elicited.

"I knew you had a strong will," he said with a slight smirk. Leaning back on the couch, he said, "I'm glad. I'd have hated the alternative."

Once again, I swallowed hard. My uncle was a dangerous man who didn't need to resort to threats to get what he wanted. Usually, he just had to tell the truth. Most of the time, the implication was enough to set his enemies on the right path. I shivered, realizing that, in that moment, he was prepared to treat me like one of them.

"What was the alternative?" I asked, braving the answer I knew but didn't want to admit.

"I'd have had some cleaning up to do," he said. Then, with a sigh, he went on, "It was always going to be like that. One decision. That's the difference between life and death. If you'd have come after me, it would have told me everything I needed to know. If that was the case, I'd have had to move on. But I couldn't leave you behind like that. Not if you'd already proven how weak willed you were."

I nodded. It made sense. Maybe it wouldn't have in a more secure world, but in Nova City, that's how things worked. You didn't leave potential enemies behind. You couldn't. Otherwise, they might grow strong enough to realize that potential. People who were soft ended up in early graves. And Jeremiah, for all his faults, was not soft. No one would ever accuse him of that unforgivable sin.

"Do you know what a Tier 7 Nexus Implant means?" he asked.

I nodded. "Seven skills," I said.

"That's the least of it," he stated, shaking his head. His bushy black beard glistened in the room's artificial light, shining almost as prominently as his bald head. "I wanted to put all the information out there, to make it public knowledge. But I was overruled."

"By who?" I couldn't help but ask, wondering who could censure my uncle.

"People more powerful than me," he stated. "It's not important. The point is that, until right now, I couldn't tell you how everything worked. Now, with you on the verge of Awakening, I can."

"Okay?"

"Just an *okay*, huh?" he said. "Your mom was like that. She just took things and rolled with whatever life threw at her. I miss her."

In the years since he'd taken me in, Jeremiah hadn't spoken about my mother very much. And it didn't take a genius to figure out why. They had been close, and the mere mention of her made the loss all the more painful. In that respect, we were more alike than I wanted to admit. The result was that I only had a child's memories of the woman. Lately, though, he'd been mentioning her more and more. Curiously, he completely ignored my deceased father—we both knew why.

"It's not just the skills," he said. "Though they're the most important part, regardless of what people will tell you. A properly leveled skill will keep you alive long after your attributes have been overwhelmed."

"What are they? Attributes, I mean. I've heard the word, and I have an idea, but . . . well, nobody's ever told me."

"Right. I always forget," he said, running his hand over his shaved head. "Three pillars. That's what constitutes personal power in this world. One—skills. At first, they're extremely generalized, but with enough work, you can evolve them into terrifying weapons."

He held up two fingers, going on, "Two—attributes. Constitution, Mind, and Mist. The first determines your physical capabilities. The second, your mental. And the third, the strength of most abilities."

Even though it was all a bit alien to me, I could easily understand the first two. However, the third was another story. Mist was the label given to the nanites—microscopic machines—that suffused everything in our world. I had learned enough history to know that that hadn't always been the case. What my uncle called the Initialization was where it had all begun. But Mist was an attribute on par with Constitution and Mind, which meant that I had a much more difficult time envisioning what it meant. I said as much, which drew a chuckle from my uncle.

"That's because you haven't Awakened yet," he said. "But that's going to change soon. Provided you agree to my terms."

"Terms? What terms?" I asked, surprised that my uncle was treating our interaction like business. "We're family."

"That's why I'm not letting you go into this without knowing precisely what you're getting into, Mirabelle," he answered. "If you take that Implant, I need to know that you're going to use it right."

"Right? How?" was my next question, though I had an inclination of what he wanted. My uncle lived a violent life, and if, as a Tier 5, he was at the top of the heap, I could only imagine the heights a Tier 7 could reach. If I took it, he'd want me to be his thug. "I don't want to be your killer."

At that, he laughed, which only made me angry. I threw a pillow at him, hissing, "It's not funny! Why are you laughing?!"

He held up a hand, catching the fluffy projectile like it had been going in slow motion. He said, "Sorry. Sorry. You were just so earnest. And coming from you, with that face . . ."

"I hate you so much right now," I muttered, crossing my arms.

"I accept that," Jeremiah stated. "But here's the thing, kid. I've got killers. Lots of them. I don't need any more. What I want is a survivor."

"What does that even mean?"

"It means that the aliens are coming in ten years," he answered. "Ten short years, and everything about this world is going to change. We can't fight it because we've already lost. What I want from you, why I want to give this Implant to you, is because I don't want you to fall under their control. I want you free. But I won't waste this on you. If you're not going to agree to my terms, I'll give it to someone else. I won't hesitate to turn them into a weapon. I'll do it, then point them right at the aliens. They'll die. We'll fail. But at least we'll take a lot of those bastards with us. Or I can give it to you, and you'll have enough power to survive. To leave this place. To make a real life."

He sighed, running both of his hands over his head before saying, "It was supposed to be for your mom, but she wouldn't take it. She said she wanted a normal life. As if there's any such thing in this fucking city."

He left his regrets unsaid, but I felt them all the same. My mother had died in a robbery gone wrong. She'd owned a small seafood stall, and she'd barely made a modest living. But that didn't stop that unaffiliated mook from trying to take what little she had. My mother had cooperated, but the man was inexperienced, nervous, and in a hurry. He hadn't meant to kill her, but that didn't stop the bullet from destroying her face. We never even had the chance to bury her—the body mongers took her before anyone could arrive, leaving only a few bystanders to tell my uncle what had happened.

If she'd have taken that Tier 7 Implant, she never would have been reduced to serving artificial seafood in a forgotten Algiers market. And even if she had chosen that route, she'd have had the power to prevent her own death. Doubtless, Jeremiah blamed himself for not forcing the Implant on her.

Then and there, I decided that I wouldn't follow in her footsteps. My memories of my mother were hazy. Indistinct. I knew I'd loved her, and in a way only a child could feel for her parent. But having heard that she'd given up the means to protect herself, to prevent me from growing up without a mother? There was a cloud of resentment growing in my heart. It wouldn't allow me to follow her path. I wanted the power to choose my own fate.

"What do you want?" I asked.

"Commitment," he said. "I've been on this planet for over a century now. Most of it fighting. I know what it takes to create a survivor. I know what skills you'll need. And most importantly, I know how to train you to get the most out of them. So, you do what I say. You take the skills I tell you to take. You train without complaint. Do that, and I'll give you the kind of opportunity most people would slaughter entire cities to obtain."

I cocked my head to the side, feeling the giant poof of hair swaying slightly at the motion. Then, I asked, "What's the catch?"

He grinned. "I know what you're thinking," he said. "You think you understand what I'm saying. You don't. It's going to be the most difficult thing you've ever done. You're going to be tested in ways you can't even imagine. But I think the hardest part for you is going to be not having control. You don't like authority."

I couldn't really argue with that. But in my defense, Nova City—at least my version of it—didn't really cater to the sorts of people who followed rules. Sure, there were plenty of people—most of the population in fact—who couldn't wait to get up and go to work at some unforgiving factory or laboratory. But me? I'd been raised by the most terrifying killer in the Garden, a place where scary people practically grew in the Silos. The mere idea of being normal was enough to make me want to vomit. I'd have chosen to be a dust fiend before I submitted to that kind of mundane existence.

And I think Jeremiah knew it, too. Otherwise, he would never have offered me the opportunity.

"Promise me you won't steer me wrong, then," I said.

"What? No concerns about your safety? Not going to make me promise you I won't put you in danger?"

I shook my head. "If what you're saying is true, I don't think that's possible," I answered with a grim smile. "And even if it was, keeping me bundled up all safe and sound would kind of defeat the purpose. That wouldn't prepare me for anything, would it?"

Expressionless, he looked at me for a long moment before saying, "I think you understand. Okay. You get the Implant, then."

Without any more preamble, he held out his hand, and the cube appeared. But it wasn't alone. Accompanying the implant were seven shards of crystal, each identically cut but in different colors. Red, blue, yellow, green, orange, black, and white, all glittering with an inner light.

"What are those?" I asked.

"Skill crystals," he said. "If I'm going to give you a Tier 7 Implant, you might as well have the skills to go with it. Like I said before, though, these are very general. You'll have to work extremely hard to turn them into anything worthwhile."

"Uh . . . okay?"

"I see you don't understand," he said. "But that's fine. This will be much easier to explain once you have an interface. So, take the Implant and place it on the back of your neck. Right at the base of your skull."

I took the cube in my hand, and I was surprised to find that it was warm to the touch—almost like it generated its own heat. I stared at it for a few seconds, just basking in the feeling I got when I looked at it. It wasn't until my uncle snapped his fingers in front of my face that I jerked back to reality.

"Sorry," I muttered.

"It's okay" was his response. "I'd be a little surprised if it didn't do that to you."

I didn't ask him to elaborate because I knew what he meant. The cube called to me on a fundamental level, and anyone who could resist such a pull would be a frightening person indeed. Instead of commenting, I followed his directions and placed the cube at the base of my skull.

The moment the cube's carved surface hit my skin, my body went rigid. I could feel the cube melt in my hands before seeping through my very pores. It wasn't unpleasant or nearly as invasive as I might've expected, but it was an entirely alien sensation. If I could've moved, I would have jerked my hand away. As it was, though, I could only sit there like a statue as the Implant invaded my body.

A searing heat erupted on the back of my neck, but the only reaction I could manage was a sharp intake of breath. My eyes watered as the smell of burnt flesh filled the air, and a web of pure agony grew from the base of my skull. In an instant, it enveloped my entire body, burning its way through my very cells.

And then, just like it had begun, it stopped.

I collapsed onto my side before rolling down to the floor. There, I looked up at my uncle. He could have caught me. It would've been easy for someone who could move like him. But he hadn't. I couldn't help but think that it was a sign of things to come. No longer would he be there to catch me when I fell. I would have to endure the consequences of my actions, uncompromised by his influence.

I don't know how long I lay there. Minutes, maybe. But it could've been as long as an hour. All the while, Jeremiah stared at me, his expression as impassive as his demeanor was relaxed. Finally, my heartbeat slowed back to a pace approaching normality, and my muscles unclenched. When they did, I stretched them out, groaning at the feeling of cramps being unkinked.

"You took that better than I expected," he said, leaning forward. "How are you feeling?"

"Like a dust fiend who hasn't had a hit in a month," I muttered, jerking my way to a sitting position.

"Don't say shit like that," he said, his tone brooking no dissent. "You have no idea what you're talking about."

"I've seen plenty of dust fiends, and—"

"Those people are victims," he growled. "And you have no clue what they're going through. So, until you do—and I pray that you never will—just don't talk about it. Got me?"

"I get you."

"Good," Jeremiah said, relaxing a little. He still reminded me of a coiled sewer serpent. Seemingly relaxed, but ready to spring out of the refuse at a moment's notice. "Then, we can move on to skills. Don't open your interface until we're finished."

Then, he handed me the first skill crystal, saying, "This is a skill called [Cybernetic Interface]. It's the only skill you'll receive that will probably never change. It will grow, but it's almost impossible to evolve. Anyone you've seen that has combat cybernetics has to have this."

"Do you?" I asked.

He nodded, saying, "I do."

"But you don't have cybernetics," I said.

"You can't see mine" was his response. "Use the crystal the same way you used the Implant."

I did, and though it wasn't nearly as intense as the Implant, it was still painful. I endured it as stoically as I could manage, and when I was finished, he handed me the next crystal. This one was for the skill [Mistwalker]. When I asked what that meant, he explained that it was a method of infiltrating technological interfaces.

"Like hacking?" I asked. "In all those old movies?"

He groaned. "Sure," he said. "If that makes it easier for you to understand, just like that."

"But—"

"Life isn't a movie, Mirabelle," Jeremiah stated. "You're not going to be sitting in front of a keyboard and jabbing random keys. That skill will allow you to remotely access most systems, and that, combined with the right expertise, will get you into anything else. What you do when you're there is up to how you've advanced the skill. And your own individual ability."

"Oh. Okay," I said. Then, I absorbed the skill crystal.

The next few were pretty self-explanatory. [Firearms], [Close Quarters Combat], and [Stealth Operations] were absorbed, one after the other. I didn't receive any influx of knowledge, and I definitely didn't feel any stronger, so I wasn't even sure they were working. But when I mentioned that, I only got a glare from my uncle, so I left it off right there.

"What is [Combat Utility]?" I asked, holding the penultimate skill crystal—a red one. The final crystal was orange.

"It's very open-ended," he said. "At first, it'll help you with all sorts of things, but we want to push it into combat medicine or triage."

"You want me to become a doctor?" I asked.

He shook his head. "No, no—not a doctor," he explained. "Combat medic. You'll never be as good as an actual healer, but you'll have enough expertise to keep you alive until you find one. That's one of your most important skills."

I nodded. I could certainly see the benefit of such a skill, so I absorbed it without complaint. Finally, I got to the last skill, which Jeremiah had labeled [Spycraft].

"It's what's going to keep you from being taken advantage of until you're strong enough to keep everyone in line," he said. "It'll let you disguise your levels, your tier, and your skills. I've never seen it taken past the first grade, but it should synergize well with your [Stealth Operations] skill. I'm hoping it'll do the same with [Mistwalker], but I don't have much experience with that one."

As I absorbed the crystal, I thought about the collection of skills he'd given me. They all seemed useful, but more than that, I could see the totality of what my uncle wanted me to become. Versatile. Deadly. Useful. And when the need arose, invisible. It made sense, given that the goal was survival.

Once I'd finished absorbing the skill, my uncle grinned. "So, how does it feel to be the highest-tiered person I've ever met?" he asked.

"Uh . . . not that different from before," I said.

He laughed. "That won't last" was his response. "But here's something no one wants to admit—people, regardless of whether or not they're identical in terms of their levels or their tiers, are not equal. One Tier 3 is not the same as another Tier 3. Do you know why?"

"Skills?"

"In part," he said, nodding. "But it's also levels. Cybernetics, too. Then there are weapons. Armor. Bio-enhancers. But more than anything else, what sets people apart is their capacity for hard work. Are you ready for hard work?"

When I saw the malicious gleam in his eye, I couldn't help but swallow hard. Still, I was committed. What's more, I knew he would give me the best chance of gaining the power my mother had refused. So, gathering my courage, I said, "Yes. I'm ready."

CHAPTER SIX

THE BAZAAR

When I first obtained my Nexus Implant, I thought I had become a superhero like in the comics I read growing up. But strength is relative. When I realized that the rest of the universe had power on a level I couldn't even conceive, it put everything into perspective. That's when I realized that the war—if it ever even was that—was lost.

—Jeremiah Braddock III

I was a little annoyed when, after all that buildup, my uncle looked out the window, saw that night had truly fallen, and said, "We'll go in the morning. Get some rest."

"But..."

He cut my complaint off with a hard-edged glance, and I went silent. Even before I'd agreed to follow his guidance, he'd often employed the kind of look that felt like a slap in the face. Some people need physical violence to make a point. My uncle, though? He could do more with a shift of his eyes than most people could accomplish with both fists. Still, that didn't stop me from huffing in annoyance as I pushed myself to my feet and dragged my way back to my bedroom.

When I got there and the door slid shut behind me, I collapsed onto my bed. For quite some time, I'd been sleeping on a discarded old couch, so suddenly having a proper bed beneath me was a welcome change. However, I was too worked up to even think about sleeping. After all, my life had just changed. I'd expected that—everyone got a Nexus Implant at my age, and that didn't come without significantly altering your life—but I had not expected things to turn so dramatically. Suddenly, I started to come to terms with the fact that, in a single night, I'd become one of most powerful people in the city.

I was a Tier 7. Even my uncle couldn't claim that, and literally everyone was terrified of him. But then I started to wonder why I didn't feel any stronger. After all, I'd seen Tier 3s punch through brick walls, and I was more than twice as powerful as them now. Shouldn't I be able to do something similar, even without any significant training?

I was just gearing up to do something stupid in order to test out my new strength when there was a knock at my door. With a sigh, I said, "Open."

The door obeyed my verbal command, sliding into the wall to reveal Heather, who was standing there and holding a tray of food. A wide, blisteringly white smile decorated her face, and I could see that the tray contained all my favorites. Jambalaya, and judging by the smell, it wasn't the kind with clumps of soy in the shape of shrimp and sausage. It was the real stuff. There was also a pile of seasoned fries made from real potatoes. And a glass bottle containing dark, fizzing lime-flavored Nova Cola. It was jam-packed with artificial sweeteners, but it had always been my favorite drink.

"You hungry?" she asked.

I sighed. "Sure" was my response. I'd never liked Heather, but it wasn't really her fault. She'd never shown me anything but kindness, and she'd always made every effort to ingratiate herself to me. In the back of my mind, though, I knew it wasn't because she liked me or wanted to be my friend. I was important to Jeremiah, and despite looking like the kind of prototypical dumb, blonde bimbo you'd find hanging out in a high-end, Bourbon Street brothel, she was smart enough to know that we came as a package deal. If she pushed me into truly hating her—as opposed to simple annoyance—I could easily turn my uncle against her. She knew that, and so, she tried her best to make sure we got along.

We didn't. I'd made my dislike abundantly clear. But she still tried, and for that, she'd at least earned some modicum of respect. Not a lot, mind you, but enough that I didn't shove the tray back into her face. Plus, you know—real jambalaya. I couldn't waste something so precious.

So, predictably, I took the tray, and after sitting at my desk—which was covered in all sorts of stickers, most of which were logos of various bands I followed—I dug in. And it was just as delightful as I'd expected it to be. Whatever other faults she might have had, the woman could cook. Maybe that was why my uncle kept her around.

That thought came with a mental roll of my eyes as I glanced in her direction and saw her abundant . . . ah . . . assets, which were barely contained in a tight tank top and a pair of shorts. That was totally the reason. But who knew? Maybe he actually liked talking to her or something. Stranger things had happened.

"How are you doing? Getting settled back in?" she asked.

"Uh . . . sure," I said between mouthfuls of delicious jambalaya. I shoved a few fries into my mouth. "It's a lot more comfortable here than in the sewers. It's the rats and the sewer vipers, you know? Oh, and all the human waste, of course."

As I continued happily munching on the food, I saw Heather's face go even paler than usual. "Oh," she said. "That must have been horrible."

I shrugged. "I guess," I said. "But it all worked out."

She sat on the bed next to me, and for a moment, she was silent, fidgeting with her fingernails. Finally, after a few seconds, she said, "I'm sorry."

"For what?" I asked, mouth full of rice, shrimp, and sausage.

"For driving you away," she said. "I never meant to make you feel unwelcome. I've only ever wanted to be your friend. The whole time you were gone, I just . . . I hardly slept. I barely ate. I was so worried about you."

That's when I really looked at her, and what I saw wasn't nearly as pretty as I remembered. She was skinnier than she'd ever been, and I had a feeling that if she lifted her shirt, I would be able to see her ribs. More than that, there were dark circles beneath her eyes that no amount of makeup could conceal. She'd made an effort, but there was a definite limit to what modern cosmetics could do. Even her blonde hair had lost some of its luster.

"Shit," I muttered.

"What?"

I shook my head. "No, it's nothing," I said. "Just starting to realize that I'm the asshole in this situation."

"What? No!" she said, looking panicked. "I pushed too hard. It's my fault. I didn't . . . I didn't mean to push you away. I'm sorry. I knew it was too soon to talk to you about this. Stupid. I'm always so stupid."

If I hadn't felt bad before, I did after that little outburst. Suddenly, I saw my actions for what they were—the tantrum of a spoiled child. Sure, I'd felt justified at the time, but running away had been a stupid decision. A hundred horrible things could have happened, and as a result, the people who cared about me would suffer. I'd never even considered how my actions would affect Jeremiah or Heather.

"Look," I said, reaching out to grip her hands. She was shaking. "You didn't do anything wrong, okay? It's me. I just wanted to . . . I don't know . . . everything here just felt so oppressive. And I needed to get away for a little while."

It really wasn't any more complicated than that. Sure, it had all started with an argument after Jeremiah refused to let me attend a Leviathan concert in Algiers, but that hadn't been the real issue. When I chose to run away, I'd only intended to do so for long enough to go to the concert. However, the freedom had gotten to me, and I had chosen to stay away for an extra day. One day turned into two, and two days turned into a week. Before long, I was living in that abandoned cistern and stealing so I could survive another day. Like that, I'd felt more alive than I ever had cooped up in my gilded cage.

"I just wanted to be free for a little bit," I said. "That's it. I just needed to get out on my own."

She looked up, and my heart broke when I saw the tears gathering around her blue eyes. "I thought it was me," she said. "You . . . y-you never liked me. I know that. I just . . . I never wanted to replace your mother or anything. I just wanted to be your friend. Like a sister. Or a cool aunt."

I gave her hands a squeeze. She really wasn't that much older than me. A decade seemed like a lot, but when compared to how old my uncle was, it was nothing. At that moment, it occurred to me that she was probably just as lonely as I ever was. After all, she left the building even less frequently than I ever had.

Heather wiped her eyes and sniffed loudly before saying, "I'm sorry. I didn't mean to put this kind of thing on you when you first got back. I know you're probably tired."

"Uh . . . yeah," I said. "It's . . . it's fine."

I didn't really know what else to say or, even if I did, how I was supposed to say it. So, after a few more awkward moments, she stood and left the room. I sat there, barely even remembering the food on my tray. I knew I needed to be better. In all the excitement, I'd forgotten the day's lesson. I needed to think about how my actions affected other people. Those innocents who'd been slaughtered by overzealous Enforcers. The three men my uncle had been forced to kill, lest the disrespect end up destabilizing his position and resulting in even more deaths. Heather, who had been so worried about me that she'd stopped eating or sleeping properly.

I'd thought I was an island, that my actions happened in a vacuum. But they didn't. Nobody's did. Often, they had unexpected consequences. And now that I was on the verge of attaining real power, I needed to think even more about the ripples of cause and effect.

As I went over it all in my head, I mechanically finished my meal. I barely tasted it, and when I was finished, I crawled into bed and fell asleep far more quickly than I could have anticipated. It felt like only a second passed before I awoke to a rough nudge on my shoulder. I looked up to see my uncle standing over me.

He said, "Up and at 'em. We've got a lot to do today."

I groaned, but I didn't argue. Instead, I threw off my synthetic-cotton blankets—Jeremiah refused to buy the real thing, calling such luxuries a waste of money—and sat up. Rubbing the sleep from my eyes, I murmured, "Like what?"

"We've got to get you kitted out," he said. "That means weapons and cybernetics. And to do that, we've got to go to the Bazaar. So, get up and get dressed. This should be an interesting day for you." He started to leave the room but stopped halfway out the door and said, "And eat something. I made eggs and grits. Real eggs, too."

"You had me at *eggs and grits*," was my grinning reply.

"That's literally everything I just . . . you know what? Whatever," he said. "Just hurry up."

As he left the room, the door slid shut behind him, and I pushed myself to my feet. After partaking of said breakfast—and savoring every last bite—I hopped in the shower, then got dressed. I chose a pair of synth-leather pants, ripped and torn in all sorts of interesting places, and a loose tank top that left a bit of my stomach bare. Over that, I wore a short synth-leather jacket, studded with metal rivets. Topping off the outfit were my new boots, as much for a sense of fashion as for the reminder that I needed to be wary of the consequences of my actions.

Finally, I was forced to do . . . something . . . with my hair. It wasn't that I was ashamed of it or anything. When everything went right, I loved it. But it was just that things rarely went right, and it ended up too frizzy, too big, or just too . . . everything. It was almost enough to make me regret getting rid of my braids.

After a lot of effort and way more fiddling than I wanted, I ended up just tying it back. Anything else would take too much time, and I was eager to experience the Bazaar. I'd heard stories about it—everyone had—but I was sure that actually experiencing what it had to offer was going to be far different than hearing a few stories.

What I did know was that it was the commercial hub of our entire world, where people bought and sold all sorts of interesting things. Without it, even the basic necessities would be out of reach—or that's what we'd learned in school. Based on my uncle's attitude, though, I had a sneaking suspicion that its usefulness in terms of the survival of everyday people had been exaggerated.

After I was finished dressing, I joined my uncle in the kitchen, where he was drinking a cup of coffee. He looked me up and down and just shook his head.

"What?" I asked, my hands on my hips as I geared up for an argument. "Something the matter with my clothes?"

He chuckled. "You're lucky you live in a climate-controlled city," he said.

"What's that mean?" I asked. "Everyone lives in the city."

"Even you don't believe that's true, do you?" he asked. "I know they pump you full of propaganda at that poor excuse for a school, but still . . . I thought you were more discerning than that. Maybe I'm giving you too much credit, though." He downed the last of his coffee, then set the cup aside as he said, "Let's go. Daylight's burning."

As I followed him out of the apartment and to the elevator, he made a point to stop and talk to everyone we passed. Most were just normal people—not even fighters—but he didn't care. To him, a local maintenance worker was just as important as one of the tribe's Operators, and Jeremiah wanted them to know how much he valued them. For my part, having seen the same thing a hundred times before, I was lost in my own thoughts. Specifically, I found myself wondering how much of what I'd learned in school I could actually trust.

My uncle had implied that it was all just propaganda, but that couldn't be true, could it? If so, someone would have said something. Jeremiah would have told me the truth, I felt sure. But looking back, was that really the case? He'd been restricted from telling me about how Nexus Implants and skills worked, so it was perfectly reasonable to expect there to have been other restrictions, as well. Whatever else I encountered, I needed to remember that I might be operating with incomplete or outright false information. Otherwise, I might end up making a fool of myself. Or worse.

Eventually, we made our way through the village-like top floor of our megabuilding and entered the elevator. It took us to the parking structure, where we quickly dismounted the elevator and went to the waiting car. Jeremiah had a whole fleet of vehicles, but he'd chosen the same sedan we'd taken the day before. After I slid into the back seat, my uncle joined me, and a moment later, we were off.

In the bright light of morning, the Garden looked different than it had the previous evening. Steam rose from the grates lining the sides of the street—the climate controllers hard at work—and there was a distinct lack of garishly dressed people. Instead, almost everyone—even the ones with wild hairstyles and multiple piercings—wore outfits appropriate for a day in the Silo or one of the factories in Algiers. It wasn't surprising. That was how almost everyone in the Garden earned a living. After all, they didn't have the advantages afforded to the people in other, wealthier districts. Or, I amended, the scions of a pseudocriminal empire.

Of course, the Operators were still a ubiquitous presence. I could see my uncle's people, the Specters, recognizable because of their predatory gaits and the bits of bright blue in their outfits. But there were other tribes represented, as well. The Bengals, with their purple and gold. The Hurricanes in green. The Cyberdogs, with their penchant for visible cybernetics. On and on it went; there were as many gangs and tribes within Nova City as there were buildings. And there were a lot of buildings, each one housing some group wanting to make a name for themselves as the city's next big thing. Most failed, and usually, explosively. But that didn't stop people from trying because the alternative was a life spent in drudgery.

Or worse, in a place like Bourbon Street. I'd never been there. Jeremiah wouldn't allow that. But I'd heard plenty of stories, and what I'd heard—even if it was exaggerated—made me want to avoid the place at all costs. But I had to admit that some of those stories made me curious, as well. I did my best to keep those feelings clamped down, though. The last thing I needed was for that kind of thing to drive my decision-making processes.

"You alright?" my uncle asked as the car skated through the streets on a cushion of Mist.

"I'm fine," I said, realizing that my cheeks were flushed just thinking about some of the things I'd heard about Bourbon Street. Or more appropriately, the people that made their living in the many, many brothels or clubs. "Just nervous, I guess."

"It's just the Bazaar," he said, completely misinterpreting my reaction. Thank God for that. I couldn't imagine being more embarrassed than if Jeremiah figured out what I'd been thinking. "You'll be fine. This is a good day. Remember that."

I nodded, but I remained silent as we traversed the city, eventually leaving the Garden and passing into Bywater. Finally, we reached our destination—a giant, circular behemoth of a building made of steel, glass, and concrete. It had a footprint to match any of the megabuildings, but at only a dozen stories tall, it was much shorter. Atop a glittering glass dome was a huge antenna that looked almost like a metal tree.

"The Dome," I muttered. It wasn't the first time I'd seen the building, but I'd never been inside. It occurred to me then that if Jeremiah hadn't given me the Tier 7 Nexus Implant, I'd have had to report to this building to receive something more mundane. Would I have qualified for something special? Or would I have been relegated to getting a Tier 2 or worse? If that had happened, would I have ended up as one of those dead-eyed pleasure slaves on Bourbon Street? Or maybe I would have been one of the mindless factory workers over in Algiers. I might have even ended up like my mother, a weak and nameless street vendor. My uncle had saved me from having to confront those possibilities, and for that, I would be eternally grateful. It only hardened my resolve to make sure he never regretted that gift.

"Come on," he said, sliding out of the back driver's-side door. I opened mine and joined him on the sidewalk, which abutted the huge concrete courtyard populated with various fountains and statues. Each one depicted a mythological deity. Zeus. Buddha. Athena. Thor. And a hundred others, all on their knees and with their arms stretched toward the sky in a welcoming posture. I heard Jeremiah mutter, "Propaganda. Fucking aliens."

"What?" I asked.

"Those are humanity's gods," he said, gesturing to the statues. "And they're practically worshipping the beings in the sky. That's what they want from us. When they come, they want us down on our knees and ready to worship them. Otherwise, they might have to work for their profits." He spat on the sidewalk, then added, "Come on. Quit gawking."

He practically dragged me through the courtyard and into one of the building's comparatively tiny entrances. I couldn't help but stare at the expansive, airy place, and I was reminded of the stories I'd heard of giant sports stadiums from the old world. Apparently, the Dome was a recreation of one of those stadiums, though I couldn't help but wonder how those comparatively unadvanced people had built such a structure. They hadn't even had Mist back then.

Finally, Jeremiah led me through the lobby, which was decorated with actual living plants, and to a hall that led into the interior of the building. There was a line, so we had to wait a few minutes before getting our turn. When we did, a bored-looking attendant took one look at us, and after Jeremiah explained that it was my first time, the woman scanned the both of us with a short, black wand before waving us through.

A few minutes, a dozen twists and turns, and a steadily rising heart rate saw us standing in front of a red-and-black obelisk. It was decorated with various carvings, the origin or meaning of which were a mystery to me, but Jeremiah didn't hesitate to place his hand on one. He said, "This is the Node that connects to the Confluence. It's how we're going to get to the Bazaar. Now, put your hand next to mine."

I did.

"And don't scream," he said.

I tried not to, but the moment the words left his mouth, I felt something snatch me around the middle and drag me away. A scream escaped my mouth, especially when I saw myself still standing there with my hand on the obelisk. Not that I had much time to study the scene because I was very quickly pulled up and out of the Dome and into the sky. A few seconds later, I was in the upper atmosphere, and only a few seconds after that, I crashed onto a polished floor.

I hadn't stopped screaming the entire time.

Jeremiah chuckled, and looking down at me, he said, "I thought I told you not to scream."

"I think I'm going to throw up," I muttered, rising to all fours.

"That'd be a neat trick, considering you don't have a physical body here," he said. "But I suppose you see new things every day. Welcome to the Bazaar. Now, get up. We've got a lot to get done, and I don't want to have to pay for an extra span of access."

CHAPTER SEVEN

EQUIPMENT EQUALS SURVIVAL

I've always thought of myself as a hard man. I was never entirely pitiless, but I could kill without much remorse. However, the moment I saw the myriad ways people had been taken advantage of after the Initialization, my heart wept. I've been fighting it ever since.

—Jeremiah Braddock III

For a second, I couldn't pull my eyes from the floor, which was made of some sort of dull-gray metal, though instead of a slick surface, it was subtly textured. Shaking my head, I blinked a few times as the nausea abated. Then, I finally raised my eyes. And what I saw was enough to elicit a gasp of surprise.

There were hundreds, if not thousands, of people around, and I could tell by some of the fashion choices that most of them had not originated in Nova City. A good number of them wore crisp suits with curiously high collars, and most had visible cybernetics. It made me feel self-conscious about my own clothing, let alone my uncle's long coat and apparent lack of mechanical parts.

"W-what . . ."

"This is the Bazaar," my uncle said, standing over me. I reached out to grab his hand, hoping to use him for leverage. However, when I did, my hand passed through his with a barely visible flicker of distortion. "Like I was trying to say, we're not really here. Your body is a projection."

"How?" I asked, looking around as I climbed to my feet. The word *room* seemed inadequate to describe the space. It was bigger than the entire Dome, and what's more, I could tell that it was only a smaller part of the whole. That's when I noticed the windows. Even as my uncle started to answer my question, I rushed away and pressed myself against the glass surface.

Outside was something I'd never expected to see. Earth loomed in front of me, blue and white with splotches of greens and browns. I gaped, unsure what to think.

"It's a satellite," I muttered.

My uncle had joined me, and with a smile I could hear in his voice, he said, "It is. A space station, actually. When I was much younger, this space was filled with lesser satellites. They governed communication, navigation, and everything else. But after the Initialization, they all went dead. The Bazaar replaced them. It's a space station the size of a city, and it's as close as the aliens are supposed to get to Earth, at least until the Integration in ten years."

"There are aliens here?" I asked, finally tearing my eyes from the view of Earth. I looked around, seeing nothing but strangely dressed humans. "Where?"

He laughed. "This is just an entry point," Jeremiah stated. "There are fourteen of them. The rest of the station is structured like a city, with residential pods for the aliens as well as more public spaces where we can conduct our business. Most people aren't aware, but there are also plenty of restricted areas where humans aren't allowed."

"What's in those areas?" I couldn't help but ask, though I didn't really expect an answer.

"No one knows," Jeremiah answered. "Weapons, maybe. Soldiers. Whatever they plan to send down there when the hundred years of Initialization are up. I don't think you're stupid enough to think it's anything good, though."

I glanced back through the window. Suddenly, the situation didn't seem so awe-inspiring. In fact, as reality set in, I felt a deep sense of dread. After all, if these aliens had the technology to build such a space station, then what chance did humanity have? How did you fight something like that?

"That look," my uncle said. "I know what you're thinking."

"You do?"

"Of course," was his response. "We're a lot alike, you and me, and my first time up here, I felt the same thing."

"And how did you get past it?" I asked.

"At first? Drinking," he stated. "Lots and lots of drinking. Then, a bunch of killing. Finally, acceptance. You're the result of that last part. I can't save humanity. Nobody can. Everyone down there is doomed. But I could save you. I can give you a chance to not only survive what's coming, but to forge a path to something better."

"Why, though? I've seen what people can do," I said. "If we all worked together, we could—"

"Look around you," he said, sweeping his arm around. "And tell me what you see."

I followed his gesture, and for a couple of minutes, I truly studied the crowd. At first, I didn't see much past my first impressions, but after a few moments, I started to see patterns. Each time one of the people in suits appeared, they'd head off toward one of the exits. Usually, along the way, they were joined by more of their kind.

"Who are the people in suits?" I asked.

"Corporate liaisons," he answered.

"Liaisons to who?"

"That's the answer," Jeremiah said. "The aliens, they couldn't legally set up shop down there." At the last, he pointed to Earth. "So, they made connections with powerful people. Most were rich before the Initialization, so they already had some infrastructure in place. But using the Mist, the alien technology, and good old-fashioned greed, they were able to create safe places for humanity. Nova City is one of those places."

"There was a price, wasn't there?"

"Of course," my uncle answered. "There's always a price, Mirabelle. Nothing comes for free. It was true in the old world, and it's even more true here. The aliens, they don't care about conquest. All they want is an increase in profits. So, as long as that's facilitated by their liaisons, they're content to just let things go the way they're going. The liaisons get their little slice of power, and the aliens get to exploit Earth and humanity for all they're worth."

He sighed, saying, "On one hand, we probably couldn't have survived without them. Or not nearly as many, at least. They're responsible for much of the technology that allows us to feed so many people. The great vertical farms that grow all the soy and corn, the drones we use to fish, and the factories that have put technology at every person's beck and call. But to do that, they've made slaves of humanity."

"What happens in ten years, though?" I asked. I didn't like the idea of a bunch of aliens exploiting humanity, but there didn't seem like there was much I could do about it. My uncle had hinted that he'd spent years—maybe even decades—fighting against them, and he'd made no real headway. But as bad as that situation was, it wasn't the end of the world. So, there had to be something else on tap.

"Clever girl," he said. "But you're not ready to know that yet. It would take hours to explain intergalactic politics, but suffice it to say that there are degrees of exploitation. On one side, there are the relatively benign aliens who run the Bazaar. So long as they get their resources, they're not going to hurt anyone more than absolutely necessary."

"And the other side?"

"Aliens who want to come in, strip-mine Earth, and take everything in one fell swoop," he said. "They won't care how many people are killed. They won't care if they leave an unlivable rock behind when they're gone. They'll come like locusts, consuming everything, then move on to the next planet when they're finished."

I narrowed my eyes. "What's a locust?" I asked.

He gave a grim chuckle. "All that, and you latch on to a bug," he said. "Locusts are insects that used to come in great swarms and ruin crops. I don't think they exist anymore. Lots of wildlife ended up like that. But you'll see."

I tried to ask more questions, but he cut me off, saying, "We only have a short time here. Let's go."

With that, he led me through the entry point, which was a strange experience. Even when I should've bumped into people, I just phased right through them. Most hardly seemed to notice, but some—usually ones wearing those strange, high-collared suits—glared at me when I got too close. One look at Jeremiah cut off any complaints, though. I wasn't sure whether they knew him or if they simply had enough experience to recognize a killer in their midst, but it was a bit funny to see indignation and anger turn to abject fear and a desire to be just about anywhere else. And I confess that, once I realized what was happening, I may have let myself drift into more than a few of them on purpose.

After all, Jeremiah's little speech had labeled them as enemies, and I was inclined to agree. At best, they were rich snobs like the ones that populated the more prosperous districts of Nova City. At worst, they were the sorts of people who would sell out their entire race for a little more power. Having a little fun at their expense was the least I could do.

But all good things must come to an end, and eventually, we made our way to the Bazaar proper. And it was a bit underwhelming, at first. It was a simple, though intimidatingly large hall with hundreds of room-sized boxes, stacked one atop the other, and there were lifts running between levels. The place was a far cry from what I'd expected, which was a space-age version of one of the markets back home, complete with fantastical aliens hawking their wares in colorful, open-air booths.

Jeremiah strode through the place with confidence, and I struggled to keep up—which, given that I didn't actually have a body, was a bit concerning. Shouldn't I be capable of any speed I could imagine? At least I didn't experience fatigue. In any case, it took us almost an hour of walking before we found our destination on the seventeenth level of a dense clump of cube-like rooms. On the door in front of us was an alien symbol, the likes of which I'd never seen.

My uncle banged on the door, and a second later, it slid open. That's when I blurted out the question that had been on my mind since the very beginning of our trek through the space station.

"Why can we touch the station itself? I thought we weren't really here," I said.

A rumbling laugh came from inside the shop, and I looked up to see the strangest creature I'd ever beheld. He mostly looked human, though his torso was a little too long, and his eyes were way too big. But what really set him apart was the fact that he had four arms. And three legs. Oh, and his skin tone was a deep burgundy. He wore a series of crisscrossed leather-looking straps across his chest and a pair of matching pants. His feet were also bare and looked more like talons than feet. Like I said—mostly human looking.

"She got all this way before asking?" the alien asked, his mouth moving completely independently of his actual words. "Next, you're going to tell me that you didn't tell her about the translation constructs."

Jeremiah rubbed the back of his neck, saying, "We were in a hurry."

Another booming laugh, and then the alien focused on me. "You are here," he said. "You're just comprised of Mist, which is contained by the station via a series of—"

"She doesn't need the details, Dexter," Jeremiah said. "Like I told you, we're in a hurry."

The alien looked disappointed, though given his strange appearance, I couldn't be sure. He recovered quickly, though, saying, "I suppose that's how it has to be, then. Come on in. I look forward to a day when you can come up here in person, old friend."

"Ten more years," Jeremiah said, leading me inside. The door slid shut behind us. "Which brings me to my niece. She's going to need an optical implant and an arsenal node."

"Budget?" the alien asked.

"Top of the line."

"Ho ho—big spender over here!" Dexter crowed, tilting his head back. He bent down to look me in the eyes, which was a distinctly unnerving experience.

"Uh . . . ever hear of personal space?" I asked, flinching away.

"Not in my line of work," Dexter stated. "Too bad I can't handle the installation. I hate leaving that up to you barbarians. Nothing for it, though."

"Just show me what you've got, Dex," Jeremiah said, rolling his hand.

Dexter went to the nearby wall, punching a series of buttons I hadn't originally seen. I wasn't even sure they'd been there before; aside from a chair and a counter, the shop had been entirely bare, as far as I could tell. That changed a second later when the walls came alive, shimmering as they revealed a series of machines. Or cybernetics. They looked strange when they weren't attached to someone, but I could recognize most of them easily enough.

He grabbed something off a nearby shelf and held it up. To me, it looked almost like a rubber sleeve, though I could see the intricate wires and circuits woven throughout the material.

"Mark Four Implant," Dexter said. "Hurk Munitions."

"Nothing from Adavant?" Jeremiah asked.

"Not unless you've got an S-grade clearance," Dexter stated. "You didn't become an admiral in the Adavant Alliance sometime within the last few weeks, did you? It feels like I would have heard about my good friend getting such an illustrious posting. Especially since Earth is quarantined right now."

Then, Jeremiah uttered the words that would make the difference in any negotiation. "Money is no object, Dex," he said. "I'll pay whatever you want. I know you have one. That's why I came here."

Dexter coughed. "No object, you say?" he said, recovering quickly. "I don't think you understand how risky moving something like an Adavant Arsenal Implant is in this climate."

"You heard what I said," Jeremiah stated. "You always ride me because I won't upgrade my implants. I haven't gotten anything for myself in almost thirty years. Do you know why?"

"Because you're cheap?"

"Because I've been saving," Jeremiah answered. "For this very moment. When I say I'm sparing no expense, I mean it. I want the best of everything you have."

"Seven million credits," Dexter said. "And I can't take a single—"

"Done," Jeremiah said.

"What?" Dexter said, clearly having expected Jeremiah to haggle. For my part, I just stood there, virtual mouth agape. Seven million credits. That was enough to set us up in King's Row, and with plenty left over. And it had bought only one implant.

"Better be some implant," I muttered.

"It is!" Dexter insisted, recovering himself. "It's the best spatial-storage implant available! Four quick-access weapon slots. Three upgradable storage nodes, each of which will contain up to three cubic meters of whatever it is you want to carry. It requires an access node to store or retrieve anything with significant mass, but that's true of any storage implant. Outside of the weapon slots, of course."

"Like I said—done," Jeremiah stated. "Now, what do you have for optics? Remember—I'm not interested in the cheap stuff you usually sell. Only the best. You know what I'm looking for. Combat HUD. Navigation. Interface assistance. Full-body integration. Everything a lone Operator might need."

"I don't have anything like that," Dexter admitted.

Jeremiah didn't blink before saying, "I suppose we're done here, then. I'll put the credits in escrow before I leave, and I expect the package to arrive before the end of the day."

He turned to leave, but the big, four-armed alien quickly rushed through the door to stand in front of him. "Wait!" he said, holding up all four hands. I was surprised to note that there were only four fingers on each of them. "Wait just a second. I get it, okay? I have a friend who deals in that kind of thing. Just come back inside, and we'll talk it out."

Jeremiah sighed. "Fine," he said, turning back around. Once everyone was back inside, the door slid shut once again. "What are you trying to sell me?"

"Kelek Infiltrator Optical Implant."

"What? A KIOI?" asked Jeremiah. "Where did you get one? Those aren't ... I mean, that's not publicly available technology."

Dexter grinned, and I saw that his teeth were jagged and sharp. I couldn't help but wonder how he managed not to cut his lips every time he spoke. "Like I said, I have a friend," he stated. "Owes me a favor. Let's just say he found it, okay?"

"In my world, they say that it fell off the back of a truck," Jeremiah said.

Dexter looked confused for a moment, but then he burst out laughing. "The translation construct tripped up a bit there," he said. "But I get it now." He shook his head. "Humans."

"How much, Dex?" Jeremiah asked.

"Seventeen million," Dexter said without any hesitation.

"That's a lot," Jeremiah responded. "More than any optical implant should cost, especially if it's hot."

"That's what it costs," Dexter said, but this time, there was a note of seriousness in his tone. I got the feeling that even if my uncle hadn't already shown his cards, there wouldn't have been any negotiation.

"Fine. Twenty-four total. Twenty-six if you can get everything to Earth's surface before the end of the day," Jeremiah said.

"I can."

"Then consider it a tip," my uncle added.

"Anything else I can do for you? Skeletal reinforcement? Claws? I have this spinal implant that can increase your speed and perception to such a degree that everyone else will look like they're moving in water. Bit tough on the nervous system, but ... well, it's a valuable trump card," Dexter went on. "I also have cloaking implants, subdermal armor, and—"

"She's only got room for two right now, Dex," Jeremiah said. "But once she levels up a bit, maybe we'll be back. Assuming she survives training."

"Here's hoping for your survival, then, young miss," Dexter said, looking me in the eyes again. "As unlikely as it probably is."

My uncle and Dexter exchanged only a few more words before we took our leave. Once we were a little away from the shop, I asked the question I'd held on to since Jeremiah had bought the arsenal implant. "How rich are you?" I asked.

"For decades after the Initialization, I went from one alien installation to the next, killing everyone and stealing anything that wasn't bolted down," he said. "I sold anything I didn't need, but I didn't spend any of the money. Not until Nova City was built, and I settled in. Even then, it was an investment. I know you've never taken much interest in what we do, but all those guns and Operators aren't just for show. Running the Garden is a business. And business has been good."

"Why didn't we move, then? I could have gone to one of those fancy schools in King's Row," I said. "Gotten a job in one of those labs where they—"

"And who do you think owns those labs?" Jeremiah asked. "Everything that happens there is tied to the aliens, and not one of the good ones like Dex who just wants to run his shop. When the Integration comes, those people are going to find out that they're no better than slaves. Even the liaisons. I don't want that for you, which is why we're here."

"I . . . I don't want that, either," I lied. It had always seemed like such a cushy life, living in King's Row or Lakeview and working in Uptown, but ultimately, it was one I'd never even considered to be attainable. Now that I knew the truth, I was glad that that kind of security had never been dangled in front of me. It would have been difficult leaving something like that behind, even when I knew what the end result would be. For a lot of people, comfortable slavery, especially when all you've ever known is luxury, was preferable to a life of freedom and hardship. Or that was what they wanted you to think, at least. For my part? I saw it for the trap it was.

Of course, I didn't really have that much room to talk about comfortable lifestyles. Compared to most people in the Garden, I was a veritable princess. I even lived in a tower. But that was going to change, according to my uncle, and if I was honest with myself, I had to admit that I couldn't wait for my grand adventure.

As we made our way through one block of cubical shops after another, my thoughts wandered. My uncle, for his part, kept his silence, clearly lost in thought. I didn't mind. Jeremiah had never been a big talker, and some of my fondest memories were when we'd simply let the silence stretch between us.

Finally, we reached our second destination, though aside from a series of glyphs on various plaques throughout the station, I couldn't tell one place from another. Luckily, Jeremiah could. We entered the next shop to find a burly minotaur, complete with sweeping horns and a bovine face. She—and judging by the stocky and muscular but undeniably feminine body, she was definitely female—had piercings in her eyebrows, ears, septum, and lip. But I only had eyes for the giant pistol on her hip. It looked like a revolver, if said revolver was made to fire actual rockets.

A high-pitched chuckle filled the room before the minotaur said, "Your little girl has good taste. I could sell you a hand cannon if you want. She's a bit scrawny to handle a weapon like that, but she might grow into it."

"Pass," Jeremiah said before I could voice my obvious desire to get my hands on just such a weapon. "How you doin', Gala?"

The minotaur woman shrugged her broad shoulders—she was showing them off by wearing a sleeveless vest that reminded me of Nora, my uncle's second-in-command. "You know how it is," she said. "Everybody wants to kill everybody else, so that's good for business."

"Any incidents?"

"The usual. The Chimeras are acting up again," she said. "But that's normal. They haven't eaten a world in a few years, so they're getting antsy. The Templars are keeping them in check, though."

The Templars. That was a designation I knew a little about. On Earth, Templars were mysterious warrior monks who habitually dressed all in white. They weren't common, but there was a temple in Uptown. I'd seen it a couple of times when I'd ventured into that district for one reason or another, but I'd never gotten close. As to the Templars themselves, I'd glimpsed one or two in my life, but I'd never been brave enough to get any closer than a couple of dozen yards. I wasn't sure if it was just superstition or if it was based in reality, but everyone said the Templars were different, that they wielded unnatural powers.

"Are these the same Templars we have on Earth?" I asked, my voice sounding small even in my own ears.

"Same organization," Jeremiah said. "Peacekeepers of the universe."

"Meddlers," Gala spat. "Always sticking their snouts where they don't belong."

Jeremiah shrugged. "Can't really argue with that," he said. "Nothing any of us can do about it, though."

"You can say that again," the minotaur woman said. "So—what can I do for you, Jeremiah? Don't tell me you lost her."

"Her?" I asked, giving my uncle the side-eye.

"She's fine," he said. "Rebecca is safe and sound back on Earth."

Gala narrowed her giant bovine eyes. "Better stay that way, too," she said. "I hate wasting good equipment on unreliable people."

"I'm so confused," I admitted. I thought I knew almost everything there was to know about my uncle, and I'd never even heard of anyone named Rebecca. "Who is Rebecca?"

"Rebecca is his rifle," Gala explained. "Silly name. Guns are clearly male. You can tell by the pseudophallic shape."

"Says the woman who named her sidearm after her first boyfriend," Jeremiah countered, rolling his eyes.

Gala patted the hand cannon at her side, saying, "Don't listen to him, Ferdinand. You're a beautiful boy with a perfect name."

"Uh . . ."

"Right," Jeremiah said, noticing my discomfort and confusion. I didn't think it was too strange that they named their guns. I mean, it was weird. No doubts there. But I was more confused by the fact that Gala's hand cannon had a name I recognized from Earth. Jeremiah didn't seem to find it as interesting as I did, though, because he immediately said, "We're looking to remedy Mirabelle's lack of firepower, Gala. I want four guns. All good quality, but appropriate for beginner to intermediate use. She's got the [Firearms] skill, but it's never been leveled."

"She knows how to shoot, though?" asked Gala.

"She does," Jeremiah said. Indeed, our megabuilding had a built-in firing range, and I'd been getting shooting lessons for years. "No practical experience, though."

"Skill should go up quickly, then," Gala said. "I recommend E-grade. It'll be a little much for her in the beginning, but she'll grow into it pretty quickly. Won't outgrow it for a while, either."

"I agree," Jeremiah said. "I need a rifle, a pistol, and a scattergun."

"Plasma, kinetic, or elemental?" Gala asked, leaning forward with her hands on the counter. The cubic shop was different from Dexter's in that its wares were clearly displayed. Some were even beneath the prominent counter separating Gala from her only two customers. I noted that the guns—mostly variations of pistols—were protected not by glass, but rather by an energy field.

"Kinetic for the rifle, plasma for the pistol, and whatever's most powerful for the scattergun," Jeremiah answered.

Gala nodded approvingly. "You're small and scrawny, but you do know your weapons," she said. "That's why I like you."

"I try," said Jeremiah, flashing a smile he rarely used, especially with strangers.

Gala went to one of the walls, selecting a rifle with a long barrel. It was constructed like any other assault rifle I'd ever seen—all sharp angles, and straight lines. Gala set it on the counter, saying, "Keugen Kinetic Rifle, E-grade. Or Kicker, which is what most people call it."

"Adjustable?"

"Of course," Gala said, picking the weapon up. She flicked a switch on the side, and the barrel extended an extra foot. A scope also folded out of the top. "Two modes. Sniper and assault. I've seen one of these boys take out a Kevorqian Rhaknar at thirty kilometers in sniper mode. One shot. Blew one of the thing's heads clean off. Assault mode packs less of a punch, but it makes up for it in rate of fire and maneuverability. Ninety-round magazine, upgradable to one twenty if you've got the skill to handle it."

"Good," said Jeremiah appreciatively. "Perfect starter weapon."

"Most people on your backwoods planet would consider this a peak weapon suitable only for seasoned warriors," Gala stated.

"We're not most people," Jeremiah said.

"Clearly" was Gala's response. Then, she went to another wall and retrieved a sleek pistol. Where the rifle had been all right angles, the pistol was shiny and curvy in all the wrong ways. "This is the Fortuin Pulse Pistol. I know it looks dainty, but—"

"No," I said before my brain could catch up to my mouth.

"Mirabelle."

"I don't like it," I said, doubling down. "It's too . . . I don't know . . ."

"She wants something big and beefy," Gala said. "Should've known. I wouldn't want that nickel-plated sissy pistol, either."

She went back to the wall and stood there for a few moments, her hands on her hips as she perused her wares. Finally, she said, "Aha! I knew I'd find the perfect one!"

Gala reached out and grabbed a weapon that looked remarkably similar to the hand cannon at her hip. It was much smaller, but it had the same revolver design. She slapped it on the counter, saying, "What do you think of this one, little girl? He looks like a Ferdinand Jr., doesn't he?"

"Uh . . . what's it do?"

"Whatever you need him to do, sweetheart," Gala said. Then, she picked the weapon back up and somehow removed the cannister. Holding it up, she said, "Adaptability. You can use any kind of round you want. Explosive. Kinetic. Stun. Plasma. You name it, this weapon can do it. Not as well as a weapon dedicated to that type of damage, but it makes up for it in versatility. That's why I love Ferdinand so much. He never lets me down."

Jeremiah, who'd been silent for a while, said, "You think it's the best tool for the job? I was thinking full plasma for the added punch. She's not going to focus on pistols."

"All the more reason for it to be versatile," Gala said. "She's not relying on it for primary damage, right? It's situational. Better to have a multi-tool, then. I'm assuming she's got an arsenal implant?"

Jeremiah nodded. "A good one, too."

"Then she's going to be able to carry plenty of ammo," Gala said. "That means she'll have a round for every occasion. A girl couldn't ask for a better accessory."

"Fine," Jeremiah said. "Not what I had planned, but it'll do. Throw in something more mundane so she can use it to skill up, yeah? And I'll leave it to you to choose the ammo. It's never been my thing, so I'd probably just be choosing at random."

Gala nodded. "Alright, so we still need a scattergun," she said. "We're looking for maximum stopping power here, aren't we?"

"Yeah. If anything gets close, she needs to be able to put it down in a hurry."

"No explosions?" Gala asked.

Jeremiah shook his head. "Close range," he reiterated.

"Elemental okay?" she asked. Jeremiah nodded. Gala immediately went to the back wall and chose a curious-looking gun. It was short and stubby, but with a barrel-like cannister attached to the bottom. She turned back and held it out for us to inspect. She said, "Macor Shock Gun. It was developed for riot suppression, but it was a little too lethal for their tastes. Turns out a billion volts of electricity is usually fatal unless someone's Tier 3 or better, and with some levels to back it up. And even if it doesn't kill, it interferes with the Mist and makes muscles spasm. You'd have to be a fully trained Tier 4 or 5 to come out of it completely unscathed. Not that there are more than two or three people on your whole planet that could be classified as fully trained. Present company excluded. Of course, for a novice, it won't be nearly so effective, but it's the kind of weapon that can grow with you."

"Perfect," Jeremiah said, nodding in approval.

"Anything else?"

"Blades," he said. "Nano edged. One long. Four short. Need an axe, too."

"No spears?"

Jeremiah shook his head. "No," he said.

"I've got just the right setup," Gala stated. "It wouldn't be up to snuff for a Quasani assassin, but for what I think you're looking for, the set should work for her. It's not cheap, though."

"It's fine."

"If you say so," Gala said. "Now—you said you needed four guns. Unless I miss my guess, you want her to follow in your footsteps?"

"I do."

"You think she can handle it?" Gala asked.

"She can" was Jeremiah's response. His tone brooked no disagreement.

"If you say so," Gala said. "Give me a second. I know what she needs."

Then, she turned to the back wall, and suddenly, a door appeared. It slid open, and she stepped through it. I couldn't see what was on the other side; instead, it was just a pervasive field of white light. A moment later, Gala returned holding a large and unadorned black case. She set it on the counter, and after Gala did something I couldn't see, the case flipped open. She wasted no time in pulling a weapon from inside.

I gasped because it was the most beautiful thing I had ever seen.

"What is it?" I asked.

"Pulsar Class Kinetic Sniper, D-grade," Jeremiah said. "Just like Rebecca."

"Rebecca's brother, maybe," Gala said with a smirk. "This strapping young man will punch a hole in a class-two combat drone from seven miles away. Farther, if you're on a big enough planet where the curvature doesn't mess with you too much. And that's with only enough skill to handle it, too." She looked at me and continued, "For someone like your uncle? You can double that."

"Uh..."

"Of course, you can't use it now," Gala said. "You could pull that trigger a thousand times, and it wouldn't do a damned thing. Call this an incentive. Train hard enough, and you can start using a real weapon."

"Is that one adjustable, too?" I asked.

She laughed. "I suppose for the right gunsmith, anything is adjustable," Gala stated. "But altering that weapon at all would be a damned shame. It's a masterpiece."

"It's a sniper rifle and a sniper rifle only, Mirabelle," my uncle stated.

"Oh."

"Look at that—she's actually disappointed!" Gala said. "Listen, little girl—versatility usually comes at a price, and in the case of a rifle, that's usually its lethality. The Keugen makes up for that by being a higher grade than you could normally use, but by the time you're of a level to use it properly, you're going to have to upgrade to more specialized equipment."

"We're almost out of time, Gala," Jeremiah said. "How much?"

"Two hundred for the lot."

Jeremiah winced. "I knew it would be expensive..."

"If that's too rich for your blood, we can always cut some corners," Gala said. "I've got a handsome little Eryanos rifle that will knock a few million off the—"

"No blood of mine is going to use trash like an Eryanos!" he growled. "You know good and well I'm going to pay. Just let me grumble a bit."

Gala grinned, displaying her flat teeth. "Grumble and groan all you want," she said. "More time for girl talk between me and Mirabelle." Then, leaning close, she said, "So, what are you going to name him? I suggest Ferdinand II. Or III, I guess. Either way, you can never go wrong with the classics."

"Uh... I... uh... I'll think about it?"

"That's what I like about you," Gala said. "You're very reasonable. Unlike that grump you call an uncle. Female guns." She snorted in derision. "As if, right?"

CHAPTER EIGHT

SECRETS

Money. Power. Influence. It's all the same thing, and its pursuit is the one constant across the entire universe. In that arena, humanity is a collection of amateurs.

—Jeremiah Braddock III

For a brief second, I was in two places at once. That disorienting feeling faded quickly, and I soon found myself pulling away from the pillar that had begun my journey into the Bazaar. For a long moment, I just stood there, my breath coming in short, shallow pants. Bending over, with my hands on my knees, I forced a long, deep breath, and over the next couple of seconds, pushed the panic from my mind.

"You did better than I did on my first time," came my uncle's voice. I looked up to see him grinning down at me. "I threw up. Of course, that might've been some bad meat. It was winter, so food was scarce, and I was eating whatever I could find."

"I feel like my brain is trying to go in two different directions," I muttered. "Is it always like that?"

"No," he said. "It'll get better as you level. Let's get back home. Hopefully, our packages will be waiting for us."

"That fast? How?"

I'd expected it to take a few days for our orders to be filled; Jeremiah had already paid, so that wouldn't be an issue, but it seemed to me like transporting something in from space should take a while. Apparently not.

"Teleportation" was his answer. "Or they call it rapid transference. It always seemed like a fancy way of saying *teleportation* to me, though. Anyway—it only works with inanimate objects, and it takes a ridiculous amount of Mist. But in this universe—and remember this because it's important—money can get you whatever you want. It cost twenty percent extra to get it sent to the roof of the building instead of to one of the designated transference centers, but that's a small price to pay if you're trying to fly under the radar."

"Oh," I said. "Okay, I guess."

After that, we wasted no time leaving the Dome. On the way out, we went a different way than how we'd entered, and I saw that the Dome was host to a wider variety of functions than I'd originally anticipated. Not only were there a multitude of human shops within the giant building, but there were also a few of the transference centers my uncle had mentioned. Of course, I wanted to stop and browse through the shops, but Jeremiah didn't want to waste the time. So, as usual, he was forced to endure my perusal of a couple of clothing boutiques. He even bought me a wicked pair of shorts, even though he complained that they were too revealing.

That was one thing I'd learned early on about Jeremiah. Even when I was little, he would do whatever he could to make me happy. Sure, he put on a gruff front, and I often felt like a prisoner in my own home, but I knew it was only because he wanted to keep me safe. And given how much money he'd just spent on my new weapons and cybernetics, I was starting to realize that my estimation of how much he cared about me was woefully inaccurate. He had just dropped a fortune on gearing me up.

After my miniature shopping spree, I asked, "Are there any cybernetic shops here?"

"A few," he stated, still pouting a bit about his schedule being thrown off. Or maybe he really did hate shopping as much as he pretended to. "But they're all shit. There are better ones in King's Row and Uptown, but they're still not as good as Dexter. It's the same with weapons. Humanity is rapidly improving, but ninety years isn't nearly long enough to catch up with the rest of the universe."

I wasn't so sure about that; ninety years seemed like a lot to me, but what did I know? My uncle was well over a hundred years old, and he looked like he was in his midforties. Obviously, aging worked a little differently when Mist was thrown into the mix. It was possible that some of the aliens out there were over a thousand years old. You could probably gain a lot of expertise in that kind of time.

We made our way back to the hover car, but we didn't really say much along the way. There was some idle small talk, but I was too distracted by our recent purchases to carry on a real conversation. Jeremiah didn't mind, and he seemed lost in his own thoughts—a common occurrence. One minute, he'd be making small talk with someone, and the next, he'd stare off into space, obviously thinking of something else entirely.

Finally, after a short trek through the city, the car pulled into our building's parking structure, and we headed toward the apartment. As always, my uncle made a point to talk to, reassure, and otherwise socialize with his people along the way. It was a special kind of torture for me. Not only was I completely disinterested in those people's lives, but I was also insanely eager to get started. After all, wasn't my life about to change? I was going to get real cybernetics. Real weapons. After spending so much time selecting my loadout, my stomach was twisting and turning in anticipation of actually using all my new toys.

Jeremiah didn't care, which meant that he soon found himself on the bad end of my most murderous glare. He didn't care about that, either, sadly enough. He was immune to my evil eye, the bastard.

Still, despite the many, many delays and detours, we eventually made it into the apartment. Just inside, I stopped as the door slid shut. My uncle, who'd kept going, turned back to me and asked, "What's going on? Something wrong?"

"No," I said. "I just . . . I don't know. It's silly and stupid, but I guess . . . I guess I just kind of expected things to be different. Dumb, right? The world hasn't changed. Just me."

After everything I'd learned over the past two days, the world just felt different. Like I'd finally opened my eyes after a lifetime of walking around in the dark. But that was just my mind playing tricks on me. Nothing was really any different. I just had a little more knowledge now. Never was that more apparent than when I laid eyes on the same boring apartment I'd known since I was a kid.

"Well, if you expected that after a little information, you're going to flip out when you finish your Awakening," he said.

"What do you mean? I thought I was already Awakened," I said, cocking my head to the side.

He shook his head. "Not until we hook up your optical implant," he said. "The KIOI is a lot more advanced than what newly Awakened usually get, but even the basic ones that don't require any skills to use end up completing the Awakening process by giving you access to your full interface."

"Okay? So, when's everything going to get here? And do we need, like, a cybernetic engineer to install it?" I asked, following him into the living room.

"Already taken care of," Jeremiah said, nodding to a series of metallic boxes in the center of the room. I have no idea how I'd missed them. "Those were brought down before we got here, and I've got a cybernetic engineer on the way from King's Row."

"Really? One of those fancy docs?" I asked. "How'd you get them to come all the way over here?"

"Like I said before, it's all about money," Jeremiah explained. "And a little intimidation, I suppose. Usually, one or the other is enough, but sometimes, you need a bit of both. Remember that."

I nodded, then went to my room to deposit my own more mundane purchases. I resisted the urge to try on my new shorts—they were made of some sort of synthetic and stretchy fabric, and they had glittering shards of neuroglass decorating the seams. The idea was that they could be programed to flash different colors based on my moods. Before my Awakening, wearing something like that hadn't been an option, but now that I was getting access to an interface? My fashion choices had just gotten infinitely more diverse.

But right then, clothes weren't the most important thing on my mind, so after tossing the bag on my bed, I went back into the living room, only to find that someone else had arrived in the short time I'd been in the back of the apartment.

The first word that came to mind when I looked at the newcomer was *prim*. Or maybe *pristine*. People in the Garden weren't exactly dirty. We took hygiene just as seriously as anyone else. But the district had a way of infecting people with its grime, giving us a very distinct look. This woman wasn't like that. Her face was impossibly clean, her skin perfectly clear, and her petite frame was wrapped in the latest upscale fashion. In theory, it was just a suit—a jacket, a nice blouse, and a knee-length skirt—but everything about it, from the material to the cut to the shoes that probably cost more than my entire wardrobe, screamed affluence.

And then there were her cybernetics. Glittering at her knuckles were exposed bits of metal, evidence that she had some sort of implant in her hands. Probably for extra control, I reasoned. Her eyes looked normal enough, but they were far too vivid of a blue to be natural. I could only imagine what they did.

Her only nod to aberrant—at least among her socioeconomic class—fashion was her jaw-length, perfectly straight hair, which was hot pink and streaked with white. It made for a striking contrast, and one for which I was fully on board. I would have to ask her where she had her hair done.

Equally striking was the contrast between her and the woman behind her. At first, I hadn't seen Nora, as strange as that might seem, considering her hulking frame and loud fashion sense, but I'd been too focused on the woman who I realized was obviously the cybernetic engineer.

"I do not usually work under such conditions, Mr. Braddock," said the surgeon. Her voice was lower pitched than I expected—almost husky. "You realize that my—"

"We won't be doing the procedures here," Jeremiah said, the interruption obviously irritating to the woman. "Relax, doc."

"My name is Dr. Cirilla Montague."

"Yeah, I'm not calling you any of that," Jeremiah said.

"It is a mouthful," agreed Nora. "Speaking of mouths, the offer still stands, cupcake."

Montague cut her eyes at Nora, looking at her in disgust. Not because she was a woman, I reasoned. Nobody cared about that kind of thing. People liked what they liked, and trying to change that was an exercise in futility that only resulted in resentment. Instead, I got the feeling that Montague considered Nora to be something of a lower life-form. Or that's how I interpreted the way she looked at my uncle's right-hand woman, at least.

"Reel it in, Nora," Jeremiah said. "You can sexually harass people on your own time."

"You got it, boss," Nora said, still grinning.

"Uh . . . hey," I said, interrupting the resulting silence.

"This is the patient?" asked Montague, looking me up and down with a clinical eye. "Any cosmetic implants I should know about?"

"No," Jeremiah stated. "Completely natural."

"I wasn't asking you, Mr. Braddock," the surgeon stated. "Be honest, girl. Any cosmetics?"

I shook my head. I knew good and well that many of the men and women of Nova City used various cosmetic implants. Some were fairly innocuous, like the ones that changed eye color or provided aesthetic enhancements to a person's body. I'd even heard about one popular "entertainer" on Bourbon Street whose whole body had undergone a striking degree of enhancement, resulting in a body so out of proportion that it barely looked human. But as much as I wished I could change certain aspects of my own body—who didn't, right?—I'd never gone so far as to get any work done.

"Good," Montague said. "Removing those things, especially when they're implanted by incompetent, barely trained butchers, can get very messy." Then, she turned toward my uncle, asking, "Where are we doing the procedure? I would like to finish as quickly as possible."

"Follow me," Jeremiah said.

Then, instead of heading toward the exit, as I'd expected, he went deeper into the apartment. When he reached a hall closet that I didn't remember ever being used for anything, he tapped a certain spot on the wall. A panel slid away, revealing a keypad, into which he punched a code. A moment later, the closet slid away, revealing a heavy door. He went through it.

"What the . . . When did this get here?" I asked, following him. Inside was a relatively compact room. The walls were lined in what looked like silver, and the most prominent decoration was a cybersurgery chair in the very center of the hidden space.

"Nora, stay outside," Jeremiah said, ignoring me. Then, when the surgeon was inside, the door slid shut, and he asked, "Will this do?"

"This is . . . it's . . . it's more advanced than my own lab," Montague said. "How did you do this? How does no one know?"

Jeremiah answered, "A man has to have his secrets, doesn't he?"

Montague wasn't listening. Instead, she'd started to inspect the walls. "This is nano-infused silver-mithril alloy," she said. "No wonder it hasn't been detected . . . but how did you get it? Who built this for you?"

Jeremiah said, "So, you're saying that it is sufficient for our purposes?"

"I could do a full-body replacement for a Tier 4 cyborg in this room," she said. "Maybe more."

"Alright, then," my uncle said. "Let's get to work."

She clearly wanted to ask more questions, but it was just as clear that Jeremiah wasn't going to answer them. So, the surgeon just nodded and began her preparations. First, she took off her jacket to reveal the cream-colored and sleeveless blouse beneath before heading to a sink in one corner, where she began to scrub her hands. Meanwhile, I was told to take off my jacket and plant myself on the chair. I did so, and a few minutes later, Montague was looming over me.

"Asleep or awake?" she asked.

"Asleep" was my uncle's immediate response. "I'll be here to make sure you don't veer off course."

I understood the question; many people in Nova City would rather go without cybernetics than put themselves entirely at someone else's mercy. And few trusted anyone enough to have someone watch their backs. As a result, the city's cybernetic engineers had developed plenty of methods to allow their patients to retain consciousness while they worked. I was lucky in that Jeremiah was there. Otherwise, I would've been too afraid I'd end up in some random bathtub, my organs ripped out and whatever cybernetics I wanted installed gone. Or worse, somewhere like Bourbon Street, with the worst kinds of implants.

"Unnecessary," Montague stated. "It would be suicide to cross a man with your reputation. Unprofitable, too."

"Just so you remember that."

She ignored his threat, instead focusing on me. "Relax," she said, putting her hand on my neck. She adjusted its position a few times, then suddenly, I felt a series of pricks as a half dozen needles pierced my skin. I didn't have much time to react because, only an instant later, I was drifting off into unconsciousness. As the darkness overtook me, I felt a wave of giddiness. When I woke up, the fun would really begin.

Later, when my eyes fluttered open, I was immediately assaulted by the bright artificial light and the gleaming walls. I squeezed them shut and took a deep breath before reopening them. I turned to see my uncle standing nearby. The doctor was nowhere to be seen.

"Is she gone already?" I asked.

"A few minutes ago," Jeremiah answered. "After she confirmed that the implants were successfully installed, there was nothing left keeping her here."

"Oh. Okay," I mumbled. "Can I have something to drink?"

"Sure," he answered. "But first, we need to boot everything up."

"How?"

"Just concentrate," he said. "There should be something that feels like a switch in your mind. That'll be your optics. Once you boot up the KIOI, it'll take care of your arsenal implant."

I closed my eyes, searching for what he'd described. A moment later, I felt it, like an incomplete circuit in my brain. Mentally, I forged a connection. When I did, I couldn't keep a gasp from escaping from between my lips.

It felt like my whole body came alive, all at once, and in a way that defied any description I might come up with. It wasn't precisely an itch or a tingle, but those were the closest I could come to putting how I felt into words. In any event, it passed in the space of a second, and my new heads-up display activated.

Not only did the HUD show mundane things like the time or direction, but it also integrated a communications package that mimicked the comm device I usually carried around. In addition, I could see that it had linked to my bank account, though I didn't have more than a few credits to my name. Finally, I could see an icon representing my arsenal implant blinking in the corner of my vision.

"You'll get used to all the information," my uncle said. "I remember going through an electromagnetic field a few years back. It disrupted my optics, and I had to wait almost a week to have it replaced. Worst week of my life. I kept asking everyone the time or for directions, and I had no idea what my cybernetics were doing. Horrible stuff."

"Should I activate the arsenal implant?" I asked.

He nodded. So, I mentally touched the appropriate icon, which brought up a simple question:

Arsenal Implant (Mark IV)—Adavant Alliance [E-grade] found. Would you like to activate? You have one (1) unused cybernetic node. [Yes] or [No]

I chose to activate it, and the moment I mentally selected the affirmative option, I became aware of something on my arm. But it was also somewhere else, too. I told Jeremiah what I was feeling, and he explained, "Quantum space. With weapons, all you have to do is mentally tag it, and you'll be able to summon and dismiss the weapon. It takes a second or two, though—less as you level the [Cybernetic Interface] skill. You've got four of those slots."

"Okay? And these other three spaces?" I asked, mentally probing them.

"Both more and less limited. That's what sets a good arsenal implant apart from a generic one. Those spaces can hold just about anything that isn't living," he stated. "Most people use them for ammo and survival gear, but it's not that uncommon for people with top-grade arsenal implants to work as couriers. But be aware of how much weight you can carry. It's based on your Constitution, so the stronger you get, the more you can shove in there. Anything more than forty pounds or so, and you'll need an access point to retrieve it, but it's great for emergency supplies and ammunition. But let's get your weapons out of the way first."

At some point, someone had brought the boxes into the cybersurgery theater, and Jeremiah quickly retrieved the top box's contents. It turned out to be the Keugen Kinetic Rifle, or the Kicker, as I'd been told was its more colloquial name. At Jeremiah's prompting, I concentrated on the rifle and was rewarded a moment later with another notification flashing across my HUD:

Kinetic Rifle—Keugen Gunsmiths (Grade E) found. Would you like to bind weapon to your Arsenal Implant? You have four (4) unused weapon slots.
[Yes] or [No]

I selected the affirmative option, and immediately, I felt the rifle at the edge of my awareness. With a thought, I dismissed it, and it disappeared. I could see a small icon representing the Kicker on my HUD, and when I selected it, the rifle appeared in my hands after only a couple of seconds.

"Whoa," I muttered, which drew a slight chuckle from my uncle. "What?"

"Nothing, Keanu," he said. "And just so you know, you can adjust your HUD however you want. I suggest you shorten your notifications and move things around when we're done here."

"Yeah, okay," I said, already thinking about what I wanted to change. I'd barely begun to explore what kind of features the KIOI had, and I was eager to test its limits. To that end, Jeremiah handed me a small chip. "What's this?"

"Operating manual," he said. "Slot that into your new information port when you've got a few extra minutes. It'll tell you what you need to know."

"I have an information port?" I asked, my hand finding a flap of artificial skin on my neck. It blended perfectly well, but I could feel the seam. When I pulled it aside, my fingers brushed against an inch-long metallic slot. An information port was one of the other things that marked a person as an adult. With it, I wouldn't have to worry about sitting in front of a screen. Instead, I could just connect directly to the information source. "I have an information port!"

"Of course," he said. "It's high quality, too, so the connection should be able to keep up with your KIOI. There's also an extendable jack in your left wrist; you'll use that to access more stationary access terminals."

"I don't—"

"But no porn," he growled. "If I find out you've been downloading questionable sims, I'm going to yank that port out of your neck. Got me?"

I swallowed hard. I hadn't intended to do any such thing. Really. I mean, nothing too shady. Unless it seemed really . . . uh . . . interesting. It wasn't like it would be anything I hadn't seen before. I mean, one stroll through the Garden, and I'd get all the education on human anatomy and mating habits I could ever need.

"I get you," I said.

"Good. Now, let's get these other weapons tagged and put away," he suggested. "Then, we'll do the ammo. I suggest keeping the different types separate until you get the hang of it."

"Okay," I said, eager to move on from the awkwardness of the previous conversation.

After that, we went through everything, and before I knew it, I had all three guns and mountains of ammunition stored in the arsenal implant. In addition, he'd had me store a nano-edged sword in the fourth slot. Once that was done, Jeremiah said, "Now, we get to the fun part. Let's open your interface."

"How?"

He gave me a level look. "Figure it out," he said.

I deflated a bit. I'd gotten a bit better at navigating my KIOI, so I had a good idea how things worked. It was insanely intuitive, probably because it was wired into my brain in such a way that it was practically a part of me. Or maybe literally part of me. I was still a bit unclear on how cybernetics worked. Either way, all I had to do was concentrate for a second, and a status page opened in front of my eyes.

Name: Mirabelle Lisa Braddock
Class: N/A (Requirements Not Met)
Level: N/A (0%)
Constitution: 3/10
Mind: 4/10
Mist: 1/10
Skills: 7/7
Cybernetic Interface: Tier 0 (1%)
Firearms: Tier 0 (0%)
Close Quarters Combat: Tier 0 (0%)
Stealth Operations: Tier 0 (0%)
Combat Utility: Tier 0 (0%)
Mistwalker: Tier 0 (0%)
Spycraft: Tier 0 (0%)

"I think it's broken," I said, a little alarmed. "My stats are, like, fractions."

"It's not broken," my uncle said. "What nobody's ever told you before is that tiers are mostly irrelevant. They only affect potential, not actual power. To realize that potential, you're going to have to work. If you want to increase your Constitution, you're going to have work out. Run. Do gymnastics. That sort of thing. For Mind, you'll have to learn. You need to do puzzles. I've found that mathematics is very effective as a training tool, and it has the added benefit of increasing the [Mistwalker] skill's progression."

"And Mist?" I asked. "How do I raise that attribute?"

"Using your skills," he said. "Mostly, it'll increase on its own, but there are a few ways we can jumpstart it. But you'll see when we start training."

"But I have so many questions!" I complained. For instance, my eyes kept flicking toward the two categories with *N/A* beside them. "How do I get a class? And what does it mean by *level*? And how is my potential determined? Like, is it just based on my tier? Or is it something else?"

"Calm down," he said, and I realized I'd thrown those questions out rapid-fire. "First, you get a class when you meet the requirements. It might be tomorrow, or it could be in ten years. And no, I'm not telling you any more than that right now. You need to focus on getting stronger. Your class will come when it comes. Second, you mostly get levels by killing things. That allows your body to naturally absorb their Mist, and once your Mist reaches a certain point, you gain a level. Finally, your potential is determined by your tier and level. Rule of thumb is that you multiply your tier—in your case, seven—by your level. So, for you, it's zero. Once you reach level one, it'll be seven. Level two, and it'll be fourteen. On and on. That number gets added to your species' baseline potential. For humans, it's ten. Again, at level one, your maximum will be seventeen. Then twenty-four. Etcetera."

"Sounds easy enough," I said, already dreaming about the day when I had a Constitution in the hundreds. If ten was the baseline potential for a human, I couldn't help but wonder what a person with twenty Constitution could do. I'd seen people perform plenty of unbelievable feats of strength, but I had always thought them the result of cybernetics. Now, I was beginning to wonder how accurate that assumption was.

"It's not," he said. "But you'll see once we start training."

"Can we start now?" I asked, finally swinging my legs off the chair and pushing myself to my feet.

Jeremiah shook his head. "No" was his answer. "We don't want to draw too much attention. Besides, this city is too safe. It'll stunt your growth."

I swallowed hard. If Nova City was too safe, I questioned what my uncle considered dangerous. Given what I'd seen from him so far, it stood to reason that whatever it was, it would eat me alive.

"For the rest of the day, I want you to study the manuals for your cybernetics and weapons," he said, handing me another few information chips. "Because tomorrow, we're getting started."

His broad grin sent a shiver up my spine, but it was accompanied by a significant wave of excitement.

CHAPTER NINE

GOODBYE, NOVA CITY

Humanity had grown soft. Pliable. Weak. The Initialization drove that point home. So many people had no idea how easy their lives really were. When society collapsed, they found out.

—Jeremiah Braddock III

"I ... thought ... you ..." I tried to get out between heaving breaths. It was a useless endeavor, so I pushed the thought to the back of my mind before redoubling my concentration on the task before me. I heaved the barbell above my head, holding it there for a brief second before dropping it to the rubber mat. I leaned forward, hands on my knees, as I caught my breath. Finally, I looked up to see my uncle standing beside Nora, who had a curious smile playing across her lips. "I thought you said we couldn't train until we left the city."

"This?" asked my uncle. "This isn't training, Mirabelle. This is just a light workout."

As I straightened back to my full height, I laced my fingers behind my head. We'd been at it for hours, as evidenced by the fact that my clothes were drenched in sweat. And I could barely stand for the wobbling of my legs.

My uncle had woken me up before the sun had even risen, and after I'd gotten dressed in a pair of sweatpants and a tank top, he'd taken me to the roof of the building, where he had a full training setup, and put me through my paces. The first bit was easy—just running through an obstacle course he used to train his Operators. But after the third time through, I'd felt the fatigue set in.

That was only the beginning, though. Next, he made me run, and more than I'd ever run at any time in my entire life. Following that was a weight lifting session with Nora, which I'd just completed.

"I think I might die," I muttered.

"Maybe!" was Nora's cheerful reply. "That's how you know you're really working!"

"I hate you. You know that, right? Like, fire-of-a-thousand-suns level of hatred."

The muscular woman crossed her arms, saying, "Well, that's just mean."

"Enough," Jeremiah stated, looking up at the sky—a weird habit, considering that if his optical interface was anything like mine, there was a clock right there. "We're done, right, Nora?"

"Yeah, boss," the woman said. "Give me a few weeks with her, and I guarantee she'll make some real gains."

"Wish I could," he said. "But we're leaving this afternoon."

"But what about—"

"Not around the kid," Jeremiah said.

"Sure, boss," Nora responded, though I could see her jaw flex at the interruption. I knew I was missing something, but I was too exhausted to care. "You want me to do anything else? I could put her through some hand-to-hand drills."

Jeremiah shook his head. "It's already going to be hard enough to hide her as it is," my uncle stated.

"Thought she took [Spycraft]," Nora said.

"She did, but it's undeveloped" was Jeremiah's response. "Until she hits the second level of Tier 1, it's basically useless. They all are. Or did you forget?"

Again, Nora's jaw flexed. She was a prideful woman, and she didn't like being talked down to. I couldn't blame her for that; my uncle was a hard man, and he didn't mince words. If someone did or said anything stupid, he wasn't going to sugarcoat his response, even when the situation called for it. Tactful, he wasn't.

"No, boss."

Jeremiah responded, "Good."

"Uh . . . am I done? I'd really like to be done now," I said, trying to relieve some of the tension in the air. All around us, there were people going through morning workouts; the training area was atop the building, and it was expansive enough to accommodate hundreds of people with varying levels of strength. Nearby, a man was doing squats with over a thousand pounds, and he wasn't struggling at all.

"Go downstairs and get cleaned up," Jeremiah ordered. "Pack whatever clothes you want to bring with you. Remember, though—it's hot down there. Hot and humid in a way you've never experienced. So, be ready to dress accordingly."

I nodded. I'd heard plenty of stories about the climate below Nova City, but having never left the city—as far as I knew, few people did—I had no context for what it might entail. I would just have to figure it out, I supposed. So, I quickly left before they decided to put me through more torturous exercises, riding the elevator down a level. A few minutes later, I was back in the apartment, where I found Heather waiting on me with some sort of green semiliquid in a tall cup.

Smiling broadly, she thrust it into my hands, saying, "Drink up! It's good for you!"

"Uh . . . what is it?" I asked.

"It's a health shake! Your uncle loves them after his workouts," she assured me.

I gave the stuff a sniff and nearly gagged. Still, I'd decided to at least try with Heather, so steeling myself, I tipped it back and drained the contents. Or I tried to. The moment the foul liquid hit my tongue, I almost gagged. Still, I was aware enough of Heather's smiling face to know that doing so would absolutely destroy her. So, I gulped it down, and when I was done, I gave her a weak smile and a thumbs-up. "That was . . . uh . . . that was great," I muttered. "Really tasty. Thanks."

"I knew you would love it!" Heather exclaimed. And before I knew it, she'd thrown her arms around me. She hugged me tightly, adding, "I'm so proud of you. I wish you didn't have to go, but Jeremiah explained everything to me. I'm going to miss you so much!"

"Uh . . . y-yeah. Me, too," I said. "But . . . I've got to . . . you know . . . pack. So . . ."

She released me. "Yeah. Right. Sorry," she said. "I'm such a ditz sometimes. Go ahead. I'm sure you have a lot to do!"

"Sure. Um . . . thanks again."

After that, I headed to my room where I quickly started packing. I still wasn't sure what I should take, so I gathered just about everything I owned—including my new boots—and shoved it into a duffel bag my uncle had provided. Then, with a thought, I threw it into my arsenal implant. It went without any issue, but I could sense that it barely fit.

"Take it out," I heard my uncle say. I turned to see him standing in the doorway.

"What?" I asked.

"The bag," he said. "Save your arsenal implant for survival supplies or ammunition. Putting anything else in there is a waste of space."

"Fine," I said, yanking the bag out of my storage.

"Follow me," Jeremiah ordered. Without checking to make sure that I was following, he turned on his heel and stalked through the apartment, ending up in an oft-forgotten back room. Inside were three huge metallic boxes. He pointed to them, saying, "Load up."

I crossed the room and read the labels. The first was ammunition for the Kicker. The second was a variety pack of rounds meant for my pistol. And the third contained the ammunition for my scattergun. Finally, a smaller box held empty magazines.

"Uh . . . what do you want me to do?"

"You can't be that dense," Jeremiah stated. "Put the rifle rounds in the magazines, which go in your first space. Second space needs to hold your pistol and scattergun ammunition. Third is for survival supplies. Or explosives, but that's probably us getting ahead of ourselves for now."

"What do you mean?" I asked.

"Skills are fluid," Jeremiah answered. "What you've got now are not what you will have for the rest of your life. Things change. Combine. Evolve. On top of that, you'll probably get a class around level ten. My point is that you need to just follow my lead. I know what I'm doing, and I won't steer you wrong."

I sighed. "Fine," I said. Even if I sometimes resented Jeremiah, I trusted him more than anyone else in the world. That might not have been saying that much, but I had the benefit of knowing two things. One, he'd already spent a fortune on me, so it stood to reason that he wanted my skills to develop properly. And second, he'd never done anything to hurt me. Sure, he'd kept me sequestered at the top of our megabuilding for years, but that was only because he wanted to ensure my safety.

But overriding everything else was the simple fact that he was the only person offering me any advice. Without him, I would be fumbling in the dark. So, until I knew more about what was going on, I had little choice but to follow his lead. Once I started figuring things out, though, I was sure that I would start to have more opinions on my own development.

"Get to work," he said, nodding at the boxes.

I let out another sigh, but I didn't complain. Instead, I went to the box containing the rifle magazines, retrieved one, then opened the crate of ammunition. Next thing I knew, I was loading rounds into the magazines. It was slow. It was tedious. And by the time an hour had passed, my fingers were so sore that they were actually bleeding. However, I persisted, and after a couple more hours, I was done.

That's when I loaded up the ammunition from the other crates before heading back to my room, where I spent another couple of hours wishing I wasn't miserably exhausted with aching fingers. I tried to distract myself by flipping on my screen, but everything just seemed so much less interesting than it had the day before. Now that I had a Nexus Implant, it felt like I should be doing something important. But there I was, trying to pretend like nothing had changed.

Finally, at around five in the afternoon, my uncle returned. After making sure that I'd loaded everything up, he said, "Okay, then. Say your goodbyes because it's time to go. Follow me."

Left unsaid was that I had no one close enough to warrant a farewell. I'd had a few acquaintances at school, but other than that, I'd lived an isolated existence. I suspected that that was by design.

Shouldering my bag, I followed Jeremiah through the apartment and, after traversing the halls, to the elevator that would lead us to the parking structure. Soon, we were on our way, passing through the city that had always been my home. It looked no different than before, with the towering buildings, ubiquitous neon lights, and lewd holographic displays. The people were unchanged, going about their lives with dogged determination. Some had just gotten off work, while others were just heading in to report for their shifts, but they all wore the same expression.

"It's resignation."

I looked up to see that Jeremiah had been watching me. "What?" I asked.

"That expression," he said. "These people, they know they'll never be more than they are right now. They trudge back and forth, going to jobs they hate, all so they can survive another day. They live a desolate mimicry of a life, completely devoid of anything more than sheer survival."

"Why?" I asked.

"What's the alternative?" was his responding question. When I didn't offer an answer, he went on, "Do you think anyone wants this? No. They didn't just wake up one day and tell themselves that they were going to be ordinary. Do you think they decided that they weren't going to try anymore? Of course not. It happens one tiny decision at a time. Death by a thousand cuts. And the whole time, you've got those assholes over in King's Row making each microdeath easier and easier. Making it more palatable. They give you all those things that make life more comfortable—the entertainment feeds, the junk food, the booze, and the drugs—and before you know it, you're stuck. You're on the downslope of your life, and there's no stopping your momentum into irrelevance."

He ran his hand over his bald head. "The Mist could have been a gift," he said. "It could have made us so much better. We could have forged a path to galactic relevance. But no. We holed up in our concrete cities, shivering in fear, even as our doom looms over us like a huge fucking shadow."

Jeremiah turned and looked at me, saying, "But not you. You're going to be what humanity should have been. You're going to survive. You're going to go out into that universe and make your mark."

In another situation, I might have made a sarcastic remark, but the feverish look in his eyes pulled me up short. So, I just nodded and looked the other way. Even as we passed by dozens of Silos—the huge, circular buildings that housed the vertical farms that fed much of Nova City—I thought about what he'd said.

Did I agree with him?

Was it a crime, just wanting to survive in comfort? My uncle clearly thought so, but I wasn't sure I blamed people for making that decision. It was a difficult world, and most people just weren't special. Even at my young age, I knew that much. I'd seen that at school. Some people—in fact, most—were meant for mundanity. Maybe that was the definition of normality.

But was the population of Nova City mired in mediocrity? Or had they sunk lower than that? More, what about the ones who could've been better? Usually, they got caught up in the same net, didn't they? Some of the classmates I knew were smart or talented enough for better lives had been destined for a life in the Silos. Or worse, in the factories that dotted Algiers. Wasn't that a waste?

Such thoughts rattled around in my brain as we left the Garden behind and descended into Algiers. The district was positioned on a lower plane than the Garden, so we were forced to follow a winding, sharply declining spiral until the car emerged onto the platform. Gone were the towering megabuildings, replaced by the blocky factories that made so many of Nova City's goods. Some things came from other cities, probably transferred via a similar system that had sent my weapons and implants down to Earth. However, that was incredibly expensive, so it was only used for the most valuable of luxuries. Those almost never made it to the Garden. Instead, we were dependent on the products that came out of Algiers.

And it was up to the task, belching out a bevy of products as well as plenty of pollution to go with it. As soon as we left the Garden behind, I smelled the heavy smog, even in the nearly airtight hover car. Garbage was piled high in every alley, and the graffiti on the walls was often covered by some unidentifiable brown sludge.

As dirty and depressing as the buildings were, the people were even worse. Gone was the colorful hair and daring fashion choices, replaced by threadbare clothes that looked like they'd never been washed. The people themselves bore smudges on their faces, and most walked with a kind of depressed apathy I'd never seen before.

Thankfully, our path took us through Algiers pretty quickly. Otherwise, I might have begun to share my uncle's pessimistic outlook. As it was, I had gained a distinctly bad taste in my mouth that had nothing to do with the decline in air quality.

Finally, we passed through the docks—a system of warehouses where goods were often stored. Most were guarded by intimidating-looking security personnel, each armed and armored with the latest military technology. Eventually, the road curved, and in front of us, I saw a looming gate.

"When we get to the gate, don't open your mouth," Jeremiah said. "Let me do the talking."

I nodded as we slowly drifted forward, finding ourselves in a line of other vehicles. Unlike Jeremiah's hover car, the ones in front of us were giant, boxy transport trucks with actual wheels.

"Where are they going?" I asked, nervously massaging the Realskin covering the arsenal implant in my forearm. It somehow simultaneously felt like authentic skin and a rubber sleeve, but it was mostly undetectable, save for a pair of tiny seams—one on my wrist and the other just below my elbow.

"To other settlements outside the city," Jeremiah stated. "And stop fiddling with your cybernetics. It's off-putting."

"I thought—"

"It doesn't matter what you thought," he said, interrupting me. "You are entirely ignorant of the workings of the world. Accept that and endeavor to remedy it."

"It's not my fault I don't know," I muttered, crossing my arms as we drifted one spot closer to the gate. "You could have told me."

"If I would have told you these things, you would have told your friends at school," he said. "And they would have told others. Before we knew what was going on, I'd have politicians from King's Row breathing down my neck for disturbing the peace. People are told what they need to know and nothing more. Get used to that because information is another form of power, and not one that the people in charge will part with lightly. Now shut up."

I thought that was entirely unfair, but I could recognize when Jeremiah was in one of his moods. He didn't seem like he wanted to hear my arguments, so I did as he asked. Slowly, we made our way to the gate, which was guarded by at least a dozen soldiers. Each one had visible cybernetics and carried high-end weaponry, the likes of which I wouldn't have even recognized if I hadn't just spent a couple of hours browsing through Gala's wares. Hers were clearly superior, at least to my eye, but the soldiers' weapons weren't that far behind. What's more, I got the sense that they were all at least Tier 2, with a smattering of Tier 3 personnel. A formidable force, assuming they were properly trained.

The driver eased the car into a blinking red rectangle of holographic light, and one of the soldiers approached. Nonchalantly carrying a submachine gun in his gleaming cybernetic hand, he wore black combat fatigues and a tactical vest. Leaning down, he motioned for the driver to activate the window. When he did, the soldier said, "What's your purpose in leaving Nova City, citizen?"

"Just a driver" was the grunted reply. He hiked his thumb over his shoulder, adding, "Ask the boss."

The soldier, who I'd just noticed had the name Valdez stitched on his vest, nodded and came to the back door. He repeated the motion, and my uncle rolled down the window. The moment he laid eyes on Jeremiah, he muttered, "Oh, shit . . ."

"There a problem?" asked my uncle.

"Uh . . . n-no, sir," the soldier stammered, his finger creeping toward the trigger.

"Keep your trigger discipline, son," Jeremiah said. "I'm taking my niece outside the city so she can see where she came from."

"Uh . . . can't let . . . you know . . . Unawakened outside the city, sir," the man stuttered.

"She got her Nexus Implant yesterday," Jeremiah said. "There's not going to be a problem, is there?"

The man glanced around, almost as if he was looking for someone else to take the responsibility away from him. Then, with a sigh, he said, "No, sir. You're cleared to head on through."

"Appreciate it."

After that, the gate slid open, revealing a wide platform that already contained a few of the transport trucks. The driver accelerated, and we took a place between a pair of hulking vehicles.

"What now?" I asked.

"Wait for it."

I was about to ask what he meant when the platform let out a rumble. A moment later, it felt like my heart had jumped into my throat because we were falling. And fast.

Wide-eyed, I glanced at my uncle, who was just smiling. I wasn't certain if that should've made me feel better or worse about the whole thing. Then, as quickly as it had begun, the platform slowed to a stop. A moment later, the trucks in front of us pulled away, revealing the landscape.

"Welcome to Louisiana," my uncle said. "Head to the safe house, Bart. No stopping. We need to get there before dark."

"Yes, sir," said the driver. Bart, apparently. I'd never even bothered to find out the man's name, and suddenly, I was a little ashamed of that fact. In any case, Bart soon accelerated, and before long, we were speeding down a paved road.

CHAPTER TEN

AN UNFAMILIAR WORLD

My training gave me an advantage, but even that wasn't enough to guarantee survival. To survive the Initialization, I had to become something more than a soldier. I had to become an unrepentant, unhesitating killer. And I did. God help me, I did.

—Jeremiah Braddock III

"It's so green," I muttered, my face practically pressing against the plasti-glass of the car's window. "How is it so green?"

Indeed, everywhere I looked was more vegetation than I'd ever seen before. In school, my class had once visited one of the Silos, and even that farming tower paled in comparison to the natural landscape stretching out to the horizon. There was also more water than I thought I'd ever see. It was dirty, brown, and looked as if anything at all could be lurking below the surface, and I can freely admit that I felt a deep sense of trepidation just from looking at that swampy abyss.

Ever since I'd found that grate, beyond which I could see the land far below Nova City, I'd thought myself worldly. Most people in the city didn't get to see such things. However, that small look at the wider world was ill preparation for what I now saw on either side of the concrete road.

Beside me, my uncle let out a chuckle. "Never gets old," he said.

"What?" I asked, not daring to tear my eyes from the marsh.

"This," he said. "Your reaction. It happens every time I bring someone down here."

"I . . . I don't understand," I said. "If all this is down here, then why do we live up there?"

To punctuate my question, I thrust my finger to the sky. The series of huge platforms that held Nova City aloft loomed over us, casting a long shadow across the swamp to the east.

"It's incredibly dangerous down here," my uncle stated.

"More than the Garden? Or worse, Algiers?" I asked.

Jeremiah said, "Immeasurably so. Up there, there are rules. But down here? There's nothing but your own power to protect you. Most people aren't up to the task. Nearly eighty percent of the Earth's population was killed before they could figure that out."

I swallowed hard, but I didn't respond. I had no concept of how many people were alive back then, but the idea of losing eighty percent of Nova City put some things into perspective. It was more people than I could count, and that was just one city. From what I'd learned in school—and from everything Jeremiah had told me—there were dozens of cities with just as many people back then. And that wasn't counting all the people who lived in rural areas. The number of dead was staggering and incomprehensible.

Such thoughts occupied my mind for the next fifteen minutes; as I stared out at the landscape, we passed a few signs of previous civilization. Crumbling and mostly submerged side roads, rusted signs, and a few decrepit buildings were all that was left. Once, I even saw a boxy vehicle, rusted and half-buried in the muck, and I was filled with a sense of loss.

It was easy to know that so many people had died. Everyone was taught as much in school. But no one had any context. More, sequestered in our towering city, we never had to see the remnants of that fallen civilization. Now, though? I couldn't escape it, and I was beginning to understand—at least on a surface level—why my uncle was the way he was. He'd lived through it, after all. He had seen everyone he knew, everyone he loved, die. It would be enough to harden anyone's heart.

And I knew he'd been a soldier even before the Initialization, and an elite one at that. How much death had he seen? How many had he killed?

"Eyes up," he muttered. My head swiveled toward him only to see that his eyes were locked on the northern side of the road. On that side, the water looked less like a swamp and more like a lake. But what did I know? Before that day, I'd never seen either up close; I was completely reliant on what I'd learned in school. Either way, I was ill-prepared for what came next.

In an explosion of mud and water, a huge shape erupted into the air. It shot forward with unnatural speed, colliding with the truck a hundred yards in front of us. The vehicle was about thirty feet long, boxy, and unlike our car, had four enormous, rubber-coated wheels. It might as well have been a plastic toy, for all the resistance it displayed.

A great metallic screech filled the air as the truck rocketed off the road, tipping over a few dozen yards into the murky water. At the same time, Bart slammed on the brakes, halting our momentum in the space of a second. When the mud and water settled, I gasped at the creature sprawled across the road.

"W-what is that thing?" I muttered.

"Gator," said my uncle, already opening his door and getting out of the car. "Ambush predators. Fast in short bursts. Extreme bite force. Very durable."

"An alligator?" I gasped. I'd learned about some of the area's native species, but my class had never gone into much depth in our studies. Given that people never left Nova City, there was no reason to know what kind of animal life lurked in the swamp below. I had always been fascinated, though, and I'd gobbled up every bit of information I could. But that information seemed to have been wholly inaccurate.

For one, the alligators in my books were supposed to have been, at most, about fifteen feet long. At most. But this one? This creature was more like the dinosaurs that had been long extinct even before the Initialization. I didn't exactly have a measuring laser handy, but if the monster was less than fifty feet long, I would have been surprised. All rigid scales, teeth, and bulging muscles, it looked quite a bit heavier than the comparatively slim creatures I'd learned about.

"You going to sit there all day? Or do you want to use some of those weapons I spent a fortune on?" my uncle asked, leaning into the car.

Suddenly, I noticed that the creature had forgotten all about the truck that had borne the brunt of its initial attack. Instead, it was looking straight at us. Or me. It was all I could do not to wet myself in fear.

Jeremiah didn't wait for me to answer. Instead, he took on a shooting stance, and a moment later, a huge rifle had appeared in his hands. It looked almost identical to the one he'd bought for me—not the Kicker, but rather the Pulsar I couldn't use yet. However, there were subtle differences between the one I had stored in my arsenal implant—most notably, that it was a bit bulkier. It also had a slightly longer barrel and a much more elaborate scope. The base of the gun was identical, though.

"I'm not going to kill it outright," he said out of the side of his mouth. "So, unless you want to get eaten, you'll pull out your weapon and go to work."

I shook the mingled fear and surprise from my mind, focusing on what I could do. Even as I did, my uncle opened up, firing a curiously quiet shot from his rifle. In a millisecond, the alligator's left front claw exploded in a shower of gore. I was surprised to see the glint of metal, as well. But the creature was a long way from stopping. In fact, it seemed even angrier than before. It darted forward with a hissing growl.

Throwing the door open, I scrambled out of the car, diving away just in time. The monster—and it had definitively graduated from animal status, by this point—crashed into the car, flipping it on end and sending it tumbling away. I couldn't worry about the vehicle's—or the driver's—fate; I needed to stop it.

Rising to one knee, I summoned the Kicker from my arsenal implant and squeezed the trigger. I was no novice to firearms; my uncle had been training me to shoot since I was little. But it didn't matter. With the huge, scaly creature looming over me, I couldn't miss. Or that's what I thought.

My shots went wide as panic threw off my aim.

"Focus!" growled my uncle from the other side of the road. He crouched there, for some reason ignored by the giant alligator. "Remember your training."

I took a deep breath, trying to push past the panic gripping my chest. My heart was beating out of control, and my hands were trembling. It was so different from practicing at the firing range. It wasn't even like when I'd run from Turk and his mooks. No—a monster the size of the alligator elicited a primal sort of fear that sapped the focus of even veteran warriors.

But I was better than that, wasn't I? Jeremiah had spent so much time and money to give me a chance at survival. He'd given me a Tier 7 Nexus Implant, which was a priceless treasure that may have been completely unique. I couldn't afford to let that go to waste. I didn't dare.

So, I took another calming breath, sighted in on what I hoped was a vulnerable spot, and fired. Short bursts. Squeeze, don't pull. Maintain a proper firing platform.

Despite its name, the Kicker had barely any recoil, which allowed me to concentrate my fire in a tight grouping. One burst after another tore into the monster's neck, and the reward was a fountain of scaly, bloody flesh. It let out another hissing roar, and as it whipped around, its long tail skidded across the swamp on the other side of the road, sending up a cascade of murky water.

I strafed, continuing my staccato firing pattern until, after a few more seconds, my magazine ran dry. With practiced precision, I dragged the magazine from its well and dropped it into my arsenal implant. A moment later, another magazine was in my hand, summoned from the same implant. I jammed it into position and chambered a round before resuming my firing pattern.

It wasn't enough, though. I was doing plenty of damage, but the monster was enormous. Even if I hit the same spot a thousand times, it would be a minor miracle if I hit anything vital. And something told me I didn't have time for that kind of strategy, anyway. I needed to change tactics.

Thankfully, the alligator was hobbled by my uncle's initial salvo, which had completely destroyed its front leg. Otherwise, it would have snapped me up in its jaws before I even had a chance to react. I wasn't going to let his efforts go to waste.

So, as I backed away—heel to toe, with continuous fire—I came up with a plan. It was stupid. Dangerous, too. And I was sure my uncle would berate me when everything was finished. I didn't think he'd let me die, but who knew what he was thinking? He'd just pitted me, a mostly untrained, barely Awakened Operator, against a monster that would give a dinosaur a run for its credits.

Maybe it was a test. If I passed, he would judge me worth his effort. If not? Well, I would be gone, and he could move on with whatever other plans he might have.

Once I was about forty yards away, I flicked a switch on the Kicker, and it transformed. The barrel elongated, and the body grew a bit bulkier, from which a scope unfolded. I sighted in on the mass of torn and bloody flesh that had been my target for the last couple of minutes. Taking another deep, steadying breath, I fired.

The bullet hit with a satisfying sound, and I was rewarded with a geyser of blood and gore. I almost celebrated right then and there, thankful that I wouldn't have to enact the rest of my plan.

And that hesitation almost cost me my life.

Moving more quickly than it had moved since tackling that first truck, it shot forward. I squealed in surprise as I narrowly darted to the side, but I kept my wits about me. Mostly. Okay, so I went a bit blank for a second, and when I came back to myself, I was in a full sprint. But it probably looked like a tactical retreat, right?

Probably not.

In any case, I soon recaptured my calm—at least as well as I could, given that there was a giant aquatic lizard that wanted to eat me—and stowed my rifle. For the next part of my plan, I needed something different. Something a bit more specialized.

I summoned Ferdinand II.

The weapon was a true hand cannon, a revolver that shot rounds almost as big around as my wrist. Which wasn't really saying much, considering how skinny I was, but it seemed abnormally big. Of course, the original Ferdinand was much more remarkable, and its rounds had probably graduated from small arms to heavy munitions, but Ferdinand II was still impressively endowed.

More importantly, I'd loaded him up with depleted atium rounds. I wasn't entirely sure what atium actually was, but it seemed expensive. And given that the rounds had been marked as explosive, that kind of said everything I needed to know about how damaging they might be.

In the time it took me to summon Ferdinand II into my hands, the alligator had recovered, and if it was angry before, it was absolutely and royally pissed off after having half of its neck turned into so much mincemeat. It charged forward, its claws digging furrows into the concrete street. I could feel the force of its bellow even before the sound overwhelmed me, but I held my ground.

Ferdinand II would pack quite a punch. I knew that. But the drawback was that he was still a pistol, and as such, he didn't have much of a range. Add to that the fact that I'd had a lot less time to practice with pistols, and I knew that I needed the alligator to come lot closer if I was going to make the shot count.

Gritting my teeth, I crouched. The smell of its breath—all rotting meat and moist grossness—washed over me. I could see its dagger-sized teeth. Its beady eyes. The scaly skin. It was a true monster, the likes of which I'd never expected to encounter. But I summoned every ounce of courage I possessed and tightened my two-handed grip on my hand cannon.

The alligator closed in, covering the few dozen yards in the space of a second. When it got close, I dove to the side, narrowly avoiding the monster's snapping jaws. Even so, I took a glancing blow from its right claw, which dragged a line of fire down my side. I let out a scream, but I couldn't let myself be deterred.

I don't know if it was my recent Awakening or luck, but I managed to twist in the air, aim, and fire in one motion. Ferdinand II kicked in my hand, but the explosive projectile flew true, burying itself in the mass of torn flesh that was the result of my efforts so far. For a brief instant, I thought I'd fired a dud.

Then the round exploded, and suddenly, I was tumbling through the air. That lasted barely a moment before my shoulder hit the concrete and I skidded across the road. My momentum took me into the murky swamp water, where I collapsed in a heap. When I finally gathered enough of my wits to sit up, I was rewarded with the sound of laughter.

My uncle was standing at the edge of the road, his hands on his hips as he beheld my handiwork.

The entire right side of the alligator's neck and much of its head was just gone. It still twitched a bit, but even I, with my lacking zoological experience, could tell that it was dead. Curiously, the massive wound revealed metallic bones.

A nearby splash made me flinch, and my head whipped around—followed quickly by Ferdinand's muzzle—to see Bart's unassuming form looming over me. His clothes were covered in muck, but he didn't seem hurt. He offered his hand, which I took. After he levered me to my feet, I looked past him to see that the car was hovering only twenty yards away, seemingly unharmed.

"What the . . ."

"Your uncle invested in quite a few defensive features," the driver said. "Pity you won't be able to take it much further."

"Huh?"

"The Mist," Bart said. "In the city, it's corralled. Controlled. But out here, it's too wild for hover cars to work. You'll have to use vehicles with traditional wheels."

"O-oh," I said. I'd never heard anything like that before, but that shouldn't have surprised me. After learning so much in the past day, I was unsurprised to find that my education had been even more inadequate than I had first suspected. I didn't know anything, and the sooner I wrapped my head around that fact, the better prepared I'd be to address the lack of knowledge.

"You did well," Bart said.

"Thanks, I guess," I said, vainly trying to wipe the muck from my pants. Why had I chosen to wear my favorite jeans? Stupidity, that's why. And now my boots were probably ruined, too. Let's not forget my hair, either, which was currently playing host to a horde of half-decayed sticks and probably an army of bacteria. Annoyed, I demanded, "Why is it so freaking hot out here?"

Bart let out a laugh. "Kind of how it is in these parts," he said. "You'll get used to it. Or not. There's a reason I stick around in Nova City most of the time. Come on."

With that, he trudged through the knee-deep water, his feet making a horrible squelching sound with every step. With a depressed sigh, I followed. As I did, my adrenaline began to abate, and I became keenly aware of how much I hurt. Like, on a scale of one to ten, it was somewhere in the three hundred range. And the wound in my side was leading the charge. With every breath came a sharp, stabbing pain that, if I was in any state to analyze the situation, would have probably been extremely alarming. As it was, it was all I could do not to openly weep, and by the time I got to the road, tears had gathered, despite my best efforts.

"Oh, that was fantastic!" my uncle said. "I'm not much of a pistol guy, but that was incredibly satisfying. I loved the way you softened it up; if you hadn't, that low-velocity round would've just bounced off its scales. Good thinking, that."

I nodded, pretending that had been my intention all along. Sure, I'd had a plan, but it had originally consisted of "shoot the same spot and hope you hit something vital." That it had worked out was pure coincidence.

"She's hurt pretty bad, boss," Bart said. "Might want to get her to the safe house sooner rather than later."

My uncle glanced at my injured side and frowned. "Shit," he said. "Right. Go get the car, Bart."

The unassuming man nodded before heading toward where the car hovered. My uncle, meanwhile, pulled a small cylinder from his pocket; it was red with white trim, and I recognized it as a med-hypo, probably loaded with some sort of antibiotic concoction. It wouldn't heal injuries, but it could stave off infection. More importantly, it would hopefully contain an anesthetic that would numb the pain lancing through my body.

Jeremiah jabbed it into my arm and depressed the button on the side. With a hiss of compressed air, it stuck me with a short needle. A second later, a comforting warmth spread throughout my body.

"Better?" he asked.

"Uh . . . yeah," I answered, my voice sounding like it was a million miles away. "A little . . . um . . . woozy, I guess."

"To be expected," Jeremiah said as the car pulled to a stop beside us. The low hum of its Mist engine was comforting. My uncle guided me inside, and a moment later, we were on our way.

Belatedly, I remembered the truck that had been knocked into the water. I asked about it, but my uncle said, "Not our problem. They're probably already dead, and if they survived, they don't need our help. We don't concern ourselves with those vermin. Traitors to humanity, the lot of them."

I didn't really agree. Everyone I'd ever met had just been trying to survive. Those soldiers and drivers might work for various corporations, but that didn't mean they weren't still people. But I knew that pointing that out would probably only set my uncle off, so I remained silent as we shot down the road.

Like that, we traveled for another couple of hours. As the sun began to dip below the horizon, Bart turned down one of the side roads. It was barely more than a dirt trail leading to the north, but he had no trouble guiding the car along the way. After another hour—during which night had truly fallen—we came to our destination.

Huge concrete walls loomed over us, atop which were dozens of armed people. Lights flooded the area, and a massive, intimidating gate barred our way.

"Welcome to Haven," said Jeremiah.

"Uh . . . what is this?" I asked as the gates opened. Bart guided the car inside the walls, and I saw a series of concrete bunkers. There was also a sizable warehouse and a dozen small houses.

"Way station," Jeremiah said. "They're all over the place if you know where to look. Not everyone wants to live in one of the megacities. Some people are too independent. If it weren't for you—or your mom before you—I would've never permanently set up in Nova City."

"Did she really die the way you said she did?" I asked suddenly, my lips loosened by the painkillers flowing through my veins.

Jeremiah sighed. "She did," he said. "Freak accident. Just a mugging gone wrong. You have no idea how many times I've wished that she took the Tier 7 from me when I offered it. She refused, though. Said she wasn't an Operator. Your father, though—he begged me for it. I almost gave it to him, too. When I saw him for what he really was, he ran to one of the corporations and told them everything he knew. Thankfully, I hadn't told him that much. He lived an unremarkable life and died the same way he lived. Good riddance."

I nodded. It wasn't the first time I'd heard my father's story, though I hadn't known about the Nexus Implant until recently. Knowing what I knew of the man, it wasn't surprising that he'd turned on Jeremiah so easily. He was a glitter fiend and a gambler, and his vices had done him in only a year or two after my mother's death. I'd never really known him, and given what I'd heard—from both Jeremiah and my mother—I didn't want to learn any more.

"Alright, let's get you patched up," Jeremiah said. "We need to be moving tomorrow."

"We're not settling here?" I asked, surprised.

"No," my uncle stated. "We're still too close to Nova City. Besides, don't you want to get in touch with your roots? Tomorrow, we're going home."

CHAPTER ELEVEN

A LONG PROCESS

> When I found out that many humans were working for the aliens, I didn't want to believe it. Even with the evidence staring me in the face, I couldn't fathom how someone could sell out their entire species. Now, I know that most people would've made the same choice. Greed is a powerful motivator.
>
> —Jeremiah Braddock III

Clutching a towel to my chest, I stared at the disgusting shower. It looked a hundred years old, and the grout between the dingy white tiles looked like it belonged in the swamps we'd left behind earlier that day. The showerhead was made of some kind of tarnished metal, and the thick block of soap lacked any of the disinfectant smell I was used to. In fact, the whole bathroom seemed like it had come from another time, primarily because everything was analog.

Gone were the sliding doors, automatic lights, and self-modulating water pressure I'd experienced back home. Instead, I had to flip an actual switch to turn on the lights, and even that got me only mixed results in the form of a flickering fluorescent bulb hanging from the ceiling by an exposed metal wire.

"That can't be safe," I muttered, taking a deep breath before discarding my towel and taking the proverbial plunge. It actually took me a moment to figure out the two knobs, but eventually, I surmised that one of them controlled hot water. The other let loose with the cold water—though it was more lukewarm than anything. But at least it was clean, which was more than I had expected.

For the next few minutes, I thoroughly scrubbed myself. I had been almost completely submerged in the fetid swamp water, so the mud and foul-smelling liquid had gotten everywhere. I wasted no time in using the harsh brick of soap to wage a minor war against the stuff, eventually attaining some semblance of cleanliness.

Once I was finished, I stepped out of the shower—and promptly slipped, barely catching myself on a nearby metal bar that was attached to the wall. Yet another difference from my bathroom back home; I'd taken the no-slip surfaces for granted—a mistake I wouldn't make again, I vowed.

After drying myself with my towel, which I'd brought from home, I took a moment to wipe the steam from the small vanity mirror. Even that, simple as it was, seemed so different from what I'd had back in Nova City. Instead of a simple reflective surface, the mirrors back home were host to a bevy of features ranging from hairstyle previews to social media integration. But as low-tech as this new one was, I viewed it as a welcome change.

However, it brought to mind a wholly different issue.

Until that moment, I hadn't really thought about how much everything had changed over the past couple of days. But looking at my reflection in the mirror, I couldn't pretend that my world hadn't come crashing down around me. Not only was the bathroom itself evidence enough of the differences but my reflection was, as well.

On the one hand, it was familiar. Light-brown skin, a dusting of freckles across my nose, and of course, my wild and curly hair. Hazel eyes. A perky nose. High cheekbones. It was the same face I'd always had. However, it had a couple of new additions—chiefly the huge bruise on my jaw and the gash across my left cheek. My uncle had insisted that they'd heal just fine, but I was inordinately terrified that the cut, in particular, would leave a scar. Images of small children running from my monstrous facade flashed through my mind.

I shook my head. That was just a silly exaggeration. Even if it scarred, it would be small. Probably completely unnoticeable. It shouldn't have mattered.

But it did.

The rest of my thin body was similarly familiar, yet battered and bruised. After my monthslong stint as a street rat, when I wasn't sure when my next meal might come along, I'd lost a good deal of weight. And I'd never really had much to lose, so I'd grown so thin that I definitely didn't look healthy.

As I stared at my reflection, I had a distressing thought. With the combination of my Awakening, a decent diet, and the training I'd already started, would I eventually end up looking like Nora? All bulging muscles and veiny mass? I shuddered at the thought. Far be it from me to judge anyone based on their appearance, but I definitely didn't want to end up like that.

I flinched at a sudden banging on the bathroom door that rattled the mirror on the wall. "You 'bout done in there? Food's getting cold," came my uncle's voice.

"One sec," I called, forcing my breathing into an even cadence. Then I muttered under my breath, "Scared me half to death."

My jumpiness was understandable, after the day I'd had. I'd killed an enormous alligator—a creature that, until that day, I wasn't even sure actually existed. Sure, I'd been taught about plenty of animals in the course of my classes, but most had seemed too fanciful to truly exist. I was half convinced that most of them—the alligator included—were mythological creatures on par with sphinxes and dragons.

"Oh God—there aren't really dragons, are there?" I questioned, staring at my reflection. If there were, I doubted a few bullets and an explosive round would do much to take one down.

After a few more seconds, I wrapped the towel around my chest and, taking another deep breath, left the bathroom. Thankfully, the hall outside was empty, so I padded down the corridor to the room that had been set aside for my uncle and me. I found the room—which was little more than a pair of cots, a metallic chest, and four walls—and dragged my duffel onto the cot I'd claimed as my own. A few minutes later, I was dressed in a pair of comfortable shorts, a black tank top emblazoned with a red Leviathan logo, and my favorite sneakers. My hair, I left completely unstyled, instead choosing to tie it back with a black band.

Once I was dressed, I left the room and found my way through the facility to a small kitchen. There, my uncle awaited. He was talking to a pair of other people—one man and one woman—who looked like they were dressed in snakeskin. Belatedly, I realized that, no, it wasn't the skin of a snake. Nor was it faux leather like was so common in Nova City. Instead, it bore a striking resemblance to the alligator we'd killed earlier that very day.

"The hero of the hour!" exclaimed the man. He had a strange mustache that was connected to his sideburns, and he wore a wide-brimmed hat studded with sharp teeth. At his hip was an honest-to-goodness sword. He thrust a tin cup into the air, exclaiming, "Hip hip hooray."

The woman—a dark-skinned brunette with strikingly high cheekbones and a strong jawline—shook her head, saying, "You are such an ass, Douglas."

"Pshaw! She slayed a true monster!" the man—Douglas—countered. "Practically a dragon, it was!"

"Ignore him," said the woman. "I'm Viola. As you heard, this idiot is Douglas."

"Um . . . I'm Mira."

Viola cut her eyes at Jeremiah, saying, "You said Mirabelle."

"That's her name," insisted my uncle.

"I've told you a thousand times I want to be called Mira!" I huffed, crossing my arms. "But you never freaking listen."

"Whatever," he muttered. Then, he pointed to the nearby stove, which looked unlike any cooking apparatus I'd ever seen before. Back home, almost everything came out of a nano-wave. But this? It was huge and bulky and square, with a giant pot of . . . something on top of it. But it did smell delicious.

"What is it?" I asked.

"Gumbo," said Douglas, puffing out his chest. "Family recipe."

"Despite it coming from this idiot," said Viola, hiking her thumb at her companion. "It really is good. We heard the boss was coming by, so he made it special."

I nodded, saying, "Uh . . . thanks." Then, as I pushed past them and gathered a bowl, I asked, "So, you live out here?"

"We do," Viola said, leaning against the counter beside me. "Everyone else here is only temporary. They'll eventually cycle back to Nova or move on to one of the other forts. Maybe even one of the other cities. Houston, maybe. Or Atlanta."

"I don't know what those names mean," I admitted, peeking into the pot. It contained some sort of brown liquid, and it had a wide variety of vegetables and something that might've been meat in it. That's when I recognized one of the shapes. "Are those . . . are those shrimp?"

"Real, freshly caught shrimp, yeah," Douglas answered. "Real okra, too. Some crab meat. We even use fresh tomatoes. You know, the kind of stuff that would cost a fortune in that city in the sky you call home. There are advantages to living down here."

It was all the convincing I needed, and I quickly grabbed the ladle and scooped a heaping portion into my bowl, which already had some rice in it. I found a spoon on the counter, and I couldn't stop myself from tasting it, right then and there. The moment the gumbo hit my tongue, I let out a moan. "Oh God. That's . . . that's the best thing I've ever tasted."

And it wasn't an exaggeration, either. It was literally the best thing I'd ever eaten. It was rich and hearty and laden with all sorts of spices for which I had no name. All I knew was that I wanted more. I devoured everything in record time, and it wasn't until I started in on my second bowl that I realized everyone was looking at me.

"What?" I asked, though with my mouth full, it was largely unintelligible.

"Nothing," a grinning Douglas said. "Eat up."

And I did. Three bowls, and I probably would've eaten more if doing so wouldn't have resulted in everything coming back up. As I ate, my uncle and the two others—who seemed like they might've been a couple, but I wasn't willing to trust my instincts in that arena—talked about things that flew right over my head. However, I did learn that Bart had already started his trip back to Nova City.

Finally, once my hunger was sated, Jeremiah guided me to another room, which was furnished with a series of chairs and an entire shelfful of books. Which was notable, considering that I'd only seen a handful of actual books in my entire life. I itched to inspect them. Or maybe steal them. To the right people, they would be worth a fortune back in Nova. Almost everything was digital, so there was no need for hard copies anymore. Clearly, the denizens of Haven didn't think like that, though. Not that I would ever sell them, of course. I'd always had a thing for real books, and I thought that such a treasure trove would qualify as the survival supplies my uncle wanted me to keep in my arsenal implant.

"So, have you checked your status since fighting the gator?" Jeremiah asked, practically falling onto a cushy leather chair.

"Uh . . ."

"Always check your status, Mirabelle," he said. "Sit down and do it now. Tell me where you've improved."

I glared at him for using my full name, but I didn't say anything. Instead, I sat on the couch adjacent to his chair and did as he told me to do. I was surprised to see that there were a couple of changes.

NAME	Mirabelle Lisa Braddock		
CLASS	N/A (Requirements Not Met)		
LEVEL	1 (3%)		
CONSTITUTION	4/17		
MIND	4/17		
MIST	2/17		
SKILLS	7/7		
SKILL NAME	Skill Tier	Modifiers	Abilities
CYBERNETIC INTERFACE	Tier 0 (7%)	None	2 Cybernetic Slots
FIREARMS	Tier 0 (9%)	None	None
CLOSE QUARTERS COMBAT	Tier 0 (2%)	None	None
STEALTH OPERATIONS	Tier 0 (0%)	None	Camouflage (F)

COMBAT UTILITY	Tier 0 (2%)	None	Triage (F)
			Basic Explosives Handling (F)
			Combat Focus (F)
			Pain Tolerance (F)
			Resistance (F)
			Foraging (F)
			Improvisation (F)
			Regeneration (F)
MISTWALKER	Tier 0 (0%)	+5% Speed (Misthack)	Mistwalk (F)
		+5% Speed (Mistwalk)	Misthack (F)
			Mistwall (F)
SPYCRAFT	Tier 0 (1%)	None	Disguise (F)
			Deception (F)

"Uh, I got level one," I said. "And some of my attributes went up. My skills aren't all at zero percent, either."

"Elaborate."

I did, noting that I'd gained one point in both Constitution and Mist. I also mentioned that my potential had expanded by seven points in each category, as well. Finally, I told him the values associated with my various skills.

"That's good," Jeremiah said. "Very good. One kill, and you've already started to grow."

The mention of growing brought to mind my previous worries about becoming a muscle-bound giant, so I asked, "Uh . . . I'm not going to end up like Nora, am I? All big and bulky?"

"No," he said. "Not unless you want to be. Nora's on so many bio-enhancers that it's a bit of a mystery how she's still alive."

"Bio-enhancers?"

"Look—that potential isn't set in stone, okay?" Jeremiah said. "You can push past it a little. When you do, you start to physically change. With Mind and Mist, those changes aren't visible, but with Constitution, you sometimes get bigger muscles. One of the ways to push those limits is bio-enhancers. They change a person's body chemistry and facilitate muscle growth. Nora's probably a good ten points past her supposed potential, and it shows."

"Oh," I said. "And I guess cybernetics do something similar, right?"

"They do," Jeremiah answered. "But you have to remember—the body has limits. Some of those limits can be exceeded, but there's always a price. For instance, look at Nora. She's big. She's strong. But because of those bio-enhancers, her life span is probably halved. She'll be lucky to be alive forty years from now."

"What's the cost of cybernetics?"

"That's a little more difficult," he said. "For one, you're limited by your skill level. You have two slots. You'll open more as you level your [Cybernetic Interface], but it takes time. So, there aren't that many people capable of reaching Singularity."

"What's that?"

"Eventually, you become more machine than living thing," Jeremiah stated. "I've seen it only once, but it was terrifying. Both for me and the man it happened to. I don't wish that on anyone—not even my worst enemies."

"Oh."

It was a troubling scenario, losing one's humanity, but I could think of plenty of situations where a person might choose to push the limits. Life was difficult, and sometimes, people had to make difficult choices just to survive.

"What's the plan, then? We're not staying here, right?" I asked, changing the subject. "Where are we going?"

"Mobile," he said. "It's where I was born. Where I lived up until the Initialization."

"And when we get there?"

"Training," Jeremiah said. "Three months. Dawn to dusk. No breaks. It's going to be hell for you, but we need to get you to a decent baseline so you can survive out here. After that, the real training begins."

"What's that mean?" I asked.

"Don't worry about that right now," my uncle said. Suddenly, a small chip appeared in his hand. He handed it to me. "Slot that. Every night, I want you to go through that."

"What's it do?" was the obvious next question.

"It's training," he said. "Similar to how we're going to train your body and physical skills, you've got to train your Mind and Mist. That chip contains a mutating set of puzzles that will become progressively more difficult. Most of them are numbers based, a lot like what you'll see when you start Mistwalking, but there are also logic puzzles, riddles, and spatial-reasoning problems."

"That doesn't sound fun at all."

"It's not meant to be" was his response. His expression hardened. "This is life-and-death, Mirabelle. I know you're looking at this as some grand adventure. That's probably my fault. But if you don't master these skills, if you don't improve, you are not going to survive. Even if by some miracle you do, you'll end up as some alien's lackey. I won't let that happen, Mirabelle. I just won't."

"I . . . I don't . . . o-okay," I said, a little taken aback by the sudden shift in his demeanor. It wasn't like I wanted that, either, but it seemed a lot more personal to him than it was for me. Which was probably accurate. After everything he'd seen and done, I felt sure that the approaching Integration—and the aliens that would inevitably come with it—was very personal. I added, "I'll start working on it tonight."

"Good. Better get started," he said. "We've got an early morning ahead of us. Now, let's get that cut in your side patched up. I'm no medic, but it'll have to do until we get to Mobile."

I nodded and lifted my shirt, exposing the back portion of my ribs. The wound didn't hurt much—not with the med-hypo's issue still coursing through my veins—but I knew it wouldn't be like that for much longer. My uncle wordlessly inspected it, then retrieved something from his own arsenal implant; it looked like a small silver gun with a cannister attached to the bottom. As he ran a nozzle along the cut, a light foam spewed from the tip, sealing the injury. After that, he told me to head back to my room, which I did. I had little desire to be around him when he was in one of his moods. My uncle was a lot of things, but sociable really wasn't one of them. On some level, I understood that there was a lot of trauma behind those moods, but on another, I didn't really have the experience to understand what that meant.

In any case, I soon found myself lying on my cot, where I followed his instructions and slotted the chip. Immediately, a number puzzle flashed before my eyes. It wasn't difficult. Just pattern recognition. And I solved it very quickly, only for it to be replaced by a logic problem. Then, once I solved that one, an equation. Another pattern-recognition puzzle, but instead of numbers, there were alien symbols. On and on it went for three hours until my mind felt like it was frying from the inside out.

But to my surprise, I wanted to keep going. There was something addictive about solving one puzzle after another. Almost like the games I used to play on the Mist screen back home. Still, I knew I needed rest, so I took the chip out of the port in my neck and set it aside before reaching over and turning off the light.

I was asleep in a matter of minutes, and my night was filled with dreams of giant alligators who gave me math problems to solve. If I failed, they would eat me. It was not a pleasant dream.

CHAPTER TWELVE

MORE COMPLICATED THAN EXPECTED

When I first gained my skills, I thought they were underwhelming. Minor increases in fire rate and damage. However, when I reached the fourth tier, I realized that I'd barely scratched the surface of what was possible.

—Jeremiah Braddock III

I awoke well before dawn. The cot wasn't very comfortable, and my dreams had been wholly terrifying. Not a great combination for a good night's rest. So, not wanting to disturb my uncle, whose snores were loud enough that I wondered if their presence had been a factor in my inability to sleep, I decided to take a few minutes to examine and adjust my interface.

The first thing I did was to move the various readouts around. The time went into the top-right corner, and right beside that was the compass readout. After a little fiddling, I was able to open a couple of other displays, as well. The most important was a tiny set of gun icons meant to represent the contents of my arsenal implant; the guns themselves weren't that important, but the numbers beside them, which were meant to indicate my stores of ammunition, were. With that, I would never unknowingly run out of ammunition.

Next, I managed to open a display to indicate my health. It wasn't represented by a number, like in some of the video games I'd played. Rather, it was a green silhouette of my body, divided into various sections. From the instruction manual, I knew that so long as the sections remained green, I was okay. If they turned yellow, I'd been damaged. Red, and I'd better find some sort of medical attention. To my surprise, everything was green except for a yellow section on my right side. But even that had begun to turn colors.

Finally, I found a way to open a square display in the top-left corner. Meant to be a minimap, it didn't show much—just the boundaries of the room—but I'd read that, as my [Cybernetic Interface] skill increased in potency, the map would expand. I had no idea how big the map could get, but it seemed silly not to use the tools at my disposal. After all, the KIOI's versatility was one of the things that set it apart; most optical interfaces weren't equipped with so many features or the ability to adapt to larger amounts of Mist.

Having taken care of my interface for now, I turned my attention to my skills. Since my Awakening, it'd felt as if I hadn't had a chance to turn around, much less truly study the transformation I'd undergone. And it was a true transformation, too—as impactful as if I'd suddenly replaced my entire body with top-end cybernetics. Now, though, with a couple of hours before dawn, I couldn't stop myself from exploring the breadth of those changes.

So, I opened my skills menu and drilled down into the submenu before focusing on my [Firearms] skill. When I did, a branching set of boxes opened up.

Tree	Firearms: Tier 0 (9%) +5% Damage (All Firearms) +2% Reload Speed (All Firearms) +2% Accuracy (All Firearms)			
Branch	Rifle: Tier 1 (7%)	Pistol: Tier 1 (2%)	Scattergun: Tier 1 (0%)	Sharpshooter: Tier 1 (9%)
Tier 1	+15% Damage (Rifle)	+15% Damage (Pistol)	+15% Damage (Scattergun)	+15% Accuracy (All Firearms)
Tier 2	+15% Range (Rifle)	+10% Accuracy (Pistol)	+15% Reload/ Ammunition Regeneration Speed (Scattergun)	+5% Damage (All Firearms)
Tier 3	Ability: Empowered Shot	Ability: Quickdraw	Ability: Double Shot	+5% Range (All Firearms)

| Tier 4 | Plasma Rifle Certification | Energy Pistol Certification | Explosive Scattergun Certification | Weapon Modification Certification |
| Tier 5 | +15% Rate of Fire (Rifle) | +25% Rate of Fire (Pistol) | +15% Accuracy (Scattergun) | Ability: Mark Target |

I read and reread the contents of the skill tree, trying to make sense of it. Then, when I couldn't figure everything out, I reopened my status to see if it might help.

NAME	Mirabelle Lisa Braddock		
CLASS	N/A (Requirements Not Met)		
LEVEL	1 (3%)		
CONSTITUTION	4/17		
MIND	5/17		
MIST	3/17		
SKILLS	7/7		
SKILL NAME	Skill Tier	Modifiers	Abilities
CYBERNETIC INTERFACE	Tier 0 (8%)	None	2 Cybernetic Slots
FIREARMS	Tier 0 (9%)	None	None
CLOSE QUARTERS COMBAT	Tier 0 (2%)	None	None
STEALTH OPERATIONS	Tier 0 (0%)	None	Camouflage (F)
COMBAT UTILITY	Tier 0 (2%)	None	Triage (F) Basic Explosives Handling (F) Combat Focus (F) Pain Tolerance (F) Resistance (F) Foraging (F) Improvisation (F) Regeneration (F)

MISTWALKER	Tier 0 (1%)	+5% Speed (Misthack) +5% Speed (Mistwalk)	Mistwalk (F) Misthack (F) Mistwall (F)
SPYCRAFT	Tier 0 (1%)	None	Disguise (F) Deception (F)

I didn't quite understand, though. I was Tier 1 in all my subskills; therefore, I should have at least seen some of the bonuses specified in the various branches of the [Firearms] tree, right? As if my interface heard my question, a message flashed before my eyes:

Bonuses applied when reaching 100% progress in current tier.

Well, that answered that, I suppose. I had a long way to go, apparently. But that wasn't a bad thing, really. If it was easy, then everyone would be so far ahead of me that there would be little chance of catching up. In any case, I started going down the list of my skills. First up was [Cybernetic Interface], which didn't have a skill tree. Instead, it simply had a description:

Cybernetic Interface—Allows the user to interface with various Mist-powered constructs. Current Progress: Tier 0 (8%).

Well, that was easy enough to understand, so I moved on to [Close Quarters Combat], which resulted in a skill tree similar to the one that came for [Firearms]:

Tree	Close Quarters Combat: Tier 0 (2%) +5% Damage (Melee) +2% Speed (Melee) +2% Accuracy (Melee)			
Branch	Pugilism: Tier 1 (0%)	Bladed Weapons: Tier 1 (0%)	Blunt Weapons: Tier 1 (0%)	Movement: Tier 1 (1%)
Tier 1	+5% Damage (Unarmed)	Nano-Blade Certification	+5% Damage (Blunt Weapons)	+2% Movement Speed

Tier 2	+10% Damage (Unarmed)	+5% Speed (Bladed Weapons)	+10% Accuracy (Blunt Weapons)	+2% Movement Speed
Tier 3	Ability: Combination Punch	Ability: Eviscerate	Ability: Pummel	Ability: Engage
Tier 4	+15% Damage (Unarmed)	+10% Accuracy (Bladed Weapons)	+10% Damage (Blunt Weapons)	+5% Movement Speed
Tier 5	Ability: Barrage	Energy Blade Certification	Ability: Mighty Swing	Ability: Disengage

I could tell that there were quite a few benefits to training that particular skill, and I was impressed with my uncle's foresight in making me learn it. I didn't particularly want to start pummeling my opponents with my hands and feet, but I also knew it would probably be necessary. Still, I didn't relish the idea of practicing it. In any case, I moved on to the next skill, [Combat Utility], and instead of seeing a skill tree, I was rewarded with a list of abilities:

Triage (F): Increases the effectiveness of rudimentary medical treatment and the accuracy of medical evaluation (5%).

Basic Explosives Handling (F): Increases the stability and yield of explosives (10%).

Combat Focus (F): When in battle, increases clarity and speed of thoughts and perception (2%).

Pain Tolerance (F): Increases the ability to withstand pain (5%).

Resistance (F): Increases resistances to disease, poison, and detrimental medical conditions (5%).

Foraging (F): Basic recognition of useful items (both synthetic and natural).

Improvisation (F): Ability to improvise basic weaponry and amenities.

Regeneration (F): Increases rate of natural healing (15%).

"Now, that's what I'm talking about," I whispered to myself, though I regretted it when I heard my uncle stir. Resolving to keep quiet a little longer, I moved on to the next skill, [Mistwalker], which I had to admit was the one that made me the most curious.

Tree	Mistwalker: Tier 0 (1%) Ability: Mistwalk (Granted upon Skill's Acquisition) Ability: Misthack (Granted upon Skill's Acquisition) Ability: Mistwall (Granted upon Skill's Acquisition)			
Branch	Mistwalk: Tier 1 (2%)	Mistwall: Tier 1 (1%)	Misthack: Tier 1 (0%)	Mist Manipulation: Tier 1 (-1%)
Tier 1	F-Grade Systems Infiltration	F-Grade System Defense	+5% Speed (Misthack)	Ability: Overcharge
Tier 2	E-Grade Systems Infiltration	E-Grade System Defense	+2% Speed (Misthack)	+2% Strength (Overcharge)
Tier 3	D-Grade Systems Infiltration	D-Grade System Defense	Ability: Breach	+2% Strength (Overcharge)
Tier 4	+2% Infiltration Stability	Ability: System Redirect	+5% Speed (Misthack)	+10% Cybernetic Efficiency
Tier 5	Ability: Bypass Trivial Defenses	+5% Increased System Defense Strength	Ability: Overload System	+5% Strength (Overcharge)

The skill tree gave me some ideas about the general purpose of the skill—at least enough that I could make some connections. I was aware that there were people who specialized in hacking the various systems that ran the world. However, I'd always thought that it was the result of years of experience and study; now, I knew that wasn't completely true. It was a skill. What's more, it was one I now possessed. Almost as if to reaffirm my understanding, I investigated the skill's abilities:

Mistwalk (F)—Thoroughly infiltrate systems via a wired connection. Expansive Access.

Misthack (F)—Quickly (and temporarily) infiltrate systems via Mist connection. Limited Access.

Mistwall (F)—A barrier between your system and any outside influence.

The explanations were a lot less descriptive than I might have hoped, but there was enough that I could piece together where each of the abilities fit. Mistwalk was for stationary systems, like those that governed a megabuilding's functions or the security system at one of the warehouses in Algiers. Meanwhile, Misthack seemed like the quick and dirty version of the ability, usable by riding the Mist in the air. Finally, Mistwall seemed like a personal firewall, shielding me from other Mistwalkers.

Or perhaps I was completely wrong. I had no real way of knowing until I actually tried to use the abilities. In any case, I had two more skills, both with associated abilities. First, I looked at [Spycraft], which gave me two abilities:

Disguise (F)—Adopt a new persona by concealing your Tier and details of your appearance.

Deception (F)—Subtly skew the facts in your favor via facial cues and the manipulation of Mist.

They were both pretty straightforward. One would allow me to conceal my identity, and the other would let me lie more effectively. However, the last seemed to smack of mind control, which didn't seem possible. What did I know, though? Mist was comprised of uncountable microscopic machines; there was no telling what they could do. Then and there, I decided to discard any notions of what was and wasn't possible. I had lived a sheltered life, and I clearly didn't know how the world worked. From what I could tell, Mist was functionally indistinguishable from the magic I had seen in video games and movies, so there probably wasn't much of a limit to what it could do.

Lastly, I inspected my final skill, [Stealth Operations]. It granted the Camouflage ability.

Camouflage (F)—Naturally use your environment for concealment.

Well, that was entirely unhelpful. Further, it seemed like the last two skills were related. I was about to dig into one of my manuals—I still hadn't really studied much about my scattergun's functionality—when I realized that my uncle was staring at me. More, light was streaming through one of the windows. I had been looking at my skills for hours.

"Find anything useful?" Jeremiah asked, guessing what I'd been doing.

"I was checking my skills and abilities," I said. "It's . . . a lot."

"It certainly is" was his response as he sat up. He wasn't wearing a shirt, so I could see the scars crisscrossing his chest. There were so many—from slashes to what looked like the puckered scars of gunshots—evidence of a life spent in the line of fire. He leaned forward, his elbows on his knees as he looked up at me, and asked, "Any questions?"

"So many," I said. "What are the differences between the different [Mistwalker] abilities? I think I have an idea, but I'm not sure." I told him my suspicions. "Is that how it is?"

"More or less," Jeremiah stated. "But if you want anything more than the broad strokes, you're going to have to go to someone else. I don't have that skill."

"What skills do you have?" I asked.

"The right ones."

"Oh, come on—I don't—"

"Don't tell anyone what your skills are," he said. "It doesn't matter if they're your friends. It doesn't matter if you trust them implicitly. With who you are and what you're going to be, there are going to be people who will do just about anything to learn your secrets. Don't give them an opening. Doing so will put your friends and family in danger."

"Oh . . . okay," I said, surprised by the vehemence in his tone. Clearly, he'd had to learn that lesson the hard way; I resolved not to put myself in that kind of situation. "I just . . . I just didn't know."

"It's okay," Jeremiah said. "But you need to understand that this world, it's a dangerous place filled with selfish people. Even the ones who seem like they're on your side can flip on you in an instant if they think it'll help them get even the tiniest bit ahead. There are only two people in this world you can trust. Yourself. And me." He sighed. "And trusting me should be stretching it."

"That . . . that sounds pretty horrible," I said. After having grown up in Nova City, I was no stranger to its pervasive attitude of self-interest. In that city, everyone was out for themselves. Perhaps they could trust family, but even then, I'd heard of plenty of sons and daughters, brothers and sisters who'd turned on their kin.

"Yeah. It does," Jeremiah said, standing and stretching. "A lot of people think it got worse after the Initialization, but I don't think that's true. When that Mist cloud hit us, I think it just exposed humanity for what it was. No more pretense. Just raw self-interest. Without consequences, people just did whatever they wanted to do. And nobody could stop them. Few even tried. Before, we were playing at civilization. Now, all that pretense has been stripped away."

I didn't respond because I really didn't have anything to contribute. Jeremiah had seen so much more of the world, so if he said that was how things were, then who was I to argue? Still, I wanted to believe that there were good people out there. Like Heather, who just wanted to be my friend, regardless of how little interest I showed in the prospect. Or Nora, who was my uncle's loyal right-hand woman. Or a hundred others with whom I had interacted over the course of my short life. Maybe my uncle just couldn't see it because he didn't want to. Or because he couldn't let himself.

"Get up and get dressed," he said. "We've got a long way to go today, and it's probably not going to be as uneventful as yesterday."

Uneventful? I'd had to battle a dinosaur-sized alligator. That didn't seem uneventful to me. I didn't get the chance to say as much because he was out of the room a second later. He hadn't even bothered to put on a shirt.

With a sigh, I pushed myself out of bed and started my morning routine. It was a mistake. My entire body felt like it had been run over by a hover car, and the wound in my side was on fire. Whatever the effect of Regeneration, it clearly wasn't enough to counteract the punishment I'd been through the day before. I shuddered to think of what kind of shape I'd have been in without it.

Groaning, I shuffled to the bathroom where I took care of my business before washing my face. I tried to do something—anything—with my hair, but ended up settling for just tying it back again. I was going to be battling across the monster-infested wilderness, not going to a party, after all. Still, I wished I had the time—or honestly, the proper expertise—to make it look decent. Maybe there was a skill for that. Oh well. Couldn't have everything, I supposed.

After that, I left the bathroom and returned to my temporary bedroom, where I got dressed in a pair of nondescript cargo pants, chunky boots, and a tank top. I'd learned my lesson on that first day, and I wasn't going to wear anything I really liked. Then, once I was ready, I shouldered my duffel, checked to make sure my arsenal implant was functioning properly, and headed to the kitchen, where I heard a bevy of voices.

When I arrived, my uncle was saying, "Standard convoy. I will be in the lead truck. Four transport trucks. And one heavy in the back. I don't see what the problem is."

Viola groaned, massaging her forehead. "The problem is that we don't have the manpower to protect four trucks," she said. "Three days ago, we sent a convoy north to Memphis. They're not supposed to be back for a week."

"And that's if nothin' happened to 'em," interjected Douglas. "Haven't heard from 'em since day before yesterday."

"That's nothing," Viola said. "Just interference in the Dead Zone."

"Dead Zone?" I asked. "What's that?"

"Nothing you need to know about yet," my uncle said.

"Oh, c'mon. It's common knowledge," Douglas said. "The girl deserves to know what's waitin' out there."

"Fine," Jeremiah sighed. "It's feeling less and less like I'm the one in charge around here."

"Sure, boss."

"Go ahead," he said. "Tell her."

Douglas beamed at me. "The Dead Zone is a strip of land, probably a hundred miles wide and five times as long that runs from what used to be central Mississippi almost all the way to Montgomery. Or what's left of it."

"I don't know what any of those places are," I admitted. "But why's it called the Dead Zone?"

"Mist is wild there. Nothing works," Viola stated. "We can send trucks through, but they're slow because we have to use solar power. The real problem is the wildlife, though. Everything's bigger and badder there."

"Bigger than that alligator?" I asked.

Douglas laughed. "That was a baby even for these parts!" he guffawed. "Up there, you got black bears the size of—"

"Enough," Jeremiah said. "She understands what it is now. No sense in scaring her."

"But—"

Jeremiah slammed his hand down on the counter, growling, "Enough!"

"Fine, fine," Douglas said, raising his hands in surrender.

"This is all well and good, but it doesn't solve the problem," Viola said, probably as much to defuse the situation as to get everything back on track. "We don't have the manpower, boss."

"Fine," Jeremiah said, running his hand across his bald head. "I'll be all the manpower you need in the lead truck. Mirabelle will ride in the back with whoever else you can spare."

"She ready for that?" asked Douglas.

"No" was my uncle's answer. "But we need to get these supplies to Mobile. Without them, people are going to start dying off. You know that. No—sometimes, we have to do what's necessary, regardless of whether or not it's the smart move."

"You're the boss," Douglas said.

"I'll get everyone moving," Viola added. "You two ought to get something to eat and stock up on provisions before you go. It's a hard trip."

As she spoke, Viola grabbed something long and yellow. She tossed it to me, and I caught it. After I did, I asked, "What is this?"

It was obviously organic, but I'd never encountered anything like it. Douglas asked, "You ain't never seen a banana before?"

"She's lived her whole life in Nova City," Jeremiah stated. "The closest she's come to fruit is Tasty Juice."

"Ugh. That stuff is neither tasty nor juice," Douglas said. "It's like Kool-Aid, but with a gallon of high-fructose corn syrup in it. You remember Kool-Aid, right? God. What I wouldn't give for—"

"Do you eat it?" I asked, skeptically eyeing the rubbery thing in my hand.

"Peel it first," Jeremiah answered.

"Oh, c'mon!" Douglas said. "I was hoping she'd just bite into it! You're absolutely no fun at all."

Jeremiah ignored him, but I shot a scathing glance his way. That shut the man up. My uncle said, "Hand it here. I'll show you."

I did, and he bent the stem and slowly peeled the yellow outer coating away to reveal something white. Then, he handed it back to me. I looked at it with a bit of suspicion, but my uncle wasn't exactly known as a practical joker. So, I took a bite. The moment I did, I was overcome with how rich the taste was.

I was no stranger to candy, so I'd had plenty of sweeter treats. But this? It was just different. And undeniably better. "Oh my God . . . it's so . . . mmm," I mumbled, my mouth full. That drew a bout of laughter from everyone in the room. I swallowed, but before I took another bite, I asked, "How come we don't have these in Nova?!"

"They do," Jeremiah said. "Just not in the Garden. Or Algiers. They're rare anywhere outside of King's Row, actually. We only have them here because there's a grove near one of my forts. It's a serious pain in the ass to harvest because the grove is infested with this tribe of semisentient monkeys that throw balls of—"

"She doesn't need to know the details, boss," Viola said.

"Oh, right. Eat up. When you're finished, meet me outside," he said to me.

I barely heard him, instead focusing on the delectable treat. In fact, I ate three more bananas—and grabbed another three for the road, shoving them into the pockets of my cargo pants—before I followed my uncle outside. In the light of day, the place was a little less drab, but the bunker-like buildings still looked like unadorned slabs of concrete. However, there was a new addition in the form of five vehicles lined up near the gate.

They were all boxy, with minimal windows and huge, knobby tires, but they had designs I recognized. The two vehicles in the front and back were clearly modified armored personal carriers, with thick slabs of pitted and dented metal lining every surface. That wasn't that uncommon a sight; I'd seen their like plenty of times in Nova City, though those were the hover-car variants. These had huge wheels that were almost as tall as me. The three trucks in the middle of the line were just as boxy, but they were made to carry goods as opposed to people. None of the vehicles were new, and they were coated in layers of rust and grime.

I crossed to where my uncle was talking to a small squad of seven men and women. All were armed with assault rifles, and all but one wore molded metal armor. I saw a few cybernetic limbs, as well. "Mirabelle," said Jeremiah. "You're in the back with these seven. I'm up front. Let's move."

"This little girl?" asked one of the women, looking me up and down. "Really? She's not even armed."

I glanced at Jeremiah, and he gave me a slight nod. I took that as permission. In an instant, I had Ferdinand II in my hand and pressing against her chin. It was a bit awkward because she was probably a head taller than me, but I made it work. Suddenly, I wished I had a hammer to cock back for dramatic effect, like in the movies that played on Nova City's entertainment feeds. That would have definitely been badass.

A moment later, the rest of the squad had shouldered their weapons, and they were pointing them at me. That seemed decidedly less badass, but I wasn't about to back down. Instead, I chose bravado.

"Think you can put me down before I make a canoe out of her head?" I growled. It wasn't nearly as intimidating as I wanted it to be, but that was probably because of my high-pitched voice. It got the point across, though. "If so, give it a try."

A tense moment followed, and I was convinced that I'd just made a huge mistake. I was terrified, but I didn't let it show. Instead, I remained stock-still, with the barrel of my hand cannon pressed firmly against the woman's chin.

Then, suddenly, she let out a chuckle. "Make a canoe out of my head," she muttered. "Seriously? That's some terrible trash talk. Where the hell did you even learn that?"

"W-what?" I asked.

"Quit playing," Jeremiah said. "We need to get on the road."

I dismissed my pistol into my arsenal implant and backed a step away. The woman looked at me for a moment, then said, "You're pretty quick, little girl. I'm Britt, and this is my squad." She rattled off some other names, but there was no way I was going to remember them, so I didn't even try. "S'pose we're going to be working together this trip. Good to know you're not completely useless."

"My name is Mira, not 'little girl,'" I said. "And thanks. I guess."

"Sure thing," she said, throwing a crooked grin in my direction. Then, to her squad, she said, "Alright, ladies—and gentlemen, I guess—mount up. Stay frosty and keep your heads on a swivel. You know what's out there."

A moment later, everyone was moving toward the armored personnel carrier in the back. As I followed, I saw my uncle move toward the front, and within a few minutes, we were off.

CHAPTER THIRTEEN

RAIDERS

Stupidity and overconfidence cost us more lives than anything else. Entire generations had been raised on games, and they all thought that their familiarity with similar systems would give them an advantage in the new world. And in a few cases, they were right. In so many others, reality soon asserted itself. Death followed.

—Jeremiah Braddock III

I sat across from Britt, trying not to let my discomfort show. But every bump in the road jostled me and threatened to throw me across the vehicle's cramped cabin. I clutched a nylon strap to keep myself in place, but all that managed to do was make me swing around like some kind of primate. To distract myself from how silly I must've looked, I studied my companions.

Britt was tall, thin, and pretty, if in a severe kind of way. Her skin was dark, but in an entirely different hue than my soft brown, and her hair, which had been shaved on one side, was straight and glossy. She had a pair of red chevrons tattooed on her cheeks, and her dark eyes seemed to take in everything. In addition to her rifle, which seemed a bit less technically advanced than the one in my arsenal implant, she carried a tomahawk at her hip. Finally, her left arm was entirely cybernetic and covered in gleaming strips of metal.

"Nice cyberware," I said, speaking up so Britt could hear me over the drone of the gasoline engine. Having never left Nova City, where all the vehicles ran on Mist, I'd never encountered anything that ran on fossil fuels.

"You like it?" asked Britt, flexing her mechanical fingers. "I can crush rocks with this bad boy. More importantly, it's got a stability enhancer. Makes aiming much easier."

I could see that. In my experience, I was much more accurate when I could rest my rifle on a bipod, but that wasn't always possible, especially in the heat of battle.

I nodded. "Makes sense," I said.

"So, you're the boss's daughter or something?" she asked.

"Niece," I said.

"What the hell are you doing out here, then?" Britt asked. "You should be cozied up in some tower, going to all the best schools. Not out here in the raider territory."

"Raider territory?"

"Bandits," she said. "That's why we usually don't send convoys out without at least twenty guards. We're light, even with the boss along for the ride. So, I hope you can hold your own, rich girl."

"I'm not rich."

"Yeah? With how fast that arsenal implant activated, I'd put it at least at mark three. Maybe better," she said. "And that kind of thing costs a lot of money. Couple that with the fact that you're the boss's daughter—"

"Niece."

"Whatever. He raised you, didn't he, princess?" Britt said, and suddenly, I started to understand that Britt knew far more about me than she'd let on. Had everything been a setup? "Makes no difference, really. The boss is the richest guy I ever heard of, and it looks like you're his pet project. So, by proxy, you're a rich girl."

"Big words, Britt," said one of the other guards with a chuckle. He was huge—at least as big as Nora, with similarly bulging muscles. The difference was that the entire left side of his face was encased in metal. "Proxy. I like it."

"Shut up, Clay," Britt growled. "Or I might just hesitate when you need me to save your life. Again. Besides, it was five letters. If that's a big word to you . . ."

"Or she might decide to skip a step and just kick your ass right now," said the last person in the passenger compartment. He was slimmer than both Britt and Clay, with cybernetic legs that clicked on the metal floor every time he moved. Two other guards were in the front seats, and another pair were atop the transport, where they were manning a pair of turrets.

"Don't threaten me with a good time, Slick," said Clay, waggling his eyebrow. "Did I tell you about this one time when I got into a fight with this chick down in Apalachicola? We were at this bar, you see? And we were both three sheets to the wind. Well, I said somethin' stupid, and—"

"And she kicked your ass," Britt said. "So, a normal day for you."

"You'd think so, wouldn't you?" said Clay. "But before I knew it, she had me pinned down in the middle of that bar. And then, out of nowhere, she shoved her tongue down my throat. We did it right then and there, and wasn't nobody there who could stop us, neither. Best sex I ever had."

"Gross," I muttered.

"You're such a pig, Clay," Britt spat.

"What?" he asked, spreading his hands wide. "I didn't do nothin' wrong! She was the aggressor! I just wanted a good tussle!"

"Still gross," I said.

"I have to agree with the princess," said Britt. She looked at me, held up her closed fist, and said, "Girl power."

"This is not what I expected this to—"

An explosion interrupted my statement, and an instant later, the side of the transport disintegrated into a fiery ball, taking Britt and Slick with it. I didn't have time to react before the transport was sent spinning through the air, and I saw Clay get thrown free. I only avoided that fate because of the death grip I had on the nylon strap.

A few seconds later, the vehicle slid to a stop on its side, and I fell atop what was left of Britt. The woman wasn't just dead. Half her body had been vaporized right down to her metal skeleton. Slick had gotten it even worse, and all that was left of him was a single metal foot, which had somehow dug into the floor.

The world spun as I tried to reorient myself. Shaking my head, I pushed myself to my knees and promptly vomited all over Britt's bisected corpse. My ears were ringing, but over that, I heard the unmistakable sound of gunfire.

So. Much. Gunfire.

It felt like I'd suddenly found myself in a war zone, which—as someone who'd spent her whole life in Nova City, where life was cheap and nobody really cared who lived or died—should have been easy for me to accept. But this was different than a few errant gunshots or a blitz from the Enforcers. It was ongoing and far more urgent than anything I'd ever experienced.

Without the Combat Focus that came from my [Combat Utility] skill, I probably would have frozen up then and there. If that had happened, I had no doubt that I would have ended up just like Britt. As it was, though, I took a few deep breaths before taking stock of my situation. And it didn't look good.

The vehicle had been turned over on its side, and because of the way it had been bent out of shape by whatever had torn a hole in it, the door in the back looked like it wasn't going to open anytime soon. Still, I rose unsteadily to my feet and stumbled in that direction. Harnessing every bit of my admittedly pitiful strength, I aimed a front kick at what looked like its weakest point. I was rewarded with a sharp pain in my foot, but the door remained firmly entrenched.

Another nearby explosion shook me to my core, and the vehicle rang like a bell. It wasn't a direct hit, but it wasn't really a miss, either. Panic overwhelmed my thoughts, and I sank to my haunches, clutching my knees and rocking back and forth as I expected the next shot to rectify that mistake.

It didn't come.

And more importantly, my Combat Focus started putting in the real work, dragging me from the quagmire of terror that had engulfed me. My breathing slowed. My stomach unclenched. And most importantly, my thoughts cleared. I slapped myself in the face, muttering, "C'mon, Mira. You're better than this. Get it the fuck together."

Another deep breath, and I started to think. How was I going to get myself out of that death trap? The door was jammed shut, which completed the compartment's status as an unadorned metal box.

What assets did I have at my disposal?

I had my rifle, but I felt certain that I couldn't get a round through the thick plating that covered the vehicle's door. And even if I could, what would such a small hole accomplish? No—the rifle was out.

Next came my scattergun. By nature, it was intended as an antipersonnel weapon, right? It would do nothing to the door and even less to the walls.

"Why couldn't I get a freaking rocket launcher?" I mumbled to myself.

But what about Ferdinand II? I had some explosive rounds, didn't I? Wasn't that precisely what I needed? I was a bit ashamed that I hadn't thought of that a little sooner, but in my defense, thinking clearly while gunfire and explosions filled the air wasn't exactly easy. And I was pretty sure I had at least a mild concussion.

Oh, and the dead bodies. That only a couple of minutes before had been walking, talking, and joking people. Yeah—not the best environment for critical thinking. Still, I ended up finding the right strategy, didn't I? That had to count for something.

Summoning Ferdinand II from my arsenal implant, I flipped the bulky cylinder open and dumped the old rounds out. After the fight with the alligator, I'd loaded it with armor-piercing rounds, hoping that if I ran into another of the enormous reptiles, I could make quick work of it. And sure, those rounds might punch a hole or two through the vehicle's armor, but I didn't see how that would get me free. So, I slipped the old bullets into my pocket before summoning the explosive-tipped rounds and slipping them into the cylinder. A moment later, I backed all the way to the other side of the compartment—which was only about ten feet—and took aim.

Then, I thought better of it.

Even if everything went perfectly, I wouldn't escape such an explosion unscathed. I needed cover. And sadly, there wasn't much of that lying around. Just a corpse that had been bisected by an explosion and a metal foot. None of that would help me out much, would it? Still, I swallowed my revulsion and dragged Britt's body—or the half that was left—and used it as a makeshift riot shield. I took aim and fired.

The resulting explosion threw me against the wall with enough force that I thought I felt a couple of ribs break. For a few seconds, the panic returned as I felt iron bands wrapping themselves around my chest, preventing me from breathing. Then, after only a few more seconds, my Combat Focus reasserted itself, and I realized that I'd just had the breath knocked out of me. More, I could tell that my Pain Tolerance had definitely taken the edge off of my broken ribs.

But I'd survived. And what's more, there was a hole in the door just big enough that I thought I could slither through it. What was left of Britt hadn't been so fortunate, and I realized that I was holding on to a strip of her combat vest, from which an unidentifiable piece of blackened flesh was clinging. I dropped it in disgust, then immediately felt guilty about it. Not that long ago, she'd been a human being. Now? Little more than a charred pile of flesh.

I'd always been under the impression that life wasn't worth much in Nova City. It seemed even cheaper in the outside world.

I couldn't let myself get distracted, though. So, pushing Britt's fate to the back of my mind, I refocused and made my way to the hole. It was taller than it was wide, so I had to contort myself to fit through. That, in turn, made the pain from my broken ribs flare up. By the time I tumbled out into the open air, I did so with all the grace of a fish on dry land. I lay there for a long moment, my ears still ringing and my body feeling like I'd just pulled double duty as Nora's punching bag.

I wasn't doing so great is my point. But I didn't have time to wallow in my pain; I had to act, and fast. Otherwise, I'd end up just like my brief companions. Climbing to my knees, I levered myself to my feet and took stock of the situation.

Chaos reigned all around me. Everywhere I looked, there was fire. The battle had done quite a number on the heavily forested area through which we'd been traveling. Trees lay on their sides, their trunks splintered and broken. The concrete that had been the road hadn't fared much better, and it was pockmarked with craters and divots. But to my surprise, the transport trucks in the center of the convoy had been unaffected. It only took a cursory glance to figure out why; around each one was a barely visible dome of blue light. Energy shields, and top-grade ones, too.

Beyond those vehicles was my uncle's transport, though he was nowhere to be seen—which scared me. Without him, there was no way I could fight off the attackers.

Speaking of which—they were everywhere. Wearing rough-spun clothing with armor stitched together from beast hides, the bandits looked entirely feral. Some sported homegrown cybernetics, but most were pure, unenhanced human beings. Armed with ancient-looking rifles and bladed weapons that looked like they'd been cobbled together from scrap, each one cut a fearsome—if primitive—figure.

Thankfully, they hadn't noticed me yet. Or not so thankfully, considering that, judging by the flickering energy shield, they were on the verge of breaking through. I couldn't let that happen. So, I stowed Ferdinand II back in my arsenal implant and summoned my rifle. Reconfiguring it into the sniper mode, I knelt down on one knee. Then, I took aim.

Without any more hesitation, I fired.

An unlucky bandit's chest exploded into a fountain of blood, gore, and bone. I barely saw it. Whether I was in shock or my Combat Focus was more effective than I expected, I smoothly shifted my focus to the next bandit, who was busy wailing on the shield with what looked to be a buzz saw blade attached to a metal pipe. It even spun. But with me sixty yards away, it didn't matter. I squeezed the trigger again, and the bullet took him just below the collarbone. On its way out, it obliterated most of his spine. And I shifted to the next target. Then the next. I took out six of them before they even knew I was there.

All good things must come to an end, though, and I'd never expected to kill them all without being noticed. When they did, there were more than a dozen of them left, and I'd pissed every single one of them off. The shields forgotten, most of them charged at me. The ones who had firearms took aim, and I ducked behind the overturned armored personnel carrier.

Taking a moment to reload, I reconfigured my weapon back into assault rifle mode. Then, keeping the personnel carrier between me and the charging horde of bandits, I retreated into the forest. Leaping over an overturned pine tree, I slid to a stop about twenty yards away from the road. From the cover of the fallen tree, I took aim.

A second or two later, the first bandits charged into view. Upon closer inspection, the woman was even more feral than I'd first thought. Dirty, with matted hair, she was covered in blue tattoos and dressed in armor that looked like it had been made from an alligator. Upon her head was a horned helmet, and she carried a rifle that looked like it was at least a century old.

I must've been a little too exposed because she noticed me straightaway. In a split second, she raised that rifle and fired, the bullets thudding into the tree and sending splinters flying into the air. I resisted the urge to duck and squeezed the trigger, sending a flurry of three-round bursts downrange. The first burst missed, pinging off the overturned vehicle, but the second and third ripped her to shreds. One round tore her arm from her shoulder, showing just how powerful my Kicker really was.

And I would need it because the moment the woman fell, she was replaced by a handful of other bandits. I laid into them without mercy, cutting them down like they were paper targets.

Paper targets that sent fountains of gore into the air. And screams. Can't forget those. Not even if I wanted to. Which I very much wished I could.

Yeah—not the best analogy.

Either way, I was so focused on my targets that I didn't even notice the pair of bandits who'd snuck up behind me. Not until I saw a club coming at me out of the corner of my eye, and by then, it was far too late for me to completely avoid it. Still, I tried to dive away, and I received another shot to the ribs for my trouble. I went skidding across the forest floor, my rifle tumbling from my grip along the way.

I gasped in agony as I collided with another tree. It felt as if someone was repeatedly stabbing me in the side, over and over again without mercy. I lay there, my breathing coming by way of shallow, ragged gasps. I was going to die. There was nothing else for it.

A chuckle filled the air, and I looked up to see the most hideous person I'd ever seen in my entire life. To this day, I have no idea if they were male or female; gender seemed unimportant next to the sheer ugliness on display. If they had a single tooth in their mouth, I would have been incredibly surprised. Lesions and sores dotted their face, and their stringy body was covered with so much dirt and mud that I could scarcely identify their skin tone.

"What's we gots here?" they said, reaching down to pick up my Kicker. "Fancy, fancy toy, yes, it is. I's makes good use o' this'n, yes, I will. I dun—"

They never finished their statement. While they'd been inspecting my rifle, I hadn't been idle. Using those brief seconds, I'd summoned my scattergun and fired, all in one motion. An arc of lightning flashed out of the barrel, frying the monstrous bandit where they stood. I didn't care. I fired again. And again. I kept firing until they were little more than smoking remnants and the cannister that held the weapon's ammunition was empty.

I tossed it aside and summoned my pistol, pointing it at the big man who'd been lagging a bit behind. He'd still caught the edges of the scattergun's issue, and he'd barely had time to climb twitchily to his feet. He raised his hand.

I didn't care.

I fired. He exploded. And I was showered with gore.

I didn't care about that, either.

At that moment, covered in blood and barely able to stand the pain coursing through my body, the only thing I really cared about was staying alive.

CHAPTER FOURTEEN

HESITATION

Everyone reacts differently to battle. Some people freeze. Others surrender to the adrenaline. Still others react indifferently. I always counted myself among the last category of people, but I sometimes wish I was the kind of person who would hesitate before killing. It would make me feel more like a human being and less like a purpose-made machine.

—Jeremiah Braddock III

Panting, I shook my head, trying to clear my mind. Growing up in Nova City, I had seen plenty of terrible things. Even having spent much of my life locked away at the top of a megabuilding, I had not been spared from the harsh realities of our world. But in all that time, I'd certainly never killed anyone. Outside of sparring with people like Nora, I had never even been in a real fight before. But now? Not only had I just exploded a person, but I'd also shot and killed a dozen more. Certainly, it didn't help that, at that very moment, I had bits and pieces of raider on my face, in my hair, and covering my body.

And I needed a minute to slow down, to process what had just happened.

Of course, that was when an explosion toward the front of the convoy told me that I didn't have even a second to collect myself. There was still a battle raging, and with all the other guards having been killed, it fell to me to help.

So, taking a deep breath, I said, "C'mon, Mira. Quit being a little bitch."

It didn't help, but then again, I wasn't sure anything but time would. So, after collecting my weapons and putting everything but the Kicker back in my arsenal implant, I just started moving, hoping that I could outpace the panic building in my chest. First, I vaulted over the fallen tree and sprinted toward the cover of the overturned armored personnel carrier. As I did, I tried to ignore the bodies all around me. My rifle had torn gaping holes in their bodies, and there wasn't so much as a twitch of life remaining within them. That was probably good because I really wasn't in any state to put anyone out of their misery.

Another explosion echoed in the distance, and a red flashing arrow on my HUD told me where it had originated. A handy feature of my KIOI, no doubt. Shouldering my rifle, I pressed myself against the truck and leaned out to take a look.

The trucks carrying the supplies were unharmed and surrounded by shimmering blue Mist shields. A steady stream of bullets, originating from the tree line, poured into the shields, but they held firm, each round disintegrated by the Mist. It wouldn't last forever, though. I was still a novice when it came to Mist tech, but even military-grade shields were power hungry and considered temporary measures. Eventually, the gunfire would make it through.

Past the trucks was the lead personnel carrier, but it looked like it was even worse shape than the one in which I had been riding. It was doubtful that my uncle had been killed; if I could survive, then he definitely would have, as well.

That's when I saw a man step out from behind the truck.

Or I was pretty sure it was a man. He was least seven feet tall, and shaped like a giant blob with arms and legs, except that his right arm had been replaced by an energy cannon. Not small arms like I'd seen back in Nova City, either. This cannon looked like it would've been at home on a tank. In his left hand, he held a huge meat cleaver; I didn't fail to notice that it was dripping with blood.

Suddenly, a huge hole erupted in the monstrous man's belly, followed closely by a crack of thunder. No—that was a gunshot. It didn't take me long to figure out where it had come from. My uncle was still alive.

Despite the gaping hole in his stomach, the giant didn't fall. Nor did he scream out in pain. Instead, he laughed. Even from across the battlefield, I could hear the deep rumble of his mirth. He grasped an earthenware jug at his waist, tipped it into his mouth, and a second later, I saw the hole knit itself back together. Another shot hit the enormous man in the shoulder, but whatever had been in that jug was still in effect because it immediately began to heal. What followed was a few more shots, all of which healed very quickly.

I reconfigured the Kicker into a sniper rifle, then took aim. I was just about to take a shot when something flashed in front of my eyes:

Jeremiah Braddock III would like to establish a voice link. Do you wish to connect?
[Yes] or [No]

I stared at it for a long second before I mentally pressed the affirmative response. A moment later, my uncle's voice erupted in my mind. "I know you think you're going to help, but leave the big asshole to me," he said, only a hint of static distorting his voice. "I've got this. Hit the other raiders at the tree line."

"Okay," I whispered, hoping he could hear me.

"Aim small, miss small," he reminded me.

It was his favorite piece of advice, and one he'd been repeating ever since I'd picked up my first firearm. To date, I still hadn't figured out what it was supposed to mean, and I suspected he didn't know, either. According to him, he'd heard it in some movie when he was younger, and it had stuck with him. But regardless of how helpful it was, the mantra did help to calm my nerves, if only because it reminded me of all the time we'd spent in the shooting range back at the megabuilding in Nova City.

Kneeling, I refocused on the tree line about seventy yards distant. The assailants were nestled among the forest's thick undergrowth, which made them difficult to see. However, my KIOI came to the rescue there, highlighting each figure as I picked them out of the thicket.

Twenty-six people, all seemingly armed with the same archaic weapons I had already seen. Twenty-six hostiles. I took aim.

My hands shook. This wasn't like before, where I'd been running on adrenaline and spurred on by surprise. Then, I'd acted in the heat of the moment, and I hadn't had time to think about the implications of my actions. Now, though, I had ample opportunity to grapple with what I was planning on doing.

And I hesitated.

I didn't want to. I knew it was wrong. I desperately wanted to start pulling that trigger. But something inside me just wouldn't allow it. I knelt there, sighted in on a figure I couldn't properly see, and I just watched.

Right up until the moment one of the Mist shields dispersed and the sound of bullets ricocheting off the metal exterior of one of the trucks dragged me out of it. With a collective roar, the group of raiders charged out from the tree line and ran through the meadow abutting the road. They looked little different from the people I'd already killed. The people whose corpses were slowly growing colder only a few feet away.

They crashed into the truck, hitting with the force of two dozen bodies and nearly tipping it over.

"Mirabelle!" came my uncle's hissing voice over the connection we'd established. "Fire!"

"I . . . I c-can't . . ."

"There are two people in that truck!" he growled. "Those raiders are going to rip them to pieces. You're the only one who can stop them. Now, put your fucking big-girl pants on and fire your fucking weapon!"

Tears made tracks through the blood on my cheeks, but something about my uncle's words tore through the panic and hesitation, leaving only grim determination behind. I didn't want to do it. But I needed to.

I fired.

Once. Twice. Over and over, mechanically moving my sight to each new target. I stopped hesitating. I stopped thinking. I just acted. And before long, there were twenty-six new corpses. Some had continued attacking the truck right up until the very end, but after a few had fallen, many of the others had turned and fled. I had shot them in the back. In the end, none were left alive. I had won.

But I didn't feel the triumphant surge of adrenaline I might have expected. Instead, I just felt numb.

In the distance, the battle between my uncle and the giant raged. I crept closer, watching as the giant slashed at Jeremiah with the meat cleaver, narrowly missing each time. As he did, my uncle's blade—a nano-edged dagger he'd actually bought for me—darted out, seven times in the space of a second. But the giant was undeterred, aiming a front kick at Jeremiah.

It connected, sending my uncle flying away. As he sailed through the air, Jeremiah twisted and summoned his rifle. He took aim and fired, taking his opponent directly in the face. Jeremiah hit the ground and rolled, coming up on his knee. He laid into the giant, one shot after another, each one tearing an enormous hole in the monstrous man's torso. Still, the giant plodded forward, aiming at Jeremiah with his arm cannon.

He let loose, and a huge ball of plasma scorched a path toward Jeremiah. It hit him in the chest, exploding with enough force to flatten the trees in a twenty-foot radius.

"No!" I screamed, raising my own rifle and firing at the giant. My bullets did nothing, thudding against the man's flesh like I was shooting a rubber ball. That didn't stop me, though. I advanced, and when my magazine was empty, I exchanged it for a fresh one. As I reloaded, I reconfigured the Kicker into an assault rifle, switched to full automatic, and opened fire.

A steady stream of bullets tore through the air, carving a series of tiny flesh wounds in the monster's neck. A few of my bullets found their mark on his face, but they did little good.

I didn't care.

When the magazine ran dry, I dismissed the Kicker and drew Ferdinand II. He was still loaded with explosive rounds, and taking a two-handed grip, I fired all eight of the remaining rounds into the monster's face. One explosion after another ripped his flesh apart, but I might as well have been throwing rocks, for all the good it did.

Whatever the case, I didn't stop. I was close enough to smell his stench, to see the fury in his misshapen face, to hear the sound of his labored breathing. Dismissing Ferdinand II, I drew the scattergun.

I opened fire. A cone of lightning, seven feet wide, erupted from the barrel, engulfing the monster. It didn't damage him. It barely even scorched his skin. But he did seize up, his muscles contracting of their own accord. I fired again. And again. Nine more times, hoping that I could overload his system.

It didn't work.

I was too outclassed. The giant had taken everything my uncle had to throw at it, and he'd come out relatively unscathed. And my efforts had been completely useless. Even as he took one shuddering step forward, I backed away, exchanging the scattergun for the Kicker, which I immediately started to reload. I never got the chance.

The giant flashed forward, dropping his cleaver, which was connected to his wrist by a thick chain, and grabbed me around the neck.

"Li'l bug," he growled, his stinking breath enveloping me as he leaned close. He sniffed. "Tasty."

I recoiled. He laughed.

But something flashed across my HUD.

Initiate Misthack?
[Yes] or [No]

With a flick of my mind, I selected the affirmative option. Immediately, my mind was swarmed by a series of numbers. More than that, time seemed to slow down; the giant's mouth stood open, as if he'd frozen midlaugh. My own body was similarly affected, but my mind was going a thousand miles an hour.

It took me only a few seconds to deduce the nature of the numbers because they were similar to the pattern-recognition puzzles I'd seen in my training. And not difficult ones, either. I blistered my way through them, and after only a few subjective seconds, I was rewarded with another message:

Misthack Successful. Options:
- **Reboot System**
- **Overcharge System**

Intuitively, probably because of the skill itself, I knew that rebooting the system would shut down any cybernetics the giant had, but only for a few seconds. By contrast, if I chose to overload the system, it would cause damage. How much? I had no idea. But I was eager to find out. I selected the second option, and time resumed at a normal pace.

"Huh?!" the giant muttered, loosening his grip. "Ow! Ow!"

He gripped his head, howling. Smoke drifted from his eyes and ears, and his arm cannon began to vibrate dangerously. I took that as my cue to leave, so I turned and sprinted down the road.

A moment later, an explosion threw me forward. I skidded across the pavement, leaving quite a bit of skin and blood in my wake. I finally tumbled to a stop, and it took me almost a full minute to shake away the disorientation. When I looked back, I saw the giant kneeling on the ground, cradling the stump of his right arm.

"Momma's gonna be so mad," he whined.

That's when my uncle decided to make an appearance. With his clothes ripped, ragged, and still smoking, he stepped up to the giant, raised his pistol, and said, "You don't have to worry about that anymore."

Then, he fired, obliterating the giant's entire head. Whatever had kept him alive so far had either run its course or been interrupted by my overload. Either way, the headless giant fell on his front, kicking up dust and debris when he hit the pavement.

And then, everything was quiet. No gunshots. No explosions. Just blessed quiet.

My uncle approached and put his hand on my shoulder. I suddenly realized I was trembling. "You did good," he said. "But it's not over." He pointed to the tree line. "Keep watch. Make sure there aren't any more. I need to check on the drivers."

I didn't say anything. Instead, I just gave him a quick nod, then turned my attention to the forest. Nothing moved, but I didn't waver. I had already stepped over the line, and I wouldn't let it all be for nothing.

Behind me, Jeremiah approached the first truck. It was the one whose shield was still intact, so he quickly passed it by. It only took him a few more seconds to deduce that everyone inside the second truck was dead. So, he went to the first, talked to the driver and her passenger, and after a couple of minutes, both vehicles had a driver.

He returned to my side and said, "We're going to ride in the lead vehicle. Come on. I don't want to be here any longer than necessary."

"W-what about them?" I asked, pointing to all the bodies, some of which were our people.

"Nothing we can do right now," he said. "In an hour, this place is going to be crawling with scavengers. And I'm not talking coyotes and rats, either. They'll come, and they'll come in force. We don't want to be here when they get here."

"We could beat them," I mumbled.

"Maybe," my uncle agreed. "But at what cost? And what if we're wrong? People need these supplies. We have a responsibility to deliver them."

He made sense, so I nodded and followed him to the lead truck. Once we were inside—with him in the front passenger's seat while I took the back—the drivers accelerated, leaving the devastation of the battlefield behind.

As far as I was concerned, we couldn't get away fast enough. To distract myself, I pulled up my status:

NAME	Mirabelle Lisa Braddock		
CLASS	N/A (Requirements Not Met)		
LEVEL	3 (71%)		
CONSTITUTION	5/31		
MIND	6/31		
MIST	4/31		
SKILLS	7/7		
SKILL NAME	Skill Tier	Modifiers	Abilities
CYBERNETIC INTERFACE	Tier 0 (24%)	None	2 Cybernetic Slots
FIREARMS	Tier 0 (31%)	+5% Damage (All Firearms) +2% Reload Speed (All Firearms) +2% Accuracy (All Firearms)	None
CLOSE QUARTERS COMBAT	Tier 0 (2%)	+5% Damage (Melee) +2% Speed (Melee) +2% Accuracy (Melee)	None
STEALTH OPERATIONS	Tier 0 (0%)	None	Camouflage (F)

COMBAT UTILITY	Tier 0 (40%)	None	Triage (F) Basic Explosives Handling (F) Combat Focus (F) Pain Tolerance (F) Resistance (F) Foraging (F) Improvisation (F) Regeneration (F)
MISTWALKER	Tier 0 (26%)	+5% Speed (Misthack) +5% Speed (Mistwalk)	Mistwalk (F) Misthack (F) Mistwall (F)
SPYCRAFT	Tier 0 (1%)	None	Disguise (F) Deception (F)

I stared at my progress, and I had to admit that it was impressive. Not only had I made a lot of headway in terms of my skills, but I'd also gained two levels and most of a third. That increased my potential to thirty-one in each attribute. On top of that, I'd actually gained a point in each category.

It was difficult to feel excited about it, though. After all, my gains were based on slaughtering dozens of people. If that was what it took to get ahead, I wasn't certain I was cut out for whatever my uncle had planned.

"You did do well," he said, turning to look back at me. It was almost as if he could read my mind. Perhaps he could; I still didn't know what kinds of skills he had. Or what existed, if I was honest. For all I knew, there was a mind reading skill out there.

"Doesn't feel like it," I said.

"It'll pass" was Jeremiah's response. "For now, keep your focus. We're not out of the woods yet."

I gave him a nod, and I fixed my attention on the wilderness through which the road cut. As I did, watching every minute detail, time passed. A few minutes, at first. Then a couple of hours. Eventually, night began to fall, and the landscape started to change. Instead of unbroken wilderness, I began to see crumbling buildings, abandoned and rusted vehicles, and in a few cases, dirty and ragged people. To a person, they were malnourished and misshapen.

"Wildlings," my uncle said. "They're the ones who don't take the Nexus Implant well. Instead of giving them access to skills, it turns them feral."

"Is there no cure?" I asked breathlessly.

"No. None."

"Poor bastards," added the driver, the first words she'd uttered since we'd set off. Then again, she'd just seen her whole convoy killed. Some of them had to have been friends. Silence was an appropriate response to that kind of trauma.

The finality of the statements cut off any further questions, and we continued along. After another few miles, a skyline loomed ahead. But the buildings weren't like the ones I'd grown up around. For one, they were smaller. For another, each building looked different than its fellows. The most curious of the cluster of buildings was a relatively squat structure that looked like it had inverted wings on the top.

"What is this place?" I asked.

"This is where I grew up," Jeremiah stated. "Welcome to Mobile, Alabama."

CHAPTER FIFTEEN

DEBTS

The journey home was a depressing one, but I had to know who had survived the Initialization. When I got there, I was unsurprised to discover that, of all my friends and family, only my sister and her son had managed to survive. Even after seeing so much death, that was a sobering thought.

—Jeremiah Braddock III

"I don't know what that means," I admitted, staring at the skyline as we drew nearer to the city. The closer we got, the more decrepit the buildings looked. The structures were crumbling remnants of a bygone age with great snaking vines covering most of their exteriors, and I suspected that it wouldn't be long before nature pulled them down altogether. That they'd managed to remain standing after so long was a minor testament to the architectural prowess of generations past.

"Mobile is the name of the city," Jeremiah said. "Alabama was the state."

"That doesn't help much," I admitted. Vaguely, the term rang a bell, but it was a memory of a lesson half learned and even less remembered.

"States were like districts," he explained. "Just bigger. It doesn't matter, though. Not anymore."

The trucks continued their approach, and in places, the road—which was curiously well-preserved—was under at least a few inches of water. The vegetation was ubiquitous, and more than once, I saw wildlife weaving between the buildings. A giant canine here, a lumbering reptile there—even a swarm of giant ratlike creatures, which Jeremiah dubbed nutria, that splashed through the water and disappeared into one of the buildings.

"They used to only be a nuisance," he said, shaking his head. "When I was little, my dad used to take us to nutria rodeos." I started to ask if they were similar to the rat fights that were so popular in Nova City, but he interrupted me, saying, "We'd set the islands in the bay on fire, and these huge swarms of nutria would come pouring off. We'd open fire. You couldn't miss. Good times."

"That's . . . that's horrible."

"They're vermin," he stated. "They spread disease, they destroy any kind of vegetation they find, and they breed so fast that even with our efforts, we could barely keep the populations in check. Sometimes, you have to do brutal things if you want to survive. That's more important now than it ever was back then, Mirabelle. Remember that."

My mind immediately went back to all the people I'd killed. I still felt guilty, but some of that had faded. After all, they'd attacked us, hadn't they? We were justified in defending ourselves.

"Why did those people attack us?" I asked.

"Survival" was his answer. "They wanted what we had. It's the only way they can live out there. I don't blame them. I've spent plenty of time as a raider myself. But just because I don't blame them doesn't mean I'm just going to lie down and die. If it makes you feel any better, these supplies are going to keep a lot of people alive over the next few months. Where we're headed, life is balanced on the edge of a knife."

"Isn't it everywhere?" I muttered.

"Yes," he answered. "That's what you need to understand about this world, Mirabelle. You've lived a sheltered life, and—"

"I've been training with guns since I was seven!" I insisted. "And besides, if I've been sheltered, that's your fault!"

"I'm not going to apologize for giving you a few years of peace," he stated. "When you get a little older, you'll understand how valuable it was. But now, you're about to step into the real world. No more training wheels. If you take nothing else from what I've told you over the past few days, it should be this: everyone has reasons for what they do. There are no good guys and bad guys— not like in those shows you like to watch on the entertainment streams. There are just people with opposing goals."

"So, you're saying that evil doesn't exist? That good is . . . what? Just a matter of perspective?" I asked, my brows furrowing. "That's stupid."

"I'm saying that nobody sets out to be evil," he said. "Do they still get there? Of course. But even then, none of the truly evil people out there really consider themselves wrong. They make compromises. We all do. And then, one day, we look up, and we've done unconscionable things. You will, too. What I'm trying to get through to you is that, when you do—and you will—make it worth it. If you're going to kill, do so for a reason. Don't just do it because you can. And never forget that, even if you hate them, your enemies are people, too."

"What does that even mean, though?" I asked. At that moment, I wasn't trying to empathize with the people I'd killed. It was easier if I just thought of them as some great enemy.

My uncle saw right through that, explaining, "The moment you start seeing your enemies as monsters, that's the moment you become one yourself. I've been there, Mirabelle. I've done things you . . . Just don't make the same mistakes I made, okay? I'm already lost. I can't change who I am now. But you can do better. You can be better."

"So, you want me to be some kind of pacifist?"

"I want you to follow your conscience," he said as we passed through the ruined city. The driver remained silent, focusing on the road and acting like she wasn't privy to our conversation. "Pacifism is for people who have the luxury of being protected by the strong. Maybe it was possible back before the Initialization. I don't know. But back then, there were laws. There were measures to protect the weak. Even then . . . it was just an excuse to justify passing the burden onto someone else. People are good at that. Governments are even better."

"What do you want from me, though? You said you wanted me to survive," I said, hardly noticing that we were slowing down. "But . . ."

"I said what I meant," Jeremiah stated. "You need to survive. I couldn't save your mom. I couldn't save your grandfather. Or your great-grandfather, either. I kept Trey alive for a couple of decades, but . . . I'm tired of failure, Mirabelle. I'm tired of losing. You have to survive. Ultimately, I don't care if you become a monster, so long as you're the monster you need to be in order to stay alive. But you need to understand that there's a cost associated with every single death. You feel that. I know you do. Just hang on to it."

The truck pulled to a stop, and the driver announced, "We're here, boss."

Jeremiah turned around and studied the landscape. Or the lack of it; instead, looming above us was a giant metal wall, at least a hundred feet tall. As I studied the corrugated surface, I saw that it had a modular design. Then it hit me—they were shipping containers stacked one atop the other.

Just when I was going to ask about the wall, it cracked apart and, like a pair of enormous double doors, swung open to reveal a village. It looked nothing like the city we'd just passed. The gray brick buildings were modest and only a couple of stories tall, but they looked well maintained.

"What is this place?" I asked.

"A free settlement," Jeremiah said. "No integration with the outside world. No Node. All built by human hands." Then, to the driver, he said, "Head on in. They won't want to leave the gate open for long."

The truck accelerated, its huge, knobby tires crunching on the loose gravel that covered the road, and as we passed through the wall, I got a good look at its structure. The doors of the gate were comprised of four shipping containers stacked atop one another and braced by metal rods. The wall itself was five times as deep and at least twice as tall. More, I couldn't help but notice the blue sheen of a Mist shield covering its entire surface.

After a couple of seconds, we emerged into the open air, and once again, I gasped in surprise. The settlement was much bigger than I'd expected, and there were plenty of people around. Most carried weapons of one sort or another, and I could see a smaller wall a half mile away.

As our small convoy drove through the settlement, I studied our surroundings. The buildings that I had dubbed simple were, in a lot of ways, more unique than the ones in Nova City. Back home, everything was built for maximum efficiency, with the goal of packing as many people into as small of a space as was possible. There was no artistry to the buildings. No creativity. Most were just concrete blocks divided into apartments.

These buildings were different, though. Not only were the construction materials varied—most were, as I'd first suspected, made of concrete bricks, but there were wooden buildings, as well. In addition, most of the buildings sported balconies lined with black iron railings. All in all, it was a strange sight for someone who'd grown up in the Garden, where most of the buildings were variations of the same overarching design.

It was also a bit disconcerting because there were considerably fewer blinking neon signs or holographic displays. It seemed like an entirely different world, and surrounded by so much unfamiliarity, I felt even more uncomfortable than I had in the wilderness. And it took me a moment to figure out why. I was a city girl, through and through, so I shouldn't have been at ease in a swamp. But in a town? It should have been familiar.

But this place wasn't, and it made me anxious.

After a couple of minutes, we turned, and I got a good view of a huge body of water. It was at least a half mile across, and the water was steadily moving. A river, then. I'd seen plenty of streams on the journey from Nova City, but this was the biggest one by a long shot.

"Brings back memories," said Jeremiah. "Used to be a cruise terminal right over there." He pointed to a cluster of buildings to his right. I had no idea what a cruise terminal was, but I didn't ask for clarification. I was too entranced by the latest strike against my utilitarian sensibilities. He pointed farther down the river at a curiously shaped building. It was like someone had taken a shallow-sloped pyramid and turned it upside down. "And that used to be a museum. Goddamn waste of money, but I guess it was well-made."

The building in front of us was unlike any of the rest of them. Instead, it looked older, and I had no trouble believing that it predated the town itself. Or the Initialization. And not by a little bit, either. The red-tile roof was sloped, with a sizable dome at the intersection of two distinct wings. A decorative facade, studded with spires and arches, gave the building a distinct flavor I'd never seen before.

But as ancient as the building looked, there were more modern characteristics, as well. For one, at each end of the building, there were towers jutting toward the sky. Atop those towers were heavy guns that looked as if they could destroy our vehicles with a single shot. And finally, the whole building was encased in a flickering blue shell of light—more Mist shields. It was a fortress.

The vehicle pulled to a stop in front of the building, and I saw the guns pointed in our direction. I swallowed hard, but my uncle said, "Get out and come with me. I have some people you need to meet."

"Um . . . okay," I said before following him out of the vehicle. Looking back at the battered truck, I had to admit that it had certainly seen better days. No trip in the wilds was without danger, even discounting the bandits we'd fought off, and the truck sported a series of dents, scratches, and even a few bite marks from overconfident beasts.

I yanked my attention back to the present and followed my uncle. As I did so, my eyes darted this way and that, noting various points of cover. I hadn't received a lot of training in combat—just plenty of time at the range—but the recent battle had given me an appreciation for knowing the terrain. Besides, I could practically feel the guns trained on us.

I followed my uncle up the steps in front of the building, where we were met by a stout, bearded man wearing a too-small tee-shirt, a pair of cargo shorts, and an old, blue, and barely-holding-it-together cap with a stylized *A* on the front. At his hip was a hand cannon not all that dissimilar from Ferdinand II, and his right hand from the elbow down was entirely mechanical.

"Took ya long nuff," he growled. Then, he hiked his thumb at a figure standing in the shadows. "Jorge and my Amigos been followin' you for the last ten miles."

"I know," my uncle said. "They're not as stealthy as they think they are." He looked past the stout—okay, he was fat—man, saying, "Didn't see you, though, Jorge. You're getting better."

"I try," said the figure, his voice strangely accented. I'd heard its like before, but there was something a little off. I just couldn't put my finger on exactly what that was. The figure stepped from the shadows, and I saw that he was cradling a huge sniper rifle. My eyes kept trying to drift away from him, and if I didn't concentrate, it was almost as if I'd forget he was even there.

"We were hit by raiders about halfway here," Jeremiah said. "And the muscle had a Tier 4 arm cannon. Mikoshi. Military-grade stuff."

"Aw, hell," said the portly man, yanking his cap off to reveal a mostly bald head. "Where the hell they get somethin' like that?"

"I don't know," my uncle answered. "But I plan to figure it out. For now, though, we need to drop these supplies and get my niece settled in. Tomorrow, we're implementing the plan."

"So soon?"

"It has to be done," Jeremiah stated. "In the meantime, we need to get Mirabelle trained up. I'm talking the full suite. You know the skills."

"I've got people who can train her," the fat man said. "I'll even put her on the right track with pistols myself." He looked at me. "Hope you're ready, 'cause you're about to have a rough couple of months."

"Six."

"What?"

"Six months," Jeremiah repeated. "The training program is six months. I'm structuring it similarly to military training. With the enhanced learning speed that comes with Awakening, she should be able to reach my goals. Then, we'll have the test."

"Better make it a coupla years," the other man said. "You've got time to get her ready."

"I can't devote that much time to this," my uncle said. "I've got an organization to run. You know that, Milo."

Milo spat, then ran his forearm over his forehead. "We can take care of her when you ain't here," he said. "Don't ya trust us?"

"Of course I do."

"Then it's settled," Milo said. "Once we get the girl somewhere to sleep, you and me—we'll adjust the schedule. When we get done, the girl's gonna be a lean, mean killin' machine. I guarantee it."

I swallowed hard, but I didn't say anything as both men—and Jorge, for that matter—fixed their gazes on me. "You ready for that?" asked my uncle. "Two years of intensive training. When you're finished, you'll—"

"Assuming she survives the tests."

"Right. After that, you'll be one of the most powerful people in Nova City," my uncle stated. "Maybe not in raw stats or the power of your skills, but you'll have adaptability on your side. At first. Eventually, you'll have the raw power to back up your versatility."

"She's gonna be a monster."

"That's the point, Milo," Jeremiah said. Then, to me, he said, "You ready?"

"Yes," I said, my voice hoarse. I'd made my decision when I'd accepted the Tier 7 implant, and nothing had happened to change my mind. I didn't like having to kill those people, but if it came down to my life or theirs, I knew which choice I would make.

Because I'd already made it. Dozens of times. And I knew I'd do the same, over and over again, because that's what survival was, at least in the world to which I had just been introduced. Maybe it would be better elsewhere, but I couldn't hold out hope for that. I needed to thrive in the environment in which I'd found myself. Anything else, and I would end up dead in some unnamed alley, just like my mother. Just like my father.

"Good," Milo said, grinning at me as he gripped my shoulder with his flesh hand. "Real good."

"Thanks, Milo," Jeremiah said. "Really. I mean it."

Again, Milo spat. "No thanks needed. Me and you, we're like family. I remember what you done for us way back when. This place, it wouldn't survive without your shipments. Food. Meds. Tech. Least we can do is train this little girl up right."

"Still—I'll remember this, Milo," Jeremiah stated. "I don't forget my debts."

"No, no, you do not," Milo agreed. "Now, go get those supplies delivered and get settled. I think Nancy's got room for ya."

"Will do," Jeremiah said with a nod. "C'mon, Mirabelle."

With that, he turned and walked away, and as I followed him back to the truck, I couldn't help but wonder what the history between my uncle and Milo was. Still, I didn't ask. My uncle didn't really like to talk about his past, and I knew that asking would just annoy him. So, we rode in silence as we made our way to a nearby warehouse, where we would unload the supplies.

CHAPTER SIXTEEN

A TENDER SIDE

I had plenty of advantages going for me. Training. Experience. Skills. But even then, I often found myself woefully outmatched when I went up against the aliens. My potential was higher, but they'd had decades to make the most out of what they had. And that made all the difference.

—Jeremiah Braddock III

After a short drive through the town, we pulled into a sizable supply depot, where a host of burly men and women were waiting to unload the supplies we'd brought. The boxes were unmarked, but my uncle told me that they contained much-needed medicine, ammunition, and foodstuffs. He also explained that, while the town was mostly self-sufficient, his support made the residents' lives much more comfortable.

"And without the ammunition," he said, leading me out of the warehouse. I scrambled to keep up as he continued, "This place would have been overrun years ago. Those bandits out there, they aren't as well armed as us. Most of them use pre-Initialization weapons. Almost useless against anybody with decent Constitution, cybernetics, or armor. But there are a lot of them."

My side twinged as I hurried to keep up. My uncle wasn't the sort to slow down, even when I was clearly injured. After the battle, my body had been riding high off of the adrenaline, but as soon as I'd started to come down to reality, the pain had set in. And it had only gotten worse as the hours dragged on. Now, every step brought with it a stab of agony. The icon on my HUD that indicated my health was uniformly yellow, and parts had even turned to orange. Any worse, and they would have been red.

My ever-observant uncle had already noticed this, and he led me to a building near the supply depot. It had a three-foot-tall red circle with a cross cutout painted on the door.

"This is a med center," he said. Pointing to the symbol, he added, "If you see that, the person inside has some kind of healing skill. Some are actual doctors. Some might be cybernetic engineers. Others could be triage specialists. But the point is that if you're outside of a megacity and you're hurt, look for a building with this symbol. They'll help you, so long as you've got the credits."

"And if I don't?"

"A gun to the head usually works," Jeremiah said. "But that's more of a last resort kind of thing. You don't want to piss off the person trying to keep you alive."

"Noted," I grunted, clutching my side.

"Hopefully, your Triage ability will eventually make this superfluous, though," he said, knocking on the door. As they waited for an answer, he explained, "It won't be as good as a real doctor, but once you advance it enough, it'll come damned close. Now, once we're in here, you need to pay attention and do exactly what she says. You could learn something."

"Uh . . . okay?"

Before I could ask anything else, the door slid open, revealing a tiny woman with canted eyes. Once, she'd probably been very pretty, with delicate features and silky hair, but now, she was so wrinkled that it was hard to tell what she might've looked like before time had its say.

"Hello, Kimiko," Jeremiah said, grinning. "Long time no see."

The tiny woman looked my uncle up and down, frowning as they engaged in some sort of nonverbal back and forth, then said, "An acceptable arrangement." She glanced at me, and I could practically feel her eyes boring into me, seeing my every secret. After a few seconds, Kimiko said, "Just her. You stay out here."

"Oh, c'mon, Kimmy—I'm not—ack!" He stopped talking and cleared his throat. After a deep breath, he said, "Seriously? You're still angry?"

The woman ignored him, then said to me, "Come, child. I will treat you inside."

I glanced at Jeremiah, and he gave me a nod, so I followed the woman inside. I had no idea what she had done to him, but I hadn't missed the note of alarm in my uncle's expression. So, I asked, "What did you do to him just then?"

"Immaterial," she said, leading me inside. The interior of the building was cramped, with only an examination table, a stool, and a couple of cabinets. "Sit."

Obviously, she wasn't the sociable type, so I didn't bother saying anything else. Instead, I just followed her directions. After that, she had me lift my shirt a couple of times so she could get to my injuries, and I was a little surprised that they weren't a lot worse than they actually were. Perhaps my [Combat Utility] had already started to pay off. Whatever the case, I watched closely as Kimiko applied a variety of salves and shots before closing the worst of my injuries with a needle and thread.

As she worked, I could feel something moving in the air; it didn't feel like a typical current, but rather, it was something else. Kimiko was halfway finished before I realized that it was Mist moving in accordance with her skills. "Wow," I muttered to myself.

Kimiko stopped what she was doing. "What did you say, child?" she asked.

"Uh . . . sorry," I said, not wanting to offend her. She seemed a bit prickly, and if I didn't know anything else, I knew not to piss off the woman who might one day hold my life in her hands. "Just . . . I haven't felt the Mist before now. It surprised me is all."

"You have a healing skill?" she asked.

I shook my head. "No" was my answer. "Well, sort of. I have [Combat Utility], and one of my abilities is Triage. I guess that counts? I'm still a little bit in the dark about how everything's supposed to work together and progress. I'll figure it out, though."

"Triage," the woman muttered to herself before going back to work. As she did, I suddenly realized that, by revealing one of my skills, I'd just done one of the things my uncle had expressly told me not to do. Swallowing hard, I hoped he would never find out. More importantly, I resolved to do better.

She only had a few more stitches before she finally wrapped my torso in bandages. After that, she directed me to lower my shirt and handed me a vial of purple liquid. "Drink that before you go to sleep. It will help aid your healing."

"Thanks," I said, settling my shirt back into place. "Do . . . I don't know—do I pay you or something?"

"No, child," she said. "I will take what I require from your guardian. You may leave now."

I blinked at the sudden dismissal, as well as her claim that she could take anything from Jeremiah. However, given that she'd briefly choked him—or maybe just caused him to cough; I was a bit fuzzy on what exactly had happened there—with nothing but her mind, I thought it was probably a good idea to just follow her directions. So, I muttered something to convey my gratitude, then left the building as quickly as I could. I didn't even realize my heart rate had spiked until I got outside and let out a deep breath.

"Unsettling, isn't she?" my uncle asked. I looked up to see him leaning against the wall of the building, his eyes trained on our surroundings. I followed his gaze, seeing that the pedestrians—and there were more than a few of them—were giving him a wide berth. Some had even crossed to the other side of the street to keep from getting too close.

"A little, I guess," I admitted. "But I feel better."

"I would expect so," he stated. "She's one of the highest-ranked doctors I know. Tier 3, if you can believe it. And all her skills are focused on medicine. If she lived in Nova City or one of the other megacities, she'd be an extremely wealthy woman."

"Oh."

He gave me a wry smile. "C'mon," he said, pushing himself off the wall and starting down the street. "I want to get you settled in. And I have a surprise for you."

That perked me up. "A surprise? What kind of surprise?" I asked, hurrying to catch up to his long-legged stride. "Is it a hover bike?"

"What? Why would I give you a hover bike? You don't even have a piloting skill," he said.

"You can use them without one," I stated. "The CB-280 Oppressor is rated for unskilled and novice pilots who—"

"No," he said. "I did not get you a fucking hover bike. Keep up."

I glared at him. Of course, I knew I didn't have any call for resentment. After all, he'd spent a not-so-small fortune on equipping me with high-tech cybernetics and firearms. Not to mention the Tier 7 Nexus Implant, which, as far as I could tell, was priceless. However, I couldn't help but feel a little annoyed; I'd made no secret about wanting a hover bike. I'd left plenty of brochures lying about the apartment, and I'd even signed Jeremiah up for one of those sketchy mailing lists that would flood his inbox with all sorts of information on all the latest models. He knew I wanted one.

And what's more, he had plenty of money. More than even I suspected, given how causally he'd bought military-grade weapons and implants for me. He could afford it. So, it didn't make any sense at all that he wouldn't buy one for me. They weren't even *that* expensive.

I kept muttering to myself about the unfairness of not getting what I wanted as I followed my uncle through the town. We attracted a fair bit of attention, a fact that I thought could be attributed to our status as outsiders. But no one bothered or approached us, probably because Jeremiah practically radiated danger wherever he went. Someone would've had to be a fool to mess with him.

At last, we reached our destination—a building with a rough white facade and a red-tile roof similar to what I'd seen on the bigger, more decorative building from before. This one had a sign, proclaiming it to be the Dew Drop Inn. Back home in Nova City, there were plenty of places that served as temporary lodging. Flophouses. No-tell motels, where people paid by the hour. Even a few high-end hotels in the more affluent districts that catered to the few wealthy outsiders who visited the city from afar. This place, it was different. It had an almost wholesome air about it—an impression aided by the hand-painted sign that bore its name.

Jeremiah wasted no time before pushing through the doors, and feeling dozens of sets of eyes on my back, I had little choice but to follow. Inside, I found a well-lit room that defied my expectations.

"So much wood," I muttered, wide-eyed as I took in the scene. "Is it real?"

In Nova, wood was expensive and rare, as much because concrete was more durable as it was because harvesting trees required people to venture outside of the city. But here, it was everywhere. Tables. A bar. Chairs. All made of polished wood, usually with bronze accents.

Jeremiah let out a chuckle, "Sure is. The original Dew Drop Inn was a restaurant, believe it or not. Franklin and Nancy just coopted the name."

He strode toward the bar, where a pretty young woman stood. She was a few years older than me, with black hair and a comfortably curvy body clad in jeans and a purple top. The rest of the inn, as far as I could tell, was mostly unoccupied. There were a couple of men sitting at a table in one of the corners and a woman sitting at the end of the bar, staring into a glass.

"Joanna," Jeremiah said with one of the most genuine smiles I'd ever seen on his face. "How are things?"

"Okay, I suppose," she said, her voice husky. "Same room as always?"

He shook his head. "Need an extra for her," he said, hiking his thumb toward me. "One of the little rooms will do. And it's long-term. At least six months. Maybe as much as a couple of years."

"Oh?" asked Joanna.

I chose that moment to introduce myself. Stepping closer to the bar, I said, "I'm Mira."

For a second, Joanna looked confused, but then, recognition dawned. "Oh—Mirabelle! This is your niece?" she asked, glancing at my uncle.

"In the flesh."

"I don't like being called by my whole name," I groused.

"Not getting what you want builds character," Jeremiah stated.

I rolled my eyes. "Whatever" was my muttered response. I was used to him ignoring my preferences about my name. Maybe one day I'd get some cool nickname, like the most famous Operators, but I had a feeling that even if that came to pass, my uncle would still call me by my full given name.

Grinning, Joanna said, "He does that to me, too. I go by Jo, but he's always called me Joanna. I like to think it's the senility setting in. He can't even remember what people prefer to be called anymore."

"What? I am not senile!" he said.

"You're like a hundred and fifty," Jo argued. "Way past the point when that kind of stuff starts to set in. The mind's the first thing to go. Or that's what they say. I'm not old, so I can't be sure."

I giggled and glanced at my uncle. "You *are* kind of ancient," I said.

Jeremiah looked back and forth between us, then with a sigh, gave up. I mentally celebrated the minor victory as he said, "Anyway—you have those rooms available, Joanna?"

Neither of us missed the emphasis on her full name. For some reason, it felt even more like a victory, and I resisted the urge to give Jo a high five. As I basked in the glow of finally putting my uncle off-balance, Jo gave him a pair of keys, and he started toward a set of stairs in the back of the room.

As we passed the woman at the end of the bar, she erupted into motion. I couldn't even track her movements before I heard the distinct blip of a plasma pistol going off. A second later, I saw a hole at least four feet wide in the wall.

Jeremiah hadn't been idle, though. Instead, he had one hand wrapped around her wrist, where he'd redirected the shot that had clearly been aimed at him, and the other around her throat. All semblance of mirth was gone from his face, replaced by cold implacability as he leaned in. I don't know what he did or how he knew it, but he growled, "Corporate scum."

Then, without further words, he flexed his hand and crushed her entire throat. Her hand went limp, and the gun clattered to the floor. But he didn't stop. Instead, he kept squeezing until he got to her spine and, with a heave, ripped it from her body.

Looking back at me, he said, "Another lesson for you, Mirabelle. Never stop until you're sure they can't come back. There are hundreds of regeneration and lifesaving skills out there, but the people who can recover from a decapitation are few and far between. Remember that."

"O-okay..."

He glanced at Jo, who hadn't moved, and said, "Sorry about the mess, Joanna. Tell your dad I'll pay for any damages."

"No problem," she said, her husky voice gaining an edge. She wasn't afraid. Instead, I got the impression that she was angry.

"Do you need me to clean it up?" was his next question.

She shook her head. "No," Jo answered. "I'm sure one of Milo's Amigos are going to be here soon enough. They'll want to look for anything that might lead us to how she got in."

"Any ideas?"

Again, his question was met with a shake of Jo's head. She said, "No. I don't recognize her, but that's not that uncommon these days. Some of the people here, they've got family in other towns. Sometimes, they visit. I just figured she was somebody like that. But I'd never seen her before a few days ago."

"That makes sense," Jeremiah said.

"It does? How does any of this make sense?" I asked.

"That's not something that concerns you right now," he answered. I started to object, but he forestalled me with a raised finger. "You're not even trained yet. Focus on that, and when the time comes, I'll tell you everything. By that point, you'll have the power to get involved if you want to."

It wasn't the response I wanted, but it was all I was going to get. So, I gave him a nod, and after that, we settled in to wait on one of Milo's Amigos to come by. Sure enough, after only five minutes or so, a swarthy, dangerous-looking man dressed in all-black fatigues stepped through the door. He gave Jeremiah a nod, but he didn't say anything before kneeling beside the body and rifling through her pockets.

"I'll leave you to it, then, Carlos," my uncle said, which earned him a grunted reply from the kneeling man. "Let me know if you need anything."

"Si, jefe."

With that, Jeremiah led me up the stairs. My room was on the first floor, but we only paused long enough for me to get a look inside before he practically dragged me to the top floor, where a much larger and more luxurious suite waited. Once we were inside, he bade me sit, then pulled a chip from his pocket.

"Here," he said. "I know your birthday isn't for another two days, but I wanted to go ahead and give this to you now. It should make your training a little easier at first."

I took the chip. "What is it?" I asked.

"Just slot it."

Wondering why he wouldn't just tell me, I rolled my eyes, but I did as he asked, sliding the chip into the slot on the side of my neck. An instant later, a notification appeared on my HUD.

Download file [Leviathan, Full Library]?
[Yes] or [No]

I gaped at the notification. Leviathan weren't a normal band whose music I could just find on the cybernet. They didn't do shows on the entertainment feeds. And they certainly didn't put their full library on a chip. As far as I knew, the only way to get access to their music was to go to one of their shows or to buy one of the bootleg recordings of one of their performances. And even those weren't all-inclusive.

I frantically confirmed the download, and a second later, almost seventy songs were listed on my HUD, most of which I'd never even heard before. Some, like "Kamikaze Parade," were little more than rumors. But there it was, listed in the ninth slot.

"H-how did you get this?" I asked, looking up at my uncle's smiling face.

"I don't know if you know this, but I'm kind of a big deal," he answered with a lopsided grin. "Happy birthday, little girl."

I couldn't stop myself from launching myself at him and throwing my arms around his broad shoulders. As I buried my face in his chest, I mumbled, "Thank you! Thank you! Thank you!" It probably wasn't terribly understandable—due to the tears and the fact that my words were muffled by his shirt—but right then, I didn't really care. In that moment, I was the happiest girl in the whole world.

CHAPTER SEVENTEEN

THE BASICS

I pity those who were born into a post-Initialization world. Sure, there's the glitz and glamour of all the new technology, but it's all an illusion. Pretty, useful things that make us that much easier to conquer and control.

—Jeremiah Braddock III

That night, I got a surprise when, as I lay in bed, I pulled up my status. It read:

NAME	Mirabelle Lisa Braddock		
CLASS	N/A (Requirements Not Met)		
LEVEL	3 (71%)		
CONSTITUTION	5/31		
MIND	6/31		
MIST	4/31		
SKILLS	7/7		
SKILL NAME	Skill Tier	Modifiers	Abilities
CYBERNETIC INTERFACE	Tier 0 (26%)	None	2 Cybernetic Slots

FIREARMS	Tier 0 (31%)	+5% Damage (All Firearms) +2% Reload Speed (All Firearms) +2% Firearms Accuracy (All Firearms)	None
CLOSE QUARTERS COMBAT	Tier 0 (2%)	+5% Damage (Melee) +2% Speed (Melee) +2% Accuracy (Melee)	None
STEALTH OPERATIONS	Tier 0 (0%)	None	Camouflage (F)
COMBAT UTILITY	Tier 0 (56%)	None	Triage (F) Basic Explosives Handling (F) Combat Focus (F) Pain Tolerance (F) Resistance (F) Foraging (F) Improvisation (F) Regeneration (F)
MISTWALKER	Tier 0 (26%)	+5% Speed (Misthack) +5% Speed (Mistwalk)	Mistwalk (F) Misthack (F) Mistwall (F)
SPYCRAFT	Tier 0 (1%)	None	Disguise (F) Deception (F)

In addition to gaining a couple of percentage points of progress in my [Cybernetic Interface] skill, I'd gotten a big jump in [Combat Utility], as well. And it didn't take long to figure out why, either. For one, I suspected that it was subtly influencing my mind. I knew that killing people—especially dozens of them—was supposed to be a traumatic experience. And it was, to a degree. I still wasn't okay with what I had done. However, I suspected that it would have been so much worse if I didn't have Combat Focus on my side. There was no PTSD-blocking ability or trait listed under the ability, but if it could keep me focused during combat, I didn't think it was that far-fetched to expect it to have out-of-combat effects, as well.

Or maybe I was just a psychopath. Either way, I didn't feel nearly as bad about what had happened on the road as I thought I should have. Of course, it would've been different if I'd been the aggressor or if I'd murdered people in cold blood; I suspected that there wasn't a skill strong enough to make me okay with that. But with the situation having been what it was? I was distressingly fine with how things had turned out.

I also expected that I'd picked up some progress from watching Kimiko work. I knew it wasn't much—after all, it'd only been a half hour, at most—but it boded well for my future. Suddenly, those abilities at the bottom of my skill trees didn't look so far away. With that in mind, I drifted off to sleep as I listened to my birthday present.

The next morning, I awoke to a banging on my door. Groggily, I dragged myself out of bed and pressed my hand against the door's control panel. It slid open to reveal my uncle, who was fully dressed and grinning from ear to ear.

"Morning, sunshine," he said. "You ready for some real training?"

"Uh . . . I . . . I guess?"

"Get dressed. Wear this," he said, shoving a bundle into my hand. I looked down to see that it was a pair of black pants and a matching shirt. A pair of boots appeared in his hands, and he handed those over, as well. "I'll get you four more sets of clothes. From now until I say you're ready, that's what you're wearing. Got it?"

"Why?"

"Because I said so," he stated. "Now, you've got fifteen minutes to get dressed and get downstairs. If you're late, that's less time you'll have to eat your breakfast."

With that, he strode away, leaving me a little taken aback. He'd never been what anyone would call a soft man, but in that brief interaction, I saw that our relationship, such as it was, had progressed into a new phase. He had discarded his status as my uncle and taken on the mantle of my trainer.

That in mind, I wasted no time in taking care of my business in the bathroom, brushing my teeth, and getting dressed. I went as quickly as I could, but even then, I barely made it downstairs in time to get a bowl of grits and a couple of fried tofu sausages. I scarfed them down in a rush, and Jeremiah led me outside.

As early as it was, the sun hadn't even begun to rise, but there were still plenty of people about. When I remarked on it, my uncle said, "These people work on a different schedule than back in the city. Nobody wants to be outside the walls after dark."

"Why not?"

"Because that's when the real monsters come out," he stated, turning and walking down the side of the street. There were a few gas-powered vehicles puttering about, but most of the traffic was on foot. "But you don't have to worry about that. For the next eight weeks, you won't leave the town. Instead, I'm putting you through basic training."

"What for? I've been shooting since I was—"

"None of that matters," he interrupted. "Your skills are too low-ranked. Your attributes are only a little better than if you hadn't been Awakened. We're going to change that. And I'm going to tell you right now—you're not going to enjoy it."

"Way to get me excited," I muttered, half to myself.

"The first four hours of your day will be spent in physical training," he said. "At first, you're going to feel like you're dying. That's fine. It's expected. Push through it, and you'll see your stats skyrocket."

"And if it's too much?" I asked, following him as he turned down a side street. A half mile away was a wide, low-slung building that I expected would be our destination.

"You will progress more slowly," he said. For a couple more minutes, we walked in silence, and when we finally reached the building, we approached a door. He stopped in front of it and turned to me. "I'm going to tell you the same thing my high school football coach told me. If you loaf, if you don't give this your very best effort, you're only cheating yourself. If you're going to spend the time doing it, if you're going to go through all the trouble to train, you may as well make the most of it. I'm not going to ride you. Nor am I going to make you do anything you don't want to do. You're almost an adult now—that Nexus Implant says that you're old enough to be your own person." He rubbed the back of his neck. "Besides, nobody can make you give something your best effort. That's on you. And only you. The only question is—do you want to be mediocre? If so, that's fine. Lots of people are. But if you want to be good, if you want to be great, it's going to take a lot of time, effort, and will."

It was one of the longest speeches my uncle had ever given me, and I took his words to heart. I knew why he'd given me the Tier 7 implant, and I had seen firsthand just how dangerous the world could be. And I suspected that the bandits were just the beginning. There were more dangerous things out there. My survival hinged on the training I was about to receive, and I was wholly committed to giving it everything I had.

"I understand," I said, my tone leaving no doubt, and my uncle led me inside.

My unflinching resolve lasted all of about thirty minutes.

"I . . . I'm . . . I'm going to die," I muttered between gasping breaths. "This . . . isn't . . . worth it."

Of course, when my instructor—a fit woman who hadn't even introduced herself before ordering me to run sprints—blew her whistle, I straightened up and ran the prescribed distance. But in my mind, I kept grumbling right up until, thirty more minutes later, she called for a brief rest.

As I gulped down water, I looked around the building. Right then, I was in a huge empty area, but within the building, there was also a wicked-looking obstacle course and an area populated by enormous metal weights. It wasn't long before I was introduced to both.

The weights weren't that bad—lifting heavy things wasn't difficult, even if it was tiring. Sure, I was disappointed when I had to use the lightest weights, but I knew I would improve. But no—the bane of my existence proved to be the obstacle course.

The thing was at least a hundred yards long, and it contained multiple sheer walls, rope bridges, tunnels through which I had to crawl, and a host of other obstacles that proved too difficult for me to overcome. But it wasn't for lack of trying. I even convinced myself that, if I was fresh, I could have finished it. Of course, in the back of my mind, I knew that just wasn't true. The reality was that I just didn't have the strength or body control to do the things I would have to do.

Which was probably the point. If it was easy, I wouldn't gain anything.

Even so, I gave it everything I had right up until my uncle called out, "Okay, that's enough!"

I'd been trying to climb a rope, and at his words, I let go and collapsed right beneath it. Closing my eyes, I tried to catch my breath, and I didn't open them until Jeremiah's voice cut through my blissful rest. "Alright, enough lazing about," he said. "We've still got a lot of work to do today. Next up is four hours of combat tactics. Then another four hours of range time. When you're done with that, I expect you to spend at least two hours working on your mind puzzles."

"R-really? That's . . . when am I going to rest?" I asked, levering myself into a sitting position.

"When you're sleeping," he said.

After that, I began a long eight weeks, during which I was pushed to my limits. Whether it was my physical conditioning, my skill with various firearms, or my mental-processing speeds, I grew by leaps and bounds. However, each time I took a step forward, the training program did, as well, so I was always just shy of mastering whatever was in front of me.

For that first week, I constantly complained, if only in my mind. I told myself that there was no shame in quitting, that I could achieve the same results with a lot less effort; if I went a little slower, it would just take longer to reach my pinnacle. It was an insidious thought, and I pushed it aside. I had to trust my uncle. If he said my current training regimen was the right way to go about things, then I would give him the benefit of the doubt.

After that, time sort of blended together. I still gave my training every ounce of concentration I possessed, but everything else just faded into the background. In a way, I felt almost like a machine—emotionless and uncompromising. Which I started to believe was due to my Combat Focus kicking in.

Or maybe it wasn't. I had no real basis for that idea, and I'd never been in any sort of comparable situation. However, it probably didn't really matter, one way or another. If I believed it was responsible, that might be enough. Kind of a placebo effect, but for my mental state.

Either way, by the end of the eight-week cycle, I was a changed woman. Not only had my stats seen marked improvement, but my skills had followed suit. After that last day, I opened my status and studied the changes:

NAME	Mirabelle Lisa Braddock		
CLASS	N/A (Requirements Not Met)		
LEVEL	3 (71%)		
CONSTITUTION	9/31		
MIND	11/31		
MIST	6/31		
SKILLS	7/7		
SKILL NAME	Skill Tier	Modifiers	Abilities
CYBERNETIC INTERFACE	Tier 1 (98%)	None	2 Cybernetic Slots
FIREARMS	Tier 1 (91%)	+5% Damage (All Firearms) +2% Reload Speed +17% Accuracy (All Firearms) +15% Damage (Rifle) +15% Damage (Pistol) +15% Damage (Scattergun)	None
CLOSE QUARTERS COMBAT	Tier 1 (4%)	+2% Movement Speed +5% Damage (Melee) +2% Speed (Melee) +2% Accuracy (Melee) +5% Damage (Unarmed) +5% Damage (Blunt Weapons)	None

STEALTH OPERATIONS	Tier 0 (0%)	None	Camouflage (F)
COMBAT UTILITY	Tier 1 (93%)	None	Triage (F) Basic Explosives Handling (F) Combat Focus (F) Pain Tolerance (F) Resistance (F) Foraging (F) Improvisation (F) Regeneration (F)
MISTWALKER	Tier 1 (27%)	+5% Speed (Misthack) +5% Speed (Mistwalk)	Mistwalk (F) Misthack (F) Mistwall (F)
SPYCRAFT	Tier 1 (31%)	None	Disguise (F) Deception (F)

All my attributes had experienced a good deal of growth. First, my Constitution had almost doubled, and because of that, I'd managed to conquer the obstacle course. However, the moment I had—which was about four weeks in—I'd been given a new goal: complete it in progressively lower times. I had continued to make progress to the point where I questioned how I'd ever struggled to complete the thing. Now, I could practically fly through it.

Of course, I had seen a couple of Milo's Amigos working on the same obstacle course, which put to rest any feelings of superiority my newfound physical prowess might have engendered. The two men didn't just complete it; I could scarcely track them as they ran through it, over and over again for almost an hour. It was a humbling display, and one I suspected had been arranged by my uncle. And it served its purpose, too. Not only did it force me to rethink my perception of my own power, but it also gave me something to shoot for.

I saw similar gains in the rest of my physical training, as well, and I soon found myself capable of lifting my own body weight like it was nothing. If I hadn't spent those eight weeks so exhausted, it would have been a euphoric feeling. As it was, I hardly had time to notice.

The same could be said for my mental training. Each day, I felt like the instructor—a short, bald man with a glorious mustache—was tasked with seeing if he could cram so much knowledge into my skull that I became a gibbering idiot. I didn't. Obviously. But more than once, it had felt like I was on the verge of breaking.

The results spoke for themselves, though. In only eight weeks, I'd learned basic combat tactics, geography, map reading, covert tactics, and most importantly of all, critical thinking. There were plenty of other topics, and we spent quite a bit of those first few days tinkering with my combat interface, but we really drilled down on subjects that would aid me in all sorts of combat scenarios.

That, as well as my nightly logic puzzles, served to increase my Mind attribute by quite a lot, and I was happy to notice an increase in my calculating power. My memory also grew a good deal sharper, which only served to increase my learning capabilities.

Finally, there was the firearms training. Before, I'd spent quite a lot of time at the firing range in my uncle's building, and I'd thought I was an expert. The first session disabused me of that notion. Sure, if I was standing still—and my targets cooperated by doing the same—I was a great shot. The moment movement was introduced to the mix, I saw just how far I had to go. On top of that, I was taught how to quickly reload and switch weapons—which, despite my top-tier arsenal implant, didn't go as quickly as my instructor wanted it to. In addition, he taught me how to effectively use cover and move in a firefight.

It was an enlightening experience, and even with how difficult it was, I very much enjoyed my time at the range. My efforts were rewarded with a huge jump in my [Firearms] skill, and by the end of the eighth week, I expected to reach the next tier fairly quickly. And I was eager to see how that would affect my damage output.

"You've done well," said my uncle. I looked up from where I'd been staring at my empty plate. I'd just eaten dinner, and with my eight weeks finished, I felt a little lost.

"Thanks," I said, giving him an exhausted smile.

"Two days," he said.

"What?"

"You've got two days," he repeated. "Do with it whatever you want. But after that, you're going to experience the roughest month of your life."

"W-what?" I asked.

"In my day, they called it hell week," Jeremiah said with a fond grin. "With your increased attributes, you should be able to handle a month. I think. We'll see, though."

Hell week? But it was a month? That definitely did not sound good. To keep myself from panicking, I asked, "What happens after that?"

"The real training," he said. "So, enjoy your two days. It'll be the last free time you have for a while."

CHAPTER EIGHTEEN

HELL MONTH

So many people refuse to understand that every great accomplishment requires incredible sacrifice. Be it time, tears, or sweat, the cost is always high. But that feeling you get when you truly accomplish something worthwhile—there's nothing like it. That feeling alone is enough to sustain you through any number of trials or tribulations.

—Jeremiah Braddock III

I had the next day to myself, so after spending two months waking up before dawn, I had every intention of sleeping in. My body, however, refused to cooperate, and I awoke at five in the morning, just like any other day. As I lay there, I felt my stomach twisting into knots. The previous couple of months had been difficult enough, and now, I was only two days away from having the difficulty ratcheted up a few notches.

But I could take it, couldn't I? My uncle wouldn't let me do it if he didn't think so, and I'd long since decided to trust his judgment. Besides, even as difficult as my training had been so far, I couldn't say that I hadn't enjoyed it. There was something altogether satisfying about looking at my status each night and seeing my numbers increase. That satisfaction was especially potent when it was accompanied by real-world examples of my improvement. I'd gone from barely being able to complete the obstacle course to breezing through, with the only difficulty coming from my own drive to go faster. And my growth hadn't been confined to that, either. My skills had been similarly affected, with almost all of them reaching Tier 1, where I saw quantifiable increases.

And I couldn't wait to see more. It was almost enough that I found myself wishing—at least a little bit—that I could just fast-forward to when I could begin my uncle's so-called hell month; it would be difficult, I was sure. In fact, I suspected that it would probably stretch my resolve to the very limits. However, I also knew that when I made it to the end, I would do so as a stronger individual. And that was enough to turn my anxiety to impatience.

First, though, I had a couple of days off, and I had no idea how to use them. Still in bed, I considered continuing with my routine. After all, I didn't want to lose any of my gains, and what's more, I knew that stopping and starting back up often made things more difficult than if I'd just kept going. So, with a sigh, I levered myself out of bed and went to the bathroom. After taking care of my business, I caught my reflection in the mirror, and I had to admit that I liked what I saw.

For one, I'd gained weight, but not in the eating-too-much-candy kind of way. Instead, I'd filled out with enough springy muscle that I actually looked healthy for a change. My time as a runaway, brief though it had been, hadn't been easy on my looks. When I'd left Nova City, my skin had been a bit spotty, my hair had been incredibly frizzy, and my features had been hollow. Now, though? I looked good. Better than I ever had before—probably a result of my increased Constitution or the Regeneration ability associated with [Combat Utility], which was proving to be one of my most valuable skills.

Or maybe that was just my vanity talking. Either way, a little training had done my body good, and I was eager to see what the future might hold.

After washing my face, I stepped out of the bathroom and selected something to wear. Instead of the fatigues I'd been wearing for the past two months, I chose a pair of tight black jeans that had rips and tears in all the right places, a white tank top with a stylized lipstick kiss on it, and a studded belt. Capping it off were the boots I'd stolen what felt like a lifetime ago. With that taken care of, I went back into the bathroom and applied a light coating of makeup and tried to arrange my hair into some semblance of order. The best I could achieve was a rough symmetry to the giant poof, which I supposed would have to do.

Dressed and ready to face the world, I headed down to the common room where Jo was serving a breakfast of eggs, grits, and bacon—all real, instead of the soy-based food we got in Nova City. That was one thing about living on the frontier: the food was light-years better than what I'd grown up eating. Perhaps that had something to do with my weight gain, as well.

"Aren't you lookin' like a million credits," Jo said, sliding a plate in front of me as I sat down. "I'm kind of jealous. You're going to put all the rest of us to shame."

Unused to compliments from anyone but Heather, my uncle's girlfriend, I fixed my eyes on the plate and said, "T-thanks. I guess."

"Want some coffee?" she asked.

"Uh . . . no," I said. "I've never liked it."

"That's because you've probably never had the real stuff," she said. "Seriously. Give it a try. I can almost guarantee you'll like it."

"Oh . . . okay," I said. "But . . . um . . . I like lots of sugar."

"Ten-four," she said with a grin before she disappeared across the room and behind the counter. A minute or two later, she returned with a steaming mug, which she set down in front of me. Crossing her arms, she said, "Give it a try."

I really didn't like being the center of anyone's attention, but what was I going to do? I didn't know anywhere else to get food, and even if I did, I didn't exactly have any credits. So, trapped as I was, I did as she asked. Lifting the cup to my mouth, I was fully prepared to make some bland comment about how it wasn't bad, but the moment the liquid hit my tongue, my eyes widened in surprise. Swallowing it, I said, "That's amazing! Where has this been all my life?!"

"Too expensive to import into Nova City. At least for the likes of us," came my uncle's voice. I turned to see him standing behind me, his hands on his hips. He looked dangerous just standing there. "Don't get used to it because this is one of the few places in this area where it's readily available. And that's only because there's a bunch of families full of real farmers attached to this town. Coffee's not usually native to this region, but it's amazing what someone with an actual [Horticulture] skill can accomplish."

"Oh . . . right," I said. "But . . . but it is really good," I added, looking at Jo almost apologetically. Jeremiah had a way of throwing a wet blanket onto any conversation. It was one of his many faults. He also snored and talked in his sleep.

Jo rolled her eyes at my uncle, sliding onto the bench across the table from me. "So, what do you have planned today? You're off, right? That's what everyone's saying."

"Uh . . . everyone?"

"You've been running around here for two months," Jo said, pushing her hair behind her ear. "People are going to talk about you. We're a decent-sized town, but in this area, we're pretty close-knit. And don't avoid my question. What do you have planned?"

"I don't know," I admitted. "Explore a little? I've barely seen any of the town, and I thought I'd . . . I don't know . . . see what it has to offer."

She broke into a wide grin. "I know! I'll be your guide," she said. "It'll be awesome. I could show you all the coolest places, and—"

"Don't you have to work?" I asked. Indeed, it felt like Jo was always working the counter, and I hadn't seen anyone else around. Of course, I knew she didn't own the place, but it felt like she was the only one who worked there.

"I get off in an hour," she said. "Mom takes over then." Her face scrunched up in concentration, and she went on, "Oh. I guess you've never seen me when

I'm not working, huh? Probably because of your weird schedule. I work the night shift and into the morning. My parents take care of things during the day."

"I guess that makes sense," I said, the mystery solved. "But you don't want to spend your time off showing me around, do you?"

"Of course I do!" Jo insisted. "We're going to be best friends. You'll see."

I glanced at my uncle, and he nodded. So, I said, "Okay. Sounds ... uh ... good, I guess. Yeah. It sounds good."

After that, I dug into my meal, eating with reckless abandon. My uncle chuckled, saying, "Slow down. It's not going anywhere."

"Sorry," I mumbled, my mouth full. I swallowed. "I'm just used to being on a schedule."

He sighed, then said, "Reminds me of my time in the army. It wasn't until later that I decided to slow down and enjoy things while I could. When I got home, I had the benefit of some of the best food in the world—you know, that's one of the things this area was known for, back then. Now, it's like pulling teeth just to get decent jambalaya."

"We ate jambalaya all the time," I said.

"That stuff in Nova City is not real jambalaya," he stated. "Everything about it is wrong. From the soy-based protein clumps that are supposed to taste like shrimp to everything else that is just wrong enough to ruin the whole thing—it is just a bad imitation. Like store-brand Cheerios."

"What are Cheerios?" I asked, a little confused. Some kind of antidepressant or something?

"Don't worry about it," Jeremiah said. "They don't exist anymore. My point is that as wondrous as the Initialization was—and it gave us so many things, making the impossible possible—we lost a lot, too. For instance, before that nanite swarm hit Earth, I was a half step from being crippled. I could get around. I could live a mostly normal life. But I was constantly in pain, and all it would take was one wrong move, and I'd have been paralyzed."

He took a mug from Jo, who'd approached without me noticing her. "Thanks," he said. Then, he continued, "But then, the Initialization came, and not only was it suddenly easy for my spine to heal back to better than it was before the injury, but it also stretched my longevity into the centuries. I'm not even middle-aged yet, and I turned one twenty last year. So, even though so many people died—and they did—I came out ahead. Suffice it to say that I've got mixed feelings about the whole thing."

"Yeah," I mumbled. "I could see that."

With that, we both went silent, and I finished my meal in peace. However, I couldn't shake the feeling that I'd gotten a brief glimpse into my uncle's tragic past. He was a man who'd lost everything, and multiple times. I felt sorry for him, which was a little disconcerting, given that he was the pillar to which my entire life had been anchored. If he was worthy of pity, then what about the rest of us?

After finishing my meal, I waited on Jo to complete her shift. As I waited, she brought me another cup of coffee, which I gratefully accepted. Once her shift was finished, she disappeared into the back to change. She emerged about twenty minutes later, grinning and looking wholly different.

"Wow," I said, looking her up and down. She wore a short miniskirt, a leather bustier, and a red studded jacket that didn't even cover her midriff. I could only pray that I looked half as cool as her.

"Wow yourself," she said. "Love those boots."

"Thanks" was my mumbled response. As confident as I was in my physical abilities, I was just as unsure when it came to social situations. In school, I'd always faded into the background where everyone just left me alone. Some of that was due to my own introverted nature, but it was also because I was Jeremiah's niece. People were afraid of him, and through the transitive property, they were scared of me, as well. That had done a number on my social prospects.

She grabbed my arm and pulled me toward the door. Or tried to, at least. With my attributes, she couldn't move me if I didn't want to be moved. "Whoa," Jo muttered. "You're . . . uh . . . you're pretty strong, huh?"

"I guess. Sorry," I said. "You caught me by surprise."

"Well, c'mon," she said, still grinning. "Let's go. I have a ton of stuff I want to show you!"

And so, I followed her out of the inn, and before I knew it, we were meandering through the town. The majority of the other pedestrians didn't seem to notice us, but every now and then, I caught someone's eyes lingering just a little longer than absolutely necessary. When I mentioned it to Jo, she just laughed.

"Are you talking about the boys?" she asked.

"Uh . . ."

Now that I thought about it, most of the people who'd noticed us were male, with a smattering of girls mixed in. And almost all of them were young, somewhere around our age.

"I guess?"

"Don't worry about it," she said. "It's good to be noticed, right? Otherwise, why would I wear this stupid jacket? It's so freaking hot!"

I mumbled some unintelligible reply, and Jo led me into a nearby market. I stopped beside a railing for a moment to take it all in. It wasn't so different from the markets in Nova City, save that the fashion seemed quite a bit different. Sure, Jo and I were dressed similarly to what would be expected in Nova City, but most of the people in the market wore decidedly less elaborate outfits. Tee-shirts. Jeans. Shorts. And flip-flops were the norm. Thankfully, there were enough people dressed like us that we didn't stick out. Not too much, at least.

The other difference was the smell. Nova had, to put it mildly, a very distinct aroma that I'd come to associate with the city. Cement and sewage, water and body odor, and a hundred other smells combined to give it its own aroma This market was different. Sure, some of the components were the same—like the body odor. But there was also the smell of sizzling meat and spices.

Finally, the goods on offer were different, as well. In Nova City, everything was sleeker. More fabricated. Soulless. But here? The goods were rough and unpolished. Utilitarian. Add to that the fact that, in Nova City, such a market would've been bathed in neon lights and the glow of a hundred holographic displays, most of which would depict something overtly sexual, and it almost felt like I'd stepped into a different world.

"What's wrong?" asked Jo.

"It's just . . . it's just so different," I said. "Back in Nova, it's just . . . it's just not like this."

"I wish I could go there," Jo said. "But it's almost impossible for someone like me to get into the city. Jeremiah's guys could probably smuggle me inside, but my parents think it's too dangerous. They've heard bad things about the city."

"It's probably worse than they know," I responded, leaning forward against the railing. "A couple days before I left, seven innocent people were killed by the Enforcers. They're, like, the elite peacekeepers. All because it was easier just to kill everyone than to figure out who set off a minor bomb."

"That's . . . that's horrible," gasped Jo.

I shrugged. "It's life in Nova," I said, trying to sound like it wasn't still bothering me. It was. A lot. I'd been the cause of that explosion, and so, at least some of the blame for those innocent people's lives rested on my shoulders. "Trust me—it's better here."

She snorted. "You only say that because you're rich," she said. She leaned over, playfully bumping against my shoulder as she said, "Most people don't just stroll in here and get whatever they want, you know."

"I'm not rich," I said. "I've got, like, forty credits to my name."

"Yeah, but Jeremiah is," Jo said. "And that's the same as you being rich. C'mon."

After that brief exchange, we set off into the market, visiting one stall after another. I quickly discovered that I couldn't afford anything, though. When we came to a booth selling Leviathan merchandise, I almost reverted to my thieving ways. None of it was high quality, but that didn't really matter. Even in Nova City, finding authentic Leviathan gear meant attending one of their shows, and given that they didn't exactly advertise on the entertainment channels, you had to travel in the right circles to even know when and where they might perform. Either way, I resisted the urge to snatch everything I could and run away.

Barely.

Okay, so I might've pocketed a tee-shirt, but in my defense, it wasn't like the guy didn't have a bunch more. If anything, I was doing him a favor by reducing his inventory costs. Or something like that. I don't know. I wanted it, and I took it. End of story.

"Did you just take that guy's shirt?" Jo asked after we'd gone a good distance from the booth.

"Uh . . . maybe?" I asked, dragging the shirt out of my arsenal implant. A couple of bullets came with it. "Shit," I muttered as they clattered to the ground.

"How?" she asked.

"Oh, I've got an arsenal implant," I said. "It's pretty high-grade, so I can store other things in there, too. I usually just use it for ammo and stuff, though."

"That is so cool," she gushed.

"Yeah," I said, returning her grin with one of my own. "It kind of is. I don't—wait . . . is that a bookstore?"

"Um . . . yeah," she said, obviously a little confused by my change of tone. "Why? Are you into books or something?"

"Do you know how rare they are?" I asked. "Like, I've only ever seen a handful of real books in my whole life. And you have a store full of them here?"

"Calm down—they're just books," Jo said, looking at me like I'd just lost my mind.

She started to say something else, but I wasn't hearing it. Instead, I was marching toward the store in question—one of the few that were actually housed in buildings as opposed to simple stalls. I went inside and gaped at the interior. Every wall was lined with books. "I think I'm in heaven," I said.

As an introvert who'd spent most of my time indoors, I'd been hard-pressed to find means of occupying my time. Sure, there were games aplenty, and the shows on the entertainment feeds were always there, but sometimes, I wanted something a little more immersive. To that end, I'd taken up reading. The books came on my personal tablet, but I didn't care all that much. The stories were what was important.

Or that's what I thought until, on my twelfth birthday, my uncle gave me a physical book. The words were the same as what I could get on my tablet, but there was just something different about holding the book in my hands. I'd been in love from the moment I laid eyes on it, and I'd begged Jeremiah to get more of them for me. Of course, there weren't many to be had, and by the time we'd left Nova City, I'd only added one other book to my tiny library. Both were sitting in my storage; I was afraid to take them out, lest I damage them outside of Nova's climate-controlled atmosphere.

"Hello there, young lady," came a gravelly voice. I looked up to see an old man standing behind the counter. With white hair, a bushy mustache, and twinkling blue eyes, he looked the part of a kindly old shopkeeper. "If you try to steal anything, my little friend's going to have something to say about it."

A clunk on the counter drew my eyes to a sawed-off scattergun; as far as I could tell, it was one of the kinetic versions, which meant that it was meant to throw a good deal of damage in a wide spread. By comparison, my own scattergun was an elemental type, and it was intended more for crowd control and disrupting cybernetics. The point was that the weapon was an overt threat, and one I didn't want to take lying down.

In an instant, Ferdinand II, loaded with explosive rounds that would rip him to shreds, was in my hand. As casually as I could, I said, "Mine's bigger, old man."

He fixed me with an impassive look, his fingers tapping against the stock of the scattergun. In the doorway, where she'd stopped dead in her tracks, Jo looked as if she was about to bolt. But I held firm. I felt positive that I could take the man out if he went for his weapon.

Then, he let out a laugh, breaking the tension. "Oh, that's fantastic!" he said. "Most everyone just runs away. But you? You really wouldn't have hesitated to shoot me, would you? No, no—don't answer. Now, what can I do for you? I can tell from your expression that you're a fellow book lover."

A second later, his weapon disappeared, telling me that he had an arsenal implant, as well. I followed suit, saying, "Yeah. This is more books than I've ever seen before, though. Like . . . where did they all come from?"

"There used to be a public library here," he said. "I was pretty young back then, but I managed to save quite a few of the books."

"Wait, you're . . . how old are you?"

"Old enough," the man said. "Now, tell me what kinds of books you like, and we'll see if we can work out a deal."

"I . . . um . . . I like the romance books," I admitted. "The ones where . . . you know . . . people fall in love and stuff."

"Don't say 'and stuff,'" he admonished. Then, he pointed to a corner of the store, saying, "Right over there. I know every book in this store, so don't get sticky fingers, you hear?"

"I won't," I said, meaning it. Besides, my uncle was rich. If I really wanted some books, he'd buy them for me. I was certain of it. So, I went to the indicated corner of the store and started to peruse the stock. And I was happy to see that there were almost forty romance novels there, each with heroic men and beautiful women on the cover. I was instantly hooked.

Jo, however, wasn't so enamored, and though she didn't say anything, she kept fidgeting like she couldn't wait to get out of there and do something more interesting. So, not wanting to force her to stick around when she clearly wanted to leave, I carefully replaced the books in question and told the shopkeeper that I'd be back the next day.

After we left the shop, we continued to browse the various stalls until I saw a pair of men harassing one of the vendors. "What's going on over there?" I asked.

"Keep moving," Jo said, ushering me past. "Those are the Tigers."

"That means literally nothing to me," I said, glancing back at the two men. Both were dressed in orange-and-blue outfits, which seemed to be about the worst combination of colors I'd ever seen, and one held a knife to the vendor's throat. Part of me wanted to head back and help sort it out, but Jo urged me along. Eventually, we found the market's exit. As we were climbing the stairs, I asked, "What was that all about? Who are those people? It looked like a shakedown."

"Because that's what it was. They're called the Tigers," she stated. "They're a gang. Sort of. They help contribute to the town's defense, so nobody wants to mess with them. But . . . they also harass vendors and charge them for protection."

"Ah," I said. So, Mobile wasn't so different from Nova City, after all. Back home, gangs did the same thing. "Well, so long as they don't mess with me . . ."

"Yeah, nobody's messing with you," she said. "Not with Jeremiah around."

"Good to know," I said. Then, I grinned and asked, "Where to next?"

CHAPTER NINETEEN

A MONTH OF HELL

After Mirabelle's mother died, I took it upon myself to raise her. At the time, her father was still around, but he couldn't even take care of himself, much less a little girl. Two years later, he was gone, too. A tragic but ultimately common tale in Nova City.

—Jeremiah Braddock III

The next day passed in much the same way, but this time, Jo introduced me to her friends. After that, we spent a pleasant day exploring the town. Not only did we revisit the market, where I bought some new clothes—after begging Jeremiah for a few extra credits—and some souvenirs, but she also showed me the ruins of an ancient fort as well as the remains of a sizable domed building, then took me on a tour of the curiously shaped high-rise that had, according to Jo, been the government's seat before the Initialization. It almost felt like a vacation—the sort of thing I'd only ever seen on the entertainment feeds where the characters of my favorite shows visited new and increasingly exotic locales. Of course, I wasn't so foolish as to believe any of those ridiculous stories represented reality, but it was a nice fantasy.

It was a new experience for me, being part of a group of friends. In school, I'd never been mistreated by my peers, but everyone there knew precisely who my uncle was. As such, they all held me at arm's length. Certainly, I'd never had any close friends. Jo showed me how different it could have been, and after taking a little while to adjust, I loved every second of it. However, all good things must come to an end, and so it was with my brief vacation from my training.

That night, I barely slept. Jeremiah hadn't minced any words about how difficult the coming month would be. He'd referred to it as hell, and I knew he wouldn't use such a word lightly. If he considered it hellish, then I had little choice but to expect the worst. So, it was with some trepidation that I found myself lying in bed, staring at the ceiling. In the corner of my HUD, I could see that I was only a few minutes from my alarm going off. Logic told me that I should just get up and face the day, but I couldn't bring myself to rise. Not until the incessant beeping of my alarm echoed inside my head.

I flicked my eyes, shutting it off with a thought, and with a groan, climbed out of bed and started getting ready for the day. I took a steaming-hot shower, then tied my hair back before getting dressed in my black fatigues and unadorned, heavy combat boots. Still, I hesitated, my nerves getting the better of me for a few moments.

But then the weight of expectations—both mine and my uncle's—settled onto my shoulders. I had been given a great gift. I had the potential to become extremely powerful. Millions of people out there would've loved to have the chance I'd been handed. What was a little discomfort next to that?

What's more, I had an inkling of what was coming. The post-Initialization world was a brutal place; there was no doubt about that. And, according to my uncle, once the Integration began, things were going to get much worse. So much so that he'd worked for the better part of a century just to give me a chance to survive. The least I could do was complete the training he'd planned for me.

With a sigh, I squared my shoulders and left my room. My steps echoed on the stairs as I descended into the common room, where I saw Jeremiah enjoying a cup of coffee with a trio of swarthy men who were each wearing camouflage fatigues. I approached and sat down next to Jeremiah. Jo appeared a few seconds later, setting a bowl of oatmeal in front of me.

"This is it?" I asked.

She shrugged and nodded at Jeremiah. "Talk to him," she said with a hint of apology in her voice.

I turned to my uncle, who said, "The next month's going to be tough for you. You don't get any creature comforts. You're barely going to sleep. And you will learn exactly what it means to be truly uncomfortable."

"W-what? Why?" I asked.

"Builds character," came the accented voice of the man across the table. I glared at him, but he didn't seem to mind. In fact, I couldn't help but notice the slight smirk playing across his face as he tucked into his own hearty breakfast.

Jeremiah filled the silence with introductions. The man who'd spoken, who was short, stout, and wearing a floppy-brimmed camouflage boonie hat, sported a thick, black mustache that matched his hair. My uncle said that his name was Angel. The other two were apparently named Diaz and Buck.

Buck was almost as tall as my uncle, but he was a lot thinner, and Diaz was average size, except for his sizable midsection. I was tempted to give them all derogatory names, at least in my head, but I figured that wouldn't be very productive.

"You're going to hate all three of them before the day's out," my uncle said. "Go ahead—eat up. We don't have any time to waste."

I wanted to ask more, but I recognized Jeremiah's tone for what it was. So, I jabbed my spoon into the tasteless brown gruel and started to eat. It was worse than I expected, but at least it was filling. After I'd finished eating, all five of us headed outside and got into an open-topped vehicle with enormous wheels and knobby tires.

"Where are we going?" I asked.

"You'll see," said my uncle, looking back at me from the passenger's seat. I was sandwiched between Potbelly and Slim. Stupid Hat was driving. Yes. Despite my earlier misgivings, I gave them names. It was easier that way. The vehicle sped off, the tires crunching on the gravelly road as we made our way through the town and eventually toward the wall. The gate opened, and we left civilization behind, heading south.

It felt so different, driving through the ruined city without a roof over my head. On the way in, I'd been surrounded by metal, and that isolation had given me a sense of security, false though I knew it probably was. But being out in the open? That was different. Scarier. I was so nervous that I kept seeing things out of the corner of my eye, but when I'd turned to try to catch a better look, nothing was there.

"You're not seeing things," said Potbelly.

"What?"

"There are things living in the city," he said, his voice bearing the same accent as Stupid Hat's. "Lots and lots of evil creatures that would just love to eat a little girl like you alive. I once saw a chupacabra swallow someone about your size whole. Remember that."

I swallowed hard. Of course, I knew he was just trying to scare me, and most of the time, I wouldn't have taken it to heart. But I was convinced I had seen movement, which only made his statement that much worse. I pushed it from my mind and tried to focus on other things as we sped down the road, dodging debris along the way. Like that, almost two hours passed until we finally pulled to a stop next to a sandy beach.

At first, I thought we'd found the ocean, but the smell of the brackish water and the fact that I could see land off to the east told me that it was more likely a protected bay. Hammering home that fact, I could see bits and pieces of an enormous bridge that had once spanned the body of water. When I looked at the water, from which tall reeds sprouted, all I could think of was that giant alligator that had attacked our convoy outside of Nova City. To distract myself from that, I studied the rest of our surroundings.

Nearby, there was an oddly shaped building that was balanced on stilts. Made of wood—which was odd in and of itself—the structure was a half dome shaped like a dodecahedron. I felt pretty sure that that wasn't normal. When I remarked on it, my uncle said, "It's a holdover from before the Initialization. It was abandoned and in a different spot, but Milo and me, we moved it over here and restored it."

"Why?" I asked.

He shrugged. "Growing up, it was a noticeable building," he stated. "I saw it every time I crossed the bay. So, when I saw that it had survived—at least mostly—I couldn't resist the urge to preserve it. Call it a keepsake of a forgotten world. But you're not here to appreciate fine architecture. You're here to have the weakness squeezed out of you."

That certainly didn't sound good, but I kept my mouth shut. My uncle continued, "At any time, you can call it. Just let one of us know that you want to quit, and it'll end. But after that, we're done."

"W-what?" I asked, not understanding.

"With the training," he answered. "You've got enough to get you through, I think. Maybe. I don't know. But something I'm sure of—if you drop out of this, you don't have the heart to keep going through the rest of what we have planned. I'll give you some money, and you can start a life back in Nova City."

"You'd abandon me?"

"What? No!" he said. "I'm not a monster, Mirabelle. We're family. If you can't do this, you can't do it. I won't judge you for it. But I also won't waste my time trying to force you into something you're not suited for. Consider this your first real test. You've already got the bare minimum I think it's going to take for you to survive the Integration. This next month, it's to see if you can endure the training necessary so that you can learn to thrive."

I bit my lip. Thriving certainly sounded good, but what did that even mean? I had the feeling that Jeremiah wanted to turn me into a warrior of some sort, but to what end, I had no clue. And he wasn't exactly sharing his plans with me.

As far as I could tell, it looked like I had a choice to make. Did I want to do the hard thing, persist through what promised to be a hellish month? Or did I want to take the easy way out? The comfortable path that would see me living a luxurious but mundane life? My heart said one thing, but my head told me something else entirely. At first, the smart choice seemed to be comfort. But my mother had gone down that road, and look where it had gotten her. Dead in a back alley. I wouldn't repeat her mistakes.

"I won't quit."

Potbelly, who was standing nearby, his hands on his hips, laughed. My uncle ignored him, saying, "Remember you said that. You're going to need that fire going forward. Remember—you can quit anytime. But if you stay, you do exactly what these three tell you to do. Otherwise, they're going to take it as quitting. Got it?"

I nodded.

He gave me a smile, which was not as reassuring as it probably should've been. Instead, I felt a shiver run up my spine. "Good luck," he said, patting me on the shoulder. Then, he turned and walked away, leaving me with Potbelly, Stupid Hat, and Slim.

As soon as my uncle got into the vehicle and drove away, Stupid Hat's voice rang out, "Alright! Let's get this show on the road. A short run ought to get you warmed up. Let's move!"

"Now, little girl!" screamed Slim as he pointed to the south along the beach. "Go!"

I jerked back to attention, and not wanting them to take my hesitation as me quitting, I took off at a jog. Of course, that wasn't good enough, and Slim, who was following along behind me, kept yelling for me to speed up. I complied, though after only a mile, I was completely out of breath. As we kept running, eventually turning around and heading back the way we'd come, I told myself that we were going to stop soon, that I was going to have an opportunity to catch my breath. But we didn't. Not for three hours. And even when we did stop, it was only so I could drop to my belly and start doing push-ups. Once my arms turned to jelly, we started running again, repeating the process a couple of hours later. Over and over again until the sun started to set.

If I thought that was going to save me, though, I had another thing coming. We kept at it through the night, only stopping for ten or fifteen minutes here or there, during which I was expected to grab as much sleep as I could. Eventually, I shifted into a daze of putting one foot in front of the other, of doing one more push-up, of following whatever directions I was given. And all the while, one of my three new least-favorite people yelled at me to go faster, to do one more push-up, to give up so they could go home.

I didn't give them the satisfaction.

Even after the sun rose again, I kept going forward. Even when they made me swim out into the bay and I felt mud and muck all over my body, I continued on. Even when one day turned to two, and two turned to three, I refused to give them the satisfaction of quitting.

I don't know if it was my attributes or my Combat Focus pushing me along. Maybe it was neither; perhaps I just had a strong will. Whatever the case, I didn't quit. Not after three days, and not after two weeks.

From time to time, my uncle would show up. He never said anything, but I knew he was there. Watching. Waiting to see if I was worth his time.

For the first few days, I kept thinking about how much longer I had left. I even counted my steps, hoping to distract myself. It didn't work, and eventually, I just lost track of everything that wasn't pushing me forward into the next minute. The next hour. The next day.

As the days wore into weeks, I barely ate. What sleep I managed to get came in short spurts and was completely inadequate. We were attacked by monsters a few times, but the three men who had become my keepers shut them down in a heartbeat.

Once, a giant snake struck, and I was too tired to even react. Potbelly, who was running behind me at the time, darted forward so quickly that I didn't even see him move, and before I knew what had happened, the snake's head had been separated from its body. Potbelly, meanwhile, was wiping the blood from a wicked-looking machete. When he saw that I'd stopped, he said, "You're not quitting are you? If not, get moving, little girl."

I shuffled back to a run, the snake attack pushed to the back of my mind alongside everything else that wasn't putting one foot in front of the other.

So it went for an entire month.

Never did I come close to quitting. Sure, more than once, I dropped from exhaustion, only to wake up some indeterminate time later to keep going, but I didn't quit. I didn't dare. Because as much as it hurt, as exhausted as I was, a powerless existence was so much worse.

Suddenly, I collided with something immovable. Predictably, with my wobbly and exhausted state being what it was, I soon found myself on the ground, and when I looked up, I saw my uncle standing over me, his fingers hooked on his belt.

"Congratulations," he said. "You passed the test. You can stop now."

Those words hit me almost as hard as the wave of exhaustion that followed. It was as if my entire body had been waiting on permission to shut down, and Jeremiah's statement had done just that. I collapsed back onto the sand, letting unconsciousness overtake me. I had done it. Now, I could rest.

CHAPTER TWENTY

A WELL-ROUNDED EDUCATION

I am not and have never been a hero. I have saved people. I live in a brutal world, and in turn, I've been forced to become a ruthless killer. Channeling that into saving people doesn't make me one of the good guys. It just means I've managed to balance the scales a little.

—Jeremiah Braddock III

"You nearly killed her," came a raspy, yet feminine voice, cutting through my unconsciousness like a knife. "She had exhausted her every reserve, and her body was feeding on its own energy. She is lucky to have survived."

My uncle's voice echoed in my ears as he said, "That was the point, Kimiko. You know better than most what that can do for a person. If all it did was—"

I groaned, trying to sit up. The muscles in my stomach tightened, and I attempted to flick my eyes open, but my body didn't seem terribly eager to obey my commands. Even when I tried to clench my fists in frustration, all I managed was a slight tremble.

I felt a soft, yet firm hand on my arm, followed by Kimiko saying, "Relax. You were completely drained. We are replenishing your reserves. Try to rest."

I could practically hear the glare in her tone, her ire obviously directed at my uncle. He had put me in danger; that much was clear. But I was still far too out of it to remember quite why I was incapable of movement. It was probably lucky, then, that I soon succumbed to my lack of energy and drifted back into unconsciousness.

Over the next few days, I only spent short spans awake, and even then, it was to varying degrees of consciousness. Sometimes, I just lay there, listening to whatever was happening around me—which was usually nothing—but other times, I was able to open my eyes. The first time I managed to force my eyes open, I saw that I was back in the doctor's office where I was lying on a cot. I had tubes hooked to my arms, and there was some sort of machine on my chest. I had no idea what any of it was, but after a few seconds of panic, I calmed down enough to remember that I had nothing to fear from my uncle or Kimiko. If they'd hooked me up to a machine, then it was because I needed it.

Still, it was uncomfortable. And anxiety inducing. But by that point, I'd become an old hand at subverting my negative mindset. Perhaps that was the whole point of the hell month in the first place—to teach me how to endure. Maybe it wasn't a test. Instead, it was possible that it was just another phase of my training.

That made me feel a bit better.

Or maybe it was the fact that soon after that revelation, I drifted back to sleep and promptly forgot it for the next few days. Either way, right?

My full recovery came as a shock when, at last, I finally opened my eyes and felt no lingering weakness. The tubes were gone. So was the machine. My uncle stood over me, and at his shoulder was the diminutive Kimiko, her face impassive. By contrast, Jeremiah's expression was filled with pride.

"Forty-two days," he said. "That's how long you were out there. I'm proud of you."

"W-what?" I muttered. "I . . . I don't understand."

That's when he explained that my hell month was a lot more open-ended than I'd been led to believe. The Amigos—the men I'd dubbed Stupid Hat, Potbelly, and Slim—had been instructed to work me until my breaking point. With minimal sleep or food, my uncle had never expected me to last the entire month, much less almost half again as long. But I had, not stopping until my body literally gave out.

"That means you have a strong will," he said, sitting on the edge of my cot. The flimsy thing felt like it was going to collapse under me, but it held strong. He patted my leg, adding, "Attributes are great. They let us do wondrous things. But without a strong will, they are entirely meaningless. Remember that. When things get hard, when you don't think you can go on, or when you're woefully overmatched—and all of that will almost assuredly happen—think back to what you just went through. It'll see you through to the other side because I can almost guarantee that, no matter what else you face, it won't be as difficult as what you just accomplished."

I told him that I still didn't quite get it, and he explained that most people couldn't have lasted more than a couple of weeks; I had exceeded that by a long shot. Then, Jeremiah told me to open my status, which I did, and I was surprised at what I found:

NAME	Mirabelle Lisa Braddock		
CLASS	N/A (Requirements Not Met)		
LEVEL	3 (71%)		
CONSTITUTION	13/31		
MIND	15/31		
MIST	7/31		
SKILLS	7/7		
SKILL NAME	Skill Tier	Modifiers	Abilities
CYBERNETIC INTERFACE	Tier 2 (10%)	None	3 Cybernetic Slots
FIREARMS	Tier 1 (91%)	+5% Damage (All Firearms) +2% Reload Speed (All Firearms) +17% Accuracy (All Firearms) +15% Damage (Rifle) +15% Damage (Pistol) +15% Damage (Scattergun)	None
CLOSE QUARTERS COMBAT	Tier 1 (4%)	+2% Movement Speed +5% Damage (Melee) +2% Speed (Melee) +2% Accuracy (Melee) +5% Damage (Unarmed) +5% Damage (Blunt Weapons)	None

STEALTH OPERATIONS	Tier 1 (1%)	None	Camouflage (F)
COMBAT UTILITY	Tier 2 (34%)	None	Triage (F) Basic Explosives Handling (F) Combat Focus (E) Pain Tolerance (E) Resistance (F) Foraging (F) Improvisation (F) Regeneration (E)
MISTWALKER	Tier 1 (27%)	+5% Speed (Misthack) +5% Speed (Mistwalk)	Mistwalk (F) Misthack (F) Mistwall (F)
SPYCRAFT	Tier 1 (31%)	None	Disguise (F) Deception (F)

I gasped in surprise. The first thing I saw was that I'd gained four points in both the Constitution and Mind attributes, putting me thoroughly into superhuman territory. In addition, I'd gained one point in Mist, which didn't seem like much until I realized that I hadn't really been working on anything that would affect it. But my attributes were just the beginning of my gains.

First, I'd finally reached Tier 2 in [Cybernetic Interface] and [Combat Utility], with the former resulting in an additional cyberware slot and the latter increasing the grade of a few of my abilities. Combat Focus, Regeneration, and Pain Tolerance had all reached E-grade, which boded well for my future prospects, I thought. It was never a bad idea to heal more quickly or be less affected by pain. And Combat Focus sort of spoke for itself. In all, though the experience wasn't one I wished to repeat, I couldn't deny that it had been effective training.

But it was only the beginning, as my uncle soon revealed that his plans for the rest of my training would take up the next eighteen months of my life. When I asked him what happened after that, he was predictably closed lipped.

Either way, it gave me something to think about as I completed my recovery. After two more days, Kimiko released me, telling me in no uncertain terms that she very much disagreed with my uncle's methods. Further, she cautioned me to "get away from that cursed man" as quickly as possible. I wanted to argue with her, but she ushered me out of the building too quickly for that.

The next few days were allocated for rest and relaxation, which meant I spent a bit more time with Jo, who continued to show me all the town's sights. She even took me to a concert, and even though the music wasn't really to my taste—it was way too twangy and not nearly loud enough—I had a great time with her and her friends. For the first time in my life, I started to feel like I actually belonged.

Of course, my miniature vacation soon came to an end, and three days after I was released by Kimiko, Jeremiah told me that I'd begin the next phase of my training the next morning. To my surprise, I was actually looking forward to it. After everything I'd already been through, I didn't think any training could really faze me anymore. So, when the day finally came, it was with anticipation—as opposed to anxiety—twisting my stomach into knots that I let my uncle escort me to an open area on the other side of the town. When we arrived, I was extremely disappointed to find Potbelly waiting for us near a sizable field.

The field itself was around a hundred yards long, with patches of knee-high grass and a variety of targets scattered throughout. Potbelly was predictably dressed in his camouflage fatigues and a matching cap. Covering his eyes were dark sunglasses that looked almost like goggles.

During my few days off, Jo had given me some background information on the so-called Amigos and the town's leader, Milo. According to her, Milo had been a teenager at the time of the Initialization, and his family had owned a farm north of the city. There, his family had employed a group of immigrant workers. When the Initialization began, they'd all banded together and, somehow, managed to survive—chiefly due to Milo learning to work with his family's former employees, which they'd always called their amigos—a label they'd worn with pride.

The rest of Milo's family, including his twin brother, were long dead, and he only had his Amigos to remind him of his past life. The men were all that was left, and they were incredibly competent, immensely loyal, and very well respected within the community.

It was almost enough to make me rethink the derogatory nicknames I'd given some of them. But then I thought about how mercilessly they'd pushed me, and I decided that a couple of less-than-flattering monikers weren't going to hurt anyone.

Whatever the case, I followed my uncle toward Potbelly, and when I arrived, my uncle told me, "Listen to him. He knows what he's talking about."

With that, he left me alone, and when he was finally gone, Potbelly said, "Let's see your rifle." I took it out and handed it to him. He inspected it for a few seconds before announcing that it was acceptable. Then, he said, "Your uncle is a sniper, so he's been teaching you how to shoot from a stationary position. I'm here to teach you about real combat."

After that, he began my instruction into close quarters battle, which, as far as I could tell, was a fancy way of saying gun fighting. He told me how to move—heel to toe, so I kept a stable upper body, how to align my sights while moving, and lastly, he stressed all the things I shouldn't do. It was a cascade of information, but thanks to my increased Mind attribute, I took it all in without any issue.

Next came the practical instruction, which saw me completing something of an obstacle course with my rifle. The goal was to shoot the targets while moving from place to place, which, after I got used to it, wasn't so difficult. Until the targets started moving. But I persisted for almost two hours until he had me switch to my hand cannon and repeat the process. Two hours later, I ended the session with my scattergun. In those six hours, I fired more rounds than I had in any one week of my entire life.

But my day wasn't finished.

With my firearms training completed, I took fifteen minutes for a meal before receiving instruction in close quarters melee combat as taught by Stupid Hat, who was predictably wearing his stupid, floppy hat. This was a lot more difficult than the firearms training because I had no real background in melee combat. Still, I enjoyed the change of pace, soaking up the instruction as well as I could.

The next segment of my day was dedicated to explosives handling. I didn't get much hands-on instruction, but I did learn about the various ways I would be able to blow someone or something up. From grenades to thermo Mist detonators, I learned about their composition and expected yield. My instructor, a short, dumpy woman named Anna, who was missing one of her hands and wore a tool belt around her waist, told me that we'd get more practical experience as I demonstrated mastery of the theoretical side of explosives handling. And I had to admit that I kind of liked the idea of creating massive explosions. But then again, who doesn't?

Finally, my day ended with an unassuming man teaching me about [Spycraft]. As I sat across from him, my eyes kept trying to slip away—the result of one of his abilities, he said. While it was active, he would be virtually unnoticed by anyone with a lower Mind attribute than him. And even people whose attributes were higher would need to pay close attention in order to notice him.

I liked the sound of that, so I paid close attention as he explained the ins and outs of disguise. According to him, disguises didn't need to be elaborate—not like in the shows on the entertainment feeds back home in Nova City. Simple ones were better. A wig and a coat could do wonders for escaping detection. However, when those failed, there were plenty of abilities available to people with higher-tiered [Spycraft] skills.

To end my day, I was put through two hours of rigorous physical training, the likes of which had occupied the first two months of my time in Mobile. At first, it was laughably easy, but I challenged myself to push harder and faster, ensuring that I always got the most out of the training.

By the time I'd finished, I was well and truly exhausted—at least from a physical standpoint. My mind, though, was still incredibly fresh, so after eating, I put myself through the same mental training as before, cycling through one number puzzle after another until, at last, I felt my eyelids start to droop, and I went to bed.

So began that phase of my training, which lasted for a full three months. It was difficult, but I had to admit that I enjoyed learning all my new skills. Plus, I found the constant uptick of my attributes and skills to be somewhat addictive; according to my uncle, who was increasingly absent as he tended to his affairs back in Nova City, that wasn't uncommon, and he'd heard rumors that that tendency for addiction was one of the reasons the system was used in the first place.

My firearms training progressed very well, and after only a month, I graduated to a virtual simulation that pitted me against Mist constructs that resembled faceless, featureless people. After I'd mastered that, Potbelly taught me how to fight indoors, which was a lot more difficult—largely because I had a habit of hesitating in doorways, which he kept referring to as the fatal funnel. He broke me of that habit by shooting me with nonlethal bullets that left huge welts all over me. By the time I finally learned that lesson, my entire body felt like a giant collective bruise. But I hit all the marks he set for me, so I decided to count it as a win, if a painful one.

Everything else went just as well, with the highlight of the three-month training period being when I finally got to go wild with the explosives I'd been learning about. That day, I had way too much fun chucking grenades and setting bombs outside the town.

The day I finished everything, my uncle returned, and after speaking to my various instructors, congratulated me on a job well done. I grinned in satisfaction and pride as I basked in his approval.

"You've got two days off," he said. "Then, we're going to have a little test."

"What? Like the hell month?" I asked.

He shook his head. "No, nothing like that," he said. "It's just a mission that needs doing. I remember my first mission, way back when I was fresh out of training. It was a simple rescue op, limited resistance. But I learned more about myself in those few hours than I ever learned in training. It'll probably be the same for you."

"Okay," I said. "What should I do until then?"

"Live," he said. "Hang out with your friends. Watch that ridiculous unicorn show you used to love. I don't know, and I don't care. But no training. I want you fresh, got it?"

I nodded. "I'll be ready," I vowed.

"Good" was his response.

CHAPTER TWENTY-ONE

A PROTECTION RACKET

I won't claim that my life since the Initialization has been all bad. I am continuously amazed by the many miraculous things that are now possible. But sometimes I feel like I'm the only one who realizes that all those miracles came at a high cost.

—Jeremiah Braddock III

Two days, all to myself. It was such a strange feeling, especially after spending months where my every minute seemed to be regulated. It felt almost decadent to wake up that first morning and not have any demands on my time. Of course, habits were what they were, and after taking care of my morning routine and having breakfast downstairs, I found myself at the training ground, where I put in a couple of hours of work. Then, I spent a little time at the range before deciding to relax back at the Dew Drop Inn.

Unsurprisingly, Jo was there to greet me. But she didn't look happy; instead, her expression was one of concern. So, I sat at the bar and asked, "What's up? Something the matter?"

She shook her head and placed a glass bottle of Nova Cola in front of me before saying, "It's nothing. Just thinking about how unfair the world is."

"In what way?" I asked, taking a sip of the carbonated and artificially sweetened beverage. It didn't really have a taste, per se. It was just sweet, but that was kind of what I wanted at that moment.

She looked around, then said, "I'll tell you when I get off. Maybe you can help or something. I don't know."

With that, I settled down to enjoy my beverage, but I couldn't deny that I was a little worried by Jo's demeanor. Normally, she was overwhelmingly chipper, so it was a bit disconcerting to see her so anxious. Whatever the case, I would soon find out what was bothering her.

An hour—and two more Nova Colas—later, Jo's mother relieved her, and she practically dragged me from the inn. We didn't stop until we reached a mostly deserted area almost a quarter mile away. We went into an alley, where there were some old crates. Sitting on one, she said, "Everything's just so fucking horrible here."

"What do you mean?" I asked, confused. Mobile obviously had its problems. It was a walled town in the middle of nowhere, and it was missing many of the comforts common to a city like Nova, but it wasn't a bad place—not as far as I was concerned, at least. I didn't say as much, though. Instead, I waited on Jo to answer my question.

"You remember those guys at the market a few months ago, right?" she asked. "The Tigers?"

"The ones wearing those horrible colors?" I asked, remembering the clashing orange and blue. The combination had practically burned my eyes, it was so horrifyingly ugly.

"I guess," she said. "But fashion issues aside, you know what they are, right? They're a gang, and they extort all the people around here. They call it protection, but if anyone doesn't pay, the Tigers send someone around to make the owners understand the need."

I nodded. "That's common in Nova, too," I said.

"Well, my mom and dad, they've been paying the Tigers for years," she said. "Nobody goes against them 'cause they help defend the city when we're attacked. But it's getting worse lately. And . . . and . . . well, there's this one guy . . . he used to be kind of nice, you know? Before he joined up. But ever since then, he's gotten worse and worse until . . . well, nowadays, he thinks he's entitled to whatever he wants."

"What's his name?"

"Jack," she said. "And . . . well, he wants me now. Told my mom and dad that unless they give me up—which they won't, obviously—they're going to have to pay extra."

"Wait—give you up? Like . . .?"

"It's exactly what it sounds like," she said. "It's why they took me off the night shift and have me working during the day now."

I looked around, suddenly feeling like I was being watched. It was meaningless paranoia, but after hearing that Jo had something of a stalker, it was understandable. "What do you want me to do?" I asked.

"I don't know," she said. "What can you do?"

"Uh . . .?"

My first thought was that I could just kill him. It wouldn't be the first person

I'd killed, and I had a feeling he wouldn't be the last, either. However, I suspected that murder would be frowned upon, by both my uncle and by Jo. So, I didn't suggest that. Instead, I said, "I don't know. Maybe I could intimidate him or something."

For a moment, Jo's expression was one of surprise, but then she let out a laugh. "You? Intimidate someone?" she said between guffaws. "Seriously?"

I crossed my arms and waited for her laughter to die down. When it did, I asked, "You finished?"

I knew I didn't cut an imposing figure, but I suppose my training had given me an inflated opinion of myself. Or rather, of how other people might see me. The reality was that I was too small and too innocent looking to frighten anyone. And I knew it.

"Sorry, sorry. I know you've been training and stuff, but . . . c'mon, Mira. You have to know that wouldn't work," she said.

I bit my lip. "Fine," I said. "What do you want me to do, then?"

"Nothing?" Jo said, seemingly confused.

"Nothing?" I echoed, also confused.

For a moment, Jo just looked at me, and then she said, "You don't have to solve my problems. You know that, don't you? Sometimes, friends just listen to one another's issues."

"Oh."

That was definitely news to me. Of course, I'd never really had many other friends—or any at all, I guess—so it stood to reason that I wouldn't know the unwritten rules of friendship. But still, it didn't make much sense to me. After all, if I could solve her problems, I wouldn't hesitate to do just that. What kind of a person would I be if I didn't? Already, I was considering enacting my first plan and just killing the guy. It would've made things so much easier.

I didn't, though. Instead, I spent the next hour listening to Jo complain about one thing or another. All the while, I made plans for how I was going to fix the Tiger issue. I'd been training for a while, so I felt confident in my abilities. If things went bad, I would just do what I had to do, but as it was, I realized I didn't have enough information to make any real decisions. So, I endeavored to rectify that lack, which was how—hours later—I found myself crouched atop a building and studying the compound where most of the Tigers were based.

I was well aware that it was probably a stupid decision, and that my uncle would certainly disapprove. But I'd been training like mad for months, and I hadn't gotten the chance to actually use any of my newfound skills. Besides, Jo had been nice to me, which was something to which I was not accustomed, and I wanted to believe that she was my friend. Because of that, I wanted to help her, and that was that, as far as I was concerned. Whether or not it was stupid didn't really matter to me.

In any case, I watched as garishly dressed mooks, some of which sported admittedly enviable mohawks, came and went from the compound. As I watched, I studied the building. It was surrounded by a low wall, maybe six or seven feet high, and looked like it had once been a warehouse of sorts. Other than that, I didn't get much information; everything else was hidden from me.

So, I waited until night had truly fallen, and I descended from my perch. Crossing the street in a sprint, I slid to a stop next to the wall. My heart pounded out of my chest—not from exertion, but rather excitement. And a little fear. But I didn't think the pair of mooks guarding the gate had seen me. Not really a surprise, given that I was wearing my black fatigues and the place wasn't exactly well lit.

I stood there for a long few moments, listening for any kind of alarm or alert, but there was nothing. So, I gathered my feet under me and leaped, grabbing the top of the wall and pulling myself up. Immediately, I saw a pair of surveillance cameras, turning in slow arcs at opposite corners of the building. When I focused on one, a menu flashed across my HUD:

Initiate Misthack?
[Yes] or [No]

I chose the affirmative response, and a pair of number puzzles appeared on my HUD. I solved them both in the blink of an eye—after spending so much time training my Mind, they were incredibly easy—resulting in another menu:

Misthack Successful. Options:
- **Reboot System**
- **Hijack System**
- **Deactivate System**

The first was useless to me, so I ignored it, but the second seemed interesting enough. It would allow me to see through the camera, which could be useful in the right circumstances. However, the last was the option I was going for. So, I selected it, then repeated the process on the other camera, barely completing the deactivation before the camera swept in my direction. Letting out a sigh of relief, I slipped down on the inside of the wall and crouched between a pile of trash and a metal dumpster. Not the best-smelling of hiding places, but it was all I could find.

As I knelt there, I saw a pair of timers in the top left of my HUD. One read seventy-five seconds, while the other read sixty. Once those timers ticked down to zero, the cameras would reactivate. So, I was on a schedule.

Glancing around to make sure the coast was clear—the Tigers didn't really believe in tight security, apparently—I darted toward the back of the building, careful to keep my steps light. Even so, they were loud in my mind, and I felt certain that, at any moment, I would be discovered. If that happened, I would have no choice but to pull out my weapons. Things would get bloody then. I didn't want that to happen, so I took extra care to remain as silent as I possibly could.

Reaching the end of the building, I peeked around the corner and saw another camera. I deactivated it the same way I'd taken care of the other two, then seeing that the coast was clear, turned the corner. Luckily, that's when I spotted my way in. Along the back side of the building ran a fire escape; accessing it would require a pretty impressive leap on my part, but over the past few months, my attributes had progressed to the point where my Constitution exceeded an Unawakened human's potential. So, I felt confident that I could make it work.

That decided, I crept forward, keeping low to the ground just in case there were any patrols I might have missed. I wouldn't avoid detection for long, but it was dark, and I was dressed all in black, so maybe it would give me enough time to react.

In any case, it was unnecessary because I reached the fire escape without issue. Then, I leaped, my fingers outstretched. For a moment, I didn't think I was going to make it, but when my fingers brushed against that rusty metal, I gripped it tightly. A moment later, I pulled myself up. There, I waited for a few seconds, my breath coming in short gasps; I hadn't really exerted myself, but my heart was going a thousand miles an hour. So, I took a few deep, calming breaths before mounting the steps of the rickety fire escape.

If I'd been any heavier, the thing might have collapsed under me. But as it was, I made it to the top without much issue, and I soon found myself next to a rusted metal door. I tried the knob, and to my surprise, it was unlocked. My first impression of the Tigers had been accurate—they really didn't care so much about security. And I was more than willing to take advantage of that fact.

I turned the knob and winced at the resultant screech of a mechanism that hadn't been used in years. It wasn't overly loud, but in my ears, it might as well have been a building-wide alarm. Still, I bit the bullet and continued the turn, opening the door only slightly to get a good look inside. Fortunately, there was no one in the hall past the door, and I slipped inside, my eyes darting around to see if there were any surprises waiting on me.

There weren't, but I heard the muffled sound of thumping music and raised voices somewhere far below me. Someone was having a party, it seemed. Or maybe it was just a normal Tuesday for the Tigers; that wouldn't have been so surprising. Many of the gangs back in Nova City were held together by desperation, drugs, alcohol, easy money, and the camaraderie that came from frequent parties. The gangs in Mobile seemed little different, from what I could tell.

I stalked further into the building, passing several rooms along the way. I felt certain that they were the gang members' quarters, but I couldn't be entirely sure. At each door, I paused to listen for evidence of any occupants. I didn't hear anything, but I wasn't so naive as to think they were entirely unoccupied. I would just have to be quick about my task and hope that nobody chose that moment to leave their bedroom.

Hurrying along, I found my way to the end of the hall. As I reached the last door, it slid open of its own accord. Acting on panicked instinct, I activated my arsenal implant and retrieved my nano-edged knife. It was only about nine inches long, and I wasn't nearly as skilled with it as I was with my firearms. But it had the advantage of being silent—a necessity at that moment.

The man in the doorway never had an opportunity to react before I slammed my blade up and into the bottom of his chin, destroying his brain in the process. He collapsed silently, held aloft by my embedded knife. Blood spilled out of the wound, coating my hand as I felt panic rising in my chest. I hadn't intended to kill anyone, but there I was, with a mook's brain shish kabobbed on my blade.

Luckily, my Combat Focus cleared my mind enough that I was soon dragging the body back and away from the doorway. It hissed shut. Looking around, I debated what to do. I could stash the body in one of the rooms, but that came with a couple of problems. First, I had no idea if any of those rooms were occupied. If the one I chose had someone inside, I'd end up with another body on my hands. And even if the room turned out to be unoccupied, the owner would eventually return. If that happened before I made my getaway, I would be burned.

No—I needed somewhere else to store the body. And I had a good idea for that. So, I started to backtrack, being extra careful to keep the man's blood from dripping onto the floor. I couldn't stop it completely, but I hoped that by flipping him over and using his shirt as a makeshift bandage, I could keep the worst of it at bay. I was only moderately successful.

In any case, I made it back to the fire escape with little difficulty, where I unceremoniously tipped the body over the edge. It landed with a sickening crunch that I did my best to ignore. A couple of minutes later, I'd descended the metal stairs and dragged the body to the corner. After deactivating the cameras again, I carried the corpse back to the dumpster and, with a sigh of relief, settled it into its new home.

It was only then that I realized just how out of my depth I was. I'd decided to infiltrate the Tigers' facility on a whim, and I'd done so completely unprepared.

All my lessons had stressed the necessity of proper preparation, but at the first opportunity to do so, I'd charged in like an untrained mook. My trainers would have been ashamed.

But the damage was already done, wasn't it? I couldn't just leave. I had no illusions about my dumpster-diving friend remaining undiscovered, and when the Tigers figured out that someone had killed one of their own, they would go on high alert. If I decided to come back another day, I'd probably face much tighter security.

Besides, Jo's problem wasn't just going away. She needed my help. Even if she hadn't asked for it, she was damned sure going to get it.

No—I had no choice but to keep going with my plan, as poorly thought out as it was.

So, I retraced my steps, doing my best to disguise the blood as I went. There wasn't that much of it on the ground, but when I got back up the fire escape and into the hall, I was confronted with a red mess. With a groan, I summoned a spare shirt from one of the extra storage spots in my arsenal implant, and I went to work cleaning it up. It took me about fifteen minutes, but I managed to do a decent job before finally moving on.

I held my breath as I activated the door at the end of the hall. It slid open, revealing an empty balcony. I crept through the doorway and peeked over the edge to see a party in full swing. There were plenty of Tigers, all identifiable by their horrendous orange-and-blue clothing, but there were quite a few unaffiliated people there, as well. The music, which had so far been little more than muffled background noise, became so loud that I could scarcely hear myself think.

As a girl who'd always appreciated loud music, that kind of thing normally didn't bother me. However, when said blaring music is horrible, it puts a decidedly different spin on it. I did my best to ignore it, turning left and following the balcony, all the while staying as low as I could so they couldn't see me from down below. My black fatigues would instantly mark me as an outsider, and then . . . well, there would be more than one dead body to worry about if that happened. Maybe even mine, depending on how competent these Tigers really were. I didn't want to find out.

I made my way to a doorway in the corner, and when I opened it, knife at the ready, I experienced my first bit of good luck. In fact, I'd hit the jackpot because the room beyond housed a security terminal. There were plenty of monitors, too, but I didn't care about them. If I could jack into the terminal, I'd have access to everything.

Stepping inside, I closed the door and locked it behind me. Wasting no time, I quickly crossed the room and popped open the port on my wrist. It had been installed at the same time as my other cybernetics, but I still hadn't had a real chance to use it. Either way, I knew how it worked. Inside was a retractable cable—seemingly metallic but feeling like plastic—with a fat connector on the end. I sat in the chair next to the terminal, pulled the cable out, and plugged the connector into the appropriate port. Instantly, a new message opened on my HUD:

Secure Terminal:
[Enter Password] or [Mistwalk]

Obviously, I didn't have a password, so I selected the second option. I didn't have much experience with Mistwalking, so I was a little surprised to be greeted by a much more elaborate number puzzle. It took me almost a minute to complete, and it included fairly advanced equations. Luckily, those were nothing new, so I completed it without issue. When I did, I gained access to the entire system.

One of the benefits of having increased my Mind attribute was that I could now process information much more quickly than ever before. So, it didn't take me long to sort through the various options and home in on the security feeds. When I did, I discovered that my previous assertion that the Tigers didn't take security very seriously was spot-on. Their laziness was my benefit, I suppose.

Over the next hour, I downloaded their files, all the while keeping an eye on the security feeds so I wouldn't be surprised. When I was finished, I felt certain that, buried somewhere within all that information, was the key to getting the Tigers off Jo's back. I just had to find it.

With that done, I quickly retreated the way I'd come, left the building, and climbed over the fence. It wasn't until I was halfway back to the inn when I started noticing all the strange looks I was getting from pedestrians. It took me far longer than it should have for me to realize what they saw—a teenage girl who was absolutely covered in blood.

Yeah—maybe I wouldn't fly as far under the radar as I'd anticipated. I could only hope that my uncle wouldn't hear about it.

CHAPTER TWENTY-TWO

BLACKMAIL

Slavery doesn't look like people imagine. It's not a bunch of prisoners walking around with collars around their necks. In reality, the bonds of slavery aren't physical. Instead, they're circumstantial. They are societal. They are cultural. Whether it's a pleasure slave on Bourbon Street, forced to take a skill that shoved them into that role, or a Rift miner in the middle of nowhere who, even if he could escape, would have nowhere to go—it's the circumstances that keep them enslaved. Getting away is usually the easy part. True escape is almost impossible.

—Jeremiah Braddock III

Whether it was luck, skill, or happenstance, I managed to make it back to my room without causing too much of a fuss. Sure, people saw all the blood, and I'm sure they were horrified. But in our world, such a state was barely even worth noting. In Nova City, it wouldn't have even warranted a second glance. Mobile was better, but only just. It was probably for the best; people who noticed such things had a habit of getting in the way of people far more powerful than them. That wouldn't end well for anybody.

Stripping out of my fatigues, I threw them into a laundry basket and quickly hopped into the shower, where I gave myself a good scrubbing. Apparently, dried blood—especially in the amounts that covered me—is surprisingly resistant to cleaning, so it took me a while to get completely clean. By the time I finished, my skin was raw enough that I felt it even through my Pain Tolerance.

Once I was clean, I dried off and inspected myself in the mirror. One thing I'd learned early on in my training was that, with my pain suppressed, I could pick up injuries and not even realize it. So, I'd been forced to make a habit of giving myself a good once-over every time I took a shower. Fortunately, I hadn't picked up anything more serious than a bruise during my extracurricular excursion. It wasn't always like that, though. More than once, I'd found cuts and gashes that had required stitches.

Pain Tolerance was useful. I couldn't deny that. But it also came with its own downsides, and I suspected that part of my training was meant to teach me how to deal with those.

With a sigh, I left the bathroom and grabbed a pair of underwear and a ripped but incredibly comfortable tee-shirt from the chest where I kept most of my clothes. After dressing, I threw myself into my bed and started in on all the data I'd pilfered from the Tigers' security terminal. Most of it was useless—just never-ending security footage—but I was surprised to find that whoever set the system up was at least organized enough to keep a record of all the members. I quickly found Jack's file and started studying it.

Apparently, he was a Tier 4, which was exceedingly rare on the frontier, and so, he'd quickly risen in the ranks. His uncommon power and quick rise had gone to his head, and there had been plenty of incidents with his peers and subordinates. It was enough that the gang's leadership had begun to question whether or not they wanted to keep him around.

As a result, he was often sent out into the wilderness to protect the gang's interests. In addition to guarding caravans to other, similar towns, the Tigers also had a few farms nearby that required security. Jack frequently drew those assignments. Not that it did much good; despite his power, he lost convoys and farms at a much higher rate than his peers. It wasn't damning evidence of malfeasance, but it gave me an avenue to investigate further. But to do so, I'd need to corner him and hack into his interface. Doing so without him figuring it out would be the difficult part.

As I lay there, my mind whirled with different possibilities. Admittedly, there was a big part of me that just wanted to kill him and be done with it. I could disappear his body with little effort, and it would solve the problem well enough. However, if my uncle had taught me anything, it was that actions often had unforeseen consequences. I'd already killed one of the Tigers. If another one went missing, it could start a chain of events I couldn't predict. At the best of times, they were a volatile group. Adding fuel to that fire was the height of recklessness, and I wanted to be better than that. So, I pushed assassination to the back of my mind, focusing on my other skills.

Briefly, I considered seducing him, like in one of those trashy books I'd recently found in the crotchety old man's bookstore. In the months since my first visit, I'd established myself as one of his best customers. I'd even learned that his name was Reuben. More importantly, I'd gained access to dozens of romance novels, most of which centered on a heroine who used her feminine wiles to solve mysteries or conduct spy missions—usually while seducing some muscle-bound bad boy with a good heart. I knew they were far from good literature, but I didn't really care.

Whatever the case, I knew I didn't have the assets to act like one of those books' protagonists. Jo, with all her curves, might've been able to pull it off; Heather definitely could have. But me? I was cuter than pretty, short, and still a little scrawny. Next to someone like Jo? I was practically invisible, and I didn't hold any illusions about gaining Jack's attention. Or anyone's, I suppose, which was kind of a depressing thought that was probably rooted more in my own insecurities than in reality, but anyway—moving on from that uncomfortable bit of introspection!

In the end, I decided that I would spend the next day following him and hope for an opportunity to do something about the situation. It wasn't the best plan in the world, but it was the best I could hope for, especially with my limited free time. So, I went to sleep with that plan in mind.

The next day, I woke up bright and early—as was my usual habit, ever since my training began—and quickly took care of my morning routine before getting dressed. Instead of my habitual black fatigues, I chose something far more nondescript. A pair of old jeans, some ratty boots, and a tee-shirt. I even managed to stuff my hair mostly under a hat, which I pulled low enough that my features weren't readily noticeable. After that, I climbed out the window—I didn't want anyone to associate this new look with me—and quickly made my way to the Tigers' compound. Once I'd climbed atop the building across the street, I settled down to watch for Jack's appearance.

Apparently, none of the Tigers—even the ones who were supposed to be on watch—were early risers, so I had a nearly six-hour wait before they began to stir. During that time, I occupied myself with various number and logic puzzles and reading the files I'd stolen from the Tigers' security terminal. The more I studied them, the more I started to notice a pattern. I don't know if I saw it because I was used to solving puzzles, but the rate at which they lost caravans was far too regular to be pure happenstance. On top of that, there was a pattern to how often their farms were attacked, too. Finally, when either of those things happened, it was never a total loss; rather, the attackers were restrained in their banditry, stealing just enough to make it worth it, but not enough to bring down the full might of the Tigers.

It all fit together far too well for it be random. Something else was at play. So, as I kept studying, I started to put the pieces together, and what I found was—well, not shocking, given what I had seen during my life in Nova City—but it was a little surprising. The attacks, apparently, had only begun after Jack had taken a leadership position, which suggested that he had something to do with it.

But it wasn't enough for an accusation. I needed more information. To that end, I waited on Jack to make an appearance. Luckily, he rose soon after his fellow Tigers, and I watched as he left the area. He was flanked by a couple of other Tigers—one male and one female. All of them were dressed in the same horrible orange and blue, with the two flunkies having mohawks. Jack, as I already knew, had more of a traditional close-cropped hairstyle, though it was dyed orange.

They turned down the street, and I waited until they were about a hundred yards away before I slipped off the roof of the building and followed. Using every trick I'd learned about [Spycraft], I kept Disguise active. I knew the ability wasn't very effective yet, but I hoped it would be enough to keep people from noticing too much about me. I was still something of a novice at tailing someone, but I kept hearing my instructor's voice in my head, reminding me of all the rules he'd given me.

After a few blocks, I turned down an alley and crossed to a parallel street. As I did, I kept my eyes from fixating on my targets, instead keeping watch via my peripheral vision. It was headache inducing, but I managed it—likely because of my comparatively high attributes. Without them, there's no way I could have kept track of everything.

Slowly, they made their way across the town and to one of the tenements where many of the poorer citizens lived. They weren't as big as the megabuildings back in Nova City, but they had the same atmosphere. Desperation filled the very air, and graffiti decorated the walls as the truly poor went about their days. Some were malnourished. Others were clearly on one drug or another. Shards from broken bottles carpeted the sidewalks, and decrepit neon signs advertised one service or another. As I glanced at one that marked a doctor's office, I suppressed a shiver. As dirty and decrepit as the storefront was, there was no way I would've ever gone there unless I had no other choice. Which was probably the case, with most of the people who lived in the area.

Of course, there were plenty of men and women of ill-repute, as well. Some were Mobile's version of Operators—garishly dressed, usually with visible cybernetics that looked cobbled together from spare parts—but others were clearly sex workers. Men and women alike, dressed in little more than a few colorful scraps, offered their services to the passersby. And given that it was just past midday, they were far from the area's best or brightest. I didn't even want to think about the life path that would lead someone to that destination.

I had nothing against sex workers, so long as they were the ones who chose that life. However, anyone who'd lived in Nova City for more than a few years knew that most of the men and women who made their livings on Bourbon Street were there out of either necessity or because someone had forced them into it, usually by nefarious means. I couldn't believe that these sex workers were in any better of a situation.

But I wasn't there to right societal wrongs, so I did my best to ignore them. Because of my Disguise ability, they hardly even noticed me. Thankfully. As much as I might empathize with their plights, I didn't want to endure their calls.

After a few more minutes, Jack and his companions stopped in front of one of the better-looking buildings. There, he exchanged a few words with his friends before heading inside. The two subordinate Tigers positioned themselves at the door, where they leaned against the wall and fingered the weapons holstered at their waists. Few people in Mobile were fortunate enough to have arsenal implants, and even those who did had inferior versions. Once again, I counted myself lucky that my uncle had seemingly endless funds with which to prop up my development.

My first instinct was to simply follow behind him, trusting that my ability would see me through. The two mooks didn't look all that attentive, and I didn't really stand out. But something inside me didn't want to trust my ability that much, so I waited a couple of minutes before slipping down the alley on the side of the building. There, I was confronted with a pair of toothless homeless men, neither of which were wearing any clothes at all. Disgusted and a little embarrassed, I hurried past them; they didn't even react to my presence, which suggested that I probably could have gone the easy way. In any case, I quickly made my way to the end of the alley and turned the corner.

The courtyard behind the building was empty, so I wasted no time in finding an open window on the second floor and climbing through it. The building was full of handholds, so it wasn't even a difficult ascent, and I soon found myself inside the tenement.

But then I recognized an issue.

I'd lost Jack. The building was six stories tall, and each floor probably held a dozen tiny apartments. If I had to go door-to-door, there was no way I'd find him before he finished whatever business he had in the building. So, using the same strategy from the night before, I hurried toward the steps and descended to the first floor. There, I swept the building until I found the maintenance office. Luckily, it was unmanned, and the building's owner had installed a security terminal to watch things while they were away. I wasted no time before jacking into the terminal via my Mistwalking ability and scanning the security feeds to track Jack to an apartment on the fourth floor. It belonged to a woman named Marissa Lopez, who was one of the few residents in the building who was completely paid up on her rent.

With a destination in mind, I found my way toward the fourth floor, passing a few addicts who'd passed out on the stairs. I stepped around them lightly, hoping that my passage would go entirely unnoticed. Finally, I reached my destination and listened at the door to Marissa Lopez's apartment. I blushed a bit when I heard the distinctive grunts and moans that told me precisely what was going on on the other side of that door.

It didn't last much longer before a particularly loud grunt announced that Jack, at least, had reached completion. I continued to listen for a few more moments, and about a minute later, I was rewarded with the sound of a woman's voice.

"Did you bring the stuff?" she asked, her voice lightly accented and a little slurred.

"You know I did, baby," came Jack's voice. I had yet to hear it before that point, but the sneering tone definitely fit the smug face I'd seen earlier. "Hold on. We'll do it together."

She mumbled something in reply, and I heard a sharp slap, followed by a sniffle and an apology. Apparently, Jack didn't have any qualms about hitting his lover, which made me dislike him even more, if that was possible. Once again, I considered just busting in and killing him. I could deal with the consequences, couldn't I?

But I restrained myself. I'd decided not to drop any more bodies, and I was going to stick with that. Even if every fiber of my being screamed at me to put the detestable man down.

I stood there for a few moments, unsure of how to proceed. It was clear that the two people had just taken some sort of drug, so it was possible that they were, even now, passed out. But if they'd taken pixie dust, the opposite would be true. The pink powder was a stimulant, after all. If I burst in and they were high on dust, I'd probably have a fight on my hands.

No—I needed more information, but I had no idea how to get it.

Stumped, I looked around until, after a few more minutes, my eyes settled on the door itself. Or rather, on the tiny camera that served as a peephole. Usually, those were one-way, but if whoever had built the tenement had been cheap, there was a chance they'd used a less expensive version. With a little tweak, I could see inside the apartment.

Maybe.

I was flying a little blind, and I was making a lot of assumptions. But I thought my plan was decent. So, I activated my Misthack ability and targeted the tiny camera. A second later, a prompt flashed across my HUD:

Intiate Misthack?
[Yes] or [No]

I chose the former and completed a childishly easy puzzle. It wasn't exactly one-two-three-four, but it wasn't that far off, either. In any case, it elicited another message:

Misthack Successful. Options:
- Reboot System
- Hijack System
- Disable System

I chose the middle option, and a square video feed settled into the right side of my HUD. It took up only about a quarter of my vision, and it looked a little distorted due to the curvature of the camera's lens. Still, I could see clearly enough to determine that Jack and his lover were both unconscious—or close enough that it didn't matter.

That made up my mind, and without further hesitation, I took control of the door via another Misthack and slid it open. Stepping inside, I was grateful to see that neither Marissa nor Jack had moved.

Now for the hard part.

I knew it was possible, based on everything I'd been taught, but I'd yet to try to Mistwalk into someone else's interface. At some point, I expected that I'd be able to do it remotely, but I was a long way from that. After watching the two naked and unconscious people for a few minutes, I was satisfied that nothing I could do would wake them up. So, kneeling beside Jack—and pointedly ignoring his nudity—I flipped open the Realskin tab on my wrist and unwound the cord that would allow me to jack into his system. Then, I felt on the side of his neck for the port that I knew would be there, and when I found a rough patch of the same artificial skin, I peeled it back and inserted my cord.

Immediately, a new message flashed across my HUD:

Personal Interface (Jack Ryder). Presence Detected. Defenses Found. Initiate Mistwalk?
[Yes] or [No]

I selected the former, expecting something similar to the security terminal into which I'd Mistwalked the day before. However, what I found was far more elaborate. There were seventeen nodes, each with their own set of logic and number puzzles. When I dove into the first, I was surprised to find that they stretched me to the limits of my abilities, and it took me almost ten minutes to clear the first node. The second went more quickly, but as I progressed from one node to the next, my mind became overtaxed, and my concentration began to waver. Sweat poured down my face, and a headache threatened to split my mind in two. But I persisted, long after the pain overwhelmed my resistances. Gritting my teeth, I cleared one node after another until, finally, the last of the defenses fell, and Jack's entire interface was opened to me.

I gasped at the access.

I could see everything. His skills. His cyberware. I could even tell precisely how close he'd come to overdosing. More importantly, underlying his conscious mind was his interface's memory. I plunged into it, and because I knew the appropriate dates, it didn't take me long to find out precisely how Jack had betrayed both the Tigers and the town. After downloading the information, I sent a jolt through his cyberware—not enough to hurt him . . . much, but just enough to jar him awake. It worked, and when he opened his eyes, he did so to the sight of Ferdinand II's barrel only inches away from his face.

"Now, Jack," I said in the calmest voice I could manage. "You have been a very bad boy."

"Who are you? What do you—"

I reached back and slammed the butt of my gun into his forehead. I didn't use all my strength, but it was satisfying nonetheless. And it shut him up, which was the point. Mostly. Causing him a good deal of pain was just a side benefit.

"No talking," I said. "Just listen. You've been selling secrets, haven't you? And not just to the bandits and raiders around here, either. You've been in touch with people in Nova City, too. And Atlanta. Now, I don't particularly care about all of that, but what I do care about is you leaving Jo alone."

"J-Jo?"

"Pretty girl. Curves. Her family runs an inn? You know who she is," I said. "So, here's the deal. You leave her alone—and I mean completely alone: no protection money, no unwanted advances, nothing. She doesn't ever need to see you or the Tigers again. And if you make that happen, I'll keep all this information to myself, yeah? Sound good?"

"Uh . . ."

I hit him again. Not because he hesitated. Just because I thought he deserved it.

"Need an answer pretty quick here," I stated. "And remember—I could have fried you just now. I can get to you anywhere. So, if you refuse . . . well, I might just have to make other arrangements. Got me?"

"O-okay!" he said, raising his hands. "Okay. I'll . . . I'll leave her alone."

"And no more selling secrets to Nova or Atlanta," I added. "I don't care about the bandits."

He quickly agreed, and I hit him again. Man, it felt good. Maybe I needed to work on that. Either way, we came to an agreement, and I left the way I'd come, feeling as if I'd really accomplished something. And I still had most of the day left to relax, so it was a pretty good day, as far as I was concerned.

CHAPTER TWENTY-THREE

THE FIRST TEST

Consequence. It is the only thing keeping humanity in check. Before the Initialization, breaking the law meant arrest, a trial, and incarceration. After, though? For the longest time, the worst parts of human nature were allowed free reign, and the whole planet suffered for it.

—Jeremiah Braddock III

The next morning, I arose, looking forward to the day ahead of me. But I was also incredibly anxious. After all, I had a test ahead of me, and I had no idea what to expect. Moreover, I didn't know how my uncle might react if I failed. Would he abandon me? Would he stop training me? Would I have to go back to the beginning and repeat the training I'd already received? It was all a mystery to me, but as far as I was concerned, the only way to ensure that I had a way forward was to pass the test, whatever it might entail.

Simple, right?

Probably not, but it was the best I could come up with. So, after taking care of my morning ablutions, I donned my normal black fatigues and headed downstairs. As I did so, I inspected my status:

NAME	Mirabelle Lisa Braddock
CLASS	N/A (Requirements Not Met)
LEVEL	3 (71%)
CONSTITUTION	16/31
MIND	17/31

MIST	9/31		
SKILLS	7/7		
SKILL NAME	Skill Tier	Modifiers	Abilities
CYBERNETIC INTERFACE	Tier 2 (91%)	None	3 Cybernetic Slots
FIREARMS	Tier 2 (12%)	+10% Damage (All Firearms) +4% Reload Speed (All Firearms) +21% Accuracy (All Firearms) +15% Damage (Rifle) +15% Damage (Pistol) +15% Damage (Scattergun)	None
CLOSE QUARTERS COMBAT	Tier 1 (79%)	+2% Movement Speed +15% Damage (Melee) +7% Speed (Melee) +5% Accuracy (Melee) +5% Damage (Unarmed) +5% Damage (Blunt Weapons)	None
STEALTH OPERATIONS	Tier 1 (3%)	None	Camouflage (F)
COMBAT UTILITY	Tier 2 (67%)	None	Triage (F) Basic Explosives Handling (F) Combat Focus (E) Pain Tolerance (E) Resistance (F) Foraging (F) Improvisation (F) Regeneration (E)

MISTWALKER	Tier 1 (35%)	+5% Speed (Misthack) +5% Speed (Mistwalk)	Mistwalk (F) Misthack (F) Mistwall (F)
SPYCRAFT	Tier 1 (39%)	None	Disguise (F) Deception (F)

I felt a wave of satisfaction when I looked at how I'd improved. Ever since my Awakening, I'd found the cycle of training and improvement to be incredibly addictive. I wouldn't go so far as to say that I lived to see those numbers go up, but it was definitely part of what kept me engaged.

During my three-month training period, I'd made incredible strides across the board. From increasing the potency of my [Firearms] and [Close Quarters Combat] skills to making progress on everything else, the differences were astounding. Not only was it nice to see a couple of tier-ups, but I'd also increased the modifiers by a significant degree. On top of that, my attributes had improved, as well, with sizable increases in all three categories. Some of my improvement had come from my self-imposed mission to blackmail Jack, but most of it was the result of three months' worth of vigorous training.

With a small smile on my face, I descended the steps and found my uncle and two of the Amigos—Potbelly and Stupid Hat—waiting for me. At some point, I fully intended to remember their real names, but for now, using the monikers I'd given them in my head was just easier. Besides, while I'd been told their names when I'd met them, I had quickly forgotten. It had gotten to the point where, if I were to ask now, I would have to admit that I'd spent months with them as my instructors, and I'd never bothered to learn their real names. And that was just too embarrassing to consider.

Thankfully, there hadn't been any instances where I needed to get their attention. And if one came up, I felt confident that I could get by with, "Hey, you!" or something like that. Yeah—probably not. But if I wanted to delude myself, I had that right.

In any case, I soon joined them at the scrubbed wooden table, sliding onto one of the bench seats. After that, Jo approached and, with a knowing nod, set a plate containing a couple of links of sausage, a biscuit, and a pile of scrambled eggs in front of me. "Thanks," I said.

"No" was her meaningful response. "Thank you."

I wanted to roll my eyes and sink into the floor. I'd regaled Jo with the tale of my exploits the day before, and once she had gotten over her fear, she had started to look at me a lot differently. Like I was a hero or something. It was incredibly uncomfortable, and more than once, I'd regretted telling her anything.

I mean—I understood why she looked at me like that. I'd basically saved her, if in a roundabout way. With the threat of exposure—or more likely, the very real demonstration that I could get to him whenever I wanted to—hanging over Jack, I felt certain that he would keep the Tigers away from Jo and the Dew Drop. And if they still came, I would make them regret it. I'd already infiltrated their compound, so it wouldn't take much to change my tactics from reconnaissance to assassination. Not that I wanted to, of course. But they didn't need to know that, did they?

After giving her a tight smile, I dug in. As I ate, my uncle said, "Seems like there might be a story there."

"Nope," I said between mouthfuls of fluffy eggs. "I'm just that good of a friend."

"Suppose this has nothing to do with you walking down the street the other day covered in blood, huh?" was his response.

I almost choked on my eggs. "W-what? No. I didn't—"

He cut his eyes at me, saying, "Don't lie. Just . . . you didn't kill anybody that matters, did you?"

"Uh . . . no?"

"Is that a question?"

"Maybe?"

He let out a long-suffering sigh before saying, "Just tell me what happened, Mirabelle."

I knew how little patience Jeremiah had for liars, so I just laid it all out there. I was confident that I'd done the right thing, even if it had gotten a lot messier than I'd anticipated. When I finished, I said, "And I'd do it again. Jack was a dick, and he deserved what he got."

"And the man you killed?"

"Him, too," I said with confidence.

To my surprise, my uncle gave a shrug, saying, "If you're convinced you did the right thing, then I won't chastise you for it. I will, however, reiterate that you need to be careful. You have no idea the time, money, and effort that has gone into training you."

"I get it," I said. "But if I see someone in trouble, I'm going to help."

"Then you're going to be one busy girl," he said. "Because we're all in trouble. Every last one of us. You need to learn to pick your battles. Sure, you say it worked out. This Jack guy is cowed. But what happens when he comes up light? Are his superiors in the Tigers going to replace him? Then, we're back to square one. Or worse, what if he calls your bluff?"

"He won't."

"Most people are cowards, so probably not. But what if he does?" Jeremiah persisted.

"I don't know," I admitted. "I guess I'll do what I said I'd do."

"And in the meantime? You already told him you were there on Jo's behalf," Jeremiah stated. "You scared him, sure. But did you go too far? Did you put his back up? Did you force him to do something he might have otherwise avoided? Like attack this inn?"

"I . . . I don't know . . ."

Truthfully, I hadn't thought through all the consequences of my actions. In fact, I'd assumed that everything was going to work out precisely how I'd dictated to Jack. The threat of exposure would keep him in line. I was sure of it.

"You did the right thing," Jeremiah said, his voice softer. "But I'm trying to make you understand that sometimes doing the right thing is actually more harmful than doing nothing. I don't think this is one of those instances, but you need to be aware of how your actions might have unintended consequences."

"I . . . okay," I said. "I'll try to do better."

"Good. That's all I can ask," my uncle responded. "Now finish your meal. You've got a big day ahead of you."

During the conversation, I'd managed to push the test out of my mind. That lasted right up until he'd mentioned my upcoming big day. So, I finished my meal in silence, then followed my uncle and the two Amigos out of the inn and to a roofless all-terrain vehicle waiting on the street. Predictably, the last Amigo was sitting in the driver's seat.

"Where are we going?" I asked, hopping into the back seat.

"Escort mission," Jeremiah said. "We're headed to one of our farms a little north of here. Once we get there, we're dropping you off. It's your job to make sure their crop gets back here safely."

"What?" I asked. "I don't know anything about—"

"This is what you've been training for," he said. "It's a nine-mile trip. You should be fine."

I sighed, knowing good and well that he wasn't going to let me off the hook. But then again, I didn't really want him to. I had been training hard, and I felt confident that he wouldn't put me into a situation where I would be overwhelmed.

Or maybe that was blind hope.

A memory of a giant alligator dominated my thoughts; back then, I'd been woefully underprepared to face that monster. And yet, Jeremiah had pitted me against it, albeit after he'd crippled the thing. The fact remained, though, that he had few issues with sending me into an overwhelming situation. Doubtless, that was how he expected me to grow.

But I had come through that, hadn't I? I could do so again. I couldn't let myself fail his test. Not this one, and not any that might come later. Not only would it probably end my training, but I didn't think I could bear his disappointment. And I knew I couldn't live with my own.

I thought about everything I'd learned, trying to come up with some kind of plan for protecting the people I was supposed to escort. However, I had no details with which to work, and until I discovered the route or the participants, it would be impossible to create a workable plan. So, with that in mind, I watched my surroundings.

We skirted the river as we went north, weaving between ruined buildings and piles of rubble. Some of them looked fresh, but others appeared to have been there for months, or even years. The vehicle was made for such rough terrain, so it had no difficulty traversing our route.

Then, as we turned, I saw something truly awe-inspiring.

In the distance, there was a huge bridge spanning the river from one bank to the other, held aloft by waist-thick cables. Some of them had been snapped, but others remained.

"Are we supposed to cross that thing?" I asked.

My uncle laughed. "That would be suicide," he said. "That bridge hasn't been safe for half a century. God knows how it's still hanging on."

In the river, below the bridge, I caught sight of something that looked suspiciously like a giant tentacle cutting through the water. "I'm guessing that part of the river isn't safe, either," I reasoned.

"Definitely not," Jeremiah said. "It's home to a river kraken. Believe me—you don't want to mess with that thing. Milo and his Amigos took a crack at it a few years back. It didn't end well for them, and the thing barely even noticed. It would take a lot more firepower than this town can muster to do anything more than annoy it."

"Uh . . . good to know," I said. Potbelly, who was sitting beside me, chuckled at my obvious apprehension, and I wanted to punch him in his stupid, fat stomach. I seethed as we continued going, turning to the west once we reached the base of the bridge. Up close, I saw that the concrete was crumbling, and the cables were in even worse condition than I'd thought. My uncle was right—it would be the height of stupidity to try crossing.

After driving on for a few hundred more yards, Jeremiah said, "Stop the jeep."

The driver, Slim, complied, and my uncle directed me to get out. I looked around. This stretch of terrain didn't look much different than any other, save that there was an old sign that seemed to have survived. It was constructed of a piece of wood stretched between two brick pillars, though the sign itself was covered in some sort of thick ivy. Kudzu, my uncle had called it.

He approached, ripping the vines away to reveal faded paint. Even with it exposed, I had to get a lot closer to read what it said. The only word I could make out was *Africatown*, whatever that meant. I asked my uncle, and he just shook his head.

"You don't know much about our history," he said. "Before the Initialization, people sometimes treated others differently according to the color of their skin. People like us, we got the worst of it."

"What? Why?" I asked.

"Tribalism, mostly. Bigotry. Stupidity. Take your pick, Mirabelle," he said. "But that's not important. With everyone struggling to survive, that kind of thing slowly fell by the wayside, replaced by other prejudices. That's not why I brought you here, though. This place, it was called Africatown because it was the last known entry point for African slaves. It was illegal by that point, and it happened more than a century before I was even born. Your ancestors escaped that fate and settled right here. Generations later, I was born."

"So . . . we were slaves?" I asked. I had vague information about the rest of the world, and I knew Africa was a continent. However, I'd never been taught anything about slavery, save for what I'd learned on the cybernet about its modern iterations. Even that, though, was sanitized, and I'd had to fill in many of the gaps with either my imagination or infrequent conversations with Nora or other members of my uncle's tribe, the Specters. To find out that my ancestors had been slaves felt like a kick to the stomach.

"They were," he said. "But they broke free. They created a life for themselves. A place they could call home. You come from survivors."

"Why are you showing me this? And I know it's not for the history lesson," I said. I felt confident that he'd only told me enough to get his point across.

"Don't let their sacrifices go to waste, Mirabelle," he said. "I know this probably isn't going to affect you. You've lived a life sequestered from the realities of your ancestry. So did I, for the most part. By the time I was born, things were a lot better. Not perfect, mind you. There was still plenty of bigotry flowing around. But if you don't take anything else from seeing this place, let it be this: We will never be slaves again. Not because of our race. Not because of our species. And certainly not because some corporate asshole wants us to work in some factory so he can impress his own overlord."

"Oh. Okay," I said, not knowing how else to respond to his miniature tirade.

He shook his head. "That really didn't have the effect I wanted it to, did it?" Jeremiah asked.

"Uh . . . I guess?" I answered. "I get it, though. Mostly."

In truth, I didn't really feel any connection with the people who'd lived in Africatown centuries before. I could feel sympathy for what they'd had to go through—and I did—but I didn't have any foundation from which I could relate.

"I guess that'll have to do," he said. "C'mon. We've got a little ways to go."

With that, we returned to the jeep and continued along our route, eventually turning off the road and following a narrow path through the woods.

We traveled north for about twenty more minutes until, at last, we reached an intimidating wall of concrete. The path led us to a fortified gate, which was guarded by a pair of Operators, one of which carried a bow, while the other was armed with a clunky-looking rifle. Both wore the blue identifying them as Specters, though I didn't recognize either of them. That wasn't so surprising, though. The Specters numbered in the tens of thousands—perhaps more because my impressions were based only on what I'd seen back in Nova—and even my uncle couldn't know every face.

After a brief exchange between my uncle and the bow-wielding guard, the gate swung open to reveal a massive field of swaying stalks. Because I recognized it from visiting one of the Silos back home, I knew it was corn. It stretched as far as I could see, and in the distance was a low-slung concrete bunker. Drones floated through the fields, misting the crops.

"Mirabelle," my uncle said. "This is Alpha Farm. You're meeting with Caleb. He's the head of security around here."

"You're not going to introduce me?" I asked.

He shook his head. "Nope" was his reply. "You need to learn to stand on your own two feet, so this is where we'll part ways. I probably won't be in Mobile when you get back, but I've already arranged the rest of your training."

"Oh. Okay," I said. "What if I fail?"

"You won't," he said. "This is a simple job. You only have to protect the shipment on the way back. You'll have plenty of help, too. This is no different than the kinds of jobs we give new recruits back home. Relax and rely on your training."

I nodded, then got out of the jeep. Before long, the vehicle had backed out of the gate, turned around, and sped off. I was watching the retreat so intently that I reacted poorly when I felt a hand on my shoulder.

With a move drilled into me by my melee-combat instructor, I grabbed the offending hand, twisted, and drew Ferdinand II from my arsenal implant. I had the barrel against a man's head before I even realized what I was doing.

"Whoa, whoa, whoa—easy now, killer," he said, his voice strained from the pressure I was putting on his wrist. "I come in peace!"

"Crap. Sorry," I said, pulling away. I kept Ferdinand II out, though. This man was a stranger, and I had no idea of his intentions. "Caleb?"

"In the flesh," he said, rubbing his wrist. "You move pretty good."

"Thanks?"

"Here. Follow me," he said. "We've been waiting on you."

With that, he set off down the path through the field at a light jog. I followed, pointedly keeping Ferdinand II out. I didn't know precisely why; I just knew that something was prickling at the back of my mind. Something wrong.

It was only when we approached the bunker that I got my answer. A dozen men and women stood around, none of which seemed to be farmers. It might've been the heavy armaments. Or the clothes. It might've even been the way they held themselves. But I was looking at a group of Operators. I only had a moment to notice that none of them wore the signature blue of the Specters before everything went horribly wrong.

I barely had time to react before they opened fire, filling the air with one round after another. I took one in the arm. Another in the thigh. And another grazed my shoulder before I managed to dive away into the cornstalks. I was up and running in half a second, heedless of my injuries.

Behind me, the fake Caleb shouted, "Get her! She came with the Wraith! If she gets away, we're done!"

I didn't stick around to hear anything else. Instead, I plunged headlong through the forest of cornstalks, using every attribute point of my Constitution to propel me faster than my pursuers. And all the while, I couldn't help but wonder whether this was the test. Or had I just gotten unlucky? Either way, a seething anger had begun to build in my chest. They'd attacked me for no reason, and with the intent to kill. If I'd been any slower, they would have succeeded, too.

But they'd made a mistake, hadn't they? They hadn't finished the job. And now, I was just pissed off enough to give them a very bad day.

CHAPTER TWENTY-FOUR

REAL-WORLD EXPERIENCE

I have killed thousands of people. Some deserved it. Others decidedly did not. All were, at least in my mind at the time, justified. But it does beg the question—why do I get to decide? What makes me special? I can kill, and I do it extremely well. But as I've proved, time and time again throughout my life, my judgement is extremely fallible. And yet, I hold so many lives in the palms of my hands. It is not fair, but then again, life never has been. The Initialization, for all its power, couldn't change that.

—Jeremiah Braddock III

My heart beat out of my chest. My breath came in ragged gasps. And my mind went blank. For the first few steps, panic overwhelmed me as I raced through the cornstalks. It only lasted a few seconds, though, before Combat Focus came into play, forcing me into rational thought. Behind me, I could hear my pursuers bearing down on me. I continued to run, putting distance between us until, at last, I broke free from the forest of corn. Luckily, no one was waiting for me.

My head swiveled to the left and right, taking stock of my situation. Due to my conditioning and relatively inflated stats, I'd managed to stretch a sizable lead between my pursuers and my position. However, I knew that wouldn't last long. There were only so many ways I could go, and anyone with half a brain could have followed the path I'd cut through the cornstalks. While I was skeptical that these people possessed much in the way of critical-thinking skills, they could certainly follow the relatively straight line of my retreat.

In front of me, the wall loomed. It was at least twenty feet high and constructed of concrete slabs. There were seams every few feet, but I wasn't certain if the shallow crevices would offer much in the way of handholds. Still, with my options being what they were, I had little choice but to give it a try.

There was only one problem, though, and it presented itself the moment I tried to begin my ascent. Whether it was adrenaline, my Pain Tolerance ability, or some combination of the two, I'd almost forgotten that I'd been shot, and more than once. My thigh was on fire, my left arm hung limp and was coated in blood, and the grazing wound I'd taken on my shoulder added enough pain to the mix that climbing the wall had started to look like an impossibility.

In the distance, I heard more shouts. I had no idea how much time I had before the group of raiders caught up with me. When they did, I'd be dead. Or worse. I wasn't so sheltered that I didn't know just how precarious my position was; I was young, reasonably pretty, and because of my wounds, vulnerable. Whatever potential I had would count for nothing if they caught me. The very best I could hope for was a quick death. Or torture. The worst didn't bear thinking about.

Gritting my teeth, I shunted the pain off to the back of my mind and resumed my efforts to climb the wall. And to my surprise, my arms and legs actually worked. Even if it came with a considerable degree of agony—and God, it hurt more than anything I'd ever experienced—I managed the climb, and far more quickly than I could have expected.

Was it my nearly superhuman attributes that had allowed it? My abilities? The so-called hell month where I'd been forced to learn how to push pain and fatigue to the side and continue moving forward? I didn't know, but whatever it was, it allowed me to reach the top just in time.

As I straddled the top of the wall, my pursuers burst into view. An instant later, gunshots rang out across the farm. Thankfully, their aim was terrible, and every one of their shots thudded into the concrete wall. Given the volume of gunfire, I couldn't point to anything but luck as to why I didn't receive another gunshot wound.

Without further hesitation, I slipped from the top of the thick wall. At first, I tried to hang from the edge and drop to the other side, but my hands were slippery with blood. And due to blood loss, I found myself increasingly exhausted. The result was that my plan never came to fruition, and I soon found myself tumbling to the ground below.

I screamed in agony as I landed on the ground, my fall cushioned by a thick carpet of fallen leaves. For a few seconds, I clutched my arm, rolling around in unbelievable pain. After a minute or so that the rational part of my brain told me I couldn't afford to lose, the pain faded to a dull ache. Knowing that my escape was only half-finished, I pushed myself to my feet. As I ran, slipping into the surrounding woods, my head pounded, and my body felt lethargic. But I kept going because I didn't have a choice. It would take the raiders some time to circle around, but when they did, my path wouldn't be difficult to follow. Not with the trail of blood I was leaving behind.

I needed a plan, and stumbling through the woods really didn't qualify.

Okay, so first things first, I needed to find somewhere safe I could hole up and heal. I had medical supplies in my arsenal implant, but using them would take time. And though I'd stretched a decent lead from my pursuers, I had no illusions about how long it would take them to find me.

With that in mind, I glanced at my minimap and, with a thought, zoomed it out as far as it could go. My immediate surroundings were detailed, but the farther the map was from my position, the hazier things got until, about two hundred yards away, the area was clouded. Whether it was luck or the fact that the area played host to thousands of streams and creeks, it didn't take me long to find what I was looking for.

The creek was little more than a shallow ditch cutting through the forest, but I hoped it would go on for miles. I stanched the blood flow as well as I could by awkwardly applying a couple of tourniquets—which, regardless of what I'd seen on the entertainment channels, was agonizingly painful. It wasn't a permanent solution, and if I left them on for too long, things would get bad. But in my situation, where a trail of blood would give away my position, it was the best I could do.

So, that taken care of, I began to make my way toward the stream. As I went, I took special care not to brush against any of the trees or foliage—a difficulty, given how thick the vegetation was. Eventually, I reached the stream, and I was just as unimpressed as I'd expected to be. A few inches deep and only a couple of yards wide, it barely qualified as a stream at all. But it was running water, which was all I really needed at that point.

So, planting myself in the center of the tiny waterway, I turned north and followed it for about an hour. As I did, my arm started going numb, and the pain, free of the effects of adrenaline, began to mount. After another hour, I judged that I'd gotten far enough away, and I left the stream behind.

The area had once been settled, as evidenced by the ruins I passed along the way. Some had clearly been houses, but little remained other than foundations and a stray wall, and even those were covered in vegetation to the point that they were barely recognizable. Still, there were some buildings that had survived better than others, and I soon found my way to what looked like it had once been a church.

Made of red-and-brown brick, one of the walls had collapsed. The roof was barely hanging on, and a spire at the top bore a rotted wooden cross. Most of the old religions were still around, and there were a couple of churches in Nova City. However, the Initialization had definitely affected the various faiths. For my part, I'd never really given any of it much thought; growing up the way I had, I hadn't been exposed to that kind of thing. Whatever the case, if God existed, I didn't think he would mind me taking shelter in one of his ruined churches.

Besides, given how weak I felt, I didn't have much of a choice in the matter. So, on unsteady legs, I stumbled into the church and collapsed in a corner that provided the most shelter. For a while, I just sat there, staring straight ahead as I caught my breath. I might have even passed out for a few minutes.

Finally, after some interminable amount of time, I regained enough of my wits to do something about my injuries. So, I painfully stripped off my shirt, leaving me in nothing but a black sports bra up top, and inspected the wounds. Thankfully, one of the bullets had barely grazed my shoulder. It had taken a decent chunk of flesh with it, but aside from the pain, it wasn't that big of a deal.

Okay—so it hurt like crazy, but with all my other injuries, it felt little worse than a beesting. Still, I cleaned it, then, after retrieving my medical kit from my arsenal implant, applied a foam bandage that hugged my shoulder like a second skin. Not only would it release antibiotics, but it would also hasten the healing process. That, combined with my Regeneration ability, would make quick work of the wound.

The others were far worse.

The wound in my arm was the most troubling. The bullet had torn most of my biceps away, which made the whole arm practically useless. I could only hope that the combination of my abilities and the advanced medical kit would keep me from experiencing permanent damage. While I could always have the arm replaced with a cybernetic equivalent, I wanted to keep my original parts as long as possible.

I hissed as I smeared healing ointment on the wound; called NuFlesh, it was specifically designed to regrow muscle and skin. Hopefully, it would work quickly. After that, I applied a foam bandage.

Next, I turned to the wound in my thigh. Unlike the others, the bullet hadn't just passed through, which meant that it was still embedded in my flesh. Not ideal, but I'd had a little training in wound management, so I was confident in fishing the thing out. I'd have to be cognizant of blood loss, but my medical kit was well stocked with everything I would need. So, I wasted no time in retrieving a pair of forceps from the kit and getting to work.

Pain was a funny thing. With all the adrenaline of battle coursing through my veins, it was easily ignored. But in that ruined church, with a pair of gleaming forceps buried in the flesh of my thigh, it hit me much harder than before. Without my abilities and training, I never could have borne it. Even with my advantages, tears streamed freely down my cheeks, and I had to bite down on the handle of my knife, lest I fill the air with my screams.

Still, I managed to retrieve the bullet, which had thankfully remained intact, and dressed my wound before passing out.

I awoke sometime after dark, and to a cacophony of noise. Outside of my hell month, I'd never really spent much time in the wilderness after dark, and during that month, it had been all I could do to keep putting one foot in front of the other, so I hadn't really noticed how loud it could get. As I sat there in that church, I had no such inhibitions on my awareness.

All around me, the shrill chirps of crickets were punctuated by the deep croaks of frogs. As a city girl, I was well used to a lack of peace and quiet, but there was a marked difference between the sounds of the forest and the urban noises to which I had grown so accustomed back in Nova City.

After inspecting my wounds and finding that they'd actually healed considerably during my bout of unconsciousness, I pushed myself to my feet. My arm still wasn't mobile, but I was happy that my wounded leg could nearly bear my weight. Not for the first time, I marveled at the power of my skills, abilities, and equipment. In my place, a normal person would have probably died. But here I was, only hours after being shot three times, and I felt confident that I could make a full recovery in a week or so. And I would be functional in only a few more hours.

But with that knowledge came a host of questions and a need to make a real plan.

My first thought was to make my way back to Mobile and warn the others there. Once Milo and his Amigos knew what was going on, they would make quick work of the bandits. It was the obvious and smart course of action.

Still, as I sat back down to rest and recover, I hesitated.

Was it all a test? Had my uncle known what I would find at that farm? And if so, how would he expect me to react? What would he want me to do?

Those were all good questions, and they were relevant enough. But even more relevant was a simmering anger clawing its way to the forefront of my mind. The bandits had shot me. They'd tried to kill me. And I'd been forced to run away. That didn't sit well. After all my training, after all the advantages I'd been afforded, retreat had been my only option.

But now?

It occurred to me that I was almost perfectly suited to hunting them.

Was that what Jeremiah would want me to do? I thought so. After all, he'd continuously preached the importance of self-reliance to me. He wanted me to survive on my own, not run to someone stronger the moment I encountered some difficulty. More than that, I knew that, were Jeremiah to be faced with the same situation, he would take care of it himself.

Could I do it, though?

On the one hand, I didn't consider myself a killer. I had been forced to do it, and on more than one occasion, but it wasn't as if I had reveled in the act. It was a necessary part of life, an inescapable facet of the world in which I lived, and I'd slowly grown to accept that. Or maybe it was just my Combat Focus influencing me. I'd long suspected that it smoothed those sorts of things out.

Besides, those raiders had probably killed the farmers, hadn't they? Innocent people who only wanted to grow food and help the people back in town. That, as much as anything, skewed my decision toward hunting down the bandits.

With that decided, I set my mind to creating a passable plan of assault. First, I would need to take a day or two to heal. After that, reconnaissance. The rest of the plan would have to wait until after I knew what I was dealing with. But for now? Now, I needed to rest. Relax. Heal.

So, I gathered my medical supplies and carefully placed everything back in the kit; it was just a black box containing various implements, vials, and tubes. I suspected it had cost my uncle almost as much as any of the rest of my equipment, and I could see why. Without it, I never would have survived. And that goal, more than anything, was my uncle's guiding light.

After putting the kit back into my arsenal implant, I retrieved some rations and a bottle of water. I had enough supplies for a couple of weeks, but after that, I would be forced to forage. I could do it. Jorge, one of the Amigos, had given me some rudimentary instruction on wilderness survival. But the last thing I wanted was to survive off of nuts, berries, and mushrooms.

For the next two days, I stayed in that church, resting and recovering. To stave off boredom, I spent most of that time training with the number and logic puzzles. I could engage with that program for hours at a time, so it was an effective and useful way to fill my time. However, in the back of my mind, my anger continued to simmer. So, by the time I judged myself ready to leave, my frustration had mounted to such a degree that I was almost eager to attack the bandits.

With such thoughts occupying my mind, I left the church behind and set off back the way I'd come.

CHAPTER TWENTY-FIVE

RECONNAISSANCE

Before the Initialization, preparation was the key to surviving any engagement. In the new world, though, it is often overlooked and discarded in favor of overwhelming power. This is a mistake, and one the world will realize once the aliens descend upon us all.

—Jeremiah Braddock III

The way back to the farm was uneventful, save that I was forced to skirt past a group of massive creatures with metal shells. From my biology classes, I recognized them as armadillos, but just like the alligator that had attacked on my first day outside of Nova City, they were far too large. Because of their increased size, coupled with the segmented metal shells, I had little choice but to assume that they had been mutated by the Mist. Perhaps most wildlife had.

In any case, they seemed completely unconcerned with my passage. Whether it was because they didn't know I was there or due to simple disinterest, I didn't know. But I wasn't going to argue with my good fortune.

My progress through the forest was slow, owing to my desire to remain undetected. I had no idea if the bandits were still looking for me, so I thought it was probably best if I took the time necessary for effective stealth. Even so, I flinched at every cracked branch and crunched leaf; I was far from an expert in moving through the wilderness, so it wouldn't have surprised me if someone heard me traipsing through the woods.

But that's why I kept the Kicker out. At least I could depend on my skills in that arena.

With the rifle clutched in my hands, I stalked toward the wall surrounding the farm. Keeping to the woods, I slowly circled around to the north, taking a counterclockwise path toward the gate. All the while, my eyes scanned my surroundings as well as the wall. It wasn't wide enough that anyone could comfortably perch atop it, but that didn't rule out cameras.

Or drones, I discovered.

The hum of a Mist engine met my ears, and I jerked to a stop. Swiveling my head, I spied the drone. Its base was about a foot wide and twice as long, and a pair of encased propellers jutted from each side, holding it aloft. A sizable lens perched in the center of the fuselage, but no weapons were in evidence.

A reconnaissance drone, then.

I brought my concentration to bear, and a prompt materialized on my HUD:

Intiate Misthack?
[Yes] or [No]

I selected the affirmative option, which brought up a simple number puzzle. The drone's defenses must have been laughable, and I easily solved the puzzle. When I did, another prompt flitted across my HUD:

Misthack Successful. Options:
- **Reboot System**
- **Hijack System**
- **Disable System**

I chose the second option, and a moment later, a new window bloomed on my HUD. It only took up a third of my vision, but splitting my attention between the drone and my surroundings was a bit disconcerting. Still, I was up to the task.

Not only was I able to see through the machine's camera, but I also took control of it. Luckily, the drone was responsive to my thoughts, so piloting it was fairly simple. Aware of the timer associated with my ability—the Misthack would only last a certain amount of time, which was dependent on a combination of its system strength and my Mist attribute; in this case, my hijack would only last a little more than a minute—I turned the drone and flew it toward the bunker.

It moved quickly, so I was able to see that most of the bandits were gathered out front of the bunker, where they were directing another group of people who were busy loading a series of trucks with crates of produce. It didn't take a genius to figure out that the laborers were the farm's residents.

With only twenty seconds left, I landed the drone atop the bunker, then repeated the Misthack, selecting to disable the system. It went dark, and I started moving. It might have been a bit of overkill, but I suspected that the drone had a preprogrammed route and that the bandits were relying on it to warn them of any intruders. So, it stood to reason that as soon as my Misthack wore off, it would return to where I'd initiated the takeover in the first place. By that point, I needed to be gone, so I dropped back farther into the woods where I didn't think anyone would notice me.

I needed a plan.

Clearly.

I was busy trying to figure out what to do when I heard a gunshot. Then another. I was moving before I even knew what I was doing, and when I reached the wall, I saw the drone, replicated my Misthack from before, and took a look at what was happening.

My heart jumped into my throat as I saw that the trucks had already been loaded, and all the laborers were kneeling in a line in front of the bunker. Two bodies lay on the ground, their brains splattered onto the gravel road.

One of the bandits laughed. Another seemed entirely disinterested, smoking a cigarette as she leaned against the wall. The others were similarly uncaring as a pudgy man raised his pistol, aimed at the next laborer in line, and fired. Another body joined the rest.

I wanted to vomit.

Sure, I had seen plenty of death. A memory of my uncle doing something very similar sprang to mind. But this was different. Turk and his mooks were Operators, if inept ones. But these people? They were civilians. Simple workers who happened to be in the wrong place at the wrong time.

My blood boiled.

I sprinted from the woods, covering the short span to the wall, and leaped. As I soared through the air, I stowed the Kicker in my arsenal implant before I thudded into the concrete barrier. My fingers held strong, grasping the top of the wall as I pulled myself up. There, I resummoned my rifle, flicked the switch to put it into sniper mode, and took aim.

Barely a second passed before the executioner's head exploded. I got another one before they scattered. My weapon swept around, looking for more targets, but these bandits weren't stupid. They'd already taken cover.

A woman poked her head out and returned fire in my general direction. Her shots went wide. Mine didn't. She fell to the ground, a massive crater in her torso. I moved on to the next one, but the rest had learned their lessons.

"C'mon," I muttered. "Poke your fucking heads out, assholes."

None complied.

The prisoners finally gathered their wits and took off, and I breathed a sigh of relief.

Until I heard a sound I would never forget. Gunshots. Dozens of them every second, all coming from the doorway of the bunker. My jaw dropped as I saw a tiny figure step out into the open. He couldn't have been more than three feet in height, but he carried a gun that was at least as long as he was tall. Belt-fed from a canister on his back, the weapon had seven rotating barrels. He didn't aim it so much as he swept the thing in a general direction and filled the air with bullets. In seconds, the farmers were dead, their bodies ripped to shreds by the powerful weapon.

Aghast at the carnage—some of the fresh corpses were unrecognizable as anything but piles of unidentifiable meat—I hesitated. Only for a second, but that was enough for the miniature man to lock his eyes on me. He swung the weapon in my direction and let loose.

I dove to the ground as he tore the wall apart. The barrage of bullets dug deep craters in the concrete, raining the dislodged pieces down on me. I rolled away, narrowly avoiding a rock that would have crushed bones. In a moment, I was up and sprinting away, following the wall to the south.

After a few more seconds, the barrage of gunfire ceased, and blessed, unnatural silence filled the air. My heart pounded out of my chest as I continued to run. Whatever plans I'd made were irrelevant after seeing the tiny man's firepower.

But intertwined with my fear was a throbbing anger. It was almost painful, thinking about how callously the little man had murdered those farmers. Stealing was understandable. Everyone was just trying to get by, and if it came down to it, taking what you needed to survive was common enough. Firing at me was justifiable. After all, they knew I was an enemy. But those farmers? They were helpless. Harmless. They should have been off-limits.

I seethed, slowing to a stop. I couldn't run away. Not after what I had seen. These people, they deserved to die—the little man with the minigun most of all.

I positioned myself at the edge of the field, where I would be partially hidden by the cornstalks. It wasn't perfect cover, and it would provide no protection. But it would at least obscure me from casual observation. Besides, I didn't intend to give my enemies the chance to react.

I could already hear them thundering through the field, snapping cornstalks along the way. There were at least three of them. Maybe more. I switched my weapon to its assault rifle configuration; I would need the rate of fire. Like that, I waited to spring my ambush.

Thirty seconds later, a man skidded out into the open, his feet throwing up clouds of dust. Then another, this one a woman. Another man. Still another man. Three more followed, and I stopped paying attention to their individual characteristics. It didn't matter. I didn't give them any silly descriptive names in my head. Enemies were enemies, and that was the only label that mattered. I don't know if I was lucky or unlucky that the small man with the big gun didn't come. If he had, I would've taken aim at him first. Now, though, I could become a more equal opportunity killer.

The six bandits approached the ruined wall, obviously looking for my corpse. I was only forty yards away, but none of them noticed me. One of them said, "He ain't here."

"Weren't no he, Billy," said one of the women. She carried no visible firearms but instead was armed with a wicked-looking machete.

"You always think the badasses is girls," the one called Billy responded.

"'Cause they usually are, ya idjit," the woman stated.

I stopped listening. Instead, I opened up in three-round bursts. The effect wasn't quite as impressive as when I used the sniper configuration of my Kicker, but at this range, it was more than adequate. Each burst took out a separate bandit, tearing through their unprotected chests with relative ease. I took out four before they even reacted.

That's when I was finally noticed.

"Over there!" screamed the bandit, pointing in my direction. "She's over—"

Five down. One to go. It happened to be the woman who'd been so sure of my sex. She dove into the cornstalks, and the burst that would have killed her thudded into the nearby rubble, kicking up dust and shattering concrete. I swore under my breath. The ambush had almost been perfect.

It didn't matter, though. I had plenty of opportunities to improve.

A coldness spread through my mind, smothering my emotions. I'd just killed quite a few people—eight, unless someone had survived what should have been a fatal wound—but I felt nothing but eagerness to finish the job. An effect of my Combat Focus, no doubt. Or maybe I was just getting used to killing. Either way, it was a boon for my current circumstances.

I rose from my kneeling position and, keeping my weapon ready, stalked down the narrow path that ran beside the wall. I knew that the woman who had escaped had probably run back to the bunker, but I wasn't going to take any chances. Nor would I leave the area before I was sure the fallen enemies were truly out of commission. My uncle and other trainers had stressed that to me; in our world, people could survive all sorts of things. So, the idea was to never count them out until you were sure they were dead.

It was a good thing, too, because I was surprised to see that, despite having gaping holes in their chests, two of my enemies had survived. One was in the middle of trying to use a med-hypo, while the other was on the edge of death. I wasted no time in plastering their brains across the rubble-strewn path, doing the same to the other unmoving men and women. No chances of survival if their heads were destroyed.

I'd just finished off the last of them when I heard a rustle in the cornstalks. I turned just in time to see a gleaming blade coming for my face. I dove to the side, rolling away and bringing my rifle to bear. The moment I took aim, the machete collided with the barrel of my Kicker, knocking it out of my hands.

"I'll kill you, you little fucking bitch!" growled the woman, bouncing on the balls of her feet. She was tall. At least six feet. And she had long arms. That, combined with her blade, meant that she had an advantage on me.

She darted forward.

Ferdinand II thundered.

She fell.

Ever since I'd upgraded my [Cybernetic Interface] to Tier 2, the time it took me to summon my weapons from my arsenal implant had been cut to a fraction of a second. And I had been practicing my quick-draw skills.

I looked down at the woman. She wasn't dead, but a good portion of her rib cage had been disintegrated by Ferdinand II's huge round. Still, she gripped her machete. It trembled as she struggled to lift it. Coughing blood, she growled, "I . . . I'll . . . kill . . . you . . ."

"You said that already," I responded before taking aim and firing. Her head exploded, and I paid her no more heed.

Reaching down, I gathered my Kicker from where it had fallen, and after inspecting the weapon, I was satisfied that it hadn't taken any damage. Not that I expected it to have; the thing was a E-grade weapon, and I didn't think a simple blade could hurt it. But it was always good to be sure.

After that, I stowed Ferdinand II and set off down the path, circling the field toward the gate. If I was going to get a good shot at the remaining few bandits—including the small guy with the huge gun—that would offer me the best view. Misthacking another drone would have been ideal, but it seemed that they'd only brought the one. And climbing to the top of the wall hadn't worked out well the last time.

Was it ideal? No. Not at all. But it was the best I could think of at the moment. And choosing a path and walking it seemed preferable to becoming mired in indecision.

Eventually, I turned the corner and began the last leg of my short journey. Before I reached the gate, I skidded to a stop and ducked into the cornstalks for cover. Creeping forward, I was careful to keep my noise to a minimum. Finally, I reached the path that led from the gate to the bunker, and I poked my head out.

Three bandits—one man and two women—stood next to the small fellow. He still held the minigun that was very nearly as big as he was, and his eyes searched the direction from which I had come. None of them were looking at me.

I took that as a sign. Flipping the Kicker back to sniper mode, I took aim at the small man. Once the reticle of my scope settled onto his chest, I took a deep breath, squeezed the trigger, and fired. The bullet thudded into him, knocking him on his back. Satisfied, I aimed at the others, taking them out one after the other in quick succession. They tried to hide, but from this direction, there was no cover.

I was just patting myself on the back when the miniature man jumped to his feet and opened fire with his minigun.

I took off into the cornstalks just in time. Behind me, the ground was destroyed by the powerful rounds. Dust filled the air, and shrapnel tore into my body. Still, I ran. Cornstalks slapped me in my face as I fled the continuous fire, but I stayed just ahead of that deadly stream of bullets.

Finally, after what felt like an eternity, the weapon ran out of ammunition. In all the confusion, I'd taken an angle that had brought me much closer to the bunker, so I could still hear the weapon spinning. And I could also hear the tiny man's high-pitched cursing.

I switched the Kicker back to its assault rifle configuration and stalked forward. I had no idea how he had survived my first shot, but I figured if I emptied an entire magazine into his head, he would go down. I didn't want to think about what would happen if such an attack failed.

I poked my head out of the corn stalks to see him trying to jam another belt of ammunition into the side port of the minigun. I didn't hesitate to take advantage of his distraction. He was only a few dozen yards away, so it wasn't difficult to put my first burst into his head.

To my dismay, they ricocheted off of his mask. He was thrown back but otherwise seemed unhurt. So, I came up with a new plan and started aiming for his gun. Specifically, the port where the belt of ammunition fed into the chamber.

Seven more bursts, half of which hit home, later, and the gun was little more than a pile of scrap. I dropped my magazine into my arsenal implant, summoning another and jamming it into the well. Before I could chamber a round, though, the small man was on me.

Screaming a wordless battle cry, he leaped into the air, a pair of hatchets in his hands. I dove forward, rolling under him, but he still managed to bury a blade in my back. Thankfully, it didn't get past my ribs. Otherwise, the strike would have destroyed my lung. As it was, it wasn't a debilitating wound. Agonizing, sure, but I was quickly growing used to that.

When I rolled to my feet, the small man had recovered from his wild but ultimately unsuccessful charge and was turning my way for another go. I chambered my round and emptied the magazine on full auto. The bullets thudded home, but to my horror, they didn't penetrate. I heard the telltale sound of bullets striking subdermal armor.

"That tickles!" he scream-laughed in his ridiculously high-pitched voice.

I dismissed the Kicker and brought Ferdinand II to bear. Its rate of fire wasn't as good as the rifle's, but it had already proven its worth a thousand times over. I fired, but even its massive rounds did little to penetrate the man's armored skin. Luckily, the sheer kinetic force of the shots threw him back almost a dozen feet, giving me time to unload everything into the seemingly invulnerable little man.

When he rose, I'd already dismissed my pistol and summoned my last resort—the scattergun. It wasn't meant for sheer damage. Rather, it was supposed to be nonlethal. Sort of. Sure, the weapon had been discontinued because it never quite met that mark, but the point remained that it was never supposed to do heavy damage. But I hoped the elemental damage would succeed where the other weapons hadn't.

He charged again, and I fired. Lightning arced from the barrel, enveloping the little man. His muscles locked up, and his momentum sent him tumbling to the ground, where he skidded to a stop. I fired again. And again.

Fifteen times, until its cannister of specially prepared Mist ammunition ran empty. He spasmed, the skin covering his subdermal armor gone. So were his clothes. Lying there and twitching, he looked like a tiny metal man.

But he wasn't dead. Not yet.

I raced forward, stowing my scattergun in my arsenal implant and summoning my final option.

I hadn't practiced much with the nano-bladed sword my uncle had bought me. Its inclusion had seemed like an afterthought at the time, but during my training, I'd learned that it was at least as high quality as the rest of my weapons. When I reached the small man, I hefted the sword above my head and brought it down in an overhand chop. The blade, its edge crackling with subtle blue Mist, hit his neck with a clang, but I was relieved to see that it had carved a small groove into the metallic surface of the bandit leader's skin.

I brought the blade down again. And again. I kept going until, at last, his head rolled free. At some point during the process, he'd died, his spine severed. But I refused to stop until I'd finished the job.

When I finally did, my shoulders sagged, and breathing hard, I looked around at the carnage. There were dead bodies—or the piles of meat that passed for them—everywhere. Some, I'd killed. Others were the bandits' victims. I felt guilty about them all.

"What a shit show," I muttered to myself before sinking to my knees. I sat there for a long time, just processing the day's events. The battle had been intense, and I'd come out on top. But the cost had been immense.

It was unavoidable, but it weighed on me all the same.

With a sigh, I heaved myself to my feet and approached the bunker. The metal door was heavy, made for security, and I wondered how the bandits had pulled off their attack. The whole farm seemed to have been well defended.

But not well enough, given that everyone was dead.

I went inside and, after sweeping the place for more bandits, found the kitchen. There, I patched myself up as best I could. The wound in my back wasn't as bad as I'd expected, but with the battle finished, my mind was free to wrap itself around the pain. I cleaned it, then awkwardly applied a foam bandage. Otherwise, I was only bruised. The injuries I'd previously sustained hadn't even broken open. That, in itself, was a minor miracle, as far as I was concerned.

All in all, I'd come through the battle in far better shape than I could have expected. I was hurt, sure, but I was still functional enough.

After taking care of myself, I went back to the door and locked it before I headed deeper into the bunker. It was a sizable building, meant to house twenty or more people. So, I found my way to one of the dorms, where I collapsed onto the bed and fell asleep.

CHAPTER TWENTY-SIX

A NECESSARY SACRIFICE

Death is a natural part of survival. Resources are finite. Everyone can't win. Sacrifices must be made at the altar of self-interest.

—Jeremiah Braddock III

I didn't sleep for long. Just a couple of hours before I jerked awake to a banging at the bunker's front door. I rolled out of bed, ignoring the pain of my many wounds as I summoned my rifle. Opening the door to the room I'd taken as my own, I peeked around the corner. Outside, the hall was straight and narrow. A perfect corridor for killing. I knelt, leaning out to aim toward the door.

Another bang. I tightened my grip.

Again. The door trembled. Something big was out there. Something strong.

Once more, something thudded against the door, and this time, it let out a metallic screech of protest. I bit my lip. It wasn't going to last much longer.

I flinched as something banged the door off the hinges. It flew down the hall, skidding to a stop only a few feet away from me. A cloud of dust hung suspended in the air, hiding my attacker. The lights flickered. I saw a shadow and squeezed the trigger.

One burst. Two bursts. Three.

The shadow was unaffected. It advanced. I fired again, but I got similar results. Either my attacker was invulnerable or my aim was off. And after all the training I'd been through, I felt confident in my ability to shoot.

My mind whirled as I tried to think of what to do, of how to win the coming fight. I came up blank. It had taken everything I had to kill the minigun-wielding miniature man. And I suspected that whatever stalked down the hall was far stronger than my previous adversary. I was going to die.

Or worse, I might be taken.

I fired again. And again. Over and over until my magazine ran empty. Still, it advanced.

I was just jamming the next magazine into the well when a familiar voice rang out, "Mirabelle? Is that you?"

I froze.

"Jeremiah?" I breathed.

Then, the light flickered again, and I saw the shadow for what it was. My uncle had finally arrived. I deflated, my muscles going slack and my shoulders slumping. It was over.

He rushed forward and knelt beside me. His hand found my shoulder, and he asked, "Are you okay?"

I looked up, and it felt like all the stress of the previous few days hit home at that very moment. Suddenly, I felt tears gathering in my eyes. I tried to hold them back. I wanted to be strong, like him. But I just couldn't stop the tide of emotion from spilling over.

"I . . . I killed . . . I tried to save them . . . but . . ."

My uncle took me in his arms and patted my back. My wounds screamed at me to tell him to stop, but I refused to listen. Instead, I sank into his embrace, burying my head in his chest, and wept like I'd never wept before.

"It's okay," he said, his hand on my back. "It's going to be okay."

I wasn't sure if I believed him.

I had killed before. I wasn't proud of it, but I'd done it. But the events of the last few days—maybe even going back to my actions in the Tigers' compound—had pushed me over the edge. Not only had I killed, but I had also been forced to watch a bunch of innocent farmers being literally ripped apart before my very eyes. I'd run through their remains. I had seen what happened to the weak and defenseless of the world.

After a few minutes, I pulled away. As I wiped my eyes, he asked, "Are you hurt?"

I let out a bitter chuckle. "You could say that," I muttered. Then, I detailed my injuries. The gunshots. The axe wound. My body had been put through the ringer, and I knew that, without proper treatment, things would get worse. I'd done what I could, but I wasn't a real medic.

"Jesus," he breathed. "I didn't think I needed to tell you not to get shot."

"Didn't exactly mean to," I muttered.

"Come on. We'll get you to Kimiko. She'll get you fixed up," he said, standing. He extended a hand, and I took it, letting him drag me to my feet. I was unsteady. Probably due to the blood loss, if I had to guess. But I managed to follow him outside and into the bright sunlight.

There were more than a dozen people waiting on us. Some, I recognized. A few Amigos were there, but so was Milo. And some others I'd seen guarding the walls of the town. Clearly, they had come expecting a fight. All they'd found were dead bodies.

"Any other survivors, hoss?" asked Milo, stepping forward. He took off his ancient blue cap and spat to the side. "Or she all that's left?"

"She's it," my uncle answered. "I'm taking her back. Secure the area. Bury the dead. Salvage what you can. We can't afford for this farm to be out of commission for long."

"Ain't that the goddamn truth," the man said, squinting up at the sun. "We'll get on it."

After that, my uncle led me to a jeep that hadn't been there during my battle and directed me to sit in the passenger's seat. I did so in a daze that continued as we took off back in the direction of Mobile. I was barely conscious, and the trip went by in a haze. Before I knew it, Jeremiah was half carrying me into Kimiko's office, where he planted me on an examination table.

The doctor herself took one look at me, then shooed my uncle outside before getting to work. I managed to retain consciousness as she undressed me, but after she jabbed me with a med-hypo, I surrendered to the unconsciousness that had been threatening to overtake me for some time.

When I awoke, it was to a strange chant.

"Mangos, mangos, mangos! I love mangos!" came an extremely high-pitched voice that could only have belonged to a little girl. I opened my eyes to see a tiny figure jumping around, waving a wooden sword in one hand and a reddish-orange fruit in another. She had a bucket on her head and, if her facial features were an indicator, was clearly related to Kimiko.

"Um . . . hey?" I said, my throat raw and my voice scratchy. I sat up, but moving even that little bit was incredibly difficult. "Who are you?"

"I'm Elie!" she announced proudly. "And you can't have my mango."

"Oh . . . okay . . ."

"Well, maybe a little," she said. "But I get most of it!"

"That's . . . um . . ."

"Okay—half!" she said, her face scrunching up. "You can have half. But you can't tell Grandma about it."

"Why is that?" I asked, a smile finding its way onto my face.

"Because."

"Because why?"

"Because I wasn't s'posed to take it," she said guiltily. Her eyes flicked back and forth conspiratorially before she added, "But it was right there. I had to take it."

That certainly seemed like a good enough reason for me, and I let out a little giggle at the young girl's antics. She certainly was a cute little thing. Maybe eight or nine, at most, with jet-black hair and a complexion to match Kimiko's.

In fact, she looked like an adorable, less severe, far younger, and much tinier version of the doctor I knew.

It was almost as if she was summoned by my thoughts when the door to the room slid open, revealing the doctor. She wore a white coat and a cold expression. To Elie, she said, "Young lady, what are you doing in here?"

"Nothing, Grandma," she said, hiding the pilfered fruit behind her back. "I was just checking on what's-her-name over there."

"Is that so?" asked Kimiko, raising an eyebrow. "And your assessment?"

"She's really nice!"

"Is that your medical opinion?" was the doctor's next question. Her lips twitched as she held back a smile. Perhaps she wasn't as stern as I'd first judged.

Elie's face scrunched up in intense concentration before she announced, "Yes!"

Kimiko laughed, and I chuckled a bit, as well, which brought a round of coughing that in turn came with a good deal of pain. Kimiko was by my side in a moment, her hand on my forehead. She said, "Elie, dear—run along. Grandma's got to work."

"I can help!" declared the little girl.

"Not now," Kimiko said. "Now, go."

Elie looked like she was going to argue, but with a dramatic sigh, she stomped out of the room. When the door closed, the doctor said, "I apologize for her. She is very independent. I don't know where she gets it."

I nodded, finally recovering from my coughing fit. "It's a mystery," I muttered.

"How are you feeling?" she asked.

"Like I was just run over by a hover car," I said. "Or maybe trampled by an alligator."

"That's expected," she said. "You pushed yourself well past your limits. With the amount of blood loss you experienced, it's a minor miracle you were still standing."

I nodded, but I didn't consider it a miracle. It was because of my [Combat Utility] skill. The abilities that came with it, chiefly Combat Focus and Regeneration, coupled with my training, had given me the ability to push through pain and fatigue. There was nothing miraculous about it.

"How long will it take me to heal?" I asked.

"I want to keep you in here for another day or two," she said. "But judging by how quickly you heal, it's probably going to be no more than a week before you're back to normal."

"That quickly?"

It certainly wasn't long, considering how many times I had been shot, which wasn't even mentioning the axe wound I'd received from the miniature man. But I definitely wasn't going to complain.

"The miracles of modern medicine," she said. "I remember life before the Initialization. Back then, the wounds you suffered would have been fatal. On the off chance that you did survive, you would have had months of recovery ahead of you. Now, it is a matter of days." She shook her head. After a few more minutes, during which she asked me various health questions and inspected my injuries, she left me alone to rest. The next two days followed a similar pattern, but I didn't see Jeremiah again until I was released from Kimiko's care.

He was waiting for me outside of the building that served as a medical center.

"You okay, then?" he asked.

"I'm fine," I said. "You could've come inside."

"I got updates from Kimiko," he stated, already walking down the sidewalk. I hustled to catch up, my wounds barely bothering me anymore. When I did, he said, "I need to apologize to you. I'm sorry. You should have never gotten caught up in that situation at the farm. But I have to ask—why didn't you contact me?"

That took me by surprise. I'd been laboring under the assumption that the entire thing had been a test, and so, I hadn't bothered sending a message to my uncle. I was beginning to suspect that I was mistaken. I said, "I thought the whole thing was part of my test."

He cut his eyes at me, saying, "I would never have sent you into that kind of a fight. You weren't ready for it."

"But you did send me."

"I made a mistake," he said. It sounded like it took every ounce of his willpower to get those words out. My uncle was good at a lot of things, but admitting that he was wrong certainly wasn't one of them.

"Nobody's perfect, I guess" was my response.

Silence stretched between us as we made our way back to the Dew Drop Inn. When we got there, I had to endure Jo's concerned questions before my uncle escorted me up to my room. Once we were there, he sat on the bed next to me and told me what they'd found.

Apparently, a group of bandits called the Bayou Boys had been growing progressively more powerful over the previous couple of years. Most of the time, they were little more than a nuisance, ambushing the odd caravan and stealing anything that wasn't nailed down. However, of late, they'd undergone a marked increase in power and displayed a far greater degree of organization.

"They don't normally come north," he said. "Usually, they stay down by the coast in Bayou La Batre. They might head a little west, but they don't mess with us."

"Yeah, clearly," I said sarcastically. "Who was the little guy?"

"Horace Lafontaine," Jeremiah said. "His mother's in charge down there. He has—or had, I suppose—a gaggle of brothers and sisters."

"He was packing some serious firepower," I said, thinking back to the minigun that had torn down a concrete wall. "Not to mention subdermal armor."

"That wasn't the half of it," my uncle stated. "That little man was filled with more cybernetics than most Operators in Nova. He was a hair's breadth from hitting the Singularity."

The Singularity. Jeremiah had explained that to me before. It was when someone's body crossed a threshold where they had so many cybernetic implants that they couldn't maintain their humanity anymore. It wasn't common—most people couldn't afford that kind of hardware—but when it happened, strange things came with it. Most people just went insane and started killing anything they saw, but others reacted in different ways. I'd heard about one woman who, after hitting the Singularity, had retreated into seclusion. The next time anyone saw her, she had become a wealthy merchant. She had been so successful that, if someone from King's Row hadn't had her killed, she might have destabilized the entire economy.

"How did he get that kind of gear?" I asked. People outside of the cities usually didn't have access to the same kind of equipment or cybernetics available to people in the cities.

"That's the million-credit question, isn't it?" he said. "That minigun of his came from off world, just like your weapons. Usually, that's not the case out here. Unless someone like me is supplying them, they should be using pre-Initialization weapons."

"The others with him were."

"But he wasn't," my uncle stated. "Neither was that big idiot that attacked us on the way here, either."

I thought back to the giant man with the arm cannon. He'd been just as invulnerable as Lafontaine, and his arm cannon had been even more devastating than the minigun. If I hadn't gotten off a lucky Misthack and fried his system, things would have turned out very differently.

I glanced at my uncle. Or maybe not. Back then, I'd gotten the feeling that he wasn't in any real danger, and I'd long thought of that attack as another test. And given that I'd emptied an entire magazine at my uncle in an enclosed hallway and he hadn't even seemed affected, I was confident that my theory held water.

"So. What now?" I asked. "Do we go after them?"

"Maybe," he said. "But for now, you need to rest. Then, you need to train. You were lucky to make it out of that alive. I'm proud of you for how well you did, but you have a long, long way to go."

I nodded, feeling a sense of pride at his approval. We made a little more small talk before he finally left me to my thoughts. The moment the door slid shut, I opened up my status to investigate my gains:

NAME	Mirabelle Lisa Braddock		
CLASS	N/A (Requirements Not Met)		
LEVEL	4 (26%)		
CONSTITUTION	17/38		
MIND	18/38		
MIST	10/38		
SKILLS	7/7		
SKILL NAME	Skill Tier	Modifiers	Abilities
CYBERNETIC INTERFACE	Tier 2 (97%)	None	3 Cybernetic Slots
FIREARMS	Tier 2 (62%)	+10% Damage (All Firearms) +4% Reload Speed (All Firearms) +21% Accuracy (All Firearms) +15% Damage (Rifle) +15% Damage (Pistol) +15% Damage (Scattergun)	None
CLOSE QUARTERS COMBAT	Tier 1 (98%)	+4% Movement Speed +15% Damage (Melee) +7% Speed (Melee) +5% Accuracy (Melee) +5% Damage (Unarmed) +5% Damage (Blunt Weapons)	None

STEALTH OPERATIONS	Tier 1 (21%)	None	Camouflage (F)
COMBAT UTILITY	Tier 2 (69%)	None	Triage (F) Basic Explosives Handling (F) Combat Focus (E) Pain Tolerance (E) Resistance (F) Foraging (F) Improvisation (F) Regeneration (E)
MISTWALKER	Tier 1 (44%)	+5% Speed (Misthack) +5% Speed (Mistwalk)	Mistwalk (F) Misthack (F) Mistwall (F)
SPYCRAFT	Tier 1 (42%)	None	Disguise (F) Deception (F)

I was very happy with my progress, considering that I'd made gains across the board. I drilled down into my submenus to check on my skill trees. What I found was that I'd made significant progress there, as well. The first one I inspected was my [Firearms] tree:

Tree	Firearms: Tier 2 (97%) +10% Damage (All Firearms) +4% Reload Speed (All Firearms) +6% Accuracy (All Firearms)			
Branch	Rifle: Tier 2 (29%)	Pistol: Tier 1 (78%)	Scattergun: Tier 1 (15%)	Sharpshooter: Tier 1 (32%)
Tier 1	+15% Damage (Rifle)	+15% Damage (Pistol)	+15% Damage (Scattergun)	+15% Accuracy (All Firearms)
Tier 2	+15% Range (Rifle)	+10% Accuracy (Pistol)	+15% Reload/ Ammunition Regeneration Speed (Scattergun)	+5% Damage (All Firearms)

Tier 3	Ability: Empowered Shot	Ability: Quickdraw	Ability: Double Shot	+5% Range (All Firearms)
Tier 4	Plasma Rifle Certification	Energy Pistol Certification	Explosive Scattergun Certification	Weapon Modification Certification
Tier 5	+15% Rate of Fire (Rifle)	+25% Rate of Fire (Pistol)	+15% Accuracy (Hipfire, Scattergun)	Ability: Mark Target

I had made sizable improvements there, which explained why my shots had begun to deal far more damage than before. I had a suspicion that, as I grew more powerful, my enemies would as well. So, if I wanted to keep up, I had to continue to progress. Next, I looked at my [Close Quarters Combat] tree.

Tree	Close Quarters Combat: Tier 1 (98%) +15% Damage (Melee) +7% Speed (Melee) +5% Accuracy (Melee)			
Branch	Pugilism: Tier 1 (13%)	Bladed Weapons: Tier 1 (72%)	Blunt Weapons: Tier 1 (15%)	Movement: Tier 2 (20%)
Tier 1	+5% Damage (Unarmed)	Nano-Blade Certification	+5% Damage (Blunt Weapons)	+2% Movement Speed
Tier 2	+10% Damage (Unarmed)	+5% Speed (Bladed Weapons)	+10% Accuracy (Blunt Weapons)	+2% Movement Speed
Tier 3	Ability: Combination Punch	Ability: Eviscerate	Ability: Pummel	Ability: Engage
Tier 4	+15% Damage (Unarmed)	+10% Accuracy (Bladed Weapons)	+10% Damage (Blunt Weapons)	+5% Movement Speed

| Tier 5 | Ability: Barrage | Energy Blade Certification | Ability: Mighty Swing | Ability: Disengage |

My gains weren't as broad in that skill tree, but I figured it was due to my preference for using firearms in actual battle. The fact that my bladed weapons were further along than the other weapon categories seemed to support that. After all, I'd never even killed anyone with my bare hands or with blunt weapons before. The movement category had progressed better than any of the rest, probably due to how much I'd been forced to run, climb, and jump. I was eager to see the ability at Tier 3, though.

Finally, I turned to the [Mistwalker] tree:

Tree	Mistwalker: Tier 1 (44%) Ability: Mistwalk (Granted upon Skill's Acquisition) Ability: Misthack (Granted upon Skill's Acquisition) Ability: Mistwall (Granted upon Skill's Acquisition)			
Branch	Mistwalk: Tier 1 (2%)	Mistwall: Tier 1 (2%)	Misthack: Tier 1 (42%)	Mist Manipulation: Tier 1 (-3%)
Tier 1	F-Grade Systems Infiltration	F-Grade System Defense	+5% Speed (Misthack)	Ability: Overcharge
Tier 2	E-Grade Systems Infiltration	E-Grade System Defense	+2% Speed (Misthack)	+2% Strength (Overcharge)
Tier 3	D-Grade Systems Infiltration	D-Grade System Defense	Ability: Breach	+2% Strength (Overcharge)
Tier 4	+2% Infiltration Stability	Ability: System Redirect	+5% Speed (Misthack)	+10% Cybernetic Efficiency
Tier 5	Ability: Bypass Trivial Defenses	+5% Increased System Defense Strength	Ability: Overload System	+5% Strength (Overcharge)

Admittedly, I was more than a little disappointed in my progress in my Mist manipulation. I'd used it quite a bit, but I'd really made any progress only in the Misthack branch. It was a little annoying, but then again, I'd received no real training in the skill. Compared to how much time I'd spent shooting or learning to fight, I'd barely even scratched the surface of that particular skill. I had high hopes that the lack would soon be remedied.

With a sigh, I lay back on my bed and went through a few logic puzzles before my injuries caught up to me. I still hadn't finished recovering, so fatigue kept creeping up and blurring my thoughts. After getting undressed, I climbed back into bed and went to sleep.

CHAPTER TWENTY-SEVEN

THE NEXT PHASE OF TRAINING

Our world, even before the Initialization, had a long history of slavery. Whether it was the African slave trade, the Jewish people being enslaved by the Egyptians, or the more modern example of slavery via incarceration, it has been a part of humanity since the very beginning. However, the wider universe's version of enslavement is far more insidious. It is the tyranny of the strong, where the sin of weakness is punished with virtual slavery. I will die before it happens to me.

—Jeremiah Braddock III

My convalescence took two weeks, and I spent much of that time with Jo and her group of closest friends. She didn't have many, but those she did have were like family to her. And as tight as we had grown, I knew I could never compete with that kind of bond. I'd been living in Mobile for quite some time now, but most of the time I still felt like a stranger in a strange land, an intruder. At heart, I was still a Nova City girl. Nothing could take that away from me.

Part of it was because, though I'd been living in Mobile for a while, I'd never really become a part of the population. Instead, because of my constant training, I was kept somewhat apart. My only real interaction with the rest of the town's residents came from my infrequent outings with Jo. Or from what I saw in the Dew Drop Inn's common room. So, as much as I enjoyed the opportunity to take a little break—that I very much needed—the morning when I was to resume my training found me eager to get on with it.

I sat next to Jeremiah, eating breakfast as he explained what I could expect. In addition to engaging in the next phase of my normal training, I would also receive much more detailed instruction in wilderness survival. He listed them off, saying, "Tracking. Foraging. Navigation. Stealth. These are all necessary if you're going to survive. To that end, you and Jorge will be spending a lot of time outside the walls. Sometimes days at a time."

"What about my other training?" I asked around a mouthful of gravy-covered biscuit. The dish was something of a specialty of the Dew Drop Inn, consisting of a creamy, white sausage gravy over fluffy biscuits. It had quickly become one of my favorites, and anytime it was served, I ended up stuffing myself until I could barely move. Luckily, my increased Constitution meant an increased metabolism, as well, so everything would get processed well before I got down to training.

"Oh, we're not letting up there," he said. "You're going to continue to the next phase of your firearms training, get further instruction into various weapons, and of course, an extended course in explosives."

I couldn't help but grin. I really did love a good explosion. But then again, what girl didn't?

"And finally, I've found you a Mistwalking tutor," he said. "It was incredibly expensive to get her to come here, but I think it'll be worth it for you."

My grin widened. Mistwalking. I'd already gotten a small taste of what it entailed, and I couldn't help but wonder what else might be possible. Of course, all the most popular programs on the entertainment network featured at least one hacker character who spent his or her time typing away at a keyboard, but with my skill, that wouldn't be necessary.

"I see you're looking forward to it."

I nodded. "I like learning new stuff," I said.

"No lingering issues from what happened at the farm?" was his next question.

I shook my head. "Not really," I answered, and against all odds, it was the truth. My ordeal at the farm had been horrific. I'd very nearly been killed. But once I had a little distance from the action, and my body had had a chance to come down from the adrenaline high, I'd realized that, as bad as it was, I didn't feel nearly as guilty about it as I might have expected. Obviously, I wished I could have saved those farmers, and I'd had more than a couple of dreams about people being ripped apart by that powerful minigun. But those issues didn't really persist into consciousness.

Was that normal? Probably not. No—definitely not, which made me think that my Combat Focus was keeping me from becoming mired in post-traumatic stress. But I wasn't going to question a good thing.

"Can I ask you something?" I asked my uncle.

"Shoot."

"How rare is that [Combat Utility] skill?" I asked.

He ran his hand over his bald head and let out a sigh. "That's a complicated question," he stated. "Do you know how most skills are earned?"

I shrugged. "Not really."

"Hard work," he said. Seeing my confusion, he went on, "Take that [Firearms] skill, for example. Most people who get that have spent years training with those weapons until the system judges that they've earned the skill. You got it at Tier 0. They would get it at Tier 1."

"Oh," I said. "What about my skills? Where did they come from?"

"A painful and tedious process where someone with the skill uses specialized equipment to make a copy," he said. "Your [Combat Utility] came from me. And to answer your question, yes—it is extraordinarily rare. It might even be unique."

"R-really?"

"Really," he said, giving me a crooked half smile. "I've told you before, Mirabelle—I wanted you to have every advantage I could give you. That skill, even though it's not as flashy as some, will help see you through. I can promise you that."

Seeing as how he had the skill—and was, in fact, probably the only person who could provide the information I wanted—I asked, "Does it help you deal with . . . you know . . . with everything?"

"It does," he said. "Before the Initialization, I had my own issues with PTSD. I'd spent so much time in war zones that I had a hard time in normal society. I spent more time in therapy than I care to admit. But once I got that skill? The issues just faded away. If I think about them, they're still there, but it's an academic sort of knowledge instead of something that really affects me."

"Did my other skills come from you?" I asked.

"Only [Firearms]," he said. "Though mine was a bit different. More focused. You might get there eventually, but for now, it's best if you're a bit more well-rounded."

"And you mentioned before that skills can evolve?" I asked, taking advantage of his talkative mood. Jeremiah rarely explained things when I asked questions, usually saying that I would find the answers when I needed them. So, I was more than willing to push for answers when he seemed uncharacteristically willing to give them.

He nodded. "Most definitely," he said. "Or did you think it'll all just plateau when you reach Tier 5 with your skills?"

"Uh . . ."

"Provided you've satisfied the requirements, your skills will have the opportunity to evolve," he said. "For instance, [Firearms] might become [Rifles], which in turn might turn into [Sniping]. Or any number of other branching paths, depending on your actions."

"Oh," I said, realizing that the world was a lot bigger than I thought it was. The bonuses from leveling my [Firearms] skill were already pretty impressive, but I had a suspicion that an evolved skill would make it look weak in comparison. Perhaps that was why my uncle could do some of the things he could do.

I couldn't help but remember the giant holes he'd blown into the hulking bandit who'd attacked us on my second day out of Nova City. My own shots had done nothing, and the only reason I'd been able to contribute at all was because of [Mistwalker] skills.

"Alright. Enough talk," Jeremiah said, standing up. "We've got work to do. Over the next six months, we're going to continue to mold you into a proper warrior."

I quickly stuffed another half biscuit into my mouth before following out of the inn, where we were met by another man who introduced himself to me as Jorge. I'd briefly met him before when we'd first arrived in Mobile, but we had never exchanged any words. He was a lean, swarthy man who wore his dark hair long. My uncle left me to his care, and he immediately led me out of the city and to the surrounding wilderness.

Once there, Jorge introduced me to woodcraft as well as basic survival training. I admit that I was a little jumpy, and considering how many times I'd encountered monstrous wildlife, I thought it was an appropriate response to being outside the gates. Still, I paid close attention while he explained which plants were edible and which ones might poison me. On top of that, he gave me some rudimentary instruction on tracking and the construction of temporary shelter.

Finally, he said, "Now we get to the fun part. You have the [Stealth Operations] skill, don't you?"

"Yes."

"Show me," he said, leaning against a tree.

I mentally activated the Camouflage ability, which drew a laugh. I crossed my arms and demanded, "It's low level, okay? It doesn't seem to work."

"Si. Si," he said, nodding along. "At your level of mastery, you need to give it a little help."

"I don't understand," I said.

"What would you do if you wanted to hide from someone and you didn't have the skill?" he asked.

"Uh . . . find a bush or something?" I asked.

"Show me."

I looked around the woods and, after spying a likely hiding place, planted myself behind some underbrush.

"Good, good," he said. "Now use the ability."

I did, and I felt something happen. On top of that, my HUD reacted to the ability's activation by overlaying a small icon above my instructor's head. It looked like an eye, but it was blinking red, which I figured probably wasn't the best sign. Then, when he glanced away, the eye stopped blinking.

"What the . . ."

The moment I muttered the two words, the icon started blinking again. So, it seemed safe to assume that it was an indicator of how well hidden I was. My KIOI had read my skill, then applied an appropriate visual aid to help me maintain stealth. Later, I would read in my manual that the eye being open meant that I couldn't hide from Jorge. If it had been closed, I would have been hidden. Suddenly, my [Stealth Operations] skill seemed a lot more powerful than it had before.

"Your skill does not hide you," he said. "It only enhances your actions. At higher levels, it may do more. Come—we will play a game."

After that, I was forced into the most anxiety-inducing game of hide-and-seek imaginable. No matter what I did, no matter where I hid, Jorge always found me. However, when he did, he always pointed out what I did wrong. A broken stick that gave away my trail here. A slight indentation where I'd stepped in soft mud there. A thousand other little things that I could have avoided.

When we were finished for the day, he made me show off my skills at building a shelter, and after that, had me forage for our dinner. My shelter was little more than a lean-to, and my foraged meal was only a few meager mushrooms, but it drove home the lessons of the day. That night, I slept in the woods.

Or at least, I tried to. Every rustle in the bushes, every chirp of a cricket, and each cry of a bird jolted me awake. It was not a restful night, and in the morning, we did it all over again. I spent the next week like that, getting a crash course in wilderness survival. Thankfully, my increased Mind attribute helped me to retain information, and my Constitution gave me incredible control over my body. So, I took to the lessons well.

On my seventh night, Jorge asked me to follow him into a nearby meadow. When we got there, I gasped at the sight before me.

A rainbow of lights danced through the air, flitting this way and that around a massive buck. When the lights drew close to the majestic creature, I saw the glint of metal on his antlers.

"Whoa," I muttered.

Beside me, Jorge said, "Remember this."

"What? Why?" I asked, still entranced by the creature in the meadow.

"You will fight beasts," he said. "Fearsome creatures that have been mutated by the Mist. But for every monster, there is something like that buck. Or those Mistflies. There is horror in this world, but there is beauty, as well. Remember that."

"I . . . I will," I said.

After that, we stayed at the edge of the meadow and watched until the buck bounded away. As I watched the thing slip into the woods, I thought about Jorge's words. My uncle was adamant that the Initialization was the worst thing that could have happened to humanity, and in a lot of ways, he was right. But there was good there, too. You just had to know where to look. That was how I interpreted the encounter and Jorge's reminder.

In any case, it wasn't long before we returned to town and the rest of my training resumed. True to my uncle's word, my [Firearms], [Close Quarters Combat], and explosives instruction built on what I'd already learned. For [Firearms], I graduated into scenario training where I would be given an objective and told to accomplish it. Usually, it boiled down to different ways to conduct an assault, but sometimes, I used some of my other skills to get creative. My instructor didn't like that, but I didn't care; if he didn't want me to hack the drones, he should've made that one of the rules of engagement.

For [Close Quarters Combat], I was finally introduced to a wide variety of weapons. And I had to admit that there was something viscerally exciting about bashing a dummy to death with a club or truncheon. Ultimately, though I did find a certain affinity for my bladed weapons, my heart remained with my various firearms.

The highlight of any day was always my explosives training, though. It was especially entertaining when we went outside the town walls for practical applications. More than once, I found my arm going numb from continuously lobbing grenades on the range that had been prepared for that purpose. Even then, it was difficult to wipe the smile from my face.

What can I say? I liked blowing stuff up.

Strangely, my least favorite part of training wasn't the difficult and brutal survival course. Nor was it getting beaten by one of the Amigos with a stick when I didn't use proper form in one of my melee drills. And I could easily ignore my fuming firearms instructor's ire. No—the one person—and subsequently, the training—I hated more than anyone else was my [Mistwalker] instructor, Helen Stone.

She was a pretty woman who had clearly been raised with a silver spoon up her ass, and she made no secret of how much better than me she thought she was. But even with my simmering hatred for the woman, I couldn't deny that the training was fruitful.

Many of her lessons were theoretical, and I learned more than I ever thought possible about the various types of systems I could infiltrate, either through Misthack or the hardwired Mistwalk. I was surprised to learn that, with many of these systems, if I approached them in the wrong way, there would be retaliation from the system in question. Apparently, it wasn't possible to just brute-force everything, which was what I'd been doing so far.

With my ever-growing Mind attribute fueling my learning speed, I memorized everything the woman taught me, and over the six-month period, I managed to earn her tolerance. Respect, even if it was grudging, would have been too much to ask. Not that I cared about what that detestable woman thought of me. As far as I was concerned, she could just go die in a fire, so long as I learned what I needed to learn.

Finally, I spent time with Kimiko, learning about how to treat various wounds. A lot of it went over my head—I had no academic foundation in medicine, after all—but the practical experience certainly helped. I hoped that if—no, when—I was injured in battle again that I would be able to put that newfound knowledge to good use.

So it went for six long months. I won't say that I was eager the entire time, but overall, I did enjoy learning new things and honing my existing skills.

At the end of that six-month period, my uncle, who had been mostly absent from Mobile, returned, and Nora came with him. Inside the Dew Drop Inn, she reached across the table and ruffled my hair, saying, "You filled out a bit. Training suits you, huh, peanut?"

I pulled away, annoyed at her habit of messing with my hair. But it didn't last, and I smiled shyly, saying, "I guess so."

"Good," Jeremiah said. "Hopefully, you can put it to good use. You've got another test in front of you, but this time, it's a bit more proactive. What do you say? Are you ready?"

"I . . . I guess so?" I said, still a little leery about any more tests. After what had happened during the last one, I thought that was understandable.

"Don't worry," he said, reading my expression. He'd always known what I was thinking. "This won't go like last time. In fact, if everything goes how we expect it to, you won't fire a single shot."

I was skeptical, but I said, "I'll do whatever it takes."

CHAPTER TWENTY-EIGHT

ANOTHER TEST

The term survival of the fittest is often misinterpreted. It doesn't mean that the strongest will inevitably emerge victorious. Rather, it favors the cunning. The adaptable. The intuitive. That is the spirit that humanity must embody if we wish to endure what's coming.

—Jeremiah Braddock III

I looked in the mirror, hating the reflection staring back at me. Reaching up, I fingered the thick, messy braids. As much as I loathed dealing with my hair, there was a part of me that wanted to start plucking the braids out and letting it poof as much as it wanted to poof. Of course, that wasn't possible. Not with my second test looming over me.

The idea was pretty simple. I was supposed to pose as a refugee from another town and get rescued by the Bayou Boys. Hopefully, they would take me to their village in Bayou La Batre, where I would use my access to acquire intelligence as to their motives, movements, and defenses. When that was done, I would slip out of the town and return overland to Mobile. The whole thing was expected to take a couple of weeks, at most. And then, I'd be back to training.

To sell my status as a refugee, my hair had been arranged in dreadlocks, and I'd donned a ripped and dirty tee-shirt. My jeans were similarly distressed, and my cheap sneakers were falling apart. In short, I looked like a young woman who'd lived her life mired in poverty. And when my uncle dropped me off in the middle of nowhere, that impression would be supported by the dirt and grime that came with any length of time in the humid wilderness of the area.

I also had [Spycraft] on my side. Using a combination of Disguise and Deception, I would bolster the ruse by masking my tier as well as my true nature. I wasn't sure what they would see when they looked at me, but when I'd showed Jo, she'd said that it was a very competent disguise. That was good enough for me.

I admit that I was a little nervous about the whole affair. Running around in Mobile and tailing oblivious gang members was one thing, but actively fooling the Bayou Boys? That was something else entirely. I knew I wouldn't be in any real danger—not unless there were multiple people around who could rival Lafontaine in power, which I doubted—but I couldn't stop a chill from going up my spine when I considered what would happen if I was wrong. The world was littered with pretty young men and women who'd turned down the wrong alley or caught the eye of someone more powerful than them.

I shook my head, saying, "You can escape if it comes to that."

Objectively, I knew it was true. My skills had grown by leaps and bounds. To reassure myself, I opened my status screen:

NAME	Mirabelle Lisa Braddock		
CLASS	N/A (Requirements Not Met)		
LEVEL	4 (27%)		
CONSTITUTION	20/38		
MIND	20/38		
MIST	13/38		
SKILLS	7/7		
SKILL NAME	Skill Tier	Modifiers	Abilities
CYBERNETIC INTERFACE	Tier 3 (6%)	None	3 Cybernetic Slots
FIREARMS	Tier 2 (97%)	+15% Damage (All Firearms) +4% Reload Speed (All Firearms) +21% Accuracy (All Firearms) +15% Damage (Rifle) +15% Range (Rifle) +15% Damage (Pistol) +10% Accuracy (Pistol) +15% Damage (Scattergun)	None

CLOSE QUARTERS COMBAT	Tier 2 (62%)	+4% Movement Speed +15% Damage (Melee) +10% Speed (Melee) +7% Accuracy (Melee) +5% Damage (Unarmed) +5% Speed (Bladed Weapons) +5% Damage (Blunt Weapons)	None
STEALTH OPERATIONS	Tier 1 (61%)	None	Camouflage (F)
COMBAT UTILITY	Tier 3 (16%)	None	Triage (E) Basic Explosives Handling (E) Combat Focus (D) Pain Tolerance (E) Resistance (E) Foraging (E) Improvisation (E) Regeneration (E)
MISTWALKER	Tier 2 (1%)	+15% Speed (Misthack) +10% Speed (Mistwalk)	Mistwalk (F) Misthack (E) Mistwall (F)
SPYCRAFT	Tier 1 (82%)	None	Disguise (F) Deception (E)

I had improved basically every facet of my tool kit. For my attributes, I'd gained three points in Constitution, two points in Mind, and three points in Mist—all huge gains that had noticeable effects on my combat ability. Not only was I stronger, faster, and more durable, but I also processed information much more quickly, and my memory had begun to approach eidetic levels. In addition, because of my increased Mist attribute, my abilities flowed much more smoothly, activating far more quickly than before. Sadly, my Mind attribute hadn't made me any wiser or given me the ability to think more critically. It only improved the mechanisms of memory and processing speed, rather than judgment and adaptability of thought. Still, I was satisfied with the results.

In terms of skills, I had progressed to the third tier of [Cybernetic Interface], albeit only barely. Apparently, progress became much more difficult to advance with higher tiers. The advancement didn't bring with it any modifiers or cybernetic slots, but I expected that to change when I got to Tier 4.

For [Firearms], I was only a few percentage points away from getting to Tier 3, but [Close Quarters Combat] had seen the most improvement, pushing forward two-thirds of a tier. Everything else had seen similar strides forward, with [Mistwalker] even making it to Tier 2, which had given me quite a boost to my speed with the associated abilities.

But the biggest improvements came from the progression of the various abilities, with a few making it to E-grade, which made them a good deal more effective. It wasn't quantified by the system, but the differences were noticeable.

To say I was happy with my progress would have been an understatement. I drilled down into the submenus and opened my skill trees, one by one. First up was the [Firearms] tree:

Tree	Firearms: Tier 2 (97%) +10% Damage (All Firearms) +4% Reload Speed (All Firearms) +6% Accuracy (All Firearms)			
Branch	Rifle: Tier 2 (95%)	Pistol: Tier 2 (14%)	Scattergun: Tier 1 (91%)	Sharpshooter: Tier 2 (12%)
Tier 1	+15% Damage (Rifle)	+15% Damage (Pistol)	+15% Damage (Scattergun)	+15% Accuracy (All Firearms)
Tier 2	+15% Range (Rifle)	+10% Accuracy (Pistol)	+15% Reload/ Ammunition Regeneration Speed (Scattergun)	+5% Damage (All Firearms)
Tier 3	Ability: Empowered Shot	Ability: Quickdraw	Ability: Double Shot	+5% Range (All Firearms)

| Tier 4 | Plasma Rifle Certification | Energy Pistol Certification | Explosive Scattergun Certification | Weapon Modification Certification |
| Tier 5 | +15% Rate of Fire (Rifle) | +25% Rate of Fire (Pistol) | +15% Accuracy (Hipfire, Scattergun) | Ability: Mark Target |

I was very excited about my progress, with my skill with rifles having progressed almost to the point of reaching the third tier. When that happened, I'd gain an ability called Empowered Shot. I had no idea what it would do, and my uncle still refused to reveal any details, but I had a suspicion that it would be a game changer, especially when I used my Kicker in its sniper configuration. Memories of Jeremiah blowing crater-sized holes in that giant, arm-cannon-wielding bandit filled my mind, and I couldn't help but grin at the idea of having that kind of firepower at my disposal.

The other [Firearms] branches hadn't progressed quite as well, but they were getting better. I suspected that, because I tended to favor my rifle, they would never quite catch up, but I was okay with that. So long as I continued to make progress, I would still grow gradually more powerful.

I moved on to my [Close Quarters Combat] tree:

Tree	Close Quarters Combat: Tier 2 (62%) +15% Damage (Melee) +10% Speed (Melee) +7% Accuracy (Melee)			
Branch	Pugilism: Tier 1 (91%)	Bladed Weapons: Tier 2 (11%)	Blunt Weapons: Tier 1 (61%)	Movement: Tier 2 (74%)
Tier 1	+5% Damage (Unarmed)	Nano-Blade Certification	+5% Damage (Blunt Weapons)	+2% Movement Speed
Tier 2	+10% Damage (Unarmed)	+5% Speed (Bladed Weapons)	+10% Accuracy (Blunt Weapons)	+2% Movement Speed

Tier 3	Ability: Combination Punch	Ability: Eviscerate	Ability: Pummel	Ability: Engage
Tier 4	+15% Damage (Unarmed)	+10% Accuracy (Bladed Weapons)	+10% Damage (Blunt Weapons)	+5% Movement Speed
Tier 5	Ability: Barrage	Energy Blade Certification	Ability: Mighty Swing	Ability: Disengage

I couldn't really argue with my progress with this skill, either. Not only had I increased the modifiers applied to my overall melee damage, but because I'd progressed a tier with bladed weapons, I'd gained quite a bit of extra speed when wielding my daggers or sword, as well. They weren't my preferred weapons, but I felt confident in their use. The one branch that really excited me was the movement category; I was close to Tier 3, which meant that I wasn't far from getting an ability called Engage. I wasn't sure what it did—again, my uncle was tight-lipped, saying that I would find out when I gained access to it—but I couldn't imagine it being anything but extremely helpful.

Finally, I turned to the enigmatic [Mistwalker] tree:

Tree	Mistwalker: Tier 2 (1%) Ability: Mistwalk (Granted upon Skill's Acquisition) Ability: Misthack (Granted upon Skill's Acquisition) Ability: Mistwall (Granted upon Skill's Acquisition) +10% Misthack Speed +10% Mistwalk Speed			
Branch	Mistwalk: Tier 1 (32%)	Mistwall: Tier 1 (2%)	Misthack: Tier 1 (56%)	Mist Manipulation: Tier 1 (-9%)
Tier 1	F-Grade Systems Infiltration	F-Grade System Defense	+5% Speed (Misthack)	Ability: Overcharge
Tier 2	E-Grade Systems Infiltration	E-Grade System Defense	+2% Speed (Misthack)	+2% Strength (Overcharge)

Tier 3	D-Grade Systems Infiltration	D-Grade System Defense	Ability: Breach	+2% Strength (Overcharge)
Tier 4	+2% Infiltration Stability	Ability: System Redirect	+5% Speed (Misthack)	+10% Cybernetic Efficiency
Tier 5	Ability: Bypass Trivial Defenses	+5% Increased System Defense Strength	Ability: Overload System	+5% Strength (Overcharge)

Just looking at the tree, I could practically feel the power buried within it. My [Mistwalker] instructor had informed me that the grades, at least in regard to system strength, were more like suggestions. I could push past them, but the further above my skill the system I was trying to infiltrate turned out to be, the more difficult it would be. Dangerous, too. At higher grades, Mistwalking meant opposing extremely powerful defenses that could fry a Mistwalker's mind at the first hint of weakness. The tier progression protected against that. If I bit off more than I could chew, though, I could end up brain dead.

Once I was finished inspecting my growth, I let out a sigh and headed downstairs to meet with Jeremiah, who would be responsible for getting me into position. When I got down into the common room, he looked up and said, "You ready?"

I nodded. "As ready as I'm going to get, I guess," I said. "It would be a lot easier if you just wanted me to go down there and kill them all."

He gave a soft chuckle, but I was only half-kidding. Given what I'd seen on the farm, I was more than prepared to do what needed to be done to the Bayou Boys. They hadn't shown any mercy to the farmers, so I didn't think they deserved any in return. In fact, the entire mission seemed like the most roundabout way to accomplish the goal. As my uncle led me outside and to a waiting jeep, I said as much.

He responded, "You only think that because you have no idea what you're talking about. Let's say you do what you want to do and head in, guns blazing. Never mind that it's extremely dangerous, but what are you going to do with the civilians? Bayou La Batre isn't home to just the Bayou Boys, you know. It's a normal town with normal people."

"Uh..."

"And then, what are you going to do with the ones who escape? Even if you can start picking them off, there will come a point when they scatter," he said. "You going to chase them all down?"

"I...uh...I didn't think about that..."

He started the vehicle and, as he pulled away from the inn, went on, "Then there are the automatic defenses to worry about. They have combat drones, you know. And I'm pretty sure your [Mistwalker] skill isn't good enough to take them down all at once. Am I wrong?"

I shook my head.

He went on, saying, "But okay. Let's say you've got some way to deal with that. I don't think you do, but you've surprised me before. So, say you've got these people at your mercy. You can kill them all if you want. Do you really want that on your conscience? Speaking as someone who's been down that road, Mirabelle...you don't. They're not some great enemy. They're just people who were born in the wrong place and are trying to do whatever they can to survive. Sure, sometimes we have to kill them. God knows I've made that choice a million times. But I want you to be better than me, Mirabelle. I want you to have the option to choose to spare them."

I nodded along. I knew Jeremiah had a body count so high I could scarcely comprehend it, so him preaching mercy wasn't exactly expected. And my first reaction was to call his plea stupid. However, it took only a moment before I understood what he meant. In the absence of choice, killing was excusable. But that didn't mean he wanted me to use it as a first option. Sometimes, it was necessary, but with this kind of a mission, if it came to that, it meant I'd made a bunch of huge mistakes.

"And finally," Jeremiah continued as we traversed the town. "Let's not forget that they're likely to have a few other Operators on the level of Lafontaine. That's not even considering Savanna, the matriarch of the clan. I'd be surprised if you could scratch the woman, much less kill her."

At last, we approached the gate, and I said, "Oh. I guess...uh...I guess doing it this way makes sense."

I didn't like admitting that I was wrong, but I couldn't deny that I hadn't thought of all the details. Perhaps that was why I wasn't the one in charge.

After that brief discussion, we remained silent as he took us on a roughly south-by-southwest track. As we went, the area became progressively swampier. Mostly, we stuck to a series of incredibly wide avenues that my uncle referred to as highways, but there were times when we were forced to go off-road. On a couple of those occasions, I was convinced that the vehicle would get bogged down, but the durable jeep managed to pull through. Finally, we reached a crumbling complex comprised of concrete-and-metal buildings. Abutting the waterway that Jeremiah referred to as a shipping channel were a series of tall but slim silos, three of which had given in to the effects of time. The rest of the buildings, like everywhere else, were slowly being reabsorbed by nature, and they'd been overtaken by the ever-present kudzu vines as well as a wide variety of other flora.

"Alright, this is where you get out," Jeremiah said. He pointed to the south. "Bayou La Batre is that way. You should run into some of their scavengers along the way, but if you don't, just... well, you know what to do. Get in, gather information, and then escape. Report back what you find."

"Simple, right?" I said, trying to convey confidence with a cocky grin. It didn't go much deeper than my expression, though. Instead, as we had made our way farther and farther south, I'd grown increasingly anxious. Now, it was almost to the point of causing my hands to shake.

"You'll be okay," he said. "I promise. You're ready for this."

"Thanks," I said.

"And if you get in trouble, remember that I'm only a call away," he said.

I felt myself blush. The incident at the farm could have been avoided entirely if I'd remembered the communication capabilities of my KIOI. I could have called in backup, and we would have made easy work of the raiders. Instead, I'd gone in half-cocked without considering the options in front of me. The results spoke for themselves. While I'd survived, things could have easily turned out very differently.

And if I'd called Jeremiah the moment I'd gotten to that church, they could have saved those farmers. I tried my best not to think about that, except to reaffirm that I wouldn't make the same mistakes again.

After making sure that I had everything I needed in my arsenal implant, I got out of the jeep and watched my uncle drive away. Suddenly, I felt alone. Again. Shaking my head, I resolved not to wallow in that fact. If I was going to move forward, I would need to learn to function without a safety net. Otherwise, I would always be dependent on Jeremiah to bail me out. So, with that in mind, I set off in the appropriate direction.

The compound—which seemed as if it had once been some sort of manufacturing plant—was desolate, but it wasn't completely uninhabited. Not only were there plenty of rodents the size of cats running around, but there were also more fearsome predators. Using Camouflage, I managed to avoid them, and the only close call I had was when I crossed paths with a mutated bobcat. It was at least three feet tall at the shoulder, bulging with muscles, and had metal tusks protruding from its mouth. I couldn't ignore the distinct gleam of metal on its paws, either.

I certainly didn't want to tangle with that creature, and so, I hunkered down and prayed that it wouldn't detect my presence. Whether I was lucky or the thing was simply disinterested, it soon passed me by. Still, I waited, nestled between a pair of bushes, for almost twenty minutes before I thought it was safe to move on.

Like that, I traversed the wilderness. Despite my high Constitution, it was slow going; the area was basically a jungle, and so, it was difficult to find a path through the thick brush. Still, I pushed ever southward until, at last, I heard something promising.

Voices. Ahead and slightly to the west.

I stalked toward the voices until I came to a long, narrow clearing where I saw a trio of figures kneeling next to a stand of huge mushrooms. They all wore homespun clothing—durable but of low quality—and wide-brimmed hats. As they worked to harvest the fungi, one of them—a woman with a scratchy voice—said, "We better hurry. It'll be dark soon."

One of the others—this one with the voice of a young man—responded, "Can't afford to leave none of this behind, Ma."

"The boy's right," said the final member of the gathering team. He was much taller than the other two, with broader shoulders. "We ain't met our quota in three weeks. This'll put us back in the green."

The woman spat, then said, "Quotas! We never used to have no goddamn quotas. Not 'til them Bayou Boys took over. Goddamn Savanna and her goddamn drones!"

I didn't think I'd get a better chance to act, so with a mental flick, I activated both Disguise and Deception before stumbling into the meadow. As soon as I did, the man whirled around, an ancient-looking double-barreled shotgun in his hands.

"Who's there?!" he demanded.

"I . . . I don't . . . my village was . . . attacked by monsters, and . . . I just barely got away . . . p-please help me," I stammered, reaching out as if he could take my hand from twenty feet away. I sniffed loudly. "Please . . . my whole family . . . is . . . is gone . . ."

I knew I was laying it on a little thick, but I hoped that my abilities would bridge the gap between my poor acting and something approaching realism. It seemed to work because the man, who looked middle-aged and had a thick beard, softened his expression. The woman wasn't so convinced, and I belatedly noted that she had a wicked-looking axe in her hands. The young man, though, was staring at me with wide eyes. They were clearly a family, given the resemblance between the three.

"Who are you? What's your name? And what village did you come from?" the woman demanded, stepping forward. Her axe seemed ready to cleave me in two.

I swallowed hard and used the backstory my uncle had given me. "Up north a little," I said. "Place called Wilmer. Or it used to be . . . nobody's left now . . ."

"Sadie..."

The woman narrowed her eyes, considering my story. I knew that the town had actually existed, and what's more, it had been decimated by a pack of mutated wolves. Some of the survivors had made it to Mobile. That, coupled with my appearance, would be enough to dissuade any disbelief. I hoped.

Finally, Sadie's expression softened, and she said, "Alright. We'll take you to town, but after that, you're on your own. We can't afford another mouth to feed."

With her acceptance of my story came the true beginning of my mission. I could only hope that it would turn out better than my last.

CHAPTER TWENTY-NINE

INFILTRATION

Every problem can't be solved at the end of a gun. Sometimes solutions require finesse. I have never been very good at those kinds of things.

—Jeremiah Braddock II

The family resumed gathering mushrooms and other edibles, leaving me mostly to my own devices. The youngest member, whose name I learned was Ethan, kept sneaking glances at me, but I pretended not to notice. At first, I thought he was just intrigued by the prospect of meeting a stranger, but it didn't take me long to realize that he had other things on his mind. Admittedly, I was a bit of a mess, but the combination of my ripped tee-shirt and jeans showed enough skin to excite him. His attention made me a bit uncomfortable, but it also made me question his standards. I looked—and more importantly, smelled—the part of a girl who'd been forced to flee through the wilderness, after all. How desperate must he have been if, even then, he found me attractive?

After another half hour, the trio finished their task, and the mother, Sadie, announced that they were headed back to town. She looked at me and asked, "Do you want to come with us? Can't guarantee it'll go good for you, but you'll be safe."

"Safe-ish," added the man. "There ain't much in the way of law down in the Bayou."

"She'll be fine," Sadie said. "Savanna don't have many rules, but she's got a soft spot for helpless girls."

"She ain't completely helpless," the man, whose name was Jasper, said. My heart jumped into my throat, and I concentrated on my arsenal implant. If things turned sour, I could have my scattergun in hand in a fraction of a second. Hopefully, the weapon's cone of lightning would be wide enough to take them all out without killing them outright. Then, he said, "She made it all the way here from Wilmer. I made that trip when I was little, and it ain't no walk in the park. She probably has a skill for concealment or somethin'. A waste for someone with only one slot, but it probably saved her life."

I resisted the urge to let out a deep sigh of relief. My abilities had held strong; he thought I was a Tier 1, which meant that I was harmless to someone like him. He was only a Tier 2 himself—just like his partner—which made him thoroughly average in terms of Awakened strength. But compared to the image I'd concocted? He might as well have been superhuman, especially considering my young age. Most teenagers hadn't had time to get the most out of their attributes.

But I wasn't most teenagers. Not only was I a Tier 7, which was, as far as I knew, uniquely powerful, but I'd spent the better part of a year in training. Even without weapons, I felt certain that I could rip the trio apart. Hopefully, it wouldn't come down to that, but if it did, I wanted it to happen out in the wilderness. If it did, I could stash the bodies and try to find another group of foragers.

"What's your name?" came a barely audible voice from beside me. I turned to see Ethan looking at me expectantly. He offered me one of his mushrooms; it was huge and red, and I recognized it as edible from my lessons with Jorge. Ethan added a question, "Are you hungry?"

"Uh . . . n-no," I said, still acting the part of a scared girl. He probably wanted to save me, the idiot. "I . . . I'm . . . uh . . . Mira."

I didn't see any issues with using my real name. After all, it wasn't as if I was famous. None of these people—nor the people in Bayou La Batre—would have any reason to know my name. So, I had chosen not to unnecessarily complicate things.

"I'm Ethan," he said, wiping his face with a dirty sleeve. It was then that I realized he was probably even younger than I had first judged. Barely a teenager, if I had to guess. I hoped I wouldn't have to kill him. If it came to that, I wasn't sure if I could pull the trigger. Taking out a bunch of mooks who wanted to kill me, I could accept. Killing a thirteen-year-old kid who wanted to help me? Yeah—that wasn't really an idea I could get behind, even if it proved necessary.

After that, my new friends and I started off toward the south. After fifteen minutes of walking, we reached a narrow footpath through the woods, which we followed for a couple of miles as it twisted and turned. As we walked, the sun dipped closer toward the horizon, and the atmosphere dimmed. The family clumped closer together, with me in the middle. Jasper took the lead, his shotgun at the ready, while Sadie, clutching her axe, brought up the rear. The area was clearly home to fearsome predators, and they were prepared to do whatever it took to get back to their town.

Even though I felt confident that I could handle myself, it was a tense journey. None of the trio made any effort at conversation, so the sounds were those native to the forest. A chirping bird. A few rustles in the nearby brush. The huffing and puffing of my companions' labored breathing. All the while, I maintained the facade of an exhausted and terrified teenage girl.

As night began to fall, we finally reached our destination in a walled town abutting a protected cove. The town itself was encircled by a rough wooden palisade, and the buildings it protected were similarly constructed, with corrugated metal roofs. Only one of the buildings within the walls was made of concrete blocks. Comprised of a single story, it had a sizable footprint that stretched at least a hundred yards in any direction.

More than anything else, what really stuck out about the town was the smell. In the Algiers district of Nova City, there were a few seafood processing plants. In the Garden, we never got their products—those were always destined for the wealthier areas, like King's Row—but every Nova citizen knew the smell. That's what the entirety of Bayou La Batre smelled like.

When he noticed my crinkled nose, Ethan said, "Sorry about the smell. That's what we do here, mostly. See those boats over there?"

I looked in the direction he'd pointed, and I saw a collection of ships, each sprouting sizable towers from their decks. From those towers stretched a series of cables, and I could see piles of sturdy netting.

"Yeah?" I said. "What are they?"

"Shrimpin' boats," he said. "Mama said that I can learn the [Shrimping] skill and work on one, so long as I take the [Fishing] skill, too. When I Awaken, I mean. That's two years from now, though."

"This town's always been about shrimpin'," Jasper interjected. "My daddy was a shrimper. My daddy's daddy was a shrimper. And before that, back before the Initialization, his daddy was, too."

"Oh," I said. "W-what about the sea monsters?"

It felt like a rational question to ask. Even in Nova City, we knew that going more than a couple of miles from the coast was tantamount to suicide, which was why we had always used drones. So, to discover that the residents of this tiny town had built their entire identities around doing just that was, to put it lightly, a surprise.

He barked a harsh laugh. "That's what the skills are for, ain't it?" he said, shouldering his shotgun. He pointed at the boats, saying, "Best shrimpers in the world, right over there. Always has been, always will be."

Jasper had said it with such finality that I couldn't really think of any way to respond. So, I remained silent as we approached a gap in the palisade, which was guarded by a handful of obvious Operators. I couldn't help but notice that they were all armed with new, pristine weapons that looked out of place in their grubby little hands.

They waved us through without even asking about my identity. Apparently, newcomers weren't a huge concern for them. Or maybe my abilities were more effective than I thought. Either way, I was soon inside the walls. The townspeople didn't seem all that different from the ones in Mobile. They were dirtier. Skinnier. And altogether less happy. But other than that, there weren't a ton of differences in the respective populations.

One thing I did notice was that a good portion of the town's residents had features like Kimiko's, with canted eyes and black hair. Later, I would learn that it was due to the area's pre-Initialization demographics, which skewed toward immigrants from a faraway country with people of that ethnicity. Vietnam, the place was called, which meant almost nothing to me.

Of course, Nova City had plenty of people who looked similar, but nobody there really cared much about race or ethnicity. We had other, far more important things to worry about. Whatever the case, it was a noticeable difference, and given that I'd come there for information, I certainly took notice. Even the smallest details could prove to be important.

I followed the family through the town, looking around as if I was impressed. The village I'd claimed had been my home had barely been more than a couple of isolated huts before being overrun by the pack of mutated wolves, so the character I had chosen to play would have been in awe of the area. I couldn't help but think that my acting skills were going to waste, though, because the family paid me no attention at all.

Except Ethan, who kept sneaking peeks at me when he thought I wasn't looking. It was almost endearing and, at first, was more than a little flattering. But I soon discovered the reason for his interest. No one in town looked like me. My skin tone set me apart as something unique. Exotic.

"Can I touch your hair?" he asked.

"W-what?" I responded, taken aback by his boldness.

He clapped his dirty hand over his mouth as if the question had slipped out all on its own. I suspected that his embarrassment had more to do with his building infatuation with me than because he thought it was a social faux pas. Whatever the case, it made me feel even more self-conscious than before. My hair had always been a touchy subject, and having him focus on it made things all the worse.

But what was I going to say? I couldn't just call him out on it. Not if I wanted to maintain the fiction of my chosen role. So, I gave him my best shy smile and said, "I-if you want to . . ."

He didn't hesitate to make good on his request, reaching out with those same dirty paws and groping the braided clump of hair. However, when his fingers brushed against it, he seemed a little disappointed, and I heard him mumble something along the lines of, "It's just hair . . ."

I wanted to make a snarky comment about how I was sorry to disappoint him, but the exchange was cut off before it could even begin when Jasper said, "This is where we part ways. I hope you find something productive to do. Savanna don't take kindly to strays who don't earn their keep."

"Oh . . ."

"We should give her someplace to stay!" suggested Ethan, and for the first time, I caught sight of something lascivious in his eyes. Something lustful. I wasn't used to people looking at me like that, but I knew the signs well enough from how, wherever Jo went, male gazes seemed to follow. Most looked at her just like Ethan was looking at me. And suddenly, the fact that he was only thirteen didn't seem to matter very much. "She can share my room!"

Sadie let out a snort. "As if I'd subject any girl to that," she said. "Besides, we ain't takin' her in. Can't feed her. Can't house her. Can't give her a job. We brought her here, and that's enough. She's on her own now."

Her lack of empathy was a little disappointing. After all, as far as they knew, I was precisely what I appeared to be—a girl who desperately needed help. That they'd chosen to cut me off wasn't surprising, but I couldn't help but feel a little disheartened by their actions. Still, it suited my mission just fine.

"Thank you for your help," I said. "I . . . I can find my own way, I think."

Sadie fixed her gaze on me, then jerked her head toward the big building by the water. She said, "If you need direction, head on over to Savanna's place. She'll get you sorted, one way or another."

"T-thanks," I said. Then, after a round of goodbyes, I hurried away, melting into the crowd. The whole time, I felt Ethan's eyes boring into my back. Or maybe my backside. I didn't want to think about which drew his interest. Instead, I wove my way through the crowd, trying to seem as unobtrusive as possible as I looked for somewhere to hole up for the night.

Fortunately, my search didn't take long, and I soon found an abandoned building near the docks. It looked like it was barely standing, but that didn't matter much to me. All I really cared about was getting a little privacy and security so I could rest before scouting out the town. And the building I chose was perfect for that.

As the sun made its final appearance for the day, I slipped into the building. Situated close to the water, it was two stories tall, but given its state of disrepair, there was absolutely no way I was going to go upstairs. Instead, I crept through the rooms on the first floor, making sure that it wasn't occupied. The last thing I needed was for some dust fiend—or whatever kind of addict they had in Bayou La Batre—to interrupt my sleep, after all.

The original purpose of the building was a mystery, but I did notice some similarities between its layout and the stores back in Mobile. So, I figured that was what it had been. However, there was no way to be sure because it had long since been picked almost entirely clean, with only half-rotted wood, a few rusty slabs of metal, and a barrel that had clearly been used to contain a fire to show that it had ever been anything but an empty shell.

I saw something out of the corner of my eye and, thanks to my training, sprang backward, narrowly avoiding something big. Something fast. It wasn't until I refocused that I saw what had tried to attack me.

"A crab?" I muttered to myself.

That seemed a bit of a misnomer because crabs weren't supposed to be the size of a hover bike. The thing was at least four feet wide, with oversize claws to match. Knowing I couldn't use my various firearms, I summoned my nano-bladed sword from my arsenal implant. Thus armed, I squared off against the creature.

Sure—I probably should have run away. That was the smart thing to do. There were likely plenty of other places I could hole up for the night. But I didn't like being pushed out by an overgrown crustacean. On top of that, I suspected that the building was probably abandoned precisely because the crab was there. After all, that first attack would have probably cut me in half if I hadn't had the advantage of my high attributes as well as my training.

Plus, I needed something to take my mind off the way Ethan had looked at me, and a fight seemed perfect for that. So, I focused on the crab, paying special attention to the metallic lining along the inner part of its claws. Doubtless, that metal was sharp.

It was one of the things I'd learned during my time under Jorge's tutelage. Much of the world's wildlife had been transformed by the Mist. A lot of the time, animals simply grew larger and more aggressive, but sometimes, like was the case with the crab before me, the stag with the metallic antlers, or the alligator with a metal skeleton, they adopted artificial components into their organic structure. Sort of a natural cybernetic.

Of course, I didn't need to know all of that to recognize one simple directive when fighting a crab—avoid the claws. Metallic or not, those things were natural weapons, especially when they were of a size to really ruin my day. So, as I faced off against the crustacean, I paid special attention to the twitching, oversize appendages.

At a stalemate, the pair of us stared at each other for a long moment. It was almost like the thing was waiting on me to make the first move, which shouldn't have been possible for an animal like that. After all, arthropods weren't exactly known for their intelligence or combat tactics, were they? This one seemed to buck that trend, though, waiting until my attention wavered slightly before it attacked.

Its claw darted out, almost too fast for me to track its movement, but at the last second, I managed to get my sword in the way. The edge clanged against the metal part of the claw as the crab clamped down and yanked it away. The sword clattered to the ground when the crab tossed it across the room. Surprised at how easily I'd been disarmed, I summoned a dagger and ducked under the crab's next attack, charging forward and stabbing at one of its eyestalks.

It skittered backward, and my dagger's blade skittered along its armored carapace. But I wasn't done. In fact, I was only just beginning. I dove back in, dipping and diving past its snapping claws as I got inside its guard. Once there, I kept up the pressure. It backed away. I followed, always attacking. Eventually, after a dozen attempted attacks, I scored my first hit.

The crab let out a hissing screech, going mad as it spun in circles. I leaped away, barely avoiding a claw that would have snapped me in two. As I watched its agonized thrashing from across the room, I came to a realization.

Even if I managed to slice its other eyestalk and blind it, my dagger—even my sword—would probably be incapable of killing it. Once, I had seen my uncle eat crab legs. It had been a rare treat, and he'd even let me try some. I'd been young enough that I couldn't really remember the taste, but the one memory of that night that still seemed fresh was the image of him cracking those claws with a tiny wooden mallet.

Could I do the same, but on a larger scale?

Dismissing my dagger, I retrieved the latest addition to my arsenal implant. It didn't have a slot of its own; instead, I kept it next to my ammunition. In fact, I'd included it on a whim, thinking that there was nothing it could do that my blades or firearms couldn't. I was wrong. In this situation, a tetsubo was precisely what I needed.

Long and, according to my uncle, resembling a baseball bat—whatever that was—it had a tapered grip and a series of knobs running along a fat barrel. It was a wicked weapon that was intended to take advantage of overwhelming strength. Nora, my uncle's hulking right-hand woman, had actually come in to show me the ins and outs of using the weapon. In her hands, it was a weapon of mass destruction. In mine? It was just adequate.

I charged forward and leaped, missing the crab's claws by barely an inch as I sailed over its head. Driven by my enhanced Constitution, I twisted in the air so that I hit the wall feetfirst. Driving with my legs, I swung down with all my might, hitting the shell with every ounce of force I could muster.

The carapace cracked beneath my tetsubo's knobby head, and I somehow managed to land atop the shell. The crab rocked and skittered about, but I maintained my balance enough to bring my weapon to bear once again.

Once.

Twice.

Three times.

That was all it took before I broke through into its soft, mushy insides. But I kept going, all the same, never stopping until the monster had ceased twitching. When I finished, I was completely covered in its viscera—which was a disgusting combination of white and yellow that smelled like rotting fish.

As I climbed off the crab, I felt my shoulders sag. I was absolutely disgusting now, and there was no way I'd be able to sneak up on anyone with the way I smelled. So, I sighed and set off to see if I could find something that passed for a shower in this village.

My search was complicated by the fact that I couldn't very well walk around town with a giant crab's guts all over me, so I ended up finding a mostly secluded spot where I could hop into the brackish water and wash off as best I could. Once I was finished, I smelled slightly less like rotting crabmeat—and more like disgusting water that was probably filled with all sorts of dangerous microbes—but at least I wasn't slimy.

After that, I set about cleaning my disgusting clothing before dressing in a pair of spare fatigues that I hoped no one would have a chance to notice. Then, I headed back to my temporary abode, set my alarm for midnight, and settled down to rest. Hopefully, I wouldn't remain in Bayou La Batre for much longer. With any luck, I could find what I needed to accomplish my mission and head back in the morning.

Yeah. Because things always went my way.

With a sigh, I curled up in the corner and tried to get as much sleep as I could.

CHAPTER THIRTY

SPY GAMES

There are more skills out there than you can imagine. Some are specialized. Others are broad. Learning to counter each and every one of them is folly. Instead, we must lean into our own strengths, lest we get lost in the weeds.

—Jeremiah Braddock III

For all that it was outwardly silent, the incessant beeping of my alarm was like a horn blaring in my mind. With a flick of thought, I turned it off, and for a moment, I considered simply going back to sleep. The fight with the crab had been more tiring than I expected. Not physically—I was well past the point where that short battle would be more than a warm-up—but rather, mentally. Still, my training hadn't been for nothing, and I quickly pushed past my tendency to procrastinate and forced myself to rise from that little corner of the building.

As soon as I did, the day's efforts caught up to me. Not only was the smell of the not-so-fresh-anymore crab strong in my nose, but my brief bath had been wholly unequal to the task of getting me clean. As a result, I felt crusty in ways I didn't even want to think about. The thick braids of my hair had grown stiff with old crab guts, and I knew it was probably too much to hope that I didn't smell like a fishery.

Even so, I was alive, and the crab wasn't. So, there was that, at least, to give my mood a little perk. Plus, if everything went right, I'd only have a day or so before I was back in Mobile and training.

It struck me then that it was kind of strange, how much enjoyment I got out of training. There was just something about seeing those numbers go up that I found addictive. But it wasn't just that, either. I liked getting better at things, seeing the improvement, day by day. Inch by inch. Minute by minute. That, as much as the changes to my status, was reason enough to look forward to training.

But first, I needed to prove that I could take it. That's what these tests were all about, after all. Making sure I had what it took to keep going. I was eager to show that my training hadn't gone to waste. So, with that in mind, I did a few light stretches, then stepped out into the salty night air.

Unsurprisingly, the village was mostly deserted, save for a handful of staggering figures who looked inebriated. However, I did catch sight of a few drones hovering near the palisade that encircled the small town. According to my uncle, there were a host of other measures in place to ensure their security. From drones to motion sensors and everything in between, it would be almost impossible to covertly infiltrate the town. Except the way I'd come, at least—and that was only possible because I looked relatively unthreatening. If my uncle—or one of the Amigos—had tried the same thing, they'd have ended up in a firefight at the gate, regardless of whether or not they had skills or abilities to hide their identities.

I crept forward, hiding in the shadows as I moved toward the village's main building, which I'd overheard Sadie refer to as the Plant, probably because that was what it had once been—a seafood processing plant. If there was intel to be had, it would be found there, I was sure. Along the way, I had to keep an eye out for errant drones—as well as the few night owls, especially around the town's lone saloon—but none of them were terribly difficult to avoid. Still, it was slow going, and almost an hour passed before I found myself pressed against the wall of the building across the street from the Plant.

I crouched low, studying the building. It was crawling with mooks of all shapes and sizes. In addition, I saw no less than eight cameras and five drones that never left the area. My experience with infiltrating the Tigers' compound had not prepared me to assault this base. At first, I panicked, thinking that my mission was impossible.

But this was just my first impression, wasn't it? I had plenty of time to watch, to wait, and to figure out what needed to be done to accomplish my goal. So, that's what I did, settling down on my haunches and watching the comings and goings.

The first thing I realized was that, though the rest of Bayou La Batre was asleep, the people in the Plant were decidedly more active. As the hours passed, I counted four different boats tying off at the docks, unloading or loading boxes, and then slipping away. What's more, from what I could see, the men and women manning those boats all wielded shinier and more impressive weapons, and many of them sported gleaming cybernetics, the likes of which I hadn't seen since leaving Nova City. And even then, I'd only seen them when someone descended into the Garden from one of the richer districts.

Or when the Enforcers made a visit.

I shuddered. No—these boats weren't manned by natives of the area. That much was abundantly clear. Something else was going on, and my task of figuring it out loomed over me even more oppressively than before. There was every chance that this test wasn't so much a test as an actual mission, after all.

Those thoughts and more flitted through my mind as I watched the building, but even when the sun started to peek above the horizon, I hadn't discovered anything new. Nor had I made any headway in my task. But a short delay was preferable to rushing in with less than perfect information. There was a time for haste, but when the situation afforded the opportunity, taking things slow and steady was almost always the best option. Nobody ever complained that they went into battle with too much information, after all.

And I did think I was in for a fight, one way or another. There were too many discrepancies. No—strange things were afoot in Bayou La Batre, and I intended to discover everything before going back to my uncle.

To that end, I slipped farther into the alley that had been my perch for the night, where I intended to change back into my disgusting clothing from the day before. Black fatigues were all well and good, but they tended to stick out, especially in a place like Bayou La Batre. Still, regardless of the necessity, I hesitated before changing. The tee-shirt, especially, was ruined, stained a dingy sort of yellow. I'd tried to wash it in the seawater, the same as I'd tried to bathe, but my efforts had been less than effective. The jeans had come mostly clean, though. Or at least the crab guts were gone, even if the smell wasn't.

I sighed, then set about the horrible task. I already felt dirty, and the horrid stench clinging to my clothes was enough to make me gag. But I pushed those minor discomforts to the back of my mind and tried to pretend I didn't smell like a fish market.

It didn't work, and I ended up heaving what little I'd eaten into the muddy alley.

All in all, it took me about fifteen minutes before I got used to the smell, and when I did, I set off back to the abandoned building where I'd killed the crab. However, when I drew close, a voice brought me up short.

"You ought not go in there, girl," a raspy voice called from behind me. I turned to see a tiny, wrinkled old woman. She carried a woven basket piled high with raw shrimp on one hunched shoulder. Her white hair was thin enough that it looked like it would blow away at the slightest breeze, and when she opened her mouth, I saw that she had scarcely more than three teeth in there. Notably, she was ethnically similar to Kimiko, which, given what I'd learned about the area, meant she was probably of Vietnamese descent. "Old Snappy lives there, and he don't take too kindly to visitors."

"O-Old Snappy?" I asked, barely remembering that I was supposed to be a terrified refugee.

"Used to be somebody's pet, believe it or not," the woman said, spittle flying from between her lips. "Grew up. Ate the owner and his family, from what I hear. By the time anybody noticed, Old Snappy was too big for anybody 'round here to kill. He don't come out of that house none too often, and when he does, he don't stray far. But he'll kill anybody who's dumb nuff to waltz in there and present him with a live meal. Best not be dumb, girl. 'S all I'm sayin'."

"I . . . I don't have anywhere else to go," I whined, seeing an opportunity. The old woman seemed kind enough, and more importantly, she wasn't accompanied by a creepy boy who wouldn't stop staring at me. Perhaps she could help me with my lack of information. Once I knew more, I would be better prepared to tackle my mission.

"Where're you from, then?" she asked. "I ain't seen you 'round here."

"Uh . . . Wilmer," I said, stating the name of the town I'd pretended to have escaped. "I came cross-country, and I didn't arrive until yesterday. But I don't have any food or anywhere to go. I don't mind working. I just . . ."

The old woman looked me up and down, then spat on the ground. "Fine," she said. "Follow me. I'll at least give you a meal and show you where you can clean up. You smell like a shrimp boat."

"I . . . I'm Mira."

"Call me Sue," said the old woman. "Now, c'mon. We ain't got all day to laze about."

"Do you want me to help?" I asked, nodding at her basket.

She looked at me like I was an idiot, then let out a cackle that was altogether too unnerving for such a diminutive woman. Then, without a word, she turned and marched away, her boots squelching in the muddy street. I hurried to follow her. As I did, I got a better look at the village.

Bayou La Batre was a lot of things, but civilized wasn't really one of them. The roads were unpaved, the buildings—especially the ones that passed for residences—were little more than hovels, and the people were dirty, smelly, and looked as if they were all in need of a good meal. Which was strange, considering how proud Jasper had been of the town's shrimping legacy. If his boasting had been any indication—as well as the impressive boats I'd seen in the harbor—the town shouldn't have had any issues with getting food. And yet, the people looked like they were starving. More, I remembered Sadie's complaints about quotas.

Something didn't add up, and I was beginning to think that it had a lot to do with the people—Operators from somewhere like Nova City, I was now certain—I had seen during the night.

I followed Sue for only a short while—after all, it wasn't a big village—until she reached a small building. Once she was there, she told me to wait while she took care of some business inside. When I complained, she looked me up and down, then said, "You stink. Nobody likes stinky people."

My jaw dropped, but she ignored my attempts at a sputtered response. Instead, she went inside, leaving me standing on a side street to await her return. As I did so, I got a few cutting glances from passersby; the whole town seemed full of early risers. I tried to ignore them, but as time wore on, I started to feel very self-conscious. Thankfully, Sue returned after only a half hour, muttering something about getting ripped off. I couldn't help but notice her basket was empty, so I assumed that she had sold the shrimp.

With that done, it wasn't long before we'd crossed the town to a small shack near the northernmost wall. She led me inside, where she said, "Strip out of those clothes, girl."

"W-what?"

"You can't wear them no more," she said. "They stink. I'll find you somethin' else. My daughter was about your size."

"O-oh . . . she won't mind if I wear her clothes?" I asked.

The old woman snorted. "Took off for the big city, she did," Sue stated. "Ain't seen her for two years. Said she was gonna be a big shot 'cause she was Tier 3. Tried to tell her different, but . . . well, she was a stubborn girl, just like her daddy."

"Uh . . ."

"Strip, I said!" she hissed. "Bathtub's in the next room. Should be some soap in there, too."

"T-thanks," I said, already taking off my clothes. I wanted to ask why I couldn't do it in the bathroom, but the old woman was insistent, and I wasn't in any position to argue. So, off my ruined clothing went, and before long, I was as naked as the day I was born. The woman barely even looked at me—thank God—before I retreated into the bathroom. Once there, I discovered precisely why she wanted me to undress out in the other room. The bathroom was tiny, and I had to hunch down just to fit inside. Still, I was relieved to find that the water worked just fine, even if I had to squat in the tub to splash myself.

Once I finished my awkward bath, I arduously unraveled my braids before going through the process of cleaning my hair. When I was done, it was frizzy and wild, but at least it was clean. I tied it back, which mitigated some of the problem, then left the bathroom to find Sue waiting outside with a clean, white towel. She handed it over, and I used it to dry off.

"You have no idea how good that feels," I said.

"You still stink" was her response as she shoved a bundle of clothing into my hands. I was relieved to find that the outfit consisted of a pair of baggy jeans and a long-sleeve shirt with a few buttons at the neck. Once I was dressed, I had to admit that the outfit was comfortable enough.

"Better," Sue said. "Now, put your shoes on. I'm going to take you to see Savanna. She'll know what to do with a stray like you."

"Savanna?" I asked. "Who's that?"

I knew she was the leader of the town, and there had been hints that she was in control of the swarm of drones that patrolled the skies above the village. However, beyond that, I didn't know anything about the woman.

"If you're lucky, she'll be your guardian angel," Sue said.

"And if I'm not lucky?" I asked.

Sue didn't answer. Instead, she just cackled and walked out the front door. I swallowed hard, and though I felt my trepidation building, I still followed. After all, I had a job to do.

Trailing after Sue, I looked up, noticing that the sun was a lot higher than I had expected. A quick glance at my clock told me that it was already midmorning. Sue's errand as well as my bath had taken far longer than I expected, and I was beginning to feel the effects of spending most of the night awake. Thankfully, due to my high Constitution attribute as well as my experiences during hell month, I had little difficulty pushing past my fatigue. It wasn't pleasant or anything, but I still managed.

Sue shuffled through the muddy streets, and I followed at her heels. Slowly, we made our way to the Plant.

"Used to be a processing plant," she explained as we drew closer to the low-slung building. "Back before I was born. Before my momma was born, too. It's old, and most of it's been replaced at one point or another. But it's saved us more times than I can count."

"Saved you? How?" I asked.

She cut her eyes at me, saying, "Them walls ain't more than a speed bump for the critters out there. They don't do nothin' more than slow 'em down. Gives us time to get inside the fort, where Savanna can protect us, see?"

"Protect you how?" I asked, eyeing the building suspiciously. With its metal-and-concrete walls, it didn't look much better fortified than the rest of the village. "Some of the . . . uh . . . critters I've seen could knock those walls down in a second."

"How, you ask? Overwhelmin' firepower," she said with a wicked gleam in her eyes and a mischievous smile playing across her creased face. "Now, c'mon. We best get you inside. If I know Savanna at all, she'll want to hear your story."

"Y-yeah," I said, and we covered the rest of the distance in a matter of moments. Finally, she led me to a nearby loading dock where men and women were busy stacking crates. We went inside, and I kept my eyes peeled for any bit of information that might indicate what was going on in the tiny town.

While I saw plenty of boxes—which was strange, in and of itself—I didn't really see anything else of note as Sue led me inside and across the building's ground floor to a set of metal stairs that led up to a catwalk that cut across the room. We crossed it, with Sue's short, shuffling steps making it take far longer than it should have, but eventually, we reached a balcony running along the far wall. At the end of the balcony was an open door leading to an office, which I surmised was our eventual destination.

Sure enough, my suspicions proved correct when Sue's path led us there. Not that I was prescient or anything—it was literally the only way we could've gone, except maybe the ladder in the opposite direction that presumably led to the roof.

Finally, we stepped inside, where we were greeted by a woman's sweet voice. "Well, well, well—what do we have here? Aren't you a pretty little thing?"

CHAPTER THIRTY-ONE

LAYERS

Before the Initialization, there were means to keep the power hungry in check. Most people were content to survive, to ensure that their loved ones were taken care of. However, there will always be those who see what someone else has and decide that it would be better off in their hands. After the Initialization gave these people the means to take what they wanted, warlords and despots became commonplace. At times, I've found myself counted among their number.

—Jeremiah Braddock III

"Where did you come from?" asked the woman, looking me up and down like I was a side of meat. I returned the favor with my own examination, and what I found was not what I'd expected. Savanna was a stout woman, with a round face and more fat than muscle on her body. Wearing a simple, mauve-colored button-up top and a pair of jeans, she was sitting behind a rough-hewn table that must've served as her desk. With short, jaw-length brown hair and a pale face that looked like it had seen everything the world had to offer, Savanna looked like a woman just past middle age. Of course, that didn't say much, given how strangely aging worked in a post-Initialization world.

"Uh . . . Wilmer," I answered, remembering my cover. "It's just north of here, and—"

"I know where Wilmer is," Savanna said. "My cousin used to live up that way. Back before the Initialization."

"Oh."

"Shame what happened there," she said. "Bears, wasn't it?"

I recognized her attempt at tripping me up, and I said, "Wolves. Big ones." To demonstrate, I held my hand up at about head height. Letting my lip quiver, I looked down as I said, "They killed my pa and my little sister, Jodi."

"And how did you get all the way down here?" Savanna asked.

I wiped at my eyes. Learning how to cry on cue hadn't been easy, but I'd recognized the necessity. I wasn't sure if it would help me when the aliens descended, but humans were sensitive to a weeping girl. With my size, I looked young enough to make it doubly effective.

"I . . . I ran," I said. "My pa held 'em off, and I . . . I just left them . . ."

It was a well-crafted backstory, complete with all the guilt that might come with a girl who'd been forced to abandon her family. That was one of the key lessons I'd been taught; when it came to adopting a new persona, it was important to understand the emotions involved. Otherwise, the performance would be shallow. And if that happened, everything would fall apart. Savanna needed to believe me; otherwise, things would get very messy. Even if I managed to escape with my life—which, given how many armed men and women I'd seen acting as laborers downstairs, wasn't a guarantee—I'd fail my mission. No—I needed to convince her that I was what I pretended to be.

Luckily, Savanna didn't seem to be the suspicious sort. Or I was a better actor than I'd given myself credit for. Either way, she stood up from her cushioned chair and approached me, her arms outstretched. Before I knew it, she'd taken me in her embrace, hugging me tightly.

"There, there, child," she cooed, patting my back. "You're safe, now. Nothin's gonna get you here."

Despite the fact that I'd come to think of her as an enemy—and she was; my firsthand experience told me that much—it felt oddly comforting with her arms around me. It shouldn't have been all that surprising. Jeremiah was a lot of things, but a hugger he wasn't. As a result, I'd been touch starved for most of my life. Heather had tried, but I'd always been too wrapped up in hating her to let it really happen.

On top of that, I'd been pushing my emotions to the back of my mind for a while now. After all, I'd been training to be a badass warrior, hadn't I? And those kinds of women didn't get all weepy at the first opportunity. Aside from a few instances where I'd just broken down, I hadn't had a good cry in some time.

And there was something about pretending to do it that brought out the real thing. Before I knew it, my fake tears had become genuine, and I buried my face in Savanna's shoulder, sobbing quietly for longer than I cared to admit.

To her credit, she didn't push me away. In her eyes, I was a distraught child, and whether it was calculated to engender loyalty or simply her maternal side coming through, she wasn't so far gone that she would refuse me the comfort she could so readily provide.

Finally, after some interminable amount of time, I pulled away, wiped my nose, and mumbled an apology, adding, "I . . . I'm sorry. I don't know what came over me."

Savanna gripped my shoulder and said, "The world is a harsh place, even harsher if we don't let ourselves deal with loss. Remember that. Emotions don't make you weak. They make you human."

I nodded. It was the exact opposite of what I'd been led to believe, but I wasn't going to argue with her—mostly because I wasn't entirely sure she was wrong. Sure, Jeremiah might have been made of stone, but that didn't make it right for me.

"Now," Savanna said, leaning against the table that served as her desk. "Tell me how you managed to make it all the way here, alone and through monster-infested wilderness."

"I . . . uh . . . I have a skill . . ."

"And what is it called?" she asked. "I feel that you've only got the one."

I nodded again, giving a sniffle that I wasn't sure was real or feigned. In any case, I said, "It's called [Hunting]. My pa gave it to me, and he taught me how to use it. It comes with Tracking, Camouflage, and Archery."

"Three abilities for one skill? That's powerful," Savanna said appreciatively. I wondered what she'd think if she knew how many benefits I got from [Combat Utility]. Perhaps that skill was even stronger than I'd previously suspected, given that it gave me eight useful abilities.

"Pa said it was," I stated. "It . . . i-it saved my life."

"It likely did," Savanna agreed. "And I think it will continue to do so."

"What? How?" I asked.

"How much do you know about Bayou La Batre?"

I shrugged. "Not much," I said. "Just that you catch shrimp."

The older woman gave a hearty laugh. "That's true enough," she acknowledged. "But it's not the whole story. Shrimp is valuable. So valuable that we can't always afford to eat it, you understand. As such, we send gathering teams out every day. They pick mushrooms and such, but every day, they have to go farther and farther. There are seven hundred people living in this village. Seven hundred mouths to feed. We always need more food."

"Oh," I said, some of the pieces falling into place. I had wondered why a village with such a prominent food source as the ocean—and the skill to extract such a bounty—had quotas on gatherers like Sadie's family. Moreover, it explained what was happening with the boats that had been constantly coming and going. Finally, it told me why she had sent the Bayou Boys to that farm.

My only real question was why Savanna was telling me. Was it all common knowledge within the village? Was my acting prowess really so impressive that she'd been put off her guard? Or did she find me so unthreatening that she didn't care what I knew? All good questions, but I suspected that I wouldn't soon get the answers.

"Which is where you come in," said Savanna.

"What can I do?" I wondered, though given my backstory, I suspected the answer.

"You're a hunter," she said. "I want you to hunt."

"Uh . . . I don't have any equipment," I lied. Savanna had no idea that I had a top-grade arsenal implant at my disposal, so she had no reason to suspect that I was armed to the teeth with powerful weaponry. In less than a second, I could draw one of my weapons and end the threat, right then and there.

But then what?

Not only would I have to escape under fire, but I was wary of unintended consequences. More than once, I'd acted without thinking things through, and because of my actions, people had died. First, those innocent bystanders back in Nova City who'd been killed because they'd had the misfortune of being in the vicinity when the Enforcers had responded to the explosions I'd set off as a distraction. Then, the gang member I'd killed while infiltrating the Tigers' compound. The latter had probably deserved it, but I still regretted that I'd had to kill him.

It was one thing to choose to take another life, but it was another thing entirely to be forced into it by bad decisions and hasty, ill-thought-out actions. It was something I was focused on avoiding; the stakes were too high for my attitude to be otherwise. Killing was sometimes necessary. I knew that. But treating life like it didn't matter at all? As my uncle had recently intimated, there was a balance to be struck between doing what was necessary and still valuing human life. Too far one way, and I'd become an unrepentant monster. Too far in the opposite direction, and I would end up either enslaved or dead. With my power—and I was growing stronger by the day—I had the burden of responsibility weighing down on me.

"That's okay," came a voice from behind me. I'd never even heard anyone approach, which was quite a feat, considering that I'd been training to avoid just that sort of thing. I turned to see a slim, yet muscular woman standing behind me. Her skin tone was a little darker than mine, and she had similar hair, which she'd arranged into a multitude of neat braids. Her features were broad and expressive, which made me immediately predisposed to liking her. A trap, I was sure. Given her silent approach, she had to have had a skill active, which made her dangerous. "I'll get you geared up."

"Uh . . . who are you?" I asked.

"Erica's our chief hunter," said Savanna. "She's like a daughter to me."

"Don't lump me in with those good-for-nothing sons you've got roaming around," Erica said with a grin. Then, noticing Savanna's tight frown, she added, "Sorry. Forgot."

"Forgot what?"

"Never mind that," Savanna said, her voice losing all pretense at friendliness. "It doesn't concern you. Erica, this is . . ."

"Mirabelle," I said, not even realizing that I'd given my whole first name, as opposed to the abbreviated version I usually preferred. When I did realize it, I almost slapped my forehead in irritation. The problem was that Savanna, in a lot of ways, reminded me of Jeremiah. She had that same air of authority hovering about her, and I must have made the subconscious connection.

"Mirabelle. Pretty name," the older woman said. "Mirabelle, this is Erica. She's going to show you the ropes and get you started doing something to help the town out. You okay with that?"

I nodded, recognizing that, if I was a hunter, I'd have an excuse to come and go as I pleased. That was valuable for when I finally made my move and needed a quick escape.

"Good, good," said a beaming Savanna. "That's very good. I hope you can be a productive member of our little town."

That was when I realized that, at some point, Sue had disappeared. Not that I minded overmuch—I wasn't really attached to the old woman—but I'd have liked to have had the opportunity to thank her. Still, it was a small town, and I was sure I'd get the chance eventually. In any case, after the introduction, it wasn't long before Savanna shooed us from her office, and Erica led me out of the building, down the village's main road, and to a house near the outskirts. Once there, we went inside, where she armed me with a rudimentary bow, a quiver containing five arrows, and a spear that was at least twice as long as I was tall.

Inspecting the giant weapon, I saw that it was made entirely of metal, which meant that it was extremely heavy. Not a problem, with my Constitution attribute, but it would've been heavy for the character I was playing. So, I feigned some difficulty with the thing, which brought a laugh from Erica.

She said, "Not your average spear, eh? See those crossbars below the blade? Meant to keep a pig from working its way up the shaft and goring you. You ever do any boar huntin' back home?"

I shook my head. My education had been expansive, so I was familiar with the concept, but I'd never actually hunted a boar. And if I had, I wouldn't have used a spear. Instead, I'd have used my rifle, preferably from far enough away that I could get a few shots in while the creature charged. Not that I could say as much to Erica, though.

"We mostly hunted deer," I said. "With the bow."

"Arrows won't do much to a pig," Erica said. "Hide's too thick, and they're too goddamn big. Got to use the spears, which means it's dangerous. You don't mind a bit of danger, do you?"

"I... uh..."

She slapped me on the shoulder, then said, "'Course you don't! The way Sue tells it, you traipsed your way across a few dozen miles of monster-infested forest. You probably ain't scared of nothin'!"

"Yeah. Right," I said, wishing my story wouldn't have included such a dangerous trek. I wasn't particularly scared, but I wasn't looking forward to facing down a giant boar, either. According to Jorge, even before the Initialization, wild boar could grow to sizes in excess of seven hundred, which, coupled with their cantankerous and territorial nature, made them incredibly dangerous. The Mist had made them much worse, doubling or even tripling their size.

She clapped me on the shoulder again and said, "Come on. You tote the spear so I can have my hands free."

"We're going now?" I asked, resting the heavy spear on my shoulder.

She looked at me like I was crazy. "Of course! I know you're all up in your feelings right now, but in my experience, the best thing to do in that situation is to focus on doin' a job. For us, that means huntin' something big and tasty. If we can get a boar, that'll feed half the town for a week, but even if all we get is a deer or somethin' like that, it'll be a good day. Now, c'mon. It's already later than I usually head out."

With that, she took off, and I had little choice but to follow my would-be mentor, all the while pretending that the spear was nearly too much weight for me to comfortably carry. It was a strange balancing act, and it took quite a bit of concentration. So, it was no surprise that my other abilities seemed to suffer a bit. Notably, as we exited the town and headed into the forest, I felt like I snapped every branch and crinkled every leaf I came upon.

"Sorry," I muttered when Erica cut her eyes at me. "It's just that the spear is really heavy."

Erica narrowed her eyes for along moment before her face softened. "Tier 1?" she asked. "Really? I don't know if I should be impressed or disappointed."

"Uh..."

"What's your Constitution?"

"Six."

"Not bad, not bad. No wonder you're struggling with the spear, though," she said. With a sigh, she added, "Nothin' for it but to move on, though." She glanced up past the canopy of oak trees, squinting at the sun. "Getting later by the minute."

Then, she resumed her path through the woods. As she did, I tried to mimic her footsteps as best I could with the restriction of the spear weighing me down, and I managed to improve a little with every passing step. It was fake growth—I could have done much better—but walking that tightrope of maintaining my facade while showing improvement was enough to give me a splitting headache. Still, I persisted, and eventually, we found our way to a snare line she'd set the day before. To my surprise, she'd managed to trap a full brace of rabbits, which she said she was keeping to herself, so long as we found bigger game.

"I've a weakness for rabbit stew," she explained. "Little bit of okra, some carrots, and potatoes . . . mmm. That's good eatin'. Nothin' better, as far as I'm concerned."

I'd never had rabbit stew, but she made it sound pretty amazing. However, I did have a little difficulty connecting the cute, fluffy bunnies to a food source, but such was the difficulty of survival that we couldn't let such thoughts affect finding our next meal. Still, a part of me wished for the days when all my meals came prepackaged and ready for the nano-wave. It wasn't good, per se—more of an acquired taste, if I was honest—but at least it didn't require me to kill animals that looked like living plushies.

So, it was with somewhat muted enthusiasm that I gathered the rabbits and strung them to hang at my waist. Erica wasn't affected by my dour mood, though. Instead, she kept her eyes out for anything that might provide enough meat to make a dent in Bayou La Batre's hunger.

It was about an hour later when that diligence proved insufficient to the task at hand.

A rustle in the nearby brush was all the warning we got before something streaked past Erica. I could only barely see it, the thing moved so fast. And that was with my inflated attributes. Erica, who felt like a Tier 2 or maybe a weak Tier 3, never had a chance to react.

She screamed as the bobcat's claws raked across her torso, threatening to disembowel her, but I was already moving. I dropped the spear, snatched an arrow from my quiver, and took aim at the feline. It skidded to a stop, giving me a good look. With mottled tawny-and-black fur, the signature stumpy tail of its species, tufted ears, and teeth that gleamed metallic, the cat was more monster than animal. And with a shoulder height that came up to my waist, it had the size to go with that label, as well.

The moment the cat slid to a stop, I let loose with my arrow, which predictably missed by half a foot. I'd been introduced to the weapon, but I'd never really practiced with it. The only reason I'd gotten as close as I had was because of my attributes. Still, a miss was a miss, and the shot had gotten the cat's attention.

It let out a hiss, then darted toward me with enough alacrity that I had only an instant to react. Diving to the side, I rolled to my feet right next to the dropped spear. As the cat skidded past me, I threw caution to the wind and picked the weapon up. With one smooth motion, I hefted it with one hand, then threw it at the cat. My aim was true, and the spear's long, broad blade drove into the bobcat's left flank.

It yowled and tried to pull away, but the spear had lodged against something that held it fast. I ran forward, grabbed the long haft, and yanked it free before plunging it forward once again. And again. With each thrust, the bobcat let out a screeching cry, but I pushed it from my mind, focusing only on making the thing dead.

My efforts were soon rewarded when, with a last heave, the creature fell to its side and breathed its last, blood-flecked breath.

The fight had only lasted a minute or two, but the stress of the life-and-death struggle had sapped my energy. As a result, I wanted to fall on my ass, right then and there. However, it only took a few seconds for me to remember Erica. Chastising myself for losing my focus, I turned to find her crumpled on the ground. She was moving, but weakly.

I rushed to her side and knelt beside her.

"Leave me," she said, coughing blood. Given her wound, that must have been incredibly painful. "Go! The cat will be back . . ."

"It's . . . it's dead," I said. "I killed it. Lucky . . . uh . . . stab. Let me see your stomach. I have an ability for emergency wound treatment."

It was the best I could come up with to explain away my Triage ability. Assuming I could save Erica's life, my role might raise some eyebrows, but I couldn't just let her bleed out. Not if I could do something about it.

Against her protests, I looked at the wound. The claws had done a number on her torso, ripping her shirt as well as her flesh apart. However, only one of the claws seemed to have pierced her abdominal wall, which was bad, sure, but it could have been worse. Feigning taking it out of my pocket, I produced a tiny aerosol can that contained a foam bandage, which I applied generously.

"W-what? How?" she asked, obviously recognizing it.

"My . . . uh . . . my pa gave it to me," I lied. "Said it was only for emergencies. This seemed like one."

"R-right . . ."

Apparently, my story was believable enough because she didn't argue. The bandage did its job, anesthetizing and disinfecting the wound as well as closing it up. Soon, Erica had regained her feet, though she did so on wobbly legs. Her eyes immediately found the slain cat.

"That . . . that's . . . how?"

"I'm a hunter," I said. "I stabbed it."

"We need to get it back to town," she said, skating past my thin story. Of course, I had a lot on my side, chiefly that I'd saved her life. She didn't seem too keen to question me about how I'd accomplished that feat. "That cat will feed . . . it must be seven hundred pounds."

"How?" I asked.

She sighed. "I presume you know how to butcher an animal?" she asked.

I nodded.

"Well, get to work, then," Erica said. "I'll help however I can, but . . ."

"No, I've got this," I said. "Just try not to move too much. I don't know how well that bandage will hold."

"Fair enough," she said, collapsing against a tree. I hoped that she was better off than she looked, and I wished that she would just head back to town. But I could also tell from her expression that any suggestion to do just that would be met with refusal. That, more than anything, told me the state of Bayou La Batre. Soon, I would put all the pieces together.

But for now, I had a cat to butcher. After borrowing Erica's hunting knife, I got down to the business at hand.

CHAPTER THIRTY-TWO

FITTING TOGETHER

The bare necessities—food, shelter, medical care—should be the last things we have to worry about. Even before the Initialization, humanity had the capability to provide the basics to each and every person in the world. The only excuse for not doing so is abject greed, laziness, and a misguided belief that we should all make our way alone. It's only gotten worse in the intervening years.

—Jeremiah Braddock III

Butchering an overgrown cat wasn't so different from butchering any other animal, so there's really no explanation for why I found it so distasteful. But meat was meat, and from everything I'd seen, Bayou La Batre was a hungry village. Erica supervised, but she was in no shape to otherwise assist, which meant that it wasn't as clean or as easy of a job as it probably should have been. But in the end, I managed it, and using the skin as a makeshift tote, I gathered as much of the meat as I could carry. Like that, we set off.

"You're stronger than you look," Erica said, clutching her wounded stomach. It was unnecessary; the foam bandage would hold until someone administered the solvent. But I didn't blame her. She'd nearly been eviscerated by an animal she could barely perceive. I'd have been a bit illogical after that, too.

I shifted the bundle on my back, saying, "I've had to carry stuff before."

"But you haven't really butchered many animals, have you?" she asked. Before I could answer, she stepped in a depression, and when she caught her balance, it must've aggravated her wound because she let out a pained hiss. I reached out quickly, offering my free hand to steady her.

"You okay?" I asked, hoping that she would forget her previous question. I didn't want her to know just how inexperienced I was in the realm of butchering a kill. If she did, my whole adopted identity would unravel.

"No. I'm definitely not," she replied through clenched teeth. "That thing almost got me. I wouldn't be here if it weren't for you."

"I just did what anybody would do," I said. "And I got lucky."

"You got stupid is what you got," she said, resuming her plodding walk. Injured as she was, the nimble gait she'd adopted during our trek into the forest was gone, replaced by a veritable stagger. "What possessed you to throw a boar spear? That thing weighs as much as you do, and it definitely ain't made for chuckin'."

"Uh . . . I panicked."

"Right," she said, cutting her eyes at me. "But you made it work, didn't you? Lucky, as you say."

"Yeah," I said. "I'm not—"

"Look," said Erica, pulling up short. "I know you're not what you're pretending to be."

"W-what? I don't—"

"Don't," she said. "Just don't. I'd rather you just refuse to respond than lie to me. You're not a hunter. You're a fighter, and unless I'm crazy, a damned good one, too. You're also not a Tier 1. I don't know how you're masking your tier, but it's got to either be a skill or something high-tech."

I started to respond, but she cut me off again, saying, "Which means you're not some refugee from an overrun village to the north. You're a spy. Or an assassin. I don't know who sent you. I don't know why. And frankly, I don't care. You saved my life, so I'm going to give you the benefit of the doubt here. But I'm going to ask you one question, Mirabelle. One question, and you'd best not lie to me. Okay?"

"I'll answer as best I can," I said. As she'd spoken, I'd focused on my arsenal implant. With a thought, I could have my nano-bladed sword out and ready. She would be dead in a second, if she said the wrong thing. I could probably even blame the bobcat, if it came down to it. It would be grisly work, setting the proper scene, but I felt confident that I could do it. Even if I didn't want to.

"Are you here to kill someone?" she asked.

I shook my head. "No" was my answer. And it was the truth, too. If I could avoid it, nobody had to die. That wasn't my mission, after all.

Erica looked at me as if she wanted to ask more but, after a couple of seconds, let out a sigh. Soon, that sigh turned into a grimace, and she said, "Okay. I'll choose to believe you."

As I shifted the bundle on my back, I wondered if the huntress realized that, right then, I was debating whether or not I should kill her. It would have been the easiest way to preserve my cover; who knew what she would do when we got back to Bayou La Batre? Would she tell Savanna? Maybe. And if she did, a whole lot more people would have to die as I made my escape.

"What are you going to do?" I asked, fishing for a reason not to end the threat, then and there, while I could guarantee I would get away with it.

My tone must have betrayed my frayed nerves because she stopped in her tracks. I noticed a tremble in her shoulders. A gleam of sweat on the back of her neck. Maybe it could be attributed to her wound, but I had a feeling that she'd come to realize precisely how much danger she was in. She had just escaped death, but now, it had returned to hover over her.

"Nothing," Erica said, her voice barely a whisper. "Nothing at all."

And I believed her. It probably wasn't the smart choice. I knew that. My uncle likely would have killed her straightaway. But I didn't want to be like him. More importantly, he didn't want me to be. Not completely. He was jaded and cynical, and all he ever saw were the worst parts of humanity. I chose to see something better. People were capable of good; I was sure of it. I decided to trust that instinct.

Of course, if it all went wrong—and I knew how likely that was—I felt confident in dealing with it. Mercy, my uncle once told me, is the prerogative of the strong.

"Okay," I said. "Good enough for me."

For a moment, I thought she was going to continue the conversation, but then, without another word, she resumed her stumbling gait through the woods. I followed close on her heels. Before my Awakening—or my training—I would have struggled with the giant bundle of meat on my back. It must have weighed two or three hundred pounds. But with my enhanced Constitution, the burden was little more than an annoyance. Still, by the time we reached the gates of Bayou La Batre, I was tired and more than fed up with carrying the awkward bundle.

For one thing, it smelled. For another, I hadn't had a proper night's rest in a few days. It wasn't enough to incapacitate me, but it certainly decreased my tolerance for annoyance. Thankfully, when we reached the village, the guards—both of which were men with crude cybernetic prosthetics and ancient rifles—rushed out to help us. Erica nearly collapsed into the first one's arms, and the second demanded to know what had happened.

"Attacked by a big cat," I said, unshouldering my bundle and tossing it on the ground at the man's feet. "We killed it, but not before it got a good swipe in on Erica."

"How?" he asked, the question more of a demand than a query.

"Together," I said. "Now, where can I take this?"

I'd intended to have Erica show me what to do with the bobcat meat, but she was already being half carried, half dragged into the village. That left me to deal with the guards alone.

"Don't know you," the man said, looking me up and down. "Where'd you come from?"

I sighed. "Up north," I said. "I have a [Hunting] skill, so Savanna sent me out with Erica. We were trying to get a boar, but we were attacked by the bobcat. She was injured. I wasn't. Not really anything else to say."

I knew my tone was a little too aggressive, but I was exhausted and annoyed. He was lucky I didn't just whip out Ferdinand II and show him what was what. Or maybe that was just my irritation talking.

"I don't think—"

"Momma don't pay you to think, Tim," came another voice. I looked up to see a man approaching from the village. With wild blond hair that seemed incapable of picking a direction it wanted to grow, a scraggly beard, and a wiry frame, he definitely cut an interesting figure. He wore a tank top and striped shorts, which showed off his cybernetic leg.

"What's it to you, Hadley?" the guard spat. "I'm a guard doin' guardin' shit. That's what your momma pays me to do."

Hadley sidled up to Tim and got into the big man's face. Somehow, even though he was shorter than the guard, he seemed to look down on him. "What's that, chief? I thought I heard a bit of a challenge in your tone there. Maybe we need to head on over to the pits and settle this, huh? It'd be like old times."

"Uh . . ."

"Oh, for God's sake," I muttered, shouldering the makeshift bundle of cat meat. "You boys are ridiculous. Can somebody please just tell me where to take this? I'm tired and hungry, and I want to make sure Erica's okay."

Hadley didn't immediately back off. Instead, he just stared at the guard for a long few seconds. Then, suddenly, he chuckled, patted the man on the chest, and said, "As you were, soldier! As you were!"

"What the . . ."

"Follow me, fair maiden!" Hadley announced, thrusting his finger into the sky. "I shan't lead you astray!"

"Really?" I asked, just as dumbfounded as the guard.

"Too much?" Hadley asked, looking crestfallen.

"Too much," I said.

"Well, I stand by it," he said. "Now, if you will?"

He thrust out his arm, clearly intending for me to take it. I rolled my eyes, then strode past him. A second later, the telltale sound of his cybernetic clomping on the muddy street announced that he was scurrying to catch up. When he did, he was panting dramatically. "Just . . . up . . . here, m'lady!" he said, pointing to a building about thirty yards ahead. I suppressed my cringe. "That's the butcher. Funny story about him. He hates me. For some reason, he got it in his head that . . . hey, wait up!"

I didn't. Instead, I pushed through the free-swinging double doors and found myself in a butcher's shop. There wasn't much there—just a couple of plucked chickens and a dressed pig carcass hanging from the ceiling, but the smell of offal and blood hung in the air, announcing that I'd found the right place. A huge man with a sizable gut stood over a table near the back of the room, a bloody cleaver in hand. I was reminded of my first real battle, when I'd helped my uncle kill the giant with the arm cannon. He, too, had carried a cleaver and wasn't all that much bigger than the man before me.

Without looking up, he bellowed, "Ain't got no meat. Rhonda's got some shrooms, but that's all."

"I have a delivery," I said, heaving the heavy bundle off my back and dropping it on the floor. Like the rest of the room, it was stained with blood. With swarms of flies dancing and darting through the air, I had to question whether the butcher's operation was sanitary. Probably not. A good thing that I didn't plan on eating anything he'd touched. With Erica out of it—and with her knowing at least part of my secret—I'd taken a chance and stored the rabbits in my arsenal implant for safekeeping. I didn't have a complete picture of the food situation in Bayou La Batre, but I didn't think it out of the question that someone would try to take my rabbits for the greater good, so I'd chosen to preempt that.

At my announcement, the big man looked up, and I saw that my initial impression of the man had been spot-on. He wasn't identical to the person I'd helped kill, but the resemblance was still there. Of course, the butcher was quite a bit older, had both arms, and didn't look quite as dumb. Still, though, given what I knew about the Bayou Boys' operations, it wasn't difficult to make the connection that the two were in some way related. The big man wore a pair of shorts, some flip-flops, and a leather apron, revealing a massive body completely covered in tattoos, some of which depicted lewd scenes. It was all I could do not to stare.

At that moment, Hadley pushed through the doors, saying, "I told you to wait up!"

"What the hell are you doin' in here, runt?" growled the butcher, looking past me.

Runt? Hadley was definitely kind of stringy, but he wasn't small. Well—compared to the butcher, he was, but that could be said of just about anybody. By comparison, I was child sized next to either one of them.

"I told you not to call me that, old man!" screamed Hadley. I turned my head just enough to see that he'd gone red in the face.

"Watch how you talk at me, boy," growled the butcher, gesturing toward Hadley with the blade. "Or you'll have two robot legs instead of just one. Got me?"

Hadley went pale. "I . . . I don't . . . momma said you wouldn't . . ."

"Your momma ain't here to protect you," the huge man spat. "Now, get the hell outa my shop. Me and this little girl's got business."

For a long second, the wiry, wild-haired man looked as if he was going to argue, but it only took one glance at that blood-covered cleaver for him to reconsider. So, without another word, he turned on his cybernetic heel and stormed out of the building, banging the doors on his way out.

"Sorry 'bout that," the butcher said, drawing my attention back in his direction. He wore an apologetic smile that revealed multiple gold teeth. "That boy's always been a disappointment. Now, is that bobcat I smell? Good eatin', that."

At first, I was impressed that he could tell what kind of meat I'd brought just from the smell, and from across the room no less, but then I realized that it was bundled in a bobcat pelt. It didn't take a genius to figure it out, I suppose.

"Yeah. Me and Erica, we killed it a coupla hours ago," I said, adopting a more rustic manner of speaking. I'd found that people were more receptive and accepting when a stranger sounded like them. Even so, I got the feeling he could see right through the ruse; I could only hope that my [Spycraft] skill would help me. I knew that such benefits weren't overtly listed by my interface, but I'd begun to suspect that my skills weren't as limited as the system said they were.

Or maybe it was just wishful thinking.

Either way, I dragged the bundle to the table, where I heaved it onto the nicked surface. Then, I opened the pelt, revealing the bloody meat. The butcher gave a broad grin, showing off a mouth gleaming with metal.

"Very nice," he said. "It ain't boar, but it'll do."

"Uh . . . what do I do? Do you pay me? Or . . . what?" I asked. I didn't care about money, but most people would. So, I had to play my role.

He reached into his pocket, then tossed something to me. I caught it easily. When I looked at it, I saw that it was a simple wooden square, marked with a series of tallies. "What is this?" I asked.

"Quota chip," he said. "With that, you can get what you need anywhere in town. Only good for a week, though, so don't let yourself get lazy. Not like that good-for-nothing runt who followed you in here." The butcher shook his head, saying, "Where I went wrong with that boy, I'll never know. It's his momma. She's too soft on 'im. Always has been. And now look at where it got us."

I wanted to know more, but I had little desire to push him. So, with a nod, I said, "Alright. Thanks."

Then, I backed out of the shop. While I did so, the man went back to his work, cutting the meat into chunks. After that, I went off in search of Erica. Not knowing where she might have been taken, I soon found my way to the town's main building, where I hoped Savanna could shed some light on things. As I went inside, I got a few curious glances from the workers and guards, but none of them stopped me. Probably a combination of a few of them recognizing me from my previous visit and my ability to look like I belonged.

It was something I'd been taught fairly early in my education. If you couldn't sneak in, the next best thing was to stroll in like you belonged there. Most people wouldn't question it.

After a couple of tense minutes, I was at Savanna's door. Inside, I heard a familiar voice complaining about being treated poorly. Savanna's response was oddly comforting as she assured Hadley that she would talk to Burton, which I assumed was the butcher's name. After a bit, I knocked on the door, and a moment later, a red-eyed Hadley answered.

"Oh. It's you," he said. "What do you want?"

"I ... uh ... I need to talk to Miss Savanna," I said.

"Miss?" he said, quirking an eyebrow in confusion.

"Mrs.? I don't know," I said. "I just need to talk to her."

"Let her in, son," Savanna ordered, and he stepped aside. She looked much the same as she had before, though she had donned a bright-orange jacket that, I swear, burned my eyeballs. I have to admit that I'd developed a definite aversion to that color, even when it wasn't paired with blue. "What do you need, Mirabelle?" she asked when I stepped inside.

"I ... well, me and Erica killed a bobcat, but she was injured," I explained. It wasn't news to Savanna, who'd obviously already heard about her hunter's fate. "Well, I took the meat to the butcher, but I don't know what to do now. I wanted to check on Erica, but I don't know where she is."

"Right," Savanna said. "Hadley, dear—please show Mirabelle where she can find Erica."

"But—"

Savanna cut him off with a simple look. Then, she said, "I don't think I stuttered, did I? Go. And Mirabelle—thank you for everything you've done. I think you're going to fit right in here."

Recognizing that as a clear dismissal, I followed a grumbling Hadley out of the office and back into the town. The village wasn't very big, so it didn't take us long to find what passed for a doctor in Bayou La Batre. I was pleased to see that a familiar white cross over a red circle, marking the practitioner as having some sort of medical skill, was painted on the door.

Inside, I found Erica, who'd been tended to by a withered old man with wire-rimmed glasses. She told me that my quick actions with the miraculous foam bandage had probably saved her life, and that the doctor was flabbergasted by the lack of infection. The prognosis was good, though she'd have to remain in his care for a few days. After that, it would take at least a month before she was back to something close to her full strength.

It was a little disappointing, given the speed of my own recovery, which made me appreciate the Regeneration ability that had come with [Combat Utility]. It wasn't as flashy as some of my other skills, but it helped in a thousand small ways. From Combat Focus to Regeneration, it filled in all the gaps to make me that much more effective.

Thankfully, Erica offered to put me up in her own home. Then, just before I left, she asked a question that made me feel like an absolute idiot. "Where's the spear?" she asked.

"Uh . . ."

"You left it, didn't you?"

"Maybe?"

"You know you're gonna have to go back out there and get it, don't you?" she said. "Because that thing was expensive. We can't just leave 'em lyin' around."

I groaned, but before I could answer, Hadley offered, "I can go with you! You need a big, strong man to protect you."

Erica laughed, which made her wince in pain. The doctor, who was hovering nearby, scolded her, but she waved him away. "First of all, you're the scrawniest one in your family," she said. "Even Horace would've been better. Second, Mira would be the one protecting you, not the other way around. You might have that fancy leg, but she's a hunter. You'd do more harm than good, Had."

He tried to argue, but Erica wasn't a pushover. In the end, he ended up leaving in a huff, mumbling about an affront to his manhood or some such.

"Sorry 'bout him," Erica said. "He's always been a bit of a white knight, if you know what I mean. The kind of guy that spends most of his time dreaming about rescuin' the fair maiden. All that white knightin' wouldn't come without a price, right? Of course the grateful wench would sleep with him. In his head, she'd be beggin' for it. He's a pig. It's only gotten worse lately, too. What with his brothers dyin'."

"What?"

"Oh—you wouldn't know," the huntress said. "Sad stuff. About a year ago—maybe a bit less—the clan's pride and joy, Lars, was killed while on patrol. Big fella, kind of stupid. He had a good heart, though. He was his momma's favorite and the spittin' image of his daddy."

Clearly, Lars was the name of the giant we'd killed on the journey from Nova to Mobile. It didn't help, having a name to put to the face. It humanized him. Not that I was terribly concerned with his fate; after all, he'd attacked us. But still, I didn't want any extra information about the people I'd killed.

"Just about killed old Burt," Erica went on. "He really loved that boy. But then Horace turned up missin', too. Killed up north by some mutated bear or some such. Wasn't even anything left of him to bury. Now, there's only Had left. The least favorite son. You'd think they'd treat him better, bein' as he's the only one left, but with Burt, it just got worse. Would be sad if Had wasn't such an ass."

"Oh."

It was strange, thinking that I'd just interacted with the parents of two people I'd killed. I hadn't really pulled the final trigger on Lars, but the giant was still dead because I'd hacked his system and overcharged his cybernetics. That had given my uncle the opening he needed to end the man's life. But with Horace, the tiny, minigun-wielding man, I was solely responsible for his death. And though I didn't regret either action, I suddenly felt a twinge of guilt at the pain I'd caused for their parents. It wasn't powerful, and it wouldn't affect my decisions or anything, but it would take an absolute monster to look into the eyes of a mother whose son you killed and feel okay with how things had turned out.

After that, the conversation petered out—partially because I wasn't the best conversationalist, but mostly because the doctor administered a med-hypo that made Erica's eyes start to droop. Soon, I started making my way through the town. Armed with my quota chip, I was able to acquire some potatoes, carrots, and a few herbs, and when I got back to Erica's place, I quickly found a sizable pot where I could make my rabbit stew.

I had some experience with cooking over an open flame—Jorge's instruction in survival was expansive—but I didn't really have the knack. So, I just cut and dressed the rabbits, cut the meat into chunks, added some water and the other ingredients I'd found, and set the whole thing to simmering over the Mist-powered stove in Erica's house. The results were . . . edible. Barely. One day, I would have to learn how to properly cook a meal.

It was so different outside of Nova City. There, everything had been cooked in a nano-wave. More than that, though, it had been prepackaged with clear instructions. I wasn't a cook, but I could follow basic directions. But outside of the city, there were no nano-waves, probably due to unstable Mist. That was the reason there weren't any hover cars, and it seemed a viable explanation for the lack of other technology I'd taken for granted.

Whatever the case, I ate my fill, and it was satisfying enough that I knew I'd go back for another shot at it in the morning. With my belly full, I finally decided to send a message to my uncle. I couldn't risk a voice communication that might be intercepted, so I sent a text-based message through the connection we'd established before I was sent on my mission. It was a simple explanation of what I'd been doing, but it ended up being a lot longer than I expected.

I might have rambled a bit. But in my defense, I was in that strange state of mind where I was simultaneously exhausted but still keyed up from the events of the day. When he responded about twenty minutes later, his answer was simple. He told me to infiltrate Savanna's office, Mistwalk into her personal terminal, and download as much information as I could get.

Simple. But not easy. I had my work cut out for me. So, I found my way to Erica's bed—I didn't think she'd mind—and fell asleep trying to figure out how I was going to accomplish the task my uncle had set for me.

CHAPTER THIRTY-THREE

MAKING A MOVE

Some people need goals. A destination that keeps them trudging toward the horizon. For me, that goal has always wavered between revenge, survival, and in the end, giving Mirabelle the means to escape the Earth's inevitable destiny.

—Jeremiah Braddock III

The next morning, I awoke to see rays of sunlight peeking between the curtains that guarded Erica's windows. Dust motes danced in the light, giving the atmosphere an ethereal cast. I lay there for a while, my head propped up with one arm, just watching the ballet play out before me. But eventually, a blinking icon at the edge of my HUD pulled me out of my reverie.

I mentally selected it, and a note I'd left for myself the night before reminded me that I had a task awaiting me. So, with a barely audible groan, I dragged myself out of Erica's bed, which had proved to be surprisingly comfortable, and stood up. That's when I realized my egregious error from the night before, when I hadn't bothered undressing or showering before getting into bed.

"Ugh," I said, stretching my top out and giving a sniff, an action that almost made me gag.

I suspected that everything else was just as ripe, though I didn't have the courage to verify my suspicions. Instead, I quickly stripped the bed down, undressed, and tossed everything into a pile. After that, I found Erica's bathroom, where I was happy to discover a brick of scented soap. Seeing that, I wasted no time before hopping into the shower.

"Oh, crap!" I squealed, hopping right back out after I'd turned the water on.

With another groan, I fiddled with the twin knobs until, at last, the water turned blessedly lukewarm. With that taken care of, I jumped back in and gave myself a vigorous scrubbing. All the previous day's grime—and more than a little blood from my kill—sloughed off and drained away, as if none of it had ever happened.

When I finished, I stepped back out of the shower—barely avoiding slipping and falling on the slick tile floor, and only then because of my enhanced attributes, which allowed me to catch myself on a nearby towel rack—and dried off. That's when I caught sight of my naked body in the mirror.

The evidence of my previous battles was apparent. There was a long, jagged scar along my ribs, a few puckered marks where I'd been shot in my shoulder and legs. And, though I hadn't realized it, I'd picked up a fresh wound on my hip. It was a thin, half-healed cut, and though it wouldn't be a problem because of my Regeneration, it did serve to highlight the necessity for me to pay better attention. With Pain Tolerance being what it was, there was every chance that I'd pick up a wound that could turn lethal without even knowing it. It was yet another thing to add to my ever-expanding list of things I needed to remember.

Shaking my head, I went searching for some clothes. Erica was taller than me, but I figured I could make do with some of her things. Of course, I had plenty of clothing in my arsenal implant, but I couldn't use any of it and maintain the facade I'd built. I hoped to finish my mission soon, but I wasn't reckless enough to take the chance that I might be discovered. Luckily, I found a pair of long cargo shorts, a blue tank top emblazoned with some logo I didn't recognize, and some clean underwear that fit reasonably well.

After dressing, I set off to discover a means of washing Erica's sheets. And my clothes. Erica seemed nice enough, but I didn't think she'd appreciate me plundering her wardrobe. Or given that I'd saved her life, maybe she wouldn't mind. Either way, I wasn't going to put it to the test.

Fortune favored me, and I found a fairly modern ion washer in the back of the small house. The machine was Mist powered, so I was familiar with its operation. Back home, the ion washers only took thirty seconds to clean an entire load of clothes, but this one took almost ten minutes, during which I took the time to go over my plans.

My first order of business was to head back out to the forest and recover the discarded boar spear and the bow I'd dropped during the fight. I also intended to do a bit more hunting, perhaps even bagging one of the boars we'd hoped to find. After all, it didn't hurt to build a little goodwill with the townspeople, and nothing would do that better than providing a thousand pounds or more of good meat.

Once I finished with that task, I hoped to spend the night scouting the Plant again. I thought I had a good idea of the comings and goings, but I wanted to verify what I'd seen by observing for at least another night. My uncle had always preached patience, and I endeavored to exemplify that trait.

My planning session was interrupted when I heard a knock at the door. Before I even knew what I was doing, I had Ferdinand II in my hand. Maybe I wasn't nearly as relaxed as I thought I was. Probably for the best, considering that, for all that it appeared to be a standard village, Bayou La Batre was still enemy territory.

"Who is it?" I called, already crossing the small house to approach the front door at an angle.

"Uh . . . it's Hadley," came the answer.

"What do you want?" I demanded, sliding against the wall next to the door. If someone kicked it in, I wouldn't get caught in the rush. Instead, being off to the side, I would be free to do what I needed to do. I tightened my grip.

"I . . . c-can you open the door, please?" he asked, his voice sounding like it had lost some of its bravado from the day before. "I just want to talk, okay? And I think I have an offer for you."

"What kind of offer?"

"The kind I can't shout through a door," he said, a note of annoyance invading his tone. "C'mon. Just let me in. I won't hurt you."

Him? Hurt me? He was, at best, a Tier 3, and I could tell from his physique that he hadn't exactly pushed himself to his limits. Sure, he could be dangerous to someone with only one skill slot, but anyone else could probably give him a run for his money. Even if I was the Tier 1 hunter I'd pretended to be, I didn't think he would pose much of a problem. That, more than anything, drove me to open the door and allow him inside. Pointedly, I hid the pistol behind my back; it wouldn't make my draw much faster than just dismissing it and relying on my arsenal implant, but I liked the way it felt in my hand. It made me feel safe, like I was the one in control.

He looked much the same as he had the day before—all messy blond hair, wiry muscle, and undeserved swagger. He wore a pair of tan cargo pants, metal-toed boots that I was a bit ashamed to say I really, really liked, and a utility vest. No shirt. Like a weirdo. To call it an eclectic outfit would have been an understatement, and that was coming from a girl who had grown up in the Garden, where fashion had long ago descended into ridiculousness.

Hadley straightened his vest and strode inside like he owned the place. After I shut the door behind him, I said, "Okay. Talk."

"Really? Aren't you gonna offer me a drink? Maybe make polite conversation?" he asked.

"What do you want?" I asked, doing my best to maintain an even tone. "You said you have an offer?"

"Maybe my offer is to bring you into the family," he said. "You know, the old-fashioned way."

He waggled his eyebrows at me. I gave him a flat stare, and he relented, "Fine. Fine. Just having a little fun. My offer is simple. You take me back with you."

"Back? Where?"

"I'm not stupid," he said. "And I have a skill that helps me out. I know you're not what you're pretending to be."

That tore it for me, and in the space of a second, I'd whipped Ferdinand II around and pressed it against his cheek. As I backed him against the wall, he held up his hands, saying, "It's fine. I'm not going to tell on you. Not unless you make me."

"What skill?" I asked, pressing the barrel into his flesh.

"It's called [None of Your Goddamn Business]," he spat, finally showing a little backbone. "Seriously? I'm not an idiot, Mira. Or whatever your real name is. I'm not going to tell you my skills. Just trust that I can tell you're not some Tier 1 with a [Hunting] skill. You're at least Tier 3. Maybe higher. I can't get a handle on it, but I know you're not what you're pretending to be. Which leaves us with a problem. But my Momma always said that every problem is just an opportunity, and I think this qualifies."

I couldn't help but notice that he seemed a lot more articulate than he had during our first meeting. Perhaps he, too, had been playing a role all along. Given the enmity his father obviously held for him, that probably wasn't a terrible idea.

But that aside, there was still the very real problem that he knew my secret. Perhaps he wasn't aware of how deep it went, but he knew enough to get me into a lot of trouble. I was prepared for the worst. In fact, I'd been paying attention to the guards and any other potential combatants ever since I'd arrived in Bayou La Batre, so I thought I had a good picture of the threat. However, that didn't mean I liked my chances against an entire town's worth of people. Or what I'd have to become if I wanted to escape with my life. I didn't fancy the notion of killing hundreds of people, regardless of whether or not it was necessary.

"What do you want?" I asked, taking a step back and letting him free. I kept my pistol out, but I chose to stop pointing it at him.

"Like I said, I figure there's only one reason someone with your skills would come here," he said. "You came from one of the other towns nearby, probably gathering information. Maybe assassination. I don't know, and I don't care. I just want out. This town, it's on its way out. In a few months, it'll be wiped off the face of the Earth. I'm sure of it."

"What makes you say that?" I asked, fishing for more information.

"Logic," Hadley stated. "I can see the writing on the wall. Those outsiders, they're going to figure it out sooner or later. They'll decide to cut out the middleman and deal directly with the shrimpers. When they do that, they won't need Momma or anybody else in Bayou La Batre. And the worst part is that the shrimpers will probably go right along with it because they'd be better off. Only reason it ain't already happened is 'cause Momma's got 'em wrapped around her little finger."

I thought about it for a second. It made sense, so long as the situation was as he described. I'd have to verify it, so my plans really hadn't changed, but I was prepared to believe him on a provisional basis.

"Okay, let's say I believe you," I said. "And just for the sake of argument, let's assume that I can give you what you want. What are you offering?"

"That wasn't enough?" he asked, clearly misjudging the value of his information.

"Not even close," I said. I saw his eyes flick toward the door, and in the space of an instant, I had Ferdinand II aimed at his head again. "Nuh-uh-uh. Let's not get any ideas, alright? Ferdinand here is kind of jumpy. He hasn't gotten to let loose in a few days."

"Ferdinand?"

I waggled my gun at him.

"Wait, you named your gun Ferdinand?" he asked, his brow scrunching in surprise. "Really?"

"Ferdinand II, actually," I said. "He has a noble lineage. So, back to our little transaction. I want information. As much as you can give me on the Plant's layout. I want to know where security terminals are. I want to know about the guards. I want to know about those drones that are always flying around. Everything."

He looked conflicted as he asked, "Are you going to kill my mom?"

I shook my head, saying, "No. Not if I can help it. That's not my job."

"Fine," he said. "I can get you a schematic of the building, and I'll mark points of interest for you. Will that work?"

I nodded, then snagged a blank nano-chip from my arsenal implant. As I handed it over, I said, "Put everything on that. Now, sit still. I have to do something before you leave."

"W-what?" he asked, taking the chip.

I didn't answer. Instead, I opened the NuSkin flap on my wrist and dragged the retractable cord out. After that, I grabbed Hadley's head, tilted it to the side, and inserted the end into the port on the side of his neck. Hadley's muscles seized up as my skill went to work. A message flashed across my HUD:

Personal Interface (Hadley Lafontaine). Presence Detected. Defenses Found. Initiate Mistwalk?
[Yes] or [No]

I selected the affirmative option, then went to work on the complex set of puzzles that guarded his system. There were forty-two of them, all arranged in a constellation of nodes. The outer band, which was comprised of twenty-eight points, was easily bypassed by solving a series of puzzles that were rendered trivial by my increased Mind attribute as well as all the practice I'd put into training myself. However, the remaining fourteen were markedly more difficult, requiring an intense level of concentration my previous usage of the skill had yet to require. In a lot of ways, the challenge was invigorating, and each one I solved sent a jolt of endorphins coursing through my brain. Finally, I broke through the last barrier, and Hadley's system opened up to me.

That's when I enacted my plan, inserting a harmless, flashing-red icon that would appear at the top of his HUD. His optical implant wasn't as complex as my KIOI, probably due to the fact that he didn't have a [Cybernetic Interface] skill. Instead, he had to rely on something far less invasive. Luckily, that meant it was easy to trick via the access given to me by my [Mistwalker] skill.

During my training with Helen, my [Mistwalker] instructor, I had learned that a good Mistrunner—her label for what she did, not mine—wasn't defined by the systems she could infiltrate. Instead, according to her, the quality of a Mistrunner was determined by the Ghosts she had at her disposal. Ghosts, I'd gone on to learn, were programs designed to do specific things. From completely destroying an entire system to causing it to glitch randomly, there were as many Ghosts as there were nanites in the air. Because they were all unique to their creators, unshareable and unable to be copied.

That meant that I'd had to learn to create some basic ones myself. The result was a small collection of mostly harmless Ghosts, the one exception being a veritable time bomb that would glitch a person's cybernetics after a certain amount of time had passed. It still wasn't finished, but I felt like I was getting much closer to making it work. Either way, I didn't think that Ghost was appropriate, given that I didn't want to disable Hadley. I just wanted him to know that I could. The threat was the point.

Thus, I infected his system with a harmless Ghost that caused an ominous blinking light in his HUD. I called it the *Red Herring*.

I pulled my consciousness away from his system and retracted my access cord back into my wrist. Then, I slapped him across the face, which brought him back to the land of the living.

"W-what? What did you do? Oh God—what does that light mean?!" he half screamed, his voice quivering with panic. I almost laughed at how high-pitched it had gotten.

"That's my insurance," I said. "Do you know what a Mistrunner is, Hadley?"

He shook his head.

"Not surprising," I stated, putting Ferdinand II away in my arsenal implant. His eyes went wide when the weapon disappeared, and I could practically read his thoughts as he wondered just how much he'd underestimated me. "A Mistrunner is, for all intents and purposes, your worst fucking nightmare. It comes from an extremely rare skill, it lets me slide right into your system and do whatever I want. I can take things out. I can put things in. I can even read your history."

"T-that's not . . . that's not possible."

He looked so terrified that I wondered if he was going to wet himself. If he did, I'd have to clean it up, lest I be forced to explain to Erica why her floor had been coated with urine. I didn't look forward to that conversation.

"I assure you that it most definitely is," I said. "That little red light in the upper-right-hand corner of your HUD will serve as a reminder. If you do something I don't like, if you go and tell your mother what I am . . . well, let's just say you'll have a very, very bad day. So will whoever has to clean up your brain matter after your skull explodes."

"Y-you can't do that."

"I can," I said. "And I will. So, here's what's going to happen. You're going to get me that information I need. In the meantime, I'm going to do what I'd already planned to do today. I'll find you tonight, and we'll figure out what we're going to do after that."

"Uh . . ."

I slapped him again, just for good measure. It felt pretty good. I have to admit, but it also made me feel a bit like a bully. After all, he had no defense against me if I chose to hurt him. And even less from his perspective, given that he thought I could explode his head with a thought. It was a little disturbing how addictive that kind of power was. Did that make me a sociopath? I hoped not.

"Got me?" I asked, pushing past those thoughts.

"I . . . uh . . . I understand," he said.

"Good," I said, patting him on the shoulder. He flinched. Maybe I had overdone it. "Now, run along. And try to act natural."

He nodded, then, after a couple of awkward seconds, left the house. I couldn't help but notice that whatever confidence he'd had was completely gone, and he looked a lot like a scurrying rodent.

Never mind that, I thought. I still had a lot to do.

So, after letting the ion washer finish, I was pleased to find that it was very effective. The bedding was spotless, and my clothing from the day before was only slightly stained. So, I redressed, made the bed, then left on my spear-hunting expedition. The guards at the gate recognized me quickly enough and waved me through, and once I was out in the woods, I stretched my Constitution attribute to its limit, sprinting through the forest. It was more of a workout than I expected, largely because the vegetation was so dense, but I made great progress, covering the ground in less than a third of the time it had taken Erica and me to cover the same distance the day before.

Predictably, when I reached the site of the fight against the cat, it had been picked clean by scavengers. However, the boar spear remained where I had dropped it. It was in pristine condition, too. The bow wasn't so lucky, and its string had snapped. Not surprising, considering the bow wasn't meant to remain strung.

Still, I gathered the bow and spear before setting off toward where I expected the boars to be. Sadly, even after a few hours of searching, I didn't find anything, so I turned back. By the time I returned to the village, the sun had already passed its zenith. Checking the time on my HUD, I was a little surprised to see that it was midafternoon.

After that, I went back to Erica's house, where I took one look at my poor attempt at rabbit stew and promptly ate one of my ration bars. It was supposed to taste like banana, but given that I'd actually had one of the fruits, I could see how far off the artificial flavoring really was. Still, it was filling. And it wasn't a mess of congealed fat and sketchy-looking vegetables. So, it had that going for it, at least.

With my belly full, I spent the rest of the afternoon wandering around the village. I thought of it as reconnaissance, but the reality was that I was just sightseeing. I was particularly interested in the shrimp boats that had just returned from a day of fishing, especially when I saw that one of them had a large gash along the side of its hull. Apparently, the tales I'd been told of sea monsters had not been exaggerated.

I sat on a nearby beach and watched as they pulled into port and started unloading the mounds of shrimp that were their catch. In Nova City, such a haul would have been worth a fortune, which told me all I really needed to know about how valuable a town like Bayou La Batre—or rather, the men and women who were experienced shrimpers—was. It lent credence to Hadley's supposition that, eventually, whoever was buying up all the shrimp would just cut out the middleman and take the town over.

As the sun set, I wondered if any of these towns would survive the Integration that was coming. My uncle had been sparse with details—I suspected he was more ignorant than he let on—but I knew that something big was coming. Something that would change the face of the Earth just as much as the Initialization had. I had a hard time believing Bayou La Batre, or any villages like it, would make it through such a tribulation.

I sat there well after night had fallen, my mind completely wrapped in speculation concerning the years to come. I was so engrossed in my own thoughts that I never saw the assassin aiming a dagger at my back.

CHAPTER THIRTY-FOUR

A LOVER'S QUARREL

I have lived a long life. Far longer than I ever thought possible. Even when I learned about Constitution's effects on the aging process, I never dreamed I would make it past a century. Sometimes, I wonder if my longevity was a blessing or a curse. I've outlived friends. Family. Lovers. I've watched them grow old, feeble, and sick. And all the while, I've remained the same. Healthy. Hearty. Hale. And whole. There are days when I wish it were otherwise.

—Jeremiah Braddock III

The knife had barely scraped my back when I reacted, reaching around and grabbing a slender wrist. I twisted, my own dagger appearing in my hand. The subtle blue energy of the nano-edge crackled in the night as I wrenched the assassin's arm and pressed a slim body into the sand, face-first. Kneeling on the small of the would-be assassin's back, I leaned close, my knife pressed against the pale flesh of a long neck.

I leaned close, hissing, "Who are you?"

"Lemme go!" came a feminine voice. The speaker sounded no older than a teenager. Beneath her black cap, I could see a few ringlets of strawberry blonde hair. "I'll cut you, bitch!"

"You're not cutting anything," I said, wrenching her arm and making her drop the knife. Still kneeling on the small of her back, I kept pressure on her captive arm. She struggled, but my grip was like iron, especially compared to hers. If she was more than a Tier 2, I would have been surprised, and her potential wasn't even close to fully developed. It was a good reminder of how far above the normal, everyday people I'd ascended.

But it took only one memory of Horace Lafontaine for me to remember that I was far from the top of the food chain. If some nobody from a hole-in-the-wall town like Bayou La Batre could give me so much trouble, how would I fare against the most powerful people in Nova City? Or even the Enforcers? It wouldn't be pretty, I was sure. They'd all had a lifetime of training to bolster their attributes and abilities, and while I'd made progress, I was still only just beginning my journey. Next to them, my potential meant nothing.

"I'm going to ask you again," I said, my voice even. It didn't reflect the pounding of my heart. "And remember, if you don't answer, I'm going to have to break your arm. So—who are you?"

"F-fuck you!" she spat.

"Wrong answer" was my calm reply. Then, I broke her arm. She screamed, but I used my leverage to push her face into the sand, muffling the sound. With the lapping of the waves and our distance from the nearest structure, I was sure that nobody would've heard it. After a few long seconds, her screams turned into sobs, and I grabbed the hair on the back of her head and dragged her face out of the sand. I asked her again, "Who are you?"

"M-my name . . . m-m-my name . . . is . . . Kacie," she sobbed. "P-please . . . d-don't hurt me . . . n-no more . . ."

I let out a subaudible groan and rolled my eyes. She was probably just a kid, and a stupid one at that. The smart thing to do would've been just to kill her, tie some heavy rocks to her body, and toss it all into the ocean where it would be eaten by crabs and other sea-born scavengers. But she was just so helpless. Her attack, as much as it had surprised me, had been ill aimed, and even if I'd let it land, it wouldn't have done much more than cause a bit of pain. I was never in mortal danger because she clearly didn't know what she was doing.

I focused a bit, and when I concentrated on her tier, which felt like it was somewhere in the middle of Tier 2, I felt even more like a bully. Sure, she'd tried to kill me, but it was like being bitten by a puppy. Without teeth. And with atrophied jaw muscles. She was harmless. Kimiko's granddaughter, Elie, would've posed more of a threat. At least she could've taken me down with weaponized cuteness.

So, I climbed off of her and said, "Get up. Now. Or I'll break your other arm."

It might've made me feel even more like a bully, but she had tried to kill me. Sure, it never would have worked, but she didn't know that. I think that entitled me to be a little harsh. Kacie scrambled to her feet, whimpering the whole time, and when she faced me, I saw that she was around my age, scrawny, and with a pale, freckled complexion. She wore a pair of denim shorts that were far too short and a tank top that she'd cut off just below her chest. The only concession she'd made to stealth was to cover her strawberry blonde hair with a black cap.

Snot trickled down her upper lip, and wet tears coated her cheeks as she cradled her broken arm.

"So—why did you try to stab me, Kacie?" I asked, casually holding my own dagger. I saw her eyes flick toward her weapon, which was still in the sand. It was a pitiful thing, poorly forged from bad metal, and it looked as if it hadn't been sharpened in years. She'd probably found it in some disused kitchen.

"'Cause you're tryin' to take my man!" she hissed, her voice cracking with another sob as she disturbed her broken arm. "He's mine, bitch! I won't let you take him!"

I narrowed my eyes. "What the hell are you talking about?" I asked, completely at a loss.

"Don't try to lie to me," she spat. "I seent you with him. He was in your house for, like, an hour!"

"My house?" I asked. Then, it hit me like a brick. "Oh. You're with Hadley."

"So, you admit it, slut?!" she growled, a feral gleam to her eye. For a moment, I thought she was going to launch herself at me. She had no weapons and only one arm, but in that moment, she seemed more like a wild animal than a rational human being. Thankfully, the pain of her broken arm chose that moment to assert itself, which saved me from having to do something I was sure I would instantly regret.

"I didn't do anything with him," I said. "We made a deal about . . . some things I need to do my job. That's all there was to it."

"And what's your job?" she demanded.

I let out a long-suffering sigh, then rolled my eyes. "How old are you, anyway? Hadley's what? At least twenty. You look like you're no older than fifteen."

"I'm eighteen!" she screeched. "Just 'cause I'm little doesn't mean I'm—"

"Fine, fine!" I said. "You're a big girl. Now, can you shut up? I don't want to have to kill you if I can help it."

That definitely closed her mouth. Until then, I think she had considered it something of a game, if a dangerous one. Given her actions, she clearly wasn't a stranger to fighting other girls. Probably winning, too, considering how she'd come after me. But even after I'd broken her arm, she obviously had not thought of herself as being in mortal danger.

"Look," I said, trying to regulate my tone. "I really, really don't want to cut your throat, okay? But I will. Don't think I won't. So, here's the deal—you're coming with me, and we're going to get this whole thing sorted out. Once that's done, I'm going to leave you to Hadley. But if I think you're a liability . . ."

I left the threat hanging in the air because I knew it would be far more effective than if I'd said what I was thinking. Kacie didn't seem too thrilled about the prospect, but after only a few seconds, she gave her consent. It was a little earlier than I'd intended to find Hadley, but with my new baggage, I didn't want to sit around and wait any longer. So, with my hand wrapped around the other girl's slender upper arm, we set off back into the village, intending to find him.

Thankfully, it didn't take long before I saw him loitering in a dark alley. Even more fortunately, Bayou La Batre had anything but a thriving nightlife. Like was common in many small towns—from what I'd been told—life ground to a halt once the sun went down. There were still some stragglers out and about, but they were either drunk or too engrossed in their own thoughts to pay much attention to a pair of harmless-looking girls. If they only knew how much devastation I could cause, they would've reacted far differently.

In any case, as soon as I saw Hadley fidgeting nervously in the alley, we crossed the muddy street and stepped into the cover of darkness provided by the narrow space. When he saw that there were two of us, his eyes widened in alarm that soon turned to confusion when he recognized my unwilling companion.

"Kacie? What are you doing here?" he demanded.

"Don't you take that tone with me!" she said, proving that she really only had one mode of communication that boiled down to various volumes of screeching. "I seen you go in her house, Had. She says it ain't what I thought, but I want to hear it from you. You cheatin' on me?"

"Uh . . . no," he said. "But you really shouldn't be here."

As he said it, he glanced at me, panic plain on his face. Doubtless, he was worried about how I was going to react.

"Why not?" the girl demanded, jutting her jaw out and cradling her broken arm. I knew it must've been agonizing, but she kept it well hidden. Maybe there was a bit more steel in her than I'd first thought.

"Because I'm leaving, Kacie," he said. "Soon. I'm not . . . I can't . . . I wish you could come with me, but—"

"Okay."

"What?" he asked, obviously surprised by her interruption. I wasn't. I saw it coming a mile away.

"I want to come with you," she said.

He glanced at me, asking, "Uh . . . is that . . . okay?"

It really wasn't, but on the other hand, I didn't have much of a choice in the matter. Sure, I could just kill them both as soon as we left town, but that didn't really appeal to me. I'd kill if I had to, but my uncle's advice hung heavy in my mind. Killing couldn't be my first option.

"Fine," I said. "So long as you've got what I asked you to get."

He nodded, then handed over the chip. I inspected it and, when I saw that nothing was out of the ordinary, slotted the thing. A smile spread across my face as I saw a detailed schematic of the building, complete with security terminals, access points, and camera locations. But there was one major problem.

"Your mother controls the drones?" I asked.

"It's . . . it's one of her skills," Hadley said, running his hand through his wild hair. "Something called [Drone Pilot]. She can control up to fifteen at a time."

"Crap," I said, glancing back out into the road.

That news really put a kink in my plans. Unless I could deal with those drones, I wasn't getting into that building undetected. Unless . . . no. It couldn't be that simple, could it? But last time I'd gone there, I'd just walked right in. Nobody had stopped me. Most barely even noticed me. If I could replicate that, then slip off to one of the security terminals, I wouldn't have to worry about the drones at all.

"Hadley, you go to that building all the time, don't you?" I asked.

He nodded. "Yeah. Why?" he said.

"Well, we're going down there right now," I said. "When we get inside, I'm going to hit the first security terminal I can find, download the information I need, then we're out of here."

"Uh . . . that's not going to work," he said. "You didn't read the whole file, did you? There's nothing on most of those terminals. Just basic, low-level stuff. Anything worth taking is going to be on the one in momma's office."

"Which I'm guessing she doesn't leave all that often."

"She doesn't," he said. "But . . . well, if I . . . I mean . . . I could probably get her out of there. I just need to give her a reason."

"And? What are you thinking?"

He didn't answer me. Instead, he glanced at Kacie, who had remained silent during our conversation. The adrenaline of the situation had started to wear off, and her arm was probably on fire. She bore it well, but there was only so much she could do without a skill to help her out. Not for the first time, I found myself thankful for [Combat Utility] and all the useful abilities that had come with it.

"Uh . . . Kacie? Do you want to get married?" he asked.

"W-what?" she blurted, her eyes widening. "Did you just propose?"

"I didn't want you to get involved, but now that you are . . ."

"Are you just askin' me to marry you 'cause you need me to do somethin'?" she demanded. I could practically hear the shriek building in the back of her throat. If Hadley said the wrong thing . . . well, it didn't bear thinking about until it actually happened. I hoped he was smarter than that.

"No!" he insisted, holding up his hands. "I just . . . I didn't want you to get hurt is all. And . . . and . . . but I've always loved you. Ever since we were little. You know that. Now, I want to get married. And . . . I guess if the announcement gets momma out of that building for the night, it'll help . . . uh . . . Mirabelle out, too. And us! Us, too! The sooner she gets what she needs, the sooner we can get out of town and start our new life in the big city."

Big city was kind of subjective, I supposed. Mobile was barely more than a village, but compared to Bayou La Batre, I guess the categorization was appropriate enough.

"Oh, Had!" she said, throwing her arm around him. She grunted when he touched the shoulder of her injured arm, but she didn't pull away. Perhaps they really did care about each other. After all, she'd tried to kill me just for talking to her man. That took love, didn't it? Or something like it, at least.

Or maybe it was just desperation. After all, in a small town like Bayou La Batre, there probably weren't a lot of choices. Perhaps Hadley was the most eligible bachelor in town, if for no other reason than a current lack of options. Either way, Kacie didn't seem to care.

After the pair of them settled down, we developed a plan. Hadley would first take Kacie to the doctor, where she would get her arm patched up and splinted. Once that was finished, they would head over to tell Savanna about their engagement. If everything went the way it was supposed to, the trio would sit down for a meal at the village's lone restaurant, which doubled as a saloon. Hadley seemed to think that it was a given that that was where they would end up, but I was a bit skeptical.

Whatever the case, the plan was set, and they went on their way. As they did so, I headed across the village to plant myself in the back alley where I'd spent most of a night observing the building. It was much the same as I remembered it, with various boats coming and going into the night, stopping only to have crates unloaded, which were soon replaced by huge baskets of shrimp. It was a well-practiced system, and I was actually a little impressed with their efficiency.

An hour and a half later, Hadley strode into the building, Kacie on his arm. I tensed up. If they were going to betray me, now would be the time. In only a few minutes, I could be facing down a dozen drones and even more angry fighters. I definitely didn't want that. Not only was it counter to my mission— I was gathering information, not assaulting the enemy position—but, in my mind, the people of Bayou La Batre had been humanized. They weren't just some faceless enemy. They were just people struggling to get by as best they could. Even Savanna, whom I'd been prepared to hate, was just doing what was right by her people.

Sure, she'd sent her sons to murder innocent people and I wouldn't forget that, but I could at least understand her motivations well enough not to hate her for what she had done. Maybe that was naive of me. I don't know, and I was in no position to examine those feelings. Instead, I watched, waiting for Hadley to escort Kacie and his mother out of the building. And sure enough, only twenty minutes later, they did just that, all three of them looking to be in good spirits. That only served to humanize them even more, and I found myself hoping against hope that I wouldn't have to kill them.

I waited for about twenty more minutes before I made my move. Avoiding the three drones I could see, I quickly crossed the muddy street to the front of the building. Without pausing, I passed through the door like I was meant to be there. My heart was pounding out of my chest as I nodded at one of the workers, giving him a tight smile. When he returned it, I almost let out a whoop of excitement, but I managed to contain myself. Barely.

The interior of the building was much as I remembered, with the first floor taking the form common to most warehouses. Workers swarmed here and there, but they were all busy enough that most of them didn't even notice me as I made my way to the stairs at the back of the building. Even when I mounted them, the busy men and women kept their minds—and more importantly, their eyes—on their tasks.

Boldly, I walked toward Savanna's office. I had just begun to think I was going to make it without any difficulties when I heard a familiar voice behind me say, "Stop. What are you doin' here, girl?"

I stopped in my tracks, then turned to see Burton, the hulking butcher, standing on the catwalk behind me. How he'd approached me without the sound betraying his presence was a mystery. Briefly, I thought about making some excuse; perhaps I could reason with him. But when he smiled, his gold teeth glittering in the building's fluorescent light, I knew that wasn't an option.

"You really want to do this here?" I asked.

He reached behind him, his massive arm far more flexible than I expected, and yanked a cleaver out of a sheath on his back. It was still bloody.

"Yeah," he said. "I kinda do."

I sighed, mourning the death of my plan. "Fine," I said. Then, I pulled my Kicker out of my arsenal implant and fired two rounds. The first went wide, crashing into one of the windows that lined the top of the outer wall. The other found his head.

It exploded, and I dismissed the weapon back from whence it had come. It all happened in the space of a second, and by the time Burton tumbled off the catwalk, I was already channeling my inner Kacie with an earsplitting shriek. "Assassin! Somebody shot Mr. Burton!" I screamed. "Help!"

CHAPTER THIRTY-FIVE

A DESPERATE ESCAPE

There are almost always an endless number of ways to solve any problem, but killing is usually the easiest.

—Jeremiah Braddock III

I sank to the metal balcony, curling in on myself in an attempt to look as devastated as possible. It was a split-second decision built around my desire to leave some of the villagers alive. Even as I watched Burton's hulking body tumbling over the edge to fall to the floor far beneath us, I wondered if my ruse would work. The shot I'd fired at the window hadn't been a miss. Instead, it was intended to set the scene of the assassination I'd just staged. The idea was simple—I would pretend that, while I was talking to Burton, someone had shot through the window and taken him out. And I was banking on my low level of apparent power and a distinct lack of weaponry to support my act.

I was taking a chance, though, and I knew it. The balcony wasn't the ideal place to take a stand, but it wasn't horrible, either. Though it didn't provide the cover I'd have hoped for, the elevation would allow me to pick off any attackers without much issue. Choosing not to take that route was a risk, but one I could wholeheartedly commit to. The people of Bayou La Batre were just people, not some great enemy that needed to be exterminated. In fact, aside from their obvious poverty, they weren't so different from the people back in Mobile. Or Nova City, come to that. No—I wouldn't engage in wholesale slaughter unless it was absolutely necessary for my survival. I'd gotten to know the people too well to go down that route.

Soon enough, the pounding of boots on metal stairs announced the arrival of a pair of Operators. One was male, while the other was female, though they looked similar enough that, initially, I had trouble telling them apart. Both were bulky, with short hair and squashed-looking faces, and I'd have been surprised if they weren't twins. The man knelt beside me, demanding, "What happened?!"

I stammered, "I . . . I don't know. I was just . . . I was just going to see Miss Savanna. And . . . then, Mr. Burton came up behind me, and . . . and . . . I heard a gunshot . . ."

For effect, I let my eyes wander to Burton's headless body, which was unmoving on the building's floor. It had already attracted a crowd. I mumbled, "Oh God . . . oh God! He's . . . h-he's dead!"

The man growled, "Pull yourself together, girl."

"Have some sympathy, Rock," said the woman, pushing him aside to kneel beside me. Her voice was strangely soothing, completely at odds with her rough appearance. The both of them were Tier 2, if my senses were anything to go by. They weren't always perfect, but ever since attaining my first level, I'd been able to get a sense for other people's relative power. Usually, I took it for granted, but after coming to Bayou La Batre, I'd begun to realize just how useful the inherent ability really was.

And given that everyone there overlooked me, I had become well aware of just how easily fooled the pseudo-ability was, as well. Idly, I wondered if there were skills with actual abilities that might cut through my Disguise ability, which was what let me conceal my true power. Probably. Even Hadley could tell that something was off, though he couldn't exactly see past the effects of the ability itself.

"Are you okay?" asked the woman, her hand on my shoulder.

Eyes downcast, I sobbed, "I . . . I . . . I didn't . . . It just happened so fast."

That's when the woman saw where I was looking and said, "Oh. Let's get her somewhere else, Rock. Miss Savanna won't mind if we use her office."

My heartbeat sped up as Rock said, "We ain't s'posed to go in there."

"I don't care," the big woman said, already dragging me to my feet. I made sure to feign unsteadiness as I clutched at her beefy arm. "Don't go lookin' down there, okay? Ain't nothin' good gonna come of it."

I tore my eyes from the grisly scene down below, but my heartbeat continued to race as she led me into Savanna's office. It hadn't gone exactly as I had expected, but I couldn't complain about the results. My goal had been to get to the leader's office—or more accurately, her terminal—and now, it seemed as if I was going to get free rein.

Once we were inside the familiar room, I hung my head, but I managed to get a good look out of the corner of my eye. Savanna's personal terminal was within arm's reach—a simple box, maybe six or seven inches wide and half as deep, embedded into the desk. I knew from my training and experiences in Nova City that sanctioned terminals functioned on their own wavelengths of Mist and were wholly impenetrable, except via a hard connection. In essence, they were similar to the implants that gave people access to skills, except with a focus on storing information rather than unlocking the potential of a body infused with Mist.

Either way, as soon as I was alone, I could get down to doing what I'd come to Bayou La Batre to do. Certainly, I'd learned a lot about how to blend into a population, but ultimately, I knew that my trip was more than just the test it had been made out to be. My uncle—or more likely, the people in Mobile—needed the information in that terminal. I had no idea what they would do with it, but then again, I didn't need to know. For now, I was just a cog in their machine.

After getting me settled into the chair behind Savanna's desk, the woman said, "My name is Teri. What's yours?"

"M-Mirabelle," I said, adding a little sniffle at the end. Already, tears were flowing down my cheeks. "I . . . is he okay?"

"Who?" asked Teri.

The man, who I assumed was her twin brother, gave a snort at that, which earned him a glare from Teri. He shrugged his shoulders, saying, "What? Nobody here actually liked Burt. He was an asshole, and I'm sure plenty of people will be happy he's gone. Besides, it was a stupid question. His head was exploded."

Before Teri could berate him, I said, "Oh. He was nice to me."

Teri looked at me like I'd just revealed the most surprising thing in the world. "Burt wasn't nice to nobody," she said.

"He was to me."

Rock started to say something, but Teri cut him off. As she rose, she said, "We need to go make sure whoever did this is gone. You okay in here?"

I nodded, saying, "I . . . I guess."

"Good," Teri said, already moving. Her brother followed her, shutting the door behind him. Like that, I'd gotten exactly what I'd needed, and I wasted no time in retrieving the cord from my wrist and jacking into the terminal's port.

Secure Terminal:
[Enter Password] or [Mistwalk]

Without a password, I had no choice but to initiate a Mistwalk. The moment I did, I felt a sharp pain in the base of my skull. I gasped, but I didn't lose my concentration. Instead, I focused on the series of nodes in front of me. There were far more than I'd ever seen before, and when I counted them, I saw that there were sixty-four points I needed to conquer before the terminal's security fell. Knowing I didn't have a lot of time, I immediately dove into the first and was relieved to see that the puzzles weren't more than I could handle. The first one fell after six minutes and forty-two seconds, which was quite a long time, considering how much I'd practiced Mistwalking in the past few months.

It didn't matter, though. I still had sixty-three to go.

Over the next forty-five minutes, I solved one puzzle after the next. Some consisted of simple logic chains, while others required full-blown mathematical proofs before they fell. Even so, I persisted, crashing through each obstacle until, at last, the system was laid bare before me. Cognizant of my time constraints, I quickly started downloading the system's contents, sequestering them into a specially constructed, quarantined section of my implant.

During training, I had made the mistake of downloading some information without partitioning it into its own section, and because of the Ghost my instructor had planted within it, I'd had to deal with a migraine as well as a weakening of my skills for the next week. After arduously purging the malicious Ghost from my implant, I had vowed not to make that same mistake again. So, I'd spent quite a lot of time partitioning a bit of my implant's storage capacity and cutting it off from the rest of my system. It was hard work, but I'd learned the necessity firsthand. If Helen had truly intended me harm, I could have been permanently incapacitated.

Never again.

By the time I finished, almost an hour had passed, and I kept eyeing the door, expecting to see Savanna or one of her mooks returning to either check on me or finish me off, depending on the results of their investigation. When none of them came, I realized that I didn't have any other reason to remain in Bayou La Batre. So, I got up and casually walked out of the office. The scene I found was a little less than ideal.

"Who are you?" came a voice from the catwalk that cut across the building. I blinked in confusion as I saw Savanna standing there, four drones hovering above her, and her son at her feet. He was battered and bruised, with blood dripping from multiple wounds. I couldn't help but notice that the drones were combat models.

"W-what?" I asked, clinging to my role. However, as I spoke, I embraced my arsenal implant and focused on my Kicker. With only a thought, it could be in my hands in a fraction of a second.

"Did you think we were stupid?" the portly woman demanded, tears streaming down her face. She kicked Hadley in the ribs. "Did you think I wouldn't find out that you'd turned my boy against me? That you killed my Burt-Burt? Who are you? Tell me, and I'll make your death quick."

I knew the jig was up. I had been found out. What I didn't know was if my sloppy killing of Burton—or Burt-Burt, as she'd called him—had been discovered or if someone like Hadley, Erica, or Kacie, all of whom knew far too much, had squealed. But regardless of how she'd figured it all out, the fact was that I needed an exit plan, and fast.

A quick glance down below, and I saw that there were dozens of mooks aiming their weapons at me. Some, I recognized from my previous trips through the building, but others were completely unfamiliar. I wasn't worried about most of them. However, there were a couple that looked like outsiders, identifiable by their higher-quality cybernetics and better weapons. From so far away, I couldn't gauge their strength, but something told me that they wouldn't be the pushovers Savanna's people would be.

"I'm going to offer you the same deal," I said, discarding my role completely. I knew I couldn't really cut an intimidating figure. Maybe if I had a mask. Or a nice hooded cloak. But for someone like Savanna, who had seen me clearly, intimidation just wasn't in the cards. So, I chose to rely on the truth. Raising my voice, I announced, "I really don't want to kill any of you. But if you make me, you'd better believe that I won't hesitate to do what's necessary."

The older woman cocked her head to the side and asked, "Are you threatening us? We got you surrounded. The building's locked down tighter than a newt's ass. You ain't gettin' out of her, little girl. The only question is how much pain you're in when you die. Now, answer my goddamn question."

The last bit was said in a menacing growl, and I knew I'd used up what time I had. So, I didn't waste a second before summoning my rifle and taking aim at one of the drones. One burst. Two bursts. Three. Two of the mechanical constructs fell from the sky, and one of them exploded. Savanna screeched in pain—maybe that was part of the skill that let her control them so completely—before the last drone opened fire. A buzz saw of gunshots filled the air, but I was already diving back into the office. I took a shot in my calf, but it only hit meat. It hurt, but it didn't lose much in the way of functionality.

I rolled back to a kneeling position and pressed myself against the wall. Luckily, I had seen a couple of gunshots hit the barrier, so I knew it could hold up and would offer decent cover. Taking a deep breath, I leaned out, but I was quickly greeted by another hail of gunfire.

With a sigh, I reconfigured my weapon into its sniper form, then leaned out and fired a shot directly at Savanna. Originally, I hadn't wanted to kill her. In fact, I was trying to avoid it at all costs. But I knew she had many more drones at her disposal, so if I wanted to make a proper retreat, I needed to cut the head off the proverbial snake. For all that I wanted to avoid it, she needed to die.

The bullet tore through the air, but just before it ripped a hole in her head, it hit a blue shield. The energy rippled, but it held. However, my skills weren't just for show, and that, combined with my high-grade rifle, meant that my shots were incredibly powerful. And even with a personal shield, momentum could be a pain in the ass to deal with.

Savanna was sent tumbling backward, and I took aim at the next drone, destroying it with a well-placed shot.

I was already sprinting forward before the drone hit the ground. As I ran, my heavy footfalls threatening to dislodge the balcony, I stowed my rifle. A hail of gunfire, arrows, and even a couple of thrown rocks followed me as I traversed the balcony, then leaped toward the window I'd shattered during the confrontation with Burton. It was already cracked and sported a decently sized hole, but I still knew my plan was going to hurt.

I hit it shoulder first and broke through, slowed by only the slightest of resistance before tumbling along the rusty roof made of corrugated metal. I skidded to a stop just as another pair of drones homed in on me, sending even more gunfire my way. I rolled to the side, but the roof was devoid of cover, so I still took a shot to my shoulder and another to my lower back. Thankfully, it missed my spine. I wasn't certain whether my Constitution could heal a severed spine, nor did I have any desire to find out firsthand.

Leaving a trail of smeared blood, I continued to roll until I hit the edge of the roof. Then, I fell, grabbing the edge of the building just in time to arrest my fall. My fingers, slippery with blood, weren't up to the task. After only an instant, my grip failed, and I fell the rest of the way. Fortunately, the building was only a couple of stories tall, so my legs were more than capable of absorbing the impact.

It still hurt, though.

Whipping my head back and forth, I took stock of the situation. With a thought, I summoned the Kicker and shouldered the weapon as I'd been taught. Then, I crept along the edge of the building until I reached the corner. Once there, I leaned out of cover, taking a quick mental snapshot of the scene before pulling back.

And it wasn't good.

There were dozens of men and women in the area, and they were coming my way. I wanted to avoid a wholesale massacre, but it was quickly becoming clear that I might not get what I wanted. That's when I looked behind me and saw the harbor.

There were a dozen huge shrimping boats at the dock, but beyond that was open water. My training had included spending quite a lot of time swimming, so I was confident in that arena. But I also knew that the ocean was home to a host of dangerous monsters. During training, I'd had one of the capable Amigos looking over my shoulder, making sure that I wouldn't be swallowed by a giant alligator or attacked by other vicious aquatic predators. If I did what I was thinking of doing, I wouldn't have that kind of safety net. I would be at the mercy of whatever horrible monsters the ocean could throw at me. But it was that or rip my way through a bunch of people whom I really didn't want to kill, and for a wide variety of reasons.

Killing would have been a much easier path to tread.

Most of the people I had encountered in Bayou La Batre were, at best, Tier 3, and there were only a few of those. The outsiders I'd glimpsed in the building were probably at that level, and they would be more difficult to take out, but I could easily kill enough of them to make my escape.

Then what, though? Was I going to solve every problem by killing people? It would get easier every time, too. I knew it would. My uncle had intimated as much. And where would I draw the line? Ten people? Twenty? A hundred? With my potential, the number could be far, far higher.

More than that, though, I'd been in Bayou La Batre for a few days. I'd met some of those people. I'd talked to them. I'd stopped looking at them as an enemy to be subdued, instead putting them in the same category as the people of Mobile. They were just trying to get by.

Once, I'd thought it a simple problem, not so dissimilar from the logic puzzles I so often completed. If someone tried to kill me, I'd kill them before they had the chance to follow through. The same went for anyone who attempted to hurt my friends or family. I had already chosen a side, especially after what had happened at that farm. The image of that tiny man ripping through those civilians wasn't one I would soon forget. I hated him for what he'd done, and initially, I'd chosen to paint all the residents of Bayou La Batre with that same brush. My short time in the village had put the lie to that categorization, though, and I'd come to realize that it was far more complicated than that. This wasn't a simple black-and-white issue where I could easily label someone an ally or an enemy.

All of that raced through my head over the course of a few seconds, and I quickly made up my mind. So, without further hesitation, I turned and sprinted toward the dock, my injuries slowing me only a little. By the time I reached the wooden platforms, the pursuit had caught up to me, and the sound of gunshots filled the air. Wood splintered behind me as I tore down the dock, and when I reached the end, I dove into the water. Kicking out, I used every point of my enhanced Constitution to propel me into deeper water.

As I did, bullets rained down on me, rendered harmless by the dozen feet of salty water. I kept swimming for a few minutes, putting ever more distance between my position and the village. After fifteen minutes, I finally surfaced, only to see that I had gone much farther than I expected. Land was only barely visible in the distance, and no pursuit dogged my path.

I had escaped.

But now, I had to worry about finding my way back to shore—and avoiding the monsters I knew dwelled within the sea. As if to highlight my plight, I felt something brush against my leg. I let out a slight yelp, but I forced myself to remain calm. Panic wouldn't help anyone.

That was all well and good, and it lasted right up until I felt something slimy wrap itself around my waist and drag me down into the water.

CHAPTER THIRTY-SIX

SACRIFICE

Once upon a time, being alone in the wilderness was a terrifying thing. But as civilization reared its ugly head, nature's sharp edge was blunted. The onset of the Mist once again changed that, bringing it back to the natural order. Once again, we have come to fear the world around us.

—Jeremiah Braddock III

Fire coursed through my veins as every nerve in my body was set alight. The agony, heedless of my Pain Tolerance, was nearly overwhelming, and as I was dragged deeper into the ocean, panic overcame rational thought. After a few seconds, though, Combat Focus came into play, and I regained enough of my wits to realize that I wasn't so much being squeezed by tentacles as I was entangled in a forest of stinging tendrils. And with every thrashing movement, I became further trapped.

It took every ounce of willpower I possessed to stop moving, to reassess my situation, and react accordingly. Somehow—probably with the help of my abilities—I managed to summon my nano-edged sword and start cutting. Every movement resulted in a cascade of agony, but I was already in so much pain that a little more didn't matter. In the past, I had been able to sink within myself and ignore pain as I put one foot in front of the other. But this was different. This agony was so all-encompassing, so insistent, that all I could do was embrace it.

And I did. Somewhere in the back of my mind where all reason had fled, I knew I couldn't escape the pain. The only way out was through, so I marshalled those stray rational thoughts and bent my will to doing just that. My blade sliced through water and tendril alike, its subtly glowing blue edge making easy work of the forest of tentacles.

The creature—and it was a monster, I was sure of it—reacted in kind. Suddenly, electric shocks arced through the tendrils, sending my muscles into spasms that almost made me drop my sword. But I held fast, redoubling my efforts at cutting myself free.

I don't know how long I bent myself to that task, but by the time I swam free, descending deep into the murky water, the pain had faded into a dull numbness and my rational mind had retreated before the sheer weight of my fight-or-flight instincts. When I was twenty or thirty feet down, I glanced up to see the monster that had attacked me.

Above me was a canopy of glowing blue tendrils, blanketing the surface in every direction and casting the water in what, in another situation, might have been a pleasant light. Throughout that tangle were corpses of fish and other sea life unfortunate enough to have found themselves in its grasp.

And at the center of it all was a bulbous mass of translucent flesh. At least fifteen feet across, it had a massive striated crest peeking just above the water, and the entire thing glowed with malevolent blue energy. If I hadn't been running so low on oxygen, I would have gaped at the monstrous thing, but as it was, if I wanted to escape its clutches, I needed to get moving.

Pushing the lingering cramps and stinging pain to the back of my mind, I kicked my legs. With my enhanced Constitution, each kick propelled me through the water as quickly as a normal person could run on dry land. On top of that, it gave me the ability to hold my breath far longer than should have been possible. The combination of the two gave me just enough of an advantage to escape the area dominated by the monster's deadly tendrils.

I don't know how far I swam, but by the time I resurfaced, the shore was little more than a thin, slightly darker strip on the horizon. Without my HUD's map and the compass that had come with it, I felt certain that I wouldn't have even noticed it in the scant silver light of the moon.

Treading water, I gulped air, thanking my uncle for pushing me into such a rigorous training program. Without it, I would have been dead a hundred times over. Not only had he given me the willpower to drag myself through that sea of stinging agony, but he had also forced me to develop my Constitution to the point where I had the means of escape. For the thousandth time since my Awakening, I had to acknowledge that my uncle knew what he was doing. Going forward, I would devote myself even more fully to the training regimen he prescribed.

But first, I needed to get to shore and take stock of my injuries. So, angling myself to the northeast, I swam toward land. In the distance, I saw the lights of Bayou La Batre, but my path would only take me farther away. For a moment, I considered going back for Hadley and Kacie, but it didn't take me long to discard that notion. Sure, Hadley had helped me, but judging by how badly he had been beaten, he had screwed up somehow. Or maybe he had betrayed me the moment things got hairy. I had no way of knowing, but I didn't think I owed him—or Kacie, who'd been dead set on killing me not that long ago—anything. Even if I could get in without being seen, which was a tall order, considering that, even in the dark, I could see Savanna's drones swarming around the village, I had no way of getting either of them out. The bottom line was that, even if they were healthy and hale, they would slow me down way too much. Their injuries further exacerbated that impossibility to the point where I'd have been a fool to even try.

It was one of those situations my uncle had so often warned me about. Was going back for Hadley the right thing to do? It probably was. But sometimes, doing the right thing had to take a back seat to doing what was necessary. Or maybe I was just making excuses so I wouldn't have to acknowledge my guilty conscience. Either way, my decision was made, and I continued the long swim to shore.

While I did, I flinched at every piece of seaweed, thinking that the tendriled monster had returned. But fortunately, it didn't seem to be hunting me. In fact, I wasn't entirely sure if the thing had a means of locomotion because during my brief observation, it hadn't moved at all, save for drifting in the current.

Not for the first time, I cursed my ignorance. Like all children in Nova City, I'd attended school, but my education had been woefully inadequate, aside from basics like reading, writing, and arithmetic. The history lessons had already proved themselves to be inaccurate, and what I'd been taught about zoology had been completely inaccurate. With a little distance, I understood the reasoning. Kids who grew up in Nova City would likely never leave, and so, they didn't need to know those things. Still, it rankled my nerves, knowing just how ill prepared I was for the wildlands outside of the city.

In an effort to distract myself from the pain still coursing through my body, I focused on such thoughts. It worked passably well, and soon, I had dragged myself ashore. When I was completely free of the salty water, I flipped onto my back and just lay there for a long few minutes, catching my breath. As I did, the full weight of my injuries pressed down on me.

Not only had I sustained whatever damage those tendrils had wrought, but I'd also been shot a couple of times. Again. That was definitely a habit I needed to break. Eventually, one of those bullets was going to hit something vital, and when that happened . . .

I didn't even want to think about taking a gutshot in the middle of a fight, and if a bullet found my heart or head, that would be the end. Probably. I was still a little fuzzy on how much my enhanced Constitution affected my durability, and I wasn't all that eager to test things out.

Either way, as I lay on that beach, I stared up at the night sky, thankful I'd made it out alive. The escape from Bayou La Batre had been difficult enough on its own, but tangling with that sea creature had hammered home precisely how far I still had to go. If random wildlife was that deadly, how strong would the aliens be after the Integration? More, what about people like my uncle? Or the Amigos? Or the Enforcers back in Nova City? Surely, they'd had all the best opportunities to enhance their power.

After a while, I dragged myself to my feet and fled into the nearby wilderness. The tree line came right up to the edge of the beach, so I soon found myself under the canopy of the semitropical forest. The ever-present kudzu, as well as the gloomy darkness, made traversal slow and difficult and the constant backtracking I did to disguise my trail made it worse. When I found a stream or a creek, I followed it for a few hundred yards before leaving it behind, hoping that it would throw off any pursuer that might stumble across the evidence of my passage. It wasn't perfect—Jorge would've called my efforts barely passable—but in my condition, it was the best I could do.

Hours later, just before the sun rose, I stumbled across an abandoned building. Due to the creeping vines that covered most of the walls and the collapse of the roof, I had no idea what the purpose of the building had been, but to me, all that mattered was that it was devoid of any signs of wildlife and the sturdy brick walls were still intact. So, after making certain the building wasn't home to some vicious monster, I settled down to make camp. More importantly, I needed to inspect my wounds.

Once I'd barricaded the lone door, I undressed and looked at my arms and legs, which were covered in angry red welts from the tangle of tendrils that had ensnared me. I had no idea how to treat such injuries, so I used a med-hypo to bolster my immune system and cleaned them as best I could with a disinfecting solution I had in my arsenal implant. Then, I turned my attention to the gunshot wound in my calf. Fortunately, though it had taken a good chunk of my calf with it, it hadn't hit the bone. So, it was a simple task to disinfect it before applying a foam bandage. Hopefully, it wouldn't scar too badly.

As I worked on my other various wounds, the effects of Combat Focus began to fade. Pain Tolerance was still in effect, but the sheer volume of stimuli I'd been subjected to had overwhelmed the ability to such an extent that, without the calm granted by Combat Focus, I would have long since fallen. With it fading a little more by the passing minute, I had a hard time keeping my mind on the task at hand.

But I managed to keep my wits about me just long enough to finish my triage, hastily eat a ration bar, and drain a bottle of fresh water before I let myself surrender to unconsciousness. As daylight came, I slept poorly, which wasn't really a surprise, given my wounds and my uncomfortable accommodations. I had lived through worse injuries. I had endured worse pain. I had been more exhausted. And I had slept in more uncomfortable places. But I had never been forced to endure all of them at once. The result was a predictably difficult bout of unconsciousness that, when I woke just after night had once again fallen, felt like I hadn't slept at all.

Even so, my wounds felt a little better, and after checking the welts, I reapplied the disinfectant before donning my customary black fatigues. After that, I engaged in some calisthenics to stretch out my overworked muscles, checked and reloaded my weaponry, then sent a message to my uncle, detailing my actions.

His reply was devoid of any judgment and was limited to a simple message: *come home.*

In the back of my mind, I'd hoped for a pickup, but I had been well aware that I wasn't likely to get one. It was a test, after all, and a trek through the wilderness—complete with all the dangers that represented—was an appropriate way to cap things off.

So, I set off, continuing as I had the night before, utilizing Jorge's teachings to conceal my path as best I could. It was slow going, and eventually, at around noon the following day, my injuries caught up to me. When I almost stumbled into a feeding canine—which I killed with a swift sword strike after it attacked—I realized that, as eager as I was to get back to civilization, I wouldn't make it there in a single day. With that thought, I found another appropriate campsite and went through my routine of treating my injuries and eating my dinner before falling into another restless sleep.

Like that, I made my way back to Mobile. Along the way, I killed a number of monsters. There were a few more wild dogs, a full-fledged wolf, a black bear, and a couple of bobcats and pumas. I even ran into a horde of squirrels with metallic teeth and red, demonic eyes, which proved to be the toughest foe I faced during the whole trip. They weren't that dangerous individually, but the swarm acted like land-bound piranhas, devouring anything that got in their way. Luckily, I ran across a half-rotted corpse of some large animal that distracted the swarm long enough for me to get away.

The most nerve-racking experience came when I had to cross a sizable creek, though. I hadn't forgotten about my experiences in the ocean, near the bay, or in the swamp on my first day outside of Nova City. Hulking alligators the size of dinosaurs; giant, bone-crushing snakes; and unnamed monsters that cast their stinging tendrils hundreds of feet in every direction—it seemed that water was the catalyst for truly dangerous predators. But I didn't have much of a choice; if I wanted to get back to Mobile, I needed to cross the thirty-foot-wide creek.

It was a harrowing experience, crossing that narrow body of water—especially when I saw a long, slim figure swimming toward me. I sped up, barely making it to shore before a giant snout, probably four feet long and sporting a mouthful of snaggled teeth, chomped down where I had been only a moment before. At first, I thought it was another alligator—its head was a similar shape—but then I realized that its body sported fins that identified it as a fish.

Which was good news because if it had been one of the scaly reptiles, it could have followed me onto the muddy bank of the creek. As it was, as soon as I was on land, the monstrous fish turned around and swam away.

Eventually, after six days of traveling through the wilderness, I approached what had once been the downtown area of the city. The buildings weren't as large as what I'd grown up with in Nova City, but after spending so much time in the area's forests, they seemed oppressively huge. What's more, I got my first sighting of people since leaving Bayou La Batre.

Or that was my first assessment. Upon further study, I wasn't sure if that categorization was wholly appropriate. They had the right general shape, but most were skeletally thin and sported a wide range of metallic additions. It was as if the same process that had transformed the wildlife had infected human beings. Later, I would find out that this was precisely what had happened. Mist was naturally corruptive, and without the guidance provided by a Nexus Implant, it mutated people just like it did with any other life-forms. They were called wildlings and were only nominally human; most people considered them on par with apes, monkeys, and other primates. After watching a pack of them—from afar—descend upon a giant possum that had wandered into their eyeline, I couldn't really argue with that assessment. They attacked with metallic claws and teeth, ripping into the poor creature like wild animals. It was simultaneously the saddest and most disgusting thing I had ever seen.

Sad because they had once been people. Either they'd received corrupted Nexus Implants or they hadn't gotten any at all and the Mist had turned them into something less than human. Disgusting because it was impossible to see a man, regardless of how much he had diverged from the path of humanity, tear a possum's intestines out with his teeth and not feel the bile rise in your throat.

I gave them a wide berth, slipping past them to approach the walled town of Mobile. When I finally reached the gate, I called out for the guards, and once my identity had been confirmed, I was let inside via a small door that led to a passage through the gate. Once inside the city, my first stop was Kimiko's medical center, where I was greeted by her granddaughter, Elie.

The little girl wore a self-serious expression as she led me to the examination room. When I was settled into place, she announced, "Granny is gonna teach me to be a healer, just like her. I wanted to be a warrior, but this is better. She says I'll get more mangoes this way."

I smiled at her and said, "I'm sure she's right."

With that, I laid back and, for the first time in what felt like forever, fully relaxed.

It didn't last long, though, because after only a couple of minutes—during which I almost fell asleep—Kimiko herself made her appearance. When I told her about my injuries, she had me strip down to my underwear before she inspected my wounds.

"You are a lucky girl," she said, her face only a couple of inches from one of the welts on my arm. I was decidedly uncomfortable with her proximity, but I wasn't going to risk angering the doctor by showing it. "Portuguese man o' war. Or the new variant of it, at least. It was deadly before the Initialization, but it's even worse now. Any weaker Constitution, and you would be dead."

"That's me," I muttered. "Lucky."

She glanced at the bandaged wound on my calf. "And you were shot again, I see," she said. "You should think about getting some subdermal armor. It would still be painful, but not as life-threatening."

I thought back to Horace Lafontaine. He'd had some kind of subdermal armor, and it had rendered him almost invulnerable to my gunshots. Going forward, that might be a good idea, provided that my uncle was willing to pay for it. Even though I had some top-notch equipment and cybernetics, I had no money of my own. Perhaps I could change that at some point.

"Yeah. That might be a good idea," I agreed.

She frowned, then mercifully produced a med-hypo and jabbed it into my neck. With a hiss of compressed air, I felt a little prick before a numbness spread across my body. Kimiko patted my shoulder, saying, "Rest now. You will feel better when you wake up."

CHAPTER THIRTY-SEVEN

PROGRESSION

So often, I went from one emergency to another, pausing only long enough to heal so that I could jump right back into the fire. It affected me more than I can say, and I regret not slowing down and living my life. After all, none of what I did mattered anyway. The bad guys are still there. The world is still ending. And there's nothing I can do about it.

—Jeremiah Braddock III

Contrary to Kimiko's instructions, I didn't immediately fall asleep. I wasn't entirely awake, either. Instead, I lay suspended in that curious place between consciousness and unconsciousness, where I was still vaguely aware of my surroundings, but I couldn't bring myself to react to anything. While in that state, my mind wandered back to my actions in Bayou La Batre, back to the many mistakes I had made. Things had turned out well enough. I had accomplished my goal. But in doing so, I'd left at least one person dead. And I had a suspicion that Hadley—not to mention Kacie—would soon follow his father, Burton, into an early grave. Savanna didn't strike me as a forgiving woman—even less so after I saw her beaten and battered son lying at her feet.

Eventually, the medication, as well as my exhaustion, caught up to me, and my mind finally surrendered to unconsciousness. My dreams were filled with inescapable sea monsters comprised of a thousand stinging tendrils, so when I awoke, it was to a massive sense of relief.

An hour later, Kimiko returned to once again check my wounds, then pronounced me healthy enough to leave the premises. So, without anything else to do, I gathered myself from the bed and left to go look for my uncle.

My first stop was the inn, though Jo's mother told me that Jeremiah wasn't around. Next, I checked the training building, only to find it empty save for a few men and women being put through their paces by the Amigos. I looked at the obstacle course with a certain fondness. For the first part of my training, it had been my bane, but it also represented my first real victory, as well. When I'd finished it for the first time, it was a sign that I could accomplish whatever I wanted, that my work would be rewarded with real progress.

After standing there for a while, I decided to get a quick workout in. I was far from healed, but I knew that if I sat around doing nothing, my muscles would grow stiff. So, taking it easy, I went through some light stretching before jogging around the building. I was pleased to see that my slow pace was still almost twice as fast as any of the new recruits. If I went all out, I could have stretched my advantage by half again as much. That, as much as anything, made me feel the same sense of accomplishment I'd felt after first conquering the obstacle course.

And I was only just beginning. When everything was said and done, when I finally completed my training, my attributes and skills would be even more impressive. Perhaps, one day, I could even rival my uncle.

An hour or so later, my injuries caught up to me, and I ended up finding my way to the edge of the building, where I sank to the polished concrete floor. Wiping sweat from my brow, I summoned a bottle of water—one of my last, which meant I would soon need to restock on provisions—from my arsenal implant. I drained the bottle, then leaned my head against the wall as I caught my breath.

As I did, I pulled up my status:

NAME	Mirabelle Lisa Braddock		
CLASS	N/A (Requirements Not Met)		
LEVEL	4 (35%)		
CONSTITUTION	22/38		
MIND	23/38		
MIST	15/38		
SKILLS	7/7		
SKILL NAME	Skill Tier	Modifiers	Abilities
CYBERNETIC INTERFACE	Tier 3 (92%)	None	3 Cybernetic Slots

FIREARMS	Tier 2 (98%)	+15% Damage (All Firearms) +4% Reload Speed (All Firearms) +21% Accuracy (All Firearms) +15% Damage (Rifle) +15% Damage (Pistol) +10% Accuracy (Pistol) +15% Damage (Scattergun)	None
CLOSE QUARTERS COMBAT	Tier 2 (63%)	+4% Movement Speed +15% Damage (Melee) +10% Speed (Melee) +7% Accuracy (Melee) +5% Damage (Unarmed) +5% Speed (Bladed Weapons) +5% Damage (Blunt Weapons)	None
STEALTH OPERATIONS	Tier 1 (97%)	None	Camouflage (F)
COMBAT UTILITY	Tier 3 (81%)	None	Triage (E) Basic Explosives Handling (E) Combat Focus (D) Pain Tolerance (E) Resistance (E) Foraging (E) Improvisation (E) Regeneration (E)

MISTWALKER	Tier 2 (19%)	+15% Speed (Misthack) +10% Speed (Mistwalk)	Mistwalk (F) Misthack (E) Mistwall (F)
SPYCRAFT	Tier 2 (1%)	None	Disguise (E) Deception (E) Observation (F)

There were a lot of small changes, a couple of much larger improvements, and one huge gain. First, my attributes had all increased. Constitution and Mist had gone up by two points apiece, while my Mind attribute had only increased by one. It didn't seem like much, but considering that it had only been a little more than a week since I'd last checked it, I was happy with the improvements.

Next, my proficiency with most of my skills had increased, as well. Most were limited to a few percentage points, but I was excited to see myself creeping ever closer to a few tier changes. Most notably, my [Firearms] skill was only a couple of percent away from reaching the third tier, when I would gain more modifiers for my weapons. I was eager to see how the individual trees had progressed, as well, but I held off on checking them for now.

The most notable increase was to my [Spycraft] skill, which had tiered up to the second level. I was surprised to see that my advancement had come with an additional ability. I opened the submenu to inspect its effect:

Observation (F)—Passive ability that increases the mind's ability to parse sensory information and notice minute details.

The moment I read the ability's description, it took effect. Suddenly, I noticed everything in my general vicinity. For instance, I could tell that one of the trainees had a blister on his right foot that was causing him to limp ever so slightly. How I knew a blister was the culprit and not a twisted ankle, I had no idea. But I knew. Just like I could tell that the temperature was a balmy eighty-one degrees, with seventy-two percent humidity. Or that the Amigo who was in charge of the training was paying close attention to me. He never looked at me, but I could tell from the way his ear twitched that he was listening. Perhaps he had a similar ability to Observation.

At first, it was all a bit overwhelming, but my Mind attribute was up to the task of categorizing everything. Soon enough, I got used to it, and when I did, it almost felt like I was some omniscient deity, like I knew everything. It wasn't true, of course. But it was an incredibly powerful ability.

Maybe that was how Hadley had discovered my secret back in Bayou La Batre. I knew that if I met someone who was masking their tier now, I would know the difference. I wouldn't be able to figure out just how powerful they were, but it was enough that I'd certainly recognize if a Tier 7 was masquerading as a Tier 1.

In all, even if my mistakes still hung over my head, it had been a profitable few days. And I was just getting started. I concentrated on my [Firearms] skill, bringing the appropriate tree up on my HUD:

Tree	**Firearms: Tier 2 (98%)** +15% Damage (All Firearms) +4% Reload Speed (All Firearms) +6% Accuracy (All Firearms)			
Branch	Rifle: Tier 2 (99%)	Pistol: Tier 2 (14%)	Scattergun: Tier 1 (91%)	Sharpshooter: Tier 2 (12%)
Tier 1	+15% Damage (Rifle)	+15% Damage (Pistol)	+15% Damage (Scattergun)	+15% Accuracy (All Firearms)
Tier 2	+15% Range (Rifle)	+10% Accuracy (Pistol)	+15% Reload/ Ammunition Regeneration Speed (Scattergun)	+5% Damage (All Firearms)
Tier 3	Ability: Empowered Shot	Ability: Quickdraw	Ability: Double Shot	+5% Range (All Firearms)
Tier 4	Plasma Rifle Certification	Energy Pistol Certification	Explosive Scattergun Certification	Weapon Modification Certification
Tier 5	+15% Rate of Fire (Rifle)	+25% Rate of Fire (Pistol)	+15% Accuracy (Hipfire, Scattergun)	Ability: Mark Target

There hadn't been much change there—just a few percentage points' worth of increase on my Rifle branch. But I'd pulled within a single point of gaining Empowered Shot. It was all I could do not to just head to the range right then and there to see if I could push it over the edge. I knew that would be pointless, though. Time at the range wasn't nearly as beneficial as the more focused training—or real-world combat scenarios. As such, just heading to the range and shooting static targets would take a week to push it to the next tier. I would just have to be patient and wait until my training resumed.

Next, I pulled up my [Close Quarters Combat] tree, and I was unsurprised to see that nothing had really changed:

Tree	Close Quarters Combat: Tier 2 (63%) +15% Damage (Melee) +10% Speed (Melee) +7% Accuracy (Melee)			
Branch	Pugilism: Tier 1 (91%)	Bladed Weapons: Tier 2 (12%)	Blunt Weapons: Tier 1 (61%)	Movement: Tier 2 (75%)
Tier 1	+5% Damage (Unarmed)	Nano-Blade Certification	+5% Damage (Blunt Weapons)	+2% Movement Speed
Tier 2	+10% Damage (Unarmed)	+5% Speed (Bladed Weapons)	+10% Accuracy (Blunt Weapons)	+2% Movement Speed
Tier 3	Ability: Combination Punch	Ability: Eviscerate	Ability: Pummel	Ability: Engage
Tier 4	+15% Damage (Unarmed)	+10% Accuracy (Bladed Weapons)	+10% Damage (Blunt Weapons)	+5% Movement Speed
Tier 5	Ability: Barrage	Energy Blade Certification	Ability: Mighty Swing	Ability: Disengage

I had gained a single percentage point in the overall skill, then another point in Bladed Weapons as well as Movement. I could only think that the combination of my fight against the bobcat and the flurry of blade strikes that had freed me from the man-of-war had been enough to push the skill that much.

Finally, I focused on my [Mistwalker] tree:

Tree	Mistwalker: Tier 2 (19%) Ability: Mistwalk (Granted upon Skill's Acquisition) Ability: Misthack (Granted upon Skill's Acquisition) Ability: Mistwall (Granted upon Skill's Acquisition) +10% Speed (Misthack) +10% Speed (Mistwalk)			
Branch	Mistwalk: Tier 1 (86%)	Mistwall: Tier 1 (2%)	Misthack: Tier 1 (82%)	Mist Manipulation: Tier 1 (-24%)
Tier 1	F-Grade Systems Infiltration	F-Grade System Defense	+5% Speed (Misthack)	Ability: Overcharge
Tier 2	E-Grade Systems Infiltration	E-Grade System Defense	+2% Speed (Misthack)	+2% Strength (Overcharge)
Tier 3	D-Grade Systems Infiltration	D-Grade System Defense	Ability: Breach	+2% Strength (Overcharge)
Tier 4	+2% Infiltration Stability	Ability: System Redirect	+5% Speed (Misthack)	+10% Cybernetic Efficiency
Tier 5	Ability: Bypass Trivial Defenses	+5% Increased System Defense Strength	Ability: Overload System	+5% Strength (Overcharge)

Even though the individual branches of the [Mistwalker] tree tended to lag quite a bit behind the overall skill, I was happy with the progress I'd made. I wasn't sure exactly how common some of those higher-graded systems were, but I definitely didn't want to need the ability to infiltrate them but find myself just a bit short. Mostly, though, I was more excited about the ability waiting for me when I hit Tier 3 on my Misthack branch.

Whatever the case, I had made a ton of progress, and I knew that I still had a long way to go. My uncle had hinted that, at some point—probably when I reached the fifth tier in a skill—I would gain the ability to evolve or combine certain skills. And I wasn't so stoic that I couldn't get excited about new and exciting abilities like that.

On top of that, when I reached level ten, I would probably gain access to a class. And while I had no idea what that really meant, I knew that it was something of a game changer, in terms of powering up. More than once, I'd wondered why, if gaining a class was such an upgrade to someone's power, my uncle didn't simply take me out into the wilderness and let me kill monsters for a few weeks. However, each time I did, I realized that I was long past questioning his methods. He knew what he was doing, and I trusted him completely with my development.

"Are you done?" came Jeremiah's familiar voice, which made me flinch in surprise.

When my heart rate had calmed down, I looked up at where he was looming over me and asked, "How long have you been standing there?"

"Long enough to see that stupid grin on your face," he said. "What'd you get?"

"Observation," I said. "It lets me—"

"I know what it is," Jeremiah stated. "But I've got to ask—if you just got one of the most overpowered sensory buffs I know of, how the hell did you let me sneak up on you? You should have heard my footsteps. My breathing. You should have felt the slight disturbance in the air, even if you didn't recognize what it meant. You should have—"

I glared at him, interrupting with, "I was distracted, okay?"

"Distracted, hmm?" he asked. "Let this be a lesson, then. No matter how powerful your abilities are—and you have some powerful ones, Mirabelle—they're only as good as the person using them. All those attributes. Those skills. The ability to notice the most minute of changes. And you still got snuck up on by a hundred-year-old man. You need to be constantly vigilant, Mirabelle. Got it?"

"I've got it," I said, chastising myself. Sure, it was unfair of him to berate me because I hadn't sensed him coming. I didn't know what skills he had, but I was certain that one of them had something to do with stealth. On top of that, he had a hundred years' worth of experience to bolster his skills. So, expecting someone like me, who'd just gained an ability like Observation, to sense him was a tall order. I knew that, but I didn't let it affect my reaction. After all, he wasn't wrong. If it wasn't him, it might be someone else. Someone just as powerful who came at me with bad intentions.

Besides, I knew that everything Jeremiah did was for my own good, even if it sometimes felt like he was holding me to a standard I'd never be able to reach.

He slid down to sit beside me, then said, "I talked to Kimiko."

"Yeah? What'd she say?"

"That you went for a little swim," Jeremiah answered. "How'd that go for you?"

"Ugh . . . that thing . . ."

I let out a little shiver, and my uncle reached over and wrapped his arm around my shoulder, pulling me close. He wasn't really much for physical affection—not since I'd gotten older—but it reminded me of when I was little, when he'd hold me and read me old stories from before the Initialization. Back when my mother was still alive.

"It's okay," he said. "Those things aren't very common. You were just unlucky to run into a big one. You know, back before the Mist came, those jellyfish were some of the most venomous creatures in the world. And even after they've been enhanced and evolved, you got out of it with only a few welts. That's impressive. Most people—even the ones who could've withstood the venom—would have panicked and died. I'm proud to find out that you're not most people."

"Thanks," I said, leaning into his chest. For a few minutes, we just sat like that, watching the trainees going about their business. I knew we must have made for an interesting sight, but I didn't care. Nor did I really think about the fact that, after spending the last couple of hours training, I was a sweaty mess. At least my uncle didn't say anything about it.

"So," he said after a while. "Do you want to talk about what you did wrong?"

I sighed, then slipped out from under his arm. Throughout my time in Bayou La Batre, I'd kept him apprised of my actions. So, he knew basically everything that had happened, which meant he also knew all the places I'd gone wrong.

"My first mistake was that I should have just stuck with that first family," I said. "I complicated things unnecessarily."

I'd had my reasons—mostly that the son creeped me out—but that shouldn't have kept me from doing what I had to do.

"Go on."

Closing my eyes, I leaned my head against the wall. "That would have kept me from having to kill that giant crab monster," I explained. "Which, even if it didn't get me caught, definitely could have."

"What about the hunting trip?"

I opened my eyes, turning my head just enough so we could lock gazes. "I'm not going to apologize for saving Erica," I said. "It probably wasn't the smart choice, but I'd make it every single time."

"Fair enough. What about the situation with your friends that you left behind?"

"Hadley and Kacie? They weren't my friends," I said. "I was just using them to get to Savanna's office. The only reason it didn't go the way I wanted it to was because the butcher chose that moment to do the same."

"You think it was a coincidence, then?" Jeremiah asked.

I shrugged. "What else could it have been?" I asked.

"Bad decisions," he said. "What would you say if I told you that the moment your friend spoke to his mother, she knew he'd betrayed her? What's more, Savanna knew it was you. She had her husband corner you on that catwalk, where they hoped you could be taken alive. To your credit, you threw a bit of a monkey wrench into that plan when you shot him in the head. You did a good job with those two subordinates, though. They believed you right up until Savanna arrived."

"W-what?" I asked, surprised to hear how much my uncle knew. "How do you know all that?"

"I was watching you, Mirabelle," he said. "Did you really think I was going to just let you run off into enemy territory all by yourself? After what happened at the farm? You're talented. You're strong. But you're only half-trained. I had your back the whole time."

"So, the mission wasn't real?" was my next question.

He let out a sigh, then ran his hand over his bald head. "It was real," he said. "None of the rest of us could've gone in there and got anything off Savanna's terminal. Not without killing everyone in the village. With any luck, they won't have any clue that you're a Mistrunner."

"So . . . I didn't do all bad?"

"No," he said. "You did better than I could've asked you to do. Like I said before, I am proud of you."

I felt my shoulders sag in relief. "What now?"

"Now, you rest," he said. "You've got a week. After that, we enter the third and final phase of your training. It's going to last almost a year, during which you won't have many opportunities to have fun. So, use this time wisely."

"I . . . I think I can handle that," I said.

CHAPTER THIRTY-EIGHT

A SHOULDER TO LEAN ON

Sometimes, I wonder how long I'll live. From my contacts within the Bazaar, I've learned that some of the most powerful people in the universe are effectively immortal. That has always seemed like a special kind of hell to me.

—Jeremiah Braddock III

I returned to my room at the Dew Drop Inn and went straight to the shower, where I spent far longer than normal just standing under the soothing cascade of hot water. Even as my muscles relaxed, I hung my head and lost myself in wondering how badly I'd messed my mission up.

I had accomplished my goal. My uncle had said that much after taking a look at the chip I'd made containing all the information I'd gleaned from Savanna's terminal. But in the process, I had killed at least one person. I wasn't so naive that I didn't think killing was sometimes necessary. I knew it was. And after backing myself into a corner, I'd had no choice but to put Burton down. And given everything I knew about the man, I couldn't really convince myself that the world wasn't a better place without him in it. But I shouldn't have put myself into a position where I had to kill him.

And then there was the question of Hadley's fate. Of Kacie's. I knew Savanna wouldn't let the betrayal go without some repercussions, but I wasn't certain if she would kill her own son. More than that, if she was going to go that far, what would she do to the family I'd followed into the village? To Erica? To Sue, the old woman who'd initially introduced me to the village head? It was possible that my infiltration, which was supposed to have been carried out without violence, could result in a half dozen deaths.

I needed to be better than that. Not just for myself, but for all the people who'd put their time into training me. I needed to think more and act less impulsively. Sure, I could trace the lines of how I'd ended up where I was, and in the moment, my actions were probably justified. Even reasonable. But every mistake compounded to throw me further off track.

For instance, if I hadn't been daydreaming on that beach, I would have seen Kacie coming, and I could have evaded her without revealing my strength. Or if I'd have gone with Sadie and her family, creepy son be damned, I could have integrated into the town without drawing Savanna's attention. That, in turn, would have kept me out of Hadley's crosshairs.

A hundred little mistakes, none big enough to kill me, but plenty to push me into situations that kept snowballing into more desperate circumstances. It would've almost been easier just to kill everyone in town. At least then I would've been in control, rather than being swept along like a leaf on a stream.

With a sigh, I shut the water off and stepped from the shower. For once, I didn't take the amenities of a modern bathroom—even if it wasn't quite as advanced as what I'd had back in Nova City—for granted. Before grabbing a fluffy white towel, I took the opportunity to inspect my body. The welts that had come from my run-in with the man-of-war were still angry, red, and puffy. By contrast, the gunshot wound in my calf had closed and was well on its way to healing completely, probably due to a combination of Kimiko's efforts as well as my own Regeneration ability. That, more than anything, hammered home just how venomous the jellyfish had been. Like my uncle had said, I was lucky to be alive.

One look at my hair was enough to elicit a groan. At some point, something had ripped some of it away. It didn't leave a bald spot—it would take more than a few strands to make an appreciable dent in my mass of hair—but it did leave everything looking a bit lopsided. I spent the next few minutes trying to wrangle it into submission, but as was so often the case, I ended up just tying it back to keep it out of the way.

Once I finished up in the bathroom, I quickly rummaged through my wardrobe, which was still inside my duffel, to find something to wear. I came up with a pair of green leggings and a black tank top, emblazoned with a giant green *V*, which was the logo of one of Nova City's top fashion houses, Verdant. I'd gotten the top on the secondhand market, and I couldn't have cared less about high fashion. However, what I did care about was the way it fit, which was perfect.

After donning my comfortable sneakers, I once again checked myself in the mirror. I wasn't completely disappointed in what I saw. Of course, I would never be a great beauty. Nor did I think I'd ever have someone like Heather's sultry looks. But I was cute enough. That had to count for something, right?

Satisfied with my appearance, I left my room and descended the steps. The moment I found my way to the common room of the inn, I heard a high-pitched squeal, and then something collided with me. I was moving before I even knew what was happening, and in an instant, I was holding someone against the wall by their throat. That's when I saw Jo's terrified expression.

"Oh, shit . . . shit, shit! I'm so sorry!" I exclaimed, letting her free. I backed away. "I didn't . . . I don't . . ."

"No," she said, massaging her throat. Her voice was scratchy. "That was my fault. I should've known better than to surprise you like that."

I looked away. "I'm still kind of wound up, I guess," I admitted. "Still, I should've been more careful."

"So? Where have you been? Can you say?" she asked.

I looked around. "Not here" was my reply. "Are you working right now? Do you know anywhere we can talk privately?"

"I have just the place," she said, grabbing me by the wrist, and in seconds, she was dragging me from the building. Of course, I could have stopped her if I wanted to, but I didn't so much mind.

After a few steps, she let go, and together, we took a left down the street and continued to walk toward the southern edge of town. As we did, I asked, "Have you had any problems from Jack?"

She shook her head. "No" was her response. "He kind of . . . uh . . . disappeared. Not that I miss him. Obviously. But nobody's seen him around for a few weeks. I talked to one of my friends, Charlie, and he said that Jack probably just screwed with the wrong guy. Maybe someone higher up in the Tigers or something. I don't know, but I'm glad he's gone. I know you said you took care of it, but there was still the chance he'd come after me, anyway. Now, with him gone, I feel like I can relax."

I nodded. I didn't see Jack's disappearance as a good thing, mostly because I knew precisely how wrong my little attempt at blackmail could go. Not for the first time, I wished I would've just killed him. Or given the evidence to one of the other Tigers. Maybe one of the Amigos would've done something. I wasn't sure how I could have done things differently, but trying to take care of it alone had probably been a mistake.

After a few minutes of walking, I followed Jo as she took a right-hand turn down a narrow side street that ended in an ancient-looking fort. The walls were only about fifteen feet high and made of crumbling red brick. There was some evidence of sentry towers made of some white stone, but they had mostly fallen.

"What is this place?" I asked as Jo led me through an unbarred gate.

"It's called Fort Condé," she said. "My mom said that it was built almost three hundred years before the Initialization."

I ran my hand along the wall, saying, "The walls are kind of short, aren't they? What would they keep out?"

"I said the same thing" was her response. "According to her, these kinds of forts weren't meant for wildlife. They had these big cannons that they used to protect the river, which was important for trade or something. I don't know. I've just always liked it for some reason. Nobody else ever comes here."

I could see why. The place looked as if it was only a stiff breeze away from falling down. However, I guess that if it had stood for more than three centuries, it probably wasn't as delicate as it looked. So, I followed her inside, and after a few twists and turns, we found ourselves in an inner courtyard that was overgrown with vegetation. All except one small area, where someone had built a stone table and a couple of benches. She led me to it and climbed up to sit on top of the table.

"So? What happened? Why are you so jumpy?" she asked.

I didn't immediately answer. Instead, I sat next to her, albeit on the actual bench, and leaned forward. For a few moments, I stared at the long grass, even reaching out to pluck a piece from the ground. Twirling it in my fingers, I said, "I think I got some people killed."

"What? Who?" she asked.

"In Bayou La Batre," I said. "It's this little village down to the south. They're responsible for some of the raids we've seen recently. Well, my job was to get into the village and gather information. But I screwed it up."

"Why did they trust you with that?" she asked.

To date, I hadn't told Jo about any of my skills. She had some ideas about them, sure, but she didn't know anything for certain. And I felt positive that if I were to tell her that I was a Tier 7, she wouldn't believe me, anyway.

"Because my uncle wanted to test me," I said. "Plus, I had all the skills to make it work. I just didn't use them right."

After that, I told her everything that had happened, leaving only the details of my skills out. I told her about meeting the family outside of the city, about Hadley and Kacie, about Erica and Sue. I even told her about the giant crab. Finally, I explained how everything had gone wrong, how I'd ended up having to kill Burt. When I got to the part about the man o' war, her jaw dropped.

"So, that's what those welts are from?" she asked, reaching out to run a finger over the puckered flesh on my arm.

I nodded. "It hurt worse than anything I've ever felt before," I said. "And I've been through plenty of pain."

"Poor thing," she said.

"Something like that," I said. "But anyway, once I got out of the water, I started hiking back here. It took me forever because I didn't want to take any of the roads. And . . . I guess I got here a couple of days ago. I've been at Kimiko's until this morning."

As I spoke, Jo nodded along, concern on her face. When it was clear I'd finished, she said, "I think you're putting too much pressure on yourself."

I shook my head. "You don't understand, Jo," I countered. "So much time and effort and money has gone into training me. That I—"

"Why you?" she asked.

"What?"

"I know your uncle's a big deal," Jo said. "Ever since I was little, he'd sweep into town, stay for a couple of days, and then run off again. I know he's rich. I know he's in with all the higher-ups, like Milo and the Amigos. But every time I ask my mom or dad about it, they just tell me to mind my own business. The most I've ever gotten from them is that he's the reason we're not like a lot of the other small towns. We're a lot better off, and it's because of him. Now, he's spent tons of money on you. He's hired tons of special trainers, like that uppity bitch Helen from room three twenty-one. Or Mistress Stone, as she insists we call her."

"She's not that bad."

Jo cut her eyes at me and said, "She sent her eggs back six times in a single day because they weren't runny enough. Six times! And then she had the audacity to complain about how slow the service was. Ugh. I was surprised dad didn't kick her out right then and there. But you know what was the worst? She doesn't like grits! I mean, seriously. She looked at me like I was trying to poison her when I offered her some. Can't trust anybody who doesn't like grits, and that's the truth."

I couldn't really dispute that simple fact. Though, because my uncle had told me so, I knew that it was a regional dish. Other parts of the world ate different things.

"Okay, she's pretty terrible," I agreed. "But she's really smart. And she's helped me a lot."

"With what, though?"

"I . . . I can't say," I said. "I'm not trying to be evasive or anything, but my uncle told me not to tell anybody any details about my skills and stuff. I accidently told Kimiko when I first got here, and . . . well, he made me run for, like, two hours straight when he found out."

Indeed, that had been one of the worst experiences of my life. After months of physical training, I could easily handle it, but back then, it had been the most horrible two hours of my life.

"Why not?"

I sighed. "Look, Jo," I said. "There's a lot going on that I don't understand, but there's one thing my uncle's told me over and over again. The Initialization was just the beginning. There's more coming. There's worse on the way. In less than ten years, the whole world's going to change, and not for the better. He's trying to prepare me for that."

Jo shook her head, asking, "What am I supposed to do with that information?"

"I . . . I don't know," I said. "But that's all I can say." I reached over and took her hand. "Just . . . just promise me that you'll take it seriously. I can tell you're only a Tier 2, and your skills are probably already filled, but you need to start working out how you're going to survive."

"Y-you're scaring me, Mira," she said.

"Good. It's a scary thing," I said. "Just promise me."

"Fine. I promise," she said. "My dad's been trying to get me to learn some basic self-defense, so I guess I'll take him up on it."

I nodded, saying, "That's . . . that's good. Really good."

We sat there for a few moments, with Jo clearly processing what I'd told her. I hadn't revealed many details, but she had clearly understood the tone of my warning well enough to take it seriously. For my part, I found myself wondering what would happen to everyone once the Integration came in a few short years. Would they all die? Would they be enslaved? Something worse? I had no idea, and I had no way of figuring any of it out. Jeremiah wasn't exactly a wellspring of information, and as far as I could tell, nobody else really knew what was coming. Not even Milo or the Amigos. Or if they did, they weren't telling me, which amounted to the same thing, as far as I was concerned.

Finally, she said, "What do you want to do now?"

"I . . . I don't know," I admitted. When I'd left my room, I'd really had no idea how I wanted to spend my miniature vacation, and that hadn't changed in the interim.

"You know what? I have an idea," she said.

"What kind of idea?" I asked, wary of the gleam in her eye.

"Well, I've noticed that you never really do anything with your hair," she said.

"I don't ever have time!" I argued, but the truth of the matter was that I'd never had anyone to teach me about those kinds of things. The best my uncle could do was put it in braids. And for better or worse, my hair wasn't like Jo's or Heather's or a lot of the other girls I'd met in my life. To put it mildly, it didn't like to cooperate.

"Well, I have a friend named Kristy," she said. "And her mom does hair. I was thinking that . . . maybe . . . I don't know—we could go and get our hair done or something?"

"I don't know . . ."

"C'mon! It'll be fun!" she insisted. "And she's really good. She can do whatever you want her to do. Like, she should be working in Nova City and doing hair on one of the shows on the entertainment feeds, she's so good."

I really didn't want to do it, but I didn't see a way out, either. Jo was clearly excited about the prospect, and I didn't want to disappoint her. So, I nodded, she squealed in delight, and before I knew it, we were heading through town to visit a hairdresser.

CHAPTER THIRTY-NINE

FUN, OR SOMETHING LIKE IT

Training is like building a pyramid. First, you need a wide, sturdy base of general competence. Then, you must narrow your focus, concentrating on the most important skills. And finally, you must choose a specialty. For me, I was always a rifleman first and everything else second.

—Jeremiah Braddock III

I looked in the mirror, my fingers snaking through the soft curls of my hair. I had no idea what the stylist had actually done, but when she'd finally given me a good look, I was floored. One side of my head was completely shaved, with only a little stubble remaining, and down the other was a cascade of tightly wound curls. Before, I'd never thought I could pull off a decent sidecut, but the stylist had put the lie to that expectation. It wasn't like what I'd seen on so many other women—or men, I suppose—who'd been blessed with straight hair, but that was fine. For the first time in my life, I actually preferred my own hair to what I saw on other people.

Especially because of the color.

My hair was stark white at the roots and fading into hot pink, and my whole look was pulled together by similarly shaded makeup. Obviously, it wasn't something I could do during a mission or while training, but for a day on the town? It was perfect.

I looked good. Like, really good. So good, in fact, that I sat there in the stylist's chair, staring at my own reflection, an expression of awe playing across my face. It wasn't until Jo spoke that the spell was broken.

"W-what?" I asked. "I . . . I wasn't listening."

"I said that I guess you like it," she repeated, grinning.

The stylist, an older woman with her hair in green braids and a complexion similar to my own, said, "Lookin' like that, the boys are never gonna leave you alone, girl."

I wasn't altogether sure how I felt about that statement. Sure, like so many girls my age, I had definitely taken notice of boys. And they'd noticed me in turn. But the idea of actually doing anything with one of them was so terrifying that I'd have rather faced another giant alligator than confront it. However, I was also inexplicably excited by the stylist's offhand comment. Yeah—I had no intention of unraveling those feelings, so I just moved right along past them.

The next few minutes passed in a daze, and before I knew it, Jo had paid the stylist. I tried to object, saying that I could pay my own way, but she wasn't having any of it. After all, she said, I had saved her from Jack. That had to be worth a favor, right? I could recognize an unwinnable argument when I saw one—even if I didn't necessarily agree—so I abandoned that particular thread.

There's just something about walking around with a fresh haircut that you're really excited about. It doesn't just give you confidence. It buoys your entire mood to the point where everything just feels so much better than before. That's what happened over the course of the rest of the day, which saw Jo and me revisiting the market, eating lunch at what she claimed was the best restaurant in town, and shopping for new clothes. Eventually, as night fell, we found our way to what Jo claimed was a local hangout for people our age.

Once upon a time, it had been a fancy hotel, as evidenced by the aged and decayed decor, but it had long since been abandoned, probably because of its proximity to the wall. When I asked Jo about it, she said, "My dad said this wasn't part of the original town, but when he was younger, they moved the walls out. He said that his parents told him that, before the Initialization, it was named after some admiral from a war they lost a long time ago."

"Why would you name something after somebody who lost?" I asked, a little confused.

She shrugged. "No clue," Jo said. "Doesn't matter, though. All those people are long gone."

I was sure she was right, but given my uncle's age, I had to amend that assumption. Was his long life a characteristic of people born before the Initialization? Or was it his enhanced Constitution? My gut told me it was the latter, but I didn't know enough to rule out the former, either.

She led me through the hotel until we ended up at a staircase, which we climbed for a few floors before exiting. By the time we reached our destination, Jo was huffing and puffing, but because of my Constitution, I wasn't even out of breath.

Still, my heart skipped a beat when I saw where we were going. The entire floor was open to the world, and because we were high enough, we could see out over the walls. In one direction lay the ruined city, but in the other was the untouched bay. However, what really caught my attention were the decorations someone had arranged.

Strings of lights, looking like fireflies, clung to the ceiling, casting everything in a soft glow. Various chairs and couches dotted the mostly open floor, and most importantly, it was full of teenagers. Some looked to be around my age, but others were clearly passed into adulthood.

Boys and girls were engaged in conversation, making out, or dancing to the beat of music blaring from sets of speakers artfully arranged throughout the floor. Everything—from the speakers to the furniture to the lighting—looked like it had seen better days, as if it had all been abandoned, but upon first inspection, it seemed clean enough.

"This is the Admiral," Jo said, sweeping her hand out. "Everybody comes here. There are drinks over there." She pointed into the corner where a man in his midtwenties was handing out cans of cheap-looking beer. "It costs a little bit to get in, but once you're here, everything's free."

"Wow."

"Impressive, right? But I bet you've got places like this all over Nova City," she said.

"Uh . . . maybe? I wouldn't know," I said before I realized what I was admitting. "I mean, yeah. We totally have places like this. But better. Yeah. Lots better."

"Right . . ."

"Okay, I don't know about any of that, okay?" I said with a sigh. "I didn't . . . you know . . . have time for this kind of thing back home."

It was another lie, but a more palatable one. The reality of it was that because of the combination of my antisocial nature and being my uncle's niece, I'd never had any friends. So, I had never been invited anywhere like the Admiral. But Jo didn't need to know that, did she? I desperately wanted her to think I was cool, and admitting I was a friendless loser didn't seem conducive to that goal.

"Yeah—I get it," she said. "With everything . . . well, I can see how you'd be too busy. But you've got a new look, and you've got a little free time now, right? So, c'mon!"

With that, she grabbed my wrist and dragged me toward a slim woman who looked like she was also in her midtwenties. She had a pair of cybernetic arms, but one of them was poorly encased in what appeared to be the cheapest version of RealSkin on the market. It wasn't ill fitting, but the texture was all wrong. To make matters worse, she'd tattooed it, probably in an attempt to cover it up; the result was one arm that was blatantly mechanical and another that looked like a combination of rubber and plastic but was covered in what should have been intricate tattoos. However, because that version of RealSkin wasn't built to take ink, it was smudged and runny, making it look like a giant blob of black ink. It was made all the worse by my new Observation ability, which made it to where I couldn't ignore just how terrible it looked.

"Note to self, don't cheap out on the fake skin," I muttered under my breath.

"What was that, little girl?" demanded the woman that I hadn't expected to hear me.

"Uh . . ."

"Leave her alone, Trixie," said Jo. "She's with me."

"And I'm supposed to care?" asked Trixie. As she spoke, I took a moment to examine her outfit. She was wearing a pair of shiny silver shorts that, if Jeremiah thought I was even thinking of going out in public wearing, he'd have locked me up for a few months. It wasn't just that they were so tight that I got a good idea of everything they were supposed to be covering. Nor was it only that they were short enough that I had underwear that offered more coverage. Rather, it was the combination of the two that made them seem so scandalous.

Of course, I'd seen more revealing clothing in Nova City, but this just seemed worse, and for reasons I couldn't adequately explain. Up top, she wore nothing but a pair of star-shaped pasties and an open vest that barely came down to her ribs. In her mechanical hands was a tapered club studded with nails, with a chain wrapped around its thickest end. Finally, her hair, which was short and arranged in a bob, and makeup were indigo, making her stand out even more.

To put it bluntly, aside from her cheap skin job, she was probably the coolest-looking person I had ever seen. While I would never have had the confidence to walk around half naked like she did, it definitely worked for her.

"I love your hair," I blurted. "And your makeup is awesome. Is it permanent? Or do you have to put it on every day?"

That took her aback, and for a few seconds, she didn't respond. Then, she grinned, saying, "Permanent. No other way to go for a lady on the go, you know what I mean?" She looked me up and down in a decidedly predatory manner, adding, "I'd be happy to get together with you when I get off. You know, to discuss fashion . . . and other things."

I swallowed hard. I could face down a mutated man o' war. I could kill dozens of dangerous mooks. I could even handle a giant idiot like Burt-Burt. But under that woman's gaze, I felt like my legs were about to give out. Obviously, I understood the implication inherent in her suggestions. I wasn't stupid. I watched movies and programs on the entertainment feeds. And while I was flattered by the attention, I'd long known that I just didn't swing that way. Still, it was difficult to remember that while she was looking at me.

That's when something snapped inside me. Suddenly, her hair didn't look so shiny. The body beneath her revealing outfit, less perfect. Her sneering face, far less enticing. And her words, entirely unpersuasive.

It actually took me a moment to realize that she had been using a skill, and when I did, my wide-eyed innocence turned into a scowl. Before I even knew what I was doing, I had my fingers around her neck, and I was squeezing. Ferdinand II was in my hand, his barrel pressed against her forehead as she futilely scrapped her cybernetic fingers against my forearms. Her efforts bore fruit in the form of a set of shallow cuts, but my Constitution was up to the task of fending off her panicked scratches.

I leaned in close, barely hearing the screams around me, and said, "If you ever try to use a skill like that on me ever again, I will kill you before you have a chance to explain yourself. You got it, Trixie?"

Tears were already flowing down her cheeks, and she tried to answer. However, because of my grip on her throat, she couldn't get the words out. So, she had to make do with a frantic nod. Satisfied, I released her. She fell to the floor, gasping for breath. Only then did the screams hit me.

"What are you doing?!" yelled Jo, who had a hold on one of my arms.

"She tried to use a skill on me," I said as calmly as I could. It came out as a snarl. "Something that tried to snake its way into my mind. I don't know what it was, but she was trying to make . . . herself and her words more attractive. I don't like it when people try to manipulate me."

As I spoke, I looked up to see that two more people—a man and a woman—had approached. Both sported cybernetics, though they were low-quality hack jobs that were barely stronger than a human limb. One carried a wicked-looking axe with a head that looked like it had once belonged to a giant buzz saw, and the other carried a club similar to the one the fallen Trixie had carried. Both were glaring at me.

"What the hell? You come to our joint and you attack us? Really? You got a death wish, little girl?" demanded the woman.

"I'm not the one on the ground," I said, keeping my voice calm as I shifted my gaze from one person to the other. "And as far as I can see, I'm the only one with a gun."

"You think that scares us?" growled the man. "We both got subdermal armor. The best in Mobile."

"So it's barely better than normal skin?" I asked. "Fine. You've got your armor. I've got Ferdinand. I think I know which one I'm betting on." To hammer my point home, I raised my pistol and gave him a good waggle. Then, I raised my voice. "Besides, I'm not in the wrong here. That woman tried to use a skill on me. Some kind of mind control. By rights, I could explode her head, and nobody could claim I was wrong to do it."

"Says you," spat the woman. "Trixie's one of us. She wouldn't do that."

"She did," I assured her. "But here's the deal—none of you can do anything about it. And yes, I see you over there with the crossbow." I glanced at the bartender, who'd crept to within range and was aiming the aforementioned weapon at me. "So, I'm going to walk out of here right now. You want to stop me, feel free. It's been a few days since I killed anybody."

As I spoke, I tried to channel my uncle's calm confidence. I wasn't certain if I could pull it off, but I really didn't want to have to kill anyone else. Not even Trixie, despite what she had just tried to do. It was bad, and she deserved punishment, but it didn't warrant a death sentence.

Probably. If I heard about her doing it again, that would be a different story altogether. I wasn't proud of my body count, but I wouldn't hesitate to add another tally to the total.

"Mira . . ."

I glanced at Jo, who looked understandably horrified. She'd wanted to take me somewhere fun, and it had ended with me pointing a gun at one of the first people I saw. Her reaction, more than anything, showed me just how different my life had become. For me, my actions were a perfectly natural response to what Trixie had tried to do. For her, it was something decidedly different. Perhaps she recognized it as necessary, but there was a good chance that she would only see the violence.

"I'm leaving now," I said, casting a challenging glare at the closest of the Admiral's mooks. "You want to figure this out, we can do it outside where nobody that doesn't deserve it will get hurt."

With that, I turned on my heel and left. With Observation, I could hear the three would-be attackers shifting from foot to foot. I could smell the urine soaking Trixie's ridiculous shorts. And I could feel the tremor of Jo's footsteps as she followed me to the stairwell.

I didn't stop until we'd reached the bottom floor of the old hotel. When I did, I turned to Jo and said, "I'm sorry. I didn't . . . I didn't want to do that. You understand that, right? I wasn't trying to—"

"Stop," she said, wiping tears from her eyes. The excitement of the encounter had clearly overwhelmed her. She sniffed. "Just stop, Mira. I get why you did it."

"What? Really? You're not going to tell me off?" I asked.

She narrowed her eyes. "That woman tried to mind rape you," she said. "And I'm sure you're not the first. Never mind that she's, like, old, and she shouldn't be even looking at us like that . . ."

"I didn't expect you to understand," I said.

"We're friends, Mira," Jo said. "I trust your judgment. I mean . . . I didn't expect you to whip out a freaking hand cannon or anything, but . . . I get it. I do. So, let's just . . . I don't know . . . let's go do something else and pretend this didn't happen."

Even as we spoke, I could hear a dozen pairs of feet pounding against the stairs behind us. We moved away, and when I looked back, I saw that most of the place's customers were leaving. Clearly, my actions had shown a light on the bouncer's predatory actions. Or maybe they were just scared. Either way, I felt certain that I'd just angered another of the town's factions.

Were they a gang, like the Tigers? Or just a group of people who were filling a void in the town's entertainment offerings for young people? I didn't know, but I wasn't sure if I cared enough to find out.

"C'mon. Let's go," I said. "We'll figure out something else to do."

"Sounds good," she said.

For the rest of the day, we just wandered around town, and Jo continued to show me the sights. An old cannon from some long-forgotten war. An overgrown park blooming with flowers she called azaleas. A decaying and decrepit house, with huge white columns and a stately look to it. On and on it went, well into the night until we ended up sitting on a concrete wall overlooking the river.

"Are you going to leave when you finish your training?" she asked, her feet dangling over the edge. We were high enough that it was mostly safe, and I was keeping an eye on the water. I trusted my Observation ability to let me know if anything big or dangerous was cutting through the water.

"I . . . I don't know," I admitted. I had always assumed I was going back to Nova City, but was that really necessary? One place was as good as any other, if I was to believe my uncle's predictions about the upcoming Integration. So, what if I did stay in Mobile? Would that be so bad? At least there, I could have a friend. I was sure that wouldn't always be the case, if I chose to travel. "What about you? Do you want to stay here?"

"It's all I've ever known."

"I know, but let's say you could go wherever you wanted," I said. "No restrictions. You could just go. What would you do? Where would you go?"

She sighed. "Well, there's this place," she said. "I've only heard about it once, and not from a reliable source. But it's this town out west, in the mountains. The person who told me about it said that's where they came from. Him and the man he was with."

"What's special about this mountain town?" I asked. I'd never even seen a mountain, save in a few movies.

"Well, it's protected by this really strong warrior," she said. "The way Stuart—that was his name—described it, it was a paradise. Nobody wanted for anything. But they were completely modern, too. As modern as any of the megacities. And Stuart would know, too. He'd been to Nova and Atlanta and a few others, too. I'd go there."

"Sounds too good to be true," I said. "What happened to this Stuart? To the guy he was with?"

"They . . . they left," she said. "It was about two years ago. They were headed south, down to this place called Miami. The way he talked about it, it wasn't a megacity, but it was supposed to be a big deal. I asked my mom and dad about it, but they'd never heard of it, either."

"Maybe they'll come back," I suggested.

"I don't know. Maybe," she said. "And when they do, I'm going to ask them to take me with them. Maybe you can do the same."

"Maybe," I said, looking out at the seemingly placid water and knowing good and well that her town in the mountains probably didn't even exist. To me, it sounded like something a disreputable person would tell an impressionable—and pretty—young girl so that he could manipulate her into coming with him. But I hoped I was wrong. "Maybe."

CHAPTER FORTY

THE BEGINNING OF THE END

There's a skill for every situation. That, as much as anything, is a source of hope. However, it is a shallow thing, mired in so much dread that it's barely even relevant. Still, I've tried to lace my natural cynicism with a thread of optimism, no matter how thin.

—Jeremiah Braddock III

Is there a story behind the new haircut?" asked my uncle, looking me up and down as I plopped down beside him. I shifted uncomfortably, glancing around the inn's common room, but I didn't see Jo anywhere. She was probably sleeping it off—the "it" being a month's worth of adventures that had been crammed into a single week. I had barely slept, and my vacation had been anything but relaxing. We had visited every part of Mobile, taking advantage of the small number of credits I'd been given by Jeremiah to great advantage. And I'd discovered quite a few things about myself along the way.

First, no matter how much alcohol I drank, I couldn't actually get drunk—a fact I discovered when she and some of her friends acquired a few cases of beer. Even while they all drank themselves into oblivion, I remained stone-cold sober, which highlighted two things. Most notably, I really, really hated the taste of beer. But perhaps more importantly, I realized that drunk people are incredibly annoying when you're the only sober one around. Still, I muscled through it, even making sure that nobody did anything too stupid.

Second, any questions about my sexuality were answered when one of Jo's friends, Lane, took an interest in me. He wasn't the most handsome boy I'd ever seen, but he wasn't far off. And he liked me! I won't go into too many details, but suffice it to say that that week brought with it quite a few firsts for me. And though I had no interest in things taking a more serious turn, I knew I'd treasure the experiences. I could only hope that I'd have enough time to explore things further.

But for now, I had my training to worry about.

"You got back two days ago, and you're just now noticing?" I asked, flicking my hand through my white-and-pink curls. "For shame."

"I noticed," he said with one of his rare smiles. "I just didn't have a chance to talk to you about it. You've been going nonstop with those new friends of yours since I got back into town."

I glanced at him, and with more hope in my voice than I wanted, asked, "Do you like it?"

His smile widened as he said, "It looks good. Not terribly practical for carrying out stealth operations, but yes, Mirabelle—I like it. Reminds me of your mother, actually. She wore her hair almost just like that when she was your age. Minus the color."

"She did?" I asked. The woman I remembered kept her hair in boring braids that let her work without getting hair everywhere, so his statement was a bit of a revelation. Perhaps I was more like my mother than I really knew.

Not that it was what I wanted, of course. She'd squandered her opportunities, opting for an average life that got her killed. She'd actively chosen to be defenseless, and she had paid the ultimate price. That wouldn't have been so bad—after all, people could do what they wanted with their own lives—if she hadn't robbed me, as well. I had grown up without parents, all because she was too afraid to take the opportunities my uncle had offered her. We might have had the same taste in hairstyles, but we were nothing alike. Not where it counted.

"Of course," he said, reaching over and flicking my hair. "I think every girl goes through the sidecut phase these days. It was a bit of a niche back in my day, but I do like it. It looks good on you."

"Thanks."

For the next couple of minutes, neither of us really said anything. I could tell by his glassy expression that Jeremiah was reading something on his HUD, so I remained silent. Instead, I studied the inn's other diners only to be disappointed when I saw that they were mostly the same crowd that ate breakfast there every morning, save for a couple of newcomers that were sitting in the corner.

One was an unassuming woman who looked average in every way. It was only because of Observation that I noticed her at all, and I suspected that the rest of the inn's occupants—with the exception of maybe Jeremiah—were entirely unaware of her presence. The other stranger was a big, beefy man with arms that looked like they were as big around as my waist. He was also in possession of the most glorious mustache I'd ever seen: thick and voluminous, it grew out of his sideburns. Wearing a bowler hat, he sat across from the woman but never actually spoke to her.

After a bit, Jo's mother appeared with a plate of eggs, bacon, and of course, grits. However, this time, the normally white grits had a bit of a yellow tint to them. When I asked about them, she said, "We got a shipment of cheese in yesterday."

"Cheese?" I asked, thinking about the yellowish goop available in Nova City. I'd never much cared for it if I was being perfectly honest. It always had a weird texture, and it tasted more artificial than other similarly manufactured food products. "Seems like a waste."

"Shut your mouth," my uncle said, the distracted look fading away. "You'd be saying something different if you knew what you were talking about."

"I've had cheese before," I said with a huff.

"You've had what passed for cheese back in Nova," he stated. "Not real cheese. Go ahead. Try it. I guarantee you won't be disappointed."

I eyed the wrong-colored grits for a few seconds before grabbing the spoon and digging in. I only got a little—after all, I was extremely skeptical—before hastily shoving the spoon into my mouth.

I think that was the moment I realized just how terrible life in Nova City really was. The flavor exploded in my mouth, overwhelming my taste buds. It wasn't the slightly chalky stuff I was used to. Rather, it was rich and savory and entirely complimentary of what was quickly becoming my favorite food.

"Ohmigod," I mumbled, the words unintelligible because I'd quickly shoveled another heaping spoonful into my mouth. "'S amazing."

Jeremiah, as well as Jo's mother, chuckled, but I didn't care that they were laughing at my expense. I just had to get as much of the bowl's contents into my stomach, and as quickly as possible. I hardly even paid attention to my surroundings as I scraped every last bit of it into my mouth. I might've broken a grits-eating record, I gobbled it down so quickly.

When I'd finally finished, I guzzled down some water to combat the salty flavors and settled into a more sedate pace as I polished the rest of my meal off. After I'd downed the last bite, my uncle gave another chuckle, saying, "I'll never get tired of seeing you so happy."

"Really?"

That came as something of a surprise to me. He wasn't the doting type. Sure, he'd always looked out for me. He had always protected me. But he'd also denied me plenty of luxuries. I might've spent my formative years confined to a tower like a fairy-tale princess, but I hadn't lived like one.

"Really."

"I . . . uh . . . I think I found my new favorite food," I said, my eyes flicking back to the corner booth. The two newcomers were still there, and my eyes still wanted to slide away from the woman. Part of that was because the big, mustachioed man was so prominent, but I was certain that there were other factors in play.

"Noticed them, huh?" Jeremiah asked, following my gaze.

"She's using a skill."

"She is. What kind do you think it is?" he asked.

I narrowed my eyes, considering it. "Probably something like [Spycraft], but it's a much higher-tiered than mine," I said. "I don't know. There's more to it, though. A lot more. I feel like I wouldn't have even noticed her if it wasn't for the fact that they're the only strangers here. And because I just got Observation."

"You're right," Jeremiah said. "The second part, I mean. Her skill is a lot more complicated than [Spycraft], though. Come on. I want you to meet them."

He stood up and, before I could object, crossed the common room to where the pair were sitting. I followed meekly, and when I arrived, the woman asked, "Did she see me?"

"She did."

"Interesting" was her response. Her voice was just as unassuming as her appearance. "I'll do it, then."

Jeremiah nodded, responding, "You can drop the skill, Vanna."

With an annoyed expression briefly disrupting her otherwise placid features, her figure shimmered, and where an unassuming person had once sat, there appeared a slim woman with dusky eyes. She was pretty, held back from being gorgeous by a sharp, overlarge nose. Her hair was midnight black, and her eyes glimmered violet, announcing the presence of her optical implant.

My jaw dropped, and I breathed, "How? My skills can't do that."

"Practice," she said with an impish smirk. "And lots of time. Believe me—you've barely scratched the surface of what your skills can do. You're probably pretty strong by the standards of this backwater, but out in the real world? You'd get eaten alive. And I've agreed to help usher you along and teach you how to survive once the training wheels come off." She gestured to the huge man across from her, adding, "Simon here, too."

I glanced at the muscular man, taking in his full appearance. If I'd ever seen anyone with more muscles, I couldn't remember it—which was saying something, considering I grew up around Nora. He had the features of a brawler, with all the lumps and misshapen pieces that came with it.

"You don't look like a Simon," I said.

"Oh?" he asked in a surprisingly genteel voice. "And what do I look like?"

I shrugged. "I don't know. Something like Brick, maybe? Or Crusher. You know, normal mook names," I answered.

"And that's what I am to you?" he asked. "A simple mook?"

"Uh . . . no?"

"Is that a question?"

"I don't—"

"Leave her alone, Simon," the woman said, grinning. "You know that's exactly what you look like. It's like you came from the Henchmen "R" Us megastore."

"Ugh. Really? That's your reference? That hasn't been relevant in a hundred years. Literally," said Simon.

"Your face isn't relevant," she muttered.

"Anyway . . . these are going to be two of your teachers for the next year," Jeremiah said.

"A year? I thought we were almost done with the training," I said, a bit of a whine in my voice. While I liked training, I was eager to see the end goal. And now, instead of only a few more months, I was in it for another year? That didn't seem fair, but I knew better than to object.

"Things change," he stated. "With Vanna and Simon available, I couldn't pass it up. They've agreed to stay here for the duration of the last phase of your training."

Vanna gestured at him with a piece of bacon, saying, "So long as you hold up your end of the bargain, we'll teach this little girl everything she needs to know."

"Consider it done," Jeremiah said.

"What are you doing for them?" I asked.

"Not your concern," he said, a predictable response. He loved me and trusted me, but he would never be the type to share unnecessary information. I'd long since gotten used to that about my uncle. "What you need to be concerned with is your schedule going forward. Check your messages."

I focused on my HUD, and sure enough, there was a blinking icon denoting an unread message. When I opened it, I saw the schedule. For the first part of every day, I would be meeting with the Mistrunner, Helen. After that, I would have classes dedicated to my various [Combat Utility] abilities; those would take up most of my day. Then, I would spend time on the firing range, running various courses for my instructors. After that, I would be trained by Simon in [Close Quarters Combat], which was his specialty. Finally, my day would end with instruction from Vanna in [Spycraft] and [Stealth Operations]. All in all, I would be going for at least fifteen hours of every day, which would leave little time for sleep, much less recreation.

"That's . . . that's a lot."

"It takes sacrifice to be the best," my uncle said. "Your skills so far, they've been relatively easy to advance. Going forward, you're going to be hitting the higher tiers. You may even evolve one or two of your skills. As that happens, things will become much more difficult. The only way to combat that difficulty is by working harder for longer. As always, though, you have a choice—if you don't think you can do it, we can head back to Nova City right now. You're prepared to survive. But if you want to thrive, know that this is still only the beginning. You will always need to continue your growth. The training will never stop."

"I'm not giving up," I said, having made my decision before he even brought it up. "I'll do whatever it takes."

"She's got a little steel in her spine," said Simon. "I like that."

"You're just looking forward to beating her up," countered Vanna.

He didn't deny it. Instead, he just gave a helpless shrug. Jeremiah ignored them both, focusing on me as he asked, "Are you sure?"

"I am."

"Well, if you're sure, then we'd better get to it, then," he said. "Come on. Helen's waiting."

I rolled my eyes, which brought a fit of giggling from both Simon and Vanna. I guess it wasn't just me that thought he was overly dramatic. Still, I hurried to follow him out of the Dew Drop Inn and into the heavily traveled street. The people of Mobile were nothing if not early risers, and we had to weave through plenty of traffic before we reached the building I dreaded the most—the once-abandoned residence Helen had recently claimed for herself. It was a small building, but since her arrival, it had gained a fresh coat of paint and all the amenities someone like her could want. My stomach knotted up the moment I laid eyes on it.

It wasn't that I disliked my [Mistwalker] training. Because it was mostly comprised of doing mathematics and solving puzzles, I actually found it very satisfying. However, I couldn't say the same for my trainer. Helen was, to put it mildly, a sour woman who clearly thought she was better than everyone else. And given what she'd shown of her abilities, I couldn't really dispute that attitude. With a flick of her mind, she could overwhelm a fort's defenses or completely disable an opponent's cybernetics. I knew this because, to train my Mistwall ability, she'd subjected me to her attacks, over and over again. To call it unpleasant would have been quite an understatement.

Even so, it was necessary. The last thing I wanted was for my own defenses to come up short when it mattered most. So, after we went inside and I settled into the seat across from the woman, the torture began. And to my surprise, it didn't let up until she called an end to our session.

"What? We're not going to do puzzles or work on my Ghosts?" I asked.

She shook her head. "You can do that on your own time," she said. "For now, you need a strong defense. I'm sure that, after meeting that harlot Vanna, you can see why."

"Huh?"

She let out a long-suffering sigh. "You did not make the connection, I take it," she said. "Fine. She uses a skill that affects the minds of anyone in a certain radius. I am sure that you felt it."

I nodded. "You're talking about the skill that made her easy to ignore?" I asked.

"I am. Mistwall is a versatile ability that does more than just shield you from other Mistrunners," she said. "It also offers some protection against mental skills like what that . . . woman uses. You will need it to function at the highest level if you are to follow her training. She is a detestable person, but she is talented enough at slinking through the shadows like a lowly thief."

"Uh-huh," I muttered.

"In any case, our allotted time has come to an end," she stated in her clipped manner of speaking. It reminded me of the doctor that had installed my cybernetics. She flicked her fingers at me. "Begone. And remember to do your training programs in your spare time. I will know if you slack off."

Using all my willpower, I managed to stay silent as I left her building. But as soon as I was out on the street, I muttered, "What free time?"

After that, I made my way to the low-slung building that contained the obstacle course, and there, I met with the same instructors who'd been teaching me for months. They were a combination of Milo's Amigos and other town residents, and they went over the various components of my [Combat Utility] skills. First, I was with Kimiko, who'd taken time out of her busy schedule to continue to teach me about emergency wound treatment. It was mostly theoretical knowledge, but soon, we would progress to more practical applications.

After that, Jorge lectured me about edible plants and animals, as well as different tricks to finding water in arid environments. He also let me in on his plans to teach me different bushcraft methods, including more advanced shelter construction and beast lore. Given how much zoological knowledge we would cover, it almost felt like I was back in school—though contrary to what I'd learned in school, I knew Jorge was teaching me accurate information.

Finally, that block of time ended with the best part—explosives handling. Again, this was taught by Anna, who took to it with her characteristic gusto. Her excitement was contagious, and besides, I really liked the idea of blowing stuff up. Not that we had that chance on the first day; that would come later, I was sure. For now, I had to be content with merely learning about different, increasingly complex compounds. She also began introducing me to different types of grenades, including ones meant more for support than actual damage.

After that came my time on the range, which saw me being taught by a trio of instructors. First came Milo, who taught me things about handling a pistol that I never even suspected I might need to know. None were big changes, but

I could see how, once I mastered the different techniques, Ferdinand II would be that much deadlier.

Next, I was instructed by one of the Amigos, Gildar. He was a short, slight man who carried a drum-fed automatic scattergun that looked as if it would knock him over the moment he fired it. To my surprise, he handled it with fluid finesse, and under his tutelage, I knew I would find new ways to use my own oft-forgotten scattergun.

The last part of that block was the first time I'd received instruction from my uncle since leaving Nova City.

"Don't get used to it," he said, standing before the rifle course. It was a combination of long-range and short-range targets, all moving and designed to force the shooter to constantly adjust, just like a real battle. "Jorge's going to take over most of the time. But when I'm in town, I'll be teaching you. Now, let's see what you've learned."

I was eager to show off, so I hit the course running. And over the next couple of minutes, I cleared the whole thing more quickly than I ever had before. I didn't miss a single target, and I skated between the different obstacles like I'd been born for it. So, I was more than a little surprised when my uncle said, "Okay, so the answer to that question is 'not much.' I should have known."

"What? I ran the course perfectly!" I insisted.

"You ran it like a drone," he said. "Like a normal soldier. You're not that, Mirabelle. Never think that you are."

"I don't understand."

"I know, but you will," he said. Then, he proceeded to break down the run, one step at a time, pointing out every single thing I did wrong. Some were easily understandable—like a misstep here or there—but others sounded like he was asking far too much from me. For instance, he spent an entire minute chastising me for leaving my toe out of cover. A single toe! I wanted to scream at him that my toe didn't matter, but he'd anticipated my outrage.

"What would happen if someone shot that toe?" he asked. "Just a single stray bullet, and you'd be limping along after that. It wouldn't stop you, right then and there. You've got too many skills and too much Constitution for that. But it would slow you down and make the next shot that much easier. Before you knew it, you would be bleeding from a dozen wounds and wondering how everything went so wrong, so quickly. That's the point, Mirabelle. You can't afford mistakes."

"Yes, sir."

"Now, do it again."

I did, and this time, I was thinking so much about all the things he'd said I did wrong that I ended up taking twice as long to clear the course. However, he didn't seem to care about the extra time, telling me that it was a better attempt.

Or rather, his exact words were "It's still shit, but it was better than last time. Go again."

And so it went until he told me it was time for me to report to Simon for my instruction in [Close Quarters Combat]. When I asked when I was supposed to eat, he tossed me a ration bar.

"So, it's like that, then?" I mumbled to myself. But I didn't waste any time before tearing into the tasteless brick, downing it with a bottle of hastily drunk water.

My time with Simon was at least as revelatory as my uncle's instruction, and he found even more fault with my melee techniques than my uncle had with my rifle handling. However, he was much nicer about it—even jovial, often grinning as I corrected my mistakes.

Finally, the end of the day loomed over me as I met with Vanna. She didn't have her skill active, so her normal appearance was on display.

"You've had some instruction in avoiding notice, have you not?" she asked.

I nodded. "A little," I said. "I'm decent at it."

She snorted. "You're an amateur until I say otherwise," Vanna said. "So, here's how we're going to play it. I'm going to give you a few tips and tricks this afternoon, but tomorrow, we're going to do things a little differently. Basically, we're going to play a little game. I'll designate some hunters—maybe some of Milo's Amigos; they're good enough for this—and you're going to be their prey. We'll start in town, but in a few months, we'll move outside. Manage to evade them and you'll get a prize. Fail and you'll be punished. What do you think about that?"

"Uh . . . what kind of prize?"

She clapped her hands together sharply, and a manic grin spread across her face. "That's the fun part! It's a surprise! Now, let's get started. You're going to need all the help you can get before tomorrow."

CHAPTER FORTY-ONE

EVERYTHING IS A TEST

Since the Initalization, I have killed thousands of people, but even before our planet was inundated by the nano-cloud we call Mist, I was a killer. I think I always had it in me, even going back to childhood. Back then, I knew I wouldn't hesitate to do what was necessary. And I only grew more certain as the years went by.

—Jeremiah Braddock III

I slipped through the crowd, focusing equally on my abilities and my surroundings. I had been on the run for two days, evading Vanna and a trio of borrowed Amigos the entire time. It was the longest I'd ever spent avoiding capture—a sign of how far I'd come if ever there was one. As I wove my way through the pedestrians, I tried to remember my lessons. The first and most important tenet was to blend in. To that end, I wore ragged, shapeless clothing, with my distinctive hair stuffed under a cap. However, other than my attire, I didn't make any other concessions to concealment. In my mind, Vanna's words kept me company:

"You know who looks suspicious? The person slinking around with hunched shoulders and wearing a hood," she said. "You know who doesn't? The girl who looks just like everyone else. Your job isn't to conceal your identity. It's to blend into the crowd. A group of people is all the camouflage you'll ever need."

Of course, that wasn't necessarily true—a fact I'd learned dozens of times over the previous six months' worth of training. Like everything else, my abilities in [Spycraft] had jumped forward by leaps and bounds, even earning me a new ability called Mimic. It was still a low-grade ability, but it had plenty of potential.

Mimic (F)—Take on the superficial appearance of another person. Combat may break the illusion.

Even though it was a relatively new ability that I'd earned only the week before, I had spent an untold number of hours exploring the possibilities. Even during my rare time off, I found myself taking on the identities of random pedestrians. It was too bad, then, that Vanna had forbidden me from using it during our frequent games, largely because she didn't want the powerful ability to become a crutch.

Sensing someone's eyes on me, I sped up just enough to step in front of the person next to me. Using the other pedestrian as moving cover, I searched the area for an appropriate hiding place. It wasn't easy; we were in a residential area, with huge, square, and blocky buildings that served as tenements. They weren't as low-class as the one in which I'd confronted Jack months before, but they were sufficiently decrepit that no one who could afford better would ever choose to make their home there.

Suddenly, I spotted an alley, and I wasted no time in using it to my advantage. When I veered off the main street, I was confronted with a familiar sight. The alley itself was narrow—maybe four or five feet across—and filled with garbage and semiconscious dustheads. Male or female, it didn't matter. They were all skeletally thin, covered in dirt, and bearing the splotchy red-and-purple bruises so common among that flavor of addict. My Triage ability told me that those marks were caused by an overabundance of Mist in a person's bloodstream, which tended to pop the vessels, resulting in the drug's trademark bruising.

Not that any of them cared. Pixie dust—or just dust, as it was colloquially known—gave its users a euphoric feeling, but when it wore off, it also rendered them insensate. Once, I might've judged them for it, but after seeing how hopeless some of their lives were, I didn't really blame them for looking for an out. Sometimes, life in our world was just too much for people to handle, and it was easier to take a snort of pixie dust and spend the next day or two in a stupor than to confront the horrors of life in a post-Initialization world.

With Observation, which had recently increased to E-grade, powering my senses, I saw everything. More than that, I couldn't ignore the smells—body odor, human waste, and garbage—or sounds. Thankfully, almost as soon as I stepped into the alley, a summer rain shower began, cutting visibility and muting the smell. I ignored the thick droplets of rain as I trotted down the alley, turning the corner when I reached the back of the building. Looking this way and that, I leaped, grabbing hold of the rickety metal fire escape and pulling myself up to the platform. After that, I raced up the switchback steps, back and forth, until I reached the roof. Once I was there, I crouched down and peeked over the edge of the building.

A smile spread across my face as I saw Lonnie, the Amigo I'd noticed following me. He was a short, stout man who, unlike the other Amigos who'd traced their lineage back to some place called Guatemala, came from native stock. He would tell anyone who would listen about his proud heritage. Of course, I didn't really believe much of what he said, but he was an amiable sort.

And besides, he was a wizard with the tomahawk he carried. He had briefly been one of my instructors, and he'd taught me the basics of the weapon. I'd had other weapons, too—from clubs to knuckle-dusters and everything in between—and I had developed a passing familiarity with most weapon types. Still, I preferred a sword. Or my rifle. Maybe Ferdinand II. The scattergun was my least favorite weapon, but I suspected that was because it hadn't really been made to do much damage. Instead, it was intended as a nonlethal alternative, which just seemed to have missed the point of weaponry, as far as I was concerned. Still, in the right situation—against a big group of lower-powered enemies—it could be lethal enough, which was its only saving grace.

Still, I'd been working with it as diligently as I had been training with my other primary weapons, resulting in marked progression. Seeing Lonnie down below, perfectly vulnerable, it made me wish I could just pull out my Kicker, throw it into its sniper configuration, and put one in the back of his skull. That would end the pursuit right then and there, wouldn't it?

Not that I wanted to kill Lonnie or anything. Not really, at least. I just wanted to win the game. Of course, violence wasn't supposed to be a part of the game, either, so half my arsenal of abilities wasn't available to me.

I pulled back—slowly, so the sudden movement wouldn't alert him—and settled down to wait. As I did, I focused on Observation, listening for his footsteps. I was a couple of hundred feet from him, but with how the ability had progressed, hearing him shouldn't have been difficult. Or that would have been the case if it weren't for all the rain.

I let out a long sigh.

I was exhausted. Hiding from Vanna and the Amigos for two straight days had kept me constantly on edge, and it was starting to catch up to me. I'd snatched a few minutes of sleep here and there, but that was a poor substitute for real rest.

Finally, after sitting there for almost an hour, I got the message I'd been looking for:

Vanna: Okay, you win this round. Meet me at the inn.

I gave a little fist pump of celebration. It felt good. Really good. I'd gotten the same feeling when I'd cleared the gauntlet, which was Simon's preferred method of testing me. Comprised of twenty fights of steadily ramping difficulty, it was one of the most exhausting things I'd ever attempted. For the first few weeks, it was all I could do to make it to the sixth or seventh fighter, but after that, I'd steadily improved. Day by day, I lasted a little longer until, after four months, I finally conquered it.

Of course, that small victory had only jump-started the next phase of my hand-to-hand training, which saw me facing different scenarios. Sometimes, I was tasked with defeating a group of fighters, but other times, I was just trying to get through them to some objective. Each day, it was something different, and it taught me the simple lesson that being able to fight was only a small part of winning an engagement. Thinking on your feet was much, much more important.

Grinning, I looked over the edge of the roof, hoping I could silently descend the fire escape and surprise Lonnie, who, last I checked, was still down below. Which was true. He was still down there. However, he was sprawled across the ground, a pool of blood mingling with the puddles of rain. His head had clearly been separated from the rest of his body.

A figure, dressed all in black, stood over him, nano-edged sword in hand. They weren't big, and despite the fact that their outfit was skintight, I couldn't tell if I was looking at a man or woman. And with my senses enhanced by Observation, that was saying something. In the couple of seconds that I spent staring at them, I realized that they were using some sort of skill.

Then, they looked up at me, their face obscured by a black mask. Even their eyes were covered by a pair of green-lensed goggles.

I froze, my breath catching in my throat.

That only lasted for a brief second before I summoned my Kicker from my arsenal implant and, in the same motion, brought it to my shoulder, took aim, and squeezed the trigger, firing a single burst in the black-clad figure's direction. The bullets tore through the air, and despite the fact that I'd spent untold hours at the range, they found nothing but the ground. Water and Lonnie's puddled blood geysered into the air as surprise filled my mind.

"I missed . . ."

Well, when at first you don't succeed, fill the air with bullets. Or something like that. That's what my rifle instructor, Jorge, kept saying. At that moment, it seemed appropriate.

One burst. Two. Three. I kept firing until my magazine ran empty, but the figure moved like lightning, their body blurring with sheer speed. They were actually dodging my shots.

Panic rising into the back of my throat, I summoned a new magazine and, after ejecting the old one, jammed it into the well. By the time I finished, the figure was three-quarters of the way up the fire escape. They weren't going up the steps, either. Instead, they were going up the outside, hopping from one railing to the next.

I swallowed hard and made a decision. I couldn't fight this person. They were too far above me. My only hope lay in retreat. But even if I turned tail and ran, there was no way I'd make it more than a handful of steps. Not with how fast they were moving.

Fortunately, I had something else up my sleeve.

Waiting until they were within a few short feet, I waited until they were between platforms before I activated an ability:

Initiate Misthack (trivial defenses detected)?
[Yes] or [No]

I selected the first option.

Misthack Iniatiated. E-Grade Defenses Overridden.

That allowed me to instantly bypass E-grade and lower systems. Luckily, the assassin—and that's what they clearly were—didn't have a particularly secure system.

Misthack Successful. Options:
- **Reboot System**
- **Overload System**
- **Breach System**

I chose to reboot the system. It all happened in the space of a fraction of a second, and when the ability hit the assassin, I heard a feminine yelp. Her body seized up, and instead of grasping the last railing, her fingers slipped on the wet metal. She fell. Seeing my opportunity, I fired a couple of bursts at her falling body, but even though my bullets hit her torso, my efforts were rendered useless due to the metallic clink of my rounds hitting subdermal armor.

Her tense body hit the ground with a thud, but the moment I saw her stirring, I knew she would soon resume her chase. After all, rebooting her system only lasted for a few seconds. After that, she would regain control of her various implants, and when she did . . .

I needed to leave, and yesterday. So, without further hesitation, I stowed my weapon and sprinted across the rooftop, not even slowing when I hit the edge. Instead, I leaped, clearing the space between buildings without any difficulty. I kept going for six more buildings; like most domiciles, they were all identical, and so, their roofs provided a perfect highway for someone with my Constitution.

At the sixth building, I skidded to a stop before the access door, aimed a kick at the lock, and sent the door flying open. I dipped inside and, taking three steps at a time, sprinted down the stairs. It didn't take me long to reach the bottom, and when I did, I quickly found the lobby and left, blending into the pedestrians.

My heart beating out of my chest, I tried to remember my training. With measured steps, I followed the flow of traffic all the way to the Dew Drop Inn, and even when I got inside, I didn't relax. I found Vanna sitting at her customary table, with Simon in his usual seat across from her. I didn't know if the two were a couple, and contrary to my normal inquisitive attitude, at that moment, I didn't really care.

Vanna grinned at me, saying, "So, you finally did it. I'm proud of you. But next time, we're going to double the number of hunters, and—"

"Never mind that," I said, slamming my hand on the table. "There was a woman. Dressed all in black. She killed Lonnie. Tried to kill me, too, but I got away. I didn't—"

Vanna's eyes flicked past me, and she said, "You didn't get away."

Even as she spoke, she rose to her feet and pushed me behind her. A moment later, she had a slender sword in her hand. Seeing her alarm, Simon wasted no time before joining her, the enormous cudgel that was his favored weapon appearing in his own hand. I followed their gazes to the inn's entrance, where the woman stood. Whatever skill she'd been using to mask her appearance was gone, and I could clearly see her feminine curves. Even so, guessing her identity would be impossible, as everything was still obscured by the black outfit.

"Step aside, Infiltrator," the woman said, her voice full of derision. "Take the thug with you. That little girl and me, we've got an issue between us."

"Can't do that, Banshee," Vanna said, holding her weapon at the ready. "You know this town's under his protection, don't you?"

"I do not fear the Wraith," the so-called Banshee said.

"You should" was all Vanna said. "Your fancy implants won't save you from him."

The Banshee gave a hollow laugh. "So everyone says," she spat. "But he's old. Slow. He can't be the—"

The wall of the inn exploded into splinters, and a moment later, the Banshee's head followed suit, erupting into a cloud of fine mist, metal shrapnel, bone, and brain matter. She fell to the floor with a loud thump.

"Tried to tell her," Vanna said.

"W-what just . . . what just happened . . ."

"Your uncle happened," she said. "Why anyone would attack anybody in this town while he's around, I have no idea. Some people must have a death wish."

"Who was she?" I asked. "Why did she kill Lonnie?"

"Looking to cause trouble for Jeremiah, no doubt," Vanna said. "But I'm proud of you. How did you get away from her?"

I told her about the short fight and how it went down. Even as I did, I heard a few more thunderous gunshots before everything went silent. A moment later, Jeremiah returned. He took one look at the dead woman and stepped over her.

"Everyone okay?" he asked.

"Your niece escaped a Banshee, Jeremiah," Vanna said, a proud smile playing across her face. "If that's not me earning my pay, I don't know what is."

"Is that so?" he asked, his eyes boring into me. I gave him a nod, and he said, "Good. Proves that the plan's working. Banshees are not to be trifled with."

"Who are they?" I asked.

"Elite Enforcers that specialize in taking down high-tiered threats," Simon said. "They take sensitive jobs. Hunt criminals. Carry out assassinations. Clear out dangerous beasts. Their members are required to pass a series of tests before they're given a place at the table."

"There were three of them in town," Jeremiah said. To Vanna, he added, "Thanks for tipping me off. As soon as I knew they were around, they weren't that hard to find."

"W-what?" I asked.

"She sent me a message," Jeremiah explained. "The same thing you should have done the moment you got away. There may come a time when you've only got yourself to depend on, but you're not there yet. You need to learn when to ask for help and when to take care of things yourself. Got it?"

"I . . . I got it."

"Good" was his response.

"How far away were you when you shot her?" I asked, something niggling at the back of my mind.

"About two hundred yards," he said. "So, not far."

That's when everything clicked for me. "On the way here, you were holding back, weren't you?" I asked. "You could have killed that big guy with the arm cannon without skipping a beat, couldn't you?"

"I could have."

"Then why didn't you? People died!" I hissed.

"People were dead before I could react," Jeremiah stated. "They laid a good trap, and before I could save the trucks, they were gone. After that, I decided to use it as a training scenario for you. Give you a taste of what it takes to survive in this world."

"It was a test."

"Everything's a test, Mirabelle," he said. "The only question is who's giving it to you. Is it your uncle, who cares about your well-being? Or is it the world? An enemy? Life is a test. Get used to it."

With that, Jeremiah turned and went back to the dead woman, where he knelt and began searching her. As it turned out, she had nothing on her. However, it was clear that she had a multitude of high-quality implants, so Jeremiah took her by the waist and slung her over his shoulder. As he left the inn, he announced, "Continue your training Mirabelle. Next time, they might send someone really dangerous."

CHAPTER FORTY-TWO

A LONG YEAR

It was ten years after the Initialization when I realized that I was a cut above the rest, but when I thought about it, it made sense. While they'd been content with defending territory or hunting down individual targets, I had been busying myself with murdering every single alien I could find. I didn't care if they posed a threat. I didn't care whether or not they were doing anything morally wrong. To me, they were all the same. Enemies, every single one of them. And I had long known how to deal with my enemies.

—Jeremiah Braddock III

It was a week after the Banshee's attack before I let myself relax and go back to normal, but that event always hovered in the back of my mind. That nameless woman served to remind me that, as much power as I had gathered, I still had a long, long way to go. She had been entirely out of my league. My shots had been completely ineffective against her. It wasn't the first time I'd encountered such a situation, either. Horace Lafontaine had been similarly protected by subdermal armor. However, I suspected that if I were to have employed the same tactics as I'd used against that tiny, minigun-wielding man, I wouldn't have left a scratch on the Banshee. She was just too far above me.

Once I came to grips with that fact, it lit a fire under me that served to push me even harder during my training. If I was dedicated before that, then I became wholly obsessed after that disastrous encounter. And over the next four months, my efforts bore fruit in monstrous gains in basically every category. Not only did my attributes progress, but each of my skills followed suit.

But that success only made my trainers push all the harder, which was how I found myself in the forests surrounding Mobile, trying to evade a relative army of Amigos. I was armed with a modified rifle that, rather than spitting out normal ammunition, fired tiny pellets that would mark my targets as being wounded. It was training, but not of one single skill. Rather, the open-ended competition was intended to force me to utilize everything I'd been taught so far.

And to my surprise, I was winning.

The Amigos were still far more skilled than I was, and most of them had well-developed abilities. However, I'd soon discovered that because of my ballooning attributes, I could easily keep up with them on a purely physical basis. It shouldn't have been surprising. Most were Tier 2, with only one or two being at Tier 3. Not only did that severely limit their potential, but it also made training that much more difficult.

It brought to mind a rare lesson from Jeremiah, this time on the nature of skills, levels, and attributes. During that hour-long conversation, he'd stressed the importance of choosing the right options when I had the opportunity to evolve my skills. However, he also covered some ground in regard to my attributes. Most notably, he had talked about training.

"It'll always be easier and more effective for you, Mirabelle," he had said. "With greater potential comes easier progression, at least in regard to your attributes. I've talked about how, when you get close to your potential, your progress slows. You have to train harder and longer to get the same gains that came so much easier when you were far away from reaching your potential. For you, so long as you keep leveling, you'll always have a long way to go. That is an advantage in that you'll probably never reach the point where progress slows down. Not like the rest of us, who end up stuck on the edge of reaching our potential. There are ways around that, like with Nora and her bio-enhancers, but they come with side effects, as well."

It made sense, then, that my attributes, which had continued to climb, had begun to exceed the lower-tiered amigos. The result was that, while I didn't put them to shame in the realm of raw ability, I did have something of an advantage. Most of the time. The sparse Tier 3 Amigos out there could still run circles around me. But I was getting there.

I dipped into a shallow gully, predictably finding a stream that I followed for a few hundred yards before leaping. Twelve feet up, I grabbed the hefty branch of an oak tree, sending a frightened squirrel—thankfully, one of the normal, noncarnivorous types—scampering away. It chittered at me angrily, but it disappeared into the forest's leafy canopy as I climbed onto the thick branch.

I wasted no time in darting down the length of the sturdy branch, my balance more than up to the task of keeping me upright, and leaping to another tree before repeating the process. Like that, I made my way through the forest, my feet never touching the ground until my path crossed my well-laid trap.

Climbing higher, I straddled the branch, hooking my foot beneath it. It was as stable of a firing platform as I was likely to find. So, I shifted my weapon off my back—it wouldn't fit in my arsenal implant—and settled in to wait for whoever was tracking me.

I hoped it was Stupid Hat with his stupid hat.

Earlier, with Observation, I'd heard someone approaching, so I'd decided to use the situation to my advantage, laying a false trail, then doubling back to set the trap. The whole thing, with my attributes, had only taken a couple of minutes. Hopefully, I hadn't missed my opportunity.

In my perch, I waited, remaining completely motionless until, finally, I heard a rustle in the nearby brush. Only moving my eyes, I focused on the appropriate area, and a few seconds later, one of the Amigos—I didn't know her name—stepped into view. Without Observation, which had quickly become one of my favorite abilities, I never would have heard her footsteps. She was clearly skilled in stealth. However, with that ability on my side, she never stood a chance. After waiting a few moments to make certain that she was alone, I fired a quick burst that took her in the chest.

She cried out, which ruined my position, but according to the rules of the game, she was counted as dead. So, I quickly used the forest of limbs to make my escape. It was a lucky thing, too, because only a second after I'd vacated my perch, a series of shots rang out, and the branch itself was rendered into splinters.

My trap had become a countertrap.

Without looking back, I doubled my speed, leaping from one branch to covering ground more quickly than most people could run. Unfortunately, none of the Amigos were normal people, and a hail of gunfire followed my path. I couldn't escape.

So, I dipped around a particularly thick hickory tree. Thrusting my back against the trunk, I focused on my hearing, and I was rewarded with the sound of the Amigo sprinting past my hiding place. Obviously, he'd assumed that I had kept moving through the canopy, but I knew my ruse wouldn't last long. So, catching the slightest glimpse of him, I activated [Mistwalker] and focused on my Misthack ability.

Misthack Successful. C-Grade defenses detected. Attempt to bypass? [Yes] or [No]

Under my breath, I swore at my luck. There was only one Amigo with those kinds of cybernetic defenses. Otherwise, I could have Misthacked my way in, disabled cybernetics, and gotten an easy kill. It was my misfortune that I'd run into Jorge himself, whom I'd learned was the highest level of all the Amigos.

In the split second that it had taken me to find his rock-solid defenses, he had whipped around, aimed his weapon at me, and fired. The shot took me in the chest, and I tumbled to the ground. The leafy undergrowth cushioned my fall. Physically, I was uninjured, but my pride had definitely taken a blow.

"Ow."

I lay there for a long moment, cycling through all the mistakes I'd made. I had done almost everything right, and as a result, I'd lasted for a full six hours this time, which was far longer than usual. Still, I'd lost. I had been killed. And my failure rankled me. After almost a minute, I opened my eyes to see Jorge standing over me. He extended a hand, and I took it. After he helped me up, he said, "What happened?"

"Didn't realize it was you," I said. "Went in for a Misthack, and I saw your C-grade defenses. Even if I'd have been successful in the hack, it would've taken me a few minutes. By then, you'd have shot me. And if I wasn't successful, I'd have been out of commission for at least a week."

That much was true. Of late, Helen had forced me to try to infiltrate higher-graded defenses, and I failed at least as often as I succeeded. But it always took a subjective eternity, and failure meant dealing with overwhelming migraines and a kind of artificial illness that made me feel weaker than I was even before my Awakening. To say I was hesitant to attempt it in the middle of a battle was an understatement.

"And what would you have done differently?" Jorge asked. I could see a flash of something in his eyes. Doubtless, he was busy messaging all the other participants in the day's training.

"I should have let you pass, then turned around and run away," I said. "Live to fight another day. Or at least wait until it was a more advantageous situation."

He nodded. "Good," he said. "The purpose of this is for you to learn, which you did."

Having said that, he turned and strode off through the woods. I scrambled to catch up, asking, "How did I do, though? I got, like, six people, right? That's pretty good, isn't it?"

"It is . . . fair," he allowed. Jorge was a lot of things, but effusive with his praise wasn't one of them. Even so, I would take what I could get, and for him, *fair* was basically a pat on the back.

After that, I silently followed Jorge for a half hour until we reached a clearing. There, I saw a series of tents and a couple of trucks with enormous knobby tires. As we approached, a couple of the Amigos—a man and a woman that looked like siblings—looked up. I couldn't help but grin at their winces; they had been two of my first victims that day. To get to them, I'd hidden in a particularly foul-smelling stagnant pool of water until they'd passed me by, only to rise to the surface and pepper them with the mostly harmless bullets. They'd never even known what hit them.

Of course, I'd picked up a few leeches for my trouble, but aside from being incredibly unpleasant, they weren't really dangerous. I'd just make sure to run by Kimiko's soon so she could give me something to prevent an infection.

Jorge wandered off, and I found a place leaning against one of the enormous tires. None of the Amigos were particularly sociable, especially with me. I suspected that they resented me for some reason, but I wasn't really interested in trying to get them to like me. When I'd asked Jeremiah about it, he'd said, "They are merely a whetstone upon which you are expected to sharpen yourself. Don't get attached."

And I had taken his advice to heart. In an abstract sense, I cared about them, but despite spending so much time with them, that feeling wasn't personal. It was the same thing I felt for any acquaintance. I wasn't one of them. They knew it, and so did I.

For the next hour, we waited until everyone returned. During that time, the Amigos packed up their gear. I had nothing to pack, and when I tried to help, I only received a glare for my troubles, so I spent my time doing number puzzles. I had to turn the difficulty up to the highest level to get any challenge, but doing so kept me from wasting my time just sitting around. Finally, everyone had returned, packed up, and piled into the trucks. I claimed a spot in one of the beds, and we set off back for town.

The Amigos chattered away among themselves, but I didn't join in. They wouldn't have wanted me to, and I didn't speak the language they used, anyway. By nightfall, we arrived back in Mobile, where I wasted no time before reporting to the training building. I had plenty of time for a workout.

Pulling a pair of shimmering, blue Misteel cuffs from my arsenal implant, I slapped them around my wrists. The moment the clasp latched, I felt my attributes plummet. The cuffs acted as a restraint by rendering the Mist within my body inert. With those cuffs on, it felt as if I'd never been Awakened at all. More importantly, it made my workouts that much more difficult.

Of course, the restraints also came with a budding panic, and I had to remind myself that I knew precisely how to escape them. It wasn't easy, but with my ever-increasing proficiency in Mist Manipulation, it was only a matter of time before I could override the effects of those restraints. Still, it wasn't a pleasant feeling, so I quickly began my workout, as much as a distraction as a quest for improvement.

I started with a few laps around the building, increasing my pace with each revolution until I was practically sprinting. Once I finished that, I went to the obstacle course, which was incredibly difficult, given my enforced limitations.

Still, I managed it as well as I could, repeating it a few times before moving to the free weights, where I put myself through a rigorous workout. By the time I finished, my every muscle felt like jelly, and I could scarcely move, my muscles were so pumped full of blood.

I went to the nearest wall and sank to my bottom before drinking a couple of bottles of water. Slowly, I regained some of my energy until, at last, I picked myself up and put myself through a lengthy stretching session.

When I'd finished, I ate a ration bar, removed the cuffs, and left the building. While I was inside training, the sun had begun to dip below the horizon, so the streets were crowded with people who were either on their way home after work or on their way out for a night on the town. With me using my abilities, none of the other pedestrians even looked at me as I walked among them. I was sweaty, stank of stagnant water and body odor, and I probably looked terrible, but no one paid any attention to me. After a few minutes, I reached my destination.

It was a strange building. Three stories tall and shaped almost like an inverted pyramid, it was slightly wider at the top than it was at the bottom. More, it abutted the river, which meant that few people chose to go there despite the energy shield that ran along the waterway's banks.

For my purposes, that made it perfect.

I quickly made my way toward the entrance, which was guarded by a huge plank of wood. I pushed it to the side, replacing it as soon as I was inside. The interior of the building was mired in deep shadow, but with Observation, that wasn't such a big problem. I couldn't really see in the dark, but in the familiar building, I didn't much need to, either.

According to my uncle, before the Initialization, the building had been some sort of museum. There had been a note of bitterness in his voice when he explained how it had been a waste of taxpayer money, too. Given that the building had been built more than a hundred years before, I didn't really have much of an opinion on the subject. But the fact that he still held something of a grudge about it was telling.

Either way, there was nothing inside to suggest its former purpose. It had been gutted, stripped down to the bare concrete walls. Even the interior partitions were gone, either rotted away or torn down so someone could get at the building's pipes. None of that mattered to me, and I soon traced a familiar path toward the stairs, which I hurriedly climbed to the roof.

Once I stepped out into the air, I took a deep breath. Up there, I could smell the nearby bay. I could see the surrounding area. And more importantly, I could be alone. For whatever reason, solitude had become very difficult for me to find. If I wasn't training, I had Jo clamoring for my attention. Sometimes, I didn't mind, but over time, it had become exhausting, largely because she never wanted to just sit still. For my part, that was exactly what I needed in order to unwind after spending most of my days in vigorous training.

So, I traversed the roof, found my favorite spot, and lay on my back. As I did so, I turned on the Leviathan file my uncle had given me and stared up at the stars.

I don't know how long I lay there. Hours, at least. And all the while, I wondered what marvels the rest of the universe held. There were aliens out there. Whole civilizations. Were they similar to human beings? Or were they completely unique? They couldn't all be bad, could they? I had no idea, but there was a part of me that wanted to find out. Perhaps, one day, I would get the chance.

By the time I started to relax, it was well into the night. More importantly, I sensed that someone had found me.

"How long have you been standing there?" I asked, not bothering to turn my head. Jeremiah hadn't tried to mask his presence, and as such, I couldn't mistake him for anyone else in the world.

"Only a few minutes," he said, finally joining me. He sat down, putting his forearms on his knees, and looked up at the stars. "What are you doing up here?"

"Decompressing," I said. "All that training, it's stressful, especially when I'm focused. After a long day, I sometimes like to come up here and just . . . unwind."

Jeremiah didn't say anything at first, which was a little surprising. I half expected him to chastise me for wasting time. But he didn't. In fact, for more than a minute, he didn't respond at all, and when he finally opened his mouth, he was on to a completely different subject. "Your friend Jack returned," he said. "And he brought some friends."

"What?" I asked. I hadn't even thought about the former Tiger in months.

"Don't worry," Jeremiah said. "We've already taken care of him. Sloppy, leaving him alive. You should have just killed him and been done with it. That's what I would have done."

"If it happened now, I would, too," I said. Despite still being uncomfortable with outright murder, my training had instilled in me the pragmatism necessary to recognize when killing was the best choice. With Jack, I'd made the mistake of mercy. And to make matters worse, it was one I couldn't rectify because he'd fled the city and disappeared into the wilderness.

"Good."

"What did you want?" I asked.

"Oh. I came up here to tell you that Nora's here," he said. "She's going to help with the rest of your training."

My eyes widened, and I couldn't suppress a grin. As much as I liked the people of Mobile—and I'd made at least one friend and more than a few acquaintances—Nora was different. Because I'd grown up with her around, she was like an aunt to me. Or a naughty big sister. I had seen her a few times since leaving Nova City, but those visits were usually limited to a day or two, at most.

"Thought you'd like that," he said. "Come on. Let's head down to the Dew Drop. She's waiting on us."

CHAPTER FORTY-THREE

THE END OF AN ERA

Good, trustworthy help is almost impossible to find. When you do, cling to it.

—Jeremiah Braddock III

I let out a little squeal when I opened the inn's front door to see Nora sitting across from a couple of Amigos. She was just as garishly dressed as ever, and if anything, her wardrobe had grown even more provocative. There was more skin on display than what was actually covered by the stretchy fabric of her leggings, which bore a series of artful slashes that exposed her muscular legs. But after spending my formative years in Nova City, I was inoculated to such things.

I raced across the common room of the Dew Drop Inn and threw my arms around Nora's neck, hugging her tightly. Until I'd laid eyes on her, I hadn't realized just how much I'd missed her familiar presence. Growing up, she had always been there with a snarky or inappropriate comment. What's more, with me mired in a sea of relative strangers, she was a familiar rock to which I could cling.

To Nora, I wasn't some mysterious girl who was being trained by the town's best Operators. Instead, I was just Mira. She had known me my whole life, and as such, she saw the side of me that was still just a teenage girl. That was refreshing, especially since my exploits had begun to make the rounds after what I'd done in the Admiral. It sometimes felt like, everywhere I went, whispers followed. Nora wouldn't be affected by any of that, I was sure.

"Whoa, there, peanut," she said, using the nickname she'd given me during my childhood, ostensibly because my head, back then, had been shaped like a nut. "Calm down."

I regained my composure and pulled away, but I couldn't keep the grin from my face. I said, "Sorry. Sorry. I'm just glad to see you."

"Naturally" was her response. "Everyone loves me."

I rolled my eyes, saying, "How long are you here? Uncle Jeremiah said—"

"I'll be around until the end of your training," she answered, shifting on the bench seat. "Sit down. Get something to eat. You look like you're down to skin and bones."

Frowning as I sat, I said, "I'll have you know that I've gained, like, thirty pounds since I saw you last."

She snorted. "You say that like it's impressive," she said. Then, she flexed her enormous biceps. "These are impressive." She reached out and wrapped her meaty fingers around my own upper arm, adding, "These, not so much. You need to start pumping some iron, little girl."

"I do."

"Not enough," Nora said. "Clearly."

Just then, my uncle sat down across from us. The pair of Amigos that Nora had been sitting with shifted down the bench to make room. As he sat, Jeremiah said, "Most people don't want to be the size of a tank, Nora."

"Everyone is wrong, then," she said without skipping a beat. She gave him a suggestive wink, adding, "If you don't believe me, maybe you and me could go have a quick tussle, boss. I promise, you'll be a convert when I get done with you."

Jeremiah coughed, then said, "I think I'll have to pass."

"Your loss," she said.

"Gross" was my response.

Nora chuckled. "Nothing gross about two adults—"

"Anyway," my uncle interrupted. "Mirabelle. Nora's going to be taking over your hand-to-hand training."

"Really? What happened to Simon?" I asked.

"Simon and Vanna have been called away," he said. "It's unavoidable. In their stead, I'll take over Vanna's lessons while Nora takes over for Simon."

"Simon Kincade?" Nora asked.

Jeremiah nodded. "He's been helping with Mirabelle's training for the past months," he explained. "His partner, Vanna, has been helping her with more subtle training."

"Simon Kincade. Now that's a hunk of meat I wouldn't mind rasslin' with," she said. "You know, I met him about four years back. I was just a little stick of a thing back then. Barely more than two hundred pounds. But he showed me some moves I'll never forget. If that little beanpole of a wife of his hadn't shown up . . ."

"Nothing would have happened," Jeremiah stated. "Simon's devoted to that woman, and in ways you probably wouldn't understand."

"What's that s'posed to mean?" Nora asked.

"That you're fundamentally incapable of monogamy," he stated. "It's not a secret. Simon's not like you. He's a one-woman kind of guy."

"Pity."

"Maybe so," Jeremiah said. "But that's how it is." Then, to me, he continued, "In any case, we're going to let you get started with Nora tomorrow, okay? I expect you to catch her up with what you've been doing."

"Alright," I said, hating that the reunion had turned to business. I wanted nothing more than to just sit around and pretend like everything hadn't changed, like we were still back in Nova City, when Nora would tease me about being so scrawny. I knew it was silly. Those days were long gone. But as much as my situation had gotten on my nerves back then, I could now look at it fondly. Especially because I'd seen some pretty horrible things since my Awakening, and there was a part of me that desperately wanted to crawl back into that cocoon of innocence. An impossibility, I was aware, but that didn't keep the idea from wrapping itself around my mind.

The rest of the evening went by without anything notable happening, save for when Jo introduced herself to Nora. When that happened, I couldn't ignore the lecherous look on the muscular woman's face. And while I let it slide in the moment, I resolved to address it soon. Which was how I found myself in the training building the next day, standing before Nora and saying, "Leave her alone, okay? She's not interested."

"Everyone's interested," Nora said. "And she's a big girl. I asked around. She's old enough, so she's fair game."

"That's gross. She's half your age," I said.

Nora shrugged her broad shoulders, then ran a hand through her short, spiky hair. "Fine" was her response. "She's off-limits until your training's over. But after that . . ."

"Not good enough," I said, planting my hands on my hips. "Off-limits for forever."

Nora narrowed her eyes, then glanced at the obstacle course. "Okay, here's the deal," she said. "If you want me to leave that fine piece of—"

"Please do not say what I think you're going to say."

Nora sighed dramatically, then said, "Fine. Okay. You are absolutely no fun. But if you want me to leave that cute little thing alone, you'd better be able to complete that course in under two minutes."

I perked up. "That it? Want me to do it right now?" I asked.

"Two minutes with me trying to stop you," she said. "In fact, that's our training for the next few weeks. You get through it, and I'll leave the girl alone. Don't and she's fair game. Got it?"

I ground my teeth together. I'd completed that obstacle course a thousand times. More, probably. And while I knew Nora would make it difficult, I felt confident enough in my abilities to accept her deal. With a nod, I said, "That works for me."

Nora's resultant grin should have told me just how big of a mistake I had made, but I was blinded by my hubris. That lasted for all of thirty seconds until, as we ran to the course, she thrust her massive fist into my stomach. I clenched up, falling to my knees and vomiting every ounce of the breakfast I'd just eaten onto the floor.

Nora stood over me, her hands on her hips as she said, "Really? I thought you'd been training. That was half-strength, and you're already on your knees. If this is all you've got, your friend's going to be eating out of the palm of my hand. Or eating something else . . ."

I pushed my nausea aside and sprang to my feet. In only a second, I was sprinting toward the obstacle course. I made it about fifteen steps before Nora kicked my legs out from under me. I'd never seen her move so quickly, but she had overtaken me without even trying. Perhaps it was going to be much more difficult than I'd thought.

That first day, I never even made it to the obstacle course. The second, I barely touched the first obstacle—a sheer wall. And on the third, I still hadn't managed to get any farther. Every time I thought I was close, Nora was there, taking the perfect actions to derail me. In the end, it took me a week before I cleared that first obstacle. Another week until I got through a quarter of the course. And a month after that before I finished the course.

That's when we started the whole thing over again, only Nora was accompanied by one of the Amigos. However, I'd gotten the hang of it all, and the additional antagonist was little more than an annoyance. In fact, even when she added a few more to the mix, I found myself clearing the course easily.

So long as I didn't lose concentration. The moment I lost focus, I would pay the price, and Nora made sure it was always incredibly painful, even if it didn't leave long-lasting damage. For those first few weeks, I hated her, but slowly, that hatred turned to appreciation as I realized just how much I was growing. Not in terms of my attributes—though those were increasing at a rapid pace—but rather, in regard to my environmental awareness as well as my proprioception. Without those ephemeral gains, I never could have completed the program she had prescribed. With them, by the end, it nearly became trivial.

If Nora's training was frustrating, I didn't have words for how I felt about my time with my uncle. I had always known he was a harsh taskmaster. I'd seen that the very first day he took me to the range back in Nova City. But he had clearly been taking it easy on me back then because his training felt like it had become more of an exercise in masochism than anything else.

"Again!" he barked through the connection in my HUD, and I scrambled from my hiding place, rubbing the injury in my shoulder. It wasn't more than a flesh wound, but it was a painful one. As I relocated, a timer counted down on my HUD. Ninety-four seconds left. I needed to find somewhere to hide. But before that, I needed to break his line of sight.

I slid down a steep slope of wet grass, skidding to a stop at the base of a small hill before slipping behind a tree. I crouched low, changing directions abruptly. When I reached an overturned and rusted-out hulk of an old vehicle, I sprinted directly away from where my uncle's last shot had originated.

Forty-two seconds.

I needed to move. I could practically feel the reticle of his scope on me. Not that he needed it. He was less than a mile away. He could have taken me out with nothing but iron sights. Fortunately, he'd limited himself to a borrowed rifle without any fancy attachments. He also wasn't using any of his abilities.

It didn't matter. We had been playing this game for weeks, and I'd yet to evade him for more than a few minutes. Usually, he encouraged me with various grazing shots when he found me. They were never life-threatening, but they definitely stung. As such, they made for a great, if abusive, motivator.

The old me would have called him a monster. But in the past couple of years, I had seen real horror. I had some idea of what kinds of monsters were out there. Without harsh training methods, I would never survive. I knew that now.

Still, that didn't make it any easier to bear.

I skidded to a stop beside the ruins of a concrete building, grabbing what had once been its corner and using it to change direction. As I did, I spied the nearby river; it was a half mile across, and if I dove into it, I felt that I could swim deep enough to evade my uncle. However, that would also put me at the mercy of all the creatures that made their home within its depths. Most notably, the river kraken that had claimed the area as its territory.

The decrepit remnants of the huge suspension bridge loomed over me, and the area's giant metal containers, rusted and mostly fallen, made for a decent cover. I sprinted between them, remembering that my uncle had said that, once upon a time, they'd held natural gas, which had been an alternative fuel source in the pre-Initialization world. Now, it was unnecessary, as almost everything ran on either Mist or solar power, with a smattering of gasoline-powered cars.

I slowed to a stop. Thirteen seconds.

Whipping my head back and forth, I didn't see anything that might offer decent cover, so I hunkered down against the rusted metal, positioning myself beneath a similarly oxidized staircase that came to a jagged stop halfway up the sizable container. It wasn't even close to perfect, but it was the best I could do.

The moment the timer expired, a shot rang out, and I took another wound on my thigh. I let out a frustrated scream as my uncle growled, "Again! You're better than this, Mirabelle!"

Summoning my determination to succeed, I rose to my feet and took off again. As I did, the timer steadily counted down. This time, I didn't get nearly as far before another shot clipped my other shoulder. A few minutes later, yet another shot hit my limping form, this time finding my uninjured thigh.

I fell to the ground, my breath coming in ragged gasps. I tried to drag myself forward, but nothing worked quite right. Finally, I heard footsteps behind me, and a moment later, my uncle said, "You did better today. Come on. Let's get you patched up so we can do it all again tomorrow."

So it went for the remainder of my final year of training. Some people would have called it torture, and in some ways, it was. Certainly, pain was my constant companion. But through that pain—and the lessons themselves, of course—I was forged into something completely new. Slowly, just like I'd managed to conquer the obstacle course, I learned to evade my uncle for progressively longer periods until, only a week before my training was supposed to be completed, I kept out of sight for long enough that he called an end to the session before I was rendered incapable of going on.

That victory tasted incredibly sweet.

Throughout that time, I continued most of my other lessons, as well, learning the ins and outs of dozens of different disciplines, from explosives to basic cybernetics repair, and everything in between. As such, my skills' proficiency increased, and my attributes drew closer to exhausting my potential.

Finally, after my last training session, I sat atop the upside-down-pyramid-shaped former museum, leaning against an old air-conditioning vent as I looked out at the bay. As I watched something huge, bestial, and imposing break free of the water miles away, I pulled up my status:

NAME	Mirabelle Lisa Braddock		
CLASS	N/A (Requirements Not Met)		
LEVEL	4 (41%)		
CONSTITUTION	27/38		
MIND	29/38		
MIST	21/38		
SKILLS	7/7		
SKILL NAME	Skill Tier	Modifiers	Abilities
CYBERNETIC INTERFACE	Tier 4 (14%)	+10% Efficiency	4 Cybernetic Slots

FIREARMS	Tier 4 (11%)	+20% Damage (All Firearms) +6% Reload Speed (All Firearms) +23% Accuracy (All Firearms) +5% Range (All Firearms) +15% Damage (Rifle) +15% Range (Rifle) +15% Damage (Pistol) +10% Accuracy (Pistol) +15% Damage (Scattergun) +15% Reload/ Ammunition Regeneration Speed (Scattergun)	Empowered Shot (E) Quickdraw (E) Double Shot (F)
CLOSE QUARTERS COMBAT	Tier 4 (6%)	+9% Movement Speed +20% Damage (Melee) +15% Speed (Melee) +9% Accuracy (Melee) +30% Damage (Unarmed) +5% Speed (Bladed Weapons) +10% Accuracy (Bladed Weapons) +5% Damage (Blunt Weapons) +10% Accuracy (Blunt Weapons)	Combination Punch (D) Eviscerate (E) Pummel (F) Engage (F)
STEALTH OPERATIONS	Tier 3 (18%)	None	Camouflage (E) Stealth (F)

COMBAT UTILITY	Tier 4 (71%)	None	Triage (D) Basic Explosives Handling (D) Combat Focus (C) Pain Tolerance (D) Resistance (E) Foraging (E) Improvisation (D) Regeneration (D)
MISTWALKER	Tier 3 (91%)	+19% Speed (Misthack) +10% Speed (Mistwalk) +15% Strength (Mistwall)	Mistwalk (D) Misthack (D) Mistwall (C) System Redirect (F) Breach (F) Overcharge (E)
SPYCRAFT	Tier 3 (88%)	None	Disguise (D) Deception (E) Observation (D)

I was extremely satisfied with my progress, not least because of how hard I knew I'd had to work for it. It told me just how difficult it was to progress; if, after years of consistent work, I'd managed to reach only Tier 4 in some of my skills, and Tier 3 in others, then other, less diligent people would be hard-pressed to match my gains. Certainly, there would be some who engaged in similar training programs, but I had to think that those would be the exception, rather than the rule. Without some of my abilities—like Combat Focus, Regeneration, and Pain Tolerance—my training regimen would have been impossible. And I had an inkling of just how rare the skill that gave me those abilities really was.

I had progressed to the fourth tier in four out of my seven skills, and those that had lagged behind were on the verge of making the jump. The only odd one out was [Stealth Operations], which, while it had progressed well, hadn't quite kept up with everything else. Still, I had plenty of time to rectify that.

The increases in my skills' tiers had come with a host of strong modifiers as well as a bevy of new abilities. To get a handle on the details of my improvement, I decided to drill down into my skill trees. The first I opened was for [Firearms], which held a special place in my heart. There was just something about shooting things that spoke to a primal part of my personality. Perhaps, given my uncle's proficiency with various firearms, it ran in my blood.

Tree	Firearms: Tier 4 (11%) +15% Damage (All Firearms) +6% Reload Speed (All Firearms) +8% Accuracy (All Firearms)			
Branch	Rifle: Tier 4 (3%)	Pistol: Tier 3 (71%)	Scattergun: Tier 3 (6%)	Sharpshooter: Tier 4 (7%)
Tier 1	+15% Damage (Rifle)	+15% Damage (Pistol)	+15% Damage (Scattergun)	+15% Accuracy (All Firearms)
Tier 2	+15% Range (Rifle)	+10% Accuracy (Pistol)	+15% Reload/ Ammunition Regeneration Speed (Scattergun)	+5% Damage (All Firearms)
Tier 3	Ability: Empowered Shot	Ability: Quickdraw	Ability: Double Shot	+5% Range (All Firearms)
Tier 4	Plasma Rifle Certification	Energy Pistol Certification	Explosive Scattergun Certification	Weapon Modification Certification
Tier 5	+15% Rate of Fire (Rifle)	+25% Rate of Fire (Pistol)	+15% Accuracy (Hipfire, Scattergun)	Ability: Mark Target

Not only had I picked up a variety of modifiers for specific types of weaponry, but I'd also gained three new abilities. The first was:

Empowered Shot (E)—Gather Mist to temporarily empower a rifle. Current modifier: 272%. Charge takes two seconds (modified by Mist Attribute). Lasts for one shot.

It was my favorite new ability, and not by a small degree. Because of its nature, it was really only useful when my Kicker was in its sniper configuration, but when I did use it, the ability allowed me to absolutely destroy targets. I suspected that my uncle had a higher-tiered version of the skill, which he'd used to kill the Banshee months before.

Next, I moved to the pistol branch's signature ability:

Quickdraw (E)—Draw (or summon from an Arsenal Implant) your weapon with alacrity. Reduces draw time by half. Fire rate increased by 25% for three seconds after drawing a pistol.

It was an incredibly useful ability, and with it, I could have Ferdinand II out and firing in record time. It had made some of the mixed-weapon courses almost trivial after I'd gained access to the ability.

The ability granted by the scattergun branch of the [Firearms] tree was:

Double Shot (F)—Doubles the effect of a scattergun, mimicking two shots.

It was a simple skill, but like Empowered Shot, I was limited in how often I could use it. If I tried to activate it more than a couple of times in succession, it did nothing. On top of that, it resulted in a brief moment of weakness that could prove deadly in battle. According to my uncle, it was tied to my Mist attribute, and as it rose, so too would I be able to use those abilities more often.

I had also gained the Weapon Modification Certification, which would let me use various attachments on my weapons. However, none of those attachments were available, so the certification was mostly forgotten.

Moving on from my [Firearms] skill tree, I opened the one pertaining to my [Close Quarters Combat] skill:

Tree	**Close Quarters Combat: Tier 4 (6%)** +20% Damage (Melee) +15% Speed (Melee) +9% Accuracy (Melee)			
Branch	Pugilism: Tier 4 (17%)	Bladed Weapons: Tier 4 (1%)	Blunt Weapons: Tier 3 (2%)	Movement: Tier 4 (21%)
Tier 1	+5% Damage (Unarmed)	Nano-Blade Certification	+5% Damage (Blunt Weapons)	+2% Movement Speed
Tier 2	+10% Damage (Unarmed)	+5% Speed (Bladed Weapons)	+10% Accuracy (Blunt Weapons)	+2% Movement Speed

Tier 3	Ability: Combination Punch	Ability: Eviscerate	Ability: Pummel	Ability: Engage
Tier 4	+15% Damage (Unarmed)	+10% Accuracy (Bladed Weapons)	+10% Damage (Blunt Weapons)	+5% Movement Speed
Tier 5	Ability: Barrage	Energy Blade Certification	Ability: Mighty Swing	Ability: Disengage

Like with the [Firearms] skill, [Close Quarters Combat] resulted in a handful of abilities, all of which were tied to reaching the third tier in an individual branch. The first was in the Pugilism branch:

Combination Punch (D)—String together a series of unarmed strikes, all in rapid succession. Each subsequent strike does double the damage of the previous. Current possible string: 4

It was easily my favorite ability in the tree, mostly because when I sparred with Nora, it was the only thing that let me hold my own, however briefly. Without it, I rarely made a dent in her durable flesh. It was unsurprising, considering that she was a wall of bio-enhanced muscle that was further strengthened by unknown cybernetics.

Next, I looked at the Bladed Weapons equivalent of Combination Punch, which was called Eviscerate.

Eviscerate (E)—Rapidly attack your enemy multiple times with a bladed weapon. All attacks will cause additional bleeding. Current possible string: 3

It was a lot like Combination Punch, but with the obvious difference of requiring a bladed weapon. However, instead of up-front damage, it seemed best suited to wearing an enemy down via blood loss. I didn't know how well that would work against someone who'd been copiously enhanced with cybernetics, but against the virtual opponents with whom I'd trained, it was incredibly effective. Plus, using my nano-sword made me feel like one of the ninjas that were so popular in the various cartoons I'd grown up watching.

Next, I turned my attention to the next ability, which was granted by my Blunt Weapons branch, called Pummel:

Pummel (F)—For a specified number of attacks (determined by Mist Attribute and ability grade) with a blunt weapon, ignore enemy armor and partially bypass Constitution. Current affected attacks: 1

Blunt weapons were admittedly my least favorite weapons, but when I'd gotten that ability, that dislike had shifted a bit. I still didn't think I'd ever truly enjoy using them, but the benefits were too strong to disregard. Being able to ignore enemy armor, like the subdermal armor I'd encountered while fighting Horace Lafontaine, could be a game changer. I was sure that there were plenty of caveats to the ability, especially because it hadn't been that difficult to obtain, but I had very limited experience with it due to only recently passing into the third tier of that branch. I was eager to test it out, though.

Lastly, I focused on the final ability associated with the [Close Quarters Combat] tree:

Engage (F)—Rapidly close with your enemy. Limit: 45 Feet

It was an extremely simple and self-explanatory ability, and one for which I had few uses. Most of the time, I wanted to keep my distance from my adversaries, and I could only think of a few very specific circumstances where I'd want to do the opposite. Still, it was nice to have the ability in my back pocket, should I ever need it. I'd practiced with it a little, but I'm honest enough to admit that it had mostly been neglected. For that specific branch, I was far more interested in the enhanced movement speed that came with increased proficiency.

Having finished up with the [Close Quarters Combat] tree, I moved on to [Mistwalker].

Tree	**Mistwalker: Tier 3 (91%)** Ability: Mistwalk (Granted upon Skill's Acquisition) Ability: Misthack (Granted upon Skill's Acquisition) Ability: Mistwall (Granted upon Skill's Acquisition) +12% Speed (Misthack) +10% Speed (Mistwalk) +15% Strength (Mistwall)			
Branch	Mistwalk: Tier 3 (89%)	Mistwall: Tier 4 (2%)	Misthack: Tier 3 (8%)	Mist Manipulation: Tier 4 (-29%)

Tier 1	F-Grade Systems Infiltration	F-Grade System Defense	+5% Speed (Misthack)	Ability: Overcharge
Tier 2	E-Grade Systems Infiltration	E-Grade System Defense	+2% Speed (Misthack)	+2% Strength (Overcharge)
Tier 3	D-Grade Systems Infiltration	D-Grade System Defense	Ability: Breach	+2% Strength (Overcharge)
Tier 4	+2% Infiltration Stability	Ability: System Redirect	+5% Speed (Misthack)	+10% Cybernetic Efficiency
Tier 5	Ability: Bypass Trivial Defenses	+5% Increased System Defense Strength	Ability: Multihack	+5% Strength (Overcharge)

Aside from the ability to infiltrate higher-grade systems or defend against increasingly dangerous threats, the tree gave me access to three abilities. The first was:

Overcharge (E)—Briefly overload an enemy's system, disabling it entirely for a short duration. Small chance of completely destroying lower-grade cybernetics. Requires physical contact.

It was the first ability I'd ever used, and I'd done so without even considering what I was doing. It had allowed my uncle to kill the giant we'd encountered when the raiders had attacked our convoy while we were first traveling to Mobile. However, I hadn't had many chances to use it since then, mostly because I couldn't find any volunteers. Without that, I had to advance it during actual combat, which was difficult, considering that it required physical contact. I could think of a few uses for the ability, but they were few and far between. The next ability was far more useful, and it had changed everything.

Breach (F)—Grants the ability to remotely upload Ghosts.

It was a simple ability, and in a lot of ways, it allowed Mishack to mimic Mistwalk. However, that mimicry was limited to the ability to upload Ghosts.

But I was fine with that because with enough creativity, Ghosts could do basically whatever I wanted them to do. Already, I'd spent an inordinate amount of time writing and rewriting Ghosts, but as many attempts as I'd made, I'd only come up with a handful of viable options. More would come, I was certain.

I moved on to the final ability granted by the tree:

System Redirect (F)—While under the influence of an enemy Mistrunner, redirect Mist attacks to nonvital systems. Protect what is important so that you may counterattack.

I'd had the chance to use the ability a few times with Helen, but she was far too strong for me to truly affect. She had told me that that was normal, and that the ability would be far more effective as I increased my proficiency, but I didn't look forward to that. In any case, it seemed like a useful ability, even if it was difficult to train.

I let out a sigh, thinking about how far I had come in the past couple of years. I was only eighteen years old, and already, I had a ridiculous amount of power. And I couldn't help but think I would soon acquire more. In time, I could be just as strong as Jeremiah. Probably stronger.

Was I ready for that?

No. But who could be? I could only keep putting one foot in front of the other and handle things as they came. Anything else, and I would get lost in the woods.

CHAPTER FORTY-FOUR

ADVENTURE

Objectively speaking, I have been on plenty of adventures. To me, though, most of them consisted of a parade death and loss. I don't recommend it to anyone, least of all someone I care about. But our world doesn't care what I want, and adventure, with all its horror, will find you, whether you like it or not. The only option is to corral what little control you can and take advantage of the situation to the best of your ability.

—Jeremiah Braddock III

Armed with all the confidence I'd earned through my copious training, I returned to the Dew Drop Inn, my head held high. When I got there, I found my uncle and Nora sitting at one of the tables, so I wasted no time in crossing the common room to join them. To my surprise, Jo soon sat down beside me.

Over the past year, we hadn't had a lot of time to hang out; I was busy with my training, and she had her job at the inn. Still, we'd found a few hours here and there, and our friendship had continued to deepen. I knew that there was a part of her that wanted it to turn into something more—I could read the signs as well as anyone, after all—but I just couldn't give her that, and not only because I wasn't attracted to women. My hesitation was also rooted in the fact that I knew she wasn't, either. Not really. At best, she would tolerate it. Instead, she just wanted to cling to me because of what I represented, because I was a way out of the town that had been her home for her entire life. I couldn't be that for her, either, so I'd kept her at arm's length, which was less than she deserved.

Even so, she was still my friend, and when I moved on, I would definitely miss her. So, I was happy that, on the eve of my final test, she'd found some time to be with me.

Glancing at Nora, I was also happy that her comments about Jo had never really held any teeth. Sure, the big woman probably found Jo attractive, but the whole situation had been designed to add a little extra motivation to my training. And it had worked, too. Even after I realized that Nora had no intentions of pursuing my friend, I was so entrenched in the training that I couldn't even begin to think about letting up.

"The woman of the hour!" Nora said, raising a chunky earthenware mug frothing with beer that had been brewed by Jo's father. It wasn't to my taste, not least because it was useless in regard to its intended purpose. No matter how much of the stuff I drank, I couldn't actually get drunk. Even when I wanted to.

"Hear, hear!"

I wanted to crawl into the nearest corner, curl up, and hope nobody ever noticed me again. It wasn't that I hated attention—I did, but that was only part of it. Rather, woven into my feeling of embarrassment was the notion that I hadn't done anything particularly noteworthy. Sure, I'd kept going well past the point when I thought my endurance would give out. However, that didn't make me special.

In fact, everything special about me had been given to me by my uncle. The Nexus Implant that had changed my life had come from him. So had my skills. My training. Everything that made me, me. To then be praised for something for which I wasn't really responsible had pushed me past my limits and into embarrassment.

Nora knew this, of course. So did Jo. I'd intimated as much to the both of them at one time or another. And in those moments of weakness, when the training had pushed me past my limits, they'd both been shoulders to cry on. That Nora brought it up now was just her way of pushing my buttons.

"Thanks," I said, feeling my cheeks warm with embarrassment.

Jo asked, "What now? Are you going on an adventure or something like in those books you always read?"

"Uh . . . I'm really not sure," I answered, glancing at my uncle. Jeremiah hadn't said anything, but I could see the tiniest of smiles on his face. He was proud of me. Others might not see it, but I knew him well enough to see that much in his reserved expression.

He spoke up, saying, "Let's not talk about that right now. This is a celebration. Today, Mirabelle completed the most difficult training regimen I could provide, and she did it by reaching far higher than I could have imagined. I'm proud of you, Mirabelle. Prouder than I've been of anything or anyone in a long, long time. Maybe ever."

"Aw," said Jo. Nora echoed her sentiment with a wide grin and another toast. I wanted to sink into my chair. Or fight monsters out in the wilderness. Maybe a giant crab, like I'd found in Bayou La Batre. Anything but accepting praise.

After that, the night became a blur of well-wishes, good food, and Nora's increasingly drunken ramblings. By comparison, my uncle remained his same reserved self, and after a few more hours, asked me to accompany him to my room. I followed obediently, and soon, we were alone. And his serious expression had come back.

"Sit, Mirabelle," he said. "We need to have a talk."

"O-okay," I said, sitting on the bed. As I did, he started to pace.

Finally, after a few awkward seconds, he asked, "What do you know about the Mist?"

"Just what you've told me," I said. "It's a galaxy-sized cloud of nanomachines that swept through and enveloped our planet ninety-something years ago. It gave us access to skills and increased attributes, as well as advanced our technology."

It was a good summary, though it didn't cover everything. For instance, left unmentioned was how it had affected the world's wildlife, making them larger and far more dangerous than ever before. The Mist also seeped into the very Earth itself, transforming mundane ore and other materials to such an extent that they gained almost mystical properties. Some, but not all—the same as the planet's wildlife.

"That's a succinct explanation," he said. "But it is incomplete."

"I know. I left out the animals and—"

"Not that," Jeremiah stated. "What I'm about to tell you is something only the elite of the elite of this world know. So, don't go running your mouth and telling everyone you meet, okay?"

"I know how to keep a secret."

"Like you did with Kimiko?" he asked, raising an eyebrow.

I quickly lowered my eyes to the floor. When I'd first gotten my Nexus Implant, he'd told me to keep my skills a secret. However, almost as soon as I'd gotten to Mobile, I'd told the doctor about a few of them. Nothing had ever come of it—she was trustworthy—but Jeremiah liked to remind me of my blunder. And if I was honest, I kept it in the forefront of my mind, as well, because I knew just how badly things could have gone if she hadn't been who she was.

"This is important, Mirabelle," he said. "I need you to acknowledge that."

"I do."

"Good. In addition to everything you just said, the Mist also resulted in something we call Rifts," he said. "Normally, they're nestled within Dead Zones, or areas of incredibly high Mist concentrations. We're not sure which comes first, the Rifts or the Dead Zones, but they always come in tandem."

"What are they?" I asked. I remembered, back before we even reached Mobile, Jeremiah discussing a Dead Zone with a couple of his subordinates, and I knew a little about it. According to that conversation, the closest Dead Zone was so named because, within its boundaries, most Mist-powered technology ceased to work due to the incredible concentration of the Mist as well as its volatile nature. Belatedly, I'd realized that the name probably had another connotation, notably that, within that Dead Zone were extremely powerful monsters that would kill anyone who ventured into the area. "The Rifts, I mean."

"Alone and untouched? Nothing," he said. "Just areas of extreme Mist fluctuation. But the denizens of the galaxy long since discovered a way to harness that energy and create portals to a series of pocket universes. Sometimes, these spaces are uninhabited. Other times, they are guarded by fierce creatures. But always, they have these."

At that, he summoned something from his own arsenal implant. It was a glowing blue crystal the size of my thumb, multifaceted, and when I looked closer, it appeared as if it contained an entire galaxy.

"W-what is that?" I breathed, my eyes wide in wonder. I had never seen anything so beautiful in all my life.

"This is what makes the entire universe work," he said. "It's called a Rift Shard, and this tiny, low-grade example is enough to power a Mist vehicle for a year. Or a small spaceship for a day or two. It's also responsible for your gear, and it's why nobody from Earth can create anything close to the technology the aliens possess. Most of humanity doesn't have access to these yet. And if the aliens have their way, we never will."

"What do you mean?" I asked, already knowing the answer. The aliens would either use us to take the planet's new resource, or they would exterminate us to take it for themselves. My uncle had already intimated as much.

"You know what I mean," he said. "There are so many alien factions in the universe. Some are content to leave us alone. Others want to protect us. But most? The overwhelming majority want to exploit humanity to varying degrees. The only reason they haven't taken over already is because of the hundred-year quarantine period between the Initialization and Integration. Once it's over, our world is fair game."

"And you don't think we can protect ourselves," I said, remembering his previous statements saying as much. "Isn't there anyone who can help us?"

"The Templars," he said. "That's why they exist. They've been recruiting on Earth for years now, but their requirements are so specific that very few have met their standards. Even fewer made it through their training. As of now, there are fewer than a hundred human Templars. Maybe half again as many trainees. They will get support from the larger organization, but it won't be enough to resist the worst of the exploitation. The best they can hope to do is keep the planet from being completely enslaved."

I sighed, trying to make sense of everything, but it was difficult for me to wrap my head around the scope of it all. My uncle went on to explain that the aliens would continue to utilize human pawns to get what they wanted, though after the Integration, those pawns would grow even more powerful than before. If the stories he'd heard from his contacts in the Bazaar were to be believed, our already unjust and unequal society would grow even more lopsided the longer the aliens were pulling the strings. Eventually, there wouldn't be room for anyone to get ahead; instead, the entire planet would have to be content being engaged in the mindless drudgery of mining Rift Shards—or harvesting other valuable materials. We would become slaves in everything but name.

"What am I supposed to do?" I asked, overwhelmed by the weight of that information. "How am I supposed to change any of that?"

"You're not."

"What?"

"It's already done," Jeremiah said. "Even now, the people in charge are bound by alliances with these predatory aliens. Sure, they could still resist, but right now, they have no reason to. It's only when it's too late that they'll realize their mistakes. Even then, they'll probably blame others. That's human nature."

I sighed, massaging the bridge of my nose. "So? Why are you telling me this now?" I asked. My uncle was a lot of things, but free with information wasn't one of them. If he was telling me this now, then he wanted something from me. And given the timing, I expected that it had something to do with my final test.

"There's a mining operation within the Dead Zone north of here," he said. "With the right skills, some aliens can slide in under the system's radar. That's what's happened up there, and they've used their superior technology and abilities to enslave a small group of people. Two generations' worth of human beings have known nothing but slavery. I want you to end the operation."

"That's it? I just go in, kill a few aliens, and—"

"It will be far more dangerous than you can imagine," he said. "But there's more. I also want you to enter the Rift. You need experience with them, and the best way to get that is to dive right in."

I didn't say anything, but I knew my discomfort with the idea was pretty apparent. I didn't mind killing a few aliens, especially after what my uncle had told me. However, the notion of going into one of these Rifts filled me with dread. Part of it was because it was all so unfamiliar, but another part of me was terrified of what I might find in there.

"Have you been in one before?" I asked.

"A few," he acknowledged. "They're all different. Some are naturalistic representations of the wilderness. Others are cities. Still others can be completely alien environments. The possibilities are nearly infinite. But so long as you adhere to your training, you will be fine. I promise. You're one of the best-trained people in this world, and you'll have everything you need to do what you need to do."

"Will you be following me like you did when I went into Bayou La Batre?" I asked.

My uncle shook his head, saying, "No. I can't get close. They'll sense me, which will bring much larger threats into the area. But you, you've got Disguise, Mimic, and Deception. You should be able to get in there without them sensing you. After that, you will be free to wreak havoc."

I lay back on the bed, saying, "This was your plan all along, wasn't it? That's why I have those skills. That's why so much of my training lately has been in evasion."

"One of the reasons, yes," he said. "Everything revolves around those Rifts, Mirabelle. Everything. If you have the tools to infiltrate them, to steal those Rift Shards right out from under their noses, you might survive long enough to escape this planet. We might find a better way to live in the universe."

"Or we could save everyone," I suggested.

"People have to want to be saved for that to work," he said. "Right now, they don't. And by the time they do, it'll be too late. Humanity is lost. Even if Earth avoids complete enslavement, it won't be a good life. They will be exploited until there's not even a memory of freedom left to seek. It's happened with other newly Integrated planets, and it'll happen here, as well. I've accepted that, and I've decided to move on. You should, too."

"I . . . I don't know if I can do that," I said, thinking about all the people in Mobile. Jo. Nora. The Amigos. Even Helen, my [Mistrunner] teacher, who'd departed the moment my training was finished. Vanna and Simon. Even those people I'd met back in Bayou La Batre. If what my uncle said was on the horizon ended up coming to pass, they would all be enslaved. I wasn't sure if I could accept that, regardless of how fruitless my uncle claimed that fighting against it was destined to be.

"You'll see," he said, running his hand over his bald head. "I didn't want to believe it, either. Not until I saw evidence with my own eyes."

"Maybe we can just agree to disagree for now," I said.

"That'll have to work" was his response. "Besides, when you get done with this training mission, I've got a surprise for you."

I definitely perked up at that. "What kind of surprise?" I asked, turning over to prop my head on my hand. "Is it a hover bike?"

He let out a long-suffering sigh. "It is not a hover bike," he stated, though there was a twinkle in his eye. "Let's just say that there's a reason I didn't get you anything big for your birthday this year. I was saving up for something extra special."

I grinned. If I was honest, I had barely even noticed when my birthday came and went. Sure, we'd had a small celebration in the common room of the inn, and I'd gotten some presents from Nora, my uncle, and Jo, but they were small things. And while I had appreciated them, I had been way too focused on my training to give them the attention they deserved. I guess that made me a bad friend. Or at least an ungrateful one. But in my defense, I'd had a lot on my mind at the time.

Jo had given me a self-styler for my hair, which turned out to be a Mist-powered machine that was shaped like a bowl. When I put it on my head, it could style my hair according to whichever templates I'd uploaded. Of course, I hadn't had time to use it, but I knew it would prove to be a valuable addition to my burgeoning beauty regimen.

Almost predictably, Nora had given me something lewd. Specifically, an all-access pass to one of the brothels on Bourbon Street in Nova City. I'd blushed furiously when I had realized what it was, but curiosity had seen me slipping it into my arsenal implant, where it would wait until I returned to the city. I didn't really intend to use it. Probably. Maybe. I mean, I'd check it out, sure. No harm in that.

Of course, there was no way I would let my uncle find out about it, though. He was a fairly progressive person, but there are some things you just don't share with the man who raised you.

Finally, Jeremiah had given me a mapmaking program that could be uploaded into my KIOI. With it, instead of the simple, two-dimensional mapping function that had come with the optical implant, I now had information on elevation, points of interest, and some details on local wildlife. It was an incredibly valuable gift, even if it wasn't quite as sexy as a new rifle or subdermal armor.

Or a hover bike.

"Well, that's it for now," Jeremiah said, his tone turning a little awkward. He really wasn't good with people. He patted my leg. "In the morning, I have some people I'm going to introduce you to, and then you're heading up north where you can finish this mission. Tonight, I want you to think of any questions you might have because once you're in the thick of the Dead Zone, communication will be impossible."

With that, he turned on his heel and slipped from the room. Alone, excitement and dread filled me, and I knew they would keep me from sleeping. So, I decided to use my time wisely, just like Jeremiah had suggested, and think of any issues that I might encounter. Eventually, though, fatigue caught up to me, and I drifted off into unconsciousness.

That night, I dreamed of Rifts that looked like black holes and tentacle-faced aliens that kept demanding I mine the Rift Shards more quickly. It was a weird dream.

CHAPTER FORTY-FIVE

PICKLE

When I stumbled upon my first Rift, I had to carve my way through two dozen aliens in order to infiltrate the breach. What I found inside was much, much worse. Not because of the Rift itself. But because of the methods used to mine it.

—Jeremiah Braddock III

The next morning, I woke up still groggy from my fitful night. However, it was only a few moments before that listlessness was replaced by excitement. Finally, at long last, I was on the verge of completing my training. I'd been in Mobile for more than two years, and in that time, I'd made incredible progress. However, until my uncle told me I was ready, I couldn't allow pride or a sense of accomplishment to creep into my mind.

I threw off my blankets and, after taking care of my business in the bathroom, dressed myself in my familiar and well-worn fatigues, boots, and a black cap to contain my hair. Once that was finished, I checked my arsenal implant, making certain that I had plenty of ammunition. Once I was satisfied, I left my room and went downstairs. Predictably, my uncle was there, though he had an unfamiliar pair of people sitting at the table with him.

The first was a slight man with narrow shoulders and a head that looked too big for his body. He wore thick-rimmed glasses and a wide-brimmed hat, but he was otherwise dressed similarly to all the town's other residents. His companion was short—maybe only an inch or two taller than me—and stocky, with the sleeves of his long sleeve shirt rolled up to reveal meaty forearms. He also had a pair of red-tinted goggles holding back his sandy-blond hair. When I reached the bottom of the stairs, the newcomers turned to look at me, and I was a little surprised to see that the stocky figure belonged to a boy who looked a year or two younger than me. He still had pudgy cheeks, for God's sake.

Taking a deep breath and ignoring the fact that both of them were staring at me, I quickly crossed the common room and sat down next to my uncle. Taking the initiative, I raised my hand in a half-hearted wave, saying, "I'm Mira."

"Remy," said the older man. Up close, I realized that he must've been six and a half feet tall, and that might have been a conservative estimate. He nodded to the thick-bodied young man, adding, "This is Pickle."

"That's not my name," the young man complained, his pudgy cheeks reddening. I wasn't sure if embarrassment or anger was the cause. His voice suggested that he was even younger than I'd thought. "It's Pick. Not Pickle. Just Pick."

"And Pick ain't a proper name, boy," Remy said, taking off his hat and running his hand through his glistening black hair. He had a curious accent, but it was one I couldn't quite place.

"Neither is Pickle!" Pick half shouted, exasperation clear in his tone. Obviously, it wasn't a new debate. He glanced at me, then back at Remy, before saying, "Please, Remy . . ."

The older man rolled his eyes, saying, "Fine. Pick it is, then. Still think it's a stupid-ass name. Besides, everybody likes pickles. Don't nobody like picks."

I was just about to ask what they were doing in Mobile when Jeremiah spoke up, saying, "Remy and Pick are going to take us up to the Dead Zone."

Remy shoveled some eggs into his mouth, asking, "You ever been in a real ship before, girl? Ain't like them silly hover cars you got back in the big city, neither. This is real flyin'."

I swallowed hard. I was aware of the existence of ships that flew between the major cities. They were huge, ungainly things that carried hundreds of tons' worth of goods at a time. But in addition to those, there were also rumored to be personal crafts that moved much more quickly. I had never seen one, and I didn't know anybody that had, so I'd always questioned their existence—especially because, according to my teachers back in school, personal travel between cities was almost nonexistent and limited solely to the ultrarich.

Clearly, that had been just as misleading as anything else I'd learned in school, making me wonder if anything they'd taught us had been true. Probably not. Miseducated people were much easier to control, after all.

"When?" I asked.

"Noon-ish," said Jeremiah. "Before then, I'm going to trust you to gather the materials you need." Suddenly, a message popped up on my HUD, telling me that my uncle had deposited a few thousand credits into my account. "There. That should cover whatever you need."

"Can the boy go?" asked Remy. "He ain't never seen a city this big. It'll do him good."

Jeremiah shrugged. "If it's okay with Mirabelle, it's okay with me," he said. Just then, Jo's mother appeared with a couple of plates, one of which she set down in front of me. It turned out that the morning's breakfast consisted of a few tortillas stuffed with potatoes, bacon, eggs, and cheese. I devoured mine in record time. Still, by the time I'd finished, Jeremiah and Remy had already left the inn, presumably to take care of something associated with my departure. Once I'd swallowed the last bite, I looked up to see Pick staring at me with wide eyes.

"What?" I asked.

"You . . . um . . . you really enjoy your food, huh?" he asked.

"That's what it's for," I said. "I spent most of my life in Nova City, so . . . you know . . ."

He narrowed his eyes. "What? Is there not enough food there or something?" he asked.

"What? No. There's plenty," I said. "Well, for most people. Some go hungry, I guess, but that's mostly because they don't want to deal with the strings attached to the food programs."

"Then why—"

"Because it's terrible," I said. "Like, imagine tasteless gruel, okay? Then add some artificial flavoring before turning it into a brick. That's what passes for food in the city. Here, everything's fresh. That makes a difference. I mean, you have had cheese, right? Like, real cheese. Not that dehydrated chalk they call cheese back in the city."

"Yes. I have had cheese," he said. "But . . . uh . . . I've got to stay away from it."

"Why?"

"Oh . . ."

His pale cheeks went red again. After a second, he mumbled something about digestive issues. I only caught those two words because of Observation. But given what he'd said, I didn't want to press the issue. So, I asked, "So, what do you do for Mr. Remy?"

"It's just Remy. He doesn't like being called mister," Pick said. "So . . . yeah, call him that. Continuously. Really get under his skin if you can."

I gave a polite chuckle, then said, "So? What do you do?"

"Oh, I'm a mechanic," he said. "Got a [Pilot] skill, too. I've still got a skill slot open, which is why we're here. Remy says that if we do this job for the Wraith, then he'll get me the [Cybernetic Engineer] skill shard. According to him, it's supposed to be rare."

I let my senses wash over him, and the feeling I got from him was that he was somewhere between Tier 2 and Tier 3, which supported his story. I could also tell by the way he held himself that he'd done at least some training of his physical characteristics, which boded well for him.

"So, you're, like, Remy's apprentice?" I asked.

"He's my stepdad," Pick said. "Or . . . I guess since Mom died, he's . . . I don't even know anymore."

My chest tightened, and I mumbled, "Sorry. Didn't know."

He shrugged, and even though I could tell he was still bothered, he said, "No worries. She's been gone for a couple of years now." Then, obviously wanting to change the subject, he said, "So, what kind of supplies do you need to get? Like, bullets and stuff? Maybe an axe or something?"

I chuckled. "Nothing like that," I stated. "I need to restock my medical kit, then get some rations. Other than that, I'm set."

"Oh."

"Don't sound so disappointed," I said, grinning at him. "You ever been to the Dead Zone before?"

"No. Remy never let me," Pick answered. "Always said it was too dangerous. But we don't actually go all the way to the Dead Zone. We only go to the edge, and even then, we've got to look out for flyers. You know, giant birds and such. Remy says he saw an eagle with a hundred-foot wingspan once, but I think he was just trying to scare me."

"That's . . . uh . . . yeah. That's pretty scary," I responded.

He shrugged. "I've seen some flyers that were close to that, but only from a distance," he said. "Back home, they're more common than down here."

"Where is home?" I asked.

"Up north," he said, gesturing in the appropriate direction. "Maybe a six-hour flight, but part of that is because we have to go around the Dead Zone. And we have to fly really slow, else we'll get tracked. Memphis is pretty close, but I've never been there. Remy says I'm not ready, whatever that means."

"If it's anything like Nova, you're not missing anything," I said. However, there was a big part of me that missed the city, if only because it was familiar. And because, despite its issues, it always felt like anything was possible there.

After that, the conversation petered out, and we left the inn behind. My first stop was Kimiko's. When I got there, I was greeted by her granddaughter, Elie. Predictably, the adorable little girl had a sack of mangos on her back. Thankfully, her toy sword and her bucket helmet had been discarded. Even more thankfully, she knew precisely where to find the supplies I needed, and I bought them without any issue, replenishing my medical kit.

Just before we were about to leave, Kimiko came into the lobby. When she saw us, she said, "Ah, just in time. It just arrived."

"What did?" I asked, confused.

"The automender your uncle ordered," she said, raising an eyebrow. "I presumed that was why you are here."

"Uh..."

"He didn't tell you, did he?" the wrinkled old woman asked. When I shook my head, she sighed. "Very well. It falls upon me to once again become your teacher. Do you know what this is?"

As she asked the question, she produced a foot-long oval capsule made of blended plastic and steel—an alloy known as plasti-steel. One side was smooth and rounded, while the other terminated in a rubberized square gasket. I could just make out seams in the surface beneath.

"Uh . . . I'm guessing the automender you just mentioned?"

"Whoa," said Pick. "Those things are worth a fortune. Remy and me, we were hired by some guys up in Saint Louis to—"

"Tales of your exploits will have to wait, young man," Kimiko said. "But he is indeed correct. This automender is worth more than your entire arsenal combined. And do you know why?"

I shook my head.

"Because it is a Mist-powered lifesaving measure," she stated. "If you are injured—and I mean truly on death's bed—you can place this upon the injury and depress this button on the side, and it will inject a swarm of Mist into the wound, mending your flesh back into place. Once it does, it will help keep everything where it is supposed to be until your natural healing takes over. But I warn you, Mirabelle—do not use it unless you have no other choice because you will not get another anytime soon."

I nodded and gingerly took the offered contraption, sending it straight into my arsenal implant. I wasn't sure if I would need such a device, but it was nice to have something so powerful in my possession. I would have to guard against panicking and using it unnecessarily. My Regeneration and Triage abilities were already powerful, so it would have to be a truly ghastly injury to require the intervention of the automender.

"Thank you," I said.

"Do not thank me," she said. "Thank your uncle. He paid very well for it. Now, begone. You're holding up the line."

I glanced behind me, but no one was there. However, rather than ask what line she was talking about, I grabbed Pick by the arm and dragged him out of Kimiko's shop.

Next, I found my way to a general store, where I bought a hundred days' worth of rations and dozens of bottles of water. If it came down to it, the water wouldn't last for long, but I hoped that it would help see me through any real crisis.

With that done, I checked and rechecked my arsenal implant to make certain that I had everything I needed, then went back to the Dew Drop Inn. As we walked, Pick gaped at the city's sights, asking me various questions about the area. I'd been there long enough that I could answer most of them without issue, but some were left unanswered due to my ignorance. He didn't seem to mind, though.

"Okay, my turn to ask you a question," I said as we closed in on the inn. "What kind of a name is Pick, anyway? Is it short for something?"

Out of the corner of my eye, I saw him blush. "It started out as Patrick," he said. "But when I was little, I couldn't say it right, so I shortened it to Pick. My mom thought it was cute, so it just kind of stuck. Then she started calling me Pickle. Which I hated, but . . . you know . . ."

"That's sweet," I said. My mother, by contrast, hadn't given me any cute nicknames. In fact, she hadn't left me with anything but a surly uncle and a deadbeat dad that ended up actually dead a couple of years later.

Pick shrugged. "I guess," he said. "Remy hates it, though. I don't know why, but he teases me about it all the time. Maybe he's just . . . I don't know . . . trying to bond with me or something. But I can't really complain. He's taught me everything I know, and he's given me a chance to succeed. I just . . ."

"You just wonder why he's got to be an asshole about it, right?" I asked.

"Something like that," he said.

"My uncle's the same way," I stated. "He's a moody jerk, and nothing I ever do is good enough for him. But he's done so much for me. And I know he loves me. So . . . I've got mixed feelings, I guess. It's probably the same with Remy, right?"

"Yeah. *Mixed feelings* sounds about right," he said as we reached the front door.

When we went inside, we had to wait a few minutes before Remy and Jeremiah returned, and in that time, Jo found me. After pouting a bit about my impending departure, she took a definite interest in Pick, which made me reevaluate the young man. Sure, he was a bit younger than me, but I couldn't deny that he had a solid, trustworthy look about him that I found appealing. And though he was short, he had plenty of muscle on his frame. It didn't surprise me, then, that Jo showed interest in him. What did surprise me was the fact that a small smile found my face when he refused to get caught up in her orbit. Of course, that frustrated her, and she ended up storming off in an annoyed huff.

Before Pick and I had a chance to resume our conversation, my uncle and his stepfather returned, announcing that it was time to leave. Obediently, we followed them outside, where one of the Amigos waited with a truck. My uncle and Remy got into the cab, while Pick and I hopped into the back.

And then we were off, leaving the town via the northernmost gate. The drive didn't last long, and before I knew it, we reached a clearing, in the middle of which was a boxy vehicle. I asked, "Is . . . is that it?"

"She's not much, but she's got it where it counts," Pick said, looking at that ship the way Jo had looked at him only an hour or so before. "Fastest thing around, and not by a little bit, either. I installed the boosters myself."

"And . . . it flies, right?" I asked skeptically. With its boxy frame, the thing looked anything but airworthy. It didn't even have wings! Instead, it was shaped like an oversize drone, and not the expensive kind.

"Of course she flies!" he exclaimed. "*The Jitterbug* is—"

"Wait, it's called *The Jitterbug*?"

"Uh . . . yeah. Remy named her."

The truck slowed to a stop before I could tease him about it, but my mind was racing with all the possibilities. As we crossed the meadow, I chose the best one, saying, "Pickle and the Jitterbug sounds like a bad band name."

"I told you my name isn't—"

"I'm just teasing," I said with a long-suffering sigh. "You don't have many friends, do you? Relax. It's just a joke. That's what friends do."

I didn't think I was qualified to give anyone a lecture on friendship, but that's where I found myself. He seemed even less experienced in that arena than I was.

"Fine. Just don't call me that," he said before hurrying ahead of me and opening *The Jitterbug*'s side hatch. It opened with a metallic clank, and I was a little alarmed to see a hunk of rust fall off.

"It's fine," I muttered to myself, wondering if I could survive a fall from a thousand feet. Probably, I thought. But it wouldn't be pleasant. I muttered, "Story of my life."

Jeremiah and Remy passed me by, both looking like they had been through the drill before, which was at least a little comforting. Finally, I worked up the nerve to hop through the hatch, and when I did, I saw a fairly empty cargo hold. The whole ship was maybe forty feet long, and most of that was taken up by the hold.

"Here," said Pick, gesturing to an uncomfortable-looking seat. "Just strap in over there and hold on. It can get kind of bumpy back here."

With that, he went into the very back, where he started fiddling with some knobs and dials. I had no idea what he was doing, so I just followed his directions and sat in the seat. Reaching up, I found some sturdy straps connected to a metal buckle, which I fastened into place, creating a harness that would hopefully help with the bumpy ride Pick had promised.

After a couple of minutes, I heard the engines come to life with a high-pitched whine. When they did, Pick returned and dragged a panel down, creating another seat right next to mine. Once he'd made sure that I was securely strapped in, he sat down and buckled his own harness into place.

"We good back there?" called Remy from the front, where he and Jeremiah sat. Pick gave him a thumbs-up, and Remy responded, saying, "Well, here we go then. Hang on, kids!"

The sound of the engines rose, and suddenly, I felt the whole ship lift off the ground. Then, a moment later, we were moving forward. I couldn't see much out of the windows in the front of the ship, but it was enough to tell me that we were going pretty damn fast. Or maybe that was just the feeling in the pit of my stomach. Either way, I suspected that we would soon reach our destination.

After that, my mission would begin. And with it, maybe the rest of my life.

CHAPTER FORTY-SIX

―

COMING IN HOT

I have lost a lot of people over the course of my life, but none hit me quite as hard as when Adelaide was killed. At the time, I thought I was accustomed to loss. Her death left a hole in my life that I never could have expected. Once I came to terms with it, I vowed to raise her daughter to be a survivor. And Mirabelle has exceeded my expectations. I can only hope that will continue because the world is destined to become more dangerous with every passing day.

—Jeremiah Braddock III

The *Jitterbug* shook, and for a moment, I expected that we were about to start falling from the sky. The only reason I thought better of it was because no one else was panicking. Jeremiah could probably survive such a fall, but I couldn't believe that Pick or Remy could make that same claim. So, if they weren't alarmed, then there was a good chance that we weren't going to crash.

Still, almost by instinct, my hand found Pick's, and I squeezed it far more firmly than I probably should have. His knuckles popped, and Observation told me that his teeth ground together in obvious pain. But he didn't cry out. Nor did he pull away. Even so, I let up as soon as I realized what I was doing. A muttered apology followed.

"It's okay," he said, glancing nervously in my direction. The tightening around his eyes told me that he was still in pain, though, and I felt a bit ashamed of myself. I should have been more responsible. If I'd kept going, I could have shattered his hand into a million pieces. I needed to be better than that.

Setting my jaw, I looked away, studying the bare cargo area. There were a few crates near the back, held in place by thick straps. "How long did you say this was going to take?" I asked, raising my voice over the hum of the Mist engines. They weren't unreasonably noisy, but they were louder than a hover car.

"A few hours," Pick said. "We have to go really slow. Maybe as many as five. It just depends on the weather. And ... uh ... the wildlife."

Images of birds with a hundred-foot wingspans filled my mind, making me wish that Pick had never even mentioned that running into such a monster was a possibility. I had no idea what we would do if we encountered one. Try to outrun it? Maybe, but I had a suspicion that *The Jitterbug* was ill-suited for such a race. Perhaps my uncle would take care of it. Or he might have expected me to. I didn't have enough information to make a guess, so I decided to ask the expert.

"What do we do if we're attacked?" I asked.

"Depends," he said. "If Remy says so, we'll fight it off. If he thinks we can't take it, he'll take evasive maneuvers. You'll want to hold on for that."

"Any weapons on the ship?"

Pick nodded, then pointed to a hatch above the door. "There's a cannon up there," he said. "We have to open the door to get a shot, but that's not a big deal. I've done it a hundred times."

I was impressed, which must've been obvious because he blushed. Again. So, I moved past it, asking, "Anything else?"

"Remy's got some guns he can control from up front," Pick explained, eager to show how knowledgeable he was. "They're powerful, too. I've seen 'em take out a patrol ship just outside of Memphis."

"Patrol ship?"

"Oh, right—you don't have those in Nova," he said. "Such a weird city 'cause it's so isolated. Guess it works for them, but ... well, the rest of the world isn't like that. Most of it, at least. In Memphis—and most of the other cities I've been to—they have a peacekeeping force that's basically an army. They send patrol ships, which are just two-man fighters, fast and light, but they pack a punch ... well, they send those out, which makes our job a lot harder."

That's when I fully grasped the fact that Remy and, by extension Pick, was a smuggler. It should have been obvious, if only because he associated with my uncle. Jeremiah didn't exactly stand on the right side of the law, so any ship's captain he hired was probably on the same page.

"But it should be okay," Pick said. "You hardly ever see anything really dangerous this far from the Dead Zone. And most of the time, the really bad stuff won't leave. It'll be fine."

I didn't really like the idea that he thought he needed to reassure me, but in the back of my mind, I appreciated it. It wasn't that I minded flying, per se. And I wasn't afraid of any monsters that might attack us. Instead, I just didn't like being cramped into a confined space without any ability to see my surroundings. It made me feel like I was trapped in a tin can, and it was a feeling I definitely did not enjoy.

But it wasn't as if I had much of a choice. So, I settled down, closed my eyes, and tried to get past my discomfort. And for a while, that worked. Pick continued to nervously babble about nothing in particular, and time passed without much happening. Then, suddenly, I heard a loud, continuous beep coming from the cockpit.

"If you ain't strapped in, you better get that way quick, fast, and in a hurry!" yelled Remy. "We got a bogey comin' in hot! Big-ass sumbitch, too!"

With my heart starting to beat out of control, I checked the straps holding me in place, and they proved to be just as well fastened as they had been upon takeoff. Glancing at Pick, I asked, "What's going on?"

"Nothing good," he replied. "Remy wouldn't have acted like that unless it was bad. We're probably going to have to fight it off."

On cue, a resounding screech cut through the ship, rattling me right down to the bone. After that, the ship banked to the left, and just in time, too. I couldn't see whatever had attacked us, but I heard the distinctive sound of claws scraping against metal. The ship went off course, twisting and turning as I gripped the straps. My stomach threatened to rebel, but I wrestled it into submission.

I felt my Combat Focus kick in, and my mind cleared. We were under attack, and judging by what I'd heard, by some sort of large bird. Other than that, I had no information.

"Pickle! Get on the cannon!" Remy shouted, jerking the joystick that controlled the ship. It responded with a corkscrewing barrel roll, and the sound of talons scraping against metal filled my ears once again. "This big bitch ain't lettin' us fly away!"

"It's Pick!" Pick shouted, unbuckling his straps. I wanted to stop him, to yell that there was no way he could keep his feet in such a situation, but he was free before I could even process what was going on. Then, when Remy banked again, Pick somehow maintained his footing. Clearly, he had some sort of ability associated with it. There was no other explanation for why he wasn't sent tumbling through the cargo hold.

Once the ship stabilized, Pick leaped, grabbing a handle on the hatch above the door, and dragged it open. When he did, a contraption unfolded, resolving itself into a manned cannon. It had a six-foot-long barrel, a square body from which snaked a series of metal tubes, and a seat, upon which Pick wasted no time in sitting. He reached up, grabbed a dangling cable, and dragged it to the port on his neck. Jabbing it into place, he pressed a button, and suddenly, the door opened.

The change in air pressure took my breath away, but my attention didn't waver. The cannon—seat and all—slid out of the ship, held in place on a far-too-thin rod. When he was outside, the thunder of the cannon joined the cacophony of screeches. It was a deep, basso report, less like a gunshot and more like someone was banging on a drum.

"Help him, Mirabelle!" Jeremiah shouted.

"I'll fall out!"

"And you'll be fine!" he yelled. "This is what you've trained for!"

Was this another test? Maybe. I knew that if I asked Jeremiah, he would claim that everything was a test. Even getting attacked by some unknown and likely monstrous avian. But he wasn't wrong. I had been training for quite some time, and I was eager to make good on my potential. So, with grim determination, I unlatched myself from the seat and, making sure I remained tethered by a single strap, pulled my way toward the door. When I reached it, I saw Pick, who was screaming wordlessly as he unloaded his cannon at an enormous bird that looked like an overgrown vulture.

Or maybe a condor.

Whatever it was, it was one of the ugliest animals I had ever seen. With a completely bald head, thick black plumage around its shoulders, and a wingspan that must've been seventy feet, the thing was a real monster.

Most disturbingly, though, was the fact that the cannon wasn't doing a damned thing. Even when Pick's shots connected—and that wasn't often—the creature shrugged them off like they were nothing. That made it an impressively durable creature, considering that Pick's missed shots dug sizable craters in the landscape below, felling trees and the ruins of buildings alike.

The condor banked toward us, and I only had a second to clench up before it made contact. As Remy evaded the flying monster, I was thrown across the cargo hold, and the only reason I didn't collide with the wall was because of my tether. Still, the sheer force involved was enough to knock the breath from my lungs. And I felt sure that the durable strap wouldn't survive much more abuse.

We needed to end the threat before that happened.

And I had just the tool for the job. After crawling back to the door, I set myself up with a clear line of sight. Then, I summoned my Kicker from my arsenal implant, configured it into its sniper mode, then took aim.

Using Empowered Shot, I counted out two seconds before squeezing the trigger. The resultant explosion of force sent me skidding backward, and the ship bucked. But my shot flew true, taking the overgrown avian directly in the rightmost wing. It squawked, and I saw blood, meat, and feathers explode.

It wobbled.

I held my breath, expecting it to fall. But to my horror, it quickly regained its altitude and turned toward us. So, from the other side of the ship, where I'd been knocked to my ass, I took aim again, used Empowered Shot, and fired.

The bullet tore into the monstrous creature in almost the exact same spot, nearly severing its wing.

But it was too late.

The huge bird, whose body was almost as big as the ship, crashed into us. Remy shouted something unintelligible, and Pick—along with the cannon—was thrown back inside. For my part, I was sent tumbling through the cargo hold once again. I heard the strap snap, and when the ship rolled, there was nothing to stop me from being thrown through the door.

As I fell, I couldn't help but think, *I knew this would happen.*

It was a fleeting thought, and there wasn't time for me to think anything else before I crashed into a tree. Limbs snapped under me, slowing me just enough that, when I finally slammed into the ground, I didn't even break any bones. It had all happened so quickly that it took a moment for my mind to catch up with the events, so I just lay there for a long moment, catching my breath.

A few seconds later, I gathered my wits enough to send a message to my uncle:

Mirabelle: I'm fine. Nothing broken. What do you want me to do?

It took Jeremiah only a few seconds to answer:

Jeremiah: Continue with the mission. You are a few days' march from your target. By the time we found a place to set down, it would be pointless to pick you up. Good luck. Let me know when you're finished.

I sighed, closing my eyes. As I lay there, I muttered, "Typical."

After a few minutes, I finally worked past my annoyance enough to sit up and inspect my body. To my surprise, I didn't seem all that injured. Sure, everything hurt. I was certain I had a few bruises. But it felt less like I'd fallen from a few hundred feet and more like I'd been through an intense sparring session with Nora.

Even so, I took my time with my examination. Triage gave me the ability to diagnose any issues or injuries, and it was coming up blank. So, once I'd gathered myself, I recovered my Kicker from where it had fallen beside me, inspected it for any damage, and once I was satisfied that it had survived the fall intact, stored it in my arsenal implant. After that, I consulted my map, then set off on a northerly track through the woods.

The first thing I noticed was that, unlike the coastal plain around Mobile, the terrain was quite hilly. It wasn't to the point where I would've called it mountainous—as if I'd ever seen a mountain at all—but it definitely wasn't quite as flat as what I was used to. As a result, the trek was a little more tiring than it probably should have been. Even so, I made pretty good time, avoiding the wildlife and carving a path through the dense forest. Sometimes figuratively, but often, literally and at the edge of my nano-bladed sword.

As I went, I passed a wide variety of abandoned buildings. Some had clearly been people's homes, once upon a time, but they had been abandoned for so long that nature had all but completely reclaimed them. More than once, I found groupings of such buildings, and I amused myself by imagining what it all had looked like in its prime. For some reason, I didn't think the people who'd lived there had been plagued by the same problems that were so prevalent in Nova City or, to a lesser extent, Mobile.

Or maybe I was completely wrong.

That first night, I sheltered in one of those buildings. Most of the interior had fallen victim to the humid air and rotted away, but there were some curious exceptions. A strangely well-preserved stuffed dog. A few rusty knives in what had once been a kitchen. A giant steel refrigerator. A few broken plastic screens. I even found a safe that had long since rusted through; it held a few gold coins and an ancient pistol. I stored both, even if I wasn't sure why.

Eventually, I settled into what had once been the bathroom and fell asleep in the still-intact porcelain tub. That night was accompanied by the same sounds I'd learned to expect. Howls from wild dogs and wolves, chirps of various insects, and the occasional roar of something far bigger filled the air. I slept fitfully, never descending into a full slumber. It was a regrettable necessity when traveling alone in the wilderness.

Thankfully, the night passed without much issue. However, after leaving the ruins of the neighborhood behind, it was only a few hours before I ran into my first problem. After hearing something coming in my direction, I scampered up a tree just in time to avoid being accosted by a pair of wildlings. One was a man, while the other was a woman. They were both naked, skeletally thin, misshapen, and cloaked in a strange blue glow that reminded me of the edge of my nano-blade.

One barked at the other, clearly trying to communicate. However, it wasn't in any language I'd ever heard. Still, the other seemed to understand, and the pair proceeded to search the area, eventually coming upon the tracks I hadn't bothered to conceal. The female raised her head to the sky and let out a howl; a few seconds later, a full twenty wildlings burst through the underbrush to surround the pair who'd found my trail. Then, they took off in the direction from which I'd come, clearly hunting me.

That told me two things. First, the next time I encountered them, I wouldn't have the luxury of waiting for them to make the first move. If it came down to it, I would need to open fire immediately, lest I be overwhelmed. Second, they weren't very intelligent. I didn't know what effect the Mist had had on them, but clearly, it had sapped some of their reasoning ability. Otherwise, they would have been able to tell that they were following my trail in the wrong direction.

It was a chilling thought, that they seemed to have devolved so thoroughly until they were little more than animals. But it was one I couldn't spend much time pondering.

After twenty minutes, I judged it safe to descend from my perch, and when I resumed my trek through the woods, I did so with quite a bit more caution, employing all the tricks I'd learned to disguise my trail. It took longer, but it was far safer.

The second night, I found what had once been a small town. A multitude of old, crumbled roads crisscrossed the area, with a handful of buildings within the town topping out at three stories. They were constructed of brick and covered with ivy, but they looked sturdy enough. So, I chose one at random and set about exploring it before settling on the top floor, where I spent another nearly sleepless night. I was used to it, though. More, my attributes allowed me to function at peak efficiency without spending much time on rest. Even so, it wasn't pleasant.

Over the next few days, I slowly traversed the wilderness, seeing more evidence of the civilization humanity had left behind. I was more than a little awed by the fact that everything was so spread out. Back in Nova, everything was piled together, and everyone lived practically on top of or below someone else. Before the Initialization, though, people had had room to breathe. To live. I wondered if the people who lived in the more affluent parts of Nova had such luxuries.

Like that, a week passed. My uncle, for all his skills and abilities, tended to look at things from his perspective. So, while he might've been capable of covering the ground in a few days, it took me quite a bit longer to find the edge of the Dead Zone. And when I did, I felt it immediately.

It was like I'd crossed an invisible boundary. On one side was normal wilderness. On the other, it was something else entirely. The first major difference was that, once I passed that line, I felt a light tingle, as if someone was running a feather along my skin. The next was that my HUD flickered. It was only a brief shudder, but it was definitely noticeable. Finally, everything seemed to have a slightly blue tint. It wasn't overt. Nor was it unpleasant. But it was there, all the same.

I took a deep breath, stepped back out of the Dead Zone, and messaged my uncle:

Mirabelle: Reached the Dead Zone. Going in. Wish me luck.

Then, without waiting for a reply, I stepped inside and began my test in earnest.

CHAPTER FORTY-SEVEN

THE DEAD ZONE

The ruins of a dead civilization haunt me. So many things that we used to take for granted have faded into memory. Even more have been forgotten entirely. Just like billions of people who were unprepared for a world in transition.

—Jeremiah Braddock III

Trekking through the Dead Zone was a novel experience. It wasn't unpleasant, just strange. However, it only took a few hundred yards for me to understand why so few people passed into the territory.

I sank back into the underbrush as I stared at an enormous turkey. I'd never actually seen one of them in person, but I'd seen videos of the birds. And instead of the twenty-pound creature the name usually referred to, this one was at least ten times that size, with wickedly curved talons and a beak that was currently ripping through the flesh of some other, unidentifiable carcass.

I sat back on my heels as I watched the monstrous bird tear into its meal, remaining as silent and unobtrusive as I could. It wasn't easy; the turkey wasn't that far away, and I suspected that it could cover the ground between us with some alacrity. Fortunately, I had plenty of experience sitting still, so I maintained my silence and stillness until it'd had its fill. Once it did, it moved away with high steps and bobbing head. Still, I remained motionless for quite some time, not wanting to draw its attention. Eventually, though, I climbed to my feet and set off to the northwest, which was where I hoped to find the Rift.

As I walked, I encountered more of the mutated wildlife, but each time, I managed to avoid clashing with them. However, each meeting further reaffirmed that the Dead Zone was an incredibly dangerous place. Not only were the animals bigger and deadlier, but even the plants had gotten in on the action, albeit far more subtly. For instance, late in the day, I realized that I'd been stumbling in circles for hours under the influence of some sort of narcotic spores. Once I knew what was going on, I was able to counteract it with a med-hypo loaded with an antidote, but it was a harsh reminder of just how bad things could go. If I'd run into a deadly predator during that episode, I would have probably died. More, I suspected that, without the increased effectiveness of medication that came with my Triage ability, the med-hypo wouldn't have been nearly as effective.

Resolving to be ever vigilant, I continued on my way.

My next potentially deadly encounter occurred on my second day in the Dead Zone. I'd camped out in a surprisingly sturdy old cabin, so I was well rested. Thankfully, I saw the snake a split second before it struck, and I was able to twist out of the way. But that didn't save me from the thing's second head. Or the third. By the fourth, I was scrambling away as fast as I could.

Frantically, I summoned my medical kit from my arsenal implant and retrieved a generic antivenom. In seconds, I'd jabbed the med-hypo into my thigh and depressed the pneumatic plunger. It unloaded with a hiss, and just in time, too. I was already feeling the effects of the venom burning through my veins. With the antivenom combatting it, it slowed to a stop and started to retreat.

That's when I took a moment to look at my adversary.

With four heads stemming from a serpentine body as big around as my thigh, the snake had mottled-green-and-brown scales. Each of its heads were poised and ready for a strike, and I heard a subdued rattle coming from its rear.

Without further hesitation, I summoned my nano-sword—mostly because my firearms would be far too loud and might attract the wrong sorts of attention. Adopting a stance I'd learned from Simon, I held the sword in front of me, the blade almost perpendicular to the ground. So, when the snake next struck, it only took a flick of my wrist to subtly knock it aside. My goal wasn't to block, but rather to redirect.

It worked, and by the time the next head came at me, I was ready. And the next after that. Once they'd cycled through once again, I went on the offensive, slicing into the thing's thick neck and using Eviscerate. The blade cut deep, only stopping when I heard the metallic ting of my sword colliding with the snake's steel spine.

I wasn't going to let that dissuade me, though. And over the next few minutes, I fell into a rhythm of parry and counterattack that eventually left the mutated snake in tatters. The extra bleeding that came with Eviscerate proved effective as the creature's movements grew ever more sluggish. Eventually, after repeated strikes, I severed one of the heads. After that, the fight resolved itself pretty quickly, though I did take a couple more bites for my trouble. Once it was finished, I treated myself with more antivenom, used an antibiotic med-hypo, then resumed my trek through the woods after applying a couple of bandages to the bites.

Over the next couple of days, I fought and killed a host of different animals. Some were little different, at least in terms of form, if not size, from what I'd learned about in school, but others were so mutated that I had trouble even identifying them, aside from a basic classification. Still, my training served me well, and with each passing hour, my edge was further sharpened by the life-and-death struggles of traversing the Dead Zone.

On the third day, I reached my destination.

I knelt at the tree line studying the vast meadow before me. It was mostly clear, but with curious flat-topped mounds scattered throughout the area. I had no idea what they were there for, nor did they really hold my attention. Not with the obvious settlement nestled on the opposite side of the clearing.

Walls that looked to have been made of metal and plastic jutted from the ground, reaching a height of thirty feet, with towers doubling that. Symbols that I interpreted as some sort of alien glyphs decorated the walls, but what really drew my attention were the robots manning the towers.

They were mostly humanoid, as far as I could tell, though they were equipped with two extra arms. And they carried weapons that didn't look so different from my Kicker. I couldn't help but wonder if they were as proficient as I was. Or, given that they were alien robots, perhaps even more so. That notion sent a shiver of fear up my spine.

After a few more minutes, I got my first glimpse of the aliens who had built the fort. And I was a little disappointed when, from a distance, it looked little different from a human. Two arms. Two legs. An otherwise normal body. However, its skin was bright red, its hair was a vivid blue, and it had pointed ears.

It was standing on one of the towers next to a robot, its eyes searching the surrounding area. Its gaze swept over me, but because I was using my various skills and abilities to remain hidden, its search proved fruitless. However, I couldn't help but hold my breath until I was sure that it hadn't seen me.

Like that, hours passed as I observed the area. It took a while, but I eventually realized that the security was quite lax. Aside from the robots, which posed an unknown threat, there was never more than one alien in the towers. It made sense, I supposed. The robots, along with the walls, would likely be more than a match for the animals in the area. And it wasn't as if there were any people about.

Other than the ones in the fort, at least.

I didn't see much of them, but the few glimpses I got were enough to set my blood to boiling. They were almost entirely naked, save for loincloths, but from what I could see, they seemed perfectly happy, with wide smiles etched upon their faces. But there was something wrong. Something I couldn't quite put my finger on.

It was just one more issue, though. First, I needed to figure out a way to deal with the robots. Then, the aliens. And finally, the people inside. After that, I would be free to confront the Rift and whatever mysteries it held. My uncle hadn't been very forthcoming about it, which he had acknowledged, only saying that every Rift was different. If I was going to delve into them, I would need to get used to adjusting according to whatever I found inside.

After a few more hours, I retreated a couple of miles away to make my camp. The aliens seemed content to remain huddled up in the fort, so I didn't think I had anything to fear from them finding me. Still, I found a decent campsite that was concealed in the ruins of an old house.

As I went about the routine of eating, cleaning up as best I could, and attending to my other needs, I gave my problems some thought. For the robots, I had what I thought was a pretty decent plan. If it worked, I could get in and out without having to wake the entire forest up with a gunfight. If it didn't, though . . . well, going loud was always an option.

For the aliens, I could only hope that they weren't more perceptive than human beings. If they weren't, I could deal with them. If their perception proved insurmountable, I always had my guns. I didn't want to get into a firefight, but sometimes, there wasn't any other way. Or at least that was what Jeremiah always said. And in this instance, it made perfect sense.

As for the people, I expected that once I dealt with the other issues, the humans would take care of themselves. I even envisioned a situation where I led them all back to Mobile, where they could find fulfilling lives. I would be hailed as a hero.

First, though, I needed to spend quite a bit more time on reconnaissance. My experiences with my previous training missions had taught me that there was no such thing as too much information. So, I went to sleep, knowing full well that I had a long few days of observation ahead of me.

And for the next four days, that's precisely what I did. I watched. I learned. And, thankfully, no real issues cropped up. The robots seemed incapable of perceiving me at a distance, and the aliens were largely disinterested. So, on the fifth night after I'd found the fort, I found myself slinking across the clearing on a mission to infiltrate the settlement.

I kept low to the ground, the high grass providing enough concealment that I felt certain that I wouldn't be seen. Not with Camouflage masking my passage. Slowly, I approached the wall, moving only a few feet every minute. If I moved too quickly, I felt certain that the robots would detect me, regardless of my skills. Thankfully, I had been well trained, and my patience proved up to the task. So, by midnight, I was pressed against the wall and looking up at one of the towers.

It was a simple thing, just a few legs, a ladder, and a covered platform, upon which was a single robot. From my reconnaissance, I knew that the aliens wouldn't send anyone out to check on things for at least another hour. I had plenty of time to enact my plan. So long as it worked, at least. I was still uncertain of whether or not it would.

I focused on the nearest robot and activated Misthack. Immediately, a message flashed across my screen:

Initiate Misthack?
[Yes] or [No]

I quickly selected the first option and, thankfully, found only trivial defenses. With practiced efficiency, I tore through the puzzles and equations until I completely overwhelmed the F-grade Mistwall. I didn't take any time to wonder why an alien civilization advanced enough to send its people to a new world would be so poorly defended. Instead, I pushed to the next prompt:

Misthack Successful. Options:
- **Reboot System**
- **Overcharge System**
- **Breach System**

The first option would give me a brief window in which I could climb the tower and physically subdue the robot. Perhaps I could have even use Mistwalk on it, which would give me a few more choices. The second option, which was intended to disable cybernetics via a pulse of destructive Mist, was even more attractive, especially if I wanted to permanently disable the sentry. But I chose the third, mostly because I'd spent my nights developing a very special Ghost for just this situation.

Breach Successful. Upload Ghost?
[Yes] or [No]

Options:
- **Sleep Mode**
- **Red Herring**
- **Buzz**
- **Time Bomb**

I had spent a good portion of my free time over the past year building and discarding various Ghosts, so I had plenty of others in my arsenal. Most were half-finished, barely effective, or unsuited to the task at hand, though. Still, I had what I needed, and I selected the very first option available to me. And as soon as I did, the robot powered down.

I couldn't help but grin. The beauty of the *Sleep Mode* Ghost was that it would remain in effect until someone either rebooted the robot's system or did damage to it. Otherwise, it would remain as stationary and unresponsive as a paperweight. Pity, then, that it was only usable on machines. Perhaps one day I would write a similar Ghost that could be used on biological entities. That would certainly make my life a lot easier. Or at least less violent.

Once I saw that my strategy for the first problem was viable, I quickly made my way around the perimeter of the fort, disabling the robots along the way. Each instance went a little more quickly until, by the last one, I could upload my Ghost in a matter of seconds. It was all too easy.

Of course, the moment that thought went through my head, I started looking for something to go wrong. I wasn't necessarily superstitious, but you can only tempt fate so much before she starts to push back. Fortunately, I wasn't immediately beset by enemies, which allowed me to move on to the next step: dealing with the aliens.

Unlike the robots, I knew this part was going to be bloody. So, after scaling the wall and dropping down on the other side, I darted into the deepest shadow I could find. It was just in time, too, because a red-hued alien soon made an appearance, turning a corner and crossing paths with the exact spot I'd just vacated.

Summoning my dagger, I waited until he passed me by before I crept up behind him. With practiced precision, I reached up, grabbed his blue hair, and swept my dagger across his throat. For good measure, I followed that up by plunging it into the base of his skull. He never got the opportunity to react, much less scream for help. Apparently, aliens were just as mortal as humans, and with the same vulnerable spots.

I dragged the deceptively heavy body into one of the shadows, then knelt down to inspect it. The alien was, indeed, very similar to a human, right down to the frozen expression of surprise on his face. And I was sure he was male, too. I checked. Call it morbid curiosity, but how often was I going to get the chance to take a peek at an alien's junk? Either way, aside from his strangely colored skin, white blood, and blue hair, he didn't seem any different than a thousand other people I'd seen in my life.

Oh, and he had pointed ears, which was strange enough, but not unheard of in places like Nova City, where people subjected themselves to all sorts of weird cosmetic surgeries. I searched him, but I didn't find anything worthwhile. Not even any cybernetics, which I found somewhat odd.

Once I was finished, I tried to hide the body as well as I could, dragging it even deeper into the shadows, before I took stock of the situation. Because of the relatively flat land, I'd been incapable of getting a good read on the fort's layout, but now that I was inside, I saw that it was a pretty bare-bones operation. There were only five windowless buildings, each made of the same metal-plastic hybrid as the walls, and looking entirely prefabricated, which they doubtless were.

I squatted next to one of the walls, thinking about my next move. Without being able to see into the buildings, I had no easy means of discerning what awaited me inside. Moreover, with only one door, I had very little chance of stealth. So, I could either go in, guns blazing, or I could just wait outside, picking them off as they exited, one by one.

Logic dictated that the latter was far and away the safest option. So, remembering the mistakes of my previous missions, I decided to remain on the smart path. Without giving it much more thought, I scaled the wall and leaped atop one of the buildings, where I settled down to wait. When I did, I got my first peek at the Rift, and I have to say that it was an impressive sight.

My first impression was that it looked like a formless blue prism, held in place by four mechanical arms that brought to mind an overturned spider. Those, according to Jeremiah's descriptions, were the stabilizers. Without them, the Rift itself would have been completely impossible. But with them? It was a doorway into a self-contained world. I had no idea what lay on the other side, but I watched as, periodically, one of the human captives, mostly naked and looking like they didn't have a care in the world, entered or exited the prism. The ones coming from the Rift carried boxes that presumably contained Rift Shards.

A few minutes passed as I studied the people I had been sent to rescue. One and all, they wore broad smiles on their faces. It didn't matter that many of them sported what looked like painful wounds. Nor did their obvious exhaustion seem to affect them. They grinned through it all, and I suspected that if I looked closer, I would see the glassy eyes so common among addicts.

An hour after I killed that first alien, another one emerged from one of the buildings. She moved with purpose as she made her way toward one of the towers, so she never saw me as I dropped down on her from the building's roof and buried my dagger in the top of her skull. After I inspected her—finding nothing—her corpse joined the other in the deep shadows between the building and the wall.

Like that, I proceeded to whittle them down throughout the night until, at last, they seemed to have caught on. I had already killed seven of them, which had obviously alerted the others enough that they sent four out to check on their comrades. This was a job for the sword.

As I had before, I killed the first by dropping down on top of him, severing his spine at the base of his skull along the way. Ripping my nano-bladed sword out of his neck, I swept it around in a wide arc, gutting the second alien. The third had his face split in two by a vicious upward swing that took him first in the jaw.

I turned on the fourth, and she scrambled away from me, clear terror in her eyes. She muttered something unintelligible, but I neither understood nor cared about what she had to say. She turned to run, but her attributes were barely better than those of an Unawakened human's. So, it was child's play to cut her down. In the space of a few seconds, I had killed four aliens.

It was not the battle I had expected.

Either way, all efforts at stealth were probably ruined, so I didn't waste any more time before stowing my blade and retrieving my Kicker from my arsenal implant. Then, I marched toward the door to the building from whence the aliens had come, and when the door slid open, I was unsurprised to see that it was empty.

I went inside, looking for a terminal, and after only a little searching through the various rooms—which looked little different from what I would expect from a human—I found one. Everything about the fort was wrong. I needed information. And the fastest way to obtain that would be the terminal. For most people, that would present a problem, given that almost all terminals had plenty of security. However, for me, it was little more than a speed bump.

I unraveled the cord concealed in my wrist, plugged it into the terminal, and using Mistwalk, quickly gained access. Once I had bypassed the terminal's security, I set about learning as much as I could. And with each file I searched, I grew more aghast at what I found.

CHAPTER FORTY-EIGHT

CONTROL

Truly effective oppression is societal sleight of hand. Provide distractions so that the oppressed do not even realize that they are the victims. In the pre-Initialization world, it came in the form of smartphones, drugs, sporting events, and social media. In our new reality, though, things are simultaneously much more overt and far more difficult to guard against.

—Jeremiah Braddock III

It took me a few minutes before I realized how strange it was that I could read the information on the terminal at all. It felt as if I had double vision. On one side, I recognized the glyphs that made up the alien language for what they were, but on the other, I understood precisely what they meant. After a while, though, I stopped worrying about how I was able to read it and focused on the content. It was disturbing enough to push any other thoughts completely out of my head.

Horror filled my mind as I discovered that the humans I had seen were no more than slaves, and they were kept in that position not by chains or whips, but by implants and skills working in conjunction. The skill, called [Worker Drone], only had one purpose: to flood the user with endorphins—or the alien equivalent—when they accomplished a task set by their masters. The implants involved supported this by causing pain when those same users refused a task, considered escape, or otherwise resisted. It was a perfect system to create unskilled and captive labor.

And the worst part? After a while, the slaves would become so addicted to doing their masters' bidding that they were incapable of thinking about anything else. Some would even forget to eat or sleep if they weren't ordered to do so. It was a detestable arrangement, and one that terrified me more than just about anything else I had seen.

You could fight aliens, bandits, and monstrous wildlife. That was the easy part. But when the invaders could so efficiently enslave a population? If you fell under their yoke, what could you do?

With visions of an enslaved humanity dancing through my mind, I continued to read, and I found that even the red-hued aliens, who were called the Castorix, were slaves to a higher master, albeit without the oppressive [Worker Drone] skill. They were only on Earth to wrangle the humans, which explained why they had been so weak. The robots I had disabled were the real guards.

I shook my head and started the download of the information. I wasn't sure whether or not my uncle already knew what was going on, but if he didn't, he definitely needed to. After a few more minutes' worth of research, I found that there was a village a few miles to the west, where more humans were kept. There, they farmed the food necessary to keep the Rift-mining operation afloat. They were also guarded by a much larger contingent of robot guards, as well as a few alien warriors. As I read, I knew I couldn't do much about that. And even if I could defeat the aliens, what then? Those people were lost. As much as I hated the situation, the combination of the [Worker Drone] skill and the implant that went with it had rendered those people into lost causes. If I really wanted to help them, I would just end their suffering, then and there.

But I didn't have that in me. On more than a few occasions, I had shown that I could kill when necessary. However, putting down an entire village was taking things a step too far for me, regardless of whether or not I considered it to be an act of mercy. I just wasn't prepared to be the person who made that choice.

Just after the download had finished, when I was busy poring over some related information, a piercing scream cut through the night. I sprang to my feet, sprinted outside, and quickly found the source of the scream. Huddled around the dead aliens was a group of enslaved humans, each naked but for the loincloths they all wore. One was clawing her arms. Another had his head tilted toward the sky as he wailed. Still others knelt beside the pile of corpses, weeping openly.

It only took me a second before I recognized that their reactions were caused by the skills and implants that had been foisted upon them, but even then, it was an incredibly difficult thing to watch. It grew even worse when one of them looked up and saw me standing at the corner of the building, mouth agape.

She shrieked, and before I knew what was going on, the entire group was sprinting toward me, rage plainly etched across their faces. I reacted on well-honed instinct, pulling my scattergun from my arsenal implant, activating Double Shot, and firing. The first pulse of the elemental discharge stopped them in their tracks, but the second fried them. Lethality, I had found, was a relative thing. What was intended as a nonlethal form of crowd control became deadly when the targets were weak enough.

And these humans who'd lived lives of enslavement were definitely weak enough. They were dead before they hit the ground.

"Shit. Shit, shit, shit!" I hissed, staring at the smoking corpses. A dozen of the people I'd hoped to save were now dead, all because I'd panicked. I had a good excuse. The reports I'd just read were enough to put anyone on edge. But those people, they couldn't have really hurt me. Not unless I stood there and took it. I didn't have to use my scattergun. I could've just leaped atop the building and fled to the Rift.

But I hadn't. And now, a dozen more people were dead. Did it matter that they were already doomed? No. Not in my mind, at least.

I bent down, my hands on my knees, and vomited the day's rations, regret enveloping my every thought. For a long few moments, I stood there, wishing I'd done things differently. Wishing I had actually thought things through. It was already done, though. I couldn't take it back. And I still had a task to complete. So, I forced myself to composure and set about searching the fort.

I didn't know whether I should be thankful or not that I didn't find anyone else. Judging by the initial group's reaction, I didn't expect a warm welcome. Nor did I want to have to kill any more people. So, I was grateful that I didn't have to figure out what to do with any remaining survivors.

I did, however, find a storage locker that contained almost a hundred Rift Shards, each almost identical to the one my uncle had shown me. I wasn't certain if they would all fit in my arsenal implant, so I left them where they were for now, intending to come back when I finished my tasks.

After that, I headed to the towers, where I found the robots just as unresponsive as ever. I knew that would eventually change, so I knelt beside the first, retrieved a small but powerful explosive charge from my arsenal implant, and set up a remote detonator before attaching it to where I thought the robot's power source would be located. Then, I repeated that process on all the other robot guards before climbing down and putting some distance between the wall and me.

Then, just before I detonated the bombs, I realized that I was making yet another mistake. I knew that the village where the rest of the humans lived—along with a lot more robots and a few alien warriors—was close enough that they would likely hear a single explosion, let alone a handful of them. If I destroyed the robots now, they would respond, and there was every chance that while I finished up inside the Rift, they would take that opportunity to surround me. If that came to pass, I wasn't going to escape the Dead Zone without a significant battle.

So, I replaced the detonator within my arsenal implant and set off through the fort toward the Rift. When I got there, I was once again mesmerized by the pulsating and formless blue prism. Up close, I could see the energy swirling in place, twisting around to form an almost hypnotic pattern. Every now and then, a bolt of blue energy would erupt from the prism only to be intercepted by one of the metallic arms that looked like nothing so much as an upside-down spider's legs. They were the Rift's stabilizers, I knew. Without them, it would be impossible.

Taking a deep breath, I said, "No time like the present."

Then, holding that breath, I stepped forward and, with a display of confidence that I didn't really feel, strode through the Rift. I felt the Mist swirl around me, then through me, and suddenly, I was somewhere else. It happened in the space of an instant, and by the time I blinked, I was in a different world.

The air was heavy with humidity, and low-slung fog carpeted the floor. More than that, though, the air tasted wrong. The atmosphere pressed down on me in a way I'd never felt on Earth, like gravity worked differently in this new space. It wasn't unpleasant, and I didn't think it would affect my combat ability overmuch, but it was noticeable, nonetheless.

I looked around, seeing that I was in an ancient corridor. Glowing red moss coated the stone walls, and curious-looking insects skittered away with my every movement. I didn't recognize any of it, further cementing the new space's alien feel. I glanced at the ceiling, and I saw a web of crisscrossing white branches that formed a dense barrier through which even light couldn't escape.

It all screamed one thing—I wasn't on Earth anymore. Nor was it a natural space. Instead, the corridor had been purposefully constructed, but by whom, I had no idea. For all I knew, the Rift had merely copied something from another world. Or it might've even transferred me across the galaxy. In that respect, my ignorance weighed on me like a heavy cloak.

Summoning my Kicker, I raised it to my shoulder and, using my well-learned techniques, slowly stepped forward. Sweeping my weapon this way and that, I tried to keep my eyes on everything all at once. But my caution proved unnecessary because, even after a hundred feet, I didn't encounter anything more dangerous than a skittering bug the size of my little toe. But with every single step, I felt a deepening sense of foreboding.

Finally, I reached the end of the corridor, which ended in a heavy wooden door that looked like it belonged in an ancient castle. Except the wood was stark white, and the iron fittings glowed a deep, unsettling green. I reached out with a tentative finger, brushing lightly against the door's handle; I knew I had to get through the door, but I was understandably trepidatious about grabbing a glowing hunk of metal. However, when my finger brushed against it, I found that it felt little different from mundane iron. Still, I quickly tapped it a few more times to be sure before finally grabbing hold of it and pulling it open to reveal a sizable room.

As I stepped through, I couldn't help but gape. The ceiling was still made of overlapping and interwoven branches, but they were in full bloom, with flowers and leaves creating a beautiful floral canopy. Floating bulbs extended from the branches, glowing with ethereal light and illuminating the room.

Around the edges were sinuous columns carved to look like great serpents, and in the center of the room floated a huge hunk of rock. Suspended in the air by nothing I could see, the four-foot-wide rock was pitted and cratered, looking as if someone had taken a chisel to its surface. It wasn't until I got closer that I saw the bits of crystal buried within the craters, and I realized that it had once held the Rift Shards the slaves had mined from the Rift. As I circled it, I saw that there were only a few left, but even as I watched, I saw that more were growing.

When I reached the other side of the floating rock, I saw a shadowy lump of fur leaning against the wall. It wasn't moving, so I judged it safe to approach. However, I kept my weapon trained on what I suspected was a creature. When I was only a few feet away, it trembled, and I let loose with a burst of gunfire. The bullets thudded into the mass, eliciting a low-pitched whine.

Whatever it was, it was still alive.

My good sense told me to retreat, but my curiosity shoved my good sense aside, taking up a position of prominence in my mind. I remained standing there, my rifle trained on the creature as I waited for it to respond. Slowly, it began to writhe. Then, the writhing became more urgent, and it started to rise. When it finally reached its feet, I had trouble comprehending precisely what it was, much less categorizing it in familiar terms. It had what looked like a hundred tendril-like legs, though they were coated in dense black fur. Its body was similar to that of the deadly jellyfish I'd encountered in the ocean, yet it was different enough to be something wholly alien. The body, just like the legs, was covered in that same dense fur. A pair of stalks, topped with what I could only guess were glistening purple eyes, jutted from what I presumed to be its head.

None of that would've been all that alarming. After all, I'd already seen some strangely mutated creatures, and I had been prepared for aliens. However, the moment it started to move, I felt a chill run up my spine. Its legs had far too many joints, and when it moved, its body bobbed up and down. I was so unnerved that, when it opened its gaping, tooth-filled mouth, I didn't hesitate to unload one burst of gunfire after another down its throat.

It screamed, the sound strikingly similar to what would come from a human, and skittered forward like an overgrown insect. I retreated, firing one burst after another. They thudded home, but the alien monster was unslowed. I didn't let up, though, and when my magazine ran dry, I reloaded with practiced alacrity before resuming my onslaught.

Suddenly, it darted toward me so fast I could hardly see it, and I barely managed to dive aside. It still clipped my legs, and it felt as if I'd been hit by a hover car. I was sent tumbling to the edge of the room, and I only barely managed to recover before the alien creature was upon me once again. At point-blank range, I fired again, this time on full automatic. The bullets tore into the creature's joint, and after that burst of sustained fire, one of its many legs was severed. Black blood burst into the air, and it stumbled to the side—less because it needed the leg and more out of surprise, I expected—narrowly missing me.

I jumped to my feet, retreating as I exchanged another spent magazine for a fresh one, and resumed my assault. A few moments later, a second leg joined the first. It had taken a couple of near misses, but I'd found my strategy. So, I bent myself to the task, using every ounce of my training to contain my bursts of fire to the appropriate targets. Within a minute, another seven legs had been severed, and the monster had begun to wobble.

Eight more, and it was barely capable of remaining upright. After that, it was only a matter of time before, finally, I finished the job of immobilizing the creature. Once I did, I took a moment to study it further. It was still a horrifying monster, especially surrounded by puddles of black blood, but it was also kind of pitiful. Seeing it writhing there, struggling to rise so it could either flee or defend itself, it wasn't difficult to label it as another animal, albeit an alien one. And I needed to put it out of its misery.

So, I reconfigured my weapon into its sniper mode, took aim, and prepared Empowered Shot. Once the ability was fully charged, I squeezed the trigger. The gunshot echoed through the room, and when the bullet hit, it tore a gaping hole in the creature's body. But still, it remained alive. So, after a few seconds—during which it mewled like the wounded animal it was—I repeated the process. That one nearly did it in, but it still took two more shots before it finally breathed its last breath.

The moment it did, I felt like collapsing. The heavy atmosphere that I'd dismissed so easily still weighed on me, and that, coupled with the rigors of fighting a monster that seemed far more durable than it should've been, had sapped me of my energy. For a moment, I thought about going back and exiting the Rift. It might've even been the smart thing to do. However, when I considered doing that, my eyes alighted on a door opposite the one from which I had entered the cavernous room.

I was certain that it hadn't been there before, which was a disturbing thought. It made me feel as if I'd just beaten a boss in one of the video games I'd played back in Nova City. Only now, this was real life with very real danger. That furry tentacle monster hadn't been a collection of pixels. It had been a flesh-and-blood creature, the likes of which I'd never encountered. So, I couldn't help but wonder: What was on the other side of that door?

I was eager to find out, but first, I needed to rest for a few minutes. I hadn't really been wounded, but fatigue could kill just as easily as an injury. With that in mind, I found a spot that hadn't been soaked in the monster's blood, sat down, and tried to regain my energy.

Because as soon as I felt up to it, I intended to explore the rest of the Rift.

CHAPTER FORTY-NINE

RESOLUTE

I don't know how the system came to be. Nor do I know much about the nature of Rifts. Because of the quarantine period between the Initialization and the Integration, specific information has always been thin on the ground. But what I do know is that it was all put into place by an altruistic race of beings whose planet had been ravaged by the galaxy-sized nano-cloud that we now call Mist. It has given us a chance. What we do with it is up to us. Everything I've ever seen from humanity tells me just how thin that chance is.

—Jeremiah Braddock III

It took me a couple of hours before I had regained enough energy to move on, and in that time, I discovered a few troubling facts. First, the monster that I'd killed had almost immediately begun to melt and turn into vapor. In my head, I imagined that it was a construct of Mist, and now that it had been killed, it was returning from whence it had come. A silly notion, perhaps, but for some reason, it felt accurate. Maybe I would one day find out whether I was right or wrong.

Second, I found a couple of corpses that had clearly belonged to the men and women who'd been forced into the Rift. They were half-eaten and partially rotted, suggesting that they had been there for a while. I didn't want to think about the kind of attitude it would take to leave your dead behind to be eaten by a furry tentacle monster. But, of course, I knew precisely what had motivated those people. It was a cycle of reward and punishment that had robbed them of every ounce of their free will, and it was a harsh reminder that slavery didn't have to look like what I'd always imagined it would. Sometimes, it was more insidious than chains or societal constraints.

Finally, I discovered a net. It was large enough to have covered the tentacle monster, made of metallic thread, and edged in hooks that I suspected would dig into the ground. Clearly, the slaves had been incapable of killing the creature and thus had been given the means to subdue it so that they could mine the Rift Shards embedded in the central hunk of rock. Given the two bodies, the process wasn't without risk, though. Having seen the monster in action, I could definitely understand their hesitation.

I searched the rest of the cavernous room, but to no avail. There was nothing there, save for the two long-dead slaves, the few pieces of the monster's skeleton that hadn't dissolved, and the net. However, I was pleased to note that the Rift Shards had continued the process of regrowth. As far as I could tell, it would take at least another week before they completely sprouted, but it was an interesting development. Moreover, it made sense of the mining operation. If the Shards regrew, the aliens would continuously send slaves in to mine the inexhaustible resource. The fact that they took time to grow just reinforced the Shards' worth.

After a few hours, I pushed those thoughts to the back of my mind and headed toward the door. Made of white wood, it was much like the one I'd previously encountered, though it was carved with elaborate whorls that sparkled with red energy. Planting myself on one side of the door, I reached over and pulled it open.

As it swung on its hinges, I clenched, waiting for some other monster to barrel through the opening. But nothing happened. Still, I remained stationary for almost a full minute before I worked up the nerve to lean out and take a peek through the doorway. What I saw nearly brought a chuckle.

It was a corridor not unlike the one leading to the Rift's exit, complete with the interwoven branches for a ceiling. Unlike that hall, though, this one was at least twice as big, with sconces along the wall that looked like they'd been grown, rather than forged. Upon those sconces sat crystals, inside of which danced purple flames that cast the entire space in an eerie, ethereal glow.

After spending a long few minutes inspecting it from the safety of the other room, I decided that I couldn't gain anything else from hesitating. So, I stepped forward, and I was immediately disgusted by the squishy sound of my boots squelching into something on the floor. I looked down, and I saw that the ground I'd thought was solid was indeed some sort of gelatinous substance.

"Gross," I muttered, picking up my foot. It came away clean, which was curious. I waited for a few more seconds to see if any other surprises presented themselves, but nothing did. So, I started forward, my feet squelching with every step. I tried to ignore the disgusting sound but to no avail. Each step came with a tremor up my spine.

Thankfully, it was only a few hundred feet to the next door, which turned out to be an exact copy of the last, and I covered that ground in a matter of minutes. It would have been much faster, but I had decided to take things slow and be as careful as I could be. My caution was for naught, though, because the corridor was as devoid of threats as the previous hall.

But that lack of danger meant that the next room likely held another foe. Or maybe even multiple creatures like the tentacle monster I had recently fought. I had no idea, and so, I took the same precautions before opening this door as I'd used with the last. When nothing came barreling through, I decided to chance a glance inside.

Floating in the center of an even larger room was a boulder, and it glittered with a thousand Rift Shards, each about twice the size of any I'd encountered before. That was all I got to see before something whipped out of the darkness, wrapped itself around my waist, and yanked me into the room.

I let out a surprised yelp, but otherwise, I didn't panic. Instead, I aimed my rifle, which I'd kept at the ready, in the vague direction I was being pulled, and fired a series of bursts. It all happened in the space of a couple of moments, and when my bullets found their mark, I was thrown to the side with far more velocity than I thought possible. I hit the wall with a dull thud, and I felt at least one rib break. But with my Combat Focus and Pain Tolerance kicking in, the injury was easily ignored as I rolled back to my feet just in time to see a fur-covered tentacle as big around as my thigh coming toward me.

I dove to the side, but the moment I committed in that direction, another one slapped me to the ground. My Kicker went flying from my hands, and yet another tentacle swept the ground, knocking it to the other side of the room. Before I could pursue it, another tentacle, this one far bigger than any of the rest, screamed toward me. In the brief second before it slammed into me, I saw that its underside was devoid of fur. Instead, it was covered in wicked hooks that looked more like the pincers of an oversize insect.

Having no desire to end up on the wrong end of those, I rolled to the side. And though I barely avoided being crushed by the sheer weight of the tentacle, I couldn't completely dodge the pincers. A pair of them latched on to my arm, easily cutting through my attribute-enhanced skin and only stopping once they reached the bone.

I screamed, and almost by instinct—or more likely, due to my extensive training—I summoned my nano-blade. As the scream turned to a snarl, I swept the blade down in an overhand attack enhanced by a hasty embrace of my Eviscerate ability. That first attack bit deep into the monstrous flesh, but that only served to make the thing panic. Before I could follow up with another strike, the monster picked me up off the ground, shook me, and then threw me into the floating boulder in the center of the room.

Somehow, I managed to angle myself such that I only skipped off the surface, but the sharp crystals dug into my back and shoulder, ripping into my flesh like I was a freshly Awakened novice rather than a seasoned fighter. I could only think that the strangely heavy atmosphere had something to do with it. Or I would have if I'd had any time to think at all. As it was, I found myself on the back foot and fighting a defensive battle.

I needed to change the paradigm if I was going to have any chance.

Fortunately, I had a weapon that I thought might give me an edge. So, the moment I rolled to a stop, I pushed myself to my feet, stowed my sword, and summoned my scattergun. It was an unassuming weapon, but I knew that it could pack quite a punch. I had no illusions about whether or not it would kill the creature. I knew it wouldn't. But it might give me the time I needed to turn the tables.

In the short couple of seconds it took me to aim my scattergun, a half dozen of the smaller tentacles had almost reached me. The larger tendril hung back, bleeding freely from where I'd cut it. That gave me hope. If a few bullets and a sword strike made it cautious, then that meant it could feel pain. And there was nothing in my arsenal better suited to dishing out pain than my scattergun.

When the searching tentacles reached me, I fired.

Lightning exploded from the barrel, arcing from one tendril to the next and creating a web of vibrant blue electricity. Then, another followed in its wake. This time, I doubled the output of the first with Double Shot.

An unholy screech filled the air, and I got my first look at the monster who owned all those tentacles. In some ways, it looked like the previous monster I'd fought within the Rift. The pieces were the same. Tentacles. A bulbous, furry body. A great, gaping mouth filled with needle-sharp teeth. But that's where the similarities ended because not only was this monster at least five times the size of the other one, it was also covered in eyestalks. And each one of them was staring at me with unrelenting hatred.

I gave it the same in return before firing my scattergun once again.

After that, I stowed my weapon and resummoned my sword before going to work on the thinner tendrils. Under the still-pulsing electrical current of my scattergun, they were incapable of more than a few twitches, and my nanosword was more than up to the task of cutting through them. So, after only a handful of seconds, four of them had been cut down to size.

But I only had eyes for the big one.

Using Engage to cover the ground, I was on top of the tentacle before it could react. Then, with a two-handed grip, I swept the slightly curved nanoblade of my sword down. It met the twitching tendril almost exactly where I'd hit it before. This time, though, it met little resistance as I sliced it in two. The severed portion flopped to the ground, and a moment later, the creature regained control of its limbs.

It screamed again, flailing the tentacles around and spraying the entire area with its black blood. I didn't care. I was already filthy, and a little blood never hurt anyone. So, I ran toward the creature, my sword trailing a bit behind me. When I drew close, I leaped. The monster tried to swat me from the air with its now-stubby tentacles, but the moment it came close, I twisted and contorted my body while using the monster's own attack as leverage. I came through the mass of tendrils unscathed, landing on the monster's body. That's when I went to work, sweeping my sword in a horizontal arc and severing a half dozen eyestalks with each attack.

Blinded, the creature panicked, bucking and rolling as it tried to throw me free. I let it, then retreated to where my Kicker had been thrown. When I spied it, I wasted no time before gathering it up and replacing it in my arsenal implant. I was sorely tempted to use it, but I had no idea if it had been damaged. Better to wait until after the fight—which I considered all but won—before making certain that it was still functional.

Instead, I stowed my sword and summoned Ferdinand II. Then, I loaded him with armor-piercing rounds, each one as big around as two of my fingers put together, and opened fire. My well-practiced aim proved flawless, and the huge rounds found a home in the monster's bulbous body. More screeches joined the fresh black blood fountaining in the air. I ignored it as I reloaded.

The creature's stubby tendrils flailed, but the movements were weak. Uncoordinated. Unless I did something horribly wrong, they were easily avoided. After relocating while reloading, I fired again, emptying the cylinder of all nine bullets. They tore the monster's furry hide to pieces, but it remained upright and alive.

So, I decided to adjust my strategy once again. This time, when Ferdinand II got a fresh set of ammunition, he was loaded with explosive rounds. My thought process was simple. The monster's hide was torn to bits, and it had long since lost its viability as natural armor, exposing the more vulnerable pieces underneath. So, that negated the explosive rounds' most glaring weakness, which was that they weren't great against armored foes. But without that armor? They could dig deep before exploding. I couldn't help but grin as I pondered the impending massacre.

So, of course, it was destined to go wrong.

At first, it went just how I'd planned, with Ferdinand II doing his job as well as I could have expected. Each round that thundered home brought with it a small localized explosion that ripped the monster apart from the inside out. But even as I killed the body, the creature revealed yet another surprise.

As I was admiring my handiwork with a tight smile, agony suddenly exploded in my leg. I hopped to the side and looked down only to see that, attached to my leg, was a creature that looked strikingly similar to a beetle, albeit one the size of my head and with overlarge mandibles. In fact, those pincers looked exactly like the ones I'd seen on the underside of the tentacle.

I stowed my weapon, reached down with both hands, forced the little monster's pincers apart, then threw it across the room. But a chittering from behind me sent a cold shiver up my spine, and without looking, I dove to the side just in time to avoid being swarmed by a few dozen more of the creatures.

Only a single glance at the furry tentacle monster's largest tendril was enough to tell me what had happened. The underside was ripped open, clearly announcing that the insects had been inside it the whole time. Now, they were free. And they seemed incredibly pissed that I'd killed their host.

I didn't have time to form a plan before the horde of insectile monsters shifted directions and skittered over me. I writhed in panic as a hundred little legs scurried over my body, and a dozen sets of pincers bit down on me. My mind went white with pain as both my Combat Focus and Pain Tolerance were overwhelmed, and I acted on learned instinct more than anything else.

Combination Punch activated as I started hammering my fists into any creature I could reach, and within a few blows, I was rewarded with the sound of shells cracking. Over and over, I punched and kicked, my limbs infused with all the strength my enhanced Constitution could muster, but each time I managed to dislodge a monster, it was soon replaced by another. And another.

I don't know how long I waged that miniature war against the overgrown insects, but eventually, the tide began to turn. And bit by bit, I started to win. Finally, at long last, I emerged from a pile of insectile carcasses, bloody, bruised, and otherwise exhausted. Bits of ragged flesh hung from my arms and legs, and I had a gaping gash across my ribs where one of them had managed to latch on. Ripping it free had dragged quite a bit of my side with it. However, I was alive. And they, decidedly, were not.

Across the room, I saw what was left of the original monster disintegrating into the Mist. I staggered to the clearest spot of the room, summoned my medical kit, and started treating my wounds. They were both better and worse than I had expected, and some of them would be sure to scar. But none were life-threatening. The alien insects' bites had been painful, sure, but they weren't deadly. Not unless they were allowed free rein.

Still, the fight had taken more out of me than I could've imagined, and I was already thinking of all the ways I could've done things better. Predictably, another door appeared, giving me just such a chance. But first, I needed to tend my wounds. And there were hundreds of Rift Shards just waiting to be harvested.

Fortunately, I'd brought plenty of medical supplies, and even more rations. I could stay in the Rift for days. Perhaps even weeks, if necessary. But if I was going to keep going, I needed to be smarter. I needed to take things more seriously. Otherwise, all my training would be for naught, and I'd end up just like those slaves had in that first room. Dead, decaying, and forgotten.

I refused to let that happen. So, I bent my mind to the task at hand, using my Triage ability to enhance my wound treatment. When I got done with that, I'd rest. Then, I would harvest the Shards. Only when I was completely healed would I move on to the next room.

It should be noted that I never once considered turning back, even when it would've probably been the smartest choice. I wasn't a quitter, after all. And the Rift had to have an end. I was resolved to find it.

CHAPTER FIFTY

DELVING THE RIFT

Sometimes, I wonder what the future will hold. But the moment I begin to make plans, I start to think about how everything else in the world turned to shit, and I find myself dreading the calamity coming our way. We cannot win. We can only hope to survive.

—Jeremiah Braddock III

I spent the next week mired in monotony as I let my wounds heal. Triage helped. As did my Regeneration ability. And my enhanced Constitution, as well. The result was that wounds that should've taken months to heal did so over the course of a few days. Certainly, I wouldn't fully recover for weeks more, and the injuries would doubtless scar, but by the end of that week, I was back to something approaching full strength.

I didn't spend that time just sitting around, though. In addition to mining the Rift Shards, which I accomplished by prying them free with my dagger, I continued to engage in physical training. It was a painful and grueling process, but without it, I felt sure that I would have to spend even more time working myself back into fighting shape.

I also spent quite a bit of time in thought. After a couple of days, I considered leaving the Rift altogether. I had already done what I'd set out to do, hadn't I? I'd gotten some experience with Rifts, and I'd dismantled the mining operation. That would mean passing my test, wouldn't it? But as I sat there, day by day, the door leading deeper into the Rift taunted me. I wanted to know what was on the other side. I wanted to test myself. The Rift Shards that would be my reward were just a bonus.

Finally, once I was satisfied that I was ready for whatever other challenges the Rift could throw at me, I found myself standing before the door that would lead deeper into the Rift. It was constructed much like the previous two, which meant that it was made of alabaster-white wood that had been carved with fanciful whorls that sparkled with red light, which in turn emanated from minuscule slivers of glowing crystal.

As I'd done before, I positioned myself to the side of the door, reached over, and pulled it open. It came ajar with the slightest creek, but the Rift was otherwise deathly silent. My heart thudded in my chest as I peeked out, and I let out a relieved breath when I saw a corridor that was much like the one I'd previously traversed. I stepped out, and remembering not to stand in the fatal funnel that was the open doorway, I crouched low. Holding my rifle in a firing position, I crept forward. Heel to toe, I covered the ground with as much alacrity as I dared.

My boots squelched in the gelatinous material of the floor, but I paid it no mind. A mistake, as it turned out, but one I couldn't predict. However, the moment the smell of burning rubber assaulted my nose, I realized what was happening. With the semisolid stuff melting the soles of my boots, I had no choice but to turn my creep into a sprint as I hurried to the next door. By that point, my feet were stinging, and the smell of melting flesh joined the aroma of burning rubber. I couldn't afford caution, so I threw my shoulder into the door and barreled into the next room.

My boots fell apart as I tumbled to the ground. Thankfully, the acidic slime had confined itself to the hall, so I was spared the agony of my body melting. However, what I found was very nearly as troubling because my tumble soon found open air. I only narrowly managed to jam my hand into a crevice before I was completely lost to the chasm I now saw stretching across the room.

As it was, I dangled there, hanging on by one hand as I looked down at the gaping abyss. I couldn't see the bottom, and the rocks that had skittered over the edge still hadn't hit the ground. Perhaps there wasn't one.

I forced my mind to something approaching placidity and, with a grunt, hauled myself up on the narrow ledge that abutted the door. It was maybe three feet across, and its twin was at least forty yards away on the other side of the chasm. How I was supposed to cross the space was a mystery, but as I stared at my latest obstacle, I couldn't help but mutter, "At least there's not another tentacle monster."

Of course, the moment I said it, I started looking around for just such a monster. The last thing I wanted was for one of the furry abominations to take me by surprise. I counted myself extremely fortunate that I hadn't lost my rifle into the abyss. If I had, I knew I would never hear the end of it from my uncle. To say nothing of losing what was probably my most potent weapon.

Seeing that there were no overt threats in the cavernous room, I stowed my rifle and decided to look around. The first thing I noticed was that, in the middle of the gap, another huge hunk of rock floated. It was almost twice as big as the one from the previous room, and the Rift Shards that decorated it were comparably larger than the ones I had tucked away in my arsenal implant. Given their size and the impending difficulty in obtaining them, I had to believe that they were that much more valuable than the others.

But even as greed threatened to overtake my mind, I realized that I had absolutely no way of harvesting the valuable shards of crystallized Mist. There was a chance that I could make the twenty-yard jump, but what if I missed? More importantly, what if I made it? I had no illusions about making a similar leap from a standstill. My Constitution gave me an incredible edge, but it would be some time before I reached that level of power.

So, I began to look for another way across, fully intending to leave the floating boulder alone. With that in mind, I walked to the closest corner of the room, where I started to inspect the walls. After only a few moments, I found that, like the ledge, the rock that made up the walls was craggy and offered the opportunity for plenty of handholds. Perhaps I could use them to climb across. I grabbed one of the most obvious chunks of jutting rock, but when I put any weight on it, it began to crumble.

"Crap," I muttered, seeing the chalklike substance crack and fall away. It was too brittle to support my weight. Maybe if I skittered across the wall like a bug, never stopping, I would be able to make it.

Or maybe the moment I got out over the cavern, it would crumble beneath my hands, and I would fall to my death. There was always that as a possibility.

Sighing, I continued inspecting the ledge and the opposite wall, but I found nothing else of interest. So, as far as I could tell, I had three choices. First, I could head back, my tail between my legs as I admitted that the Rift had beaten me. That option, I discarded almost immediately, partially because I had no desire to, once again, traverse that hall of acidic ooze. But my reticence to retreat was also mired in my competitive nature; I simply didn't want to admit defeat.

My second option was that I could take a flying leap and hope my enhanced Constitution would see me through. This had the added benefit of allowing me to harvest the room's Rift Shards. And it seemed far more straightforward than the final possibility, which would see me climbing across the wall. It was a risky plan in that, if I stopped moving even for a second, my handholds would crumble and I would fall. Of course, I might fall, anyway, regardless of how quickly I moved.

Kneeling next to the ledge, I ran my hand along the boundaries of the chasm. I felt incredibly smooth rock, meaning I couldn't add another option to the mix. Climbing down to the bottom and then back up on the other side seemed to be an impossibility. Even if there was a bottom, which I doubted.

While I gave it some thought, I sat down, stripped off what was left of my boots, and inspected my feet. They were both better and worse than I expected. On the one hand, the bottoms of my feet were a mass of blisters. But on the other, they were already scabbing over. I knew that it would only take hours before they were completely healed, largely due to my overworked Regeneration ability combined with my Constitution.

So, leaning against the wall, I stretched my legs out and enjoyed a tasteless ration bar while I waited for them to heal. As I did, I tossed my ruined boots over the edge. Thankfully, I'd had the presence of mind to pack an extra pair in my arsenal implant, though my reasoning didn't include the possibility of them being destroyed by acidic slime. Instead, I'd brought two sets in case one became soaked through; I could leave one out to dry while wearing the other. But now? Having a replacement set of boots was a godsend.

But it was my last pair, so I knew I'd have to be careful. Yeah—not a great chance of that, especially when I was considering whether I should try a twenty-yard leap of faith or channel my inner spider girl and scramble across a wall while my handholds crumbled beneath my fingers. So, careful didn't really seem like it was in the cards.

"I should just go back," I said to myself, my voice echoing slightly in the cavernous room. Leaning back against the wall, I closed my eyes and tried to think of anything but the itching that came along with my healing feet. Finally, after a couple of hours, it all faded away, and I looked down to see that, while they were still red, the blisters had faded. I just shook my head and said, "God, I'm glad for Regeneration."

In fact, I was thankful for all the abilities that had come with my [Combat Utility] skill. They were all incredibly useful, and I would've been dead a hundred times over without them. Not to mention the effect they had on my training; without Combat Focus, Regeneration, and Pain Tolerance, I wouldn't have even made it through my hell month, much less the more focused training that followed. Not for the first time, I found myself grateful that my uncle had invested so much time and effort into giving me enough power to forge my own path, even if I still wasn't sure what that path might end up being.

But that was a thought for another time. For now, I had a chasm to cross. I should probably admit that I never truly considered heading back. Not when I had a task before me.

So, I chose the wall.

My decision was based on the fact that, after traversing the obstacle course hundreds, if not thousands of times, I felt confident in my climbing ability. And given that I'd survived Nora's interference, I was pretty sure I could make it across. Of course, pretty sure shouldn't have been enough to push me into doing it, but I absolutely refused to go back. Not now. So, without further hesitation, I began my climb.

At first, everything went fine. While recovering, I'd taken a few minutes to study the area closest to the ledge, so I had most of the first ten yards mapped out. I knew where to find the best handholds, so it was child's play to scramble across. However, the issues started to present themselves when I found uncharted territory. Suddenly, I had to spend precious milliseconds searching for my next handhold. Fortunately, I had Observation on my side; without it, there was absolutely no way I could've made it. And even with the sense-sharpening ability working at full capacity, I found the handholds crumbling beneath my fingers on more than one occasion.

Sweat beaded on my forehead—not from exertion, but rather from the stress—as I skittered across the wall. Finally, after a little more than a minute of intense focus, I leaped to the ledge on the other side. I sank to my knees, my breath coming in shallow pants as I tried to steady myself against the wall. I was so caught up in it that I never even noticed the ledge crumbling.

Not until it was almost too late.

A crack shattered my brief reverie, and I cast a panicked look in the appropriate direction. That's when I saw a great chunk of the rocky ledge break free. Combat Focus wrapped itself around my mind, and I was moving before I even fully realized the danger before me. And just before the final bit of the ledge crumbled beneath my feet, I leaped, and at the last moment, I felt my fingers tighten around the door's green-glowing iron handle.

For the second time in the last few hours, I hung there, my feet dangling over the yawning chasm and my heart in my throat. Gritting my teeth, I hauled myself up until I could get enough leverage to open the door. As it swung outward, something burst through the doorway only to fly into the chasm below. A dozen more shapes followed, moving so quickly that I could only get the vaguest sense of their shape, which was something akin to a rodent, albeit one with glistening black scales and a size more comparable to a wild dog.

So, I guess they were unholy abominations that weren't like rodents at all.

Whatever the case, as I hung from that open door, none of them came even close to me. And they certainly couldn't fly. After a few seconds, during which a hundred of the things came sprinting through the door, the deluge petered out, replaced by the oppressive silence I had come to associate with the Rift. Still, I waited for a couple more minutes—hanging from the door wasn't difficult for me—before I chanced a peek through the doorway.

It opened into a blessedly empty hall, so after making certain that the floor wasn't covered in acidic goop, I wrangled myself inside, where I collapsed in a heap.

It was yet another mistake.

The click-clack of tiny clawed feet was all the warning I had before something slammed into me. I reacted on instinct, grabbing at the missile and digging my fingers into a scaly body. I ripped it free of where it was steadily trying to dig itself through my torso and tossed it across the corridor where it collided with the wall. I heard bones crunch, and the creature fell to the ground with a mewling hiss.

I didn't pay it any more attention as I glanced down the corridor to see another wave of the dog-sized lizard-rats screaming toward me. In a brief second, my scattergun was in my hand. I took aim, activated Double Shot, and fired. Lightning burst forth from the barrel, then arced from one creature to the next. Another pulse, and they skidded to a stop, piling up on one another.

I fired again. And again. Over and over, I sent one pulse of electricity after another through those disgusting creatures. After the third or fourth shot, I saw smoke rising from their bodies. I kept going until, at last, my weapon's ammunition cannister went dry. Mechanically, I switched it out for another, then dismissed my scattergun when I didn't see any further motion.

Still tense, I drew my rifle and crept forward. By the time I reached the pile of lizard-rat corpses, they had begun to disintegrate into Mist, but the smell remained. It was like a mixture of burnt rubber, rancid meat, and hot garbage, all rolled into one, and it was all I could do not to gag as I picked my way past them.

When I drew within ten yards of the door, it flew open, and another cascade of monstrous reptilian rodents came pouring out. I didn't hesitate to open fire on full auto, cutting down the first wave with my first magazine. Rather than reload, I exchanged it for my scattergun and repeated my previous strategy; the rest of the monsters were dead within two pulses.

The door slammed shut of its own accord, sending a chill up my spine.

I could easily see the pattern. Once every minute, the door would open, and a bunch of monsters would come screaming out, which meant I only had a few seconds before the Rift tried to overwhelm me again. And I wasn't going to let that happen. In fact, I had a surprise for whatever was on the other side of that door.

I was tired. I was in pain. And, more than anything, I really didn't want to get up close and personal with those monstrous lizard-rats. So, I strode toward the door, planted myself on the side, and summoned my trump card.

It was a device of my own making. An end-of-training project, in a lot of ways. It looked a lot like a soda can, only it wasn't covered in a garish logo, and it didn't sport some impossibly buxom mascot. Instead, it was all business. More importantly, it was filled to the brim with an explosive compound that would, when detonated, fill a hundred-foot radius with scorching plasma.

Reaching over, I opened the door with one hand while pressing the grenade's timer with another. Then, I tossed it inside before slamming the door shut once again. I just had time to pull my hand back before an explosion shook the entire Rift, blowing the door from its hinges and filling half the hall with liquid flames.

For my part, I held my head in my hands as I squeezed my eyes shut against the heat. Even so, I could feel my skin blistering with the rapid rise in temperature. But it was nothing compared to what the next room's denizens felt.

Hundreds of agonized screams filled the air as, presumably, an entire room's worth of those hideous creatures burned alive. What's more, a different sound soon joined the cacophony, but where the others were high-pitched whines and hisses, this one was a basso rumbling that rattled my bones.

As soon as I felt the fire die down, I summoned my rifle and slipped into the room. What I saw was a massacre of smoking corpses. Hundreds, if not thousands, of the creatures were dead, piled high in heaps of broiled flesh. But my eyes were immediately drawn to a bigger, still-moving figure on the other side of the room.

I commanded the Kicker into its sniper configuration, took aim, then used Empowered Shot before squeezing the trigger. The bullet took the creature, which was a bear-sized version of the other monsters, in the shoulder. It would've been a head shot, but the thing twitched to the side at the last second. Still, the shot was rewarded with a fountain of blood, scales, and meaty flesh.

I repeated the process, but once again, I missed my intended target. My shot skidded off its broad back, taking a hunk of muscle with it. That's when the monster's eyes found me.

It charged, its claws digging into the ground as it covered the distance with enviable alacrity. I fired again, but the bullet went wide, thudding into the faraway wall. As the hulking monster drew closer, I dove to the side, reconfiguring my weapon into the assault rifle mode, and by the time I rolled back to my feet, I was already firing.

Each burst found a home in the monster's thick, scaled body, but it didn't seem injured. In fact, if anything, it appeared even more formidable. A red mist burst forth from its hide, and it turned to face me. Its eyes, of which there were six, all glowed in a similar hue. Its jaw hung open, revealing multiple rows of sharp triangular teeth. Its forked tongue flicked out, tasting the air.

I fired again.

The creature blurred, avoiding my burst of fire altogether, then, before I could react, it was on top of me. I screamed as it bit down on my shoulder, its teeth ripping through my flesh with ease. My fingers spasmed, and my weapon clattered to the ground. But Combat Focus wouldn't let me panic.

Activating Combination Punch, I hammered my fist into the monster's head. Once. Twice. Three times. It yanked, trying to pull away, but I hit it again. Bones cracked beneath my fist, and the creature released me. It skittered away, and I collapsed to the ground. Its bite had gone deep, severing tendons and ripping muscles; I couldn't move my right arm, and I was bleeding profusely. If I let the monster escape, it would only return once I'd weakened enough that I couldn't resist.

As it retreated, I used Engage and moved so quickly that it was almost a teleport. My fist, again powered by Combination Punch, found a home on its skull. It reared, but its momentum sent it rocketing into the wall. I followed with dogged determination, aiming a second punch at its injured head.

In a last-ditch effort, it raked its claws at me, but I took the blow without flinching. Even as its claws scraped across my ribs, ripping the flesh from my torso, another punch landed. Then another. And another after that. Each one dazed it further until, at last, it began to spasm as the damage overwhelmed its brain.

I kept going.

Screaming with primal rage, I continued to rain one punch after another into the monster's crushed skull. I didn't stop until its head had turned to mush and the Rift had already begun its reclamation process.

Finally, I sagged against the floor, the weight of my injuries overwhelming my rage until, at last, I let myself collapse. Dimly, I tried to summon medical supplies to treat my injuries, but the combination of the exhaustion as well as the blood loss had already darkened my vision. Unconsciousness, I knew, was on the horizon. So, I summoned a med-hypo, jammed it into my thigh, and depressed the pneumatic plunger. It hissed as it delivered its medicated payload, and just before I surrendered to unconsciousness, I had the presence of mind to hope that it would be enough to stave off any issues until I awoke.

Just before I fell asleep, though, one thought skittered through my mind.

I had won. I had lived. And that fearsome monster had died. That was something, at least.

CHAPTER FIFTY-ONE

THE PRICE OF WINNING

Every victory comes at a price. Sometimes, that price can be paid in advance, via preparation and training. But most of the time, the true cost doesn't present itself until we've already committed to the game.

—Jeremiah Braddock III

I lay back, breathing hard as the giant scaled rodent dissipated into motes of Mist that then dissolved into the too-heavy air. Even though Pain Tolerance was still in full effect, my entire body was in agony. The worst of it was confined to my shoulder, which was completely immobile, but the various other injuries I had sustained were almost as bad.

Through gritted teeth, I growled, "If only I would've passed out . . ."

For a moment, I'd thought that was where I was headed, but a deep breath had sent tendrils of agony to wrap around my body, preventing me from letting unconsciousness overtake me. Until I took care of my wounds, I would have no solace.

So, after a few minutes where I tried to work myself up to it, I finally decided to push myself to a seated position. I did so with a scream of pure pain, but with tears in my eyes, I kept going until I was upright. Summoning an anesthetic med-hypo, I slammed the injector into my least-injured thigh and let numbness spread through my body. Once it did, I bent myself to the task of removing my clothing. With how gravely I had been injured, I knew I would never manage to undress in a conventional manner, so I grabbed a pair of scissors from my medical kit and committed to the task of slicing my clothes to ribbons. My work took longer than I expected, but in the end, I found myself peeling the clothing off in layers, taking some skin and drying blood along with it. Even with my pain-dampening ability and the anesthetic working against it, the torment was nearly overwhelming. But I persisted until I was naked but for a pair of black underwear.

My body was scraped raw, with bite and claw marks everywhere. But I knew my shoulder was the worst of the bunch. Without quick intervention, it would never heal properly. So, I grabbed a capsule from my medical kit, pressed it against the wound, and depressed a big blue button. Immediately, the contents of the capsule went to work, invading my wound and resetting everything in the proper place.

The automender was a miracle of modern medicine, and it only had one purpose—to use Mist to reset bones, reattach ligaments, and seal muscle fibers back together. It accomplished that purpose with aplomb. However, it was incredibly expensive, even for my uncle, and once expended, the hunk of plasti-steel was useless. It was, as Kimiko had said, only for emergency use. Even that would've been impossible if I didn't have my Triage ability; without that or some other comparable ability, the automender would be unusable.

Considering that my arm was only hanging on by a few thin ligaments that had somehow managed to survive, I thought my situation qualified as an emergency, so I hadn't hesitated before using it.

The process took almost twenty minutes, and it was not a pleasant experience. The anesthetic helped. So did my Pain Tolerance. But no abilities or drugs could ever mask the feeling of having your insides twisted and turned and reattached. Idly, I wondered which hurt more—the rending teeth of the now-dissipated monster or the automender. Even when the capsule beeped, letting me know that it was finished, I still hadn't come to an answer.

I threw the capsule aside, then went to work on my other injuries. First, I cleaned them. Then, I administered targeted antibiotic injections. Finally, I sealed them with foam bandages. All in all, the treatment of my wounds cost a veritable fortune, but it was difficult to regret it when, without that treatment, I would never make it out of the Rift alive.

But that was a worry for later because, as soon as my wounds had been treated, I slumped to the side and let unconsciousness overtake me. This time, I didn't wake up for almost ten hours, and when I did, I felt as if I'd been in a fight against a bear-sized lizard-rodent. Which was accurate.

Groaning, I forced myself upright, then checked my various injuries. Fortunately, my Regeneration as well as my treatment had worked wonders. And while it would still be some time before I was back to a hundred percent, I'd made quite a bit of headway. So, after making certain that things hadn't gotten worse, I dressed in my spare set of fatigues. Then, I got down to the business of eating. My body needed plenty of fuel if it was going to heal, and though the ration bars weren't exactly tasty, they were packed with all the nutrients necessitated by my healing body. I choked them down with a smile on my face. Figuratively. Literally, I was grimacing in mingled pain and disgust.

Once my hunger was sated, I found a corner of the room and took care of my biological necessities before settling back down to heal and think about my situation. And while things were looking up in terms of my injuries, my circumstances were decidedly grim. For one, both ledges in the previous room had crumbled into dust, which meant the only way out was for me to attempt the leap I'd shied away from in the beginning. Twenty yards didn't really seem like much until you considered trying to make it in a single jump. Then, it felt insurmountable.

Of course, I knew it probably wasn't. With a running start and my enhanced Constitution, I felt pretty good about making it. The problem really showed itself when I thought about the second leap, which would be just as long, but from a standstill. Of making that jump, I was far less confident.

As I thought, I looked around the room. Predictably, it had another floating boulder that contained Rift Shards that were half again as large as were available in the chasm room. However, I didn't make an immediate move to harvest them. Instead, I spent the next few days healing, eating, and resting. To occupy my mind, I continuously went through my puzzles, making better progress than ever before. But eventually, even that lost its luster. I wanted to move. I needed to make progress. I needed to see what awaited on the other side of the door that led even deeper into the Rift.

It was another week before I could move my arm, and a further four days before I regained full range of motion. Two more days after that, I could do so without pain. During all that time, I kept up my routine, steadily incorporating physical exercises into the mix. It was a curious period for me. On the one hand, it felt almost like a waste of time. And it was. I could think of a thousand things I could've been doing that would have resulted in more progress. However, it also taught me a valuable lesson about optimal recovery. I learned to listen to my body and use what it said to inform how hard I pushed myself, but even more importantly, I learned to take pride in my efforts. Just like lifting a few extra pounds brought a sense of accomplishment, so too did lifting my arm an additional inch. It might have been even more powerful because the effort involved made recovery one of the most difficult things I had ever done.

Eventually, the combination of my rations starting to run low and my recovery finishing up pushed me into making a decision. Either I needed to go back and risk jumping across the chasm, or I needed to keep going and hope the end of the Rift came with an exit.

The leap didn't seem quite so difficult as it had in the beginning because, during my recovery, I'd incorporated jumping into my training. And if I did everything right, I could just make it. Of course, that wasn't enough to engender confidence, but it was a step in the right direction. If it came down to it, I would give myself about a fifty percent chance of making it, which was a little better than I probably should have expected. Or maybe I was just being optimistic for once.

Either way, I felt like I'd made my choice the moment I had entered the Rift. Either I was going to finish what I'd started, or I was going to die trying. And considering how poorly the last two rooms had gone, the latter seemed far more likely.

In a lot of ways, I knew it was probably a bad idea. After all, I didn't have a death wish. But I also knew I was being tested, and not just by my uncle. I was testing myself, too. I had spent the last few years engaged in constant training. I had pushed myself to my limit on multiple occasions. And now, I needed the validation that would come with completing my exploration of the Rift. Otherwise, it would all feel as if I had wasted my time.

None of that was really the case. Rationally, I knew that. But reason doesn't always prevail. Sometimes, emotions get the better of us. So it was with the Rift, which was how I ended up standing before the next door, the floating boulder having been mined of its Rift Shards, with all my weapons loaded and my rifle in my hands.

Without further ado, I slipped to the side and, reaching out, opened the door. Fortunately, no horde of ratlike reptiles came pouring through, so I took a quick glance into the next hall. And I was surprised to see that it was far grander than any that had come before. The ceilings were nearly twice as high, the walls nearly three times as far apart, and the glowing lights far more vibrant. When I finally stepped inside—after first making sure that I wasn't going to melt my feet on gelatinous acid—I felt as if I was stepping into another world.

I was so entranced that I hardly noticed the tiny flecks of light drifting lazily along the hall's subtle air currents as they descended from the ceiling. And when I did notice them, I stared in awe at the beautiful bioluminescent display. They looked a lot like the Mistflies I'd seen in the forests around Mobile, only they weren't flying. Instead, they merely fell, drifting down from the ceiling to create an ethereal display of natural beauty.

And then one of them hit my upturned face, and a tormented scream ripped itself from my throat. Pain lanced through my entire body as I was racked by an agonizing seizure. My every muscle cramped all at once, and I fell to the floor where I couldn't stop myself from writhing in pain. Then another hit me. And another. I felt like I was bathed in fire, though, once my Combat Focus kicked in, I was aware enough to note that nothing was actually burning. The effect, according to the senses that came with Triage, seemed purely neurological.

Not that the information helped me to overcome the deluge of pain. I lost all control as I flopped around on the floor. Every few seconds, one of the motes fell upon me, extending my torment for that much longer. Before, I thought I knew what agony was, but my experience with those devilish lights put the lie to my previous understanding.

I had been stung by a deadly jellyfish. I had been shot multiple times. And I'd had my arm nearly bitten off. But none of it compared to what I felt in that hall, largely because I was powerless to stop it. There's a certain agony to being helpless, and it was one that, convulsing there on that floor, I felt incredibly keenly.

Slowly, I managed to gather enough control to turn my head and look at the door leading back the way I had come, but I was distraught to find that it had disappeared completely. Not surprising, considering that the doors didn't present themselves until I'd dealt with the room's challenge, but distressing because, in the back of my mind that was still sheltered from the agony, I had hoped to drag myself back into the other room.

But no. That was no longer an option. Instead, I would have to crawl my way to the other end of the hall. Suddenly, the distance, which had felt trivial when I could traverse it on my feet, seemed entirely insurmountable. I very nearly lost myself to despair at that thought. But somehow, I managed to gather my wits and, with convulsing fingers, drag myself forward an inch that felt like a mile.

Then two.

Three.

It took a hellish eternity, but eventually, those inches turned into feet, and those feet turned into yards. Bit by bit, I dragged myself through that hall, and all the while, the motes of light continued to fall upon me. Like that, I crawled through hell, and when I finally reached the next door, I had forgotten what the lack of pain felt like.

Then, the moment I touched the door, it stopped. I collapsed to the ground, my muscles still spasming. But I was blessedly free of the agony that had been coursing through my body.

Slowly, my mind embraced the lack of pain, and after some interminable amount of time, I pushed myself to my feet. I felt a degree of soreness I hadn't felt since the end of my hell month, and even that had been couched in exhaustion. Now, though, I was wide-awake—almost energized—so I could feel every ache to its fullest extent.

I glanced back into the hall to see that, only a few scant feet away, the motes of light danced in the air, looking almost eager to inflict more pain upon me. And they continued all the way to the other end of the hall. Whatever else happened, I wouldn't make it back the way I had come—not without enduring the same pain all over again. I wasn't certain I could force myself to do that. Not now that I was free.

That knowledge only served to fortify the decision I'd already made. Onward was the only option left to me. So, once my muscles unknotted and I felt that I'd recovered, I flattened myself against the wall and opened the door. The moment it was open, I heard a series of loud thuds, and when I looked in the appropriate direction, I saw a handful of long black spikes protruding from the wall.

"What the . . ."

I leaned out, only for an instant, but even that was nearly enough to get me killed. I jerked back just in time to avoid ending up with a bunch of black quills in my head. That was enough for me to remember my tactical training.

Until now, the Rift had only been populated by animalistic monsters, so I'd mostly disregarded the training I'd undergone to help fight other armed combatants, but whatever was in there—my brief glance hadn't yielded any results—was not so dissimilar from a man with a gun. So, I chose to use the tactics I'd been taught to combat such a situation.

Mentally reaching into my arsenal implant, I retrieved a pair of grenades. With the first, I pulled the pin, then tossed it inside. A moment later, a loud bang preceded a blinding flash of light. With that, I repeated the action with the second grenade; it erupted, as well, but instead of a flash-bang or the incendiary I'd used against the lizard-rodents, this one was packed full of tiny metal shards. When it exploded, I was rewarded with a series of shrieks.

I waited a few seconds, then tossed another flash-bang inside, and when it detonated, I rushed into the room and searched for the closest cover. I found none, but then again, I didn't really need it. With my Kicker in hand, I ran forward, searching for my targets. There were nine of them, and they were all still disoriented by my last grenade.

The creatures were vaguely humanoid, almost as if someone had crossed rodents, human beings, and lizards. They had elongated snouts reminiscent of alligators, ears like rodents, and torsos that reminded me of people. However, their entire bodies were covered in green scales, and they had long, thin tails like rats. At the ends of those tails were rapidly regrowing spikes that looked distressingly similar to the ones I'd seen embedded in the wall.

I opened fire.

Fortunately, these creatures were a lot less durable than the giant lizard-rodent I'd fought in the previous room, and my bullets tore through them with relative ease. Still, they didn't go down without a fight. The moment I started shooting, the entire group whipped their tails forward, throwing those spikes in my direction. Most went wide by a fair margin, but a few came distressingly close. One found its way home, clipping my left arm.

I ignored it as I continued what had rapidly become a massacre. Circling the huge floating boulder in the center of the room, I made quick work of the remaining creatures, and soon, I found myself alone but for the corpses, which were rapidly dissipating into motes of Mist.

Of course, I remained on my guard for any other threats that might present themselves, but to my surprise, nothing did. More importantly, instead of another door, I found the same formless blue prism I'd used to enter the Rift. It didn't take a genius to figure out that it was an exit. Or maybe it led to the next level of the Rift, if such a thing existed. Were there Rifts inside of Rifts? I realized that I had no idea, and my ignorance was definitely a hinderance. Still, there was nothing to be done about it.

So, with my way clear, I turned my attention back to the floating boulder. It was of a size with the previous one, though instead of a multitude of Rift Shards, it only had a single one. And it was the size of my head. Nestled atop the boulder, it was one of the most beautiful things I had ever seen. So, I wasted no time in climbing to the top and using my dagger to pry it free. Once I did, I held it in my hands—curiously, it was nearly weightless—and stared into its depths. As I did, I was beset by the feeling that I was looking at an entire miniature galaxy, and it took me a couple of moments to tear my attention away and store it in my arsenal implant.

Thankfully, despite its size being on the edge of what I could store outside of an access point, it went in without any issues. And so, after treating my latest wound by applying a foam bandage, I stepped up to the prism-like gateway and, taking a deep breath, stepped through.

After a brief moment of disorientation, I found myself standing in the bright light of a midday sun. And I was surrounded by robots as well as red-hued aliens, a few of them looking and feeling like actual warriors.

"Crap," I muttered to myself as a couple dozen weapons were trained in my direction.

CHAPTER FIFTY-TWO

THE IMPORTANCE OF PREPARATION

I know that, sooner or later, my lifestyle will catch up to me. It may happen tomorrow or a hundred years from now, but it will eventually happen. That's one of the reasons I chose to train Mirabelle. Even when I'm dead and gone, I hope that she can be my legacy. I hope that she can be better than I've ever been.

—Jeremiah Braddock III

A huge red alien with a musculature that would have excited Nora to no end stepped forward and barked a rasping series of words I couldn't understand. But with him gesturing at me with his massive axe, the threat was clear. My eyes shifted from one entity to the next. Six identical robots, each carrying a rifle not dissimilar from my Kicker, and half again as many aliens. Some of the accompanying aliens were like the axe-wielding leader, with muscles on top of muscles, but others held their weapons tentatively. I quickly surmised that they weren't much—if any—better than the ones I'd already slain. If the leader and his ilk were warriors, the others were more like caretakers.

Or slave drivers.

Either way, they didn't seem all that threatening to me. Not unless I stood still and let them shoot me, which was the last thing I intended to do.

Even as the leader continued his rasping orders, I summoned my detonator. It was a small device, maybe three inches long, with a pair of buttons. One would disarm the bombs I hoped were still attached to the robots' power supplies. The other would detonate them. I wasted no time in pressing the latter, and to my enormous satisfaction, I was rewarded with a series of sizable explosions.

I didn't take any time to appreciate them, though. Instead, the moment I hit the detonator, I was moving to my right. I got three steps before I felt like I'd been slapped with the world's largest pillow. I lost my footing and went flying through the air. I twisted so that when I hit the ground, I did so with a roll that eventually brought me back to my feet.

Summoning my Kicker from my arsenal implant, I darted to one of the nearby buildings to take cover. Crouching at the intersection of a pair of prefabricated walls, I leaned out and took in the sight of my handiwork.

And it was glorious.

Aliens—mostly the caretakers, I noted, but there were two of the warriors, as well—sprawled on the ground, bleeding from a dozen wounds. White blood pooled beneath their still bodies, evidence of their ignominious deaths. Of the robots, there was no sign, but that wasn't surprising. So long as no one had removed the charges, their fate was sealed. I'd made those explosives myself, and I knew they packed enough force to punch through the side of a tank. I knew because I'd done just that with my first batch, much to the delight of my explosives instructor, Anna, who had a habit of clapping and cheering like a child while we were testing my creations. I understood her feelings, though. There just wasn't anything quite like a good, solid explosion. Or six.

But as happy as I was to appreciate my handiwork, the battle was far from won. The leader had only been thrown forward to sprawl on his face, but as he picked himself up, he looked none the worse for wear. In fact, he just seemed angry. The remaining four warriors were similarly unaffected, though they all looked a bit disoriented. I decided to take advantage of that.

Squeezing the Kicker's trigger, I fired a burst that took one of them directly in the head. White blood sprayed as the alien's head exploded, and I moved on to the next. This time, because she was forewarned by my previous shot, my burst of bullets went wide of my intended target. Instead of hitting her in the head, her shoulder erupted in a spray of white blood and viscera. She screamed, but I didn't hesitate to shift my sights to the third. And after I got similar results, the fourth.

Finally, I fired at the leader, the bullets taking him in the chest. To my surprise, though, they thudded against his muscles with no discernable damage. That's when he locked his eyes on me and, with a roar, sprinted in my direction. I unloaded the rest of my magazine, but to little effect.

And then he was on top of me.

His axe, which glimmered with blue energy much like my nano-bladed sword, whistled through the air as he swung it with inhuman strength. I ducked and rolled away, dismissing my Kicker as I did. With a metallic clang, his weapon smashed into the building's corner, carving a huge chunk out of the strange material. He screamed something unintelligible as he aimed a kick in my direction. I didn't have the leverage to dodge, so I had no choice but to tense up and take the kick.

His foot hit me with the force of a sledgehammer, and for the second time since I'd left the Rift, my comparatively small body went flying. I twisted and turned, summoning Ferdinand II as I sailed through the air. Then, just before I hit the ground, I fired. Ferdinand II barked, sending his explosive payload in the direction of the warrior, who was tugging on his axe, trying to dislodge it from the building. The round hit him in the forehead, detonating with a small, contained explosion that sent him sprawling to the ground.

For my part, I hit the ground on my back, which knocked the breath from my lungs. Even as I struggled to breathe, I knew I couldn't stop, so I rolled to the side and pushed myself to my feet. Dismissing Ferdinand II to reload my Kicker, I very nearly missed the club coming for my face.

At the last second, I leaned back, and the knobby metal weapon barely skipped across my forehead. My vision went momentarily white, but I kept my wits about me well enough to continue backing away. I felt the wind of a narrowly missed swing, and then, after only a second, my sight returned.

And it was just in time to see one of the wounded warriors looming over me. Discarding my plan to reload my rifle, I summoned my nano-sword instead. I dodged the alien's overhand swing, then swept my blade across her torso. It bit deep, not stopping until it hit her vertebrae, and when I pulled it free, strikingly human-looking entrails fell free with a wet plop.

She screamed, dropping her club to grasp at her innards, but I pushed her from my mind. She wouldn't be much of a threat going forward. Gut wounds weren't immediately fatal, but it was difficult to swing a melee weapon when your insides had become your outsides. So, I turned my attention to another one of the recovering warriors whose arm I'd almost severed with my second volley and activated Engage to rapidly close the gap.

I was on him before he could react, and my nano-bladed sword descended upon his other arm, cutting through it with surprising ease. I finished him off with a horizontal swing that sent his head flying from his shoulders.

As I turned my attention to the second-to-last warrior, rain began to fall in great, fat droplets. I ignored it as I saw the male alien taking aim with a small pistol. I resummoned Ferdinand II, and before he could even squeeze his trigger, I'd already sent two explosive rounds into his face, thanks to Quickdraw.

They weren't nearly as effective as I'd hoped, likely because the warrior had a decent Constitution attribute, but it was enough to send him skidding across the increasingly wet ground. I used Engage again to close the ground between us, and before he could recover, I'd started hacking him to pieces, using Eviscerate to make sure that, even if I didn't kill him immediately, he'd die soon enough. It was unnecessary because, after only three swings, I'd sliced through his frantic defenses and into his chest. Once his heart and lungs were exposed, I wasted no time before cutting them free.

A deep growl cut through my bloodlust, and I looked up to see the leader—with his shirt burnt through and his face blistered from where I'd shot him—glaring at me. He said something to me, but I still couldn't understand it. My lack of a response only served to infuriate him even more.

He hefted his axe, which he'd managed to rip free of the building. In the driving rain, I stood my ground, the thick white blood of his companions dripping from my sword. I could recognize a challenge when I saw one. I could respect it, too. After all, I'd just killed everyone in the alien's party. What's more, I knew from the files I'd read before jumping into the Rift that he and the other aliens had little more choice than the humans they'd enslaved. At best, they were hired hands. At worst, they were something akin to indentured servants. Either way, they didn't deserve to die.

Except that they'd invaded my planet and were complicit in the worst kind of slavery. Whole generations had lived and died under their horrible regime. It didn't matter that they hadn't had a choice. They had still done it. And because of that, I had few regrets concerning my actions.

He charged, his heavy footsteps splashing in the rapidly accumulating water. I tightened my two-handed grip on my nano-bladed sword, shifting one foot slightly behind the other as I turned my body. And then, he reached me.

His axe cut through the air in a diagonal cut aimed at my shoulder. I swayed to the side, letting it pass within a half inch of my chest, then whipped my sword out. Eviscerate activated, and I used my superior speed to cut him four times in quick succession. None of the wounds were deep, but influenced by my ability, they bled profusely.

The red alien let out another roar and redirected his axe into a horizontal swing that he intended to cut me in two at the waist. I leaped, clearing the axe at the last possible moment, then used his shoulder for leverage to spring over his head. I twisted and flipped, my sword once again whipping out to cut into his scalp. When I landed behind him, I stabbed forward, the nano-blade piercing him through the side. Like lightning, I withdrew, and a spurt of white blood followed.

He didn't stop, though, swinging around and aiming a backhanded blow at my face. I ducked under it, then rolled to safety. I regained my feet, and my sword darted out, slicing through his vulnerable hamstrings.

As the enraged but flagging alien turned again, I sprang backward, then backed away. I watched as he glared at me. He was bleeding from a half dozen cuts, and his blood had begun to pool beneath him, staining the puddles of rainwater milky white. He growled something in his foreign language. I ignored him, shifting back into my stance.

He came at me again because, in the end, he had no choice. He couldn't retreat, or his masters would punish him. He couldn't hesitate, or he would bleed out. Even though he knew he was outmatched, the only option open to him was to keep at me. So, that's precisely what he did.

And for a few more minutes, he made a good showing. He even managed to clip me a couple of times. But his attacks were weak and rendered ineffective by his blood loss. They were no more than flesh wounds, and I bore them easily.

In the end, the fight came to a close anticlimactically when he fell to his knees and pitched forward onto his face. The blood loss from a dozen profusely bleeding wounds had finally done him in. I had won.

But I didn't feel good about my victory. How could I? It had been nothing but a slaughter. Sighing, I whipped my sword out, sending the white blood flying, before I dismissed my weapon. Over the next few minutes, I inspected the bodies of my assailants, but I found nothing of worth. So, I retreated into one of the buildings where I treated my wounds. Nothing was serious, so I made do with a med-hypo and a few foam bandages.

When I emerged from the building, I felt exhausted. Not physically. I'd had plenty of rest, and most of my injuries were mere annoyances. Sure, they hurt a little, but I'd grown used to pain, especially lately. Instead, my fatigue was purely mental. It felt like I'd been living on the ragged edge for months, if not years, and I just wanted to take a few days—maybe a month or so—and rest. Being in the field was a lot different from even the most intense training, and the Rift had ratcheted the difficulty up by at least a few notches.

But I suppose that was the point of it all. My uncle had sent me in there, likely with the express purpose of forcing me to find my limits. I still hadn't, but I had come very, very close. Especially in the corridor of pain that had preceded the final room. I never wanted to revisit anything like that ever again.

I knew I probably would, though.

Before that, however, I had to remember that I was still in enemy territory. For one, I didn't know if the nearby settlement had any other alien warriors to send after me. If they did, I felt confident in taking care of them, but that wouldn't be the case if I was unfocused. I was just about to leave when I remembered a recent lesson I'd learned.

A little more than a year before, I'd let Jack live. And that had very nearly come back to bite me. My uncle had taken care of it, but after doing so, he'd chastised me for leaving such a blatant loose end dangling in the wind. I had resolved to never do that again. And yet, here I was, about to make the same mistake all over again, except on a much larger scale.

As much as I wanted to be gone from the area, I still needed to rid the region of the alien menace. So, with tired determination, I rigged the Rift stabilizers with explosives, which I detonated as I left the fort and set myself on a course toward the village. It was only a couple of miles, and the forest wasn't nearly as thick as it was farther to the south, so I made good time. When the village came into view, I settled down into a concealing thicket, where I decided to watch for a bit before making my move.

What I saw was disgusting. Everywhere I looked, I saw people—human beings—being treated like little more than animals. I could scarcely watch the horrid scene, and with each passing second, my resolve firmed. After a couple of hours, during which the rain had continued to fall and the sun had begun to dip below the horizon, I decided to make my move.

Summoning my Kicker, I quickly reconfigured it into its sniper mode. Then, I took a prone firing position and sighted in on my first red-skinned target. I fired, not even waiting to see his head explode before quickly adjusting my sights to another target. That one went down a moment later, and I moved on to the next. Then the next after that. One after another, I assassinated the aliens until thirty-two bodies decorated the village.

As the aliens dropped, the dirty and bedraggled human slaves wailed and screamed, falling to their knees and pulling out their hair. I ignored them. As much as I wished I could save them, they were already lost. My actions weren't about that. Instead, I'd killed the aliens so I could stop the injustice. Certainly, I knew that the human slaves would likely die. But that was a price to my conscience I was willing to pay. I even managed to convince myself that I was doing them a favor. After all, what they had wasn't really a life.

I almost believed it, too.

So, it was with a heavy heart and a significantly increased body count that I retreated back into the woods and started the long trek back to Mobile. I could only hope that when I returned, I would have a little time to make peace with what I'd just done. I didn't mind killing aliens. Even if they never had much of a choice, they were still invaders. But I couldn't help but wonder if I should have just included the humans in my massacre.

And that thought terrified me. I didn't want to become the sort of person who could kill people rather than give them a chance to live a better life. But I knew that if things continued along the way they were going, that would be my inevitable destination.

CHAPTER FIFTY-THREE

THE GRIEVING TEMPLAR

I was doomed the moment I was born. The deck was always stacked against me. A young, black man growing up in the Deep South. No father. No money. Just a burning desire to escape. I turned to the army, not because I wanted to fight, but because it was the only option open to me. And as it turned out, I was a born killer. Sometimes, I wonder if I would've ever discovered that if I'd have been born under different circumstances.

—Jeremiah Braddock III

After traveling for a few hours, I finally decided to take refuge in a huge decrepit building that was surrounded by acres of concrete. The building itself was confined to one level, but the ceilings were high enough that it could've housed a couple of stories. Ivy and other vegetation covered its crumbling facade, but because of the paved surroundings, only a few trees had managed to take hold in the area. The result was a mostly open space, populated only by the rusted-out hulks of a handful of ancient cars.

As I approached it, I couldn't help but wonder what the building's original purpose had been. Perhaps my uncle would know. Either way, I advanced with appropriate caution, holding my rifle in a firing position. During my time in the wilderness, I had been surprised often enough that even an apparently empty lot couldn't lull me into a sense of security. As it happened, my caution was unnecessary, and I reached the building's entrance unmolested.

I stepped inside, sweeping my weapon around as I studied the interior. The roof was still intact, so the worst of the rain remained outside. However, the humidity had done a number on the place, resulting in an entire ecosystem of fungi and creeping vines. I heard the skittering of rodents, as well, but through Observation, I determined that none of them were large enough to truly threaten me. So, I continued inside.

I wasn't certain if it was due to my enhanced Constitution, the effects of Observation, or some side benefit of my optical implant, but I'd developed the ability to see in the dark, albeit not as well as I could in daylight. A good thing, too, because the only light entering the building came from the open entrance, and even that was muted by the overcast and rainy day. Because of that night vision, though, I got a good look at the building's interior, and what I saw was baffling.

Along the front were a series of rotted tables, topped by plastic screens. I approached one, and I was a little surprised to see a thin plastic bag. Further inspection of the area only served to confuse me more because upon the table was a metal rack, empty but for a couple of sealed tins a few inches long. At the other end of the table was a box with a glass front, inside of which were soda cans.

That, as much as anything else, told me that the building had been some sort of shop. Perhaps it had been an indoor market, though the sheer size of the building suggested a multitude of purposes. Maybe it was something like the King's Row mall back in Nova City, which housed hundreds of shops. That mall was vertically constructed, but with so much land available, it was understandable that pre-Initialization architects would've chosen to build out rather than up. With that explanation in mind, I moved farther into the building.

I spent the next couple of hours exploring the place, but I didn't find anything of note. Just some old, useless screens, a few tires, and a few rusted-out tools. It had clearly been abandoned for decades, and it looked it. However, my inspection did yield results in the form of an isolated place for me to sleep.

Judging by the still-intact porcelain toilets, the room had been a public bathroom. However, because it only had one entrance, it was a perfect place to hole up for the night. So, once I barricaded the heavy metal door, I rechecked my wounds from the previous battle, cleaned up, and devoured a brick-like ration bar. It didn't go down easily because I'd been fantasizing about my nightly meals back in the Dew Drop Inn. I'd taken them for granted of late, and as I chewed on the tasteless nutrient brick, I resolved to change that.

After I was fed and my wounds were treated, I hung my wet clothes up to dry. I knew they wouldn't completely dry out overnight, but I hoped they would come close because I didn't have any spares. Not after getting repeatedly torn up in the Rift.

Once that was done, I decided to take a look at my status, and I was surprised to find that all of my skills were on the verge of reaching the fifth tier. In addition, I'd managed to gain a few levels, as well. As a result, I felt it wouldn't be long before I finally attained level ten and got to choose a class. That, though, was a thought for another day. As happy as I was to see the progression, I knew I needed time to decompress.

Leaning against the wall, I took a little time to just think. Usually, I spent any free time I had doing puzzles or furthering my training, but for once, I just wanted to relax—at least as well as I could while camping in an ancient and abandoned building. With a flick of my eyes, I searched my KIOI's memory and selected the audio file my uncle had given me for my sixteenth birthday. Even as the first Leviathan track began, I let out a long, exhausted sigh.

When my uncle had given me the file, he'd told me that it would help me to get through my training. And at first, he was right. When I was running sprints or trying to improve my time on the obstacle course, it certainly acted as a distraction from the pain and fatigue. However, the longer I kept it up, the more I'd come to realize that distractions were detrimental. If I was going to get the most out of my training, I needed to focus on it fully, to eke every last benefit I could out of my time spent. After all, when you're dealing in seconds or inches, the slightest improvement can be the difference between life and death.

And given how close I'd come to dying in the Rift, my focus had been well applied. Going forward, I would only be less inclined to distraction because I knew the price that came with waning focus.

For now, though, I just relaxed. I listened. And despite the up-tempo beat and the thrashing guitar solos, it was strangely soothing. Eventually, sometime around the second loop through the file, I fell asleep, and I didn't wake until the next morning. It was the most refreshing night of sleep I'd had in months, so I rose from the floor, optimistic about the coming days.

Even the taste—or lack thereof—of another ration bar wasn't enough to dampen my mood as I went about my morning ablutions. It'd been weeks since I'd really felt clean, and I knew that, with the coming journey, it would likely be weeks more before I got back to Mobile and had a proper shower. Perhaps I could find a likely stream along the way.

After engaging in a few calisthenics meant to get my blood pumping, I removed the barricade from the door and exited the room, then the building. Thankfully, the thunderstorm had passed in the night. However, after only twenty minutes of trekking through the wilderness, I began to wish that the rainfall had stuck around. Without it, the heat had become oppressive, made even more so by the climbing humidity. I did my best to ignore it, but within an hour, my clothes were soaked with sweat.

So it went for the next two days while I made my way out of the Dead Zone. I made good time, only stopping when absolutely necessary, and I was relieved when, on the third day, I stepped across that almost invisible line and into normal territory. Looking back, I saw the same vaguely blue tint that I'd grown so accustomed to, and it felt as if someone had lifted a weight off my shoulders. I'd almost forgotten the heavy atmosphere, but now that it was gone, it seemed all the more oppressive.

The moment I was clear of the Dead Zone, I sent my uncle a message, letting him know that my mission had been successful, but he didn't respond. That wasn't abnormal, and given that I was in the middle of a test, I never really expected him to answer. However, I wanted to keep him apprised of my progress, just in case he'd started to worry.

I turned back around and kept going, eventually coming across a mostly intact highway. At probably twenty-five feet wide, it was cracked, and in places, the concrete was crumbling, but it made traversal a good deal easier than it would've been if I'd continued trekking through the forest.

However, on the second day after finding the road, I came upon an issue in the form of a convoy of unfamiliar trucks heading north. With Observation, I heard them coming long before they saw me, so I dove off the road and into the nearby brush. I managed to hide just in time because, only a few moments later, a huge, armored carrier rumbled past. I held my breath as I saw that it was manned by men and women who looked strikingly similar to the Enforcers back in Nova City.

Seven more vehicles passed by. Five cargo trucks and one more personnel carrier, the last of which sported a wicked-looking cannon on top. They were well prepared for whatever issues the wildlife might present. As I watched them roll past, I wondered how I would fare against such a force. There were dozens of Enforcers, each armed and armored, and a pair of cannons that I suspected would pack quite a punch. Even if I could take them, it wouldn't be a fight I would seek.

Not unless I had a few weeks to prepare, plan, and observe. Otherwise, any attack would be doomed to failure.

Once I was sure they were long gone, I continued along my way. It was two days later that I encountered an issue. Night had already fallen, and I was looking for somewhere to camp for the night when I stumbled upon a village of wildlings. At first, I took them for half-decayed corpses because they were sprawled across the road, but further inspection was enough to establish their identity as the feral, mutated humans. Even as I settled down to watch them, they started to rise, one after the other until they were all milling around aimlessly.

Until one let out a barking yell, silencing them and getting their attention. I looked at the apparent leader, and I saw that the wildling in question was a tall, skeletally thin figure with gaunt cheeks. The left side of his face was a mass of scars, and his eye was completely missing. His hair grew in ragged clumps, but what drew my eye was what looked like a tattoo on his left pectoral.

Never mind that I hadn't seen any other wildlings with tattoos. They were the unfortunate creatures who had never had the opportunity to get a Nexus

Implant. Without that guiding force, the Mist had twisted them into feral monsters. So, when did the creature get a tattoo?

Using my tried-and-true hiding method, I'd taken up a position in the boughs of a sprawling oak tree, so I didn't think they would discover me. Still, I kept my rifle at hand.

"Please do not kill him," came a soft voice from behind me.

I started, nearly falling from the branch. The leaves rustled, attracting some attention from the wildlings on the ground, but I was well concealed. Besides, I wasn't really concerned with the threats down below. I was far more worried about whoever had just spoken to me. Still, I managed to mostly maintain my composure as I turned my head to see a man crouching behind me.

He wasn't much bigger than me, though he had much broader shoulders. His hair was even wilder than mine, and he had a great, bushy beard. He also looked almost as dirty as the unfortunate wildlings below us, except that his outfit—which was completely white—was spotless. I didn't need to see any more to know precisely what I was looking at.

A Templar, if one who'd clearly seen better days.

I'd only ever seen them from afar, but even with my sheltered upbringing, I knew what they were. Elite warriors who used Mist in strange and terrifying ways, Templars were considered something akin to sorcerers. Before I'd begun my training, I'd thought that part a myth. Certainly, I knew they were probably powerful, but some of the stories I'd heard—some claimed there were Templars who could throw fireballs and manipulate the wind—were so unbelievable that they were patently ridiculous.

But then I'd started my training, and I had seen what even my skills could do. Even as my body, Mind, and abilities grew stronger, my skepticism about what was possible faded away.

I was about to say something when he held a finger up to his lips, prompting silence. I whipped my head back to the wildlings, and I saw that they were directly under us. The tattooed leader sniffed the air a few times, but then he and the others moved on. After that, I remained motionless for a long while, just to make sure that they were truly gone.

Finally, after twenty minutes, the Templar said, "You may relax. The Unfortunates have fled the area."

I turned my attention back in his direction, and I asked, "You're a Templar, right? Who are you? Why are you here? And why did you sneak up on me?"

"You snuck up on me," he said with a kindly smile, displaying blindingly white teeth. Clearly, his lack of hygiene didn't extend to his mouth. Then, he pointed up at the tree's higher branches, adding, "I was up there when you disturbed my watch."

"Your watch?"

"The leader of the Unfortunate Ones," he said. "He was once my apprentice. I had high hopes for him, but alas, the Mist took him."

"What are you talking about?" I asked, more than a little confused.

"I see that you are unaware of our customs," the Templar said. "I am Frederick, and if you would share a meal with me, I will tell you what I can."

It was probably a bad idea. After all, I was alone, and no matter how much I focused on the man, I couldn't discern his tier. Of course, Observation told me that he was powerful, but beyond that, I knew nothing. However, I was intrigued, and more importantly, I was tired of eating ration bars. So, with a nod, I said, "Lead the way, Freddie."

He cocked his head to the side, then cracked a small smile. "Freddie. I like that," he said. Then, without waiting for a response, he leaped down from the limb and started walking to the west. I hopped down and followed behind him.

We walked for almost an hour, during which time the sun began to slip below the horizon. I was a little trepidatious about walking through the forest at night, but Freddie seemed okay with it. So, I followed without complaint. Finally, we reached a small shack; it was a fresh construction made of logs, suitable for a single person, but it looked sturdy enough. Freddie didn't stop before heading inside and, a moment later, emerged with a sizable cast-iron cauldron.

"Come," he said. "Let us check the traps."

He set off without my consent, and with a sigh, I followed. A few minutes later, we reached the first of his traps, which had captured a wild hare. It was a mundane, unmutated creature, and I was reminded of the rabbit stew I'd tried to cook back in Bayou La Batre. Hopefully, Freddie knew more about cooking than I did. Over the next thirty minutes, night truly fell, and we gathered three more rabbits. Once Freddie had extracted the creatures from his snare lines, he reset them, and then we headed back to his shack. Once there, we gutted and skinned the creatures before he threw the meat into the cauldron. He must have had an arsenal implant or something of the like because he quickly produced a few jugs of water and enough vegetables to populate the stew. In no time at all, he had it simmering over an open flame in front of the shack.

Through it all, he said little, and I took my cues from him, remaining silent, as well. Eventually, the stew finished cooking, and he ladled it into a couple of earthenware bowls he produced from thin air. I was just about to ask him about it when he said, "I suppose you want to know what is going on." He gestured with his spoon, saying, "Eat and I will tell you what I can of my order. Perhaps that will make sense of things for you."

I nodded, then dipped my own spoon into the stew. When I slipped it into my mouth, I was pleasantly surprised by the flavor. It wasn't great, but it was hearty and much better than the nutrient bricks I'd been eating of late. I quickly shoveled another spoonful into my mouth as Freddie began his explanation.

"The Templars do not use Nexus Implants," he said. "We learn to manipulate the Mist on our own."

"How?"

"Meditation," he said. "Cultivation. It's a whole . . . process that takes a decade or more before it bears fruit. I cannot and will not explain it now."

"Fair enough," I muttered, shoving another spoonful of rabbit stew into my mouth. It was definitely a lot better than my poor attempt.

"The process is not without its dangers," he said. "The initial stages, they are not possible in tame environments. To make it work, we must be inundated in wild Mist."

"Like in the Dead Zone or a Rift," I guessed.

"You have been in the Dead Zone? You have seen a Rift?" he asked.

"Yes and yes," I said. "The Dead Zone felt like someone had thrown a weighted blanket over me. The Rift was more oppressive."

"So, you went inside," he mused. "Impressive."

I shrugged, eating more stew. When I swallowed, I said, "I guess. It wasn't fun, I'll tell you that much."

"Nor should it be," the man said, scratching his dirty beard. "But yes, our new initiates are subjected to the environment inside a Dead Zone. Or, if possible, a Rift. This does not come without risk, though. Few have strong enough spirits to withstand the wild Mist, and they succumb to it, becoming like those Unfortunate Ones we saw earlier."

"So, you drag some kids into a Dead Zone, and they either learn what you're trying to teach them or they turn into wildlings," I said. "You and my uncle would definitely get along. Similar training methods."

"Is that so?" he said. "Would you like some more stew?"

I looked down to see that I'd finished my bowl, so I nodded and handed it back to him. While he served me a second helping, I asked, "That tall one back there, the one with the tattoo—you said he was your apprentice, right?"

"His name was Elijah," Freddie said. "And he was a promising young man. All signs pointed to him breaking through and becoming a true Initiate. The Mist had other plans, and almost a year ago, he became as you saw him. A true loss."

With that, he stood, adding, "Stay in the cabin if you like. I may see you again before you depart."

Before I could respond, he strode off into the night, leaving me alone. Briefly, I considered following him, but I decided against that idea. He clearly wanted to be alone, so who was I to take that from him? I would be content to eat his stew and sleep in his cabin, and then, in the morning, I would be on my way. I wanted to know more about the Templars, but if I had learned nothing else, it was that we didn't always get what we wanted.

CHAPTER FIFTY-FOUR

THE JOURNEY HOME

I have made so many mistakes over the course of my long life, but with Mirabelle, I feel like I've finally gotten something right. Only time will tell, though.

—Jeremiah Braddock III

Eager to be on my way, I left that shack before dawn the next morning. Freddie hadn't returned during the night, and I suspected that he wouldn't be back anytime soon. As intrigued as I was, I found that I was okay with that. I wasn't certain if he'd been telling me the truth or if he was crazy, but I found his presence unnerving enough that I was eager to leave before he came back. So, in the predawn darkness, I left that shack behind.

As I traversed the forest, I kept all my senses trained on my surroundings. I had seen enough of the wilderness that the last thing I wanted was to stumble onto something truly dangerous. Fortunately, though, my trek was uneventful, and I soon reached the road I'd left behind the day before.

Looking around, I found plenty of evidence of the wildlings. A sharpened stick here. A pile of excrement there. A scrap of a blanket. I even found a crude doll made of twigs, reminding me that the wildling population wasn't just confined to adults. There were children there, as well. Thinking about those poor souls growing up as little more than animals broke my heart into a million pieces.

Shaking my head, I continued along the road at an easy jog. At one point, it would've been tiring, but with my Constitution, I could keep it up all day and then some. In fact, I was fairly certain that, at that speed, so long as I ate and drank, I wouldn't exhaust my reserves of energy for a long, long while. It served as a poignant reminder of just how much I'd changed over the previous couple of years.

After a few hours, when the sun had truly begun to rise, the road turned into a crumbling bridge meant to traverse a wide but shallow creek. One look at the murky water told me that it wasn't safe to drink, so I eschewed refilling my water bottles in favor of crossing it as quickly as possible. Of course, just after I reached the midway point, I was attacked by a mud-covered giant frog whose tongue lashed out at me with barely fathomable speed.

Fortunately, I'd been well trained, and I was experienced enough that I was on my guard. The moment I saw motion, I summoned my nano-bladed sword from my arsenal implant. The frog was enormous and probably weighed twice as much as I did, so its tongue was as big around as my arm. But with a quick swipe, my sword went through it just fine. The monstrous animal let out a screeching wail before dipping back into the water and swimming away. After that, it was easy to track by the blood staining the water.

Keeping my sword out, I waded through the creek and to the other side before crawling up the steep, muddy bank and back into the trees. A few minutes later, I found the road once again and continued on my way. Like that, I traveled for another week, passing the remnants of a long-dead society along the way. I saw huge buildings reminiscent of the enormous market in which I'd briefly found shelter, rotted homes that must have once been quaint, and a host of rusted behemoths that had once been cars. I even found a knot of twisting and turning bridges at the intersection of two huge highways.

While I traveled, I wondered at the nature of the fallen civilization. Were their lives so much different than ours? Did they have to worry about overbearing threats like the aliens or even the Enforcers back in Nova City? Or had their lives been peaceful? Did they spend most of their lives toiling for someone else's benefit? Or were they truly free? I had no idea, but wondering about it was an interesting way to pass the time.

Of course, I usually didn't make it very far before having to evade some monster, which, as much as anything else, served to remind me why everything was abandoned. Most of them were variations on animals I'd already encountered, though usually with a twist. Some were just bigger. Others, like a six-legged coyote, had extra limbs. Still others were adorned with various metal fins, spikes, fangs, or claws. The one thing they all had in common was that they were incredibly dangerous, though.

My training served me well, and I was able to avoid most of them. However, even with my abilities—both trained and granted from my skills—I had to fight at least a few times each day. Invariably, I would always start with my sword, largely because I wanted to avoid drawing attention with the sound of my gunshots, but a couple of times, I was forced to go all out. One of those instances occurred when I was accosted by a giant snapping turtle that had planted itself across the half-flooded road where it was basking in the sun.

I tried to go around, but the moment the truck-sized creature caught my scent, it refused to let me pass. So, after narrowly avoiding its lightning-quick snapping jaws, which splintered the trunk of an oak tree like it was nothing, I shifted my efforts from evasion to termination. I quickly learned, however, that the monstrous animal was probably the toughest creature I'd ever faced. Not only was its shell harder than concrete, but my sword skated off its pebbled skin without even leaving a mark.

Next, I tried Ferdinand II, who was loaded with armor-piercing rounds. They penetrated the thing's skin, but the wounds they left behind were shallow and mostly cosmetic. They barely even bled. After that, I tried my sniper-configured Kicker, but it was similarly ineffective. The scattergun stunned the turtle for a brief second, but it quickly recovered. Finally, I decided to use the tetsubo I'd used to train my blunt-weapons abilities, and with the use of Pummel, I finally made headway.

The ability had the distinctive characteristic of ignoring armor, so the monster's shell and thick hide were little impediment to my attacks. However, just because I could finally damage the thing didn't mean I was out of the woods, and I spent the next two hours sneaking in a hit every now and then as I avoided its snapping beak. Eventually, the wounds started to pile up, and at last, I shattered its skull.

I had a similarly difficult time when I was forced to fight a giant, man-sized hawk that kept trying to swoop in and snatch me up in its talons. It almost caught me the first time, but Observation proved its worth, and I narrowly avoided its attack. With its efforts thwarted, the huge bird banked and flew away to the west.

Or that's what I thought. I realized the error of my ways when, an hour later, it returned the moment I started to relax. Like that, the thing stalked me well into the night until, at last, I managed to slice a piece of its wing off and send it plummeting to the ground. I was on it in a heartbeat, and I quickly hacked it apart.

It was not an elegant kill, but then again, it rarely was. If there was one lesson I'd learned since that first time I'd killed another living creature, it was that forcibly taking something's life was almost never clean. It was tragic, messy, and undignified. But in a lot of cases, especially for me, it was also very necessary. So it was with the hawk, which was an unquestionably beautiful creature. Less so when its feathers were marred by its own blood. I was saddened to have had to kill it.

Slowly, I continued south, drawing ever closer to Mobile. At the same time, I was approaching the rest of my life. With my test finished, my formal training was over. I would finally be integrated into Jeremiah's plans. And while I wasn't sure what that entailed, I found myself eager to prove that I could hold my own.

My training had awakened a competitive streak within me, and I wanted to show my uncle that I could pull my own weight.

Finally, after a week's worth of travel, I started seeing familiar landmarks. I even passed the town of Wilmer, which had been ravaged by wolves. Nothing of the small town was left, save for the abandoned remnants of a couple of huts and a single old building that might have once been the settlement's central structure. There were no people left, though, and anything of value had been stripped from the area by bandits and scavengers.

Or maybe wildlings. I had no real way of knowing. Nor did I care. Not when I was so close to home. So, I only gave the place a cursory search before moving on. It was another day before I saw the old skyline of Mobile, with its abandoned and crumbling buildings, including the squat, winged structure that had once been the seat of the government. Curiously, I hadn't come across any patrols.

That should have been my first hint that something was wrong. The Amigos were almost always out and about, and I should have long since run into them. But there was nothing.

As I drew closer, I saw snaking tendrils of smoke twisting through the air over where I knew the town to be. Suddenly, I remembered my uncle's lack of responses to my many attempts to contact him. At the time, I'd thought he was still testing me, but now? With the absence of the Amigos and the smoke on the horizon, I couldn't help but think that something had gone horribly wrong.

I picked up the pace, transforming my easy jog into something that covered far more ground. It still wasn't terribly taxing, but it was more dangerous in that I couldn't really examine my surroundings. Ultimately, that almost got me killed.

A glint in the distance was all the warning I got before a bullet tore through the air, aimed straight at my chest. As I dove to the side, the gunshot echoed across the landscape. The ground erupted into a cloud of dust and old concrete as I took cover.

The other sniper was about a quarter mile away and nestled on the top floor of a four-story redbrick building, and I had taken refuge behind a pile of rubble to the side of the road. Looking around, I summoned my Kicker from my arsenal implant, then shifted it into its sniper configuration. I didn't take aim, though. The other sniper knew where I was, and at that distance, the only way they wouldn't kill me the moment I stuck my head out was if they were incredibly bad at their job.

"Staying alive means assuming that your opponent is competent," my uncle had once taught me. And I'd taken those words to heart. So, I scanned my surroundings, marking potential cover as I plotted my route. I had the advantage of knowing precisely where the sniper was, so my strategy wasn't so different than what I'd used during my training with Jeremiah. Only this time, instead of a simple scrape, I'd get a bullet through my chest if I failed.

That made all the difference.

My heart started beating faster, and for once, my Combat Focus didn't kick in. It actually took me a moment to realize that it hadn't because I didn't need it. I was used to life-and-death struggle. I had prepared for it. I'd spent hundreds of hours training for just such a situation, and I no longer needed to lean on my ability as a crutch.

I took a deep breath, then, keeping low, sprinted from my position. I knew precisely which path to take to avoid giving the other sniper a proper shot, and I slid into cover a few seconds later. I only stayed there for a few seconds before relocating to the next obstruction. Then the next. Over and over until I felt confident that I'd evaded the sniper's view.

But it wasn't enough just to escape. I needed answers.

So, I started to circle around their position. I flitted from one position to the other, always staying out of sight as I flanked the redbrick building until, at last, I could approach from behind. As quietly as I could, I leaped to a second-story window, where I grabbed the ledge and pulled myself through. I silently rolled to my feet, scanning the area for any threats. There were none, so I quickly found my way to the stairwell.

Taking it one step at a time, I mounted the stairs. A few steps up, my caution bore fruit in the form of my discovery of a mine. It was a thin metal disc, out of which was thrown a barely perceptible beam of red-hued light. A trip wire, I recognized, and at ankle height. I stepped over it.

A second later, I realized my mistake, so I went back, and using my Basic Explosives Handling ability, which enhanced my training to such an extent that I could disarm ithe mine with relative ease, I deactivated the mine and tucked it away in my arsenal implant. Then, I moved on to the third floor, which I spent a few minutes clearing. It could have been quicker, given that most of the inner walls had crumbled or rotted away, but I was being thorough. This time, my caution proved unnecessary, and I soon found myself back in the stairwell, where I found another mine, which I disarmed and pocketed like I had the first.

Before long, I was standing before the door leading to the fourth floor, which was where I had seen the sniper. I knelt there for a few moments, just letting my senses take everything in. Observation gave me some ideas about what lay on the other side of the door, but it was, at best, an incomplete picture. Nothing short of going in there was going to give me anything more.

I bit my lip, then took a long, deep breath before twisting the knob and pushing the door ajar. Thankfully, it opened without a sound, which allowed me to perform a cursory scan of the floor. What I saw was more than a little disconcerting.

Six figures milled around near the window where I had seen the sniper, who was still aiming in the direction they'd last seen me. So, seven enemies in total, which wasn't terribly intimidating. Or it wouldn't have been if I hadn't recognized their black-and-white uniforms, which marked them as Nova City Enforcers.

I stared at them, my mouth dropping open. It didn't make sense. Nova City was more than a day's worth of travel from Mobile. There was no reason for them to be here. But they were. Nothing could change that.

So, with no ability to change what I couldn't change, I summoned my scattergun from my arsenal implant, took aim, and pulled the trigger. Lightning arced from the barrel, enveloping the entire group and sending them into seizures. I used Double Shot when I fired again, giving them a second and third dose of electricity. The weapon had been designed specifically for crowd suppression, and unlike had so often been the case, these Enforcers had the Constitutions to let it properly do its job. They dropped to the ground, still alive but unable to move.

So, in the space of a few scant milliseconds, I stowed my scattergun and summoned my Kicker. Taking aim at the prone forms, I opened fire. Six bursts, six corpses. Given that they were busy watching a seldom-used road leading to a relatively small town, I suspected that they weren't exactly the best the Enforcers had to offer. In any case, they couldn't pose a threat if they were dead.

Finally, I focused on the sniper, who was still twitching as she stared at me with undisguised malice. Blood-flecked drool coated her chin from where, presumably, she'd bitten her tongue. I noticed everything, cataloging it even as I activated my Misthack ability.

Initiate Misthack (trivial defenses detected)?
[Yes] or [No]

I selected the affirmative option, which prompted another notification.

Misthack Initiated. D-Grade Defenses Overridden.

Instantly, I bypassed her defenses, which opened up a new menu:

Misthack Successful. Options:
- **Reboot System**
- **Overload System**
- **Breach System**

I chose the first option, which briefly deactivated her implants, including her interface. She went slack as her various cybernetics lost power. For most people, it wouldn't be that huge of a loss. But for an Enforcer? She likely had a half dozen high-grade cybernetics throughout her body, and with them deactivated, she could scarcely move.

But it was only temporary, so I moved quickly, rushing to her side where I initiated a Mistwalk and infiltrated her system via a hard connection. Within a few seconds, I'd overridden any inherent defenses and exposed every weakness in her system. Then, I started turning things off permanently. By the time the reboot cycled, I had bricked her whole system.

And there was a lot there. Subdermal armor. Top-of-the-line optics that were almost as good as my KIOI. An arsenal implant with weapon slots. A military-grade cybernetic leg. The list went on and on. The woman was almost a full android, which made my efforts all the more effective. To a normal person without any cybernetics? I would have been severely limited. But with her? I could disable her almost completely.

"W-what did you do?" she stammered, her words slurred and her eyes wide and unseeing. They were implants, as well, so when I'd deactivated them, it had rendered her blind.

"I'm going to ask you some questions," I said. "You're going to answer them. If you don't, I'm going to make whatever time you have left extremely unpleasant. And don't bother lying. When I'm connected to you like this, I can tell if you're being dishonest."

Of course, that was, itself, a lie. But she didn't need to know that. Mistrunners were uncommon enough that most people would believe basically anything we claimed. Besides, if I really wanted to, I could delve into her memory and figure things out for myself. Interrogation was more of a time-saver than an absolute necessity.

"I . . . I won't . . ."

I put my finger on her quivering lips, saying, "Shhh. Don't talk until I ask you the questions, okay? What's going on? Why is there smoke coming from Mobile?"

Her wide eyes darted around as panic gripped her. She couldn't see, but that didn't seem to matter. I asked her again, accentuating the question by reactivating her optics. As my uncle often said, you could sometimes catch more flies with honey than with vinegar.

"Who are you?" she asked, focusing on me.

"Doesn't matter," I said. "Now, talk. Or I'll blind you again."

"We . . . w-we came for him."

"Who?" I asked.

"The Wraith," she said. "We . . . we had an informant. Someone who told us his schedule. Where he'd be. We bombarded the city. And . . . and we . . . we finally got him. He killed almost a hundred of us . . . some of the best we had, but . . . but he's gone now. The Wraith is dead."

CHAPTER FIFTY-FIVE

YOU CAN NEVER GO HOME AGAIN

I've always known that I wouldn't go without a fight. All I can hope is that when my life catches up to me, there won't be too much collateral damage.

—Jeremiah Braddock III

"Dead?" I muttered. "You . . . you're lying . . ."

But I knew she wasn't. I could see it in her eyes, in her expression. My uncle was gone. Dead. Somehow, they had gotten to him.

In the back of my mind, I considered the possibility that she was simply mistaken. After all, it would have taken more than a squad of Enforcers to kill Jeremiah. But then again, a hundred of their best didn't sound like a small squad. And she had mentioned bombardment. But maybe he'd just tricked them. Or she was ill-informed.

So, looking for confirmation of my denial, I delved into her memory. And what I found was, in a word, disturbing. The Enforcers had been told where they could find Jeremiah, and they'd spared no expense in taking him out. Seven gunships had been sent to shell Mobile into oblivion, but even with the town having crumbled all around him, Jeremiah was still alive. Wounded, but still alive. That lasted until the Enforcers had swarmed him, taking heavy losses along the way. But eventually, they'd strung him up and hacked him to pieces. Even that hadn't killed him. Not immediately, at least. He'd hung there for almost a week—little more than a few chunks of his torso and a head—before finally succumbing. It was the most horrible thing I had ever seen, and when I retracted my cord, tears were flowing freely down my cheeks.

"W-what are you going to do to me?" came the woman's voice.

In that split second, my anger ignited. Suddenly, I didn't care about the morality of killing a helpless prisoner. Against what I had seen in her memory banks, such concerns held no water. Before I even knew what I was doing, my fists were descending on her face. I didn't use proper form. Nor did I activate any of my abilities. But even so, I pummeled her until there was nothing left but a mass of still-quivering and bloody flesh where her face had once been. It was unrecognizable, but she was still alive.

I quickly took care of that, too, smothering her until she went still.

It didn't help, though. It did nothing to assuage my grief.

I'm not sure how long I knelt beside that nameless Enforcer, but by the time my tears ran dry, night had fallen. More importantly, my resolve had stiffened, and I had established a plan. There were more Enforcers around, which was something I intended to change. I wouldn't suffer the continued existence of anyone who'd had a hand in my uncle's death. Maybe he deserved it. Certainly, he had never been an angel, and I suspected that I only knew a fraction of the things he had done. But that didn't matter. Not to me. He was the man who'd raised me. The man who had given me everything. He'd loved me like a daughter, and it had taken his death for me to realize that he had been the father I had never really had. I'd loved him.

And now he was gone.

Whatever else my training had given me, it had bestowed upon me the ability to avenge that death, and I intended to use those skills appropriately. So, I picked myself up off the floor and mechanically went through the Enforcers' equipment. There was nothing quite as high quality as my own gear, but it was good enough that I decided to take it all with me. I didn't worry about maintaining their dignity as I stripped them all down to their own skin, piling their clothes, equipment, and spare ammunition into one of the corners. Then, I went to work on their bodies, cutting them into pieces, which I threw into their own pile. When I was finished, they'd been reduced to so much meat and bone.

I didn't have the time nor the inclination to bury them, and what's more, I knew that someone would eventually come to relieve them. When they got there, I wanted to send them all a message. The dismembered bodies would do that just fine.

Logic dictated that I should hide my presence, but I wasn't in any mood for reason. Instead, I wanted to scare them. To make them wonder what kind of monster had gotten their friends and colleagues. I wanted them to dread the day that same monster would come for them. I told myself it was because fearful people made mistakes, but the reality of it was that I just wanted revenge. I needed them to suffer.

Once I'd finished with that, I gathered the equipment, putting as much of it in my arsenal implant as I could, then bundling the rest so I could carry it on my back. Then, I set off through the ruins of the old city, moving away until I found myself nearing the Africatown sign my uncle had shown me what felt like a lifetime before. Nearby, there was an old building that had once been a church; it was all far enough away from the city proper that I felt confident that I could shelter there unmolested. So, after depositing the equipment inside, I settled down for a few minutes to review the files I had downloaded from the Enforcer's memory.

There wasn't much there. Apparently, the individual Enforcers were on a need-to-know kind of system, and the one I'd interrogated hadn't needed to know much. Still, I got some basic information about numbers, locations, and suspected pockets of survivors. There were distressingly few; the rest of the city's occupants had been killed during the Enforcers' bombardment or their subsequent assault and occupation. I could only hope that some of my friends had managed to survive.

But I didn't expect it.

Once I'd internalized the information, marking everything on my map, I left the old church behind. I had some hunting to do.

I covered the ground in a hurry, flitting from one deepening shadow to the next as night began to fall. In the past, I'd avoided being out after the sun went down, but now, with the help of Observation, I found that I didn't mind so much. The darkness fit my mood as well as my purpose as I methodically made my way toward my first target—another sniper's nest nestled in the top floor of another of the abandoned city's buildings. I didn't approach it directly. Instead, I set up in a much taller building almost a mile away. From there, I settled down into a firing position, my Kicker in its sniper configuration, and I waited.

It didn't take long for me to notice movement in one of the windows. Just a glimmer of motion, and I knew where my targets were. I focused in, my scope magnifying the area until it felt like I was on top of them. I counted four in my line of sight. All but the sniper seemed distracted and disinterested, which I expected to take advantage of. I shifted my sights from one figure to the next in quick succession, going through the motions of my attack. I needed to be quick. I had to be perfect. Nothing else would do.

Channeling my copious training, I took aim at the sniper, concentrated on Empowered Shot, waited the prescribed two seconds, and then fired. Before the bullet even hit home, I moved to my next target and fired again. The sniper's head exploded, but I ignored it, moving to the third. I moved like a well-programmed drone, my motions smooth and perfect. And a moment later, all four Enforcers were dead.

A few gunshots rang out, but the shooter had neither the ability nor the knowledge to hit me from so far away. So, I settled down to wait. It took a further hour, but eventually, I caught sight of another Enforcer who'd been hidden behind a wall. My view was brief, but I didn't hesitate before putting a bullet through his head. After that, silence reigned.

Again, I waited, forcing myself not to think about why I was doing what I was doing. If I just didn't think about it, I could almost pretend that Jeremiah was still alive. He was just away. Off doing whatever it was that he did when he wasn't around me. But that could only last for a few minutes before my stomach tightened, and I remembered the images attached to the files I'd downloaded from that Enforcer's memory. My uncle's familiar face, slack and bloody, with only a spine and a little bit of his chest dangling beneath him . . .

To distract myself, I trained my attention on my surroundings, focusing everything I had on Observation. That's when I saw a pair of Enforcers, dressed in closer-fitting outfits than the ones I'd dealt with before, approaching my position. They moved like shadows across the landscape, and if I hadn't been flaring my ability, I'd have never noticed them. But now that I had, I knew precisely what to do.

I shifted my focus to the first, who was clearly a woman. Then, I embraced Empowered Shot, waited two seconds, then fired. The shot took her in the chest, and she was thrown from her feet. However, it didn't result in the fountain of gore I'd learned to expect. So, I repeated the process, putting another bullet in her before she even had the opportunity to react. Even then, she was still moving, albeit slowly. The third shot put a stop to that, but by the time she was dead, the second figure had disappeared.

"Crap," I muttered, searching for the other assassin. In another situation, I might have panicked, but after everything I'd discovered, I felt too numb. So, when the assassin burst through the window, aiming a kick at my face, I reacted calmly. My arm darted up, knocking the kick aside, and he went flying past me. As I turned, he skidded across the floor, adopting a fighting stance.

"Who are you?" he demanded. He was wearing a black mask that matched his suit, but because of the skintight nature of the outfit, I could recognize all the hallmarks of masculinity. Any other time, I might've blushed at just how little it hid. But now, I just aimed my rifle at him and squeezed the trigger.

To my surprise, he blurred to the side, dodging my first burst, then darted to the other as I adjusted my aim. I fired again, but he moved so quickly that I could hardly track him. Luckily, Misthack was too fast, even for him.

Initiate Misthack (trivial defenses detected)?
[Yes] or [No]

With a flick of my mind, I selected the first option. As I did, the assassin reached me and aimed another kick in my direction. I ducked under it, moving to the next prompt:

Misthack Initiated. E-Grade Defenses Overridden.

I blocked a jab, then narrowly avoided a right hook as I waited the second it took for the Misthack to complete. Once it did, another prompt bloomed on my HUD:

Misthack Successful. Options:
- **Reboot System**
- **Overload System**
- **Breach System**

I selected Overload, and midkick, his body began to convulse. Smoke rose from the seams of his suit, and his momentum took him to the floor. He hit with a thud, scattering debris and dust.

I put up my rifle, exchanging it for my nano-sword. Then standing over him, I brought the blade down without ceremony or an ounce of regret. It took four hacking slashes before I separated his head from his body, but he died from the first swing. The other three just felt appropriate.

After searching his body—and finding nothing except his outfit, which I took—I cut his body to pieces, then relocated to my next position, which was about half a mile away. Once I was there, I repeated the process, taking out another sniper's nest. It only took one volley, and I wasn't stalked by any more Banshees, but it worked out much the same way as the first. So, I moved on to a third after that. By the end of the night, I'd taken out four nests and one more set of assassins.

Considering that a job well done, I retreated back to the old church, deposited the gear I'd pilfered, and set up the mines at the church's entrance. Then, I settled down to eat, rest, and prepare for the next night. However, at some point, I started crying again, and I didn't stop for hours more. By the time my tears ran dry, I was exhausted enough that sleep soon overtook me, and I slept through the rest of the day.

When I awoke that evening, I couldn't remember any of my dreams, but I still had a deep sense of loss and foreboding; I wasn't sure if it was due to the realities of the day before or some unremembered dream. Either way, I had a job to do and a plan for how I intended to accomplish it.

The previous night, I'd decimated the outer band of the Enforcers' defenses. Those sniper's nests would be replaced, but I didn't care. I just wanted them to know what I had done so that they'd be concentrating on enemy snipers. While they did that, I would dress in one of their uniforms and use my abilities to adopt a new identity so I could infiltrate their base, which was located in the former museum where I'd spent so much time staring out at the bay.

So, I quickly found the least bloody uniform, which happened to have belonged to that second assassin I'd killed, cleaned it as best I could, then slipped it on. It fit just as snugly on me as it had on him, and if I hadn't been so focused on the job before me, I might've been a little embarrassed. It was the sort of thing Nora would wear, though she would've subjected it to a few artful rips and tears before dying it some garish color.

I shook my head, hoping that she was still alive. Perhaps she'd already gone back to Nova City.

Once I was dressed, I used Mimic to take on the appearance of that very first sniper and Disguise to bring my apparent tier down to three. It wasn't perfect—Hadley had proven that much back in Bayou La Batre—but I hoped it would keep me from being looked at too closely. And if not, I had plenty of firepower at my disposal.

Again, I set off into the night, harnessing my enhanced Constitution to cover the ground extremely quickly. Once I reached the ruins of the old city, I took all necessary caution as I navigated toward Mobile. Along the way, I passed a couple of new sniper's nests, but I left them alone. I had bigger fish to fry, but when I'd finished with the base, I had every intention of coming back to finish the job.

It was interesting to me that, for all their apparent diligence, they didn't even know when I was right on top of them. I suppose there was something to be said for the fact that I'd spent over two years in the area, much of that training with incredibly talented people, like the Amigos or my uncle, who were hunting me. By contrast, evading those Enforcer teams was child's play.

Still, I knew the price of overconfidence, so I maintained my focus as I slowly made my way toward the reverse-pyramid-shaped building in the distance. My first real obstacle should have been the wall that encircled the town, but when I reached it, I was disturbed to see that it had been breached in multiple places. The concrete-filled storage containers that had once been stacked together had been melted into so much slag. So, my route was unimpeded, and I quickly stepped through the first gap I found.

When I did, I was confronted with a scene of absolute destruction. Everywhere I looked, buildings had crumbled and fallen. It didn't matter if it was a tenement, a more affluent home, or the seat of the local government—everything had been destroyed. It was difficult to imagine that anyone might have survived. But still, I picked my way through the rubble until I found myself facing what was left of the Dew Drop Inn.

It had fared a little better than its surroundings, which was both a blessing and a curse. A blessing because it was recognizable, but a curse because it allowed me to see what had happened to the proprietors—including Jo. I approached and knelt beside my friend's half-buried corpse. From the waist up, she didn't look much different from when I'd left. But below her navel was nothing but debris. Her eyes stared unseeing into the night sky. She had been dead for days. A week, maybe.

Once again, the tears came, and I was filled with so much guilt and regret. The last time I had seen her, she'd stormed off because Pick was paying more attention to me than to her. But now? She was gone, just like my uncle. Just like everyone else, it seemed. By the time my tears had dried up, my mind had refocused, and my resolve had been reaffirmed. I was going to kill every last one of them.

I wanted to do something for her body. Bury it. Burn it. Something. But I couldn't spare the time. Nor did I think it really mattered. Whatever Jo had once been, her corpse was just a hunk of meat now. And nothing I could do would ever change that. So, I rose and left the Dew Drop Inn behind as I made my way to the Enforcers' base.

When it finally came into view, I couldn't help but gasp at the sight. It swarmed with personnel—far more than I could've expected. There were hundreds of them, most dressed in the same black-and-white uniform I'd seen before. A few wore body-hugging outfits similar to mine, and the others gave these assassins a wide berth. I intended to use that to my advantage.

Taking a breath, I prepared to approach. I kept telling myself that my abilities were all the camouflage I needed, that no one would look at me twice. But it was still nerve-racking to contemplate just strolling up to the enemy's base. Still, I was wholly committed. It was either this or set up somewhere nearby and start picking them off, one by one—a losing strategy if ever there was one. No—I needed to get inside first. I needed information.

Calming myself, I rose from where I'd been crouching and started forward. I got one step before my eyes found something that made me stumble. Just in front of the building was a ten-foot pole, atop which was my uncle's disembodied head. Until that moment, I'd convinced myself that he might still be alive, that the Enforcer's memories had been false. But with the evidence staring me in the face, there was no denying it.

Jeremiah was gone. I was on my own. And the longer I looked at it, the more I came to one simple conclusion: they had fucked with the wrong family.

CHAPTER FIFTY-SIX

AVENGER

Revenge is pointless. I would know because, in my life, I've let it dictate my choices far more often than I care to admit. But even after I got what I thought I wanted, it was never fulfilling. I never came out the other side better than I was before. I just had a higher body count.

—Jeremiah Braddock III

The night wore on, and still, I couldn't move from where I'd taken cover. Instead, I stared ahead at what was left of my uncle. So many memories flitted through my mind, each more impactful than the last. But one, above all, stuck with me longer than the rest. It was a day after my mother's funeral, and Jeremiah had found me sitting on the edge of his building's roof, just staring out at the city. At the time, I didn't have any tears left, but my grief had pressed down on me with palpable weight. Jeremiah sat beside me, but he didn't say anything. Instead, he just put his arm around my shoulders and pulled me close. Like that, we sat for hours. Neither of us spoke. There were no stories of my mother's wasted life. Nor did he offer any meaningless platitudes. He just held me, comforting me the only way he knew how.

But even then, I knew that his actions came from experience. There was a connection between us. He'd lost so much in his life, so he knew—better than anybody else, probably—exactly what I was feeling.

Kneeling there behind a pile of rubble and looking up at what was left of him, I needed my uncle's comfort more than ever before. But he wasn't there, and he never would be again. I was all alone.

Finally, my grief gave way to anger. In turn, that anger became action as I slipped from behind that mound of rubble and confidently approached the building. In some ways, it was much the same as it ever was, a concrete behemoth of a structure with three levels of tapered walls. However, in other ways, it was wholly different—chiefly, that it was swarming with Enforcers, many of which felt extremely powerful. It was a reminder that the sniper's nests I'd encountered before were poor representations of the danger involved. I couldn't let myself care, though. Not with my uncle's death so fresh in my mind.

The other key difference was that the Enforcers had mounted a series of automated cannons along the roof. Anyone who led an assault on that position would be subjected to an incredible amount of firepower. It was good, then, that I had [Spycraft] on my side, concealing my identity and letting me blend into the crowd. Still, I knew that, regardless of whether or not I looked like I belonged, I had to act the part, as well, lest I draw too much of the wrong kind of attention. If they could kill my uncle, then I knew I wouldn't stand a chance.

Striding forward, I passed Jeremiah's corpse—or what was left of it—without a second glance. I didn't need to look at it again. The image was burned into my mind, and it was one I wouldn't soon forget. I mounted the steps, pushing past a pair of Enforcers. For a second, one of them—a woman—looked as if she was going to question me, but then the other reached out and grabbed her arm. Out of the corner of my eye, I saw him shake his head. It seemed that the Banshee's uniform put me into a position of some power; I intended to use that to my advantage.

As I stepped inside the building, I was once again surprised by how much things had changed. There were Enforcers everywhere. Some were clumped into groups, conversing about one thing or another, while others were clustered around various screens, obviously monitoring the area. A brief glance told me that they were taking the loss of the sniper teams seriously, and that they were watching their replacements. Clearly, they hoped to catch me in the act; it was a good thing, then, that I had no intention of going back for them anytime soon. Eventually, sure. But not yet. I had other things to accomplish first.

Channeling my training, I fully sank into the persona I'd stolen. Acting like I belonged was not an easy task, especially considering that my every instinct was screaming at me to pull out my rifle, switch to full automatic, and open up on the crowd of Enforcers. Complicating matters was the reality that, with every passing second, I fully expected someone to see through the ruse comprised of my various abilities. Surprisingly, though, that didn't happen, and I was able to reach the stairs unhindered.

So began my search through the building. I went floor by floor, never stopping for long enough for anyone to grow suspicious until, at last, I found what I needed. The terminal was on the fourth floor, and it wasn't the first I had seen. However, sequestered in a seemingly forgotten corner, it was curiously unattended. The entire floor seemed deserted, in fact. Which suited me just fine. After checking the area once more, I approached the security terminal and dragged the cord from my wrist, connecting without hesitation.

A sudden spike of pain lanced through my mind, and my body went completely limp. Even as I collapsed, I heard footsteps approaching from nearby. I couldn't move, so all I saw was feet, but I heard the Enforcers' voices.

"How did she get in?" asked one.

Another answered, "I have no idea. Are we sure she's not one of ours? Looks like a Banshee."

"Look closer, Edie. It's a skill," said the first.

"Oh. Oh!" the second one exclaimed. "It's almost seamless . . ."

I stopped listening. Instead, I shunted the pain into the back of my mind and concentrated on my connection to the terminal. Clearly, I had underestimated their defenses, and I'd paid the price when they proved too much for me to handle. However, only a small portion of the backlash had managed to get past my Mistwall, which meant that I still had some degree of control. I intended to use it to my advantage.

First, I embraced Mistwalk, which resulted in the following prompt:

Security Terminal (#7). Presence Detected. Defenses Found. Initiate Mistwalk?
[Yes] or [No]

I mentally slammed on the affirmative option, which resulted in the most complex set of defenses I'd ever seen. Before, the most formidable Mistwall I'd encountered had been comprised of sixty-four nodes, but this one had nearly four hundred. But I couldn't let that dissuade me. If I didn't get through it, and quickly, I would end up just like my uncle. So, I bent the entirety of my mind to the task, solving one puzzle after the next, all in quick succession. As I did, time felt meaningless. I barely even noticed the two Enforcers searching me. Nor did I pay any attention to their calls for backup. I only had room for one goal—solve the next puzzle.

Like that, I tore through the Mistwall, and the moment I felt that last defense fall, the pain in the back of my mind dissipated, and the security terminal opened up to me. Immediately, I deactivated the autoturrets before starting the download of the terminal's memory banks into the partitioned portion of my own mind. As it began, I once again took notice of my surroundings.

And it didn't look good.

There were a dozen Enforcers, two of which were dressed in the skintight suits that I now knew marked them as Banshees. They felt dangerous, too. Lying on the floor, I listened as they discussed what to do with me.

"Restrain her, then put her down with the others," one suggested. "She might be useful."

Another said, "I say we put a few bullets in her head while we can. You saw what happened to the sniper teams."

"She took them by surprise, and . . ."

I stopped listening. Instead, the moment the download finished, I used Misthack, targeting the most dangerous of the bunch. He was a burly Tier 5 that felt almost as strong as my uncle. But he was also sporting a wide variety of cybernetic parts, which meant that he was extremely vulnerable to me.

After initiating the Misthack and bypassing his defenses, I used Breach before uploading one of my favorite Ghosts. I called it *Time Bomb*, and it was the Ghost I'd spent the most time developing. The product of almost a year's worth of work, its purpose was simple in that it was meant to cause cybernetics to glitch out by varying the flow of Mist to said implants. One second, it would overload a person's optics, blinding them with far too much information, then the next, it would completely cut a cybernetic arm off from the Mist. And it would continue to loop, faster and faster until the victim was incapacitated.

And the best part? It could spread from one victim to the next via ambient Mist exchange. I'd never used it to its fullest extent, mostly because it took hours to spread. But once it reached a critical mass, it was unstoppable—at least in an enclosed space. The only caveat was that it wasn't lethal, in and of itself. But I had a plan for that, too.

So, I uploaded the Ghost, then repeated the actions on all twelve of my would-be captors. Meanwhile, someone roughly yanked my cord out of the security terminal and bound my wrists behind my back. A moment later, they hauled me to my feet. I feigned semiconsciousness, banking on them believing that I was still under the effects of my Mistwalk's backlash.

One of the Enforcers threw me over his shoulder, and I did my best not to tense up as I was carried across the room and to the stairs. Eventually, we found our way down to the basement, where I was immediately strapped to a chair. A couple of minutes later, I was left alone, so I opened my eyes to take in my surroundings.

And they were bleak.

Given its size, the room might as well have been a closet. In the corner, water dripped from an exposed pipe, and a single light bulb dangled from the ceiling. It flickered every few seconds, creating a strobing sensation. Otherwise, the room was bare.

I waited there for almost forty-five minutes until, at last, the room's heavy, rusted door opened, admitting a single figure. I had no idea if they were male or female because, when I tried to focus on them, my eyes seemed to lose focus, blurring my vision to such an extent that their features were completely obscured. When they spoke, their voice was similarly masked, sounding feminine and masculine in equal measure.

As the door clanged shut, they said, "Interesting. Even now, you maintain your disguise. A high-grade skill, then. What is it?"

I didn't answer, which they must have expected because they didn't skip a beat before asking, "Who are you? Who sent you? And why did you kill my people?"

"I'm nobody," I mumbled, purposefully slurring my words. I hoped that it would cause them to underestimate me. "And I didn't kill anyone."

At first, the figure didn't say anything. Then, they knelt in front of me and, with one outstretched finger, traced a line along my jaw. "I do not believe you," they said. "Twenty-four dead. You hunted them, likely so that we would concentrate on the outer defenses and allow you to infiltrate this temporary base. Once you did, you immediately found a security terminal. Are you from Atlanta? Did Whitehand send you?"

I had no idea who that was, and even if I had, I had other things on my mind. So, I concentrated on the task at hand. Using Misthack, I quickly broke through her defenses and uploaded *Time Bomb*. The more originators I had, the better. Soon, it would spread to everyone in the base. When it did, I intended to make my move.

"I confess," they said. "I had hoped you would be cooperative. We could use someone like you. With certain restraints, of course. But I'm sure you wouldn't find a Slave Implant too taxing."

My heart sped up. "W-what?" I asked, my panic rising. I knew all about Slave Implants. Everyone in Nova City did. Bourbon Street was full of people who'd either sold themselves into slavery or had it forced upon them. And I knew that was only a small sample. There were almost certainly plenty of others who'd fallen under that particular spell.

"Oh, yes," they said. "Waste not, am I right? I'm certain you understand. Whoever your employer is has doubtless made copious use of those sorts of implants. None of us ever think we'll find ourselves subject to the whims of another, but alas . . . that's the way the world works, isn't it? I only wish we had them here."

They stood, then continued, "Perhaps we will work together in the future. I do so love a competent subordinate."

Then, without another word, they turned and left the room. However, a moment later, they were replaced by a big, burly woman with arms almost as big as Nora's. I only had a moment to recognize the stun baton in her hand before she jammed it into my side. Immediately, my entire body locked up as wave after wave of electricity coursed through me.

My torturer didn't ask any questions. Nor did she threaten me. Instead, she just kept jamming that baton into my side, a wicked and cruel grin painted across her face. Perhaps I'd killed someone she held dear. Or maybe she was just a sadistic person who enjoyed torturing people. I had no way of knowing. In fact, I stopped caring after only a few minutes, and by the time those minutes turned into more than an hour, I could barely think at all.

Like that, I spent four hours. All the while, my Ghost kept spreading through the base until, at last, it bore fruit. My torturer had clearly grown tired of doing the same thing over and over again, so she grabbed my jaw and forced my mouth open. Then, she moved to shove the baton inside.

She never got the chance because, suddenly, her cybernetic arm twitched and flung itself to the side. The baton went flying into the wall, where it shattered into three pieces.

"What the . . ."

The burly woman never got the chance to say anything else because as her eyes rolled up into her head, her jaws clamped shut, and she started to seize. Apparently, *Time Bomb* had finally erupted, and it worked a lot faster than I'd expected. Seeing that the woman was out of it, I launched myself backward with enough force that the chair broke apart. Dipping down, I slid my bound hands under my feet. As I stood, I summoned my nano-bladed dagger and, after a little awkwardness, managed to cut through my metallic shackles. Once my hands were free, I approached my prone torturer, then unceremoniously stomped on her head until it became an unrecognizable lump of flesh and bloody hair.

I might have taken some of my frustrations out on her, but in my defense, she deserved it. Either way, it was not the cleanest of kills, and I was completely okay with that.

Once I was finished, I removed a charge from my arsenal implant, then stuck it to the wall. It wasn't the strongest explosive I had at my disposal, but it would get the job done. Then, I stepped up to the door before cracking it open and peeking out. My caution was unnecessary because, even though there was a guard, he was convulsing on the floor. I didn't bother killing him. The Ghost wouldn't last forever, but it would keep doing its thing for long enough.

I stepped over his quivering form, then took stock. Despite visiting the building quite often in the past, I'd never been to the basement. Regardless, the layout didn't seem complicated, and I soon commenced a search of the premises, mostly for the others one of the Enforcers who'd captured me had referenced. If there were survivors, I wanted to find them.

Gradually, I explored the basement until, at last, I came to a room containing a trio of bodies. I recognized two of them. Pick and Remy were unmistakable. I stood there for a long moment, just staring at the scene in disgust. I hadn't known Pick for long, but he had been nice to me. And now, just like everyone else, he was dead.

Suddenly, I noticed movement. It was a simple rise and fall of his chest, but it was a clear sign of life. I raced forward and knelt beside him. My hand found his neck as I checked for a pulse; he was alive, if only barely. So, I retrieved my medical kit from my arsenal implant and went to work; after I had administered an adrenaline-laced med-hypo, his eyes flew open.

"Mira?" he said with a sharp intake of air. "W-what? What are you doing here? Please, you have to go . . . they're going to come . . . back . . ."

"What happened?" I asked.

"It was . . . it was that woman," he said. "She . . . s-she betrayed us all. She told the Enforcers where to find Jeremiah, and once they had . . . confirmed his presence, they started shelling us with heavy artillery. Everyone . . . died. They're all . . . oh God . . . they're all gone . . ."

He was babbling—probably because of the synthetic adrenaline I'd used to wake him up. But I needed information almost as much as I needed him conscious. So, I asked, "What woman? Was it a Banshee? Was it Helen?"

I don't know why I jumped straight to the Mistrunner who'd been my instructor, except that she had always acted as if she was better than all of us. She was easy to hate, and therefore, it wasn't difficult to imagine that she was the betrayer.

"No," he said. "It was the big one. The . . . the one who followed the Wraith around . . . N-nora . . ."

"What? No . . . you . . . that's not possible," I gasped. Nora was completely loyal to my uncle. There was no way she had betrayed him. I was prepared to call Pick a liar until he grabbed my hand and placed a shard on my palm.

"It's all there," he said. "I was . . . I wanted to get out, to show it to you so you would know . . . Slot it and see for yourself."

I shook my head. I didn't need to see some shard. I knew Nora. She was my friend. Practically family. I knew she wouldn't intentionally hurt my uncle. But even as those thoughts raced through my mind, I reached up, flipped the patch of Realskin that covered my port, and slotted the shard into place.

CHAPTER FIFTY-SEVEN

ACTIONS AND CONSEQUENCES

Trust is the most difficult gift I've ever had to give. It goes against my every instinct, trusting another person. Because I know just how selfish, self-centered, and dishonest people can be. And I can't shake the feeling that, eventually, that'll be the end of me.

—Jeremiah Braddock III

Mouth agape, I watched the video on the shard. There was no sound, but I didn't need it, either. All I needed was to see Nora shaking hands with one of the Enforcers. I had no idea if money had been exchanged or if there was some other reason behind her betrayal, but I didn't care. I had all the evidence I needed.

But I went further, delving into the files I'd downloaded from the security terminal. And what I saw painted a very telling picture. Gradually, I gathered the various pieces until I could fit them together into a coherent explanation. Even after I'd examined everything a few times over, I wasn't certain that I wanted to know what I now knew.

"It was my fault," I muttered, retrieving the shard from my port. I handed it back to Pick, who'd remained silent the whole time, and he made it disappear. Obviously, he had something like an arsenal implant, though I suspected that it was far more limited in scope than the one I depended on so heavily. Either way, I wasn't really thinking about his kit. Instead, I was wholly focused on all the mistakes I had made.

The first, and the one that had kicked off the whole thing, was taking the

Tier 7 Nexus Implant in the first place. The moment I had, my uncle's fate had been sealed. He just hadn't known it yet.

"What are you talking about?" asked Pick, his throat raspy. Absentmindedly, I retrieved a bottle of water from my own arsenal implant and handed it over. He greedily downed the liquid as I thought about how I was going to answer his question.

"The only reason they didn't kill my uncle sooner was because they knew he had what they wanted," I said, not wanting to get into specifics. I wanted to trust Pick, but what I'd just discovered told me just how dangerous that was. "They just didn't know where it was. When he gave it to me, they had no reason to keep him alive anymore. Nora told them. She painted a target on his back."

"That doesn't make it your fault," he said, shifting to a more upright position. "I don't know what it was, but—"

"Then, he disappeared with me," I went on. "Dipped under their radar. They wanted to find him, but they had no idea where to look. Not until Jack came to them. I could have killed him. I had every reason to. Plenty of opportunity. But I chose to let him live. And he disappeared; nobody knew that he'd gone to tell the Enforcers that my uncle was here in Mobile."

Pick didn't know the whole story there, so he remained silent. I could tell, though, that he wanted to dispute my claim. To rob me of blame. I refused to let him. So, I continued, saying, "But Uncle Jeremiah, he was always hard to pin down. One day, he'd be here, and the next, he would be gone. So, they turned to Nora, who . . . insisted on training me. I thought it was because she wanted to help me. I thought she cared about me. But . . . b-but she just wanted to be here so she could let them know when my uncle was around. And she did."

I took a deep breath as tears flowed down my cheeks. They weren't driven by sadness, though. Instead, they were based on anger. With myself for setting the whole thing in motion. With Nora for her betrayal. With Jack for being an unrelenting scumbag. The Enforcers because they were the instrument by which everyone had been killed. Even the people of Mobile like the Amigos, who were supposed to have protected the civilians.

I clenched my hands into fists until my knuckles went white. "They laid in wait," I said. "Just . . . just waiting for an opportunity, and when Nora told them he was there, they let loose. Now, everybody's gone. Dead. Because of me."

"You couldn't have known . . ."

"But I did!" I half screamed. "I did. I knew . . . I knew they would be after us. My uncle said it a hundred times. He went on and on about how selfish people were. But I let Jack live. I trusted Nora. And everyone else paid the price . . ."

"I . . . I don't know what you want me to say . . ."

Nothing. There was nothing Pick could say that would make me feel any better. The only thing that might assuage my guilt was to continue with my original plan. Fortunately, my *Time Bomb* Ghost had had plenty of time to spread and affect most of the base, which would clear the way for me to exact revenge.

Or at least part of it. But Nora was already gone, and dealing with her would be a task for another day. For now, I needed to put one proverbial foot in front of the other, lest I become enmeshed in so much guilt that I couldn't force myself to move. If that happened, I would die, and all of Jeremiah's sacrifices would have been for nothing.

So, I stood, wiped the tears from my cheeks, and asked, "Can you walk?"

Pick nodded. "I can, but not very fast," he said.

I reached down and helped him up. With that done, we both left the room; when we passed the prone Enforcer, I quickly ended his life with a decisive sword stroke and gathered his pistol, which I handed to Pick. "I hope you can use that," I said. "Cover my back. Shouldn't be many of them still upright, but some of them might've been powerful enough to resist my Ghost."

Stepping forward, I placed a series of demolition charges on load-bearing pillars and walls. I was no expert, but I'd received a little training on how to best bring a building down. I put it to good use as I rigged the entire basement to blow. Then, we moved up to the first floor, which received much the same treatment. However, we also ran across a few groups of Enforcers. I didn't go out of my way to kill them, mostly because I wasn't sure how much longer my Ghost would last. If I stopped to execute every one of them, I'd run out of time. It was better, then, to bring the building down on their heads.

Like that, Pick and I finished placing every demolition charge I had in my arsenal implant. I was aware that it was probably overkill, but I figured it was better to use too many than too few. This was a job that needed to be finished the first time because I knew I wouldn't get a second chance.

Finally, after finishing on the fourth floor, we descended the stairs and quickly found our way to the entrance. I could've done it quicker by myself, but Pick refused to be left alone. Probably for good reason, given his lack of pertinent combat skills and the recent trauma he had been through. Understandable as it was, though, I couldn't help but become a little annoyed when we took long enough that, when we passed the groups of Enforcers on the first floor, they'd begun to stir. The Ghost, I knew, wouldn't last much longer.

"Stay behind me," I said, approaching the doors. At one point, they'd been glass, but after the Initialization, that had been replaced. Then, those replacements had been further reinforced by the Enforcers. So, I had no idea what was waiting on the other side. I retrieved the detonator for the charges from my arsenal implant, then handed it to Pick, saying, "If there's anyone out there, I want you to run to cover as soon as I engage. The moment you're clear, bring the building down."

"What about you?" he asked, watching as I checked my various weapons. I knew they were all still fully loaded, but it never hurt to double-check.

"Don't worry about me," I stated, holding my Kicker. "Just bring it down. Don't hesitate. I don't want to have a bunch of Enforcers flooding out of the building while I'm trying to deal with whatever's out there."

"Might not be anyone out there," he said.

"There is."

"How do you know?" he asked, gesturing to the solid doors.

"Intuition," I lied. In fact, using Observation, I'd already heard movement. And given that everyone else was dead, it didn't take much logic to come to the conclusion that there were some Enforcers out there. I had no idea how they'd avoided being infected by my Ghost, but at this point, it didn't matter.

I asked if he was ready, and I received a nervous nod. He gripped his pilfered pistol so hard that his knuckles had turned white. With the other hand, he clung to the detonator like his life depended on it. And it did. Without that, we'd be overwhelmed.

Not for the first time, I wished I'd have just gone to the top of the building and started picking people off. It was a losing strategy, not least because of the sheer advantage in numbers the Enforcers had, but at least it would have been more straightforward. Besides, I wasn't entirely sure I wanted to live in a world where everyone I knew and loved was either dead or a traitor.

But I was committed now, for better or worse. And I wasn't burdened by some naive desire to keep my body count to a minimum anymore. That lesson had been an expensive one, but I had learned it well. Leaving enemies alive was a recipe for disaster.

So, I took a deep breath, slid to the side of the closest door, then reached over to open it. The moment I did, the air was filled with dozens of gunshots. I'd expected as much, so I didn't even flinch as I summoned a flash-bang and tossed it outside. I quickly followed it up with a smoke grenade, then relocated to another one of the doors. By the time I reached it, the air outside the building was obscured by a thick white smoke that cut visibility down to a couple of feet.

For them, at least.

For me, with Observation on my side, it wasn't very effective. I darted out of the building, strafing to my left as I peppered the area with one burst from my Kicker after another. I couldn't really see much, but with all my senses working at a superhuman level, I knew precisely where my enemies were. Each burst found its mark, and I was rewarded with a series of grunts, a couple of groans, and even one startled scream. It was music to my ears.

To my surprise, the area was occupied by a dozen Enforcers, each one at least Tier 3. Most were Tier-3. And there were even a handful of Tier-5's out there. Knowing what I faced, there was no way I was going to underestimate them.

I continued my assault until I reached the cover of a sizable pile of rubble. I crouched behind it, summoning another grenade from my arsenal implant.

Then, I tossed it into the smoke. However, it exploded harmlessly well before it hit the ground; clearly, they'd deployed a drone system to take care of any more grenades. That meant I'd have to finish things manually.

I didn't mind that. As much as I loved explosions, there was something visceral about ripping someone apart with bullets.

Knowing that the Enforcers were homing in on me, I shot off a couple more bursts before relocating. As I moved, I stayed low, exchanging a spent magazine for a fresh one as I slid behind an overturned and burned-out skeleton of a car. I was just about to pop up to continue my assault when my instincts went wild. I don't know if it was my Combat Focus, Observation, or simple battle experience, but in that split second, I knew that if I didn't move, I was going to lose my head. So, I ducked and rolled away; my caution was rewarded when I heard a sword clang against the metal wreck.

I gathered myself just in time to block the next attack—an overhand slash meant to cleave me in two—with my Kicker. I kicked out at my assailant's knee, but she—and the figure definitely belonged to a woman—pulled her leg back at the last moment. Then, she aimed a jab at my face. I tilted my head forward, taking the punch in my forehead; the resulting impact hurt like crazy, but it was just pain. I knew there would be no real damage.

I used that brief moment to fire off a burst that took my attacker in the stomach. She staggered backward, which gave me plenty of room to take aim and fire at her head. Even at such close range, it didn't explode like I might have expected. Instead, I heard a distinctly metallic clang of subdermal armor. However, whether the bullets penetrated or not was largely irrelevant because the impact staggered her even further. As she fell against the car's remains, I unloaded my entire magazine into her. And even her subdermal armor couldn't hold up to that. She dropped dead before my magazine ran dry.

But the damage was done. During my brief battle, the smoke had begun to clear, and the rest of the Enforcers had homed in on my location. I dove back into cover just in time to avoid a hail of gunfire. I hunkered down, but the car's metal was thin enough that it couldn't block everything. After only a second, I felt the bite of a gunshot in my shoulder. Then another in my calf. I covered my head and curled into a ball, but the barrage of gunfire was ceaseless. The car was quickly torn to pieces, and my injuries began to mount.

As I lay there, my body bleeding and my end drawing near, I couldn't help but feel bitter. After everything I had been through, I still wasn't strong enough. My uncle had given me everything, and yet, I hadn't lasted a single month after the conclusion of my training. Certainly, there were good reasons. Few people in the world could have stood up to an entire battalion of Enforcers. But then again, I had every advantage, didn't I? And I had squandered that.

In that moment, I remembered all the times I'd slacked off. I thought about all the poor decisions I'd made. All the mistakes that had led me there. It was enough that I came very close to just giving up. I was already dead, wasn't I? I just needed to wake up and realize it.

Suddenly, I thought about my uncle. Not about his life. Instead, I thought about his death. He'd fought to the very end. They'd had to literally tear him limb from limb to kill him. And even then, when he was only a head with a bit of a spine attached, he hadn't immediately succumbed. More than that, he'd never given in. He had never stopped fighting. So, what kind of a person would I be if I didn't do the same?

My fingers tightened on my rifle's grip, and I focused on Observation. Even as my wounds—usually from ricocheting bullets—continued to pile up, I ignored them. Instead, I focused on my assailants. On their footsteps. Their smells. The subtle shifts in the air that came from their movements.

Two squads. Four on the left. Five on the right. All Tier 3 or better, mostly armed with rifles or submachine guns and backed up by the skills to use them. But they hadn't worked like I had. They'd trained, sure. That much was clear. But they hadn't spent the better part of three years pushing themselves to the very limits of their endurance.

I had. I was better than them. It was time I showed them how much of a mistake they'd made by messing with me and my family. And even if I ended up dying, I wasn't going to go down without a fight.

So, I stowed my rifle and summoned my nano-sword. Then, even as the gunfire continued, I found the leftmost target, who turned out to be a slender man in one of the Banshee uniforms. I used Engage, and in a blink of an eye, I'd covered the thirty feet between us. Even amid the gunfire, I heard his gasp as my blade descended, cutting into his neck. I kicked out with every ounce of strength I possessed, and he went tumbling through the air, leaving a spray of blood in his wake. I knew from experience that it was a fatal wound.

I was moving again before any of the other Enforcers could react, and I got similar results with the next man in line. With the third, I changed tactics, slicing at his knees and gripping him by the back of his shirt before slamming my blade through his spine. By then, the rest of the Enforcers had reacted, but because I was using him as a riot shield, their bullets never reached me.

I dismissed my nano-bladed sword and replaced it with Ferdinand II. I whipped my arm around the bullet-riddled human shield and rapidly fired into my next victim. My pistol was loaded with armor-penetrating rounds, so the Enforcer's subdermal armor was largely useless. The bullets took her in the chest, but they didn't have enough penetrating power to come out the other side, so they just rattled around inside. She didn't survive the onslaught.

Rushing forward, I rammed into the last member of the leftmost squad. He let out a surprised scream as I trampled him, and I made a point to stomp down on his throat along the way. It took two blows to crush his spine.

I was just about to turn my attention to the next squad when something rammed into me. My human shield went skidding across the rubble-strewn ground. I lost my grip on my pistol, as well.

Pushing away, I suddenly felt the barrel of a gun on the back of my head, followed by a familiar voice, "Nuh-uh-uh. Let's not get too feisty."

I splayed my fingers and stopped struggling as a knee dug into my neck shoving my cheek into the gravelly ground. I didn't need to look up to recognize the voice as belonging to the apparent leader of the Enforcers. Not only were they capable of concealing their identity from me, but they'd snuck up on me, as well.

"What do we do, boss?" came a gruff voice. The other squad was still alive and well. My gambit hadn't been successful. However, instead of going out with a blaze of glory, I'd been taken prisoner. And given that the leader had already threatened me with a Slave Implant, I didn't think they'd execute me. No—I was too valuable for that.

"I need you to—"

Suddenly, a deafening sound swept through the area, followed closely by a shock wave that sent my captor sprawling. Because I was already on the ground, I managed to escape the worst of it, but even then, it rattled my bones. A split second later, a billowing cloud of dust and debris filled the air.

I couldn't help but smile. Pick, it seemed, had finally come through and brought the building down.

CHAPTER FIFTY-EIGHT

LIMITS

Death is always a possibility. I knew it when I was a soldier, and it's even more likely now that I've made so many powerful enemies. Sometimes, it feels like the whole world's out to get me. But that's okay. I'm out to get them, too.

—Jeremiah Braddock III

I dragged myself to my feet, and after I summoned my rifle, took aim at a prone figure. A moment later, they were filled with holes. I moved to the next, repeating my actions. As I shot, the dust began to settle, revealing the rubble-strewn landscape where the building had once stood. My demolition charges had done their job well, and I knew that it would be a miracle if anyone inside had survived.

And that suited me just fine. With the death of everyone I loved, my anger and desire for revenge left little room for doubts or mercy. I didn't care that those people were only doing a job, that they were just doing what they had to do to survive. I was well aware that the true enemy was the system of oppression against which my uncle had spent his life fighting. However, you can't shoot a concept. You can't blow up an economic system. You can't stab oppression in the eye. But those soldiers? I could do all of that and more to them.

I advanced, searching the dust-clogged area for the other Enforcers, but visibility was down to only a few feet. In addition, my other senses had been overloaded by the explosion, so Observation was almost useless. So, it wasn't surprising when one of those Enforcers charged out of the dust cloud, aiming a wicked-looking axe at my head.

I was more than ready for it. In fact, my muscles were practically twitching in anticipation of the coming conflict, so I was moving before he even got close. I ducked as I darted forward, my shoulder hitting his midsection with the force of a runaway car, and I sent him sprawling to the ground. He was quick to recover, though, and though he lost his axe along the way, his fists soon found their way to my back, where they descended, one blow after another, with the force of a sledgehammer.

I grunted in barely felt pain, then aimed a Combination Punch at his ribs. The first blow landed with a dull thud, but the second much-more-powerful punch brought with it the sound of cracking bones. The third shattered them altogether. His own assault slowed as he let out a wet cough. Disgusted, I pushed him away.

The Enforcer stumbled and fell on his back. My stomach fluttered, and a grim smile crept upon my face as I heard him gasp in pain. I didn't want to torture anyone, but I wasn't going to go out of my way to spare my enemies any agony, either. I stepped forward and planted a kick into the man's injured side. Like all the Banshees', his face was covered by a black mask, and his eyes were concealed behind green-lensed goggles, but it wasn't difficult to hear the sob escape from between his lips. The idea that he was crying brought a little joy back into my life.

I kicked him again.

Then, dismissing my rifle, I drew my nano-bladed sword. It took four rapid strikes to sever his head; the Enforcers were stronger than most of Nova City's Operators, but the Banshees were on another level entirely, at least in terms of toughness. In skills, they left a lot to be desired, which was probably the only reason I was still alive.

The moment I finished the man off, I raised my head and searched the area. There were two more Enforcers and the blurry leader left, so I knew I wasn't out of the woods. The leader alone was sure to be a dangerous opponent. I thought the nano-sword was my best bet; the rifle was too unwieldy, the pistol had too few rounds, and the scattergun would barely even slow them down.

For a few seconds, I remained still, my sword held out in front of me, and just listened. The ringing in my ears had abated, but my hearing was a long way off from being back to normal. With Observation, it was still more sensitive than it would've been for an Unawakened person. So, when I heard a light scuff of a boot against rock coming from my right, I responded immediately.

I raised my sword just in time to intercept one of the other Banshee's blades. He moved so quickly that I could scarcely track his movements, so the only reason I managed to avoid being decapitated was the fact that I'd started moving before I could even see him. The two weapons clashed with a loud clang, and the force of the blow surprised me by sending me skidding almost a foot backward. I recovered quickly, though, aiming a sweeping kick at the man's leg. He lifted his foot, but I adjusted my kick accordingly, and a second later, he lost his balance. I was on him in an instant, bringing my sword down in a vicious overhand strike that he tried to block.

It didn't work the way he expected, and the force of my attack nearly tore his sword from his hands. It snapped back, cutting into his masked face and drawing a startled and pained scream. I quickly reversed my nano-edged blade in an upswing that clipped the side of his head, carving through a good portion of his skull. Bits of his brain went with it.

Apparently, he hadn't invested in high-grade subdermal armor like his colleagues had. That was his mistake. Still, he must've had decent Constitution because, even missing a chunk of his brain, he was still alive. I ended that a moment later, cleaving his spasming head in two.

For some reason, seeing that brought my uncle to mind. He'd still been alive when they'd put his head on a pike. I wondered how long that had lasted. Hours? Maybe days? I had been gone for a while, so I had no idea how long it had been since the Enforcers had taken over.

I stalked forward through the dust cloud; only a couple of minutes had passed since the explosion, and I hoped to use that to my advantage. With any luck, the leader would still be dazed. If they weren't, I didn't know if I could handle them.

Luck, as it turned out, wasn't with me because a pair of shapes soon materialized out of the cloud of dust. One was blurry, and the other was dressed in the now-familiar uniform of the Banshees. However, the blurry form of the leader flickered in and out of focus, revealing her true form.

Unlike the other Banshees, she wore no mask. No goggles. Instead, her head was bare, showing off luxurious blonde hair that she wore in a thick braid and a face that looked like it belonged on a fashion model. Her body followed suit, bearing all the curves one would expect from someone with that kind of face. I knew none of it was real. Nobody was that perfect. She'd clearly had plenty of work done.

Armed with a rifle, the other figure was a male, though he maintained his anonymity via the same mask all the other Banshees wore. Still, he was broad shouldered and extremely muscular, which made me think of Simon, my old melee-combat instructor. Thankfully, he and Vanna had gotten out well before the Enforcers had descended upon Mobile. Hopefully, they were still alive and well.

"You are an annoying little shit, you know that?" said the woman, discarding her blurry disguise with a sneer. "All this, and for what? To avoid the kind of life most people can only dream of? Do you know what kind of salary you would've gotten? The kinds of perks? You would've been the envy of every woman in Nova City!"

"And all it would've cost me was my freedom, right?" I responded, keeping my voice even. It wouldn't do to show too much emotion. "Just a little Slave

Implant. Isn't that what you promised me? Doesn't sound like a great deal to me."

"I don't think you understand—"

I never let her finish. Instead, I used Engage to close the gap between us. I swung my sword at her face, but she predictably blocked it with one of the long daggers that suddenly appeared in her hands. But the blow barely held a fraction of my strength, which allowed me to easily pivot and aim a real attack at the muscular man beside her. It took him by complete surprise, but he managed to raise his rifle just in time to obstruct the path of my nano-blade. Still, it sliced through the metal weapon with ease to carve a furrow into his chest. If he hadn't been equipped with subdermal armor, he would've died, then and there.

Annoyed, I hopped back, narrowly avoiding a pair of slicing daggers. I put a few steps' worth of distance between my position and the leader, but she pursued doggedly. I kept backing away as I blocked one attack after another. The woman was fast—probably faster than me—but I'd been sparring against superior fighters since the very beginning. So, I held my own, looking for my chance to strike.

It came a moment later when, now ten or fifteen feet away, the other Enforcer recovered enough to draw a pistol from his own arsenal implant. As he aimed at me, I darted to the side, then used Engage again. But he'd seen that trick, so he was ready for my sweeping overhand strike. What he wasn't ready for was the foot he soon found planted in his chest. My kick sent him sprawling, and I summoned Ferdinand II, aimed, and shot a pair of rounds into his chest.

The weapon was still loaded with armor-piercing rounds, so his subdermal armor—especially weakened as it was by my sword strike—wasn't much use. The bullets tore through him and rattled around in his chest cavity, destroying his organs. I didn't stop to admire what would soon become a kill, though, because I knew that the leader would soon be upon me. I leaped forward, climbing atop a waist-high mound of rubble, then sprang backward in a back-flip to avoid the dagger strike I'd felt coming from behind.

As I sailed through the air, I aimed Ferdinand II and discharged the remaining rounds in quick succession. To my surprise, though, the blonde woman spun around wickedly fast and slapped the bullets from the air with her daggers. When I landed, skidding to a stop, she was glaring at me with legitimate hatred.

"You killed them all," she growled. "They were my friends."

"Yeah, well . . . you killed my uncle."

She stopped in her tracks. "Uncle?" she wondered. Then, as if she finally understood who was standing across from her, her eyes widened. "You're the girl."

"I'm a girl. Not sure if I'm *the* girl," I responded, already switching my now-empty weapon out for my nano-sword. I was tempted to use my rifle, but she was close enough that I didn't want to risk it. After all, she'd blocked Ferdinand II's issue without much trouble; it stood to reason that she would do the same with any rounds my Kicker might spit out. And if she managed that, I would have no choice but to summon my nano-sword, anyway. However, the brief lag of doing so might give her the opening she needed. So, I decided to skip ahead. Besides, I suspected that bullets would only be so effective against someone like her. Not unless I had skills like my uncle had had.

"You're the Tier 7, aren't you?" she asked. "The one he gave the stolen Nexus Implant to."

"No idea what you're talking about," I lied. I knew there was no way she could know for sure one way or the other, what with my Mimic, Disguise, and Deception abilities all still going full tilt. "I'm just a local girl who doesn't like big-city bullies coming in and killing my fucking friends and family."

"You're her," the woman persisted. "I know it. Please, just come back to Nova with me. We won't even have to use a Slave Implant. You'll be richer than—"

I didn't want to hear whatever else she had to say, so I tuned her out as I leaped forward. My sword darted out, but it was quickly intercepted by her dagger. That was okay because I kept everything under complete control. In the beginning, I'd swung my sword like a club. But now? I knew it was a surgical weapon that didn't need my full strength behind it. So, exercising every ounce of training I'd received, I altered the course of my blade, aiming at it at her face with an upward sweep. She reacted well, throwing her head back to avoid the worst of it, but my strike still flew true, slicing through her chin, up her cheek, and across her nose. Blood spurted, and she let out an agonized scream.

I knew it probably wasn't so much the pain of the cut, which was shallow enough that it wasn't even close to life-threatening. Instead, a woman like her, who'd spent countless credits to perfect her look, had to be a vain creature. And now I'd ruined the masterpiece that was her face. It felt good, seeing the fury in her eyes. It was laced with horror and humiliation.

"You'll pay for that, you little bitch!" she screeched, going on the offensive, covering the distance between us in the blink of an eye. Suddenly, she was upon me, her long daggers dashing and darting, slicing and stabbing as she discarded all pretense of trying to take me alive.

I did the best I could, deflecting most of her attacks with subtle blocks and parries. Over and over, our blades clashed together, but as the seconds wore on, I came to the horrifying conclusion that she was better than me. Not just in technique. Not just in raw attributes. Instead, she had the mindset that only came with years of pushing herself to the very edge of death against increasingly challenging opponents. It made my own training seem paltry by comparison.

But even though I was entirely outmatched, I didn't give up. However, determination can only take a girl so far, and soon, one of her daggers found its way to my arm, slashing through my biceps. It was the beginning of the end, and we both knew it. With a grin rendered macabre by the bloody wound on her face, the woman redoubled her efforts. Suddenly, she seemed like she was moving twice as fast.

Or I was just moving that slowly.

Either way, I couldn't keep up. I tried to retreat, backing away until my heels brushed against an overturned and burned-out car. My mind whirled as I tried to think of a way out, some ability or skill. But with all my training, with everything I'd done so far, it wasn't enough. And with that realization crashing into my mind, I hesitated for the briefest of instants, and the woman's dagger slipped past my guard to slam into my gut.

It felt like time stood still.

Her smile widened, revealing blood-streaked teeth. I tried to aim my sword at her, but her other dagger darted out, slicing through the tendons on my wrist. My fingers went slack, and the hilt of my sword tumbled from my hand. It hit the ground with a subdued clatter.

I wouldn't give up, though. I couldn't. I didn't have it in me. Balling my other hand into a fist, I activated Combination Punch, but when I aimed it at her wounded face, it was weak. Ineffectual. My body sagged in defeat, but I kept struggling, clawing at the hand clutching the dagger in my belly. It was useless, though.

"All that potential," the woman growled. "Wasted on a useless piece of trash like you. It should have gone to someone worthwhile. Someone better."

I couldn't argue with her, and not just because the words wouldn't come when I summoned them. The mere fact that I was dying was all the evidence anyone needed to verify her claim.

She leaned close, and with a sneer, said, "You are—"

Her sentence was cut off by a loud gunshot, and I saw her head jerk to the side. Another shot soon followed, this one hitting her neck. And another after that. They kept going until, at last, she was driven away. The moment she released the dagger, I felt my strength return. I was still wounded—potentially mortally—but I still had a lot of fight left in me. I gripped the hilt of the dagger and ripped it free.

That's when the realization hit me. She'd used some sort of ability to drain my strength. It was the only thing that made any sense.

I glanced at the origin of the gunshots to see Pick standing there, his face covered in so much dust that he was barely recognizable. In quivering hands, he held the pistol he'd gotten on our way out of the base.

I wheeled on the woman. The gunshots had driven her to the ground, but when I looked at her, she wasn't that injured. The one that had hit her head had clearly rung her bell, but none of them had gotten past her subdermal armor. Still, she was dazed. She might've even had a concussion. If I was going to end the fight, I had a very limited opportunity.

So, I summoned my Kicker, which I was forced to hold with one hand, reconfigured it into its sniper mode, and activated my Empowered Shot ability. In the two seconds it took to charge, the woman visibly recovered and started to climb to her feet. But it wasn't enough. Just as I pulled the trigger, she looked up. Raising her palm to me, she started to say something.

I never found out what she meant to say because the bullet, empowered by my ability, tore into her head, exploding it like an overripe melon. The moment I confirmed that she was dead, I sank to the ground, overwhelmed by my injuries. I had a dozen cuts. A useless hand. A stab wound through my gut. And I'd used every ounce of energy I had.

But even with all that, I gave a sigh of relief. We had won the first battle in my quest for revenge.

CHAPTER FIFTY-NINE

THE LAST STEP

I hope Mirabelle can be the person I failed to become. That's what it's all about. Giving her the opportunity to live a life where she doesn't have to constantly look over her shoulder. It might be a pipe dream, but it is my fervent hope that, despite giving her the tools to become the perfect soldier, she can one day leave all that behind. I couldn't, but my failures are my own. She's better than me in every way. I just hope she can realize it before she lets the world corrupt her.

—Jeremiah Braddock III

"We can't stay here," Pick said, looking around. The dust had begun to settle, but it still gave plenty of cover. "That explosion will have been heard for miles. And these weren't the only ones around."

At first, I didn't hear him. Instead, I was too focused on my own self-pity. I might have killed that woman, but she had still beaten me. Without Pick, I would have died, my mission unfulfilled and my uncle's sacrifices completely wasted. After a few seconds, I said, "Thank you for the assist."

"Didn't you hear me?" he asked, panic clear in his voice. He reached down to offer his hand. I took it, and he helped me to my feet, which elicited a groan on my part.

I clutched my stomach, saying, "I really need to get some armor or something. Here. Hold this."

I summoned my medical kit from my arsenal implant and handed him the box. Then, without thinking, I unzipped the one-piece Banshee uniform I'd been wearing and, with a gasp, dragged it down my torso. The pain of it detaching from the wound in my stomach was almost unbearable, but I gritted my teeth and pushed through it. Looking up, I saw a blushing Pick, who was looking everywhere but at me. That's when I realized that I'd just taken my top off in front of a boy.

Suddenly, the pain in my stomach couldn't hold a candle to my embarrassment. Of course, I was still wearing a black sports bra, so I was decent enough. But still, if Pick was going to be sticking around—and that was anything but certain—I was going to have learn a little modesty.

For both our sakes.

Pushing my embarrassment to the side, I reached out, opened the medical kit, and retrieved a couple of med-hypos. One was loaded with an anesthetic that would numb the pain of my wound while the other was filled with a coagulant that would stop the bleeding. I pressed the anesthetic against my stomach and pressed the plunger. With a pneumatic hiss, it delivered its payload, and I sighed as I felt near-instant relief. I used the coagulant next, which slowed the bleeding to a seep before using some of the anesthetic pads in the medical kit to clean the area. Finally, I retrieved a canister containing the last of my foam bandages, which I applied to the area.

The whole process was much more difficult than it should've been, complicated by the fact that I couldn't use one of my hands. The tendons had been completely severed, so it just hung limp and useless. But it wasn't bleeding overly much, so I treated it with a simple anesthetic wipe and a more conventional bandage that I hoped would also serve to keep it stationary. Once all that was done, I arduously pulled my top back into place and told Pick that I was good to go.

"Are you sure? That wound in your stomach . . ."

"I'm fine," I said, pulling my Kicker back out of my arsenal implant. I was lucky in that it had been my left hand that had been injured, so it wouldn't affect my lethality very much. Propping the weapon on my forearm wasn't ideal, but I'd been trained to make do.

With that done, we quickly vacated the area. As we did so, we passed what had once been Kimiko's shop, and I was horrified to see a tiny hand extending from beneath tons of rumble. It was still gripping a wooden sword.

Tears crept down my cheeks, but I didn't dare stop. Even if it was only the replacement sniper teams, I knew there were plenty of Enforcers still in the area. And I was far from prepared to combat them. There was every chance that, even if I did everything right, I'd never make it out of the area alive.

But then again, that was my life now.

No more safety nets. No more uncle watching over my shoulder. It was just me now. And I would need to use everything I'd been taught if I was going to survive.

Or more importantly, if I was going to get revenge.

Because I hadn't forgotten who'd betrayed my uncle. Certainly, I felt a good deal of lingering guilt. If I hadn't taken the Tier 7 Nexus Implant, none of it would have happened. However, Nora—my uncle's trusted right-hand woman—had knowingly and intentionally betrayed him to the Enforcers. Without her say-so, they never would've known when he was in Mobile. In fact, I suspected that they never would have even known I had the implant at all. Because of her actions, countless people had died.

And I intended to make her pay.

But first, I needed to get somewhere safe so I could rest and recuperate. Gradually, Pick and I traversed the ruined city, and I got a good, up-close-and-personal look at what the Enforcers had done. Everywhere I turned, there were destroyed buildings and evidence of dead bodies. Some, like with little Elie, were evidenced by a body part sticking out of the rubble. For others, all that was left were bloodstains. But during that trek, I didn't see another living soul.

Fortunately, I remembered my previous reconnaissance well enough to trace a path through the area, and soon, we'd made our way past the wall and out of the city. As we pushed northward, Pick grew ever more nervous.

"You're not scared of the beasts?" he asked, clutching his pistol tightly.

"Not really," I said, keeping my proverbial eye on everything all at once. I had been trained to pay attention to my surroundings, and with Observation providing plenty of information, I would know well before anything attacked us. Already, we'd passed a few animals, but none of them had attacked. "I've seen worse."

As we made our way north, the anesthetic I'd used to numb the pain of my wound began to wear off, but I did my best to ignore it. Still, by the time we finally reached the church where I'd made camp the last few days, the agony was starting to become overwhelming.

Pick noticeably relaxed when we got inside and I closed the door, though he was more than a little alarmed at the pile of equipment I'd stashed in the corner.

"How many people did you kill?" he breathed.

"A lot," I said, not wanting to get into my actual kill count. I knew the number. Even though they were my enemies, I couldn't forget the act of taking another person's life. Still, I kept that information to myself, as much to keep him from looking at me like a monster as to fool myself into thinking of them as a statistic in my brain instead of once-living people. I'm not really sure it worked on either level.

After making sure that nothing in my temporary shelter had changed, I stepped outside—to Pick's protests—and went about gathering some sticks. It took a few minutes to find appropriate materials, but when I got back, I set about the unenviable task of creating a splint for my hand. The bandages helped keep it stationary, but even then, it painfully flopped around every time I moved.

Once I was done, I asked Pick to step outside so I could have some privacy as I inspected my other wounds. He complied, but I saw that he was trembling the whole time. I would have to be quick; my companion might've saved my life, but he definitely wasn't cut out for this kind of thing.

After undressing down to my underwear, I spent the next twenty minutes treating my many wounds. Most of them were shallow cuts administered by the blonde woman's knives, but there were a few more serious injuries, as well. I did the best I could, administering the last couple of med-hypos in my kit before bandaging everything up. From experience, I knew it would be enough; my Regeneration was one of my strongest abilities, and it had been put to work enough times that I could easily predict how well it would function.

Finally, after putting my clothes back on—this time, my fatigues—I stuck my head outside and told Pick that he could come back in. When he did, his eyes were wild, and I noticed him flinching at every sound. His caution was probably warranted, considering that night had begun to fall. Soon, all the area's most dangerous predators would be out and about, and for all his good qualities, Pick didn't seem like much of a fighter.

I barred the door behind him, then went to the back of the room. Once there, I dragged a Mist-powered lantern from my arsenal implant and turned it on, bathing the room in light. Normally, because of Observation, I didn't really need it, but Pick didn't have my advantages in that respect.

Sitting down, I took a couple of ration bars from my arsenal implant and offered him one, asking, "Hungry?"

He nodded, then took it, settling in a few feet away from me. I handed him a bottle of water, as well, and began to mechanically consume my own ration bar. It was the same tasteless brick I'd grown accustomed to, but it felt good to get something into my stomach. I knew my body would need the energy if I was going to heal properly.

Pick did the same, and when he was finished, he leaned back against the brick wall and let out a long sigh. Then, he started to sob.

I didn't blame him. Pick had lost just as much as I had—maybe more—and, unlike me, he didn't have the benefit of training to see him through. No Combat Focus to soothe his psyche. No [Firearms] or [Close Quarters Combat] to make him feel in control. As a result, he must've felt like he was being dragged along a mighty river of terrible circumstance, and it was all he could do to keep his head above the water.

In some ways, I felt similar. But for my part, I knew I had options. I had the skills to make my own way. I just wasn't sure exactly which way that was going to be. My first thought was to head back to Nova City. After all, Nora was there, and I desperately wanted to get my revenge. It was also familiar territory. I might've lived a sheltered life before my Awakening, but I still knew the city passably well. Or at least I thought I did.

But was going back to Nova a good idea? Surely, if Nora knew I was alive, she would expect me. Then again—I felt it was fairly likely that she thought I'd been killed right alongside my uncle. Anything that could kill someone like Jeremiah would have no trouble with me.

Which was one of the reasons I hesitated to head to Nova City. I was aware that it had taken the full might of the Enforcers to take down my uncle, and to do so, they'd been perfectly okay with killing thousands of innocent people. So, what would they do to me if they discovered I was in town? It was a valid concern, and to distract myself from making a decision, I opened my status page for the first time since right after I'd left the Dead Zone. When I did, I got an incredible surprise.

You have reached level 10. Please choose a class from the following options:

What followed was a list of at least a hundred different choices. My mouth fell open as I read each of them. Some were self-explanatory, like {Combat Medic} or {Courier}. The first would increase my abilities in wound treatment, while the second would expand my storage capabilities. However, others seemed more esoteric, like {Mind Mage}, which gave a vague description involving manipulating people's thoughts. Aside from a brief moment where I imagined myself commanding Nora to jump off the roof of a megabuilding, I found myself shying away from that one. Sure, it might end up being powerful, but it hit a little too close to the enslavement I'd witnessed around the Rift. I wanted nothing to do with making people do anything against their will, except maybe at the end of my rifle.

After spending about an hour perusing the options, during which time Pick finally settled down and fell asleep only a few inches away from the Mist lamp, I narrowed it down to a handful of choices.

The first was {Sniper}, which had the following description:

{Sniper}—You are an expert at striking from afar. Requirements: Rifle Mastery (Tier 5), [Stealth Operations] (Tier 5), [Combat Utility] (or equivalent) (Tier 5). Abilities Granted: Silenced Shot, Relocate, Obliterate Target

It certainly seemed like an incredibly powerful class, and I felt almost certain that it was the one my uncle had chosen. I was almost as sure that he'd evolved it at some point, even if no one had ever confirmed that that was even a possibility. I almost chose it the moment I saw it, but I forced myself to patience. Jeremiah would have wanted me to examine all my options before making a well-reasoned, logical choice. So, I moved on to the next, which was called {Avenger}:

{Avenger}—You are a defender of the weak and avenger of the slain. Requirements: [Close Quarters Combat] (Tier 5), [Firearms] (Tier 5), Vow of Revenge. Abilities Granted: Impugn, Interrogate, Righteous Blow

Again, it was obviously a strong choice, and it didn't take a genius to figure out that it had come from my recent experiences. However, I couldn't help but wonder if my previous choices contributed to the class option becoming available. It wasn't listed as a requirement, but it still felt right. I moved on to the next option, which was {Spy}:

{Spy}—You are the shadow in the night, a thorn in your enemy's side. Requirements: [Spycraft] (Tier 5), [Combat Utility] (Tier 5). Abilities Granted: Misdirection, Mental Fortress, Sneak Attack

Both the {Avenger} class as well as {Spy} seemed well suited to my current mission of revenge, but I wondered if they would be as useful after I'd accomplished what I'd set out to do. Perhaps. I kept going, looking at the next option, {Mistrunner}:

{Mistrunner}—You are the perfect weapon, adept with a variety of weapons and a deft manipulator of Mist. Requirements: [Firearms] (Tier 5), [Close Quarters Combat] (Tier 5), [Combat Utility] (Tier 5), [Spycraft] or [Stealth Operations] (Tier 5), [Mistwalker] (Tier 5). Abilities Granted: None (some abilities or skills may be lost or evolved)

"What the hell?" I muttered. The class's requirements were off the charts and far more restrictive than any of the others, but it didn't even grant any abilities. And I was more than a little concerned with the last line, which said that I may lose some of my abilities or skills. Of course, it also said that they might evolve, which calmed me down a little. Still, it seemed like something was definitely up with that class description.

Or maybe I was just thinking about things from the wrong perspective. Perhaps the system didn't think about balance when offering classes. Just because something had high requirements didn't mean it was powerful. But then there was that description, which seemed to describe exactly what Jeremiah had intended me to become. Certainly, he'd talked a lot about survival, but it wasn't an accident that almost all my skills had combat applications.

To him, survival meant being the biggest and baddest warrior around. Anything else would result in me being manipulated and used, if not outright killed.

With a sigh, I moved to the last class option on my short list:

{Operator}—A master of combat, you can fill most roles. Requirements: [Firearms] (Tier 5), [Close Quarters Combat] (Tier 5), [Combat Utility] (Tier 5). Abilities Granted: Bombardment, Treatment, Bulletstorm

That seemed more in line with what I'd expected. I did think it was curious that two of the class's names were part of the common vernacular. Most of the fighters in Nova City were generically referred to as Operators, while even Helen, my [Mistwalker] teacher had been described as a Mistrunner. And I felt positive that none of them had the actual class. Helen, in particular, seemed like she'd never held a gun in her life, much less possessed the skill slots or the experience to progress all the way to Tier 5 in those skills. I thought it much more likely that those terms had been adopted because someone—probably the aliens—had leaked them to the population.

Or maybe it was all just a coincidence. Either way, it didn't matter. I needed to make a choice, and I knew that that decision would affect my future in a wide variety of ways. I sighed, leaning back against the wall as I decided to give the other dozens of classes an in-depth look, but as the hours passed by, I came to realize that none of them could hold a candle to the ones that had made my short list.

So, I reexamined my choices, starting with {Sniper}. It was a strong class, but it seemed a little limited. Sure, in one specific situation—a long-range firefight—it would be fantastic, but it wouldn't really help me with anything else. {Avenger} and {Spy} suffered from similar issues in that for very specific situations, I would be very capable. But in most other circumstances, they would do nothing for me. If I chose those, it would be on me to pick and choose how I wanted to assert myself.

In theory, picking my battles sounded like a smart strategy. And it was. However, I knew from experience that fights had a way of finding you, regardless of whether or not you wanted them. If that happened after I chose {Sniper}, {Avenger}, or {Spy}, they wouldn't really help me.

By comparison, both {Mistrunner} and {Operator} looked like well-rounded, jack-of-all-trades classes, though given the requirements, I didn't think the master-of-none part of that saying would apply. If nothing else, my uncle had taught me that system-related things were rarely fair. Some people, for better or worse, were simply superior. And the moment I'd taken that Tier 7 Nexus Implant, I'd established myself as one of them. The following years of training had further supplemented that status, and now, I was seeing the results.

Which was why my eyes kept going to {Mistrunner}. With those requirements, it seemed tailor-made for me. Six skills, all at Tier 5. How many people in the universe could boast that combination? I wasn't sure, but I knew there couldn't be more than a few on Earth. And that, as much as a growing certainty in the back of my mind, was why I chose {Mistrunner}.

When I did, a piercing spike of pain erupted in the back of my neck, and it was so intense that I immediately went into shock and passed out. An hour later—judging by the clock on my HUD—I woke with a start that brought a snort of disapproval from the still-sleeping Pick. I shook my head, rubbing the back of my neck, and inspected the messages that had greeted me upon awakening.

You have chosen the class {Mistrunner}.

Merging skills: [Spycraft] and [Stealth Operations], resulting in [Infiltration]. Disguise lost. All other abilities maintained or evolved.

Merging skills: [Firearms] and [Close Quarters Combat], resulting in [Combat]. Quickdraw, Mighty Swing, and Eviscerate lost. All other abilities maintained.

Evolving skill: [Cybernetic Interface] into [Cybernetic Mastery].

Evolving skill: [Mistwalker] into [Mistrunner].

Evolving skill: [Combat Utility] into [Fieldcraft].

My mouth fell open. Just like that, I'd opened two more skill slots. However, I'd lost three abilities. Most notably, I'd lost Disguise and Eviscerate. The loss of Quickdraw didn't really hurt because I'd barely ever used it. And with Mighty Swing, I hadn't even realized I had reached a level of mastery to get the ability, much less used it. So, as much as I felt the sting of losing the abilities, it wasn't enough to wrangle my excitement from opening two completely new skill slots. Or from evolving three other skills.

I opened my status to inspect the changes for myself, though:

NAME	Mirabelle Lisa Braddock		
CLASS	MISTRUNNER		
LEVEL	10 (0%)		
CONSTITUTION	38/80		
MIND	35/80		
MIST	34/80		
SKILLS	5/7		
SKILL NAME	Skill Tier	Modifiers	Abilities
CYBERNETIC MASTERY	Tier 1 (0%)	100% Efficiency	6 Cybernetic Slots
COMBAT	Tier 1 (0%)	+50% Damage (All) +50% Speed (Melee) +50% Accuracy (All) +25% Range (Firearms) +50% Reload Speed (Firearms)	Empowered Shot (D) Double Shot (E) Combination Punch (D) Pummel (E) Engage (E) Disengage (F) Mark Target (F) Barrage (F)
INFILTRATION	Tier 1 (0%)	+15% Stealth Effectiveness	Stealth (E) Camouflage (E) Deception (E) Mimic (E) Observation (D)
MISTRUNNER	Tier 1 (0%)	+25% Speed (Misthack) +25% Speed (Mistwalk) +50% Strength (Mistwall) +50% Breach Range	Mistwalk (D) Misthack (D) Mistwall (C) System Redirect (F) Disable Cybernetics (F) Overcharge (E)

FIELDCRAFT	Tier 1 (0%)	+25% Combat Effectiveness	Triage (D) Basic Explosives Handling (D) Combat Focus (C) Pain Tolerance (D) Resistance (E) Foraging (E) Improvisation (D) Regeneration (D)
OPEN			
OPEN			

Immediately after I opened my status, I had a warning flash across my HUD. It said:

Warning: You have recently lost two (2) skills. Replace them within sixty-two (62) days (Earth or Planet 2341-M) or you will forfeit the potential and any attributes exceeding your new, lower potential.

"Crap," I muttered to myself. I wasn't in danger of losing any attributes, but I still didn't want to chance it. It seemed that I needed to head to the Bazaar soon and find someone who could sell some skills to me. That, as much as my desire for revenge, made up my mind. Nova City was the closest place with access to the Bazaar, and what's more, I already knew the way. Hopefully, it wouldn't take me long to get back.

Or maybe I was just making excuses to do what I already wanted to do. Either way, my mind was made up. I would head back to Nova City, visit the Bazaar, then find a way to take my revenge on Nora and anyone else who might've been responsible for the deaths of my uncle, Jo, and all the rest of the innocent people who'd been killed.

Before that, though, I needed to rest and recover as best I could. After, I would take the first steps of the rest of my life. I settled back down against the wall, closed my eyes, and fell asleep. That night, I dreamed of revenge.

ABOUT THE AUTHOR

Nicholas Searcy began writing on Royal Road with the fantasy series Death: Genesis. However, he's since branched out into science fiction with the Mistrunner series. A resident of Alabama, as well as being an avid football and baseball fan, he enjoys kicking back and reading a good book, writing all sorts of stories, and spending time with family.

DISCOVER
STORIES UNBOUND

PodiumAudio.com

www.ingramcontent.com/pod-product-compliance
Ingram Content Group UK Ltd.
Pitfield, Milton Keynes, MK11 3LW, UK
UKHW041433180426
11947UKWH00007B/405